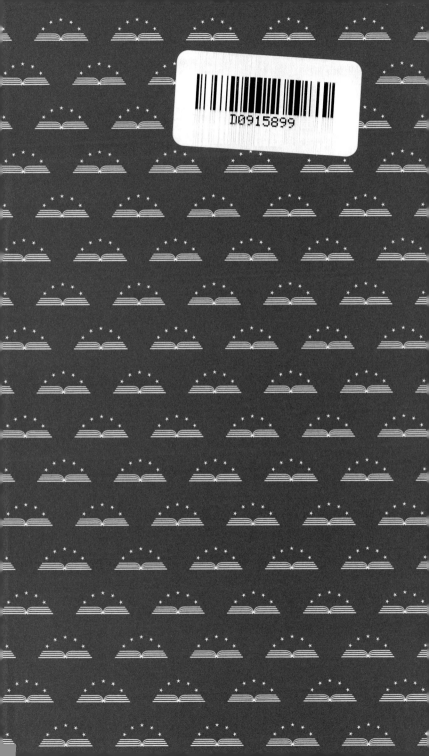

Library of America, a nonprofit organization,
champions our nation's cultural heritage
by publishing America's greatest writing in
authoritative new editions and providing resources
for readers to explore this rich, living legacy.

OCTAVIA E. BUTLER

OCTAVIA E. BUTLER

KINDRED
FLEDGLING
COLLECTED STORIES

Gerry Canavan
& Nisi Shawl
editors

THE LIBRARY OF AMERICA

Contents

Introduction

BY NISI SHAWL

With this first volume of Octavia Estelle Butler's work, the Library of America kicks off its canonization of discomfort. In journals and notes to herself Butler wrote about wanting to publish what she called "Yes books," books that went gloriously beyond readers' expectations of excitement and adventure to make her heroes victors against overwhelming odds. Yet most of her fiction wound up being about compromise, negotiation, and accepting the unacceptable. All is nuance, balance, and wide-eyed intersubjectivity. In Butler's universe there are no heroic victors. There are no outright winners, nor any losers without at least one admirable trait.

Though the stealth fantasy story "Crossover" was her first professional publication, *Kindred* is most readers' introduction to Octavia's oeuvre. It's required reading for hundreds of high school and college courses. So the first thing a lot of people learn about this author is her unflinchingness. *Kindred* is a firsthand account of the evils of chattel slavery written in the voice of a twentieth-century Black woman. As you read this novel you're not only faced with vivid examples of America's historical systematization of cruelty, you're given their context: the leeway that plantation owner Rufus Weylin saw himself granting when he "allowed" Dana Franklin—the novel's protagonist and narrator—to read to his mother, the distinction-without-a-difference between feeding enslaved children from a pig trough and out of bowls on dirt floors.

Dana accepts the beatings and threats inherent to enslavement in order to ensure her survival. She learns over and over again the many ways she doesn't dare fight back. She realizes survival, for her, is not about winning. Halfway through the novel, Dana pimps out her unwilling great-grandmother to Weylin; she is ashamed of what she's doing, but she does it anyway. Because the alternative is nonexistence.

The existence of *Fledgling*'s hero, Shori Matthews, is equally fraught. As a genetically engineered predator, a member of the vampire-like, human-appearing Ina species, Shori can and does take people's lives, can and does bind them to her service with her addictive venom. Most of Shori's ethical quandaries arise from an abundance of power rather than the lack of it that Dana confronts. Once again, though, the path forward for Octavia's protagonist lies through negotiation, accommodation, and empathy.

Kindred is typically the first book by Octavia Estelle Butler that people read. *Fledgling* is the last book she wrote. It should not have been. There are many series-worthy narrative arcs left deliberately uncompleted in the novel, such as the romantic relationship just beginning to develop between Shori and the Ina male Daniel Gordon, and clues dropped when Shori learns about Ina creation myths that suggest the Ina will eventually depart for other planets. Shori's relative youth—at fifty-three years of age she's still an adolescent, since the Ina age more slowly than humans—is another sign of how long and brilliantly Octavia's account of her life could have shone, through multiple dawns.

Additional proof: while preparing this volume its editors had access to a previously unpublished excerpt from "Asylum," a *Fledgling* sequel in progress at the time of Octavia's untimely death.

It's impossible for me, even fourteen years later, to write of that tragedy without my eyes filling, my heart bruising, my hands wringing themselves into regret-drenched knots. Octavia was my friend. I was not with her when she died. I could not prevent it, could not cushion her fall to the ice-coated sidewalk outside her home, could not perfuse her lovely brain with healing thoughts and drain away the explosions of blood filling her precious head.

All I can do now is read what she wrote for us and find within her pages that same blood, coursing purposefully through the veins of her works.

It's there. Sometimes figuratively, as in the genealogy Dana Franklin traces back to Rufus Weylin's act of rape. Sometimes literally, as in the sustenance the Ina take from their human symbionts.

It's everywhere. In her introduction to *Bloodchild and Other Stories* (also included here) Octavia notes, "I am essentially a novelist." But though she confesses in the same introduction to hating to write them, Octavia's short stories carry their fair share of the sanguine substance that appears to have fascinated her, whether in actual or metaphorical form. Most of the blood is literal in the gorily tender "Bloodchild," which Octavia often referred to as her "pregnant man story." But there are family links—blood ties—between the alien, insectile Tlic and their human hosts as well. "The Evening and the Morning and the Night" is about allegorical ties of blood, too, and makes additional references to a genetic disorder. For "Near of Kin" and "Childfinder," the narrative again focuses on the definition of blood denoting lineage.

When reading "Speech Sounds" and two other essays in this volume, I stretch the blood symbolism even further: "Lost Races of Science Fiction" examines blood-as-ethnicity, and the ways in which difference has been used to bar participation in the imaginative genres. "The Monophobic Response" links reluctance to bridge the barriers of blood with humanity's anxieties concerning extraterrestrial life. In "Speech Sounds" I see an embryonic family relationship between its hero, Rye, and the children she takes into her care during the story's near-future apocalypse.

I want to find as much of Octavia in her work as I can. Her body, her blood . . .

Have I disturbed you? Is what I'm saying too close to blasphemy? Good. I value disturbance as an Octavian quality. I cherish her evocation of it in myself and others.

Unlike the devil's advocates and ostentatiously controversial "edgelords" clogging Internet forums and other sites of public discourse, Octavia eschewed creating controversy merely for thrills. There are reasons, good reasons, behind the choice she makes, for instance, to give Shori the appearance of an eleven-year-old girl with the sexual appetite of an adult woman. Story logic demands that Noah, the narrator of "Amnesty," experience both the accidental atrocities perpetrated on her by aliens and her intentional torture at the hands of other humans. The disquiet Octavia's stories elicit is far from gratuitous. It is intrinsic to her work—so intrinsic that she spared not even herself.

Most authors, it has been said, hate the act of writing itself, though we love having written. Octavia admitted that she disliked writing short stories, but she loved writing everything else. In her variously titled instructions-to-wannabe-authors essay published here as "Furor Scribendi," she points out that "so much of writing is fun," and in her afterword to "Positive Obsession" she admits that reading and writing are pretty much all she ever does. Yet in "Speech Sounds" she robs her characters of the ability to communicate with words. The hero of "The Book of Martha," a woman working on her fifth novel, sacrifices a pleasurable and satisfying literary career to save us from ourselves. If it was necessary for the outcome of whatever thought experiments she was conducting within her fictional frameworks, Octavia destroyed the sources of her own comfort without hesitation.

Strong emotions, she counseled me, are the best basis for stories. What do you fear? What do you loathe? What would you give anything to rescue and protect and preserve for eternity? Write about that, she told her students.

Octavia feared parasitic insects—as do I. "Bloodchild" is born of her close, careful study of what she feared, and of her courage in examining its imperatives and internal justifications. It's a tour de force, an ingenious, Alexander Calder–caliber balancing of tension, terror, hope, and delight. Inspired by Octavia's example and moved to action by her urging, I wrote about a mother and daughter dealing with a nationwide infestation of plague-carrying head lice. Their love of and trust in one another mirrors the relationship I perceived between me and Octavia, a relationship that while deep was by no means unique.

Octavia helped me, yes. And she helped many others as well. She knew what she was doing when she loaned us money, listened to us, scolded us, praised us, invited us into her home and her thoughts and, I believe, her heart. She was reproducing.

Octavia was an immense influence on the genre; authors who never had the joy of meeting her can nevertheless testify to the lasting lessons taught by her direct style and ferocious, no-holds-barred story lines. Those who, like myself, were fortunate to meet and become even more familiar with her are still discovering how much she gave us.

Then there are those inhabiting the space between these inner and outer circles, those who were closer to Octavia than readers and more distant than luncheon dates and hiking pals. For these, Octavia made a special effort. Despite crippling shyness she spoke publicly, gave interviews, appeared on panels, taught classes. Multiple Hugo and Nebula Award–winner Ted Chiang was a student of Octavia's at the Clarion Writers' Workshop. Andrea Hairston, winner of the Carl Brandon Kindred, Carl Brandon Parallax, and Philip K. Dick awards was a student of Octavia's at the Clarion West Writers' Workshop. Kij Johnson, Kathleen Alcala, Sheree Renee Thomas, Cat Rambo, Ann Leckie, Benjamin Rosenbaum, and editor Gordon Van Gelder were among the many other acclaimed authors enrolled in Octavian classes.

Those with more powerful critical chops than I possess will make marvelous sense of the writing world's record of Octavia's lineage. They will trace the passing along of characteristic phrases and practices; uncover shared archetypes and common concerns; and reflect on her brilliance, her grace, her stubborn discipline, and on how these personal traits also became part of her literary legacy, the passing on of her blood, her writerly DNA. In that worthy endeavor, they'll have no abler guide than my co-editor, Gerry Canavan. Gerry's notes and chronology enhance this volume and make it essential to us who truly wish to understand what we had in Octavia Butler.

And to what we still have. For as she said herself in her afterword to the only memoir she would ever write, the essay titled by her preference "Positive Obsession," "I have no doubt at all that the best and the most interesting part of me is my fiction."

Here it is for you: Octavia's favorite Octavian-ness, in all its thrilling welter of tension and glory of unease. Enjoy.

KINDRED

To Victoria Rose,
friend and goad

Prologue

I LOST AN arm on my last trip home. My left arm.

And I lost about a year of my life and much of the comfort and security I had not valued until it was gone. When the police released Kevin, he came to the hospital and stayed with me so that I would know I hadn't lost him too.

But before he could come to me, I had to convince the police that he did not belong in jail. That took time. The police were shadows who appeared intermittently at my bedside to ask me questions I had to struggle to understand.

"How did you hurt your arm?" they asked. "Who hurt you?" My attention was captured by the word they used: Hurt. As though I'd scratched my arm. Didn't they think I knew it was gone?

"Accident," I heard myself whisper. "It was an accident."

They began asking me about Kevin. Their words seemed to blur together at first, and I paid little attention. After a while, though, I replayed them and suddenly realized that these men were trying to blame Kevin for "hurting" my arm.

"No." I shook my head weakly against the pillow. "Not Kevin. Is he here? Can I see him?"

"Who then?" they persisted.

I tried to think through the drugs, through the distant pain, but there was no honest explanation I could give them—none they would believe.

"An accident," I repeated. "My fault, not Kevin's. Please let me see him."

I said this over and over until the vague police shapes let me alone, until I awoke to find Kevin sitting, dozing beside my bed. I wondered briefly how long he had been there, but it didn't matter. The important thing was that he was there. I slept again, relieved.

Finally, I awoke feeling able to talk to him coherently and understand what he said. I was almost comfortable except for the strange throbbing of my arm. Of where my arm had been. I moved my head, tried to look at the empty place . . . the stump.

Then Kevin was standing over me, his hands on my face turning my head toward him.

He didn't say anything. After a moment, he sat down again, took my hand, and held it.

I felt as though I could have lifted my other hand and touched him. I felt as though I had another hand. I tried again to look, and this time he let me. Somehow, I had to see to be able to accept what I knew was so.

After a moment, I lay back against the pillow and closed my eyes. "Above the elbow," I said.

"They had to."

"I know. I'm just trying to get used to it." I opened my eyes and looked at him. Then I remembered my earlier visitors. "Have I gotten you into trouble?"

"Me?"

"The police were here. They thought you had done this to me."

"Oh, that. They were sheriff's deputies. The neighbors called them when you started to scream. They questioned me, detained me for a while—that's what they call it!—but you convinced them that they might as well let me go."

"Good. I told them it was an accident. My fault."

"There's no way a thing like that could be your fault."

"That's debatable. But it certainly wasn't your fault. Are you still in trouble?"

"I don't think so. They're sure I did it, but there were no witnesses, and you won't co-operate. Also, I don't think they can figure out how I could have hurt you . . . in the way you were hurt."

I closed my eyes again remembering the way I had been hurt —remembering the pain.

"Are you all right?" Kevin asked.

"Yes. Tell me what you told the police."

"The truth." He toyed with my hand for a moment silently. I looked at him, found him watching me.

"If you told those deputies the truth," I said softly, "you'd still be locked up—in a mental hospital."

He smiled. "I told as much of the truth as I could. I said I was in the bedroom when I heard you scream. I ran to the living room to see what was wrong, and I found you struggling to free your arm from what seemed to be a hole in the wall. I went to help you. That was when I realized your arm wasn't just stuck, but that, somehow, it had been crushed right into the wall."

"Not exactly crushed."

"I know. But that seemed to be a good word to use on them —to show my ignorance. It wasn't all that inaccurate either. Then they wanted me to tell them how such a thing could happen. I said I didn't know . . . kept telling them I didn't know. And heaven help me, Dana, I don't know."

"Neither do I," I whispered. "Neither do I."

The River

THE TROUBLE began long before June 9, 1976, when I became aware of it, but June 9 is the day I remember. It was
my twenty-sixth birthday. It was also the day I met Rufus—the
day he called me to him for the first time.

Kevin and I had not planned to do anything to celebrate my
birthday. We were both too tired for that. On the day before,
we had moved from our apartment in Los Angeles to a house
of our own a few miles away in Altadena. The moving was celebration enough for me. We were still unpacking—or rather, I
was still unpacking. Kevin had stopped when he got his office
in order. Now he was closeted there either loafing or thinking
because I didn't hear his typewriter. Finally, he came out to
the living room where I was sorting books into one of the big
bookcases. Fiction only. We had so many books, we had to try
to keep them in some kind of order.

"What's the matter?" I asked him.

"Nothing." He sat down on the floor near where I was working. "Just struggling with my own perversity. You know, I had
half-a-dozen ideas for that Christmas story yesterday during
the moving."

"And none now when there's time to write them down."

"Not a one." He picked up a book, opened it, and turned
a few pages. I picked up another book and tapped him on the
shoulder with it. When he looked up, surprised, I put a stack
of nonfiction down in front of him. He stared at it unhappily.

"Hell, why'd I come out here?"

"To get more ideas. After all, they come to you when you're
busy."

He gave me a look that I knew wasn't as malevolent as it
seemed. He had the kind of pale, almost colorless eyes that
made him seem distant and angry whether he was or not. He
used them to intimidate people. Strangers. I grinned at him
and went back to work. After a moment, he took the nonfiction to another bookcase and began shelving it.

I bent to push him another box full, then straightened quickly
as I began to feel dizzy, nauseated. The room seemed to blur

and darken around me. I stayed on my feet for a moment holding on to a bookcase and wondering what was wrong, then finally, I collapsed to my knees. I heard Kevin make a wordless sound of surprise, heard him ask, "What happened?"

I raised my head and discovered that I could not focus on him. "Something is wrong with me," I gasped.

I heard him move toward me, saw a blur of gray pants and blue shirt. Then, just before he would have touched me, he vanished.

The house, the books, everything vanished. Suddenly, I was outdoors kneeling on the ground beneath trees. I was in a green place. I was at the edge of a woods. Before me was a wide tranquil river, and near the middle of that river was a child splashing, screaming . . .

Drowning!

I reacted to the child in trouble. Later I could ask questions, try to find out where I was, what had happened. Now I went to help the child.

I ran down to the river, waded into the water fully clothed, and swam quickly to the child. He was unconscious by the time I reached him—a small red-haired boy floating, face down. I turned him over, got a good hold on him so that his head was above water, and towed him in. There was a red-haired woman waiting for us on the shore now. Or rather, she was running back and forth crying on the shore. The moment she saw that I was wading, she ran out, took the boy from me and carried him the rest of the way, feeling and examining him as she did.

"He's not breathing!" she screamed.

Artificial respiration. I had seen it done, been told about it, but I had never done it. Now was the time to try. The woman was in no condition to do anything useful, and there was no one else in sight. As we reached shore, I snatched the child from her. He was no more than four or five years old, and not very big.

I put him down on his back, tilted his head back, and began mouth-to-mouth resuscitation. I saw his chest move as I breathed into him. Then, suddenly, the woman began beating me.

"You killed my baby!" she screamed. "You killed him!"

I turned and managed to catch her pounding fists. "Stop it!" I shouted, putting all the authority I could into my voice. "He's alive!" Was he? I couldn't tell. Please God, let him be alive. "The boy's alive. Now let me help him." I pushed her away, glad she was a little smaller than I was, and turned my attention back to her son. Between breaths, I saw her staring at me blankly. Then she dropped to her knees beside me, crying.

Moments later, the boy began breathing on his own—breathing and coughing and choking and throwing up and crying for his mother. If he could do all that, he was all right. I sat back from him, feeling light-headed, relieved. I had done it!

"He's alive!" cried the woman. She grabbed him and nearly smothered him. "Oh, Rufus, baby . . ."

Rufus. Ugly name to inflict on a reasonably nice-looking little kid.

When Rufus saw that it was his mother who held him, he clung to her, screaming as loudly as he could. There was nothing wrong with his voice, anyway. Then, suddenly, there was another voice.

"What the devil's going on here?" A man's voice, angry and demanding.

I turned, startled, and found myself looking down the barrel of the longest rifle I had ever seen. I heard a metallic click, and I froze, thinking I was going to be shot for saving the boy's life. I was going to die.

I tried to speak, but my voice was suddenly gone. I felt sick and dizzy. My vision blurred so badly I could not distinguish the gun or the face of the man behind it. I heard the woman speak sharply, but I was too far gone into sickness and panic to understand what she said.

Then the man, the woman, the boy, the gun all vanished.

I was kneeling in the living room of my own house again several feet from where I had fallen minutes before. I was back at home—wet and muddy, but intact. Across the room, Kevin stood frozen, staring at the spot where I had been. How long had he been there?

"Kevin?"

He spun around to face me. "What the hell . . . how did you get over there?" he whispered.

"I don't know."

"Dana, you . . ." He came over to me, touched me tentatively as though he wasn't sure I was real. Then he grabbed me by the shoulders and held me tightly. "What happened?"

I reached up to loosen his grip, but he wouldn't let go. He dropped to his knees beside me.

"Tell me!" he demanded.

"I would if I knew what to tell you. Stop hurting me."

He let me go, finally, stared at me as though he'd just recognized me. "Are you all right?"

"No." I lowered my head and closed my eyes for a moment. I was shaking with fear, with residual terror that took all the strength out of me. I folded forward, hugging myself, trying to be still. The threat was gone, but it was all I could do to keep my teeth from chattering.

Kevin got up and went away for a moment. He came back with a large towel and wrapped it around my shoulders. It comforted me somehow, and I pulled it tighter. There was an ache in my back and shoulders where Rufus's mother had pounded with her fists. She had hit harder than I'd realized, and Kevin hadn't helped.

We sat there together on the floor, me wrapped in the towel and Kevin with his arm around me calming me just by being there. After a while, I stopped shaking.

"Tell me now," said Kevin.

"What?"

"Everything. What happened to you? How did you . . . how did you move like that?"

I sat mute, trying to gather my thoughts, seeing the rifle again leveled at my head. I had never in my life panicked that way—never felt so close to death.

"Dana." He spoke softly. The sound of his voice seemed to put distance between me and the memory. But still . . .

"I don't know what to tell you," I said. "It's all crazy."

"Tell me how you got wet," he said. "Start with that."

I nodded. "There was a river," I said. "Woods with a river running through. And there was a boy drowning. I saved him. That's how I got wet." I hesitated, trying to think, to make sense. Not that what had happened to me made sense, but at least I could tell it coherently.

I looked at Kevin, saw that he held his expression carefully neutral. He waited. More composed, I went back to the beginning, to the first dizziness, and remembered it all for him —relived it all in detail. I even recalled things that I hadn't realized I'd noticed. The trees I'd been near, for instance, were pine trees, tall and straight with branches and needles mostly at the top. I had noticed that much somehow in the instant before I had seen Rufus. And I remembered something extra about Rufus's mother. Her clothing. She had worn a long dark dress that covered her from neck to feet. A silly thing to be wearing on a muddy riverbank. And she had spoken with an accent—a southern accent. Then there was the unforgettable gun, long and deadly.

Kevin listened without interrupting. When I was finished, he took the edge of the towel and wiped a little of the mud from my leg. "This stuff had to come from somewhere," he said.

"You don't believe me?"

He stared at the mud for a moment, then faced me. "You know how long you were gone?"

"A few minutes. Not long."

"A few seconds. There were no more than ten or fifteen seconds between the time you went and the time you called my name."

"Oh, no . . ." I shook my head slowly. "All that couldn't have happened in just seconds."

He said nothing.

"But it was real! I was there!" I caught myself, took a deep breath, and slowed down. "All right. If you told me a story like this, I probably wouldn't believe it either, but like you said, this mud came from somewhere."

"Yes."

"Look, what did you see? What do you think happened?"

He frowned a little, shook his head. "You vanished." He seemed to have to force the words out. "You were here until my hand was just a couple of inches from you. Then, suddenly, you were gone. I couldn't believe it. I just stood there. Then you were back again and on the other side of the room."

"Do you believe it yet?"

He shrugged. "It happened. I saw it. You vanished and you reappeared. Facts."

"I reappeared wet, muddy, and scared to death."

"Yes."

"And I know what I saw, and what I did—my facts. They're no crazier than yours."

"I don't know what to think."

"I'm not sure it matters what we think."

"What do you mean?"

"Well . . . it happened once. What if it happens again?"

"No. No, I don't think . . ."

"You don't know!" I was starting to shake again. "Whatever it was, I've had enough of it! It almost killed me!"

"Take it easy," he said. "Whatever happens, it's not going to do you any good to panic yourself again."

I moved uncomfortably, looked around. "I feel like it could happen again—like it could happen anytime. I don't feel secure here."

"You're just scaring yourself."

"No!" I turned to glare at him, and he looked so worried I turned away again. I wondered bitterly whether he was worried about my vanishing again or worried about my sanity. I still didn't think he believed my story. "Maybe you're right," I said. "I hope you are. Maybe I'm just like a victim of robbery or rape or something—a victim who survives, but who doesn't feel safe any more." I shrugged. "I don't have a name for the thing that happened to me, but I don't feel safe any more."

He made his voice very gentle. "If it happens again, and if it's real, the boy's father will know he owes you thanks. He won't hurt you."

"You don't know that. You don't know what could happen." I stood up unsteadily. "Hell, I don't blame you for humoring me." I paused to give him a chance to deny it, but he didn't. "I'm beginning to feel as though I'm humoring myself."

"What do you mean?"

"I don't know. As real as the whole episode was, as real as I know it was, it's beginning to recede from me somehow. It's becoming like something I saw on television or read about—like something I got second hand."

"Or like a . . . a dream?"

I looked down at him. "You mean a hallucination."

"All right."

"No! I know what I'm doing. I can see. I'm pulling away from it because it scares me so. But it was real."

"Let yourself pull away from it." He got up and took the muddy towel from me. "That sounds like the best thing you can do, whether it was real or not. Let go of it."

The Fire

I

I TRIED.

I showered, washed away the mud and the brackish water, put on clean clothes, combed my hair . . .

"That's a lot better," said Kevin when he saw me.

But it wasn't.

Rufus and his parents had still not quite settled back and become the "dream" Kevin wanted them to be. They stayed with me, shadowy and threatening. They made their own limbo and held me in it. I had been afraid that the dizziness might come back while I was in the shower, afraid that I would fall and crack my skull against the tile or that I would go back to that river, wherever it was, and find myself standing naked among strangers. Or would I appear somewhere else naked and totally vulnerable?

I washed very quickly.

Then I went back to the books in the living room, but Kevin had almost finished shelving them.

"Forget about any more unpacking today," he told me. "Let's go get something to eat."

"Go?"

"Yes, where would you like to eat? Someplace nice for your birthday."

"Here."

"But . . ."

"Here, really. I don't want to go anywhere."

"Why not?"

I took a deep breath. "Tomorrow," I said. "Let's go tomorrow." Somehow, tomorrow would be better. I would have a night's sleep between me and whatever had happened. And if nothing else happened, I would be able to relax a little.

"It would be good for you to get out of here for a while," he said.

"No."

"Listen . . ."

"No!" Nothing was going to get me out of the house that night if I could help it.

Kevin looked at me for a moment—I probably looked as scared as I was—then he went to the phone and called out for chicken and shrimp.

But staying home did no good. When the food had arrived, when we were eating and I was calmer, the kitchen began to blur around me.

Again the light seemed to dim and I felt the sick dizziness. I pushed back from the table, but didn't try to get up. I couldn't have gotten up.

"Dana?"

I didn't answer.

"Is it happening again?"

"I think so." I sat very still, trying not to fall off my chair. The floor seemed farther away than it should have. I reached out for the table to steady myself, but before I could touch it, it was gone. And the distant floor seemed to darken and change. The linoleum tile became wood, partially carpeted. And the chair beneath me vanished.

2

When my dizziness cleared away, I found myself sitting on a small bed sheltered by a kind of abbreviated dark green canopy. Beside me was a little wooden stand containing a battered old pocket knife, several marbles, and a lighted candle in a metal holder. Before me was a red-haired boy. Rufus?

The boy had his back to me and hadn't noticed me yet. He held a stick of wood in one hand and the end of the stick was charred and smoking. Its fire had apparently been transferred to the draperies at the window. Now the boy stood watching as the flames ate their way up the heavy cloth.

For a moment, I watched too. Then I woke up, pushed the boy aside, caught the unburned upper part of the draperies and pulled them down. As they fell, they smothered some of the flames within themselves, and they exposed a half-open window. I picked them up quickly and threw them out the window.

The boy looked at me, then ran to the window and looked

out. I looked out too, hoping I hadn't thrown the burning cloth onto a porch roof or too near a wall. There was a fireplace in the room; I saw it now, too late. I could have safely thrown the draperies into it and let them burn.

It was dark outside. The sun had not set at home when I was snatched away, but here it was dark. I could see the draperies a story below, burning, lighting the night only enough for us to see that they were on the ground and some distance from the nearest wall. My hasty act had done no harm. I could go home knowing that I had averted trouble for the second time.

I waited to go home.

My first trip had ended as soon as the boy was safe—had ended just in time to keep me safe. Now, though, as I waited, I realized that I wasn't going to be that lucky again.

I didn't feel dizzy. The room remained unblurred, undeniably real. I looked around, not knowing what to do. The fear that had followed me from home flared now. What would happen to me if I didn't go back automatically this time? What if I was stranded here—wherever here was? I had no money, no idea how to get home.

I stared out into the darkness fighting to calm myself. It was not calming, though, that there were no city lights out there. No lights at all. But still, I was in no immediate danger. And wherever I was, there was a child with me—and a child might answer my questions more readily than an adult.

I looked at him. He looked back, curious and unafraid. He was not Rufus. I could see that now. He had the same red hair and slight build, but he was taller, clearly three or four years older. Old enough, I thought, to know better than to play with fire. If he hadn't set fire to his draperies, I might still be at home.

I stepped over to him, took the stick from his hand, and threw it into the fireplace. "Someone should use one like that on you," I said, "before you burn the house down."

I regretted the words the moment they were out. I needed this boy's help. But still, who knew what trouble he had gotten me into!

The boy stumbled back from me, alarmed. "You lay a hand on me, and I'll tell my daddy!" His accent was unmistakably southern, and before I could shut out the thought, I began wondering whether I might be somewhere in the South. Somewhere two or three thousand miles from home.

If I was in the South, the two- or three-hour time difference would explain the darkness outside. But wherever I was, the last thing I wanted to do was meet this boy's father. The man could have me jailed for breaking into his house—or he could shoot me for breaking in. There was something specific for me to worry about. No doubt the boy could tell me about other things.

And he would. If I was going to be stranded here, I had to find out all I could while I could. As dangerous as it could be for me to stay where I was, in the house of a man who might shoot me, it seemed even more dangerous for me to go wandering into the night totally ignorant. The boy and I would keep our voices down, and we would talk.

"Don't you worry about your father," I told him softly. "You'll have plenty to say to him when he sees those burned draperies."

The boy seemed to deflate. His shoulders sagged and he turned to stare into the fireplace. "Who are you anyway?" he asked. "What are you doing here?"

So he didn't know either—not that I had really expected him to. But he did seem surprisingly at ease with me—much calmer than I would have been at his age about the sudden appearance of a stranger in my bedroom. I wouldn't even have still been in the bedroom. If he had been as timid a child as I was, he would probably have gotten me killed.

"What's your name?" I asked him.

"Rufus."

For a moment, I just stared at him. "Rufus?"

"Yeah. What's the matter?"

I wished I knew what was the matter—what was going on! "I'm all right," I said. "Look . . . Rufus, look at me. Have you ever seen me before?"

"No."

That was the right answer, the reasonable answer. I tried to make myself accept it in spite of his name, his too-familiar face. But the child I had pulled from the river could so easily have grown into this child—in three or four years.

"Can you remember a time when you nearly drowned?" I asked, feeling foolish.

He frowned, looked at me more carefully.

"You were younger," I said. "About five years old, maybe. Do you remember?"

"The river?" The words came out low and tentative as though he didn't quite believe them himself.

"You do remember then. It was you."

"Drowning . . . I remember that. And you . . . ?"

"I'm not sure you ever got a look at me. And I guess it must have been a long time ago . . . for you."

"No, I remember you now. I saw you."

I said nothing. I didn't quite believe him. I wondered whether he was just telling me what he thought I wanted to hear—though there was no reason for him to lie. He was clearly not afraid of me.

"That's why it seemed like I knew you," he said. "I couldn't remember—maybe because of the way I saw you. I told Mama, and she said I couldn't have really seen you that way."

"What way?"

"Well . . . with my eyes closed."

"With your—" I stopped. The boy wasn't lying; he was dreaming.

"It's true!" he insisted loudly. Then he caught himself, whispered, "That's the way I saw you just as I stepped in the hole."

"Hole?"

"In the river. I was walking in the water and there was a hole. I fell, and then I couldn't find the bottom any more. I saw you inside a room. I could see part of the room, and there were books all around—more than in Daddy's library. You were wearing pants like a man—the way you are now. I thought you were a man."

"Thanks a lot."

"But this time you just look like a woman wearing pants."

I sighed. "All right, never mind that. As long as you recognize me as the one who pulled you out of the river . . ."

"Did you? I thought you must have been the one."

I stopped, confused. "I thought you remembered."

"I remember seeing you. It was like I stopped drowning for

a while and saw you, and then started to drown again. After that Mama was there, and Daddy."

"And Daddy's gun," I said bitterly. "Your father almost shot me."

"He thought you were a man too—and that you were trying to hurt Mama and me. Mama says she was telling him not to shoot you, and then you were gone."

"Yes." I had probably vanished before the woman's eyes. What had she thought of that?

"I asked her where you went," said Rufus, "and she got mad and said she didn't know. I asked her again later, and she hit me. And she never hits me."

I waited, expecting him to ask me the same question, but he said no more. Only his eyes questioned. I hunted through my own thoughts for a way to answer him.

"Where do you think I went, Rufe?"

He sighed, said disappointedly, "You're not going to tell me either."

"Yes I am—as best I can. But answer me first. Tell me where you think I went."

He seemed to have to decide whether to do that or not. "Back to the room," he said finally. "The room with the books."

"Is that a guess, or did you see me again?"

"I didn't see you. Am I right? Did you go back there?"

"Yes. Back home to scare my husband almost as much as I must have scared your parents."

"But how did you get there? How did you get here?"

"Like that." I snapped my fingers.

"That's no answer."

"It's the only answer I've got. I was at home; then suddenly, I was here helping you. I don't know how it happens —how I move that way—or when it's going to happen. I can't control it."

"Who can?"

"I don't know. No one." I didn't want him to get the idea that he could control it. Especially if it turned out that he really could.

"But . . . what's it like? What did Mama see that she won't tell me about?"

"Probably the same thing my husband saw. He said when

I came to you, I vanished. Just disappeared. And then reappeared later."

He thought about that. "Disappeared? You mean like smoke?" Fear crept into his expression. "Like a ghost?"

"Like smoke, maybe. But don't go getting the idea that I'm a ghost. There are no ghosts."

"That's what Daddy says."

"He's right."

"But Mama says she saw one once."

I managed to hold back my opinion of that. His mother, after all . . . Besides, I was probably her ghost. She had had to find some explanation for my vanishing. I wondered how her more realistic husband had explained it. But that wasn't important. What I cared about now was keeping the boy calm.

"You needed help," I told him. "I came to help you. Twice. Does that make me someone to be afraid of?"

"I guess not." He gave me a long look, then came over to me, reached out hesitantly, and touched me with a sooty hand.

"You see," I said, "I'm as real as you are."

He nodded. "I thought you were. All the things you did . . . you had to be. And Mama said she touched you too."

"She sure did." I rubbed my shoulder where the woman had bruised it with her desperate blows. For a moment, the soreness confused me, forced me to recall that for me, the woman's attack had come only hours ago. Yet the boy was years older. Fact then: Somehow, my travels crossed time as well as distance. Another fact: The boy was the focus of my travels —perhaps the cause of them. He had seen me in my living room before I was drawn to him; he couldn't have made that up. But I had seen nothing at all, felt nothing but sickness and disorientation.

"Mama said what you did after you got me out of the water was like the Second Book of Kings," said the boy.

"The what?"

"Where Elisha breathed into the dead boy's mouth, and the boy came back to life. Mama said she tried to stop you when she saw you doing that to me because you were just some nigger she had never seen before. Then she remembered Second Kings."

I sat down on the bed and looked over at him, but I could

read nothing other than interest and remembered excitement in his eyes. "She said I was what?" I asked.

"Just a strange nigger. She and Daddy both knew they hadn't seen you before."

"That was a hell of a thing for her to say right after she saw me save her son's life."

Rufus frowned. "Why?"

I stared at him.

"What's wrong?" he asked. "Why are you mad?"

"Your mother always call black people niggers, Rufe?"

"Sure, except when she has company. Why not?"

His air of innocent questioning confused me. Either he really didn't know what he was saying, or he had a career waiting in Hollywood. Whichever it was, he wasn't going to go on saying it to me.

"I'm a black woman, Rufe. If you have to call me something other than my name, that's it."

"But . . ."

"Look, I helped you. I put the fire out, didn't I?"

"Yeah."

"All right then, you do me the courtesy of calling me what I want to be called."

He just stared at me.

"Now," I spoke more gently, "tell me, did you see me again when the draperies started to burn? I mean, did you see me the way you did when you were drowning?"

It took him a moment to shift gears. Then he said, "I didn't see anything but fire." He sat down in the old ladder-back chair near the fireplace and looked at me. "I didn't see you until you got here. But I was so scared . . . it was kind of like when I was drowning . . . but not like anything else I can remember. I thought the house would burn down and it would be my fault. I thought I would die."

I nodded. "You probably wouldn't have died because you would have been able to get out in time. But if your parents are asleep here, the fire might have reached them before they woke up."

The boy stared into the fireplace. "I burned the stable once," he said. "I wanted Daddy to give me Nero—a horse I liked. But he sold him to Reverend Wyndham just because Reverend

Wyndham offered a lot of money. Daddy already has a lot of money. Anyway, I got mad and burned down the stable."

I shook my head wonderingly. The boy already knew more about revenge than I did. What kind of man was he going to grow up into? "Why did you set this fire?" I asked. "To get even with your father for something else?"

"For hitting me. See?" He turned and pulled up his shirt so that I could see the crisscross of long red welts. And I could see old marks, ugly scars of at least one much worse beating.

"For Godsake . . . !"

"He said I took money from his desk, and I said I didn't." Rufus shrugged. "He said I was calling him a liar, and he hit me."

"Several times."

"All I took was a dollar." He put his shirt down and faced me.

I didn't know what to say to that. The boy would be lucky to stay out of prison when he grew up—if he grew up. He went on,

"I started thinking that if I burned the house, he would lose all his money. He ought to lose it. It's all he ever thinks about." Rufus shuddered. "But then I remembered the stable, and the whip he hit me with after I set that fire. Mama said if she hadn't stopped him, he would have killed me. I was afraid this time he would kill me, so I wanted to put the fire out. But I couldn't. I didn't know what to do."

So he had called me. I was certain now. The boy drew me to him somehow when he got himself into more trouble than he could handle. How he did it, I didn't know. He apparently didn't even know he was doing it. If he had, and if he had been able to call me voluntarily, I might have found myself standing between father and son during one of Rufus's beatings. What would have happened then, I couldn't imagine. One meeting with Rufus's father had been enough for me. Not that the boy sounded like that much of a bargain either. But, "Did you say he used a whip on you, Rufe?"

"Yeah. The kind he whips niggers and horses with."

That stopped me for a moment. "The kind he whips . . . who?"

He looked at me warily. "I wasn't talking about you."

I brushed that aside. "Say blacks anyway. But . . . your father whips black people?"

"When they need it. But Mama said it was cruel and disgraceful for him to hit me like that no matter what I did. She took me to Baltimore City to Aunt May's house after that, but he came and got me and brought me home. After a while, she came home too."

For a moment, I forgot about the whip and the "niggers." Baltimore City. Baltimore, Maryland? "Are we far from Baltimore now, Rufe?"

"Across the bay."

"But . . . we're still in Maryland, aren't we?" I had relatives in Maryland—people who would help me if I needed them, and if I could reach them. I was beginning to wonder, though, whether I would be able to reach anyone I knew. I had a new, slowly growing fear.

"Sure we're in Maryland," said Rufus. "How could you not know that."

"What's the date?"

"I don't know."

"The year! Just tell me the year!"

He glanced across the room toward the door, then quickly back at me. I realized I was making him nervous with my ignorance and my sudden intensity. I forced myself to speak calmly. "Come on, Rufe, you know what year it is, don't you?"

"It's . . . eighteen fifteen."

"When?"

"Eighteen fifteen."

I sat still, breathed deeply, calming myself, believing him. I did believe him. I wasn't even as surprised as I should have been. I had already accepted the fact that I had moved through time. Now I knew I was farther from home than I had thought. And now I knew why Rufus's father used his whip on "niggers" as well as horses.

I looked up and saw that the boy had left his chair and come closer to me.

"What's the matter with you?" he demanded. "You keep acting sick."

"It's nothing, Rufe. I'm all right." No, I was sick. What was I going to do? Why hadn't I gone home? This could turn out to

be such a deadly place for me if I had to stay in it much longer.
"Is this a plantation?" I asked.

"The Weylin plantation. My daddy's Tom Weylin."

"Weylin . . ." The name triggered a memory, something
I hadn't thought of for years. "Rufus, do you spell your last
name, W-e-y-l-i-n?"

"Yeah, I think that's right."

I frowned at him impatiently. A boy his age should certainly
be sure of the spelling of his own name—even a name like this
with an unusual spelling.

"It's right," he said quickly.

"And . . . is there a black girl, maybe a slave girl, named
Alice living around here somewhere?" I wasn't sure of the girl's
last name. The memory was coming back to me in fragments.

"Sure. Alice is my friend."

"Is she?" I was staring at my hands, trying to think. Every
time I got used to one impossibility, I ran into another.

"She's no slave, either," said Rufus. "She's free, born free like
her mother."

"Oh? Then maybe somehow . . ." I let my voice trail
away as my thoughts raced ahead of it fitting things together.
The state was right, and the time, the unusual name, the girl,
Alice . . .

"Maybe what?" prompted Rufus.

Yes, maybe what? Well, maybe, if I wasn't completely out of
my mind, if I wasn't in the middle of the most perfect hallucination I'd ever heard of, if the child before me was real and was
telling the truth, maybe he was one of my ancestors.

Maybe he was my several times great grandfather, but still
vaguely alive in the memory of my family because his daughter had bought a large Bible in an ornately carved, wooden
chest and had begun keeping family records in it. My uncle
still had it.

Grandmother Hagar. Hagar Weylin, born in 1831. Hers was
the first name listed. And she had given her parents' names as
Rufus Weylin and Alice Green-something Weylin.

"Rufus, what's Alice's last name?"

"Greenwood. What were you talking about? Maybe what?"

"Nothing. I . . . just thought I might know someone in
her family."

"Do you?"

"I don't know. It's been a long time since I've seen the person I'm thinking of." Weak lies. But they were better than the truth. As young as the boy was, I thought he would question my sanity if I told the truth.

Alice Greenwood. How would she marry this boy? Or would it be marriage? And why hadn't someone in my family mentioned that Rufus Weylin was white? If they knew. Probably, they didn't. Hagar Weylin Blake had died in 1880, long before the time of any member of my family that I had known. No doubt most information about her life had died with her. At least it had died before it filtered down to me. There was only the Bible left.

Hagar had filled pages of it with her careful script. There was a record of her marriage to Oliver Blake, and a list of her seven children, their marriages, some grandchildren . . . Then someone else had taken up the listing. So many relatives that I had never known, would never know.

Or would I?

I looked over at the boy who would be Hagar's father. There was nothing in him that reminded me of any of my relatives. Looking at him confused me. But he had to be the one. There had to be some kind of reason for the link he and I seemed to have. Not that I really thought a blood relationship could explain the way I had twice been drawn to him. It wouldn't. But then, neither would anything else. What we had was something new, something that didn't even have a name. Some matching strangeness in us that may or may not have come from our being related. Still, now I had a special reason for being glad I had been able to save him. After all . . . after all, what would have happened to me, to my mother's family, if I hadn't saved him?

Was that why I was here? Not only to insure the survival of one accident-prone small boy, but to insure my family's survival, my own birth.

Again, what would have happened if the boy had drowned? Would he have drowned without me? Or would his mother have saved him somehow? Would his father have arrived in time to save him? It must be that one of them would have saved him somehow. His life could not depend on the actions of his un-conceived descendant. No matter what I did, he would have to survive to father Hagar, or I could not exist. That made sense.

But somehow, it didn't make enough sense to give me any comfort. It didn't make enough sense for me to test it by ig-noring him if I found him in trouble again—not that I could have ignored *any* child in trouble. But this child needed special care. If I was to live, if others were to live, he must live. I didn't dare test the paradox.

"You know," he said, peering at me, "you look a little like Alice's mother. If you wore a dress and tied your hair up, you'd look a lot like her." He sat down companionably beside me on the bed.

"I'm surprised your mother didn't mistake me for her then," I said.

"Not with you dressed like that! She thought you were a man at first, just like I did—and like Daddy did."

"Oh." That mistake was a little easier to understand now.

"Are you sure you aren't related to Alice yourself?"

"Not that I know of," I lied. And I changed the subject abruptly. "Rufe, are there slaves here?"

He nodded. "Thirty-eight slaves, Daddy said." He drew his bare feet up and sat cross-legged on the bed facing me, still examining me with interest. "You're not a slave, are you?"

"No."

"I didn't think so. You don't talk right or dress right or act right. You don't even seem like a runaway."

"I'm not."

"And you don't call me 'Master' either."

I surprised myself by laughing. "Master?"

"You're supposed to." He was very serious. "You want me to call you black."

His seriousness stopped my laughter. What was funny, any-way? He was probably right. No doubt I was supposed to give him some title of respect. But "Master"?

"You have to say it," he insisted. "Or 'Young Master' or . . . or 'Mister' like Alice does. You're supposed to."

"No." I shook my head. "Not unless things get a lot worse than they are."

The boy gripped my arm. "Yes!" he whispered. "You'll get into trouble if you don't, if Daddy hears you."

I'd get into trouble if "Daddy" heard me say anything at all. But the boy was obviously concerned, even frightened for me. His father sounded like a man who worked at inspiring fear. "All right," I said. "If anyone else comes, I'll call you 'Mister Rufus.' Will that do?" If anyone else came, I'd be lucky to survive.

"Yes," said Rufus. He looked relieved. "I still have scars on my back where Daddy hit me with the whip."

"I saw them." It was time for me to get out of this house. I had done enough talking and learning and hoping to be transported home. It was clear that whatever power had used me to protect Rufus had not provided for my own protection. I had to get out of the house and to a place of safety before day came —if there was a place of safety for me here. I wondered how Alice's parents managed, how they survived.

"Hey!" said Rufus suddenly.

I jumped, looked at him, and realized that he had been saying something—something I had missed.

"I said what's your name?" he repeated. "You never told me."

Was that all? "Edana," I said. "Most people call me Dana."

"Oh, no!" he said softly. He stared at me the way he had when he thought I might be a ghost.

"What's wrong?"

"Nothing, I guess, but . . . well, you wanted to know if I had seen you this time before you got here the way I did at the river. Well, I didn't see you, but I think I heard you."

"How? When?"

"I don't know how. You weren't here. But when the fire started and I got so scared, I heard a voice, a man. He said, 'Dana?' Then he said, 'Is it happening again?' And someone else—you—whispered, 'I think so.' I heard you!"

I sighed wearily, longing for my own bed and an end to questions that had no answers. How had Rufus heard Kevin and me across time and space? I didn't know. I didn't even have time to care. I had other more immediate problems.

"Who was the man?" Rufus asked.

"My husband." I rubbed a hand across my face. "Rufe, I have to get out of here before your father wakes up. Will you show me the way downstairs so that I don't awaken anyone?"

"Where will you go?"

"I don't know, but I can't stay here." I paused for a moment wondering how much he could help me—how much he would help me. "I'm a long way from home," I said, "and I don't know when I'll be able to get back there. Do you know of anyplace I could go?"

Rufus uncrossed his legs and scratched his head. "You could go outside and hide until morning. Then you could come out and ask Daddy if you could work here. He hires free niggers sometimes."

"Does he? If you were free and black, do you think you'd want to work for him?"

He looked away from me, shook his head. "I guess not. He's pretty mean sometimes."

"Is there someplace else I could go?"

He did some more thinking. "You could go to town and find work there."

"What's the name of the town?"

"Easton."

"Is it far?"

"Not so far. The niggers walk there sometimes when Daddy gives them a pass. Or maybe . . ."

"What?"

"Alice's mother lives closer. You could go to her, and she could tell you the best places to go to get work. You could stay with her too, maybe. Then I might see you again before you go home."

I was surprised he wanted to see me again. I hadn't had much contact with children since I'd been one myself. Somehow, I found myself liking this one, though. His environment had left its unlikable marks on him, but in the ante bellum South, I could have found myself at the mercy of someone much worse —could have been descended from someone much worse.

"Where can I find Alice's mother?" I asked.

"She lives in the woods. Come on outside, and I'll tell you how to get there."

He took his candle and went to the door of his room. The room's shadows moved eerily as he moved. I realized suddenly how easy it would be for him to betray me—to open the door and run away or shout an alarm.

Instead, he opened the door a crack and looked out. Then he turned and beckoned to me. He seemed excited and pleased, and only frightened enough to make him cautious. I relaxed, followed him quickly. He was enjoying himself—having an adventure. And, incidentally, he was playing with fire again, helping an intruder to escape undetected from his father's house. His father would probably take the whip to both of us if he knew.

Downstairs, the large heavy door opened noiselessly and we stepped into the darkness outside—the near darkness. There was a half-moon and several million stars lighting the night as they never did at home. Rufus immediately began to give me directions to his friend's house, but I stopped him. There was something else to be done first.

"Where would the draperies have fallen, Rufe? Take me to them."

He obeyed, taking me around a corner of the house to the side. There, what was left of the draperies lay smoking on the ground.

"If we can get rid of this," I said, "can you get your mother to give you new draperies without telling your father?"

"I think so," he said. "They hardly talk to each other anyway."

Most of the remnants of the drapes were cold. I stamped out the few that were still edged in red and threatening to flame up again. Then I found a fairly large piece of unburned cloth. I spread it out flat and filled it with smaller pieces and bits of ash and whatever dirt I scooped up along with them. Rufus helped me silently. When we were finished, I rolled the cloth into a tight bundle and gave it to him.

"Put it in your fireplace," I told him. "Watch to see that it all burns before you go to sleep. But, Rufe . . . don't burn anything else."

He glanced downward, embarrassed. "I won't."

"Good. There must be safer ways of annoying your father. Now which way is it to Alice's house?"

3

He pointed the way, then left me alone in the silent chilly night. I stood beside the house for a moment feeling frightened and lonely. I hadn't realized how comforting the boy's presence had been. Finally, I began walking across the wide grassy land that separated the house from the fields. I could see scattered trees and shadowy buildings around me. There was a row of small buildings off to one side almost out of sight of the house. Slave cabins, I supposed. I thought I saw someone moving around one of them, and for a moment, I froze behind a huge spreading tree. The figure vanished silently between two cabins—some slave, probably as eager as I was to avoid being caught out at night.

I skirted around a field of some grassy waist-high crop I didn't even try to identify in the dim light. Rufus had told me his short cut, and that there was another longer way by road. I was glad to avoid the road, though. The possibility of meeting a white adult here frightened me, more than the possibility of street violence ever had at home.

Finally, there was a stand of woods that looked like a solid wall of darkness after the moonlit fields. I stood before it for several seconds wondering whether the road wouldn't be a better idea after all.

Then I heard dogs barking—not too far away by their sound —and in sudden fear, I plunged through a tangle of new young growth and into the trees. I wondered about thorns, poison ivy, snakes . . . I wondered, but I didn't stop. A pack of half-wild dogs seemed worse. Or perhaps a pack of tame hunting dogs used to tracking runaway slaves.

The woods were not as totally dark as they had seemed. I could see a little after my eyes grew accustomed to the dimness. I could see trees, tall and shadowy—trees everywhere. As I walked on, I began to wonder how I could be sure I was still going in the right direction. That was enough. I turned around —hoping that I still knew what "around" meant, and headed back toward the field. I was too much of a city woman.

I got back to the field all right, then veered left to where Rufus had said there was a road. I found the road and followed it, listening for the dogs. But now, only a few night birds and insects broke the silence—crickets, an owl, some other bird I had no name for. I hugged the side of the road, trying to suppress my nervousness and praying to go home.

Something dashed across the road so close to me that it almost brushed my leg. I froze, too terrified even to scream, then realized that it was just some small animal that I had frightened—a fox, perhaps, or a rabbit. I found myself swaying a little, swaying dizzily. I collapsed to my knees, desperately willing the dizziness to intensify, the transferal to come . . .

I had closed my eyes. When I opened them, the dirt path and the trees were still there. I got up wearily and began walking again.

When I had been walking for a while, I began to wonder whether I had passed the cabin without seeing it. And I began to hear noises—not birds or animals this time, not anything I could identify at first. But whatever it was, it seemed to be coming closer. It took me a ridiculously long time to realize that it was the sound of horses moving slowly down the road toward me.

Just in time, I dove into the bushes.

I lay still, listening, shaking a little, wondering whether the approaching horsemen had seen me. I could see them now, dark, slowly moving shapes going in a direction that would eventually take them past me on toward the Weylin house. And if they saw me, they might take me along with them as their prisoner. Blacks here were assumed to be slaves unless they could prove they were free—unless they had their free papers. Paperless blacks were fair game for any white.

And these riders were white. I could see that in the moonlight as they came near. Then they turned and headed into the woods just a few feet from me. I watched and waited, keeping absolutely still until they had all gone past. Eight white men out for a leisurely ride in the middle of the night. Eight white men going into the woods in the area where the Greenwood cabin was supposed to be.

After a moment of indecision, I got up and followed them, moving carefully from tree to tree. I was both afraid of them and glad of their human presence. Dangerous as they could be to me, somehow, they did not seem as threatening as the dark shadowy woods with its strange sounds, its unknowns.

As I had expected, the men led me to a small log cabin in a moonlit clearing in the woods. Rufus had told me I could reach the Greenwood cabin by way of the road, but he hadn't told me the cabin sat back out of sight of the road. Maybe it didn't. Maybe this was someone else's cabin. I half hoped it was because if the people inside this cabin were black, they were almost certainly in for trouble.

Four of the riders dismounted and went to hit and kick the door. When no one answered their pounding, two of them began trying to break it down. It looked like a heavy door —one more likely to break the men's shoulders than it was to give. But apparently the latch used to keep it shut wasn't heavy. There was a sound of splintering wood, and the door swung inward. The four men rushed in with it, and a moment later, three people were shoved, almost thrown out of the cabin. Two of them—a man and woman—were caught by the riders outside who had dismounted, apparently expecting them. The third, a little girl dressed in something long and light colored, was allowed to fall to the ground and scramble away, ignored by the men. She moved to within a few yards of where I lay in the bushes near the edge of the clearing.

There was talk in the clearing now, and I began to distinguish words over the distance and through the unfamiliar accents.

"No pass," said one of the riders. "He sneaked off."

"No, Master," pleaded one of those from the cabin—clearly a black man speaking to whites. "I had a pass. I had . . ."

One of the whites hit him in the face. Two others held him, and he sagged between them. More talk.

"If you had a pass, where is it?"

"Don't know. Must have dropped it coming here."

They hustled the man to a tree so close to me that I lay flat on the ground, stiff with fear. With just a little bad luck, one of the whites would spot me, or, in the darkness, fail to spot me and step on me.

The man was forced to hug the tree, and his hands were tied to prevent him from letting go. The man was naked, apparently dragged from bed. I looked at the woman who still stood back beside the cabin and saw that she had managed to wrap herself in something. A blanket, perhaps. As I noticed it, one of the whites tore it from her. She said something in a voice so soft that all I caught was her tone of protest.

"Shut your mouth!" said the man who had taken her blanket. He threw it on the ground. "Who the hell do you think you are, anyway?"

One of the other men joined in. "What do you think you've got that we haven't seen before?"

There was raucous laughter.

"Seen more and better," someone else added.

There were obscenities, more laughter.

By now, the man had been securely tied to the tree. One of the whites went to his horse to get what proved to be a whip. He cracked it once in the air, apparently for his own amusement, then brought it down across the back of the black man. The man's body convulsed, but the only sound he made was a gasp. He took several more blows with no outcry, but I could hear his breathing, hard and quick.

Behind him, his child wept noisily against her mother's leg, but the woman, like her husband, was silent. She clutched the child to her and stood, head down, refusing to watch the beating.

Then the man's resolve broke. He began to moan—low gut-wrenching sounds torn from him against his will. Finally, he began to scream.

I could literally smell his sweat, hear every ragged breath, every cry, every cut of the whip. I could see his body jerking, convulsing, straining against the rope as his screaming went on and on. My stomach heaved, and I had to force myself to stay where I was and keep quiet. Why didn't they stop!

"Please, Master," the man begged. "For Godsake, Master, please . . ."

I shut my eyes and tensed my muscles against an urge to vomit.

I had seen people beaten on television and in the movies. I had seen the too-red blood substitute streaked across their backs and heard their well-rehearsed screams. But I hadn't lain nearby and smelled their sweat or heard them pleading and praying, shamed before their families and themselves. I was probably less prepared for the reality than the child crying not far from me. In fact, she and I were reacting very much alike. My face too was wet with tears. And my mind was darting from one thought to another, trying to tune out the whipping. At one point, this last cowardice even brought me something useful. A name for whites who rode through the night in the ante bellum South, breaking in doors and beating and otherwise torturing black people.

Patrols. Groups of young whites who ostensibly maintained order among the slaves. Patrols. Forerunners of the Ku Klux Klan.

The man's screaming stopped.

After a moment, I looked up and saw that the patrollers were untying him. He continued to lean against the tree even when the rope was off him until one of the patrollers pulled him around and tied his hands in front of him. Then, still holding the other end of the rope, the patroller mounted his horse and rode away half-dragging his captive behind him. The rest of the patrol mounted and followed except for one who was having some kind of low-voiced discussion with the woman. Evidently, the discussion didn't go the way the man wanted because before he rode after the others, he punched the woman in the face exactly as her husband had been punched earlier. The woman collapsed to the ground. The patroller rode away and left her there.

The patrol and its stumbling captive headed back to the road, slanting off toward the Weylin house. If they had gone back exactly the way they came, they would have either gone over me or driven me from my cover. I was lucky—and stupid for having gotten so close. I wondered whether the captive black man belonged to Tom Weylin. That might explain Rufus's friendship with the child, Alice. That is, if this child was Alice. If this was the right cabin. Whether it was or not, though, the woman, unconscious and abandoned, was in need of help. I got up and went over to her.

The child, who had been kneeling beside her, jumped up to run away.

"Alice!" I called softly.

She stopped, peered at me through the darkness. She was Alice, then. These people were my relatives, my ancestors. And this place could be my refuge.

4

"I'm a friend, Alice," I said as I knelt and turned the unconscious woman's head to a more comfortable-looking position. Alice watched me uncertainly, then spoke in a small whispery voice.

"She dead?"

I looked up. The child was younger than Rufus—dark and slender and small. She wiped her nose on her sleeve and sniffed.

"No, she's not dead. Is there water in the house?"

"Yeah."

"Go get me some."

She ran into the cabin and returned a few seconds later with a gourd dipper of water. I wet the mother's face a little, washed blood from around her nose and mouth. From what I could see of her, she seemed to be about my age, slender like her child, like me, in fact. And like me, she was fine-boned, probably not as strong as she needed to be to survive in this era. But she was surviving, however painfully. Maybe she would help me learn how.

She regained consciousness slowly, first moaning, then crying out, "Alice! Alice!"

"Mama?" said the child tentatively.

The woman's eyes opened wider, and she stared at me. "Who are you?"

"A friend. I came here to ask for help, but right now, I'd rather give it. When you feel able to get up, I'll help you inside."

"I said who are you!" Her voice had hardened.

"My name is Dana. I'm a freewoman."

I was on my knees beside her now, and I saw her look at my blouse, my pants, my shoes—which for unpacking and working around the house happened to be an old pair of desert boots. She took a good look at me, then judged me.

"A runaway, you mean."

"That's what the patrollers would say because I have no papers. But I'm free, born free, intending to stay free."

"You'll get me in trouble!"

"Not tonight. You've already had your trouble for tonight." I hesitated, bit my lip, then said softly, "Please don't turn me away."

The woman said nothing for several seconds. I saw her glance over at her daughter, then touch her own face and wipe away blood from the corner of her mouth. "Wasn't going to turn you 'way," she said softly.

"Thank you."

I helped her up and into the cabin. Refuge then. A few hours of peace. Perhaps tomorrow night, I could go on behaving like the runaway this woman thought I was. Perhaps from her, I could learn the quickest, safest way North.

The cabin was dark except for a dying fire in the fireplace, but the woman made her way to her bed without trouble.

"Alice!" she called out.

"Here I am, Mama."

"Put a log on the fire."

I watched the child obey, her long gown hanging dangerously near hot coals. Rufus's friend was at least as careless with fire as he was.

Rufus. His name brought back all my fear and confusion and longing to go home. Would I really have to go all the way to some northern state to find peace? And if I did, what kind of peace would it be? The restricted North was better for blacks than the slave South, but not much better.

"Why did you come here?" the woman asked. "Who sent you?"

I stared into the fire frowning. I could hear her moving around behind me, probably putting on clothing. "The boy," I said softly. "Rufus Weylin."

The small noises stopped. There was silence for a moment. I knew I had taken a risk telling her about Rufus. Probably a foolish risk. I wondered why I had done it. "No one knows about me but him," I continued.

The fire began to flare up around Alice's small log. The log cracked and sputtered and filled the silence until Alice said, "Mister Rufe won't tell." She shrugged. "He never tells nothing."

And there in her words was a reason for the risk I had taken. I hadn't thought of it until now, but if Rufus was one to tell what he shouldn't, Alice's mother should know so that she could either hide me or send me away. I waited to see what she would say.

"You sure the father didn't see you?" she asked. And that had to mean that she agreed with Alice, that Rufus was all right. Tom Weylin had probably marked his son more than he knew with that whip.

"Would I be here if the father had seen me?" I asked.

"Guess not."

I turned to look at her. She wore a gown now, long and white like her daughter's. She sat on the edge of her bed watching me. There was a table near me made of thick smooth planks, and a bench made from a section of split log. I sat down on the bench. "Does Tom Weylin own your husband?" I asked.

She nodded sadly. "You saw?"

"Yes."

"He shouldn't have come. I told him not to."

"Did he really have a pass?"

She gave a bitter laugh. "No. He won't get one either. Not to come see me. Mister Tom said for him to choose a new wife there on the plantation. That way, Mister Tom'll own all his children."

I looked at Alice. The woman followed my gaze. "He'll never own a child of mine," she said flatly.

I wondered. They seemed so vulnerable here. I doubted that this was their first visit from the patrol, or their last. In a place like this, how could the woman be sure of anything. And then there was history. Rufus and Alice would get together somehow.

"Where are you from?" asked the woman suddenly. "The way you talk, you not from 'round here."

The new subject caught me by surprise and I almost said Los Angeles. "New York," I lied quietly. In 1815, California was nothing more than a distant Spanish colony—a colony this woman had probably never heard of.

"That's a long way off," said the woman.

"My husband is there." Where had that lie come from? And I had said it with all the longing I felt for Kevin who was now too far away for me to reach through any effort of my own.

The woman came over and stood staring down at me. She looked tall and straight and grim and years older.

"They carried you off?" she asked.

"Yes." Maybe in a way I had been kidnapped.

"You sure they didn't get him too?"

"Just me. I'm sure."

"And now you're going back."

"Yes!" fiercely, hopefully. "Yes!" Lie and truth had merged.

There was silence. The woman looked at her daughter, then back at me. "You stay here until tomorrow night," she said. "Then there's another place you can head for. They'll let you have some food and . . . oh!" She looked contrite. "You must be hungry now. I'll get you some . . ."

"No, I'm not hungry. Just tired."

"Get into bed then. Alice, you too. There's room for all of us there . . . now." She went to the child and began brushing off some of the dirt Alice had brought in from outside. I saw her close her eyes for a moment, then glance at the door. "Dana . . . you said your name was Dana?"

"Yes."

"I forgot the blanket," she said. "I left it outside when . . . I left it outside."

"I'll get it," I said. I went to the door and looked outside. The blanket lay where the patroller had thrown it—on the ground not far from the house. I went over to pick it up, but just as I reached it, someone grabbed me and swung me around. Suddenly, I was facing a young white man, broad-faced, dark-haired, stocky, and about half-a-foot taller than I was.

"What in hell . . . ?" he sputtered. "You . . . you're not the one." He peered at me as though he wasn't sure. Apparently, I looked enough like Alice's mother to confuse him—briefly. "Who are you?" he demanded. "What are you doing here?"

What to do? He held me easily, barely noticing my efforts to pull away. "I live here," I lied. "What are *you* doing here?" I thought he'd be more likely to believe me if I sounded indignant.

Instead, he slapped me stunningly with one hand while he held me with the other. He spoke very softly. "You got no manners, nigger, I'll teach you some!"

I said nothing. My ears still rang from his blow, but I heard him say,

"You could be her sister, her twin sister, almost."

That seemed to be a good thing for him to think, so I kept silent. Silence seemed safest anyway.

"Her sister dressed up like a boy!" He began to smile. "Her runaway sister. I wonder what you're worth."

I panicked. Having him catch and hold me was bad enough. Now he meant to turn me in as a runaway . . . I dug the nails of my free hand into his arm and tore the flesh from elbow to wrist.

Surprise and pain made the man loosen his grip on me slightly, and I wrenched away.

I heard him yell, heard him start after me.

I ran mindlessly toward the cabin door only to find Alice's mother there barring my way.

"Don't come in here," she whispered. "Please don't come in here."

I had no chance to go in. The man caught me, pulled me backward, threw me to the ground. He would have kicked me, but I rolled aside and jumped to my feet. Terror gave me speed and agility I never knew I had.

Again I ran, this time for the trees. I didn't know where I was going, but the sounds of the man behind me sent me zigzagging on. Now I longed for darker denser woods that I could lose myself in.

The man tackled me and brought me down hard. At first, I lay stunned, unable to move or defend myself even when he began hitting me, punching me with his fists. I had never been beaten that way before—would never have thought I could absorb so much punishment without losing consciousness.

When I tried to scramble away, he pulled me back. When I tried to push him away, he hardly seemed to notice. At one point, I did get his attention though. He had leaned down close to me, pinning me flat on my back. I raised my hands to his face, my fingers partly covering his eyes. In that instant, I knew I could stop him, cripple him, in this primitive age, destroy him.

His eyes.

I had only to move my fingers a little and jab them into the soft tissues, gouge away his sight and give him more agony than he was giving me.

But I couldn't do it. The thought sickened me, froze my hands where they were. I had to do it! But I couldn't . . .

The man knocked my hands from his face and moved back

from me—and I cursed myself for my utter stupidity. My chance was gone, and I'd done nothing. My squeamishness belonged in another age, but I'd brought it along with me. Now I would be sold into slavery because I didn't have the stomach to defend myself in the most effective way. Slavery! And there was a more immediate threat.

The man had stopped beating me. Now he simply kept a tight hold on me and looked at me. I could see that I had left a few scratches on his face. Shallow insignificant scratches. The man rubbed his hand across them, looked at the blood, then looked at me.

"You know you're going to pay for that, don't you?" he said.

I said nothing. Stupidity was what I would pay for, if anything.

"I guess you'll do as well as your sister," he said. "I came back for her, but you're just like her."

That told me who he probably was. One of the patrollers —the one who had hit Alice's mother, probably. He reached out and ripped my blouse open. Buttons flew everywhere, but I didn't move. I understood what the man was going to do. He was going to display some stupidity of his own. He was going to give me another chance to destroy him. I was almost relieved.

He tore loose my bra and I prepared to move. Just one quick lunge. Then suddenly, for no reason that I could see, he reared above me, fist drawn back to hit me again. I jerked my head aside, hit it on something hard just as his fist glanced off my jaw.

The new pain shattered my resolve, sent me scrambling away again. I was only able to move a few inches before he pinned me down, but that was far enough for me to discover that the thing I had hit my head on was a heavy stick—a tree limb, perhaps. I grasped it with both bands and brought it down as hard as I could on his head.

He collapsed across my body.

I lay still, panting, trying to find the strength to get up and run. The man had a horse around somewhere. If I could find it . . .

I dragged myself from beneath his heavy body and tried to stand up. Halfway up, I felt myself losing consciousness, falling back. I caught hold of a tree and willed myself to stay conscious. If the man came to and found me nearby, he would kill me. He would surely kill me! But I couldn't keep my hold on the tree. I fell, slowly it seemed, into a deep starless darkness.

5

Pain dragged me back to consciousness. At first, it was all I was aware of; every part of my body hurt. Then I saw a blurred face above me—the face of a man—and I panicked.

I scrambled away, kicking him, clawing the hands that reached out for me, trying to bite, lunging up toward his eyes. I could do it now. I could do anything.

"Dana!"

I froze. My name? No patroller would know that.

"Dana, look at me for Godsake!"

Kevin! It was Kevin's voice! I stared upward, managed to focus on him clearly at last. I was at home. I was lying on my own bed, bloody and dirty, but safe. Safe!

Kevin lay half on top of me, holding me, smearing himself with my blood and his own. I could see where I had scratched his face—so near the eye.

"Kevin, I'm sorry!"

"Are you all right now?"

"Yes. I thought . . . I thought you were the patroller."

"The what?"

"The . . . I'll tell you later. God, I hurt, and I'm so tired. But it doesn't matter. I'm home."

"You were gone two or three minutes this time. I didn't know what to think. You don't know how good it is to have you back again."

"Two or three minutes?"

"Almost three minutes. I watched the clock. But it seemed to be longer."

I closed my eyes in pain and weariness. It hadn't just seemed longer to me. I had been gone for hours and I knew it. But at that moment, I couldn't have argued it. I couldn't have argued anything. The surge of strength that helped me to fight when I thought I was fighting for my life was gone.

"I'm going to take you to the hospital," said Kevin. "I don't know how I'm going to explain you, but you need help."

"No."

He got up. I felt him lift me.

"No, Kevin, please."

"Listen, don't be afraid. I'll be with you."

"No. Look, all he did was hit me a few times. I'll be all right." Suddenly I had strength again, now that I needed it. "Kevin, I went from here the first time, and this second time. And I came back here. What will happen if I go from the hospital and come back there?"

"Probably nothing." But he had stopped. "No one who sees you leave or come back will believe it. And they wouldn't dare tell anybody."

"Please. Just let me sleep. That's all I need really—rest. The cuts and bruises will heal. I'll be fine."

He took me back to the bed, probably against his better judgment, and put me down. "How long was it for you?" he asked.

"Hours. But it was only bad at the end."

"Who did this to you?"

"A patroller. He . . . he thought I was a runaway." I frowned. "I have to sleep, Kevin. I'll make more sense in the morning, I promise." My voice trailed away.

"Dana!"

I jumped, tried to refocus my attention on him.

"Did he rape you?"

I sighed. "No. I hit him with a stick—knocked him out. Let me sleep."

"Wait a minute . . ."

I seemed to drift away from him. It became too much trouble for me to go on listening and trying to understand, too much trouble to answer.

I sighed again and closed my eyes. I heard him get up and go away, heard water running somewhere. Then I slept.

6

I was clean when I awoke before dawn the next morning. I was wearing an old flannel nightgown that I hadn't worn since Kevin and I were married and that I'd never worn in June. On one side of me was a canvas tote bag containing a pair of pants, a blouse, underclothing, a sweater, shoes, and

the biggest switchblade knife I had ever seen. The tote bag
was tied to my waist with a length of cord. On the other side
of me lay Kevin, still asleep. But he woke up when I kissed
him.

"You're still here," he said with obvious relief, and he
hugged me, reminding me painfully of a few bruises. Then he
remembered, let me go, and switched on the light. "How do
you feel?"

"Pretty well." I sat up, got out of bed, managed to stand up
for a moment. Then I got back under the cover. "I'm healing."

"Good. You're rested, you're healing, now you can tell me
what the hell happened to you. And what's a patroller? All I
could think of was the Highway Patrol."

I thought back to my reading. "A patroller is . . . was a
white man, usually young, often poor, sometimes drunk. He
was a member of a group of such men organized to keep the
blacks in line."

"What?"

"Patrollers made sure the slaves were where they were supposed to be at night, and they punished those who weren't.
They chased down runaways—for a fee. And sometimes they
just raised hell, had a little fun terrorizing people who weren't
allowed to fight back."

Kevin leaned on one elbow and looked down at me. "What
are you talking about? Where were you?"

"In Maryland. Somewhere on the Eastern Shore if I understood Rufus."

"Maryland! Three thousand miles away in . . . in what? A
few minutes?"

"More than three thousand miles. More than any number
of miles." I moved to relieve pressure on an especially tender
bruise. "Let me tell you all of it."

I remembered it for him in detail as I had the first time.
Again, he listened without interrupting. This time when I finished, he just shook his head.

"This is getting crazier and crazier," he muttered.

"Not to me."

He glanced at me sidelong.

"To me, it's getting more and more believable. I don't like it.
I don't want to be in the middle of it. I don't understand how

it can be happening, but it's real. It hurts too much not to be. And . . . and my ancestors, for Godsake!"

"Maybe."

"Kevin, I can show you the old Bible."

"But the fact is, you had already seen the Bible. You knew about those people—knew their names, knew they were Marylanders, knew . . ."

"What the hell is that supposed to prove! That I was hallucinating and weaving in the names of my ancestors? I'd like to give you some of this pain that I must still be hallucinating."

He put an arm over my chest, resting it on unbruised flesh. After a while, he said, "Do you honestly believe you traveled back over a century in time and crossed three thousand miles of space to see your dead ancestors?"

I moved uncomfortably. "Yes," I whispered. "No matter how it sounds, no matter what you think, it happened. And you're not helping me deal with it by laughing."

"I'm not laughing."

"They were my ancestors. Even that damn parasite, the patroller, saw the resemblance between me and Alice's mother."

He said nothing.

"I'll tell you . . . I wouldn't dare act as though they weren't my ancestors. I wouldn't let anything happen to them, the boy or girl, if I could possibly prevent it."

"You wouldn't anyway."

"Kevin, take this seriously, please!"

"I am. Anything I can do to help you, I'll do."

"Believe me!"

He sighed. "It's like you just said."

"What?"

"I wouldn't dare act as though I didn't believe. After all, when you vanish from here, you must go someplace. If that place is where you think it is—back to the ante bellum South —then we've got to find a way to protect you while you're there."

I moved closer to him, relieved, content with even such grudging acceptance. He had become my anchor, suddenly, my tie to my own world. He couldn't have known how much I needed him firmly on my side.

"I'm not sure it's possible for a lone black woman—or even a black man—to be protected in that place," I said. "But if you have an idea, I'll be glad to hear it."

He said nothing for several seconds. Then he reached over me into the canvas bag and brought out the switchblade. "This might improve your chances—if you can bring yourself to use it."

"I've seen it."

"Can you use it?"

"You mean, *will* I use it."

"That too."

"Yes. Before last night, I might not have been sure, but now, yes."

He got up, left the room for a moment, and came back with two wooden rulers. "Show me," he said.

I untied the cord of the canvas bag and got up, discovering sore muscles as I moved. I limped over to him, took one of the rulers, looked at it, rubbed my face groggily, and in a sudden slashing motion, drew the ruler across his abdomen just as he was opening his mouth to speak.

"That's it," I said.

He frowned.

"Kevin, I'm not going to be in any fair fights."

He said nothing.

"You understand? I'm a poor dumb scared nigger until I get my chance. They won't even see the knife if I have my way. Not until it's too late."

He shook his head. "What else don't I know about you?"

I shrugged and got back into bed. "I've been watching the violence of this time go by on the screen long enough to have picked up a few things."

"Glad to hear it."

"It doesn't matter much."

He sat down next to where I lay. "What do you mean?"

"That most of the people around Rufus know more about real violence than the screenwriters of today will ever know."

"That's . . . debatable."

"I just can't make myself believe I can survive in that place. Not with a knife, not even with a gun."

He took a deep breath. "Look, if you're drawn back there

again, what can you do but try to survive? You're not going to just let them kill you."

"Oh, they won't kill me. Not unless I'm silly enough to resist the other things they'd rather do—like raping me, throwing me into jail as a runaway, and then selling me to the highest bidder when they see that my owner isn't coming to claim me." I rubbed my forehead. "I almost wish I hadn't read about it."

"But it doesn't have to happen that way. There were free blacks. You could pose as one of them."

"Free blacks had papers to prove they were free."

"You could have papers too. We could forge something . . ."

"If we knew what to forge. I mean, a certificate of freedom is what we need, but I don't know what they looked like. I've read about them, but I've never seen one."

He got up and went to the living room. Moments later, he came back and dumped an armload of books on the bed. "I brought everything we had on black history," he said. "Start hunting."

There were ten books. We checked indexes and even leafed through some of the books page by page to be sure. Nothing. I hadn't really thought there would be anything in these books. I hadn't read them all, but I'd at least glanced through them before.

"We'll have to go to the library then," said Kevin. "We'll go today as soon as it's open."

"If I'm still here when it opens."

He put the books on the floor and got back under the cover. Then he lay there frowning at me. "What about the pass Alice's father was supposed to have?"

"A pass . . . that was just written permission for a slave to be somewhere other than at home at a certain time."

"Sounds like just a note."

"It is," I said. "You've got it! One of the reasons it was against the law in some states to teach slaves to read and write was that they might escape by writing themselves passes. Some did escape that way." I got up, went to Kevin's office and took a small scratch pad and a new pen from his desk and the large atlas from his bookcase.

"I'm going to tear Maryland out," I told him as I returned.

"Go ahead. I wish I had a road atlas for you. The roads in it wouldn't exist in those days but it might show you the easiest way through the country."

"This one shows main highways. Shows a lot of rivers too, and in eighteen fifteen there were probably not many bridges." I looked closely at it, then got up again.

"What now?" asked Kevin.

"Encyclopedia. I want to see when the Pennsylvania Railroad built this nice long track through the peninsula. I'd have to go into Delaware to pick it up, but it would take me right into Pennsylvania."

"Forget it," he said. "Eighteen fifteen is too early for railroads."

I looked anyway and found that the Pennsylvania Railroad hadn't even been begun until 1846. I went back to bed and stuffed the pen, the map, and the scratch pad into my canvas bag.

"Tie that cord around you again," said Kevin.

I obeyed silently.

"I think we may have missed something," he said. "Getting home may be simpler for you than you realize."

"Getting home? Here?"

"Here. You may have more control over your returning than you think."

"I don't have any control at all."

"You might. Listen, remember the rabbit or whatever it was that you said ran across the road in front of you?"

"Yes."

"It scared you."

"Terrified me. For a second, I thought it was . . . I don't know, something dangerous."

"And your fear made you dizzy, and you thought you were coming home. Does fear usually make you dizzy?"

"No."

"I don't think it did this time either—at least not in any normal way. I think you were right. You did almost come home. Your fear almost sent you home."

"But . . . but I was afraid the whole time I was there. And I was scared half out of my mind while that patroller was beating me. But I didn't come home until I'd knocked him out —saved myself."

"Not too helpful."

"No."

"But look, was your fight with the patroller really over? You said you were afraid that if he found you there, passed out, he'd kill you."

"He would have, for revenge. I fought back, actually hurt him. I can't believe he'd let me get away with that."

"You may be right."

"I am right."

"The point is, you believe you are."

"Kevin . . ."

"Wait. Hear me out. You believed your life was in danger, that the patroller would kill you. And on your last trip, you believed your life was in danger when you found Rufus's father aiming a rifle at you."

"Yes."

"And even with the animal—you mistook it for something dangerous."

"But I saw it in time—just as a dark blur, but clearly enough to see that it was small and harmless. And I see what you're saying."

"That you might have been better off if your animal had been a snake. Your danger then—or assumed danger—might have sent you home before you ever met the patroller."

"Then . . . Rufus's fear of death calls me to him, and my own fear of death sends me home."

"So it seems."

"That doesn't really help, you know."

"It could."

"Think about it, Kevin. If the thing I'm afraid of isn't really dangerous—a rabbit instead of a snake—then I stay where I am. If it is dangerous, it's liable to kill me before I get home. Going home does take a while, you know. I have to get through the dizziness, the nausea . . ."

"Seconds."

"Seconds count when something is trying to kill you. I wouldn't dare put myself in danger in the hope of getting home before the ax fell. And if I got into trouble by accident, I wouldn't dare just wait passively to be saved. I might wind up coming home in pieces."

"Yes . . . I see your point."

I sighed. "So the more I think about it, the harder it is for me to believe I could survive even a few more trips to a place like that. There's just too much that could go wrong."

"Will you stop that! Look, your ancestors survived that era —survived it with fewer advantages than you have. You're no less than they are."

"In a way I am."

"What way?"

"Strength. Endurance. To survive, my ancestors had to put up with more than I ever could. Much more. You know what I mean."

"No, I don't," he said with annoyance. "You're working yourself into a mood that could be suicidal if you're not careful."

"Oh, but I'm talking about suicide, Kevin—suicide or worse. For instance, I would have used your knife against that patroller last night if I'd had it. I would have killed him. That would have ended the immediate danger to me and I probably wouldn't have come home. But if that patroller's friends had caught me, they would have killed me. And if they hadn't caught me, they would probably have gone after Alice's mother. They . . . they may have anyway. So either I would have died, or I would have caused another innocent person to die."

"But the patroller was trying to . . ." He stopped, looked at me. "I see."

"Good."

There was a long silence. He pulled me closer to him. "Do I really look like that patroller?"

"No."

"Do I look like someone you can come home to from where you may be going?"

"I need you here to come home to. I've already learned that."

He gave me a long thoughtful look. "Just keep coming home," he said finally. "I need you here too."

The Fall

I THINK KEVIN was as lonely and out of place as I was when I met him, though he was handling it better. But then, he was about to escape.

I was working out of a casual labor agency—we regulars called it a slave market. Actually, it was just the opposite of slavery. The people who ran it couldn't have cared less whether or not you showed up to do the work they offered. They always had more job hunters than jobs anyway. If you wanted them to think about using you, you went to their office around six in the morning, signed in, and sat down to wait. Waiting with you were winos trying to work themselves into a few more bottles, poor women with children trying to supplement their welfare checks, kids trying to get a first job, older people who'd lost one job too many, and usually a poor crazy old street lady who talked to herself constantly and who wasn't going to be hired no matter what because she only wore one shoe.

You sat and sat until the dispatcher either sent you out on a job or sent you home. Home meant no money. Put another potato in the oven. Or in desperation, sell some blood at one of the store fronts down the street from the agency. I had only done that once.

Getting sent out meant the minimum wage—minus Uncle Sam's share—for as many hours as you were needed. You swept floors, stuffed envelopes, took inventory, washed dishes, sorted potato chips (really!), cleaned toilets, marked prices on merchandise . . . you did whatever you were sent out to do. It was nearly always mindless work, and as far as most employers were concerned, it was done by mindless people. Nonpeople rented for a few hours, a few days, a few weeks. It didn't matter.

I did the work, I went home, I ate, and then slept for a few hours. Finally, I got up and wrote. At one or two in the morning, I was fully awake, fully alive, and busy working on my novel. During the day, I carried a little box of No Doz. I kept awake with them, but not very wide awake. The first thing

49

Kevin ever said to me was, "Why do you go around looking
like a zombie all the time?"

He was just one of several regular employees at an auto-parts
warehouse where a group of us from the agency were doing an
inventory. I was wandering around between shelves of nuts,
bolts, hubcaps, chrome, and heaven knew what else checking
other people's work. I had a habit of showing up every day and
of being able to count, so the supervisor decided that zombie
or not, I should check the others. He was right. People came in
after a hard night of drinking and counted five units per clearly-
marked, fifty-unit container.

"Zombie?" I repeated looking up from a tray of short black
wires at Kevin.

"You look like you sleepwalk through the day," he said. "Are
you high on something or what?"

He was just a stock helper or some such bottom-of-the-
ladder type. He had no authority over me, and I didn't owe
him any explanations.

"I do my work," I said quietly. I turned back to the wires,
counted them, corrected the inventory slip, initialed it, and
moved down to the next shelf.

"Buz told me you were a writer," said the voice that I
thought had gone away.

"Look, I can't count with you talking to me." I pulled out a
tray full of large screws—twenty-five to a box.

"Take a break."

"Did you see that agency guy they sent home yesterday? He
took one break too many. Unfortunately, I need this job."

"Are you a writer?"

"I'm a joke as far as Buz is concerned. He thinks people
are strange if they even read books. Besides," I added bitterly,
"what would a writer be doing working out of a slave market?"

"Keeping herself in rent and hamburgers, I guess. That's
what I'm doing working at a warehouse."

I woke up a little then and really looked at him. He was an
unusual-looking white man, his face young, almost unlined,
but his hair completely gray and his eyes so pale as to be almost colorless. He was muscular, well-built, but no taller than
my own five-eight so that I found myself looking directly into
the strange eyes. I looked away startled, wondering whether

I had really seen anger there. Maybe he was more important in the warehouse than I had thought. Maybe he had some authority . . .

"Are you a writer?" I asked.

"I am now," he said. And he smiled. "Just sold a book. I'm getting out of here for good on Friday."

I stared at him with a terrible mixture of envy and frustration. "Congratulations."

"Look," he said, still smiling, "it's almost lunch time. Eat with me. I want to hear about what you're writing."

And he was gone. I hadn't said yes or no, but he was gone.

"Hey!" whispered another voice behind me. Buz. The agency clown when he was sober. Wine put him into some kind of trance, though, and he just sat and stared and looked retarded—which he wasn't, quite. He just didn't give a damn about anything, including himself. He drank up his pay and walked around in rags. Also, he never bathed. "Hey, you two gonna get together and write some books?" he asked, leering.

"Get out of here," I said breathing as shallowly as possible.

"You gonna write some poor-nography together!" He went away laughing.

Later, at one of the round rusting metal tables in the corner of the warehouse that served as the lunch area, I found out more about my new writer friend. Kevin Franklin, his name was, and he'd not only gotten his book published, but he'd made a big paperback sale. He could live on the money while he wrote his next book. He could give up shitwork, hopefully forever . . .

"Why aren't you eating?" he asked when he stopped for breath. The warehouse was in a newly built industrial section of Compton, far enough from coffee shops and hot dog stands to discourage most of us from going out to eat. Some people brought their lunches. Others bought them from the catering truck. I had done neither. All I was having was a cup of the free dishwater coffee available to all the warehouse workers.

"I'm on a diet," I said.

He stared at me for a moment, then got up, motioned me up. "Come on."

"Where?"

"To the truck if it's still there."

"Wait a minute, you don't have to . . ."

"Listen, I've been on that kind of diet."

"I'm all right," I lied, embarrassed. "I don't want anything."

He left me sitting there, went to the truck, and came back with a hamburger, milk, a small wedge of apple pie.

"Eat," he said. "I'm still not rich enough to waste money, so eat."

To my own surprise, I ate. I hadn't intended to. I was caffeine jittery and surly and perfectly capable of wasting his money. After all, I'd told him not to spend it. But I ate.

Buz sidled by. "Hey," he said, low-voiced. "Porn!" He moved on.

"What?" said Kevin.

"Nothing," I said. "He's crazy." Then, "Thanks for the lunch."

"Sure. Now tell me, what is it you write?"

"Short stories, so far. But I'm working on a novel."

"Naturally. Have any of your stories sold?"

"Some. To little magazines no one ever heard of. The kind that pay in copies of the magazine."

He shook his head. "You're going to starve."

"No. After a while, I'll convince myself that my aunt and uncle were right."

"About what? That you should have been an accountant?"

I surprised myself again by laughing aloud. The food was reviving me. "They didn't think of accounting," I said. "But they would have approved of it. It's what they would call sensible. They wanted me to be a nurse, a secretary, or a teacher like my mother. At the very best, a teacher."

"Yes." He sighed. "I was supposed to be an engineer, myself."

"That's better, at least."

"Not to me."

"Well anyway, now you have proof that you were right."

He shrugged and didn't tell me what he would later—that his parents, like mine, were dead. They had died years before in an auto accident still hoping that he might come to his senses and become an engineer.

"My aunt and uncle said I could write in my spare time if I wanted to," I told him. "Meanwhile, for the real future, I was to take something sensible in school if I expected them

to support me. I went from the nursing program into a secretarial major, and from there to elementary education. All in
two years. It was pretty bad. So was I."

"What did you do?" he asked. "Flunk out?"

I choked on a piece of pie crust. "Of course not! I always got
good grades. They just didn't mean anything to me. I couldn't
manufacture enough interest in the subjects to keep me going.
Finally, I got a job, moved away from home, and quit school. I
still take extension classes at UCLA, though, when I can afford
them. Writing classes."

"Is this the job you got?"

"No, I worked for a while at an aerospace company. I was
just a clerk-typist, but I talked my way into their publicity
office. I was doing articles for their company newspaper and
press releases to send out. They were glad to have me do it
once I showed them I could. They had a writer for the price of
a clerk-typist."

"Sounds like something you could have stayed with and
moved up."

"I meant to. Ordinary clerical work, I couldn't stand, but
that was good. Then about a year ago, they laid off the whole
department."

He laughed, but it sounded like sympathetic laughter.

Buz, coming back from the coffee machine muttered,
"Chocolate and vanilla porn!"

I closed my eyes in exasperation. He always did that. Started
a "joke" that wasn't funny to begin with, then beat it to death.
"God, I wish he'd get drunk and shut up!"

"Does getting drunk shut him up?" asked Kevin.

I nodded. "Nothing else will do it."

"No matter. I heard what he said this time."

The bell rang ending the lunch half-hour, and he grinned.
He had a grin that completely destroyed the effect of his eyes.
Then he got up and left.

But he came back. He came back all week at breaks, at lunch.
My daily draw back at the agency gave me money enough to
buy my own lunches—and pay my landlady a few dollars—but
I still looked forward to seeing him, talking to him. He had
written and published three novels, he told me, and outside
members of his family, he'd never met anyone who'd read one

of them. They'd brought so little money that he'd gone on taking mindless jobs like this one at the warehouse, and he'd gone on writing—unreasonably, against the advice of saner people. He was like me—a kindred spirit crazy enough to keep on trying. And now, finally . . .

"I'm even crazier than you," he said. "After all I'm older than you. Old enough to recognize failure and stop dreaming, so I'm told."

He was a prematurely gray thirty-four. He had been surprised to learn that I was only twenty-two.

"You look older," he said tactlessly.

"So do you," I muttered.

He laughed. "I'm sorry. But at least it looks good on you."

I wasn't sure what "it" was that looked good on me, but I was glad he liked it. His likes and dislikes were becoming important to me. One of the women from the agency told me with typical slave-market candor that he and I were "the weirdest-looking couple" she had ever seen.

I told her, not too gently, that she hadn't seen much, and that it was none of her business anyway. But from then on, I thought of Kevin and I as a couple. It was pleasant thinking.

My time at the warehouse and his job there ended on the same day. Buz's matchmaking had given us a week together.

"Listen," said Kevin on the last day, "you like plays?"

"Plays? Sure. I wrote a couple while I was in high school. One-acters. Pretty bad."

"I did something like that myself." He took something from his pocket and held it out to me. Tickets. Two tickets to a hit play that had just come to Los Angeles. I think my eyes glittered.

"I don't want you to get away from me just because we won't be co-workers any more," he said. "Tomorrow evening?"

"Tomorrow evening," I agreed.

It was a good evening. I brought him home with me when it was over, and the night was even better. Sometime during the early hours of the next morning when we lay together, tired and content in my bed, I realized that I knew less about loneliness than I had thought—and much less than I would know when he went away.

2

I decided not to go to the library with Kevin to look for forgeable free papers. I was worried about what might happen if Rufus called me from the car while it was moving. Would I arrive in his time still moving, but without the car to protect me? Or would I arrive safe and still, but have trouble when I returned home—because this time the home I returned to might be the middle of a busy street?

I didn't want to find out. So while Kevin got ready to go to the library, I sat on the bed, fully dressed, stuffing a comb, a brush, and a bar of soap into my canvas bag. I was afraid I might be trapped in Rufus's time for a longer period if I went again. My first trip had lasted only a few minutes, my second a few hours. What was next? Days?

Kevin came in to tell me he was going. I didn't want him to leave me alone, but I thought I had done enough whining for one morning. I kept my fear to myself—or I thought I did.

"You feel all right?" he asked me. "You don't look so good."

I had just had my first look in the mirror since the beating, and I didn't think I looked so good either. I opened my mouth to reassure him, but before I could get the words out, I realized that something really was wrong. The room was beginning to darken and spin.

"Oh no," I moaned. I closed my eyes against the sickening dizziness. Then I sat hugging the canvas bag and waiting.

Suddenly, Kevin was beside me holding me. I tried to push him away. I was afraid for him without knowing why. I shouted for him to let me go.

Then the walls around me and the bed beneath me vanished. I lay sprawled on the ground under a tree. Kevin lay beside me still holding me. Between us was the canvas bag.

"Oh God!" I muttered, sitting up. Kevin sat up too and looked around wildly. We were in the woods again, and it was day this time. The country was much like what I remembered from my first trip, though there was no river in sight this time.

"It happened," said Kevin. "It's real!"

I took his hand and held it, glad of its familiarity. And yet I wished he were back at home. In this place, he was probably better protection for me than free papers would have been, but I didn't want him here. I didn't want this place to touch him except through me. But it was too late for that.

I looked around for Rufus, knowing that he must be nearby. He was. And the moment I saw him, I knew I was too late to get him out of trouble this time.

He was lying on the ground, his body curled in a small knot, his hands clutching one leg. Beside him was another boy, black, about twelve years old. All Rufus's attention seemed to be on his leg, but the other boy had seen us. He might even have seen us appear from nowhere. That might be why he looked so frightened now.

I stood up and went over to Rufus. He didn't see me at first. His face was twisted with pain and streaked with tears and dirt, but he wasn't crying aloud. Like the black boy, he looked about twelve years old.

"Rufus."

He looked up, startled. "Dana?"

"Yes." I was surprised that he recognized me after the years that had passed for him.

"I saw you again," he said. "You were on a bed. Just as I started to fall, I saw you."

"You did more than just see me," I said.

"I fell. My leg . . ."

"Who are you?" demanded the other boy.

"She's all right, Nigel," said Rufus. "She's the one I told you about. The one who put out the fire that time."

Nigel looked at me, then back at Rufus. "Can she fix your leg?"

Rufus looked at me questioningly.

"I doubt it," I said, "but let me see anyway." I moved his hands away and as gently as I could, pulled his pants leg up. His leg was discolored and swollen. "Can you move your toes?" I asked.

He tried, managed to move two toes feebly.

"It's broken," commented Kevin. He had come closer to look.

"Yes." I looked at the other boy, Nigel. "Where'd he fall from?"

"There." The boy pointed upward. There was a tree limb hanging high above us. A broken tree limb.

"You know where he lives?" I asked.

"Sure. I live there too."

The boy was probably a slave, I realized, the property of Rufus's family.

"You sure do talk funny," said Nigel.

"Matter of opinion," I said. "Look, if you care what happens to Rufus, you'd better go tell his father to send a . . . a wagon for him. He won't be walking anywhere."

"He could lean on me."

"No. The best way for him to go home is flat on his back —the least painful way, anyhow. You go tell Rufus's father that Rufus broke his leg. Tell him to send for the doctor. We'll stay with Rufus until you get back with the wagon."

"You?" He looked from me to Kevin, making no secret of the fact that he didn't find us all that trustworthy. "How come you're dressed like a man?" he asked me.

"Nigel," said Kevin quietly, "don't worry about how she's dressed. Just go get some help for your friend."

Friend?

Nigel gave Kevin a frightened glance, then looked at Rufus.

"Go, Nigel," whispered Rufus. "It hurts something awful. Say I said for you to go."

Nigel went, finally. Unhappily.

"What's he afraid of?" I asked Rufus. "Will he get into trouble for leaving you?"

"Maybe." Rufus closed his eyes for a moment in pain. "Or for letting me get hurt. I hope not. It depends on whether anybody's made Daddy mad lately."

Well, Daddy hadn't changed. I wasn't looking forward to meeting him at all. At least I wouldn't have to do it alone. I glanced at Kevin. He knelt down beside me to take a closer look at Rufus's leg.

"Good thing he was barefoot," he said. "A shoe would have to be cut off that foot now."

"Who're you?" asked Rufus.

"My name's Kevin—Kevin Franklin."

"Does Dana belong to you now?"

"In a way," said Kevin. "She's my wife."

"Wife?" Rufus squealed.

I sighed. "Kevin, I think we'd better demote me. In this time . . ."

"Niggers can't marry white people!" said Rufus.

I laid a hand on Kevin's arm just in time to stop him from saying whatever he would have said. The look on his face was enough to tell me he should keep quiet.

"The boy learned to talk that way from his mother," I said softly. "And from his father, and probably from the slaves themselves."

"Learned to talk what way?" asked Rufus.

"About niggers," I said. "I don't like that word, remember? Try calling me black or Negro or even colored."

"What's the use of saying all that? And how can you be married to him?"

"Rufe, how'd you like people to call you white trash when they talk to you?"

"What?" He started up angrily, forgetting his leg, then fell back. "I am not trash!" he whispered. "You damn black . . ."

"Hush, Rufe." I put my hand on his shoulder to quiet him. Apparently I'd hit the nerve I'd aimed at. "I didn't say you were trash. I said how'd you like to be called trash. I see you don't like it. I don't like being called nigger either."

He lay silent, frowning at me as though I were speaking a foreign language. Maybe I was.

"Where we come from," I said, "it's vulgar and insulting for whites to call blacks niggers. Also, where we come from, whites and blacks can marry."

"But it's against the law."

"It is here. But it isn't where we come from."

"Where do you come from?"

I looked at Kevin.

"You asked for it," he said.

"You want to try telling him?"

He shook his head. "No point."

"Not for you, maybe. But for me . . ." I thought for a moment trying to find the right words. "This boy and I are liable to have a long association whether we like it or not. I want him to know."

"Good luck."

"Where do you come from?" repeated Rufus. "You sure don't talk like anybody I ever heard."

I frowned, thought, and finally shook my head. "Rufe, I want to tell you, but you probably won't understand. We don't understand ourselves, really."

"I already don't understand," he said. "I don't know how I can see you when you're not here, or how you get here, or anything. My leg hurts so much I can't even think about it."

"Let's wait then. When you feel better . . ."

"When I feel better, maybe you'll be gone. Dana, tell me!"

"All right, I'll try. Have you ever heard of a place called California?"

"Yeah. Mama's cousin went there on a ship."

Luck. "Well, that's where we're from. California. But . . . it's not the California your cousin went to. We're from a California that doesn't exist yet, Rufus. California of nineteen seventy-six."

"What's that?"

"I mean we come from a different time as well as a different place. I told you it was hard to understand."

"But what's nineteen seventy-six?"

"That's the year. That's what year it is for us when we're at home."

"But it's eighteen nineteen. It's eighteen nineteen everywhere. You're talking crazy."

"No doubt. This is a crazy thing that's happened to us. But I'm telling you the truth. We come from a future time and place. I don't know how we get here. We don't want to come. We don't belong here. But when you're in trouble, somehow you reach me, call me, and I come—although as you can see now, I can't always help you." I could have told him about our blood relationship. Maybe I would if I saw him again when he was older. For now, though, I had confused him enough.

"This is crazy stuff," he repeated. He looked at Kevin. "You tell me. Are you from California?"

Kevin nodded. "Yes."

"Then are you Spanish? California is Spanish."

"It is now, but it will be part of the United States eventually, just like Maryland or Pennsylvania."

"When?"

"It will become a state in eighteen fifty."

"But it's only eighteen nineteen. How could you know . . . ?" He broke off, looked from Kevin to me in confusion. "This isn't real," he said. "You're making it all up."

"It's real," said Kevin quietly.

"But how could it be?"

"We don't know. But it is."

He thought for a while looking from one to the other of us. "I don't believe you," he said.

Kevin made a sound that wasn't quite a laugh. "I don't blame you."

I shrugged. "All right, Rufe. I wanted you to know the truth, but I can't blame you for not being able to accept it either."

"Nineteen seventy-six," said the boy slowly. He shook his head and closed his eyes. I wondered why I had bothered to try to convince him. After all, how accepting would I be if I met a man who claimed to be from eighteen nineteen—or two thousand nineteen, for that matter. Time travel was science fiction in nineteen seventy-six. In eighteen nineteen—Rufus was right—it was sheer insanity. No one but a child would even have listened to Kevin and me talk about it.

"If you know California's going to be a state," said Rufus, "you must know some other things that are going to happen."

"We do," I admitted. "Some things. Not very much. We're not historians."

"But you ought to know everything if it already happened in your time."

"How much do you know about seventeen nineteen, Rufe?"

He stared at me blankly.

"People don't learn everything about the times that came before them," I said. "Why should they?"

He sighed. "Tell me something, Dana. I'm trying to believe you."

I dug back into the American history that I had learned both in and out of school. "Well, if this is eighteen nineteen, the President is James Monroe, right?"

"Yeah."

"The next President will be John Quincy Adams."

"When?"

I frowned, calling back more of the list of Presidents I had memorized for no particular reason when I was in school. "In eighteen twenty-four. Monroe had—will have—two terms."

"What else?"

I looked at Kevin.

He shrugged. "All I can think of is something I got from those books we looked through last night. In eighteen twenty, the Missouri Compromise opened the way for Missouri to come into the Union as a slave state and Maine to come in as a free state. Do you have any idea what I'm talking about, Rufus?"

"No, sir."

"I didn't think so. Have you got any money?"

"Money? Me? No."

"Well, you've seen money, haven't you?"

"Yes, sir."

"Coins should have the year they were made stamped on them, even now."

"They do."

Kevin reached into his pocket and brought out a handful of change. He held it out to Rufus and Rufus picked out a few coins. "Nineteen sixty-five," he read, "nineteen sixty-seven, nineteen seventy-one, nineteen seventy. None of them say nineteen seventy-six."

"None of them say eighteen-anything either," said Kevin. "But here." He picked out a bicentennial quarter and handed it to Rufus.

"Seventeen seventy-six, nineteen seventy-six," the boy read. "Two dates."

"The country's two hundred years old in nineteen seventy-six," said Kevin. "Some of the money was changed to commemorate the anniversary. Are you convinced?"

"Well, I guess you could have made these yourself."

Kevin took back his money. "You might not know about Missouri, kid," he said wearily. "But you'd have made a good Missourian."

"What?"

"Just a joke. Hasn't come into fashion yet."

Rufus looked troubled. "I believe you. I don't understand, like Dana said, but I guess I believe."

Kevin sighed. "Thank God."

Rufus looked up at Kevin and managed to grin. "You aren't as bad as I thought you'd be."

"Bad?" Kevin looked at me accusingly.

"I didn't tell him anything about you," I said.

"I saw you," said Rufus. "You were fighting with Dana just before you came here, or . . . it looked like fighting. Did you make all those marks on her face?"

"No, he didn't," I said quickly. "And he and I weren't fighting."

"Wait a minute," said Kevin. "How could he know about that?"

"Like he said." I shrugged. "He saw us before we got here. I don't know how he does it, but he's done it before." I looked down at Rufus. "Have you told anyone else about seeing me?"

"Just Nigel. Nobody else would believe me."

"Good. Best not to tell anyone else about us now either. Nothing about California or nineteen seventy-six." I took Kevin's hand and held it. "We're going to have to fit in as best we can with the people here for as long as we have to stay. That means we're going to have to play the roles you gave us."

"You'll say you belong to him?"

"Yes. I want you to say it too if anyone asks you."

"That's better than saying you're his wife. Nobody would believe that."

Kevin made a sound of disgust. "I wonder how long we'll be stuck here," he muttered. "I think I'm getting homesick already."

"I don't know," I said. "But stay close to me. You got here because you were holding me. I'm afraid that may be the only way you can get home."

3

Rufus's father arrived on a flat-bed wagon, carrying his familiar long rifle—an old muzzleloader, I realized. With him in the wagon was Nigel and a tall stocky black man. Tom Weylin was tall himself, but too lean to be as impressive as his massive slave. Weylin didn't look especially vicious or depraved. Right now, he only looked annoyed. We stood up as he climbed down from the wagon and came to face us.

"What happened here?" he asked suspiciously.

"The boy has broken his leg," said Kevin. "Are you his father?"

"Yes. Who are you?"

"My name's Kevin Franklin." He glanced at me, but caught himself and didn't introduce me. "We came across the two boys right after the accident happened, and I thought we should stay with your son until you came for him."

Weylin grunted and knelt to look at Rufus's leg. "Guess it's broken all right. Wonder how much that'll cost me."

The black man gave him a look of disgust that would surely have angered him if he had seen it.

"What were you doing climbing a damn tree?" Weylin demanded of Rufus.

Rufus stared at him silently.

Weylin muttered something I didn't quite catch. He stood up and gestured sharply to the black man. The man came forward, lifted Rufus gently, and placed him on the wagon. Rufus's face twisted in pain as he was lifted, and he cried out as he was lowered into the wagon. Kevin and I should have made a splint for that leg, I thought belatedly. I followed the black man to the wagon.

Rufus grabbed my arm and held it, obviously trying not to cry. His voice was a husky whisper.

"Don't go, Dana."

I didn't want to go. I liked the boy, and from what I'd heard of early nineteenth-century medicine, they were going to pour some whiskey down him and play tug of war with his leg. And he was going to learn brand new things about pain. If I could give him any comfort by staying with him, I wanted to stay.

But I couldn't.

His father had spoken a few private words with Kevin and was now climbing back up onto the seat of the wagon. He was ready to leave and Kevin and I weren't invited. That didn't say much for Weylin's hospitality. People in his time of widely scattered plantations and even more widely scattered hotels had a reputation for taking in strangers. But then, a man who could look at his injured son and think of nothing but how much the doctor bill would be wasn't likely to be concerned about strangers.

"Come with us," pleaded Rufus. "Daddy, let them come."

Weylin glanced back, annoyed, and I tried gently to loosen Rufus's grip on me. After a moment, I realized that Weylin was looking at me—staring hard at me. Perhaps he was seeing my resemblance to Alice's mother. He couldn't have seen me clearly enough or long enough at the river to recognize me now as the woman he had once come so near shooting. At first, I stared back. Then I looked away, remembering that I was supposed to be a slave. Slaves lowered their eyes respectfully. To stare back was insolent. Or at least, that was what my books said.

"Come along and have dinner with us," Weylin told Kevin. "You may as well. Where were you going to stay the night, anyway?"

"Under the trees if necessary," said Kevin. He and I climbed onto the wagon beside the silent Nigel. "Not much choice, as I told you."

I looked at him, wondering what he had told Weylin. Then I had to catch myself as the black man prodded the horses forward.

"You, girl," Weylin said to me. "What's your name?"

"Dana, sir."

He turned to stare at me again, this time as though I'd said something wrong. "Where do you come from?"

I glanced at Kevin, not wanting to contradict anything he had said. He gave me a slight nod, and I assumed I was free to make up my own lies. "I'm from New York."

Now the look he was giving me was really ugly, and I wondered whether he'd heard a New York accent recently and found mine a poor match. Or was I saying something wrong? I hadn't said ten words to him. What could be wrong?

Weylin looked sharply at Kevin, then turned around and ignored us for the rest of the trip.

We went through the woods to a road, and along the road past a field of tall golden wheat. In the field, slaves, mostly men, worked steadily swinging scythes with attached wooden racks that caught the cut wheat in neat piles. Other slaves, mostly women, followed them tying the wheat into bundles. None of them seemed to pay any attention to us. I looked around for a white overseer and was surprised not to see one. The Weylin house surprised me too when I saw it in daylight. It wasn't white. It had no columns, no porch to speak of. I was almost disappointed. It was a red-brick Georgian Colonial, boxy but handsome in a quiet kind of way, two and a half stories high with dormered windows and a chimney on each end. It wasn't big or imposing enough to be called a mansion. In Los Angeles, in our own time, Kevin and I could have afforded it.

As the wagon took us up to the front steps, I could see the river off to one side and some of the land I had run through a few hours—a few years—before. Scattered trees, unevenly cut grass, the row of cabins far off to one side almost hidden by the trees, the fields, the woods. There were other buildings lined up beside and behind the house opposite the slave cabins. As we stopped, I was almost sent off to one of these.

"Luke," said Weylin to the black man, "take Dana around back and get her something to eat."

"Yes, sir," said the black man softly. "Want me to take Marse Rufe upstairs first?"

"Do what I told you. I'll take him up."

I saw Rufus set his teeth. "I'll see you later," I whispered, but he wouldn't let go of my hand until I spoke to his father.

"Mr. Weylin, I don't mind staying with him. He seems to want me to."

Weylin looked exasperated. "Well, come on then. You can wait with him until the doctor comes." He lifted Rufus with no particular care, and strode up the steps to the house. Kevin followed him.

"You watch out," said the black man softly as I started after them.

I looked at him, surprised, not sure he was talking to me. He was.

"Marse Tom can turn mean mighty quick," he said. "So can the boy, now that he's growing up. Your face looks like maybe you had enough white folks' meanness for a while."

I nodded. "I have, all right. Thanks for the warning."

Nigel had come to stand next to the man, and I realized as I spoke that the two looked much alike, the boy a smaller replica of the man. Father and son, probably. They resembled each other more than Rufus and Tom Weylin did. As I hurried up the steps and into the house, I thought of Rufus and his father, of Rufus becoming his father. It would happen some day in at least one way. Someday Rufus would own the plantation. Someday, he would be the slaveholder, responsible in his own right for what happened to the people who lived in those half-hidden cabins. The boy was literally growing up as I watched —growing up because I watched and because I helped to keep him safe. I was the worst possible guardian for him—a black to watch over him in a society that considered blacks subhuman, a woman to watch over him in a society that considered women perennial children. I would have all I could do to look after myself. But I would help him as best I could. And I would try to keep friendship with him, maybe plant a few ideas in his mind that would help both me and the people who would be his slaves in the years to come. I might even be making things easier for Alice.

Now, I followed Weylin up the stairs to a bedroom—not the same one Rufus had occupied on my last trip. The bed was bigger, its full canopy and draperies blue instead of green. The room itself was bigger. Weylin dumped Rufus onto the bed, ignoring the boy's cries of pain. It did not look as though Weylin was trying to hurt Rufus. He just didn't seem to pay any attention to how he handled the boy—as though he didn't care.

Then, as Weylin was leading Kevin out of the room, a red-haired woman hurried in.

"Where is he?" she demanded breathlessly. "What happened?"

Rufus's mother. I remembered her. She pushed her way into the room just as I was putting Rufus's pillow under his head.

"What are you doing to him?" she cried. "Leave him alone!" She tried to pull me away from her son. She had only one reaction when Rufus was in trouble. One wrong reaction.

Fortunately for both of us, Weylin reached her before I forgot myself and pushed her away from me. He caught her, held her, spoke to her quietly.

"Margaret, now listen. The boy has a broken leg, that's all. There's nothing you can do for a broken leg. I've already sent for the doctor."

Margaret Weylin seemed to calm down a little. She stared at me. "What's she doing here?"

"She belongs to Mr. Kevin Franklin here." Weylin waved a hand presenting Kevin who, to my surprise, bowed slightly to the woman. "Mr. Franklin is the one who found Rufus hurt," Weylin continued. He shrugged. "Rufus wanted the girl to stay with him. Can't do any harm." He turned and walked away. Kevin followed him reluctantly.

The woman may have been listening as her husband spoke, but she didn't look as though she was. She was still staring at me, frowning at me as though she was trying to remember where she'd seen me before. The years hadn't changed her much, and, of course, they hadn't changed me at all. But I didn't expect her to remember. Her glimpse of me had been too brief, and her mind had been on other things.

"I've seen you before," she said.

Hell! "Yes, ma'am, you may have." I looked at Rufus and saw that he was watching us.

"Mama?" he said softly.

The accusing stare vanished, and the woman turned quickly to attend him. "My poor baby," she murmured, cradling his head in her hands. "Seems like everything happens to you, doesn't it? A broken leg!" She looked close to tears. And there was Rufus, swung from his father's indifference to his mother's sugary concern. I wondered whether he was too used to the contrast to find it dizzying.

"Mama, can I have some water?" he asked.

The woman turned to look at me as though I had offended her. "Can't you hear? Get him some water!"

"Yes, ma'am. Where shall I get it?"

She made a sound of disgust and rushed toward me. Or at least I thought she was rushing toward me. When I jumped out of her way, she kept right on going through the door that I had been standing in front of.

I looked after her and shook my head. Then I took the chair that was near the fireplace and put it beside Rufus's bed. I sat down and Rufus looked up at me solemnly.

"Did you ever break your leg?" he asked.

"No. I broke my wrist once, though."

"When they fixed it, did it hurt much?"

I drew a deep breath. "Yes."

"I'm scared."

"So was I," I said remembering. "But . . . Rufe, it won't take long. And when the doctor is finished, the worst will be over."

"Won't it still hurt after?"

"For a while. But it will heal. If you stay off it and give it a chance, it will heal."

Margaret Weylin rushed back into the room with water for Rufus and more hostility for me than I could see any reason for.

"You're to go out to the cookhouse and get some supper!" she told me as I got out of her way. But she made it sound as though she were saying, "You're to go straight to hell!" There was something about me that these people didn't like—except for Rufus. It wasn't just racial. They were used to black people. Maybe I could get Kevin to find out what it was.

"Mama, can't she stay?" asked Rufus.

The woman threw me a dirty look, then turned gentler eyes on her son. "She can come back later," she told him. "Your father wants her downstairs now."

More likely, it was his mother who wanted me downstairs now, and possibly for no more substantial reason than that her son liked me. She gave me another look, and I left the room. The woman would have made me uncomfortable even if she'd liked me. She was too much nervous energy compacted into too small a container. I didn't want to be around when she exploded. But at least she loved Rufus. And he must have been used to her fussing over him. He hadn't seemed to mind.

I found myself in a wide hallway. I could see the stairs a few feet away and I started toward them. Just then, a young black girl in a long blue dress came out of a door at the other end of the hall. She came toward me, staring at me with open curiosity. She wore a blue scarf on her head and she tugged at it as she came toward me.

"Could you tell me where the cookhouse is, please?" I said when she was near enough. She seemed a safer person to ask than Margaret Weylin.

Her eyes opened a little wider and she continued to stare at me. No doubt I sounded as strange to her as I looked.

"The cookhouse?" I said.

She looked me over once more, then started down the stairs without a word. I hesitated, finally followed her because I didn't know what else to do. She was a light-skinned girl no older than fourteen or fifteen. She kept looking back at me, frowning. Once she stopped and turned to face me, her hand tugging absently at her scarf, then moving lower to cover her mouth, and finally dropping to her side again. She looked so frustrated that I realized something was wrong.

"Can you talk?" I asked.

She sighed, shook her head.

"But you can hear and understand."

She nodded, then plucked at my blouse, at my pants. She frowned at me. Was that the problem, then—hers and the Weylins'?

"They're the only clothes I have right now," I said. "My master will buy me some better ones sooner or later." Let it be Kevin's fault that I was "dressed like a man." It was probably easier for the people here to understand a master too poor or too stingy to buy me proper clothing than it would be for them to imagine a place where it was normal for women to wear pants.

As though to assure me that I had said the right thing, the girl gave me a look of pity, then took my hand and led me out to the cookhouse.

As we went, I took more notice of the house than I had before—more notice of the downstairs hall, anyway. Its walls were a pale green and it ran the length of the house. At the front, it was wide and bright with light from the windows beside and above the door. It was strewn with oriental rugs of different sizes. Near the front door, there was a wooden bench, a chair, and two small tables. Past the stairs the hall narrowed and at its end, there was a back door that we went through.

Outside was the cookhouse, a little white frame cottage not far behind the main house. I had read about outdoor kitchens and outdoor toilets. I hadn't been looking forward to either. Now, though, the cookhouse looked like the friendliest place I'd seen since I arrived. Luke and Nigel were inside eating from wooden bowls with what looked like wooden spoons. And there were two younger children, a girl and boy, sitting on the floor eating with their fingers. I was glad to see them there because I'd read about kids their age being rounded up and fed from troughs like pigs. Not everywhere, apparently. At least, not here.

There was a stocky middle-aged woman stirring a kettle that hung over the fire in the fireplace. The fireplace itself filled one whole wall. It was made of brick and above it was a huge plank from which hung a few utensils. There were more utensils off to one side hanging from hooks on the wall. I stared at them and realized that I didn't know the proper names of any of them. Even things as commonplace as that. I was in a different world.

The cook finished stirring her kettle and turned to look at me. She was as light-skinned as my mute guide—a handsome middle-aged woman, tall and heavy-set. Her expression was grim, her mouth turned down at the corners, but her voice was soft and low.

"Carrie," she said. "Who's this?"

My guide looked at me.

"My name is Dana," I said. "My master's visiting here. Mrs. Weylin told me to come out for supper."

"Mrs. Weylin?" The woman frowned at me.

"The red-haired woman—Rufus's mother." I didn't quite catch myself in time to say Mister Rufus. I didn't really see why I should have to say anything. How many Mrs. Weylins were there on the place anyway?

"Miss Margaret," said the woman, and under her breath, "Bitch!"

I stared at her in surprise thinking she meant me.

"Sarah!" Luke's tone was cautioning. He couldn't have heard what the cook said from where he was. Either she said it often, or he had read her lips. But at least now I understood that it was Mrs. Weylin—Miss Margaret—who was supposed to be the bitch.

The cook said nothing else. She got me a wooden bowl, filled it with something from a pot near the fire, and handed it to me with a wooden spoon.

Supper was corn meal mush. The cook saw that I was looking at it instead of eating it, and she misread my expression.

"That's not enough?" she asked.

"Oh, it's plenty!" I held my bowl protectively, fearful that she might give me more of the stuff. "Thank you."

I sat down at the end of a large heavy table across from Nigel and Luke. I saw that they were eating the same mush, though theirs had milk on it. I considered asking for milk on mine, but I didn't really think it would help.

Whatever was in the kettle smelled good enough to remind me that I hadn't had breakfast, hadn't had more than a few bites of dinner the night before. I was starving and Sarah was cooking meat—probably a stew. I took a bite of the mush and swallowed it without tasting it.

"We get better food later on after the white folks eat," said Luke. "We get whatever they leave."

Table scraps, I thought bitterly. Someone else's leftovers. And, no doubt, if I was here long enough, I would eat them and be glad to get them. They had to be better than boiled meal. I spooned the mush into my mouth, quickly fanning away several large flies. Flies. This was an era of rampant disease. I wondered how clean our leftovers would be by the time they reached us.

"Say you was from New York?" asked Luke.

"Yes."

"Free state?"

"Yes," I repeated. "That's why I was brought here." The words, the questions made me think of Alice and her mother. I looked at Luke's broad face, wondering whether it would do any harm to ask about them. But how could I admit to knowing them—knowing them years ago—when I was supposed to be new here? Nigel knew I had been here before, but Sarah and Luke might not. It would be safer to wait—save my questions for Rufus.

"People in New York talk like you?" asked Nigel.

"Some do. Not all."

"Dress like you?" asked Luke.

"No. I dress in what Master Kevin gives me to dress in." I wished they'd stop asking questions. I didn't want them to make me tell lies I might forget later. Best to keep my background as simple as possible.

The cook came over and looked at me, at my pants. She pinched up a little of the material, feeling it. "What cloth is this?" she asked.

Polyester double knit, I thought. But I shrugged. "I don't know."

She shook her head and went back to her pot.

"You know," I said to her back, "I think I agree with you about Miss Margaret."

She said nothing. The warmth I'd felt when I came into the room was turning out to be nothing more than the heat of the fire.

"Why you try to talk like white folks?" Nigel asked me.

"I don't," I said, surprised. "I mean, this is really the way I talk."

"More like white folks than some white folks."

I shrugged, hunted through my mind for an acceptable explanation. "My mother taught school," I said, "and . . ."

"A nigger teacher?"

I winced, nodded. "Free blacks can have schools. My mother talked the way I do. She taught me."

"You'll get into trouble," he said. "Marse Tom already don't like you. You talk too educated and you come from a free state."

"Why should either of those things matter to him? I don't belong to him."

The boy smiled. "He don't want no niggers 'round here talking better than him, putting freedom ideas in our heads."

"Like we so dumb we need some stranger to make us think about freedom," muttered Luke.

I nodded, but I hoped they were wrong. I didn't think I had said enough to Weylin for him to make that kind of judgment. I hoped he wasn't going to make that kind of judgment. I wasn't good at accents. I had deliberately decided not to try to assume one. But if that meant I was going to be in trouble every time I opened my mouth, my life here would be even worse than I had imagined.

"How can Marse Rufe see you before you get here?" Nigel asked.

I choked down a swallow of mush. "I don't know," I said. "But I wish to heaven he couldn't!"

4

I stayed in the cookhouse when I finished eating because it was near the main house, and because I thought I could make it from the cookhouse into the hall if I started to feel dizzy—just in case. Wherever Kevin was in the house, he would hear me if I called from the hallway.

Luke and Nigel finished their meal and went to the fireplace to say something privately to Sarah. At that moment, Carrie, the mute, slipped me bread and a chunk of ham. I looked at it, then smiled at her gratefully. When Luke and Nigel took Sarah out of the room with them, I feasted on a shapeless sandwich. In the middle of it, I caught myself wondering about the ham, wondering how well it had been cooked. I tried to think of something else, but my mind was full of vaguely remembered horror stories of the diseases that ran wild during this time. Medicine was just a little better than witchcraft. Malaria came from bad air. Surgery was performed on struggling wide-awake patients. Germs were question marks even in the minds of many doctors. And people casually, unknowingly ingested all kinds of poorly preserved ill-cooked food that could make them sick or kill them.

Horror stories.

Except that they were true, and I was going to have to live with them for as long as I was here. Maybe I shouldn't have eaten the ham, but if I hadn't, it would be the table leavings later. I would have to take some chances.

Sarah came back with Nigel and gave him a pot of peas to shell. Life went on around me as though I wasn't there. People came into the cookhouse—always black people—talked to Sarah, lounged around, ate whatever they could put their hands on until Sarah shouted at them and chased them away. I was in the middle of asking her whether there was anything I could do to help out when Rufus began to scream. Nineteenth-century medicine was apparently at work.

The walls of the main house were thick and the sound seemed to come from a long way off—thin high-pitched screaming. Carrie, who had left the cookhouse, now ran back in and sat down beside me with her hands covering her ears.

Abruptly, the screaming stopped and I moved Carrie's hands gently. Her sensitivity surprised me. I would have thought she would be used to hearing people scream in pain. She listened for a moment, heard nothing, then looked at me.

"He probably fainted," I said. "That's best. He won't feel the pain for a while."

She nodded dully and went back out to whatever she had been doing.

"She always did like him," remarked Sarah into the silence. "He kept the children from bothering her when she was little."

I was surprised. "Isn't she a few years older than he is?"

"Born the year before him. Children listened to him though. He's white."

"Is Carrie your daughter?"

Sarah nodded. "My fourth baby. The only one Marse Tom let me keep." Her voice trailed away to a whisper.

"You mean he . . . he sold the others?"

"Sold them. First my man died—a tree he was cutting fell on him. Then Marse Tom took my children, all but Carrie. And, bless God, Carrie ain't worth much as the others 'cause she can't talk. People think she ain't got good sense."

I looked away from her. The expression in her eyes had gone from sadness—she seemed almost ready to cry—to anger. Quiet, almost frightening anger. Her husband dead, three children sold, the fourth defective, and her having to thank God for the defect. She had reason for more than anger. How amazing that Weylin had sold her children and still kept her to cook his meals. How amazing that he was still alive. I didn't think he would be for long, though, if he found a buyer for Carrie.

As I was thinking, Sarah turned and threw a handful of something into the stew or soup she was cooking. I shook my head. If she ever decided to take her revenge, Weylin would never know what hit him.

"You can peel these potatoes for me," she said.

I had to think a moment to remember that I had offered my help. I took the large pan of potatoes that she was handing me and a knife and a wooden bowl, and I worked silently, sometimes peeling, and sometimes driving away the bothersome flies. Then I heard Kevin outside calling me. I had to make myself put the potatoes down calmly and cover them with a cloth Sarah had left on the table. Then I went to him without haste, without any sign of the eagerness or relief I felt at having him nearby again. I went to him and he looked at me strangely.

"Are you all right?"

"Fine now."

He reached for my hand, but I drew back, looking at him. He dropped his hand to his side. "Come on," he said wearily. "Let's go where we can talk."

He led the way past the main house away from the slave cabins and other buildings, away from the small slave children who chased each other and shouted and didn't understand yet that they were slaves.

We found a huge oak with branches thick as separate trees spread wide to shade a large area. A handsome lonely old tree. We sat beside it putting it between ourselves and the house. I settled close to Kevin, relaxing, letting go of tension I had hardly been aware of. We said nothing for a while, as he leaned back and seemed to let go of tensions of his own.

Finally, he said, "There are so many really fascinating times we could have gone back to visit."

I laughed without humor. "I can't think of any time I'd like to go back to. But of all of them, this must be one of the most dangerous—for me anyway."

"Not while I'm with you."

I glanced at him gratefully.

"Why did you try to stop me from coming?"

"I was afraid for you."

"For me!"

"At first, I didn't know why. I just had the feeling you might be hurt trying to come with me. Then when you were here, I realized that you probably couldn't get back without me. That means if we're separated, you're stranded here for years, maybe for good."

He drew a deep breath and shook his head. "There wouldn't be anything good about that."

"Stay close to me. If I call, come quick."

He nodded, and after a while said, "I could survive here, though, if I had to. I mean if . . ."

"Kevin, no ifs. Please."

"I only mean I wouldn't be in the danger you would be in."

"No." But he'd be in another kind of danger. A place like this would endanger him in a way I didn't want to talk to him about. If he was stranded here for years, some part of this place would rub off on him. No large part, I knew. But if he survived here, it would be because he managed to tolerate the life here. He wouldn't have to take part in it, but he would have to keep quiet about it. Free speech and press hadn't done too well in the ante bellum South. Kevin wouldn't do too well either. The place, the time would either kill him outright or mark him somehow. I didn't like either possibility.

"Dana."

I looked at him.

"Don't worry. We arrived together and we'll leave together."

I didn't stop worrying, but I smiled and changed the subject. "How's Rufus? I heard him screaming."

"Poor kid. I was glad when he passed out. The doctor gave him some opium, but the pain seemed to reach him right through it. I had to help hold him."

"Opium . . . will he be all right?"

"The doctor thought so. Although I don't know how much a doctor's opinion is worth in this time."

"I hope he's right. I hope Rufus has used up all his bad luck just in getting the set of parents he's stuck with."

Kevin lifted one arm and turned it to show me a set of long bloody scratches.

"Margaret Weylin," I said softly.

"She shouldn't have been there," he said. "When she finished with me, she started on the doctor. 'Stop hurting my baby!'"

I shook my head. "What are we going to do, Kevin? Even if these people were sane, we couldn't stay here among them."

"Yes we can."

I turned to stare at him.

"I made up a story for Weylin to explain why we were here —and why we were broke. He offered me a job."

"Doing what?"

"Tutoring your little friend. Seems he doesn't read or write any better than he climbs trees."

"But . . . doesn't he go to school?"

"Not while that leg is healing. And his father doesn't want him to fall any farther behind than he already is."

"Is he behind others his age?"

"Weylin seemed to think so. He didn't come right out and say it, but I think he's afraid the kid isn't very bright."

"I'm surprised he cares one way or the other, and I think he's wrong. But for once Rufus's bad luck is our good luck. I doubt that we'll be here long enough for you to collect any of your salary, but at least while we're here, we'll have food and shelter."

"That's what I thought when I accepted."

"And what about me?"

"You?"

"Weylin didn't say anything about me?"

"No. Why should he? If I stay here, he knows you stay too."

"Yes." I smiled. "You're right. If you didn't remember me in your bargaining, why should he? I'll bet he won't forget me though when he has work that needs to be done."

"Wait a minute, you don't have to work for him. You're not supposed to belong to him."

"No, but I'm here. And I'm supposed to be a slave. What's a slave for, but to work? Believe me, he'll find something for me to do—or he would if I didn't plan to find my own work before he gets around to me."

He frowned. "You want to work?"

"I want to . . . I have to make a place for myself here. That means work. I think everyone here, black and white, will resent me if I don't work. And I need friends. I need all the friends I can make here, Kevin. You might not be with me when I come here again. If I come here again."

"And unless that kid gets a lot more careful, you will come here again."

I sighed. "It looks that way."

"I hate to think of your working for these people." He shook his head. "I hate to think of you playing the part of a slave at all."

"We knew I'd have to do it."

He said nothing.

"Call me away from them now and then, Kevin. Just to re-mind them that whatever I am, they don't own me . . . yet."

He shook his head again angrily in what looked like a refusal, but I knew he'd do it.

"What lies did you tell Weylin about us?" I asked him. "The way people ask questions around here, we'd better make sure we're both telling the same story."

For several seconds, he said nothing.

"Kevin?"

He took a deep breath. "I'm supposed to be a writer from New York," he said finally. "God help us if we meet any New Yorkers. I'm traveling through the South doing research for a book. I have no money because I drank with the wrong people a few days ago and was robbed. All I have left is you. I bought you before I was robbed because you could read and write. I thought you could help me in my work as well as be of use otherwise."

"Did he believe that?"

"It's possible that he did. He was already pretty sure you could read and write. That's one reason he seemed so suspicious and mistrustful. Educated slaves aren't popular around here."

I shrugged. "So Nigel has been telling me."

"Weylin doesn't like the way you talk. I don't think he's had much education himself, and he resents you. I don't think he'll bother you—I wouldn't stay here if I did. But keep out of his way as much as you can."

"Gladly. I plan to fit myself into the cookhouse if I can. I'm going to tell Sarah you want me to learn how to cook for you."

He gave a short laugh. "I'd better tell you the rest of the story I told Weylin. If Sarah hears it all, she might teach you how to put a little poison in my food."

I think I jumped.

"Weylin was warning me that it was dangerous to keep a slave like you—educated, maybe kidnapped from a free state —as far north as this. He said I ought to sell you to some trader heading for Georgia or Louisiana before you ran away and I lost my investment. That gave me the idea to tell him I planned to sell you in Louisiana because that was where my journey ended—and I'd heard I could make a nice profit on you down there.

"That seemed to please him and he told me I was right

—prices were better in Louisiana if I could hold on to you until I got you there. So I said educated or not, you weren't likely to run away from me because I'd promised to take you back to New York with me and set you free. I told him you didn't really want to leave me right now anyway. He got the idea."

"You make yourself sound disgusting."

"I know. I think I was trying to at the end—trying to see whether anything I did to you could make me someone he wouldn't want anywhere near his kid. I think he did cool a little toward me when I said I'd promised you freedom, but he didn't say anything."

"What were you trying to do? Lose the job you'd just gotten?"

"No, but while I was talking to him, all I could think was that you might be coming back here alone someday. I kept trying to find the humanity in him to reassure myself that you would be all right."

"Oh, he's human enough. If he were of a little higher social class, he might even have been disgusted enough with your bragging not to want you around. But he wouldn't have had the right to stop you from betraying me. I'm your private property. He'd respect that."

"You call that human? I'm going to do all I can to see that you never come here alone again."

I leaned back against the tree, watching him. "Just in case I do, Kevin, let's take out some insurance."

"What?"

"Let me help you with Rufus as much as I can. Let's see what we can do to keep him from growing up into a red-haired version of his father."

5

But for three days I didn't see Rufus. Nor did anything happen to bring on the dizziness that would tell me I was going home at last. I helped Sarah as well as I could. She seemed to warm up to me a little and she was patient with my ignorance of cooking. She taught me and saw to it that I ate better. No more corn meal mush once she realized I didn't like it. ("Why didn't you say something?" she asked me.) Under her direction,

I spent God knows how long beating biscuit dough with a hatchet on a well-worn tree stump. ("Not so hard! You ain't driving nails. Regular, like this . . .") I cleaned and plucked a chicken, prepared vegetables, kneaded bread dough, and when Sarah was weary of me, helped Carrie and the other house servants with their work. I kept Kevin's room clean. I brought him hot water to wash and shave with, and I washed in his room. It was the only place I could go for privacy. I kept my canvas bag there and went there to avoid Margaret Weylin when she came rubbing her fingers over dustless furniture and looking under rugs on well-swept floors. Differences be damned, I did know how to sweep and dust no matter what century it was. Margaret Weylin complained because she couldn't find anything to complain about. That, she made painfully clear to me the day she threw scalding hot coffee at me, screaming that I had brought it to her cold.

So I hid from her in Kevin's room. It was my refuge. But it was not my sleeping place.

I had been given sleeping space in the attic where most of the house servants slept. It apparently never occurred to anyone that I should sleep in Kevin's room. Weylin knew what kind of relationship Kevin was supposed to have with me, and he made it clear that he didn't care. But our sleeping arrangement told us that he expected discretion—or we assumed it did. We co-operated for three days. On the fourth day, Kevin caught me on my way out to the cookhouse and took me to the oak tree again.

"Are you having trouble with Margaret Weylin?" he asked.

"Nothing I can't handle," I said, surprised. "Why?"

"I heard a couple of the house servants talking, just saying vaguely that there was trouble. I thought I should find out for sure."

I shrugged, said, "I think she resents me because Rufus likes me. She probably doesn't want to share her son with anyone. Heaven help him when he gets a little older and tries to break away. Also, I don't think Margaret likes educated slaves any better than her husband does."

"I see. I was right about him, by the way. He can barely read and write. And she's not much better." He turned to face me squarely. "Did she throw a pot of hot coffee on you?"

I looked away. "It doesn't matter. Most of it missed anyway."

"Why didn't you tell me? She could have hurt you."

"She didn't."

"I don't think we should give her another chance."

I looked at him. "What do you want to do?"

"Get out of here. We don't need money badly enough for you to put up with whatever she plans to do next."

"No, Kevin. I had a reason for not telling you about the coffee."

"I'm wondering what else you haven't told me."

"Nothing important." My mind went back over some of Margaret's petty insults. "Nothing important enough to make me leave."

"But why? There's no reason for . . ."

"Yes there is. I've thought about it, Kevin. It isn't the money that I care about, or even having a roof over my head. I think we can survive here together no matter what. But I don't think I have much chance of surviving here alone. I've told you that."

"You won't be alone. I'll see to it."

"You'll try. Maybe that will be enough. I hope so. But if it isn't, if I do have to come here alone, I'll have a better chance of surviving if I stay here now and work on the insurance we talked about. Rufus. He'll probably be old enough to have some authority when I come again. Old enough to help me. I want him to have as many good memories of me as I can give him now."

"He might not remember you past the day you leave here."

"He'll remember."

"It still might not work. After all, his environment will be influencing him every day you're gone. And from what I've heard, it's common in this time for the master's children to be on nearly equal terms with the slaves. But maturity is supposed to put both in their 'places.'"

"Sometimes it doesn't. Even here, not all children let themselves be molded into what their parents want them to be."

"You're gambling. Hell, you're gambling against history."

"What else can I do? I've got to try, Kevin, and if trying means taking small risks and putting up with small humiliations now so that I can survive later, I'll do it."

He drew a deep breath and let it out in a near whistle. "Yeah.

I guess I don't blame you. I don't like it, but I don't blame you."

I put my head on his shoulder. "I don't like it either. God, I hate it! That woman is priming herself for a nervous breakdown. I just hope she doesn't have it while I'm here."

Kevin shifted his position a little and I sat up. "Let's forget about Margaret for a moment," he said. "I also wanted to talk to you about that . . . that place where you sleep."

"Oh."

"Yes, oh. I finally got up to see it. A rag pallet on the floor, Dana!"

"Did you see anything else up there?"

"What? What else should I have seen?"

"A lot of rag pallets on the floor. And a couple of cornshuck mattresses. I'm not being treated any worse than any other house servant, Kevin, and I'm doing better than the field hands. Their pallets are on the ground. Their cabins don't even have floors, and most of them are full of fleas."

There was a long silence. Finally, he sighed. "I can't do anything for the others," he said, "but I want you out of that attic. I want you with me."

I sat up and stared down at my hands. "You don't know how I've wanted to be with you. I keep imagining myself waking up at home some morning—alone."

"Not likely. Not unless something threatens you or endangers you during the night."

"You don't know that for sure. Your theory could be wrong. Maybe there's some kind of limit on how long I can stay here. Maybe a bad dream would be enough to send me home. Maybe anything."

"Maybe I should test my theory."

That stopped me. I realized he was talking about endangering me himself, or at least making me believe my life was in danger—scaring the hell out of me. Scaring me home. Maybe.

I swallowed. "That might be a good idea, but I don't think you should have mentioned it to me—warned me. Besides . . . I'm not sure you could scare me enough. I trust you."

He covered one of my hands with his own. "You can go on trusting me. I won't hurt you."

"But . . ."

"I don't have to hurt you. I can arrange something that will scare you before you have time to think about it. I can handle it."

I accepted that, began to think maybe he really could get us home. "Kevin, wait until Rufus's leg is healed."

"So long?" he protested. "Six weeks, maybe more. Hell, in a society as backward as this, who knows whether the leg will heal at all?"

"Whatever happens, the boy will live. He still has to father a child. And that means he'll probably have time to call me here again, with or without you. Give me the chance I need, Kevin, to reach him and make a haven for myself here."

"All right," he said sighing. "We'll wait awhile. But you won't do your waiting in that attic. You're moving into my room tonight."

I thought about that. "All right. Getting you home with me when I go is the one thing more important to me than staying with Rufus. It's worth getting kicked off the plantation for."

"Don't worry about that. Weylin doesn't care what we do."

"But Margaret will care. I've seen her using that limited reading ability of hers on her Bible. I suspect that in her own way, she's a fairly moral woman."

"You want to know how moral she is?"

His tone made me frown. "What do you mean?"

"If she chases me any harder, she and I will wind up playing a scene from that Bible she reads. The scene between Potiphar's wife and Joseph."

I swallowed. *That woman!* But I could see her in my mind's eye. Long thick red hair piled high on her head, fine smooth skin. Whatever her emotional problems, she wasn't ugly.

"I'm moving in tonight, all right," I said.

He smiled. "If we're quiet about it, they might not even bother to notice. Hell, I saw three little kids playing in the dirt back there who look more like Weylin than Rufus does. Margaret's had a lot of practice at not noticing."

I knew which children he meant. They had different mothers, but there was a definite family resemblance between them. I'd seen Margaret Weylin slap one of them hard across the face. The child had done nothing more than toddle into her path. If she was willing to punish a child for her husband's sins, would she be any less willing to punish me if she knew that I was where she wanted to be with Kevin? I tried not to think about it.

"We still might have to leave," I said. "No matter what these people have to accept from each other, they might not be willing to tolerate 'immorality' from us."

He shrugged. "If we have to leave, we leave. There's a limit to what you should put up with even to get your chance with the boy. We'll work our way to Baltimore. I should be able to get some kind of job there."

"If we go to a city, how about Philadelphia?"

"Philadelphia?"

"Because it's in Pennsylvania. If we leave here, let it be for a free state."

"Oh. Yes, I should have thought of that myself. Look . . . Dana, we might have to go to one of the free states, anyway." He hesitated. "I mean if it turns out we can't get home the way we think we can. I'll probably become an unnecessary expense to Weylin when Rufus's leg heals. Then we'd have to make a home for ourselves somewhere. That probably won't happen, but it's a possibility."

I nodded.

"Now let's go get whatever belongs to you out of that attic." He stood up. "And, Dana, Rufus says his mother is going out visiting today. He'd like to see you while she's gone."

"Why didn't you tell me sooner? A start finally!"

Later that day, as I was mixing some corn-bread batter for Sarah, Carrie came to get me. She made a sign to Sarah that I had already learned to understand. She wiped the side of her face with one hand as though rubbing something off. Then she pointed to me.

"Dana," said Sarah over her shoulder, "one of the white folks wants you. Go with Carrie."

I went. Carrie led me up to Rufus's room, knocked, and left me there. I went in and found Rufus in bed with his leg sandwiched between the two boards of a wooden splint and held straight by a device of rope and cast iron. The iron weight looked like something borrowed from Sarah's kitchen— a heavy little hooked thing I'd once seen her hang meat on to roast. But it apparently served just as well to keep Rufus's leg in traction.

"How are you feeling?" I asked as I sat down in the chair beside his bed.

"It doesn't hurt as much as it did," he said. "I guess it's getting well. Kevin said . . . Do you care if I call him Kevin?"

"No, I think he wants you to."

"I have to call him Mr. Franklin when Mama is here. Anyway, he said you're working with Aunt Sarah."

Aunt Sarah? Well, that was better than Mammy Sarah, I supposed. "I'm learning her way of cooking."

"She's a good cook, but . . . does she hit you?"

"Of course not." I laughed.

"She had a girl in there a while back, and she used to hit her. The girl finally asked Daddy to let her go back to the fields. That was right after Daddy sold Aunt Sarah's boys, though. Aunt Sarah was mad at everybody then."

"I don't blame her," I said.

Rufus glanced at the door, then said low-voiced, "Neither do I. Her boy Jim was my friend. He taught me how to ride when I was little. But Daddy sold him anyway." He glanced at the door again and changed the subject. "Dana, can you read?"

"Yes."

"Kevin said you could. I told Mama, and she said you couldn't."

I shrugged. "What do you think?"

He took a leather-bound book from under his pillow. "Kevin brought me this from downstairs. Would you read it to me?"

I fell in love with Kevin all over again. Here was the perfect excuse for me to spend a lot of time with the boy. The book was *Robinson Crusoe*. I had read it when I was little, and I could remember not really liking it, but not quite being able to put it down. Crusoe had, after all, been on a slave-trading voyage when he was shipwrecked.

I opened the book with some apprehension, wondering what archaic spelling and punctuation I would face. I found the expected f's for s's and a few other things that didn't turn up as often, but I got used to them very quickly. And I began to get into *Robinson Crusoe*. As a kind of castaway myself, I was happy to escape into the fictional world of someone else's trouble.

I read and read and drank some of the water Rufus's mother had left for him, and read some more. Rufus seemed to enjoy it. I didn't stop until I thought he was falling asleep. But even then, as I put the book down, he opened his eyes and smiled.

"Nigel said your mother was a school teacher."

"She was."

"I like the way you read. It's almost like being there watching everything happen."

"Thank you."

"There's a lot more books downstairs."

"I've seen them." I had also wondered about them. The Weylins didn't seem to be the kind of people who would have a library.

"They belonged to Miss Hannah," explained Rufus obligingly. "Daddy was married to her before he married Mama, but she died. This place used to be hers. He said she read so much that before he married Mama, he made sure she didn't like to read."

"What about you?"

He moved uncomfortably. "Reading's too much trouble. Mr. Jennings said I was too stupid to learn anyway."

"Who's Mr. Jennings?"

"He's the schoolmaster."

"Is he?" I shook my head in disgust. "He shouldn't be. Listen, do you think you're stupid?"

"No." A small hesitant no. "But I read as good as Daddy does already. Why should I have to do more than that?"

"You don't have to. You can stay just the way you are. Of course, that would give Mr. Jennings the satisfaction of thinking he was right about you. Do you like him?"

"Nobody likes him."

"Don't be so eager to satisfy him then. And what about the boys you go to school with? It is just boys, isn't it—no girls?"

"Yeah."

"Well look at the advantage they're going to have over you when you grow up. They'll know more than you. They'll be able to cheat you if they want to. Besides," I held up *Robinson Crusoe*, "look at the pleasure you'll miss."

He grinned. "Not with you here. Read some more."

"I don't think I'd better. It's getting late. Your mother will be home soon."

"No she won't. Read."

I sighed. "Rufe, your mother doesn't like me. I think you know that."

He looked away. "We have a little more time," he said. "Maybe you'd better not read though. I forget to listen for her when you read."

I handed him the book. "You read me a few lines."

He accepted the book, looked at it as though it were his enemy. After a moment, he began to read haltingly. Some words stopped him entirely and I had to help. After two painful paragraphs, he stopped and shut the book in disgust. "You can't even tell it's the same book when I read it," he said.

"Let Kevin teach you," I said. "He doesn't believe you're stupid, and neither do I. You'll learn all right." Unless he really did have some kind of problem—poor vision or some learning disability that people in this time would see as stubbornness or stupidity. Unless. What did I know about teaching children? All I could do was hope the boy had as much potential as I thought he did.

I got up to go—then sat down again, remembering another unanswered question. "Rufe, what ever happened to Alice?"

"Nothing." He looked surprised.

"I mean . . . the last time I saw her, her father had just been beaten because he went to see her and her mother."

"Oh. Well, Daddy was afraid he'd run off, so he sold him to a trader."

"Sold him . . . does he still live around here?"

"No, the trader was headed south. To Georgia, I think."

"Oh God." I sighed. "Are Alice and her mother still here?"

"Sure. I still see them—when I can walk."

"Did they have any trouble because I was with them that night?" That was as near as I dared to come to asking what had happened to my would-be enslaver.

"I don't think so. Alice said you came and went away quick."

"I went home. I can't tell when I'm going to do that. It just happens."

"Back to California?"

"Yes."

"Alice didn't see you go. She said you just went into the woods and didn't come back."

"That's good. Seeing me vanish would have frightened her." Alice was keeping her mouth closed too then—or her mother was. Alice might not know what happened. Clearly there were things that even a friendly young white could not be told. On the other hand, if the patroller himself hadn't spread the word about me or taken revenge on Alice and her mother, maybe he was dead. My blow could have killed him, or someone could have finished him after I went home. If they had, I didn't want to know about it.

I got up again. "I have to go, Rufe. I'll see you again whenever I can."

"Dana?"

I looked down at him.

"I told Mama who you were. I mean that you were the one who saved me from the river. She said it wasn't true, but I think she really believed me. I told her because I thought it might make her like you better."

"It hasn't that I've noticed."

"I know." He frowned. "Why doesn't she like you? Did you do something to her?"

"Not likely! After all, what would happen to me if I did something to her?"

"Yeah. But why doesn't she like you?"

"You'll have to ask her."

"She won't tell me." He looked up solemnly. "I keep thinking you're going to go home—that somebody will come and tell me you and Kevin are gone. I don't want you to go. But I don't want you to get hurt here either."

I said nothing.

"You be careful," he said softly.

I nodded and left the room. Just as I reached the stairs, Tom Weylin came out of his bedroom.

"What are you doing up here?" he demanded.

"Visiting Mister Rufus," I said. "He asked to see me."

"You were reading to him!"

Now I knew how he happened to come out just in time to catch me. He had been eavesdropping, for Godsake. What

had he expected to hear? Or rather, what had he heard that
he shouldn't have? About Alice, perhaps. What would he
make of that? For a moment my mind raced, searching for
excuses, explanations. Then I realized I wouldn't need them.
I would have met him outside Rufus's door if he had stayed
long enough to hear about Alice. He had probably heard me
addressing Rufus a little too familiarly. Nothing worse. I had
deliberately not said anything damaging about Margaret because I thought her own attitude would damage her more in
her son's eyes than anything I could say. I made myself face
Weylin calmly.

"Yes, I was reading to him," I admitted. "He asked me to
do that too. I think he was bored lying in there with nothing
to do."

"I didn't ask you what you thought," he said.

I said nothing.

He walked me farther from Rufus's door, then stopped and
turned to look hard at me. His eyes went over me like a man
sizing up a woman for sex, but I got no message of lust from
him. His eyes, I noticed, not for the first time, were almost as
pale as Kevin's. Rufus and his mother had bright green eyes. I
liked the green better, somehow.

"How old are you?" he asked.

"Twenty-six, sir."

"You say that like you're sure."

"Yes, sir. I am."

"What year were you born?"

"Seventeen ninety-three." I had figured that out days ago
thinking that it wasn't a part of my personal history I should
hesitate over if someone asked. At home, a person who hesitated over his birthdate was probably about to lie. As I spoke
though, I realized that here, a person might hesitate over his
birthdate simply because he didn't know it. Sarah didn't know
hers.

"Twenty-six then," said Weylin. "How many children have
you had?"

"None." I kept my face impassive, but I couldn't keep myself
from wondering where these questions were leading.

"No children by now?" He frowned. "You must be barren
then."

I said nothing. I wasn't about to explain anything to him. My fertility was none of his business, anyway.

He stared at me a little longer, making me angry and uncomfortable, but I concealed my feelings as well as I could.

"You like children though, don't you?" he asked. "You like my boy."

"Yes, sir, I do."

"Can you cipher too—along with your reading and writing?"

"Yes, sir."

"How'd you like to be the one to do the teaching?"

"Me?" I managed to frown . . . managed not to laugh aloud with relief. Tom Weylin wanted to buy me. In spite of all his warnings to Kevin of the dangers of owning educated, Northern-born slaves, he wanted to buy me. I pretended not to understand. "But that's Mr. Franklin's job."

"Could be your job."

"Could it?"

"I could buy you. Then you'd live here instead of traveling around the country without enough to eat or a place to sleep."

I lowered my eyes. "That's for Mr. Franklin to say."

"I know it is, but how do you feel about it?"

"Well . . . no offense, Mr. Weylin, I'm glad we stopped here, and as I said, I like your son. But I'd rather stay with Mr. Franklin."

He gave me an unmistakable look of pity. "If you do, girl, you'll live to regret it." He turned and walked away.

I stared after him believing in spite of myself that he really felt sorry for me.

That night I told Kevin what had happened, and he wondered too.

"Be careful, Dana," he said, unwittingly echoing Rufus. "Be as careful as you can."

6

I was careful. As the days passed, I got into the habit of being careful. I played the slave, minded my manners probably more than I had to because I wasn't sure what I could get away with. Not much, as it turned out.

Once I was called over to the slave cabins—the quarter—to watch Weylin punish a field hand for the crime of answering back. Weylin ordered the man stripped naked and tied to the trunk of a dead tree. As this was being done—by other slaves —Weylin stood whirling his whip and biting his thin lips. Suddenly, he brought the whip down across the slave's back. The slave's body jerked and strained against its ropes. I watched the whip for a moment wondering whether it was like the one Weylin had used on Rufus years before. If it was, I understood completely why Margaret Weylin had taken the boy and fled. The whip was heavy and at least six feet long, and I wouldn't have used it on anything living. It drew blood and screams at every blow. I watched and listened and longed to be away. But Weylin was making an example of the man. He had ordered all of us to watch the beating—all the slaves. Kevin was in the main house somewhere, probably not even aware of what was happening.

The whipping served its purpose as far as I was concerned. It scared me, made me wonder how long it would be before I made a mistake that would give someone reason to whip me. Or had I already made that mistake?

I had moved into Kevin's room, after all. And though that would be perceived as Kevin's doing, I could be made to suffer for it. The fact that the Weylins didn't seem to notice my move gave me no real comfort. Their lives and mine were so separate that it might take them several days to realize that I had abandoned my place in the attic. I always got up before they did to get water and live coals from the cookhouse to start Kevin's fire. Matches had apparently not been invented yet. Neither Sarah nor Rufus had ever heard of them.

By now, the manservant Weylin had assigned to Kevin ignored him completely, and Kevin and his room were left to me. It took us twice as long to get a fire started, and it took me longer to carry water up and down the stairs, but I didn't care. The jobs I had assigned myself gave me legitimate reason for going in and out of Kevin's room at all hours, and they kept me from being assigned more disagreeable work. Most important to me, though, they gave me a chance to preserve a little of 1976 amid the slaves and slaveholders.

After washing and watching Kevin bloody his face with the straight razor he had borrowed from Weylin, I would go down to help Sarah with breakfast. Whole mornings went by without my seeing either of the Weylins. At night, I helped clean up after supper and prepare for the next day. So, like Sarah and Carrie, I rose before the Weylins and went to bed after them. That gave me several days of peace before Margaret Weylin discovered that she had another reason to dislike me.

She cornered me one day as I swept the library. If she had walked in two minutes earlier, she would have caught me reading a book. "Where did you sleep last night?" she demanded in the strident accusing voice she reserved for slaves.

I straightened to face her, rested my hands on the broom. How lovely it would have been to say, *None of your business, bitch!* Instead, I spoke softly, respectfully. "In Mr. Franklin's room, ma'am." I didn't bother to lie because all the house servants knew. It might even have been one of them who alerted Margaret. So now what would happen?

Margaret slapped me across the face.

I stood very still, gazed down at her with frozen calm. She was three or four inches shorter than I was and proportionately smaller. Her slap hadn't hurt me much. It had simply made me want to hurt her. Only my memory of the whip kept me still.

"You filthy black whore!" she shouted. "This is a Christian house!"

I said nothing.

"I'll see you sent to the quarter where you belong!"

Still I said nothing. I looked at her.

"I won't have you in my house!" She took a step back from me. "You stop looking at me that way!" She took another step back.

It occurred to me that she was a little afraid of me. I was an unknown, after all—an unpredictable new slave. And maybe I was a little too silent. Slowly, deliberately, I turned my back and went on sweeping.

I kept an eye on her, though, without seeming to. After all, she was as unpredictable as I was. She could pick up a candlestick or a vase and hit me with it. And whip or no whip, I wasn't going to stand passively and let her really hurt me.

But she made no move toward me. Instead, she turned and

rushed away. It was a hot day, muggy and uncomfortable. No one else was moving very fast except to wave away flies. But Margaret Weylin still rushed everywhere. She had little or nothing to do. Slaves kept her house clean, did much of her sewing, all her cooking and washing. Carrie even helped her put her clothes on and take them off. So Margaret supervised— ordered people to do work they were already doing, criticized their slowness and laziness even when they were quick and industrious, and in general, made trouble. Weylin had married a poor, uneducated, nervous, startlingly pretty young woman who was determined to be the kind of person she thought of as a lady. That meant she didn't do "menial" work, or any work at all, apparently. I had no one to compare her to except her guests who seemed, at least, to be calmer. But I suspected that most women of her time found enough to do to keep themselves comfortably busy whether they thought of themselves as "ladies" or not. Margaret, in her boredom, simply rushed around and made a nuisance of herself.

I finished my work in the library, wondering all the while whether Margaret had gone to her husband about me. Her husband, I feared. I remembered the expression on his face when he had beaten the field hand. It hadn't been gleeful or angry or even particularly interested. He could have been chopping wood. He wasn't sadistic, but he didn't shrink from his "duties" as master of the plantation. He would beat me bloody if he thought I had given him reason, and Kevin might not even find out until too late.

I went up to Kevin's room, but he wasn't there. I heard him when I passed Rufus's room and I would have gone in, but a moment later, I heard Margaret's voice. Repelled, I went back downstairs and out to the cookhouse.

Sarah and Carrie were alone when I went in, and I was glad of that. Sometimes old people and children lounged there, or house servants or even field hands stealing a few moments of leisure. I liked to listen to them talk sometimes and fight my way through their accents to find out more about how they survived lives of slavery. Without knowing it, they prepared me to survive. But now I wanted only Sarah and Carrie. I could say what I felt around them, and it wouldn't get back to either of the Weylins.

"Dana," Sarah greeted me, "you be careful. I spoke for you today. I don't want you making me out to be a liar!"

I frowned. "Spoke for me? To Miss Margaret?"

Sarah gave a short harsh laugh. "No! You know I don't say no more to her than I can help. She's got her house, and I got my kitchen."

I smiled and my own trouble receded a little. Sarah was right. Margaret Weylin kept out of her way. Talk between them was brief and confined usually to meal planning.

"Why do you dislike her so if she doesn't bother you?" I asked.

Sarah gave me the look of silent rage that I had not seen since my first day on the plantation. "Whose idea you think it was to sell my babies?"

"Oh." She had not mentioned her lost children since that first day either.

"She wanted new furniture, new china dishes, fancy things you see in that house now. What she had was good enough for Miss Hannah, and Miss Hannah was a real lady. Quality. But it wasn't good enough for white-trash Margaret. So she made Marse Tom sell my three boys to get money to buy things she didn't even need!"

"Oh." I couldn't think of anything else to say. My trouble seemed to shrink and become not worth mentioning. Sarah was silent for a while, her hands kneading bread dough automatically, maybe with a little more vigor than necessary. Finally she spoke again.

"It was Marse Tom I spoke to for you."

I jumped. "Am I in trouble?"

"Not by anything I said. He just wanted to know how you work and are you lazy. I told him you wasn't lazy. Told him you didn't know how to do some things—and, girl, you come here not knowing how to do *nothing*, but I didn't tell him that. I said if you don't know how to do something, you find out. And you work. I tell you to do something, I know it's going to be done. Marse Tom say he might buy you."

"Mr. Franklin won't sell me."

She lifted her head a little and literally looked down her nose at me. "No. Guess he won't. Anyway, Miss Margaret don't want you here."

I shrugged.

"Bitch," muttered Sarah monotonously. Then, "Well, greedy and mean as she is, at least she don't bother Carrie much."

I looked at the mute girl eating stew and corn bread left over from the table of the whites. "Doesn't she, Carrie?"

Carrie shook her head and kept eating.

"Course," said Sarah, turning away from the bread dough, "Carrie don't have nothing Miss Margaret wants."

I just looked at her.

"You're caught between," she said. "You know that don't you?"

"One man ought to be enough for her."

"Don't matter what ought to be. Matters what is. Make him let you sleep in the attic again."

"Make him!"

"Girl . . ." She smiled a little. "I see you and him together sometimes when you think nobody's looking. You can make him do just about anything you want him to do."

Her smile surprised me. I would have expected her to be disgusted with me—or with Kevin.

"Fact," she continued, "if you got any sense, you'll try to get him to free you now while you still young and pretty enough for him to listen."

I looked at her appraisingly—large dark eyes set in a full unlined face several shades lighter than my own. She had been pretty herself not long ago. She was still an attractive woman. I spoke to her softly. "Were you sensible, Sarah? Did you try when you were younger?"

She stared hard at me, her large eyes suddenly narrowed. Finally, she walked away without answering.

7

I didn't move to the quarter. I took some cookhouse advice that I'd once heard Luke give to Nigel. "Don't argue with white folks," he had said. "Don't tell them 'no.' Don't let them see you mad. Just say 'yes, sir.' Then go 'head and do what you want to do. Might have to take a whippin' for it later on, but if you want it bad enough, the whippin' won't matter much."

There were a few whip marks on Luke's back, and I'd twice heard Tom Weylin swear to give them company. But he hadn't. And Luke went about his business, doing pretty much as he pleased. His business was keeping the field hands in line. Called the driver, he was a kind of black overseer. And he kept this relatively high position in spite of his attitude. I decided to develop a similar attitude—though with less risk to myself, I thought. I had no intention of taking a whipping if I could avoid it, and I was sure Kevin could protect me if he was nearby when I needed him.

Anyway, I ignored Margaret's ravings and continued to disgrace her Christian house.

And nothing happened.

Tom Weylin was up early one morning and he caught me stumbling, still half-asleep, out of Kevin's room. I froze, then made myself relax.

"Morning, Mr. Weylin."

He almost smiled—came as near to smiling as I'd ever seen. And he winked.

That was all. I knew then that if Margaret got me kicked out, it wouldn't be for doing a thing as normal as sleeping with my master. And somehow, that disturbed me. I felt almost as though I really was doing something shameful, happily playing whore for my supposed owner. I went away feeling uncomfortable, vaguely ashamed.

Time passed. Kevin and I became more a part of the household, familiar, accepted, accepting. That disturbed me too when I thought about it. How easily we seemed to acclimatize. Not that I wanted us to have trouble, but it seemed as though we should have had a harder time adjusting to this particular segment of history—adjusting to our places in the household of a slaveholder. For me, the work could be hard, but was usually more boring than physically wearing. And Kevin complained of boredom, and of having to be sociable with a steady stream of ignorant pretentious guests who visited the Weylin house. But for drop-ins from another century, I thought we had had a remarkably easy time. And I was perverse enough to be bothered by the ease.

"This could be a great time to live in," Kevin said once. "I keep thinking what an experience it would be to stay in it—go

West and watch the building of the country, see how much of
the Old West mythology is true."

"West," I said bitterly. "That's where they're doing it to the
Indians instead of the blacks!"

He looked at me strangely. He had been doing that a lot
lately.

Tom Weylin caught me reading in his library one day. I was
supposed to be sweeping and dusting. I looked up, found him
watching me, closed the book, put it away, and picked up my
dust cloth. My hand was shaking.

"You read to my boy," he said. "I let you do that. But that's
enough reading for you."

There was a long silence and I said tardily, "Yes, sir."

"In fact, you don't even have to be in here. Tell Carrie to do
this room."

"Yes, sir."

"And stay away from the books!"

"Yes, sir."

Hours later in the cookhouse, Nigel asked me to teach him
to read.

The request surprised me, then I was ashamed of my surprise. It seemed such a natural request. Years before, Nigel had
been chosen to be Rufus's companion. If Rufus had been a
better student, Nigel might already know how to read. As it
was, Nigel had learned to do other things. At a husky thirteen,
he could shoe a horse, build a cabinet, and plot to escape to
Pennsylvania someday. I should have offered to teach him to
read long before he asked me.

"You know what's going to happen to both of us if we get
caught?" I asked him.

"You scared?" he asked.

"Yes. But that doesn't matter. I'll teach you. I just wanted to
be sure you knew what you were getting into."

He turned away from me, lifted his shirt in the back so that I
could see his scars. Then he faced me again. "I know," he said.

That same day, I stole a book and began to teach him.

And I began to realize why Kevin and I had fitted so easily
into this time. We weren't really in. We were observers watching a show. We were watching history happen around us. And
we were actors. While we waited to go home, we humored the

people around us by pretending to be like them. But we were poor actors. We never really got into our roles. We never forgot that we were acting.

This was something I tried to explain to Kevin on the day the children broke through my act. It suddenly became very important that he understand.

The day was miserably hot and muggy, full of flies, mosquitoes and the bad smells of soapmaking, the outhouses, fish someone had caught, unwashed bodies. Everybody smelled, black and white. Nobody washed enough or changed clothes often enough. The slaves worked up a sweat and the whites sweated without working. Kevin and I didn't have enough clothes or any deodorant at all, so often, we smelled too. Surprisingly, we were beginning to get used to it.

Now we were walking together away from the house and the quarter. We weren't heading for our oak tree because by then, if Margaret Weylin saw us there, she sent someone with a job for me. Her husband may have stopped her from throwing me out of the house, but he hadn't stopped her from becoming a worse nuisance than ever. Sometimes Kevin countermanded her orders, claiming that he had work for me. That was how I got a little rest and gave Nigel some extra tutoring. Now, though, we were headed for the woods to spend some time together.

But before we got away from the buildings, we saw a group of slave children gathered around a tree stump. These were the children of the field hands, children too young to be of much use in the fields themselves. Two of them were standing on the wide flat stump while others stood around watching.

"What are they doing?" I asked.

"Playing some game, probably." Kevin shrugged.

"It looks as though . . ."

"What?"

"Let's get closer. I want to hear what they're saying."

We approached them from one side so that neither the children on the tree stump nor those on the ground were facing us. They went on with their play as we watched and listened.

"Now here a likely wench," called the boy on the stump. He gestured toward the girl who stood slightly behind him. "She cook and wash and iron. Come here, gal. Let the folks see you." He drew the girl up beside him. "She young and strong," he continued. "She worth plenty money. Two hundred dollars. Who bid two hundred dollars?"

The little girl turned to frown at him. "I'm worth more than two hundred dollars, Sammy!" she protested. "You sold Martha for five hundred dollars!"

"You shut your mouth," said the boy. "You ain't supposed to say nothing. When Marse Tom bought Mama and me, we didn't say nothing."

I turned and walked away from the arguing children, feeling tired and disgusted. I wasn't even aware that Kevin was following me until he spoke.

"That's the game I thought they were playing," he said. "I've seen them at it before. They play at field work too."

I shook my head. "My God, why can't we go home? This place is diseased."

He took my hand. "The kids are just imitating what they've seen adults doing," he said. "They don't understand . . ."

"They don't have to understand. Even the games they play are preparing them for their future—and that future will come whether they understand it or not."

"No doubt."

I turned to glare at him and he looked back calmly. It was a what-do-you-want-me-to-do-about-it kind of look. I didn't say anything because, of course, there was nothing he could do about it.

I shook my head, rubbed my hand across my brow. "Even knowing what's going to happen doesn't help," I said. "I know some of those kids will live to see freedom—after they've slaved away their best years. But by the time freedom comes to them, it will be too late. Maybe it's already too late."

"Dana, you're reading too much into a kids' game."

"And you're reading too little into it. Anyway . . . anyway, it's not their game."

"No." He glanced at me. "Look, I won't say I understand how you feel about this because maybe that's something I can't understand. But as you said, you know what's going to happen. It already has happened. We're in the middle of history. We surely can't change it. If anything goes wrong, we might have all we can do just to survive it. We've been lucky so far."

"Maybe." I drew a deep breath and let it out slowly. "But I can't close my eyes."

Kevin frowned thoughtfully. "It's surprising to me that there's so little to see. Weylin doesn't seem to pay much attention to what his people do, but the work gets done."

"You think he doesn't pay attention. Nobody calls you out to see the whippings."

"How many whippings?"

"One that I've seen. One too goddamn many!"

"One is too many, yes, but still, this place isn't what I would have imagined. No overseer. No more work than the people can manage . . ."

". . . no decent housing," I cut in. "Dirt floors to sleep on, food so inadequate they'd all be sick if they didn't keep gardens in what's supposed to be their leisure time and steal from the cookhouse when Sarah lets them. And no rights and the possibility of being mistreated or sold away from their families for any reason—or no reason. Kevin, you don't have to beat people to treat them brutally."

"Wait a minute," he said. "I'm not minimizing the wrong that's being done here. I just . . ."

"Yes you are. You don't mean to be, but you are." I sat down against a tall pine tree pulling him down beside me. We were in the woods now. Not far to one side of us was a group of Weylin's slaves who were cutting down trees. We could hear them, but we couldn't see them. I assumed that meant they couldn't see us either—or hear us over the distance and their own noise. I spoke to Kevin again.

"You might be able to go through this whole experience as an observer," I said. "I can understand that because most of the time, I'm still an observer. It's protection. It's nineteen seventy-six shielding and cushioning eighteen nineteen for me. But now and then, like with the kids' game, I can't maintain the distance. I'm drawn all the way into eighteen nineteen, and I don't know what to do. I ought to be doing something though. I know that."

"There's nothing you could do that wouldn't eventually get you whipped or killed!"

I shrugged.

"You . . . you haven't already done anything, have you?"

"Just started to teach Nigel to read and write," I said. "Nothing more subversive than that."

"If Weylin catches you and I'm not around . . ."

"I know. So stay close. The boy wants to learn, and I'm going to teach him."

He raised one leg against his chest and leaned forward looking at me. "You think someday he'll write his own pass and head North, don't you?"

"At least he'll be able to."

"I see Weylin was right about educated slaves."

I turned to look at him.

"Do a good job with Nigel," he said quietly. "Maybe when you're gone, he'll be able to teach others."

I nodded solemnly.

"I'd bring him in to learn with Rufus if people weren't so good at listening at doors in that house. And Margaret is always wandering in and out."

"I know. That's why I didn't ask you." I closed my eyes and saw the children playing their game again. "The ease seemed so frightening," I said. "Now I see why."

"What?"

"The ease. Us, the children . . . I never realized how easily people could be trained to accept slavery."

8

I said good-bye to Rufus the day my teaching finally did get me into trouble. I didn't know I was saying good-bye, of course—didn't know what trouble was waiting for me in the cookhouse where I was to meet Nigel. I thought there was trouble enough in Rufus's room.

I was there reading to him. I had been reading to him regularly since his father caught me that first time. Tom Weylin didn't want me reading on my own, but he had ordered me to read to his son. Once he had told Rufus in my presence, "You ought to be ashamed of yourself! A nigger can read better than you!"

"She can read better than you too," Rufus had answered.

His father had stared at him coldly, then ordered me out of the room. For a second I was afraid for Rufus, but Tom Weylin left the room with me.

"Don't go to him again until I say you can," he told me.

Four days passed before he said I could. And again he chastised Rufus before me.

"I'm no schoolmaster," he said, "but I'll teach you if you can be taught. I'll teach you respect."

Rufus said nothing.

"You want her to read to you?"

"Yes, sir."

"Then you got something to say to me."

"I . . . I'm sorry, Daddy."

"Read," said Weylin to me. He turned and left the room.

"What exactly are you supposed to be sorry for?" I asked when Weylin was gone. I spoke very softly.

"Talking back," said Rufus. "He thinks everything I say is talking back. So I don't say very much to him."

"I see." I opened the book and began to read.

We had finished *Robinson Crusoe* long ago, and Kevin had chosen a couple of other familiar books from the library. We had already gone through the first, *Pilgrim's Progress*. Now we were working on *Gulliver's Travels*. Rufus's own reading was improving slowly under Kevin's tutoring, but he still enjoyed being read to.

On my last day with him, though, as on a few others, Margaret came in to listen—and to fidget and to fiddle with Rufus's hair and to pet him while I was reading. As usual, Rufus put his head on her lap and accepted her caresses silently. But today, apparently, that was not enough.

"Are you comfortable?" she asked Rufus when I had been reading for a few moments. "Does your leg hurt?" His leg was not healing as I thought it should have. After nearly two months, he still couldn't walk.

"I feel all right, Mama," he said.

Suddenly, Margaret twisted around to face me. "Well?" she demanded.

I had paused in my reading to give her a chance to finish. I lowered my head and began to read again.

About sixty seconds later, she said, "Baby, you hot? You want me to call Virgie up here to fan you?" Virgie was about ten—one of the small house servants often called to fan the whites, run errands for them, carry covered dishes of food between the cookhouse and the main house, and serve the whites at their table.

"I'm all right, Mama," said Rufus.

"Why don't you go on?" snapped Margaret at me. "You're supposed to be here to read, so read!"

I began to read again, biting off the words a little.

"Are you hungry, baby?" asked Margaret a moment later. "Aunt Sarah's just made a cake. Wouldn't you like a piece?"

I didn't stop this time. I just lowered my voice a little and read automatically, tonelessly.

"I don't know why you want to listen to her," Margaret said to Rufus. "She's got a voice like a fly buzzing."

"I don't want no cake, Mama."

"You sure? You ought to see the fine white icing Sarah put on it."

"I want to hear Dana read, that's all."

"Well, there she is, reading. If you can call it that."

I let my voice grow progressively softer as they talked.

"I can't hear her with you talking," Rufus said.

"Baby, all I said was . . ."

"Don't say nothing!" Rufus took his head off her lap. "Go away and stop bothering me!"

"Rufus!" She sounded hurt rather than angry. And in spite of the situation, this sounded like real disrespect to me. I stopped reading and waited for the explosion. It came from Rufus.

"Go away, Mama!" he shouted. "Just leave me alone!"

"Be still," she whispered. "Baby, you'll make yourself sick."

Rufus turned his head and looked at her. The expression on his face startled me. For once, the boy looked like a smaller replica of his father. His mouth was drawn into a thin straight line and his eyes were coldly hostile. He spoke quietly now as Weylin sometimes did when he was angry. "You're making me sick, Mama. Get away from me!"

Margaret got up and dabbed at her eyes. "I don't see how you can talk to me that way," she said. "Just because of some nigger . . ."

Rufus just looked at her, and finally she left the room.

He relaxed against his pillows and closed his eyes. "I get so tired of her sometimes," he said.

"Rufe . . . ?"

He opened weary, friendly eyes and looked at me. The anger was gone.

"You'd better be careful," I said. "What if your mother told your father you talked to her that way?"

"She never tells." He grinned. "She'll be back after while to bring me a piece of cake with fine white icing."

"She was crying."

"She always cries. Read, Dana."

"Do you talk to her that way often?"

"I have to, or she won't leave me alone. Daddy does it too."

I took a deep breath, shook my head, and plunged back into *Gulliver's Travels.*

Later, as I left Rufus, I passed Margaret on her way back to his room. Sure enough, she was carrying a large slice of cake on a plate.

I went downstairs and out to the cookhouse to give Nigel his reading lesson.

Nigel was waiting. He already had our book out of its hiding place and was spelling out words to Carrie. That surprised me because I had offered Carrie a chance to learn with him, and she had refused. Now though, the two of them, alone in the cookhouse, were so involved in what they were doing that they didn't even notice me until I shut the door. They looked up then, wide-eyed with fear. But they relaxed when they saw it was only me. I went over to them.

"Do you want to learn?" I asked Carrie.

The girl's fear seemed to return and she glanced at the door.

"Aunt Sarah's afraid for her to learn," said Nigel. "Afraid if she learns, she might get caught at it, and then be whipped or sold."

I lowered my head, sighed. The girl couldn't talk, couldn't communicate at all except in the inadequate sign language she had invented—a language even her mother only half-understood. In a more rational society, an ability to write would be of great help to her. But here, the only people who could read her writing would be those who might punish her for being able to write. And Nigel. And Nigel.

I looked from the boy to the girl. "Shall I teach you, Carrie?" If I did and her mother caught me, I might be in more trouble than if Tom Weylin caught me. I was afraid to teach her both for her sake and for mine. Her mother wasn't a woman I wanted to offend or to hurt, but my conscience wouldn't let me refuse her if she wanted to learn.

Carrie nodded. She wanted to learn all right. She turned away from us for a moment, did something to her dress, then turned back with a small book in her hand. She too had stolen from the library. Her book was a volume of English history illustrated with a few drawings which she pointed out to me.

I shook my head. "Either hide it or put it back," I told her. "It's too hard for you to begin with. The one Nigel and I are using was written for people just starting to learn." It was an old speller—probably the one Weylin's first wife had been taught from.

Carrie's fingers caressed one of the drawings for a moment. Then she put the book back into her dress.

"Now," I said, "find something to do in case your mother comes in. I can't teach you in here. We'll have to find someplace else to meet."

She nodded, looking relieved, and went over to sweep the other side of the room.

"Nigel," I said softly when she was gone, "I surprised you when I came in here, didn't I?"

"Didn't know it was you."

"Yes. It could have been Sarah, couldn't it?"

He said nothing.

"I teach you in here because Sarah said I could, and because the Weylins never seem to come out here."

"They don't. They send us out here to tell Sarah what they want. Or to tell her to come to them."

"So you can learn here, but Carrie can't. We might have trouble no matter how careful we are, but we don't have to ask for it."

He nodded.

"By the way, what does your father think of my teaching you?"

"I don't know. I didn't tell him you was."

Oh God. I took a shaky breath. "But he does know, doesn't he?"

"Aunt Sarah probably told him. He never said nothing to me though."

If anything went wrong, there would be blacks to take their

revenge on me when the whites finished. When would I ever go home? *Would* I ever go home? Or if I had to stay here, why couldn't I just turn these two kids away, turn off my conscience, and be a coward, safe and comfortable?

I took the book from Nigel and handed him my own pencil and a piece of paper from my tablet. "Spelling test," I said quietly.

He passed the test. Every word right. To my surprise as well as his, I hugged him. He grinned, half-embarrassed, half-pleased. Then I got up and put his test paper into the hot coals of the hearth. It burst into flames and burned completely. I was always careful about that, and I always hated being careful. I couldn't help contrasting Nigel's lessons with Rufus's. And the contrast made me bitter.

I turned to go back to the table where Nigel was waiting. In that moment, Tom Weylin opened the door and stepped in.

It wasn't supposed to happen. For as long as I had been on the plantation, it had not happened—no white had come into the cookhouse. Not even Kevin. Nigel had just agreed with me that it didn't happen.

But there stood Tom Weylin staring at me. He lowered his gaze a little and frowned. I realized that I was still holding the old speller. I'd gotten up with it in my hand and I hadn't put it down. I even had one finger in it holding my place.

I withdrew my finger and let the book close. I was in for a beating now. Where was Kevin? Somewhere inside the house, probably. He might hear me if I screamed—and I would be screaming shortly, anyway. But it would be better if I could just get past Weylin and run into the house.

Weylin stood squarely in front of the door. "Didn't I tell you I didn't want you reading!"

I said nothing. Clearly, nothing I could say would help. I felt myself trembling, and I tried to be still. I hoped Weylin couldn't see. And I hoped Nigel had had the sense to get the pencil off the table. So far, I was the only one in trouble. If it could just stay that way . . .

"I treated you good," said Weylin quietly, "and you pay me back by stealing from me! Stealing my books! Reading!"

He snatched the book from me and threw it on the floor. Then he grabbed me by the arm and dragged me toward the door. I managed to twist around to face Nigel and mouth the words, "Get Kevin." I saw Nigel stand up.

Then I was out of the cookhouse. Weylin dragged me a few feet, then pushed me hard. I fell, knocked myself breathless. I never saw where the whip came from, never even saw the first blow coming. But it came—like a hot iron across my back, burning into me through my light shirt, searing my skin . . .

I screamed, convulsed. Weylin struck again and again, until I couldn't have gotten up at gunpoint.

I kept trying to crawl away from the blows, but I didn't have the strength or the co-ordination to get far. I may have been still screaming or just whimpering, I couldn't tell. All I was really aware of was the pain. I thought Weylin meant to kill me. I thought I would die on the ground there with a mouth full of dirt and blood and a white man cursing and lecturing as he beat me. By then, I almost wanted to die. Anything to stop the pain.

I vomited. And I vomited again because I couldn't move my face away.

I saw Kevin, blurred, but somehow still recognizable. I saw him running toward me in slow motion, running. Legs churning, arms pumping, yet he hardly seemed to be getting closer.

Suddenly, I realized what was happening and I screamed—I think I screamed. He had to reach me. He had to!

And I passed out.

The Fight

W E NEVER really moved in together, Kevin and I. I had
a sardine-can sized apartment on Crenshaw Boulevard
and he had a bigger one on Olympic not too far away. We both
had books shelved and stacked and boxed and crowding out
the furniture. Together, we would never have fitted into either
of our apartments. Kevin did suggest once that I get rid of
some of my books so that I'd fit into his place.

"You're out of your mind!" I told him.

"Just some of that book-club stuff that you don't read."

We were at my apartment then, so I said, "Let's go to your
place and I'll help you decide which of your books you don't
read. I'll even help you throw them out."

He looked at me and sighed, but he didn't say anything
else. We just sort of drifted back and forth between our two
apartments and I got less sleep than ever. But it didn't seem to
bother me as much as it had before. Nothing seemed to bother
me much. I didn't love the agency now, but, on the other hand,
I didn't kick the furniture in the morning anymore, either.

"Quit," Kevin told me. "I'll help you out until you find a
better job."

If I hadn't already loved him by then, that would have done
it. But I didn't quit. The independence the agency gave me
was shaky, but it was real. It would hold me together until
my novel was finished and I was ready to look for something
more demanding. When that time came, I could walk away
from the agency not owing anybody. My memory of my aunt
and uncle told me that even people who loved me could demand more of me than I could give—and expect their demands to be met simply because I owed them.

I knew Kevin wasn't that way. The situation was completely
different. But I kept my job.

Then about four months after we'd met, Kevin said, "How
would you feel about getting married?"

I shouldn't have been surprised, but I was. "You want to
marry me?"

"Yeah, don't you want to marry me?" He grinned. "I'd let you type all my manuscripts."

I was drying our dinner dishes just then, and I threw the dish towel at him. He really had asked me to do some typing for him three times. I'd done it the first time, grudgingly, not telling him how much I hated typing, how I did all but the final drafts of my stories in longhand. That was why I was with a blue-collar agency instead of a white-collar agency. The second time he asked, though, I told him, and I refused. He was annoyed. The third time when I refused again, he was angry. He said if I couldn't do him a little favor when he asked, I could leave. So I went home.

When I rang his doorbell the next day after work, he looked surprised. "You came back."

"Didn't you want me to?"

"Well . . . sure. Will you type those pages for me now?"

"No."

"Damnit, Dana . . . !"

I stood waiting for him to either shut the door or let me in. He let me in.

And now he wanted to marry me.

I looked at him. Just looked, for a long moment. Then I looked away because I couldn't think while I was watching him. "You, uh . . . don't have any relatives or anything who'll give you a hard time about me, do you?" As I spoke, it occurred to me that one of the reasons his proposal surprised me was that we had never talked much about our families, about how his would react to me and mine to him. I hadn't been aware of us avoiding the subject, but somehow, we'd never gotten around to it. Even now, he looked surprised.

"The only close relative I've got left is my sister," he said. "She's been trying to marry me off and get me 'settled down' for years. She'll love you, believe me."

I didn't, quite. "I hope she does," I said. "But I'm afraid my aunt and uncle won't love you."

He turned to face me. "No?"

I shrugged. "They're old. Sometimes their ideas don't have very much to do with what's going on now. I think they're still waiting for me to come to my senses, move back home, and go to secretarial school."

"Are we going to get married?"

I went to him. "You know damn well we are."

"You want me to go with you when you talk to your aunt and uncle?"

"No. Go talk to your sister if you want to. Brace yourself though. She might surprise you."

She did. And braced or not, he wasn't ready for his sister's reaction.

"I thought I knew her," he told me afterward. "I mean, I did know her. But I guess we've lost touch more than I thought."

"What did she say?"

"That she didn't want to meet you, wouldn't have you in her house—or me either if I married you." He leaned back on the shabby purple sofa that had come with my apartment and looked up at me. "And she said a lot of other things. You don't want to hear them."

"I believe you."

He shook his head. "The thing is, there's no reason for her to react this way. She didn't even believe the garbage she was handing me—or didn't used to. It's as though she was quoting someone else. Her husband, probably. Pompous little bastard. I used to try to like him for her sake."

"Her husband is prejudiced?"

"Her husband would have made a good Nazi. She used to joke about it—though never when he could hear."

"But she married him."

"Desperation. She would have married almost anybody." He smiled a little. "In high school, she and this friend of hers spent all their time together because neither of them could get a boy friend. The other girl was black and fat and homely, and Carol was white and fat and homely. Half the time, we couldn't figure out whether she lived at the girl's house or the girl lived with us. My friends knew them both, but they were too young for them—Carol's three years older than I am. Anyway, she and this girl sort of comforted each other and fell off their diets together and planned to go to the same college so they wouldn't have to break up the partnership. The other girl really went, but Carol changed her mind and trained to become a dental assistant. She wound up marrying the first dentist she ever worked for—a smug little reactionary twenty years older than she was. Now she lives in a big house in La Cañada and quotes clichéd bigotry at me for wanting to marry you."

I shrugged, not knowing what to say. I-told-you-so? Hardly. "My mother's car broke down in La Cañada once," I told him. "Three people called the police on her while she was waiting for my uncle to come and get her. Suspicious character. Five-three, she was. About a hundred pounds. Real dangerous."

"Sounds like the reactionary moved to the right town."

"I don't know, that was back in nineteen sixty just before my mother died. Things may have improved by now."

"What did your aunt and uncle say about me, Dana?"

I looked at my hands, thinking about all they had said, paring it down wearily. "I think my aunt accepts the idea of my marrying you because any children we have will be light. Lighter than I am, anyway. She always said I was a little too 'highly visible.'"

He stared at me.

"You see? I told you they were old. She doesn't care much for white people, but she prefers light-skinned blacks. Figure that out. Anyway, she 'forgives' me for you. But my uncle doesn't. He's sort of taken this personally."

"Personally, how?"

"He . . . well, he's my mother's oldest brother, and he was like a father to me even before my mother died because my father died when I was a baby. Now . . . it's as though I've rejected him. Or at least that's the way he feels. It bothered me, really. He was more hurt than mad. Honestly hurt. I had to get away from him."

"But, he knew you'd marry some day. How could a thing as natural as that be a rejection?"

"I'm marrying you." I reached up and twisted a few strands of his straight gray hair between my fingers. "He wants me to marry someone like him—someone who looks like him. A black man."

"Oh."

"I was always close to him. He and my aunt wanted kids, and they couldn't have any. I was their kid."

"And now?"

"Now . . . well, they have a couple of apartment houses over in Pasadena—small places, but nice. The last thing my uncle said to me was that he'd rather will them to his church than leave them to me and see them fall into white hands. I think that was the worst thing he could think of to do to me. Or he thought it was the worst thing."

"Oh hell," muttered Kevin. "Look, are you sure you still want to marry me?"

"Yes. I wish . . . never mind, just yes. Definitely, yes."

"Then let's go to Vegas and pretend we haven't got relatives."

So we drove to Las Vegas, got married, and gambled away a few dollars. When we came home to our bigger new apartment, we found a gift—a blender—from my best friend, and a check from *The Atlantic* waiting for us. One of my stories had finally made it.

2

I awoke.

I was lying flat on my stomach, my face pressed uncomfortably against something cold and hard. My body below the neck rested on something slightly softer. Slowly, I became aware of sunlight and shadow, of shapes.

I lifted my head, started to sit up, and my back suddenly caught fire. I fell forward, hit my head hard on the bare floor of the bathroom. My bathroom. I was home.

"Kevin?"

I listened. I could have looked around, but I didn't want to.

"Kevin?"

I got up, aware that my eyes were streaming muddy tears, aware of the pain. God, the pain! For several seconds, all I could do was lean against the wall and bear it.

Slowly, I discovered that I wasn't as weak as I had thought. In fact, by the time I was fully conscious, I wasn't weak at all. It was only the pain that made me move slowly, carefully, like a woman three times my age.

I could see now that I had been lying with my head in the bathroom and my body in the bedroom. Now I went into the bathroom and turned on the water to fill the tub. Warm water. I don't think I could have stood hot. Or cold.

My blouse was stuck to my back. It was cut to pieces, really, but the pieces were stuck to me. My back was cut up pretty badly too from what I could feel. I had seen old photographs of the backs of people who had been slaves. I could remember the scars, thick and ugly. Kevin had always told me how smooth my skin was . . .

I took off my pants and shoes and got into the tub still wearing my blouse. I would let the water soften it until I could ease it from my back.

In the tub, I sat for a long while without moving, without thinking, listening for what I knew I would not hear elsewhere in the house. The pain was a friend. Pain had never been a friend to me before, but now it kept me still. It forced reality on me and kept me sane.

But Kevin . . .

I leaned forward and cried into the dirty pink water. The skin of my back stretched agonizingly, and the water got pinker.

And it was all pointless. There was nothing I could do. I had no control at all over anything. Kevin might as well be dead. Abandoned in 1819, Kevin *was* dead. Decades dead, perhaps a century dead.

Maybe I would be called back again, and maybe he would still be there waiting for me and maybe only a few years would have passed for him, and maybe he would be all right . . . But what had he said once about going West watching history happen?

By the time my wounds had softened and my rag of a blouse had come unstuck from them, I was exhausted. I felt the weakness now that I hadn't felt before. I got out of the tub and dried myself as best I could, then stumbled into the bedroom and fell across the bed. In spite of the pain, I fell asleep at once.

The house was dark when I awoke, and the bed was empty except for me. I had to remember why all over again. I got up stiffly, painfully, and went to find something that would make me sleep again quickly. I didn't want to be awake. I barely wanted to be alive. Kevin had gotten a prescription for some pills once when he was having trouble sleeping.

I found what was left of them. I was about to take two of them when I got a look at myself in the medicine cabinet mirror. My face had swollen and was puffy and old-looking. My hair was in tangled patches, brown with dirt and matted with blood. In my semihysterical state earlier, I had not thought to wash it.

I put the pills down and climbed back into the tub. This time I turned on the shower and somehow managed to wash my hair. Raising my arms hurt. Bending forward hurt. The shampoo that got into my cuts hurt. I started slowly, wincing, grimacing. Finally I got angry and moved vigorously in spite of the pain.

When I looked passably human again, I took some aspirins. They didn't help much, but I was sane enough now to know that I had something to do before I could afford to sleep again.

I needed a replacement for my lost canvas bag. Something that didn't look too good for a "nigger" to be carrying. I finally settled on an old denim gym bag that I'd made and used back in high school. It was tough and roomy like the canvas bag, and faded enough to look properly shabby.

I would have put in a long dress this time if I'd had one. All I had, though, were a couple of bright filmy evening dresses that would have drawn attention to me, and, under the circumstances, made me look ridiculous. Best to go on being the woman who dressed like a man.

I rolled up a couple of pairs of jeans and stuffed them into the bag. Then shoes, shirts, a wool sweater, comb, brush, tooth paste and tooth brush—Kevin and I had really missed those—two large cakes of soap, my washcloth, the bottle of aspirins—if Rufus called me while my back was sore, I would need them—my knife. The knife had come back with me because I happened to be wearing it in a makeshift leather sheath at my ankle. I didn't know whether to be glad or not that I hadn't had a chance to use it against Weylin. I might have killed him. I had been angry enough, frightened enough, humiliated enough to try. Then if Rufus called me again, I would have to answer for the killing. Or maybe Kevin would have to answer for it. I was suddenly very glad that I had left Weylin alive. Kevin was in for enough trouble. And, too, when I saw Rufus again—if I saw him again—I would need his help. I wouldn't be likely to get it if I had killed his father—even a father he didn't like.

I stuffed another pencil, pen, and scratch pad into the bag. I was slowly emptying Kevin's desk. All my things were still packed. And I found a compact paperback history of slavery in America that might be useful. It listed dates and events that I should be aware of, and it contained a map of Maryland.

The bag was too full to close completely by the time everything was in, but I tied it shut with its own rope drawstring, and tied the drawstring around my arm. I couldn't have stood anything tied around my waist.

Then, incongruously, I was hungry. I went to the kitchen and found half-a-box of raisins and a full can of mixed nuts. To my surprise, I finished both, then slept again easily.

It was morning when I awoke, and I was still at home. My back hurt whenever I moved. I managed to spray it with an ointment Kevin had used for sunburn. The whip lacerations hurt like burns. The ointment cooled them and seemed to help. I had the feeling I should have used something stronger, though. Heaven knew what kind of infection you could get from a whip kept limber with oil and blood. Tom Weylin had ordered brine thrown onto the back of the field hand he had whipped. I could remember the man screaming as the solution hit him. But his wounds had healed without infection.

As I thought of the field hand, I felt strangely disoriented. For a moment, I thought Rufus was calling me again. Then I realized that I wasn't really dizzy—only confused. My memory of a field hand being whipped suddenly seemed to have no place here with me at home.

I came out of the bathroom into the bedroom and looked around. Home. Bed—without canopy—dresser, closet, electric light, television, radio, electric clock, books. Home. It didn't have anything to do with where I had been. It was real. It was where I belonged.

I put on a loose dress and went out to the front yard. The tiny blue-haired woman who lived next door noticed me and wished me a good morning. She was on her hands and knees digging in her flower garden and obviously enjoying herself. She reminded me of Margaret Weylin who also had flowers. I had heard Margaret's guests compliment her on her flowers. But, of course, she didn't take care of them herself . . .

Today and yesterday didn't mesh. I felt almost as strange as I had after my first trip back to Rufus—caught between his home and mine.

There was a Volvo parked across the street and there were powerlines overhead. There were palm trees and paved streets. There was the bathroom I had just left. Not a hole-in-the-ground privy toilet that you had to hold your breath to go into, but a bathroom.

I went back into the house and turned the radio on to an all-news station. There, eventually, I learned that it was Friday, June 11, 1976. I'd gone away for nearly two months and come back yesterday—the same day I left home. Nothing was real.

Kevin could be gone for years even if I went after him today and brought him back tonight.

I found a music station and turned the radio up loud to drown out my thinking.

The time passed and I did more unpacking, stopping often, taking too many aspirins. I began to bring some order to my own office. Once I sat down at my typewriter and tried to write about what had happened, made about six attempts before I gave up and threw them all away. Someday when this was over, if it was ever over, maybe I would be able to write about it.

I called my favorite cousin in Pasadena—my father's sister's daughter—and had her buy groceries for me. I told her I was sick and Kevin wasn't around. Something about my tone must have reached her. She didn't ask any questions.

I was still afraid to leave the house, walking or driving. Driving, I could easily kill myself, and the car could kill other people if Rufus called me from it at the wrong time. Walking, I could get dizzy and fall while crossing the street. Or I could fall on the sidewalk and attract attention. Someone could come to help me—a cop, anyone. Then I could be guilty of taking someone else back with me and stranding them.

My cousin was a good friend. She took one look at me and recommended a doctor she knew. She also advised me to send the police after Kevin. She assumed that my bruises were his work. But when I swore her to silence, I knew she would be silent. She and I had grown up keeping each other's secrets.

"I never thought you'd be fool enough to let a man beat you," she said as she left. She was disappointed in me, I think.

"I never thought I would either," I whispered when she was gone.

I waited inside the house with my denim bag always nearby.

The days passed slowly, and sometimes I thought I was waiting for something that just wasn't going to happen. But I went on waiting.

I read books about slavery, fiction and nonfiction. I read everything I had in the house that was even distantly related to the subject—even *Gone With the Wind*, or part of it. But its version of happy darkies in tender loving bondage was more than I could stand.

Then, somehow, I got caught up in one of Kevin's World War II books—a book of excerpts from the recollections of concentration camp survivors. Stories of beatings, starvation, filth, disease, torture, every possible degradation. As though the Germans had been trying to do in only a few years what the Americans had worked at for nearly two hundred.

The books depressed me, scared me, made me stuff Kevin's sleeping pills into my bag. Like the Nazis, ante bellum whites had known quite a bit about torture—quite a bit more than I ever wanted to learn.

3

I had been at home for eight days when the dizziness finally came again. I didn't know whether to curse it for my own sake or welcome it for Kevin's—not that it mattered what I did.

I went to Rufus's time fully clothed, carrying my denim bag, wearing my knife. I arrived on my knees because of the dizziness, but I was immediately alert and wary.

I was in the woods either late in the day or early in the morning. The sun was low in the sky and surrounded as I was by trees, I had no reference point to tell me whether it was rising or setting. I could see a stream not far from me, running between tall trees. Off to my opposite side was a woman, black, young—just a girl, really—with her dress torn down the front. She was holding it together as she watched a black man and a white man fighting.

The white man's red hair told me who he must be. His face was already too much of a mess to tell me. He was losing his fight—had already lost it. The man he was fighting was his size with the same slender build, but in spite of the black man's slenderness, he looked wiry and strong. He had probably been conditioned by years of hard work. He didn't seem much affected when Rufus hit him, but he was killing Rufus.

Then it occurred to me that he might really be doing just that—killing the only person who might be able to help me find Kevin. Killing my ancestor. What had happened here seemed obvious. The girl, her torn dress. If everything was as it seemed, Rufus had earned his beating and more. Maybe he had grown up to be even worse than I had feared. But no matter what he was, I needed him alive—for Kevin's sake and for my own.

I saw him fall, get up, and be knocked down again. This time, he got up more slowly, but he got up. I had a feeling he'd done a lot of getting up. He wouldn't be doing much more.

I went closer, and the woman saw me. She called out something I didn't quite understand, and the man turned his head to look at her. Then he followed her gaze to me. Just then, Rufus hit him on the jaw.

Surprisingly, the black man stumbled backward, almost fell. But Rufus was too tired and hurt to follow up his advantage. The black man hit him one more solid blow, and Rufus collapsed. There was no question of his getting up this time. He was out cold.

As I approached, the black man reached down and caught Rufus by the hair as though to hit him again. I stepped up to the man quickly. "What will they do to you if you kill him?" I said.

The man twisted around to glare at me.

"What will they do to the woman if you kill him?" I asked.

That seemed to reach him. He released Rufus and stood straight to face me. "Who's going to say I did anything to him?" His voice was low and threatening, and I began to wonder whether I might wind up joining Rufus unconscious on the ground.

I made myself shrug. "You'll say yourself what you did if they ask you right. So will the woman."

"What are you going to say?"

"Not a word if I can help it. But . . . I'm asking you not to kill him."

"You belong to him?"

"No. It's just that he might know where my husband is. And I might be able to get him to tell me."

"Your husband . . . ?" He looked me over from head to foot. "Why you go 'round dressed like a man?"

I said nothing. I was so tired of answering that question that I wished I had risked going out to buy a long dress. I looked down at Rufus's bloody face and said, "If you leave him here now, it will be a long while before he can send anyone after you. You'll have time to get away."

"You think you'd want him alive if you was her?" He gestured toward the woman.

"Is she your wife?"

"Yeah."

He was like Sarah, holding himself back, not killing in spite of anger I could only imagine. A lifetime of conditioning could be overcome, but not easily. I looked at the woman. "Do you want your husband to kill this man?"

She shook her head and I saw that her face was swollen on one side. "While ago, I could have killed him myself," she said. "Now . . . Isaac, let's just get away!"

"Get away and leave *her* here?" He stared at me, suspicious and hostile. "She sure don't talk like no nigger I ever heard. Talks like she been mighty close with the white folks—for a long time."

"She talks like that 'cause she comes from a long way off," said the girl.

I looked at her in surprise. Tall and slender and dark, she was. A little like me. Maybe a lot like me.

"You're Dana, aren't you?" she asked.

"Yes . . . how did you know?"

"He told me about you." She nudged Rufus with her foot. "He used to talk about you all the time. And I saw you once, when I was little."

I nodded. "You're Alice, then. I thought so."

She nodded and rubbed her swollen face. "I'm Alice." And she looked at the black man with pride. "Alice Jackson now."

I tried to see her again as the thin, frightened child I remembered—the child I had seen only two months before. It was impossible. But I should have been used to the impossible

by now—just as I should have been used to white men prey-
ing on black women. I had Weylin as my example, after all.
But somehow, I had hoped for better from Rufus. I wondered
whether the girl was pregnant with Hagar already.

"My name was Greenwood when you saw me last," Alice
continued. "I married Isaac last year . . . just before Mama
died."

"She died then?" I caught myself visualizing a woman my
age dying, even though I knew that was wrong. But still, the
woman must have died fairly young. "I'm sorry," I said. "She
tried to help me."

"She helped lot of folks," said Isaac. "She used to treat this
little no-good bastard better than his own people treated him."
He kicked Rufus hard in the side.

I winced and wished I could move Rufus out of his reach.
"Alice," I said, "wasn't Rufus a friend of yours? I mean . . .
did he just grow out of the friendship or what?"

"Got to where he wanted to be more friendly than I did,"
she said. "He tried to get Judge Holman to sell Isaac South to
keep me from marrying him."

"You're a slave?" I said to Isaac, surprised. "My God, you'd
better get out of here."

Isaac gave Alice a look that said very clearly, *You talk too
much*. Alice answered the look.

"Isaac, she's all right. She got a whipping once for teaching
a slave how to read. Tom Weylin was the one whipped her."

"I want to know what she's going to do when we leave,"
said Isaac.

"I'm going to stay with Rufus," I told him. "When he comes
to, I'm going to help him home—as slowly as possible. I'm not
going to tell him where you went because I won't know."

Isaac looked at Alice, and she tugged at his arm. "Let's go!"
she urged.

"But . . ."

"You can't whip everybody! Let's go!"

He seemed on the verge of going when I said, "Isaac, if
you want me to, I can write you a pass. It doesn't have to be
to where you're really going, but it might help you if you're
stopped."

He looked at me with no trust at all, then turned and walked away without answering.

Alice hesitated, spoke softly to me. "Your man went away," she said. "He waited a long time for you, then he left."

"Where did he go?"

"Somewhere North. I don't know. Mister Rufe knows. You got to be careful, though. Mister Rufe gets mighty crazy sometimes."

"Thank you."

She turned and followed Isaac, leaving me alone with the unconscious Rufus—alone to wonder where she and Isaac would go. North to Pennsylvania? I hoped so. And where had Kevin gone? Why had he gone anywhere? What if Rufus wouldn't help me find him? Or what if I didn't stay in this time long enough to find him? Why couldn't he have waited . . . ?

4

I knelt down beside Rufus and rolled him over onto his back. His nose was bleeding. His split lip was bleeding. I thought he had probably lost a few teeth, but I didn't look closely enough to be sure. His face was a lumpy mess, and he would be looking out of a couple of black eyes for a while. All in all, though, he probably looked worse off than he was. No doubt he had some bruises that I couldn't see without undressing him, but I didn't think he was badly hurt. He would be in some pain when he came to, but he had earned that.

I sat on my knees, watching him, first wishing he would hurry and regain consciousness, then wanting him to stay unconscious so that Alice and her husband could get a good start. I looked at the stream, thinking that a little cold water might bring him around faster. But I stayed where I was. Isaac's life was at stake. If Rufus was vindictive enough, he could surely have the man killed. A slave had no rights, and certainly no excuse for striking a white man.

If it was possible, if Rufus was in any way still the boy I had known, I would try to keep him from going after Isaac at all. He looked about eighteen or nineteen now. I would be able to bluff and bully him a little. It shouldn't take him long to realize that he and I needed each other. We would be taking turns helping each other now. Neither of us would want the other to hesitate. We would have to learn to co-operate with each other —to make compromises.

"Who's there?" said Rufus suddenly. His voice was weak, barely audible.

"It's Dana, Rufe."

"Dana?" He opened his swollen eyes a little wider. "You came back!"

"You keep trying to get yourself killed. I keep coming back."

"Where's Alice?"

"I don't know. I don't even know where we are. I'll help you get home, though, if you'll point the way."

"Where did she go?"

"I don't know, Rufe."

He tried to sit up, managed to raise himself about six inches before he fell back, groaning. "Where's Isaac?" he muttered. "That's the son-of-a-bitch I want to catch up with."

"Rest awhile," I said. "Get your strength back. You couldn't catch him now if he was standing next to you."

He moaned and felt his side gingerly. "He's going to pay!"

I got up and walked toward the stream.

"Where are you going?" he called.

I didn't answer.

"Dana? Come back here! Dana!"

I could hear his increasing desperation. He was hurt and alone except for me. He couldn't even get up, and I seemed to be abandoning him. I wanted him to experience a little of that fear.

"*Dana!*"

I dug the washcloth out of my denim bag, wet it, and took it back to him. Kneeling beside him, I began wiping blood from his face.

"Why didn't you tell me that's where you were going?" he said petulantly. He was panting and holding his side.

I watched him, wondering how much he had really grown up.

"Dana, say something!"

"I want you to say something."

He squinted at me. "What?" I was leaning close to him, and I caught a whiff of his breath when he spoke. He had been drinking. He didn't seem drunk, but he had definitely been drinking. That worried me, but there was nothing I could do about it. I didn't dare wait until he was completely sober.

"I want you to tell me about the men who attacked you," I said.

"What men? Isaac . . ."

"The men you were drinking with," I improvised. "They were strangers—white men. They got you drinking, then tried to rob you." Kevin's old story was coming in handy.

"What in hell are you talking about? You know Isaac Jackson did this to me!" The words came out in a harsh whisper.

"All right, Isaac beat you up," I agreed. "Why?"

He glared at me without answering.

"You raped a woman—or tried to—and her husband beat you up," I said. "You're lucky he didn't kill you. He would have if Alice and I hadn't talked him out of it. Now what are you going to do to repay us for saving your life?"

The bewilderment and anger left his face, and he stared at me blankly. After a while, he closed his eyes and I went over to rinse my washcloth. When I got back to him, he was trying—and failing—to stand up. Finally, he collapsed back panting and holding his side. I wondered whether he was hurt more than he appeared to be—hurt inside. His ribs, perhaps.

I knelt beside him again and wiped the rest of the blood and dirt from his face. "Rufe, did you manage to rape that girl?"

He looked away guiltily.

"Why would you do such a thing? She used to be your friend."

"When we were little, we were friends," he said softly. "We grew up. She got so she'd rather have a buck nigger than me!"

"Do you mean her husband?" I asked. I managed to keep my voice even.

"Who in hell else would I mean!"

"Yes." I gazed down at him bitterly. Kevin had been right. I'd been foolish to hope to influence him. "Yes," I repeated. "How dare she choose her own husband. She must have thought she was a free woman or something."

"What's that got to do with it?" he demanded. Then his voice dropped to almost a whisper. "I would have taken better care of her than any field hand could. I wouldn't have hurt her if she hadn't just kept saying no."

"She had the right to say no."

"We'll see about her rights!"

"Oh? Are you planning to hurt her more? She just helped me save your life, remember?"

"She'll get what's coming to her. She'll get it whether I give it to her or not." He smiled. "If she ran off with Isaac, she'll get plenty."

"Why? What do you mean?"

"She did run off with Isaac, then?"

"I don't know. Isaac figured I was on your side so he didn't trust me enough to tell me what they were going to do."

"He didn't have to. Isaac just attacked a white man. He's not going back to Judge Holman after doing that. Some other nigger might, but not Isaac. He's run away, and Alice is with him, helping him to escape. Or at least, that's the way the Judge will see it."

"What will happen to her?"

"Jail. A good whipping. Then they'll sell her."

"She'll be a slave?"

"Her own fault."

I stared at him. Heaven help Alice and Isaac. Heaven help me. If Rufus could turn so quickly on a life-long friend, how long would it take him to turn on me?

"I don't want her being sold South, though," he whispered. "Her fault or not, I don't want her dying in some rice swamp."

"Why not?" I asked bitterly. "Why should it matter to you?"

"I wish it didn't."

I frowned down at him. His tone had changed suddenly. Was he going to show a little humanity then? Did he have any left to show?

"I told her about you," he said.

"I know. She recognized me."

"I told her everything. Even about you and Kevin being married. Especially about that."

"What will you do, Rufe, if they bring her back?"

"Buy her. I've got some money."

"What about Isaac?"

"To hell with Isaac!" He said it too vehemently and hurt his side. His face twisted in pain.

"So you'll be rid of the man and have possession of the woman just as you wanted," I said with disgust. "Rape rewarded."

He turned his head toward me and peered at me through swollen eyes. "I begged her not to go with him," he said quietly. "Do you hear me, *I begged her!*"

I said nothing. I was beginning to realize that he loved the woman—to her misfortune. There was no shame in raping a black woman, but there could be shame in loving one.

"I didn't want to just drag her off into the bushes," said Rufus. "I never wanted it to be like that. But she kept saying no. I could have had her in the bushes years ago if that was all I wanted."

"I know," I said.

"If I lived in your time, I would have married her. Or tried to." He began trying to get up again. He seemed stronger now, but in pain. I sat watching him, but not helping. I was not eager for him to recover and go home—not until I was sure what story he would tell when he got there.

Finally, the pain seemed to overwhelm him and he lay down again. "What did that bastard do to me?" he whispered.

"I could go and get help for you," I said. "If you tell me which way to go."

"Wait." He caught his breath and coughed and the coughing hurt him badly. "Oh God," he moaned.

"I think you've got broken ribs," I said.

"I wouldn't be surprised. I guess you'd better go."

"All right. But, Rufe . . . white men attacked you. You hear?"

He said nothing.

"You said people would be going after Isaac anyway. All right then, so be it. But let him—and Alice—have a chance. They've given you one."

"It won't make any difference whether I tell or not. Isaac's a runaway. They'll have to answer for that, no matter what."

"Then your silence won't matter."

"Except to give them the start you want them to have."

I nodded. "I do want them to have it."

"You'll trust me, then?" He was watching me very closely. "If I say I won't tell, you'll believe me?"

"Yes." I paused for a moment. "We should never lie to each other, you and I. It wouldn't be worthwhile. We both have too much opportunity for retaliation."

He turned his face away from me. "You talk like a damn book."

"Then I hope Kevin did a good job of teaching you to read."

"You . . . !" He caught my arm in a grip I could have broken, but I let him hold on. "You threaten me, I'll threaten you. Without me, you'll never find Kevin."

"I know that."

"Then don't threaten me!"

"I said we were dangerous to each other. That's more a reminder than a threat." Actually, it was more a bluff.

"I don't need reminders or threats from you."

I said nothing.

"Well? Are you going to go get some help for me?"

Still I said nothing. I didn't move.

"You go through those trees," he said pointing. "There's a road out there, not too far away. Go left on the road and then just follow it until you come to our place."

I listened to his directions knowing that I would use them sooner or later. But we had to have an understanding first, he and I. He didn't have to admit that we had one. He could keep his pride if that was what he thought was at stake. But he did have to behave as though he understood me. If he refused, he was going to get a lot more pain now. And maybe later when Kevin was safe and Hagar had at least had a chance to be born —I might never find out about that—I would walk away from Rufus and leave him to get out of his own trouble.

"Dana!"

I looked at him. I had let my attention wander.

"I said she'll . . . they'll get their time. White men attacked me."

"Good, Rufe." I laid a hand on his shoulder. "Look, your father will listen to me, won't he? I don't know what he saw last time I went home."

"He doesn't know what he saw either. Whatever it was, he's seen it before—that time at the river—and he didn't believe it then, either. But he'll listen to you. He might even be a little afraid of you."

"That's better than the other way around. I'll get back as quickly as I can."

5

The road was farther away than I had expected. As it got darker—the sun was setting, not rising—I tore pages from my scratch pad and stuck them on trees now and then to mark my trail. Even then I worried that I might not be able to find my way back to Rufus.

When I reached the road, I pulled up some bushes and made a kind of barricade speckled with bits of white paper. That would stop me at the right place when I came back—if no one moved it meanwhile.

I followed the road until it was dark, followed it through woods, through fields, past a large house much finer than Weylin's. No one bothered me. I hid behind a tree once when two white men rode past. They might not have paid any attention to me, but I didn't want to take the chance. And there were three black women walking with large bundles balanced on their heads.

"'Evenin'," they said as I passed them.

I nodded and wished them a good evening. And I walked faster, wondering suddenly what the years had done to Luke and Sarah, to Nigel and Carrie. The children who had played at selling each other might already be working in the fields now. And what would time have done to Margaret Weylin? I doubted that it had made her any easier to live with.

Finally, after more woods and fields, the plain square house was before me, its downstairs windows full of yellow light. I was startled to catch myself saying wearily, "Home at last."

I stood still for a moment between the fields and the house and reminded myself that I was in a hostile place. It didn't look alien any longer, but that only made it more dangerous, made me more likely to relax and make a mistake.

I rubbed my back, touched the several long scabs to remind myself that I could not afford to make mistakes. And the scabs forced me to remember that I had been away from this place for only a few days. Not that I had forgotten—exactly. But it was as though during my walk I had been getting used to the idea that years had passed for these people since I had seen them last. I had begun to feel—feel, not think—that a great deal of time had passed for me too. It was a vague feeling, but it seemed right and comfortable. More comfortable than trying to keep in mind what was really happening. Some part of me had apparently given up on time-distorted reality and smoothed things out. Well, that was all right, as long as it didn't go too far.

I continued on toward the house, mentally prepared now, I hoped, to meet Tom Weylin. But as I approached, a tall thin shadow of a white man came toward me from the direction of the quarter.

"Hey there," he called. "What are you doing out here?" His long steps closed the distance between us quickly, and in a moment, he stood peering down at me. "You don't belong here," he said. "Who's your master?"

"I've come to get help for Mister Rufus," I said. And then, feeling suddenly doubtful because he was a stranger, I asked, "This is still where he lives, isn't it?"

The man did not answer. He continued to peer at me. I wondered whether it was my sex or my accent that he was trying to figure out. Or maybe it was the fact that I hadn't called him sir or master. I'd have to begin that degrading nonsense again. But who was this man, anyway?

"He lives here." An answer, finally. "What's wrong with him?"

"Some men beat him. He can't walk."

"Is he drunk?"

"Uh . . . no, sir, not quite."

"Worthless bastard."

I jumped a little. The man had spoken softly, but there was no mistaking what he had said. I said nothing.

"Come on," he ordered, and led me into the house. He left me standing in the entrance hall and went to the library where I supposed Weylin was. I looked at the wooden bench a few steps from me, the settee, but although I was tired, I didn't sit down. Margaret Weylin had once caught me sitting there tying my shoe. She had screamed and raged as though she'd caught me stealing her jewelry. I didn't want to renew my acquaintance with her in another scene like that. I didn't want to renew my acquaintance with her at all, but it seemed inevitable.

There was a sound behind me and I turned in quick apprehension. A young slave woman stood staring at me. She was light-skinned, blue-kerchiefed, and very pregnant.

"Carrie?" I asked.

She ran to me, caught me by the shoulders for a moment, and looked into my face. Then she hugged me.

The white stranger chose that moment to come out of the library with Tom Weylin.

"What's going on here?" demanded the stranger.

Carrie moved away from me quickly, head down, and I said, "We're old friends, sir."

Tom Weylin, grayer, thinner, grimmer-looking than ever, came over to me. He stared at me for a moment, then turned to face the stranger. "When did you say his horse came in, Jake?"

"About an hour ago."

"That long . . . you should have told me."

"He's taken that long and longer before."

Weylin sighed, glanced at me. "Yes. But I think it might be more serious this time. Carrie!"

The mute woman had been walking away toward the back door. Now, she turned to look at Weylin.

"Have Nigel bring the wagon around front."

She gave the half-nod, half-curtsey that she reserved for whites and hurried away.

Something occurred to me as she was going and I spoke to Weylin. "I think Mister Rufus might have broken ribs. He wasn't coughing blood so his lungs are probably all right, but it might be a good idea for me to bandage him a little before you move him." I had never bandaged anything worse than a cut finger in my life, but I did remember a little of the first aid I had learned in school. I hadn't thought to act when Rufus broke his leg, but I might be able to help now.

"You can bandage him when we get him here," said Weylin. And to the stranger, "Jake, you send somebody for the doctor."

Jake took a last disapproving look at me and went out the back door after Carrie.

Weylin went out the front door without another word to me and I followed, trying to remember how important it was to bandage broken ribs—that is, whether it was worth "talking back" to Weylin about. I didn't want Rufus badly injured, even though he deserved to be. Any injury could be dangerous. But from what I could remember, bandaging the ribs was done mostly to relieve pain. I wasn't sure whether I remembered that because it was true or because I wanted to avoid any kind of confrontation with Weylin. I didn't have to touch the scabs on my back to be conscious of them.

A tall stocky slave drove a wagon around to us and I got on the back while Weylin took the seat beside the driver. The driver glanced back at me and said softly, "How are you, Dana?"

"Nigel?"

"It's me," he said grinning. "Grown some since you seen me last, I guess."

He had grown into another Luke—a big handsome man bearing little resemblance to the boy I remembered.

"You keep your mouth shut and watch the road," said Weylin. Then to me, "You've got to tell us where to go."

It would have been a pleasure to tell him where to go, but I spoke civilly. "It's a long way from here," I said. "I had to pass someone else's house and fields on my way to you."

"The judge's place. You could have got help there."

"I didn't know." And wouldn't have tried if I had known. I wondered, though, whether this was the Judge Holman who would soon be sending men out to chase Isaac. It seemed likely.

"Did you leave Rufus by the side of the road?" Weylin asked.

"No, sir. He's in the woods."

"You sure you know where in the woods?"

"Yes, sir."

"You'd better."

He said nothing else.

I found Rufus with no particular difficulty and Nigel lifted him as gently and as easily as Luke once had. On the wagon, he held his side, then he held my hand. Once, he said, "I'll keep my word."

I nodded and touched his forehead in case he couldn't see me nodding. His forehead was hot and dry.

"He'll keep his word about what?" asked Weylin.

He was looking back at me, so I frowned and looked perplexed and said, "I think he has a fever as well as broken ribs, sir."

Weylin made a sound of disgust. "He was sick yesterday, puking all over. But he would get up and go out today. Damn fool!"

And he fell silent again until we reached his house. Then, as Nigel carried Rufus inside and up the stairs, Weylin steered me into his forbidden library. He pushed me close to a whale-oil lamp, and there, in the bright yellow light, he stared at me silently, critically until I looked toward the door.

"You're the same one, all right," he said finally. "I didn't want to believe it."

I said nothing.

"Who are you?" he demanded. "What are you?"

I hesitated not knowing what to answer because I didn't know how much he knew. The truth might make him decide I was out of my mind, but I didn't want to be caught in a lie.

"Well!"

"I don't know what you want me to say," I told him. "I'm Dana. You know me."

"Don't tell me what I know!"

I stood silent, confused, frightened. Kevin wasn't here now. There was no one for me to call if I needed help.

"I'm someone who may have just saved your son's life," I said softly. "He might have died out there sick and injured and alone."

"And you think I ought to be grateful?"

Why did he sound angry? And why shouldn't he be grateful? "I can't tell you how you ought to feel, Mr. Weylin."

"That's right. You can't."

There was a moment of silence that he seemed to expect me to fill. Eagerly, I changed the subject. "Mr. Weylin, do you know where Mr. Franklin went?"

Oddly, that seemed to reach him. His expression softened a little. "Him," he said. "Damn fool."

"Where did he go?"

"Somewhere North. I don't know. Rufus has some letters from him." He gave me another long stare. "I guess you want to stay here."

He sounded as though he was giving me a choice, which was surprising because he didn't have to. Maybe gratitude meant something to him after all.

"I'd like to stay for a while," I said. Better to try to reach Kevin from here than go wandering around some Northern city trying to find him. Especially since I had no money, and since I was still so ignorant of this time.

"You got to work for your keep," said Weylin. "Like you did before."

"Yes, sir."

"That Franklin comes back, he'll stop here. He came back once—hoping to find you, I think."

"When?"

"Last year sometime. You go up and stay with Rufus until the doctor comes. Take care of him."

"Yes, sir." I turned to go.

"That seems to be what you're for, anyway," he muttered.

I kept going, glad to get away from him. He had known more about me than he wanted to talk about. That was clear from the questions he hadn't asked. He had seen me vanish twice now. And Kevin and Rufus had probably told him at least something about me. I wondered how much. And I wondered what Kevin had said or done that made him a "damn fool."

Whatever it was, I'd learn about it from Rufus. Weylin was too dangerous to question.

6

I sponged Rufus off as best I could and bandaged his ribs with pieces of cloth that Nigel brought me. The ribs were very tender on the left side. Rufus said the bandage made breathing a little less painful, though, and I was glad of that. But he was still sick. His fever was still with him. And the doctor didn't come. Rufus had fits of coughing now and then, and that seemed to be agonizing to him because of his ribs. Sarah came in to see him—and to hug me—and she was more alarmed at the marks of his beating than at his ribs or his fever. His face was black and blue and deformed-looking with its lumpy swellings.

"He will fight," she said angrily. Rufus opened his puffy slits of eyes and looked at her, but she went on anyway. "I've seen him pick a fight just out of meanness," she said. "He's out to get himself killed!"

She could have been his mother, caught between anger and concern and not knowing which to express. She took away the basin Nigel had brought me and returned it full of clean cool water.

"Where's his mother?" I asked her softly as she was leaving.

She drew back from me a little. "Gone."

"Dead?"

"Not yet." She glanced at Rufus to see whether he was listening. His face was turned away from us. "Gone to Baltimore," she whispered. "I'll tell you 'bout it tomorrow."

I let her go without questioning her further. It was enough to know that I would not be suddenly attacked. For once, there would be no Margaret to protect Rufus from me.

He was thrashing about weakly when I went back to him. He cursed the pain, cursed me, then remembered himself enough to say he didn't mean it. He was burning up.

"Rufe?"

He moved his head from side to side and did not seem to hear me. I dug into my denim bag and found the plastic bottle of aspirin—a big bottle nearly full. There was enough to share.

"Rufe!"

He squinted at me.

"Listen, I have medicine from my own time." I poured him a glass of water from the pitcher beside his bed, and shook out two aspirin tablets. "These could lower your fever," I said. "They might ease your pain too. Will you take them?"

"What are they?"

"They're called aspirin. In my time, people use them against headache, fever, other kinds of pain."

He looked at the two tablets in my hand, then at me. "Give them to me."

He had trouble swallowing them and had to chew them up a little.

"My Lord," he muttered. "Anything tastes that bad must be good for you."

I laughed and wet a cloth in the basin to bathe his face. Nigel came in with a blanket and told me the doctor was held up at a difficult childbirth. I was to stay the night with Rufus.

I didn't mind. Rufus was in no condition to take an interest in me. I would have thought it would be more natural, though, for Nigel to stay. I asked him about it.

"Marse Tom knows about you," said Nigel softly. "Marse Rufe and Mister Kevin both told him. He figures you know enough to do some doctoring. More than doctoring, maybe. He saw you go home."

"I know."

"I saw it too."

I looked up at him—he was a head taller than me now—and saw nothing but curiosity in his eyes. If my vanishing had frightened him, the fear was long dead. I was glad of that. I wanted his friendship.

"Marse Tom says you s'pose to take care of him and you better do a good job. Aunt Sarah says you call her if you need help."

"Thanks. Thank her for me."

He nodded, smiled a little. "Good thing for me you showed up. I want to be with Carrie now. It's so close to her time."

I grinned. "Your baby, Nigel? I thought it might be."

"Better be mine. She's my wife."

"Congratulations."

"Marse Rufe paid a free preacher from town to come and say the same words they say for white folks and free niggers. Didn't have to jump no broomstick."

I nodded, remembering what I'd read about the slaves' marriage ceremonies. They jumped broomsticks, sometimes backward, sometimes forward, depending on local custom; or they stood before their master and were pronounced husband and wife; or they followed any number of other practices even to hiring a minister and having things done as Nigel had. None of it made any difference legally, though. No slave marriage was legally binding. Even Alice's marriage to Isaac was merely an informal agreement since Isaac was a slave, or had been a slave. I hoped now that he was a free man well on his way to Pennsylvania.

"Dana?"

I looked up at Nigel. He had whispered my name so softly I had hardly heard him.

"Dana, was it white men?"

Startled, I put a finger to my lips, cautioning, and waved him away. "Tomorrow," I promised.

But he wasn't as co-operative as I had been with Sarah. "Was it Isaac?"

I nodded, hoping he would be satisfied and let the subject drop.

"Did he get away?"

Another nod.

He left me, looking relieved.

I stayed up with Rufus until he managed to fall asleep. The aspirins did seem to help. Then I wrapped myself in the blanket, pulled the room's two chairs together in front of the fireplace, and settled in as comfortably as I could. It wasn't bad.

The doctor arrived late the next morning to find Rufus's fever gone. The rest of his body was still bruised and sore, and his ribs still kept him breathing shallowly and struggling not to cough, but even with that, he was much less miserable. I had gotten him a breakfast tray from Sarah, and he had invited me to share the large meal she had prepared. I ate hot biscuits with butter and peach preserve, drank some of his coffee, and had a little cold ham. It was good and filling. He had the eggs, the rest of the ham, the corn cakes. There was too much of everything, and he didn't feel like eating very much. Instead, he sat back and watched me with amusement.

"Daddy'd do some cussin' if he came in here and found us eating together," he said.

I put down my biscuit and reined in whatever part of my mind I'd left in 1976. He was right.

"What are you doing then? Trying to make trouble?"

"No. He won't bother us. Eat."

"The last time someone told me he wouldn't bother me, he walked in and beat the skin off my back."

"Yeah. I know about that. But I'm not Nigel. If I tell you to do something, and he doesn't like it, he'll come to me about it. He won't whip you for following *my* orders. He's a fair man."

I looked at him, startled.

"I said fair," he repeated. "Not likable."

I kept quiet. His father wasn't the monster he could have been with the power he held over his slaves. He wasn't a monster at all. Just an ordinary man who sometimes did the monstrous things his society said were legal and proper. But I had seen no particular fairness in him. He did as he pleased. If you told him he wasn't being fair, he would whip you for talking back. At least the Tom Weylin I had known would have. Maybe he had mellowed.

"Stay," said Rufus. "No matter what you think of him, I won't let him hurt you. And it's good to eat with someone I can talk to for a change."

That was nice. I began to eat again, wondering why he was in such a good mood this morning. He had come a long way from his anger the night before—from threatening not to tell me where Kevin was.

"You know," said Rufus thoughtfully, "you still look mighty young. You pulled me out of that river thirteen or fourteen years ago, but you look like you would have been just a kid back then."

Uh-oh. "Kevin didn't explain that part, I guess."

"Explain what?"

I shook my head. "Just . . . let me tell you how it's been for me. I can't tell you why things are happening as they are, but I can tell you the order of their happening." I hesitated, gathering my thoughts. "When I came to you at the river, it was June ninth, nineteen seventy-six for me. When I got home, it was still the same day. Kevin told me I had only been gone a few seconds."

"Seconds . . . ?"

"Wait. Let me tell it all to you at once. Then you can have all the time you need to digest it and ask questions. Later, on that same day, I came to you again. You were three or four years older and busy trying to set the house afire. When I went home, Kevin told me only a few minutes had passed. The next morning, June tenth, I came to you because you'd fallen out of a tree. . . . Kevin and I came to you. I was here nearly two months. But when I went home, I found that I had lost only a few minutes or hours of June tenth."

"You mean after two months, you . . ."

"I arrived home on the same day I had left. Don't ask me how. I don't know. After eight days at home, I came back here." I faced him silently for a moment. "And, Rufe, now that I'm here, now that you're safe, I want to find my husband."

He absorbed this slowly, frowning as though he was translating it from another language. Then he waved vaguely toward his desk—a new larger desk than he had had on my last visit. The old one had been nothing more than a little table. This one had a roll-top and plenty of drawer space both above and below the work surface.

"His letters are in the middle drawer there. You can have them if you want them. They have his addresses . . . But Dana, you're saying while I've been growing up, somehow, time has been almost standing still for you."

I was at the desk hunting through the cluttered drawer for the letters. "It hasn't stood still," I said. "I'm sure my last two visits here have aged me quite a bit, no matter what my calendar at home says." I found the letters. Three of them—short notes on large pieces of paper that had been folded, sealed with sealing wax, and mailed without an envelope. "Here's my Philadelphia address," Kevin said in one. "If I can get a decent job, I'll be here for a while." That was all, except for the address. Kevin wrote books, but he'd never cared much for writing letters. At home he tried to catch me in a good mood and get me to take care of his correspondence for him.

"I'll be an old man," said Rufus, "and you'll still come to me looking just like you do now."

I shook my head. "Rufe, if you don't start being more careful, you'll never live to be an old man. Now that you're grown up, I might not be able to help you much. The kind of trouble you get into as a man might be as overwhelming to me as it is to you."

"Yes. But this time thing . . ."

I shrugged.

"Damnit, there must be something mighty crazy about both of us, Dana. I never heard of anything like this happening to anybody else."

"Neither have I." I looked at the other two letters. One from New York, and one from Boston. In the Boston one, he was talking about going to Maine. I wondered what was driving him farther and farther north. He had been interested in the West, but Maine . . . ?

"I'll write to him," said Rufus. "I'll tell him you're here. He'll come running back."

"I'll write him, Rufe."

"I'll have to mail the letter."

"All right."

"I just hope he hasn't already taken off for Maine."

Weylin opened the door before I could answer. He brought in another man who turned out to be the doctor, and my leisure time was over. I put Kevin's letters back into Rufus's desk —that seemed the best place to keep them—took away the breakfast tray, brought the doctor the empty basin he asked for, stood by while the doctor asked Weylin whether I had any sense or not and whether I could be trusted to answer simple questions accurately.

Weylin said yes twice without looking at me, and the doctor asked his questions. Was I sure Rufus had had a fever? How did I know? Had he been delirious? Did I know what delirious meant? Smart nigger, wasn't I?

I hated the man. He was short and slight, black-haired and black-eyed, pompous, condescending, and almost as ignorant medically as I was. He guessed he wouldn't bleed Rufus since the fever seemed to be gone—bleed him! He guessed a couple of ribs were broken, yes. He rebandaged them sloppily. He guessed I could go now; he had no more use for me.

I escaped to the cookhouse.

"What's the matter with you?" asked Sarah when she saw me.

I shook my head. "Nothing important. Just a stupid little man who may be one step up from spells and good luck charms."

"What?"

"Don't pay any attention to me, Sarah. Do you have anything for me to do out here? I'd like to stay out of the house for a while."

"Always something to do out here. You have anything to eat?"

I nodded.

She lifted her head and gave me one of her down-the-nose looks. "Well, I put enough on his tray. Here. Knead this dough."

She gave me a bowl of bread dough that had risen and was ready to be kneaded down. "He all right?" she asked.

"He's healing."

"Was Isaac all right?"

I glanced at her. "Yes."

"Nigel said he didn't think Marse Rufe told what happened."

"He didn't. I managed to talk him out of it."

She laid a hand on my shoulder for a moment. "I hope you stay around for a while, girl. Even his daddy can't talk him out of much these days."

"Well, I'm glad I was able to. But look, you promised to tell me about his mother."

"Not much to tell. She had two more babies—twins. Sickly little things. They lingered awhile, then died one after the other. She almost died too. She went kind of crazy. The birth had left her pretty bad off anyhow—sick, hurt inside. She fought with Marse Tom, got so she'd scream at him every time she saw him—cussin' and goin' on. She was hurtin' most of the time, couldn't get out of bed. Finally, her sister came and got her, took her to Baltimore."

"And she's still there?"

"Still there, still sick. Still crazy, for all I know. I just hope she stays there. That overseer, Jake Edwards, he's a cousin of hers, and he's all the mean low white trash we need around here."

Jake Edwards was the overseer then. Weylin had begun hiring overseers. I wondered why. But before I could ask, two house servants came in and Sarah deliberately turned her back to me, ending the conversation. I began to understand what had happened later, though, when I asked Nigel where Luke was.

"Sold," said Nigel quietly. And he wouldn't say anything more. Rufus told me the rest.

"You shouldn't have asked Nigel about that," he told me when I mentioned the incident.

"I wouldn't have, if I'd known." Rufus was still in bed. The doctor had given him a purgative and left. Rufus had poured the purgative into his chamber pot and ordered me to tell his father he'd taken it. He had had his father send me back to him so that I could write my letter to Kevin. "Luke did his work," I said. "How could your father sell him?"

"He worked all right. And the hands would work hard for him—mostly without the cowhide. But sometimes he didn't show much sense." Rufus stopped, began a deep breath, caught himself and grimaced in pain. "You're like Luke in some ways," he continued. "So you'd better show some sense yourself, Dana. You're on your own this time."

"But what did he do wrong? What am I doing wrong?"

"Luke . . . he would just go ahead and do what he wanted to no matter what Daddy said. Daddy always said he thought he was white. One day maybe two years after you left, Daddy got tired of it. New Orleans trader came through and Daddy said it would be better to sell Luke than to whip him until he ran away."

I closed my eyes remembering the big man, hearing again his advice to Nigel on how to defy the whites. It had caught up with him. "Do you think the trader took him all the way to New Orleans?" I asked.

"Yeah. He was getting a load together to ship them down there."

I shook my head. "Poor Luke. Are there cane fields in Louisiana now?"

"Cane, cotton, rice, they grow plenty down there."

"My father's parents worked in the cane fields there before they went to California. Luke could be a relative of mine."

"Just make sure you don't wind up like him."

"I haven't done anything."

"Don't go teaching nobody else to read."

"Oh."

"Yes, oh. I might not be able to stop Daddy if he decided to sell you."

"Sell me! He doesn't own me. Not even by the law here. He doesn't have any papers saying he owns me."

"Dana, don't talk stupid!"

"But . . ."

"In town, once, I heard a man brag how he and his friends had caught a free black, tore up his papers, and sold him to a trader."

I said nothing. He was right, of course. I had no rights—not even any papers to be torn up.

"Just be careful," he said quietly.

I nodded. I thought I could escape from Maryland if I had to. I didn't think it would be easy, but I thought I could do it. On the other hand, I didn't see how even someone much wiser than I was in the ways of the time could escape from Louisiana, surrounded as they would be by water and slave states. I would have to be careful, all right, and be ready to run if I seemed to be in any danger of being sold.

"I'm surprised Nigel is still here," I said. Then I realized that might not be a very bright thing to say even to Rufus. I would have to learn to keep more of my thoughts to myself.

"Oh, Nigel ran away," said Rufus. "Patrollers brought him back, though, hungry and sick. They had whipped him, and Daddy whipped him some more. Then Aunt Sarah doctored him and I talked Daddy into letting me keep him. I think my job was harder. I don't think Daddy relaxed until Nigel married Carrie. Man marries, has children, he's more likely to stay where he is."

"You sound like a slaveholder already."

He shrugged.

"Would you have sold Luke?"

"No! I liked him."

"Would you sell anyone?"

He hesitated. "I don't know. I don't think so."

"I hope not," I said watching him. "You don't have to do that kind of thing. Not all slaveholders do it."

I took my denim bag from where I had hidden it under his bed, and sat down at his desk to write the letter, using one of his large sheets of paper with my pen. I didn't want to bother dipping the quill and steel pen on his desk into ink.

"Dear Kevin, I'm back. And I want to go North too . . ."

"Let me see your pen when you're finished," said Rufus.

"All right."

I went on writing, feeling myself strangely near tears. It was as though I was really talking to Kevin. I began to believe I would see him again.

"Let me see the other things you brought with you," said Rufus.

I swung the bag onto his bed. "You can look," I said, and continued writing. Not until I was finished with the letter did I look up to see what he was doing.

He was reading my book.

"Here's the pen," I said casually, and I waited to grab the book the moment he put it down. But instead of putting it down, he ignored the pen and looked up at me.

"This is the biggest lot of abolitionist trash I ever saw."

"No it isn't," I said. "That book wasn't even written until a century after slavery was abolished."

"Then why the hell are they still complaining about it?"

I pulled the book down so that I could see the page he had been reading. A photograph of Sojourner Truth stared back at me solemn-eyed. Beneath the picture was part of the text of one of her speeches.

"You're reading history, Rufe. Turn a few pages and you'll find a white man named J. D. B. De Bow claiming that slavery is good because, among other things, it gives poor whites someone to look down on. That's history. It happened whether it offends you or not. Quite a bit of it offends me, but there's nothing I can do about it." And there was other history that he must not read. Too much of it hadn't happened yet. Sojourner Truth, for instance, was still a slave. If someone bought her from her New York owners and brought her South before the Northern laws could free her, she might spend the rest of her life picking cotton. And there were two important slave children right here in Maryland. The older one, living here in Talbot County, would be called Frederick Douglass after a name change or two. The second, growing up a few miles south in Dorchester County, was Harriet Ross, eventually to be Harriet Tubman. Someday, she was going to cost Eastern Shore plantation owners a huge amount of money by guiding three hundred of their runaway slaves to freedom. And farther down in Southampton, Virginia, a man named Nat Turner was biding his time. There were more. I had said I couldn't do anything to change history. Yet, if history could be changed, this book in the hands of a white man—even a sympathetic white man—might be the thing to change it.

"History like this could send you down to join Luke," said Rufus. "Didn't I tell you to be careful!"

"I wouldn't have let anyone else see it." I took it from his hand, spoke more softly. "Or are you telling me I shouldn't trust you either?"

He looked startled. "Hell, Dana, we have to trust each other. You said that yourself. But what if my daddy went through that bag of yours. He could if he wanted to. You couldn't stop him."

I said nothing.

"You've never had a whipping like he'd give you if he found that book. Some of that reading . . . He'd take you to be another Denmark Vesey. You know who Vesey was?"

"Yes." A freedman who had plotted to free others violently.

"You know what they did to him?"

"Yes."

"Then put that book in the fire."

I held the book for a moment, then opened it to the map of Maryland. I tore the map out.

"Let me see," said Rufus.

I handed him the map. He looked at it and turned it over. Since there was nothing on the back but a map of Virginia, he handed it back to me. "That will be easier to hide," he said. "But you know if a white man sees it, he'll figure you mean to use it to escape."

"I'll take my chances."

He shook his head in disgust.

I tore the book into several pieces and threw it onto the hot coals in his fireplace. The fire flared up and swallowed the dry paper, and I found my thoughts shifting to Nazi book burnings. Repressive societies always seemed to understand the danger of "wrong" ideas.

"Seal your letter," said Rufus. "There's wax and a candle on the desk there. I'll send the letter as soon as I can get to town."

I obeyed inexpertly, dripping hot wax on my fingers.

"Dana . . . ?"

I glanced at him, caught him watching me with unexpected intensity. "Yes?"

His eyes seemed to slide away from mine. "That map is still bothering me. Listen, if you want me to get that letter to town soon, you put the map in the fire too."

I turned to face him, dismayed. More blackmail. I had

thought that was over between us. I had hoped it was over; I needed so much to trust him. I didn't dare stay with him if I couldn't trust him.

"I wish you hadn't said that, Rufe," I told him quietly. I went over to him, fighting down anger and disappointment, and began putting the things that he had scattered back into my bag.

"Wait a minute." He caught my hand. "You get so damned cold when you're mad. Wait!"

"For what?"

"Tell me what you're mad about."

What, indeed? Could I make him see why I thought his blackmail was worse than my own? It was. He threatened to keep me from my husband if I did not submit to his whim and destroy a paper that might help me get free. I acted out of desperation. He acted out of whimsy or anger. Or so it seemed.

"Rufe, there are things we just can't bargain on. This is one of them."

"You're going to tell me what we can't bargain on?" He sounded more surprised than indignant.

"You're damn right I am." I spoke very softly. "I won't bargain away my husband or my freedom!"

"You don't have either to bargain."

"Neither do you."

He stared at me with at least as much confusion as anger, and that was encouraging. He could have let his temper flare, could have driven me from the plantation very quickly. "Look," he said through his teeth, "I'm trying to help you!"

"Are you?"

"What do you think I'm doing? Listen, I know Kevin tried to help you. He made things easier for you by keeping you with him. But he couldn't really protect you. He didn't know how. He couldn't even protect himself. Daddy almost had to shoot him when you disappeared. He was fighting and cursing . . . at first Daddy didn't even know why. I'm the one who helped Kevin get back on the place."

"You?"

"I talked Daddy into seeing him again—and it wasn't easy. I may not be able to talk him into anything for you if he sees that map."

"I see."

He waited, watching me. I wanted to ask him what he would do with my letter if I didn't burn the map. I wanted to ask, but I didn't want to hear an answer that might send me out to face another patrol or earn another whipping. I wanted to do things the easy way if I could. I wanted to stay here and let a letter go to Boston and bring Kevin back to me.

So I told myself the map was more a symbol than a necessity anyway. If I had to go, I knew how to follow the North Star at night. I had made a point of learning. And by day, I knew how to keep the rising sun to my right and the setting sun to my left.

I took the map from Rufus's desk and dropped it into the fireplace. It darkened, then burst into flame.

"I can manage without it, you know," I said quietly.

"No need for you to," said Rufus. "You'll be all right here. You're home."

7

Isaac and Alice had four days of freedom together. On the fifth day, they were caught. On the seventh day, I found out about it. That was the day Rufus and Nigel took the wagon into town to mail my letter and take care of some business of their own. I had heard nothing of the runaways and Rufus seemed to have forgotten about them. He was feeling better, looking better. That seemed to be enough for him. He came to me just before he left and said, "Let me have some of your aspirins. I might need them the way Nigel drives."

Nigel heard and called out, "Marse Rufe, you can drive. I'll just sit back and relax while you show me how to go smooth over a bumpy road."

Rufus threw a clod of dirt at him, and he caught it, laughing, and threw it back just missing Rufus. "See there?" Rufus told me. "Here I am all crippled up and he's taking advantage."

I laughed and got the aspirins. Rufus never took anything from my bag without asking—though he could have easily done so.

"You sure you feel well enough to go to town?" I asked as I gave them to him.

"No," he said, "but I'm going." I didn't find out until later that a visitor had brought him word of Alice and Isaac's capture. He was going to get Alice.

And I went to the laundry yard to help a young slave named Tess to beat and boil the dirt out of a lot of heavy smelly clothes. She had been sick, and I had promised her I would help. My work was still pretty much whatever I wanted it to be. I felt a little guilty about that. No other slave—house or field—had that much freedom. I worked where I pleased, or where I saw that others needed help. Sarah sent me to do one job or another sometimes, but I didn't mind that. In Margaret's absence, Sarah ran the house—and the house servants. She spread the work fairly and managed the house as efficiently as Margaret had, but without much of the tension and strife Margaret generated. She was resented, of course, by slaves who made every effort to avoid jobs they didn't like. But she was also obeyed.

"Lazy niggers!" she would mutter when she had to get after someone.

I stared at her in surprise when I first heard her say it. "Why should they work hard?" I asked. "What's it going to get them?"

"It'll get them the cowhide if they don't," she snapped. "I ain't goin' to take the blame for what they don't do. Are you?"

"Well, no, but . . ."

"I work. You work. Don't need somebody behind us all the time to make us work."

"When the time comes for me to stop working and get out of here, I'll do it."

She jumped, looked around quickly. "You got no sense sometimes! Just talk all over your mouth!"

"We're alone."

"Might not be alone as we look. People listen around here. And they talk too."

I said nothing.

"You do what you want to do—or think you want to do. But you keep it to yourself."

I nodded. "I hear."

She lowered her voice to a whisper. "You need to look at some of the niggers they catch and bring back," she said. "You need to see them—starving, 'bout naked, whipped, dragged, bit by dogs. . . . You need to see them."

"I'd rather see the others."

"What others?"

"The ones who make it. The ones living in freedom now."

"If any do."

"They do."

"Some say they do. It's like dying, though, and going to heaven. Nobody ever comes back to tell you about it."

"Come back and be enslaved again?"

"Yeah. But still . . . This is dangerous talk! No point to it anyway."

"Sarah, I've seen books written by slaves who've run away and lived in the North."

"Books!" She tried to sound contemptuous but sounded uncertain instead. She couldn't read. Books could be awesome mysteries to her, or they could be dangerous time-wasting nonsense. It depended on her mood. Now her mood seemed to flicker between curiosity and fear. Fear won. "Foolishness!" she said. "Niggers writing books!"

"But it's true. I've seen . . ."

"Don't want to hear no more 'bout it!" She had raised her voice sharply. That was unusual, and it seemed to surprise her as much as it surprised me. "Don't want to hear no more," she repeated softly. "Things ain't bad here. I can get along."

She had done the safe thing—had accepted a life of slavery because she was afraid. She was the kind of woman who might have been called "mammy" in some other household. She was the kind of woman who would be held in contempt during the militant nineteen sixties. The house-nigger, the handkerchief-head, the female Uncle Tom—the frightened powerless woman who had already lost all she could stand to lose, and who knew as little about the freedom of the North as she knew about the hereafter.

I looked down on her myself for a while. Moral superiority. Here was someone even less courageous than I was. That comforted me somehow. Or it did until Rufus and Nigel drove into town and came back with what was left of Alice.

It was late when they got home—almost dark. Rufus ran into the house shouting for me before I realized he was back. "Dana! Dana, get down here!"

I came out of his room—my new refuge when he wasn't in it—and hurried down the stairs.

"Come on, come on!" he urged.

I said nothing, followed him out the front door not knowing what to expect. He led me to the wagon where Alice lay bloody, filthy, and barely alive.

"Oh my God," I whispered.

"Help her!" demanded Rufus.

I looked at him, remembering why Alice needed help. I didn't say anything, and I don't know what expression I was wearing, but he took a step back from me.

"Just help her!" he said. "Blame me if you want to, but help her!"

I turned to her, straightened her body gently, feeling for broken bones. Miraculously, there didn't seem to be any. Alice moaned and cried out weakly. Her eyes were open, but she didn't seem to see me.

"Where will you put her?" I asked Rufus. "In the attic?"

He lifted her gently, carefully, and carried her up to his bedroom.

Nigel and I followed him up, saw him place the girl on his bed. Then he looked up at me questioningly.

"Tell Sarah to boil some water," I told Nigel. "And tell her to send some clean cloth for bandages. Clean cloth." How clean would it be? Not sterile, of course, but I had just spent the day cooking clothes in lye soap and water. That surely got them clean.

"Rufe, get me something to cut these rags off her."

Rufus hurried out, came back with a pair of his mother's scissors.

Most of Alice's wounds were new, and the cloth came away from them easily. Those that had dried and stuck to the cloth, I left alone. Warm water would soften them.

"Rufe, have you got any kind of antiseptic?"

"Anti-what?"

I looked at him. "You've never heard of it?"

"No. What is it?"

"Never mind. I could use a salt solution, I guess."

"Brine? You want to use that on her back?"

"I want to use it wherever she's hurt."

"Don't you have anything in your bag better than that?"

"Just soap, which I intend to use. Find it for me, will you?

Then . . . hell, I shouldn't be doing this. Why didn't you take her to the doctor?"

He shook his head. "The judge wanted her sold South—for spite, I guess. I had to pay near twice what she's worth to get her. That's all the money I had, and Daddy won't pay for a doctor to fix niggers. Doc knows that."

"You mean your father just lets people die when maybe they could be helped?"

"Die or get well. Aunt Mary—you know, the one who watches the kids?"

"Yes." Aunt Mary didn't watch the kids. Old and crippled, she sat in the shade with a switch and threatened them with gory murder if they happened to misbehave right in front of her. Otherwise, she ignored them and spent her time sewing and mumbling to herself, contentedly senile. The children cared for each other.

"Aunt Mary does some doctoring," said Rufus. "She knows herbs. But I thought you'd know more."

I turned to look at him in disbelief. Sometimes the poor woman barely knew her name. Finally I shrugged. "Get me some brine."

"But . . . that's what Daddy uses on field hands," he said. "It hurts them worse than the beating sometimes."

"It won't hurt her as badly as an infection would later."

He frowned, came to stand protectively close to the girl. "Who fixed up your back?"

"I did. No one else was around."

"What did you do?"

"I washed it with plenty of soap and water, and I put medicine on it. Here, brine will have to be my medicine. It should be just as good." Please, heaven, let it be as good. I only half knew what I was doing. Maybe old Mary and her herbs weren't such a bad idea after all—if I could be sure of catching her in one of her saner moments. But no. Ignorant as I knew I was, I trusted myself more than I trusted her. Even if I couldn't do any more good than she could, I was at least less likely to do harm.

"Let me see your back," said Rufus.

I hesitated, swallowed a few indignant words. He spoke out of love for the girl—a destructive love, but a love, nevertheless. He needed to know that it was necessary to hurt her more and that I had some idea what I was doing. I turned my back to him and raised my shirt a little. My cuts were healed or nearly healed.

He didn't speak or touch me. After a moment, I put my shirt down.

"You didn't get the big thick scars some of the hands get," he observed.

"Keloids. No, thank God, I'm not subject to them. What I've got is bad enough."

"Not as bad as she'll have."

"Get the salt, Rufe."

He nodded and went away.

8

I did my best for Alice, hurt her as little as possible, got her clean and bandaged the worst of her injuries—the dog bites.

"Looks like they just let the dogs chew on her," said Rufus angrily. He had to hold her for me while I cleaned the bites, gave them special attention. She struggled and wept and called for Isaac, until I was almost sick at having to cause her more pain. I swallowed and clenched my teeth against threatening nausea. When I spoke to Rufus, it was more to calm myself than to get information.

"What did they do with Isaac, Rufe? Give him back to the judge?"

"Sold him to a trader—fellow taking slaves overland to Mississippi."

"Oh God."

"He'd be dead if I'd spoken up."

I shook my head, located another bite. I wanted Kevin. I wanted desperately to go home and be out of this. "Did you mail my letter, Rufe?"

"Yeah."

Good. Now if only Kevin would come quickly.

I finished with Alice and gave her, not aspirins, but sleeping pills. She needed rest after days of running, after the dogs and the whipping. After Isaac.

Rufus left her in his bed. He simply climbed in beside her.

"Rufe, for Godsake!"

He looked at me, then at her. "Don't talk foolishness. I'm not going to put her on the floor."

"But . . ."

"And I'm sure not going to bother her while she's hurt like this."

"Good," I said relieved, believing him. "Don't even touch her if you can help it."

"All right."

I cleaned up the mess I had made and left them. Finally, I made my way to my pallet in the attic, and lay down wearily.

But tired as I was, I couldn't sleep. I thought of Alice, and then of Rufus, and I realized that Rufus had done exactly what I had said he would do: Gotten possession of the woman without having to bother with her husband. Now, somehow, Alice would have to accept not only the loss of her husband, but her own enslavement. Rufus had caused her trouble, and now he had been rewarded for it. It made no sense. No matter how kindly he treated her now that he had destroyed her, it made no sense.

I lay turning, twisting, holding my eyes closed and trying first to think, then not to think. I was tempted to squander two more of my sleeping pills to buy myself relief.

Then Sarah came in. I could see her vaguely outlined in the moonlight that came through the window. I whispered her name, trying not to awaken anyone.

She stepped over the two children who slept nearest to me and made her way over to my corner. "How's Alice?" she asked softly.

"I don't know. She'll probably be all right. Her body will anyway."

Sarah sat down on the end of my pallet. "I'd have come in to see her," she said, "but then I'd have to see Marse Rufe too. Don't want to see him for a while."

"Yeah."

"They cut off the boy's ears."

I jumped. "Isaac?"

"Yeah. Cut them both off. He fought. Strong boy, even if he didn't show much sense. The judge's son hit him, and he struck back. And he said some things he shouldn't have said."

"Rufus said they sold him to a Mississippi trader."

"Did. After they got through with him. Nigel told me 'bout it—how they cut him, beat him. He'll have to do some healing 'fore he can go to Mississippi or anywhere else."

"Oh God. All because our little jackass here drank too much and decided to rape somebody!"

She hushed me with a sharp hiss. "You got to learn to watch what you say! Don't you know there's folks in this house who love to carry tales?"

I sighed. "Yes."

"You ain't no field nigger, but you still a nigger. Marse Rufe can get mad and make things mighty hard for you."

"I know. All right." Luke's being sold must have frightened her badly. He used to be the one who hushed her.

"Marse Rufe keeping Alice in his room?"

"Yes."

"Lord, I hope he'll let her 'lone. Tonight, anyway."

"I think he will. Hell, I think he'll be gentle and patient with her now that he's got her."

"Huh!" A sound of disgust. "What'll you do now?"

"Me? Try to keep the girl clean and comfortable until she gets well."

"I don't mean that."

I frowned. "What do you mean?"

"She'll be in. You'll be out."

I stared at her, tried to see her expression. I couldn't, but I decided she was serious. "It's not like that, Sarah. She's the only one he seems to want. And me, I'm content with my husband."

There was a long silence. "Your husband . . . was that Mister Kevin?"

"Yes."

"Nigel said you and him was married. I didn't believe it."

"We kept quiet about it because it's not legal here."

"Legal!" Another sound of disgust. "I guess what Marse Rufe done to that girl is legal."

I shrugged.

"Your husband . . . he'd get in trouble every now and then 'cause he couldn't tell the difference 'tween black and white. Guess now I know why."

I grinned. "I'm not why. He was like that when I married

him—or I wouldn't have married him. Rufus just sent him a letter telling him to come back and get me."

She hesitated. "You sure Marse Rufe sent it?"

"He said he did."

"Ask Nigel." She lowered her voice. "Sometimes Marse Rufe says what will make you feel good—not what's true."

"But . . . he'd have no reason to lie about it."

"Didn't say he was lyin'. Just said ask Nigel."

"All right."

She was silent for a moment, then, "You think he'll come back for you, Dana, your . . . husband?"

"I know he will." He would. Surely he would.

"He ever beat you?"

"No! Of course not!"

"My man used to. He'd tell me I was the only one he cared about. Then, next thing I knew, he'd say I was looking at some other man, and he'd go to hittin'."

"Carrie's father?"

"No . . . my oldest boy's father. Miss Hannah, her father. He always said he'd free me in his will, but he didn't. It was just another lie." She stood up, joints creaking. "Got to get some rest." She started away. "Don't you forget now, Dana. Ask Nigel."

"Yes."

9

I asked Nigel the next day, but he didn't know. Rufus had sent him on an errand. When Nigel saw Rufus again, it was at the jail where Rufus had just bought Alice.

"She was standing up then," he said remembering. "I don't know how. When Marse Rufe was ready to go, he took her by the arm, and she fell over and everybody around laughed. He had paid way too much for her and anybody could see she was more dead than alive. Folks figured he didn't have much sense."

"Nigel, do you know how long it would take a letter to reach Boston?" I asked.

He looked up from the silver he was polishing. "How would

I know that?" He began rubbing again. "Like to find out
though—follow it and see." He spoke very softly.

He said things like that now and then when Weylin gave him
a hard time, or when the overseer, Edwards, tried to order him
around. This time, I thought it was Edwards. The man had
stomped out of the cookhouse as I was going in. He would
have knocked me down if I hadn't jumped out of his way. Nigel
was a house servant and Edwards wasn't supposed to bother
him, but he did.

"What happened?" I asked.

"Old bastard swears he'll have me out in the field. Says I
think too much of myself."

I thought of Luke and shuddered. "Maybe you'd better take
off some time soon."

"Carrie."

"Yes."

"Tried to run once. Followed the Star. If not for Marse
Rufe, I would have been sold South when they caught me."
He shook his head. "I'd probably be dead by now."

I went away from him not wanting to hear any more about
running away—and being caught. It was pouring rain outside,
but before I reached the house I saw that the hands were still
in the fields, still hoeing corn.

I found Rufus in the library going over some papers with his
father. I swept the hall until his father left the room. Then I
went in to see Rufus.

Before I could open my mouth, he said, "Have you been up
to check on Alice?"

"I'll go in a moment. Rufe, how long does it take for a letter
to go from here to Boston?"

He lifted an eyebrow. "Someday, you're going to call me
Rufe down here and Daddy is going to be standing right behind you."

I looked back in sudden apprehension and Rufus laughed.
"Not today," he said. "But someday, if you don't remember."

"Hell," I muttered. "How long?"

He laughed again. "I don't know, Dana. A few days, a week,
two weeks, three . . ." He shrugged.

"His letters were dated," I said. "Can you remember when
you received the one from Boston?"

He thought about it, finally shook his head. "No, Dana, I just didn't pay any attention. You better go look in on Alice."

I went, annoyed, but silent. I thought he could have given me a decent estimate if he had wanted to. But it didn't really matter. Kevin would receive the letter and he could come to get me. I couldn't really doubt that Rufus had sent it. He didn't want to lose my good will anymore than I wanted to lose his. And this was such a small thing.

Alice became a part of my work—an important part. Rufus had Nigel and a young field hand move another bed into Rufus's room—a small low bed that could be pushed under Rufus's bed. We had to move Alice from Rufus's bed for his comfort as well as hers, because for a while, Alice was a very young child again, incontinent, barely aware of us unless we hurt her or fed her. And she did have to be fed—spoonful by spoonful.

Weylin came in to look at her once, while I was feeding her.

"Damn!" he said to Rufus. "Kindest thing you could do for her would be to shoot her."

I think the look Rufus gave him scared him a little. He went away without saying anything else.

I changed Alice's bandages, always checking for signs of infection, always hoping not to find any. I wondered what the incubation period was for tetanus or—or for rabies. Then I tried to make myself stop wondering. The girl's body seemed to be healing slowly, but cleanly. I felt superstitious about even thinking about diseases that would surely kill her. Besides, I had enough real worries just keeping her clean and helping her grow up all over again. She called me Mama for a while.

"Mama, it hurts."

She knew Rufus, though. Mister Rufus. Her friend. He said she crawled into his bed at night.

In one way, that was all right. She was using the pot again. But in another . . .

"Don't look at me like that," said Rufus when he told me. "I wouldn't bother her. It would be like hurting a baby."

Later it would be like hurting a woman. I suspected that wouldn't bother him at all.

As Alice progressed, she became a little more reserved with him. He was still her friend, but she slept in her trundle bed all night. And I ceased to be "Mama."

One morning when I brought her breakfast, she looked at me and said, "Who are you?"

"I'm Dana," I said. "Remember?" I always answered her questions.

"No."

"How do you feel?"

"Kind of stiff and sore." She put a hand down to her thigh where a dog had literally torn away a mouthful. "My leg hurts."

I looked at the wound. She would have a big ugly scar there for the rest of her life, but the wound still seemed to be healing all right—no unusual darkening or swelling. It was as though she had just noticed this specific pain in the same way she had just noticed me.

"Where is this?" she asked.

The way she was just really noticing a lot of things. "This is the Weylin house," I said. "Mister Rufus's room."

"Oh." She seemed to relax, content, no longer curious. I didn't push her. I had already decided I wouldn't. I thought she would return to reality when she was strong enough to face it. Tom Weylin, in his loud silence, clearly thought she was hopeless. Rufus never said what he thought. But like me, he didn't push her.

"I almost don't want her to remember," he said once. "She could be like she was before Isaac. Then maybe . . ." He shrugged.

"She remembers more every day," I said. "And she asks questions."

"Don't answer her!"

"If I don't, someone else will. She'll be up and around soon."

He swallowed. "All this time, it's been so good . . ."

"Good?"

"She hasn't hated me!"

10

Alice continued to heal and to grow. She came down to the cookhouse with me for the first time on the day Carrie had her baby.

Alice had been with us for three weeks. She might have been twelve or thirteen mentally now. That morning, she had told

Rufus she wanted to sleep in the attic with me. To my surprise, Rufus had agreed. He hadn't wanted to, but he had done it. I thought, not for the first time, that if Alice could manage to go on not hating him, there would be very little she couldn't ask of him. If.

Now, slowly, cautiously, she followed me down the stairs. She was weak and thinner than ever, looking like a child in one of Margaret Weylin's old dresses. But boredom had driven her from her bed.

"I'll be glad when I get well," she muttered as she paused on a step. "I hate to be like this."

"You're getting well," I said. I was a little ahead of her, watching to see that she did not stumble. I had taken her arm at the top of the stairs, but she had tried to pull away.

"I can walk."

I let her walk.

We got to the cookhouse just as Nigel did, but he was in a bigger hurry. We stood aside and let him rush through the door ahead of us.

"Huh!" said Alice as he went by. "'Scuse me!"

He ignored her. "Aunt Sarah," he called, "Aunt Sarah, Carrie's having pains!"

Old Mary had been the midwife of the plantation before her age caught up with her. Now, the Weylins may have expected her to go on doctoring the slaves, but the slaves knew better. They helped each other as best they could. I hadn't seen Sarah called to help with a birth before, but it was natural that she should be called to this one. She dropped a pan of corn meal and started to follow Nigel out.

"Can I help?" I asked.

She looked at me as though she'd just noticed me. "See to the supper," she said. "I was going to send somebody in to finish cooking, but you can, can't you?"

"Yes."

"Good." She and Nigel hurried away. Nigel had a cabin away from the quarter, not far from the cookhouse. A neat wood-floored brick-chimneyed cabin that he had built for himself and Carrie. He had shown it to me. "Don't have to sleep on rags up in the attic no more," he'd said. He'd built a bed and two chairs. Rufus had let him hire his time, work for other whites in the area, until he had money enough to buy the things he couldn't make. It had been a good investment for Rufus. Not only did he get part of Nigel's earnings, but he got the assurance that Nigel, his only valuable piece of property, was not likely to run away again soon.

"Can I go see?" Alice asked me.

"No," I said reluctantly. I wanted to go myself, but Sarah didn't need either of us getting in her way. "No, you and I have work to do here. Can you peel potatoes?"

"Sure."

I sat her down at the table and gave her a knife and some potatoes to peel. The scene reminded me of my own first time in the cookhouse when I had sat peeling potatoes until Kevin called me away. Kevin might have my letter by now. He almost surely did. He might already be on his way here.

I shook my head and began cutting up a chicken. No sense tormenting myself.

"Mama used to make me cook," said Alice. She frowned as though trying to remember. "She said I'd have to be cooking for my husband." She frowned again, and I almost cut myself trying to watch her. What was she remembering?

"Dana?"

"Yes?"

"Don't you have a husband? I remember once . . . something about you having a husband."

"I do. He's up North now."

"He free?"

"Yes."

"Good to marry a freeman. Mama always said I should."

Mama was right, I thought. But I said nothing.

"My father was a slave, and they sold him away from her. She said marrying a slave is almost bad as being a slave." She looked at me. "What's it like to be a slave?"

I managed not to look surprised. It hadn't occurred to me that she didn't realize she was a slave. I wondered how she had explained her presence here to herself.

"Dana?"

I looked at her.

"I said what's it like to be a slave?"

"I don't know." I took a deep breath. "I wonder how Carrie is doing—in all that pain, and not even able to scream."

"How could you not know what it's like to be a slave. You are one."

"I haven't been one for very long."

"You were free?"

"Yes."

"And you let yourself be made a slave? You should run away."

I glanced at the door. "Be careful how you say things like that. You could get into trouble." I felt like Sarah, cautioning.

"Well it's true."

"Sometimes it's better to keep the truth to yourself."

She stared at me with concern. "What will happen to you?"

"Don't worry about me, Alice. My husband will help me get free." I went to the door to look out toward Carrie's cabin. Not that I expected to see anything. I just wanted to distract Alice. She was getting too close, "growing" too fast. Her life would change so much for the worse when she remembered. She would be hurt more, and Rufus would do much of the hurting. And I would have to watch and do nothing.

"Mama said she'd rather be dead than be a slave," she said.

"Better to stay alive," I said. "At least while there's a chance to get free." I thought of the sleeping pills in my bag and wondered just how great a hypocrite I was. It was so easy to advise other people to live with their pain.

Suddenly, she threw the potato she had been peeling into the fire.

I jumped, looked at her. "Why'd you do that?"

"There's things you ain't saying."

I sighed.

"I'm here too," she said. "Been here a long time." She narrowed her eyes. "Am I a slave too?"

I didn't answer.

"I said am I a slave?"

"Yes."

She had risen half off the bench, her whole body demanding that I answer her. Now that I had, she sat down again heavily, her back and shoulders rounded, her arms crossed over her stomach hugging herself. "But I'm supposed to be free. I was free. Born free!"

"Yes."

"Dana, tell me what I don't remember. Tell me!"

"It will come back to you."

"No, you tell—"

"Oh, hush, will you!"

She drew back a little in surprise. I had shouted at her. She probably thought I was angry—and I was. But not at her. I wanted to pull her back from the edge of a cliff. It was too late though. She would have to take her fall.

"I'll tell you whatever you want to know," I said wearily. "But believe me, you don't want to know as much as you think you do."

"Yes I do!"

I sighed. "All right. What do you want to know?"

She opened her mouth, then frowned and closed it again. Finally, "There's so much . . . I want to know everything, but I don't know where to start. Why am I a slave?"

"You committed a crime."

"A crime? What'd I do?"

"You helped a slave to escape." I paused. "Do you realize that in all the time you've been here, you never asked me how you were hurt?"

That seemed to touch something in her. She sat blank-faced for several seconds, then frowned and stood up. I watched her carefully. If she was going to have hysterics, I wanted her to have them where she was, out of sight of the Weylins. There were too many things she could say that Tom Weylin in particular would resent.

"They beat me," she whispered. "I remember. The dogs, the rope . . . They tied me behind a horse and I had to run, but I couldn't . . . Then they beat me . . . But . . . but . . ."

I walked over to her, stood in front of her, but she seemed to look through me. She had that same look of pain and confusion she'd had when Rufus brought her from town.

"Alice?"

She seemed not to hear me. "Isaac?" she whispered. But it was more a soundless moving of her lips than a whisper. Then,

"*Isaac!*" An explosion of sound. She bolted for the door. I let her take about three steps before I grabbed her.

"Let go of me! Isaac! *Isaac!*"

"Alice, stop. You'll make me hurt you." She was struggling against me with all her feeble strength.

"They cut him! They cut off his ears!"

I had been hoping she hadn't seen that. "Alice!" I held her by the shoulders and shook her.

"I've got to get away," she wept. "Find Isaac."

"Maybe. When you can walk more than ten steps without getting tired."

She stopped her struggles, stared at me through streaming tears. "Where'd they send him?"

"Mississippi."

"Oh Jesus . . ." She collapsed against me, crying. She would have fallen if I hadn't held her and half-dragged and half-carried her back to the bench. She sat slumped where I put her, crying, praying, cursing. I sat with her for a while, but she didn't tire, or at least, she didn't stop. I had to leave her to finish preparing supper. I was afraid I would anger Weylin and get Sarah into trouble if I didn't. There would be trouble enough in the house now that Alice had her memory back, and somehow, it had become my job to ease troubles—first Rufus's, now Alice's—as best I could.

I finished the meal somehow, though my mind wasn't on it. There was the soup that Sarah had left simmering; fish to fry; ham that had been rock-hard before Sarah soaked it, then boiled it; chicken to fry and corn bread and gravy to make; Alice's forgotten potatoes to finish; bread to bake in the little brick oven alongside the fireplace; vegetables, including salad; a sugary peach dessert—Weylin raised peaches; a cake that Sarah had already made, thank God; and both coffee and tea. There would be company to help eat it all. There usually was. And they would all eat too much. It was no wonder the main medicines of this era were laxatives.

I got the food ready, almost on time, then had to hunt down the two little boys whose job it was to ferry it from cookhouse to table and then serve it. When I found them, they wasted some time staring at the now silent Alice, then they grumbled because I made them wash. Finally, my washhouse friend Tess, who also worked in the main house, ran out and said, "Marse Tom say get food on the table!"

"Is the table set?"

"Been set! Even though you didn't say nothin'."

Oops. "I'm sorry, Tess. Here, help me out." I thrust a

covered dish of soup into her hands. "Carrie is having her baby now and Sarah's gone to help her. Take that in, would you?"

"And come back for more?"

"Please."

She hurried away. I had helped her with the washing several times—had done as much of it as I could myself recently because Weylin had casually begun taking her to bed, and had hurt her. Apparently, she paid her debts.

I went out to the well and got the boys just as they were starting a water fight.

"If you two don't get yourselves into the house with that food . . . !"

"You sound just like Sarah."

"No I don't. You know what she'd be saying. You know what she'd be doing too. Now move! Or I'll get a switch and really be like her."

Dinner was served. Somehow. And it was all edible. There may have been more of it if Sarah had been cooking, but it wouldn't have tasted any better. Sarah had managed to overcome my uncertainty, my ignorance of cooking on an open hearth, and teach me quite a bit.

As the meal progressed and the leftovers began to come back, I tried to get Alice to eat. I fixed her a plate but she pushed it away, turned her back to me.

She had sat either staring into space or resting her head on the table for hours. Now, finally, she spoke.

"Why didn't you tell me?" she asked bitterly. "You could have said something, got me out of his room, his bed . . . Oh Lord, his bed! And he may as well have cut my Isaac's ears off with his own hand."

"He never told anyone Isaac beat him."

"Shit!"

"It's true. He never did because he didn't want you to get hurt. I know because I was with him until he got back on his feet. I took care of him."

"If you had any sense, you would have let him die!"

"If I had, it wouldn't have kept you and Isaac from being caught. It might have gotten you both killed though if anyone guessed what Isaac had done."

"Doctor-nigger," she said with contempt. "Think you know

so much. Reading-nigger. *White-nigger!* Why didn't you know enough to let me die?"

I said nothing. She was getting angrier and angrier, shouting at me. I turned away from her sadly, telling myself it was better, safer for her to vent her feelings on me than on anyone else.

Along with her shouting now, I could hear the thin faint cries of a baby.

11

Carrie and Nigel named their thin, wrinkled, brown son, Jude. Nigel did a lot of strutting and happy babbling until Weylin told him to shut up and get back to work on the covered passageway he was supposed to be building to connect the house and the cookhouse. A few days after the baby's birth, though, Weylin called him into the library and gave him a new dress for Carrie, a new blanket, and a new suit of clothes for himself.

"See," Nigel told me later with some bitterness. "'Cause of Carrie and me, he's one nigger richer." But before the Weylins, he was properly grateful.

"Thank you, Marse Tom. Yes, sir. Sure do thank you. Fine clothes, yes, sir . . ."

Finally he escaped back to the covered passageway.

Meanwhile, in the library, I heard Weylin tell Rufus, "You should have been the one to give him something—instead of wasting all your money on that worthless girl."

"She's well!" Rufus answered. "Dana got her well. Why do you say she's worthless?"

"Because you're going to have to whip her sick again to get what you want from her!"

Silence.

"Dana should have been enough for you. She's got some sense." He paused. "Too much sense for her own good, I'd say, but at least she wouldn't give you trouble. She's had that Franklin fellow to teach her a few things."

Rufus walked away from him without answering. I had to get away from the library door where I had been eavesdropping very quickly as I heard him approach. I ducked into the dining room and came out again just as he was passing by.

"Rufe."

He gave me a look that said he didn't want to be bothered, but he stopped anyway.

"I want to write another letter."

He frowned. "You've got to be patient, Dana. It hasn't been that long."

"It's been over a month."

"Well . . . I don't know. Kevin could have moved again, could have done anything. I think you should give him a little more time to answer."

"Answer what?" asked Weylin. He'd done what Rufus had predicted—come up behind us so silently that I hadn't noticed him.

Rufus glanced at his father sourly. "Letter to Kevin Franklin telling him she's here."

"She wrote a letter?"

"I told her to write it. Why should I do it when she can?"

"Boy, you don't have the sense you—" He cut off abruptly. "Dana, go do your work!"

I left wondering whether Rufus had shown lack of sense by letting me write the letter—instead of writing it himself—or by sending it. After all, if Kevin never came back for me, Weylin's property was increased by one more slave. Even if I proved not to be very useful, he could always sell me.

I shuddered. I had to talk Rufus into letting me write another letter. The first one could have been lost or destroyed or sent to the wrong place. Things like that were still happening in 1976. How much worse might they be in this horse-and-buggy era? And surely Kevin would give up on me if I went home without him again—left him here for more long years. If he hadn't already given up on me.

I tried to put that thought out of my mind. It came to me now and then even though everything people told me seemed to indicate that he was waiting. Still waiting.

I went out to the laundry yard to help Tess. I had come to almost welcome the hard work. It kept me from thinking. White people thought I was industrious. Most blacks thought I was either stupid or too intent on pleasing the whites. I thought I was keeping my fears and doubts at bay as best I could, and managing to stay relatively sane.

I caught Rufus alone again the next day—in his room this time where we weren't likely to be interrupted. But he wouldn't listen when I brought up the letter. His mind was on Alice. She was stronger now, and his patience with her was gone. I had thought that eventually, he would just rape her again—and again. In fact, I was surprised that he hadn't already done it. I didn't realize that he was planning to involve me in that rape. He was, and he did.

"Talk to her, Dana," he said once he'd brushed aside the matter of my letter. "You're older than she is. She thinks you know a lot. Talk to her!"

He was sitting on his bed staring into the cold fireplace. I sat at his desk looking at the clear plastic pen I had loaned him. He'd used half its ink already. "What the hell have you been writing with this?" I asked.

"Dana, listen to me!"

I turned to face him. "I heard you."

"Well?"

"I can't stop you from raping the woman, Rufe, but I'm not going to help you do it either."

"You want her to get hurt?"

"Of course not. But you've already decided to hurt her, haven't you?"

He didn't answer.

"Let her go, Rufe. Hasn't she suffered enough because of you?" He wouldn't. I knew he wouldn't.

His green eyes glittered. "She'll never get away from me again. Never!" He drew a deep breath, let it out slowly. "You know, Daddy wants me to send her to the fields and take you."

"Does he?"

"He thinks all I want is a woman. Any woman. So you, then. He says you'd be less likely to give me trouble."

"Do you believe him?"

He hesitated, managed to smile a little. "No."

I nodded. "Good."

"I know you, Dana. You want Kevin the way I want Alice. And you had more luck than I did because no matter what happens now, for a while he wanted you too. Maybe I can't ever have that—both wanting, both loving. But I'm not going to give up what I can have."

"What do you mean, 'no matter what happens now'?"

"What in hell do you think I mean? It's been five years! You want to write another letter. Did you ever think maybe he threw the first letter out? Maybe he got like Alice—wanted to be with one of his own kind."

I said nothing. I knew what he was doing—trying to share his pain, hurt me as he was hurting. And of course, he knew just where I was vulnerable. I tried to keep a neutral expression, but he went on.

"He told me once that you two had been married for four years. That means he's been here away from you even longer than you've been together. I doubt if he'd have waited as long as he did if you weren't the only one who could get him back to his home time. But now . . . who knows. The right woman could make this time mighty sweet to him."

"Rufe, nothing you say to me is going to ease your way with Alice."

"No? How about this: You talk to her—talk some sense into her—or you're going to watch while Jake Edwards beats some sense into her!"

I stared at him in revulsion. "Is that what you call love?"

He was on his feet and across the room to me before I could take another breath. I sat where I was, watching him, feeling frightened, and suddenly very much aware of my knife, of how quickly I could reach it. He wasn't going to beat me. Not him, not ever.

"Get up!" he ordered. He didn't order me around much, and he'd never done it in that tone. "Get up, I said!"

I didn't move.

"I've been too easy on you," he said. His voice was suddenly low and ugly. "I treated you like you were better than the ordinary niggers. I see I made a mistake!"

"That's possible," I said. "I'm waiting for you to show me I made a mistake."

For several seconds, he stood frozen, towering over me, glaring down as though he meant to hit me. Finally, though, he relaxed, leaned against his desk. "You think you're white!" he muttered. "You don't know your place any better than a wild animal."

I said nothing.

"You think you own me because you saved my life!"

And I relaxed, glad not to have to take the life I had saved —glad not to have to risk other lives, including my own.

"If I ever caught myself wanting you like I want her, I'd cut my throat," he said.

I hoped that problem would never arise. If it did, one of us would do some cutting all right.

"Help me, Dana."

"I can't."

"You can! You and nobody else. Go to her. Send her to me. I'll have her whether you help or not. All I want you to do is fix it so I don't have to beat her. You're no friend of hers if you won't do that much!"

Of hers! He had all the low cunning of his class. No, I couldn't refuse to help the girl—help her avoid at least some pain. But she wouldn't think much of me for helping her this way. I didn't think much of myself.

"Do it!" hissed Rufus.

I got up and went out to find her.

She was strange now, erratic, sometimes needing my friendship, trusting me with her dangerous longings for freedom, her wild plans to run away again; and sometimes hating me, blaming me for her trouble.

One night in the attic, she was crying softly and telling me something about Isaac. She stopped suddenly and asked, "Have you heard from your husband yet, Dana?"

"Not yet."

"Write another letter. Even if you have to do it in secret."

"I'm working on it."

"No sense in you losing your man too."

Yet moments later for no reason that I could see, she attacked me, "You ought to be ashamed of yourself, whining and crying after some poor white trash of a man, black as you are. You always try to act so white. White nigger, turning against your own people!"

I never really got used to her sudden switches, her attacks, but I put up with them. I had taken her through all the other stages of healing, and somehow, I couldn't abandon her now. Most of the time, I couldn't even get angry. She was like Rufus. When she hurt, she struck out to hurt others. But she had been hurting less as the days passed, and striking out less. She was healing emotionally as well as physically. I had helped her to heal. Now I had to help Rufus tear her wounds open again.

She was at Carrie's cabin watching Jude and two other older babies someone had left with her. She had no regular duties yet, but like me, she had found her own work. She liked children, and she liked sewing. She would take the coarse blue cloth Weylin bought for the slaves and make neat sturdy clothing of it while small children played around her feet. Weylin complained that she was like old Mary with the children and the sewing, but he brought her his clothing to be mended. She worked better and faster than the slave woman who had taken over much of old Mary's sewing—and if she had an enemy on the plantation, it was that woman, Liza, who was now in danger of being sent to more onerous work.

I went into the cabin and sat down with Alice before the cold fireplace. Jude slept beside her in the crib Nigel had made for him. The other two babies were awake lying naked on blankets on the floor quietly playing with their feet.

Alice looked up at me, then held up a long blue dress. "This is for you," she said. "I'm sick of seeing you in them pants."

I looked down at my jeans. "I'm so used to dressing like this, I forget sometimes. At least it keeps me from having to serve at the table."

"Serving ain't bad." She'd done it a few times. "And if Mister Tom wasn't so stingy, you'd have had a dress a long time ago. Man loves a dollar more than he loves Jesus."

That, I believed literally. Weylin had dealings with banks. I knew because he complained about them. But I had never known him to have any dealings with churches or hold any kind of prayer meeting in his home. The slaves had to sneak away in the night and take their chances with the patrollers if they wanted to have any kind of religious meeting.

"Least you can look like a woman when your man comes for you," Alice said.

I drew a deep breath. "Thanks."

"Yeah. Now tell me what you come here to say . . . that you don't want to say."

I looked at her, startled.

"You think I don't know you after all this time? You got a look that says you don't want to be here."

"Yes. Rufus sent me to talk to you." I hesitated. "He wants you tonight."

Her expression hardened. "He sent *you* to tell me that?"

"No."

She waited, glaring at me, silently demanding that I tell her more.

I said nothing.

"Well! What did he send you for then?"

"To talk you into going to him quietly, and to tell you you'd be whipped this time if you resist."

"Shit! Well, all right, you told me. Now get out of here before I throw this dress in the fireplace and light it."

"I don't give a damn what you do with that dress."

Now it was her turn to be startled. I didn't usually talk to her that way, even when she deserved it.

I leaned back comfortably in Nigel's homemade chair. "Message delivered," I said. "Do what you want."

"I mean to."

"You might look ahead a little though. Ahead and in all three directions."

"What are you talking about?"

"Well, it looks as though you have three choices. You can go to him as he orders; you can refuse, be whipped, and then have him take you by force; or you can run away again."

She said nothing, bent to her sewing and drew the needle in quick neat tiny stitches even though her hands were shaking. I bent down to play with one of the babies—one who had forgotten his own feet and crawled over to investigate my shoe. He was a fat curious little boy of several months who began trying to pull the buttons off my blouse as soon as I picked him up.

"He go' pee all over you in a minute," said Alice. "He likes to let go just when somebody's holding him."

I put the baby down quickly—just in time, as it turned out.

"Dana?"

I looked at her.

"What am I going to do?"

I hesitated, shook my head. "I can't advise you. It's your body."

"Not mine." Her voice had dropped to a whisper. "Not mine, his. He paid for it, didn't he?"

"Paid who? You?"

"You know he didn't pay me! Oh, what's the difference? Whether it's right or wrong, the law says he owns me now. I don't know why he hasn't already whipped the skin off me. The things I've said to him . . ."

"You know why."

She began to cry. "I ought to take a knife in there with me and cut his damn throat." She glared at me. "Now go tell him that! Tell him I'm talking 'bout killing him!"

"Tell him yourself."

"Do your job! Go tell him! That's what you for—to help white folks keep niggers down. That's why he sent you to me. They be calling you mammy in a few years. You be running the whole house when the old man dies."

I shrugged and stopped the curious baby from sucking on my shoe string.

"Go tell on me, Dana. Show him you the kind of woman he needs, not me."

I said nothing.

"One white man, two white men, what difference do it make?"

"One black man, two black men, what difference does that make?"

"I could have ten black men without turning against my own."

I shrugged again, refusing to argue with her. What could I win?

She made a wordless sound and covered her face with her hands. "What's the matter with you?" she said wearily. "Why you let me run you down like that? You done everything you could for me, maybe even saved my life. I seen people get lock-jaw and die from way less than I had wrong with me. Why you let me talk about you so bad?"

"Why do you do it?"

She sighed, bent her body into a "c" as she crouched in the chair. "Because I get so mad . . . I get so mad I can taste it in my mouth. And you're the only one I can take it out on—the only one I can hurt and not be hurt back."

"Don't keep doing it," I said. "I have feelings just like you do."

"Do you want me to go to him?"

"I can't tell you that. You have to decide."

"Would you go to him?"

I glanced at the floor. "We're in different situations. What I'd do doesn't matter."

"*Would you go to him?*"

"No."

"Even though he's just like your husband?"

"He isn't."

"But . . . All right, even though you don't . . . don't hate him like I do?"

"Even so."

"Then I won't go either."

"What will you do?"

"I don't know. Run away?"

I got up to leave.

"Where you going?" she asked quickly.

"To stall Rufus. If I really work at it, I think I can get him to let you off tonight. That will give you a start."

She dropped the dress to the floor and came out of her chair to grab me. "No, Dana! Don't go." She drew a deep breath, then seemed to sag. "I'm lying. I can't run again. I can't. You be hungry and cold and sick out there, and so tired you can't walk. Then they find you and set dogs on you . . . My Lord, the dogs . . ." She was silent for a moment. "I'm going to him. He knew I would sooner or later. But he don't know how I wish I had the nerve to just kill him!"

12

She went to him. She adjusted, became a quieter more sub-dued person. She didn't kill, but she seemed to die a little.

Kevin didn't come to me, didn't write. Rufus finally let me write another letter—payment for services rendered, I supposed—and he mailed it for me. Yet another month went by, and Kevin didn't reply.

"Don't worry about it," Rufus told me. "He probably did move again. We'll be getting a letter from him in Maine any day now."

I didn't say anything. Rufus had become talkative and happy, openly affectionate to a quietly tolerant Alice. He drank more than he should have sometimes, and one morning after he'd really overdone it, Alice came downstairs with her whole face swollen and bruised.

That was the morning I stopped wondering whether I should ask him to help me go North to find Kevin. I wouldn't have expected him to give me money, but he could have gotten me some damned official-looking free papers. He could even have gone with me, at least to the Pennsylvania State Line. Or he could have stopped me cold.

He had already found the way to control me—by threatening others. That was safer than threatening me directly, and it worked. It was a lesson he had no doubt learned from his father. Weylin, for instance, had known just how far to push Sarah. He had sold only three of her children—left her one to live for and protect. I didn't doubt now that he could have found a buyer for Carrie, afflicted as she was. But Carrie was a useful young woman. Not only did she work hard and well herself, not only had she produced a healthy new slave, but she had kept first her mother, and now her husband in line with no effort at all on Weylin's part. I didn't want to find out how much Rufus had learned from his father's handling of her.

I longed for my map now. It contained names of towns I could write myself passes to. No doubt some of the towns on it didn't exist yet, but at least it would have given me a better idea of what was ahead. I would have to take my chances without it.

Well, at least I knew that Easton was a few miles to the north, and that the road that ran past the Weylin house would take me to it. Unfortunately, it would also take me through a lot of open fields—places where it would be nearly impossible to hide. And pass or no pass, I would hide from whites if I could.

I would have to carry food—johnnycake, smoked meat, dried fruit, a bottle of water. I had access to what I needed. I had heard of runaway slaves starving before they reached freedom, or poisoning themselves because they were as ignorant as I was about which wild plants were edible.

In fact, I had read and heard enough scare stories about the fate of runaways to keep me with the Weylins for several days longer than I meant to stay. I might not have believed them, but I had the example of Isaac and Alice before me. Fittingly, then, it was Alice who gave me the push I needed.

I was helping Tess with the wash—sweating and stirring dirty clothes as they boiled in their big iron pot—when Alice came to me, crept to me, looking back over her shoulder, her eyes wide with what I read as fear.

"You look at this," she said to me, not even glancing at Tess who had stopped pounding a pair of Weylin's pants to watch us. She trusted Tess. "See," she said. "I been looking where I wasn't s'pose to look—in Mister Rufe's bed chest. But what I found don't look like it ought to be there."

She took two letters from her apron pocket. Two letters, their seals broken, their faces covered with my handwriting.

"Oh my God," I whispered.

"Yours?"

"Yes."

"Thought so. I can read some words. Got to take these back now."

"Yes."

She turned to go.

"Alice."

"Yeah?"

"Thanks. Be careful when you put them back."

"You be careful too," she said. Our eyes met and we both knew what she was talking about.

I left that night.

I collected the food and "borrowed" one of Nigel's old hats, to pull down over my hair—which wasn't very long, luckily. When I asked Nigel for the hat, he just looked at me for a long moment, then got it for me. No questions. I didn't think he expected to see it again.

I stole a pair of Rufus's old trousers and a worn shirt. My jeans and shirts were too well known to Rufus's neighbors, and the dress Alice had made me looked too much like the dresses every other slave woman on the place wore. Besides, I had decided to become a boy. In the loose shabby, but definitely male clothing I had chosen, my height and my contralto voice would get me by. I hoped.

I packed everything I could into my denim bag and left it in its place on my pallet where I normally used it as a pillow. My freedom of movement was more useful to me now than it had ever been. I could go where I wanted to and no one said,

"What are you doing here? Why aren't you working?" Everyone assumed I was working. Wasn't I the industrious stupid one who always worked?

So I was left alone, allowed to make my preparations. I even got a chance to prowl through Weylin's library. Finally, at day's end, I went to the attic with the other house servants and lay down to wait until they were asleep. That was my mistake.

I wanted the others to be able to say they saw me go to bed. I wanted Rufus and Tom Weylin to waste time looking around the plantation for me tomorrow when they realized they hadn't seen me for a while. They wouldn't do that if some house servant—one of the children, perhaps—said, "She never went to bed last night."

Overplanning.

I got up when the others had been quiet for some time. It was about midnight, and I knew I could be past Easton before morning. I had talked to others who had walked the distance. Before the sun rose, though, I'd have to find a place to hide and sleep. Then I could write myself a pass to one of the other places whose names and general locations I had learned in Weylin's library. There was a place near the county line called Wye Mills. Beyond that, I would veer northeast, slanting toward the plantation of a cousin of Weylin's and toward Delaware to travel up the highest part of the peninsula. In that way, I hoped to avoid many of the rivers. I had a feeling they were what would make my trip long and difficult.

I crept away from the Weylin house, moving through the darkness with even less confidence than I had felt when I fled to Alice's house months before. Years before. I hadn't known quite as well then what there was to fear. I had never seen a captured runaway like Alice. I had never felt the whip across my own back. I had never felt a man's fists.

I felt almost sick to my stomach with fear, but I kept walking. I stumbled over a stick that lay in the road and first cursed it, then picked it up. It felt good in my hand, solid. A stick like this had saved me once. Now, it quenched a little of my fear, gave me confidence. I walked faster, moving into the woods alongside the road as soon as I passed Weylin's fields.

The way was north toward Alice's old cabin, toward the

Holman plantation, toward Easton which I would have to skirt. The walking was easy, at least. This was flat country with only a few barely noticeable rolling hills to break the monotony. The road ran through thick dark woods that were probably full of good places to hide. And the only water I saw flowed in streams so tiny they barely wet my feet. That wouldn't last, though. There would be rivers.

I hid from an old black man who drove a wagon pulled by a mule. He went by humming tunelessly, apparently fearing neither patrollers nor any other dangers of the night. I envied his calmness.

I hid from three white men who rode by on horseback. They had a dog with them, and I was afraid it would smell me and give me away. Luckily, the wind was in my favor, and it went on its way. Another dog found me later, though. It came racing toward me through a field and over a rail fence, barking and growling. I turned to meet it almost without thinking, and clubbed it down as it lunged at me.

I wasn't really afraid. Dogs with white men frightened me, or dogs in packs—Sarah had told me of runaways who had been torn to pieces by the packs of dogs used to hunt them. But one lone dog didn't seem to be much of a threat.

As it turned out, the dog was no threat at all. I hit it, it fell, then got up and limped away yelping. I let it go, glad I hadn't had to hurt it worse. I liked dogs normally.

I hurried on, wanting to be out of sight if the dog's noise brought people out to investigate. The experience did make me a little more confident of my ability to defend myself, though, and the natural night noises disturbed me less.

I reached the town and avoided what I could see of it—a few shadowy buildings. I walked on, beginning to tire, beginning to worry that dawn was not far away. I couldn't tell whether my worrying was legitimate or came from my desire to rest. Not for the first time, I wished I had been wearing a watch when Rufus called me.

I pushed myself on until I could see that the sky really was growing light. Then, as I looked around wondering where I could find shelter for the day, I heard horses. I moved farther from the road and crouched in a thick growth of bushes, grasses, and young trees. I was used to hiding now, and no more afraid than I had been when I'd hidden before. No one had spotted me yet.

There were two horsemen moving slowly up the road toward me. Very slowly. They were looking around, peering through the dimness into the trees. I could see that one of them was riding a light colored horse. A gray horse, I saw as it drew closer, a . . .

I jumped. I managed not to gasp, but I did make that one small involuntary movement. And a twig that I hadn't noticed snapped under me.

The horsemen stopped almost in front of me, Rufus on the gray he usually rode, and Tom Weylin on a darker animal. I could see them clearly now. They were looking for me—already! They shouldn't even have known yet that I was gone. They couldn't have known—unless someone told them. Someone must have seen me leaving, someone other than Rufus or Tom Weylin. They would simply have stopped me. It must have been one of the slaves. Someone had betrayed me. And now, I had betrayed myself.

"I heard something," said Tom Weylin.

And Rufus, "So did I. She's around here somewhere."

I shrank down, tried to make myself smaller without moving enough to make more noise.

"Damn that Franklin," I heard Rufus say.

"You're damning the wrong man," said Weylin.

Rufus let that go unanswered.

"Look over there!" Weylin was pointing away from me, pointing into the woods ahead of me. He headed his horse over to investigate what he had seen—and frightened out a large bird.

Rufus's eyes were better. He ignored his father and headed straight for me. He couldn't have seen me, couldn't have seen anything other than a possible hiding place. He plunged his horse into the bushes that hid me, plunged it in to either trample me or drive me out.

He drove me out. I threw myself to one side away from the horse's hooves.

Rufus let out a whoop and swung down literally on top of me. I fell under his weight, and the fall twisted my club out of my hand, set it in just the right position for me to fall on.

I heard my stolen shirt tear, felt the splintered wood scrape my side . . .

"She's here!" called Rufus. "I've got her!"

He would get something else too if I could reach my knife. I twisted downward toward the ankle sheath with him still on top of me. My side was suddenly aflame with pain.

"Come help me hold her," he called.

His father strode over and kicked me in the face.

That held me, all right. From far away, I could hear Rufus shout—strangely soft shouting—"You didn't have to do that!"

Weylin's reply was lost to me as I drifted into unconsciousness.

13

I awoke tied hand and foot, my side throbbing rhythmically, my jaw not throbbing at all. The pain there was a steady scream. I probed with my tongue and found that two teeth on the right side were gone.

I had been thrown over Rufus's horse like a grain sack, head and feet hanging, blood dripping from my mouth onto the familiar boot that let me know it was Rufus I rode with.

I made a noise, a kind of choked moan, and the horse stopped. I felt Rufus move, then I was lifted down, placed in the tall grass beside the road. Rufus looked down at me.

"You damn fool," he said softly. He took his handkerchief and wiped blood from my face. I winced away, tears suddenly filling my eyes at the startlingly increased pain.

"Fool!" repeated Rufus.

I closed my eyes and felt the tears run back into my hair.

"You give me your word you won't fight me, and I'll untie you."

After a while, I nodded. I felt his hands at my wrists, at my ankles.

"What's this?"

He had found my knife, I thought. Now he would tie me again. That's what I would have done in his place. I looked at him.

He was untying the empty sheath from my ankle. Just a piece of rough-cut, poorly sewn leather. I had apparently lost the

knife in my struggle with him. No doubt, though, the shape of
the sheath told him what it had held. He looked at it, then at
me. Finally, he nodded grimly and, with a sharp motion, threw
the sheath away.

"Get up."

I tried. In the end, he had to help me. My feet were numb
from being tied, and were just coming back to painful life. If
Rufus decided to make me run behind his horse, I would be
dragged to death.

He noticed that I was holding my side as he half-carried me
back to his horse, and he stopped to move my hand and look
at the wound.

"Scratch," he pronounced. "You were lucky. Going to hit
me with a stick, were you? And what else were you going to
do?"

I said nothing, thought of him sending his horse charging
over the spot I had barely leaped from in time.

As I leaned against his horse, he wiped more blood from
my face, one hand firmly holding the top of my head so that I
couldn't wince away. I bore it somehow.

"Now you've got a gap in your teeth," he observed. "Well, if
you don't laugh big, nobody'll notice. They weren't the teeth
right in front."

I spat blood and he never realized that I had made my comment on such good luck.

"All right," he said, "let's go."

I waited for him to tie me behind the horse or throw me
over it grain-sack fashion again. Instead, he put me in front of
him in the saddle. Not until then did I see Weylin waiting for
us a few paces down the road.

"See there," the old man said. "Educated nigger don't mean
smart nigger, do it?" He turned away as though he didn't expect an answer. He didn't get one.

I sat stiffly erect, holding my body straight somehow until
Rufus said, "Will you lean back on me before you fall off! You
got more pride than sense."

He was wrong. At that moment, I couldn't manage any
pride at all. I leaned back against him, desperate for any support I could find, and closed my eyes.

He didn't say anything more for a long while—not until we were nearing the house. Then,

"You awake, Dana?"

I sat straight. "Yes."

"You're going to get the cowhide," he said. "You know that."

Somehow, I hadn't known. His gentleness had lulled me. Now the thought of being hurt even more terrified me. The whip, again. "No!"

Without thinking about it or intending to do it, I threw one leg over and slid from the horse. My side hurt, my mouth hurt, my face was still bleeding, but none of that was as bad as the whip. I ran toward the distant trees.

Rufus caught me easily and held me, cursing me, hurting me. "You take your whipping!" he hissed. "The more you fight, the more he'll hurt you."

He? Was Weylin to whip me, then, or the overseer, Edwards?

"Act like you've got some sense!" demanded Rufus as I struggled.

What I acted like was a wild woman. If I'd had my knife, I would surely have killed someone. As it was, I managed to leave scratches and bruises on Rufus, his father, and Edwards who was called over to help. I was totally beyond reasoning. I had never in my life wanted so desperately to kill another human being.

They took me to the barn and tied my hands and raised whatever they had tied them to high over my head. When I was barely able to touch the floor with my toes, Weylin ripped my clothes off and began to beat me.

He beat me until I swung back and forth by my wrists, half-crazy with pain, unable to find my footing, unable to stand the pressure of hanging, unable to get away from the steady slashing blows . . .

He beat me until I tried to make myself believe he was going to kill me. I said it aloud, screamed it, and the blows seemed to emphasize my words. He would kill me. Surely, he would kill me if I didn't get away, save myself, *go home!*

It didn't work. This was only punishment, and I knew it. Nigel had borne it. Alice had borne worse. Both were alive and healthy. I wasn't going to die—though as the beating went on, I wanted to. Anything to stop the pain! But there was nothing. Weylin had ample time to finish whipping me.

I was not aware of Rufus untying me, carrying me out of the barn and into Carrie's and Nigel's cabin. I was not aware of him directing Alice and Carrie to wash me and care for me as I had cared for Alice. That, Alice told me about later—how he demanded that everything used on me be clean, how he insisted on the deep ugly wound in my side—the scratch—being carefully cleaned and bandaged.

He was gone when I awoke, but he left me Alice. She was there to calm me and feed me pills that I saw were my own inadequate aspirins, and to assure me that my punishment was over, that I was all right. My face was almost too swollen for me to ask for salt water to wash my mouth. After several tries, though, she understood and brought it to me.

"Just rest," she said. "Carrie and me'll take care of you as good as you took care of me."

I didn't try to answer. Her words touched something in me, though, started me crying silently. We were both failures, she and I. We'd both run and been brought back, she in days, I in only hours. I probably knew more than she did about the general layout of the Eastern Shore. She knew only the area she'd been born and raised in, and she couldn't read a map. I knew about towns and rivers miles away—and it hadn't done me a damned bit of good! What had Weylin said? That educated didn't mean smart. He had a point. Nothing in my education or knowledge of the future had helped me to escape. Yet in a few years an illiterate runaway named Harriet Tubman would make nineteen trips into this country and lead three hundred fugitives to freedom. What had I done wrong? Why was I still slave to a man who had repaid me for saving his life by nearly killing me. Why had I taken yet another beating. And why . . . why was I so frightened now —frightened sick at the thought that sooner or later, I would have to run again?

I moaned and tried not to think about it. The pain of my body was enough for me to contend with. But now there was a question in my mind that had to be answered.

Would I really try again? Could I?

I moved, twisted myself somehow, from my stomach onto my side. I tried to get away from my thoughts, but they still came.

See how easily slaves are made? they said.

I cried out as though from the pain of my side, and Alice came to ease me into a less agonizing position. She wiped my face with a cool damp cloth.

"I'll try again," I said to her. And I wondered why I was saying it, boasting, maybe lying.

"What?" she asked.

My swollen face and mouth were still distorting my speech. I would have to repeat the words. Maybe they would give me courage if I said them often enough.

"I'll try again." I spoke as slowly and as clearly as I could.

"You rest!" Her voice was suddenly rough, and I knew she had understood. "Time enough later for talking. Go to sleep."

But I couldn't sleep. The pain kept me awake; my own thoughts kept me awake. I caught myself wondering whether I would be sold to some passing trader this time . . . or next time . . . I longed for my sleeping pills to give me oblivion, but some small part of me was glad I didn't have them. I didn't quite trust myself with them just now. I wasn't quite sure how many of them I might take.

14

Liza, the sewing woman, fell and hurt herself. Alice told me all about it. Liza was bruised and battered. She lost some teeth. She was black and blue all over. Even Tom Weylin was concerned.

"Who did it to you?" he demanded. "Tell me, and they'll be punished!"

"I fell," she said sullenly. "Fell on the stairs."

Weylin cursed her for a fool and told her to get out of his sight.

And Alice, Tess, and Carrie concealed their few scratches and gave Liza quiet meaningful glances. Glances that Liza turned away from in anger and fear.

"She heard you get up in the night," Alice told me. "She got up after you and went straight to Mister Tom. She knew better than to go to Mister Rufe. He might have let you go. Mister Tom never let a nigger go in his life."

"But why?" I asked from my pallet. I was stronger now, but Rufus had forbidden me to get up. For once, I was glad to obey. I knew that when I got up, Tom Weylin would expect me to work as though I were completely well. Thus, I had missed Liza's "accident" completely.

"She did it to get at me," said Alice. "She would have liked it better if I had been the one slipping out at night, but she hates you too—almost as much. She figures I would have died if not for you."

I was startled. I had never had a serious enemy—someone who would go out of her way to get me hurt or killed. To slaveholders and patrollers, I was just one more nigger, worth so many dollars. What they did to me didn't have much to do with me personally. But here was a woman who hated me and who, out of sheer malice, had nearly killed me.

"She'll keep her mouth shut next time," said Alice. "We let her know what would happen to her if she didn't. Now she's more scared of us than of Mister Tom."

"Don't get yourselves into trouble over me," I said.

"Don't be telling us what to do," she replied.

15

The first day I was up, Rufus called me to his room and handed me a letter—from Kevin to Tom Weylin.

"Dear Tom," it said, "There may be no need for this letter since I hope to reach you ahead of it. If I'm held up, however, I want you—and Dana—to know that I'm coming. Please tell her I'm coming."

It was Kevin's handwriting—slanted, neat, clear. In spite of the years of note taking and longhand drafts, his writing had never gone to hell the way mine had. I looked blankly at Rufus.

"I said once that Daddy was a fair man," he said. "You all but laughed out loud."

"He wrote to Kevin about me?"

"He did after . . . after . . ."

"After he learned that you hadn't sent my letters?"

His eyes widened with surprise, then slowly took on a look

of understanding. "So that's why you ran. How did you find out?"

"By being curious." I glanced at the bed chest. "By satisfying my curiosity."

"You could be whipped for snooping through my things."

I shrugged, and small pains shot through my scabby shoulders.

"I never even saw that they had been moved. I'll have to watch you better from now on."

"Why? Are you planning to hide more lies from me?"

He jumped, started to get up, then sat back down heavily and rested one polished boot on his bed. "Watch what you say, Dana. There are things I won't take, even from you."

"You lied," I repeated deliberately. "You lied to me over and over. *Why*, Rufe?"

It took several seconds for his anger to dissolve and be replaced by something else. I watched him at first, then looked away, uncomfortably. "I wanted to keep you here," he whispered. "Kevin hates this place. He would have taken you up North."

I looked at him again and let myself understand. It was that destructive single-minded love of his. He loved me. Not the way he loved Alice, thank God. He didn't seem to want to sleep with me. But he wanted me around—someone to talk to, someone who would listen to him and care what he said, care about him.

And I did. However little sense it made, I cared. I must have. I kept forgiving him for things . . .

I stared out the window guiltily, feeling that I should have been more like Alice. She forgave him nothing, forgot nothing, hated him as deeply as she had loved Isaac. I didn't blame her. But what good did her hating do? She couldn't bring herself to run away again or to kill him and face her own death. She couldn't do anything at all except make herself more miserable. She said, "My stomach just turns every time he puts his hands on me!" But she endured. Eventually, she would bear him at least one child. And as much as I cared for him, I would not have done that. I couldn't have. Twice, he had made me lose control enough to try to kill him. I could get that angry with him, even though I knew the consequences of killing him.

He could drive me to a kind of unthinking fury. Somehow, I couldn't take from him the kind of abuse I took from others. If he ever raped me, it wasn't likely that either of us would survive.

Maybe that was why we didn't hate each other. We could hurt each other too badly, kill each other too quickly in hatred. He was like a younger brother to me. Alice was like a sister. It was so hard to watch him hurting her—to know that he had to go on hurting her if my family was to exist at all. And, at the moment, it was hard for me to talk calmly about what he had done to me.

"North," I said finally. "Yes, at least there I could keep the skin on my back."

He sighed. "I never wanted Daddy to whip you. But hell, don't you know you got off easy! He didn't hurt you nearly as much as he's hurt others."

I said nothing.

"He couldn't let a runaway go without some punishment. If he did, there'd be ten more taking off tomorrow. He was easy on you, though, because he figured your running away was my fault."

"It was."

"It was your own fault! If you had waited . . ."

"For what! You were the one I trusted. I did wait until I found out what a liar you were!"

He took the charge without anger this time. "Oh hell, Dana . . . all right! I should have sent the letters. Even Daddy said I should have sent them after I promised you I would. Then he said I was a damn fool for promising." He paused. "But that promise was the only thing that made him send for Kevin. He didn't do it out of gratitude to you for helping me. He did it because I had given my word. If not for that, he would have kept you here until you went home. If you're going to go home this time."

We sat together in silence for a moment.

"Daddy's the only man I know," he said softly, "who cares as much about giving his word to a black as to a white."

"Does that bother you?"

"No! It's one of the few things about him I can respect."

"It's one of the few things about him you should copy."

"Yeah." He took his foot off the bed. "Carrie's bringing a tray up here so we can eat together."

That surprised me, but I just nodded.

"Your back doesn't hurt much, does it?"

"Yes."

He stared out the window miserably until Carrie arrived with the tray.

16

I went back to helping Sarah and Carrie the next day. Rufus said I didn't have to, but as tedious as the work was, I could stand it easier than I could stand more long hours of boredom. And now that I knew Kevin was coming, my back and side didn't seem to hurt as much.

Then Jake Edwards came in to destroy my new-found peace. It was amazing how much misery the man could cause do-ing the same job Luke had managed to do without hurting anyone.

"You!" he said to me. He knew my name. "You go do the wash. Tess is going to the fields today."

Poor Tess. Weylin had tired of her as a bed mate and passed her casually to Edwards. She had been afraid Edwards would send her to the fields where he could keep an eye on her. With Alice and I in the house, she knew she could be spared. She had cried with the fear that she would be spared. "You do ev-erything they tell you," she wept, "and they still treat you like a old dog. Go here, open your legs; go there, bust your back. What they care! I ain't s'pose to have no feelin's!" She had sat with me crying while I lay on my stomach sweating and hurt-ing and knowing I wasn't as bad off as I thought I was.

I would be a lot worse off now, though, if I obeyed Ed-wards. He had no right to give me orders, and he knew it. His authority was over the field hands. But today, Rufus and Tom Weylin had gone into town leaving Edwards in charge, leaving him several hours to show us how "important" he was. I'd heard him outside the cookhouse trying to bully Nigel. And I'd heard Nigel's answer, first placating—"I'm just doing what Marse Tom told me to do." Finally threatening—"Marse Jake, you put your hands on me, you go' get hurt. Now that's all!"

Edwards backed off. Nigel was big and strong and not one to make idle threats. Also, Rufus tended to back Nigel, and Weylin tended to back Rufus. Edwards had cursed Nigel, then come into the cookhouse to bother me. I had neither the size nor the strength to frighten him, especially now. But I knew what a day of washing would do to my back and side. I'd had enough pain, surely.

"Mr. Edwards, I'm not supposed to be washing. Mister Rufus told me not to." It was a lie, but Rufus would back me too. In some ways, I could still trust him.

"You lyin' nigger, you do what *I* tell you to do!" Edwards loomed over me. "You think you been whipped? You don't know what a whippin' is yet!" He carried his whip around with him. It was like part of his arm—long and black with its lead-weighted butt. He dropped the coil of it free.

And I went out, God help me, and tried to do the wash. I couldn't face another beating so soon. I just couldn't.

When Edwards was gone, Alice came out of Carrie's cabin and began to help me. I felt sweat on my face mingling with silent tears of frustration and anger. My back had already begun to ache dully, and I felt dully ashamed. Slavery was a long slow process of dulling.

"You stop beatin' them clothes 'fore you fall over," Alice told me. "I'll do this. You go back to the cookhouse."

"He might come back," I said. "You might get in trouble." It wasn't her trouble I was worried about; it was mine. I didn't want to be dragged out of the cookhouse and whipped again.

"Not me," she said. "He knows where I sleep at night."

I nodded. She was right. As long as she was under Rufus's protection, Edwards might curse her, but he wouldn't touch her. Just as he hadn't touched Tess—until Weylin was finished with her . . .

"Thanks, Alice, but . . ."

"Who's that?"

I looked around. There was a white man, gray-bearded and dusty, riding around the side of the main house toward us. I thought at first that it was the Methodist minister. He was a friend and sometime dinner guest of Tom Weylin in spite of Weylin's indifference to religion. But no children gathered around this man as he rode. The kids always mobbed the minister—and his wife too when he brought her along. The couple dispensed candy and "safe" Bible verses ("Servants, be obedient to them that are your masters . . ."). The kids got candy for repeating the verses.

I saw two little girls staring at the gray-bearded stranger, but no one approached him or spoke to him. He rode straight back to us, stopped, sat looking at both of us uncertainly.

I opened my mouth to tell him the Weylins weren't home, but in that moment, I got a good look at him. I dropped one of Rufus's good white shirts into the dirt and stumbled over to the fence.

"Dana?" he said softly. The question mark in his voice scared me. Didn't he know me? Had I changed so much? He hadn't, beard or no beard.

"Kevin, get down. I can't reach you up there."

And he was off the horse and over the laundry yard fence, pulling me to him before I could take another breath.

The dull ache in my back and shoulders roared to life. Suddenly, I was struggling to get away from him. He let me go, confused.

"What the . . . ?"

I went to him again because I couldn't keep away, but I caught his arms before he could get them around me. "Don't. My back is sore."

"Sore from what?"

"From running away to find you. Oh, Kevin . . ."

He held me—gently now—for several seconds, and I thought if we could just go home then, at that moment, everything would be all right.

Finally, Kevin stood back from me a little, looked at me without letting me go. "Who beat you?" he asked quietly.

"I told you, I ran away."

"Who?" he insisted. "Was it Weylin again?"

"Kevin, forget it."

"Forget . . . ?"

"Yes! Please forget it. I might have to live here again someday." I shook my head. "Hate Weylin all you want to. I do. But don't do anything to him. Let's just get out of here."

"It was him then."

"Yes!"

He turned slowly and stared toward the main house. His face was lined and grim where it wasn't hidden by the beard. He looked more than ten years older than when I had last seen him. There was a jagged scar across his forehead—the remnant of what must have been a bad wound. This place, this time, hadn't been any kinder to him than it had been to me. But what had it made of him? What might he be willing to do now that he would not have done before?

"Kevin, please, let's just go."

He turned that same hard stare on me.

"Do anything to them and I'll suffer for it," I whispered urgently. "Let's go! Now!"

He stared at me a moment longer, then sighed, rubbed his hand across his forehead. He looked at Alice, and because he didn't speak to her, just kept looking, I turned to look at her too.

She was watching us—watching dry-eyed, but with more pain than I had ever seen on another person's face. My husband had come to me, finally. Hers would not be coming to her. Then the look was gone and her mask of toughness was in place again.

"You better do like she says," she told Kevin softly. "Get her out of here while you can. No telling what our 'good masters' will do if you don't."

"You're Alice, aren't you?" asked Kevin.

She nodded as she would not have to Weylin or Rufus. They would have gotten a dull dry "yes, sir." "Used to see you 'round here sometimes," she said. "Back when things made sense."

He made a sound, not quite a laugh. "Was there ever such a time?" He glanced at me, then back at her again, comparing. "Good Lord," he murmured to himself. Then to her, "You going to be all right here, finishing this work by yourself?"

"Go' be fine," she said. "Just get her out of here."

He finally seemed convinced. "Get your things," he told me.

I almost told him to forget about my things. Extra clothing, medicine, tooth brush, pens, paper, whatever. But here, some of those things were irreplaceable. I climbed the fence, went to the house and up to the attic as quickly as I could and stuffed everything into my bag. Somehow, I got out again without being seen, without having to answer questions.

At the laundry yard fence, Kevin waited, feeding something to his mare. I looked at the mare, wondering how tired she was. How far could she carry two people before she had to rest? How far could Kevin go before he had to rest? I looked at him as I reached him and could read weariness now in the dusty lines of his face. I wondered how fast he had traveled to reach me. When had he slept last?

For a moment, we stood wasting time, staring at each other. We couldn't help it—I couldn't anyway. New lines and all, he was so damned beautiful.

"It's been five years for me," he said.

"I know," I whispered.

Abruptly, he turned away. "Let's go! Let's put this place behind us for good."

Please, God. But not very likely. I turned to say good-bye to Alice, called her name once. She was beating a pair of Rufus's pants, and she kept beating them with no break in her rhythm to indicate that she had heard me.

"Alice!" I called louder.

She did not turn, did not stop her beating and beating of those pants, though I was certain now that she heard me. Kevin laid a hand on my shoulder and I glanced at him, then again at her. "Good-bye, Alice," I said, this time not expecting any answer. There was none.

Kevin mounted and helped me up behind him. As we headed away, I leaned against Kevin's sweaty back and waited for the regular thump of her beating to fade. But we could still hear it faintly when we met Rufus on the road.

Rufus was alone. I was glad of that, at least. But he stopped a few feet ahead of us, frowning, deliberately blocking our way.

"Oh hell," I muttered.

"You were just going to leave," Rufus said to Kevin. "No thanks, nothing at all, just take her and go."

Kevin stared at him silently for several seconds—stared until Rufus began to look uncomfortable instead of indignant.

"That's right," Kevin said.

Rufus blinked. "Look," he said in a milder tone, "look, why don't you stay for dinner. My father will be back by then. He'd want you to stay."

"You can tell your father—!"

I dug my fingers into Kevin's shoulder, cutting off the rush of words before they became insulting in content as well as in tone. "Tell him we were in a hurry," Kevin finished.

Rufus did not move from blocking our path. He looked at me.

"Good-bye, Rufe," I said quietly.

And without warning, with no perceptible change in mood, Rufus turned slightly and trained his rifle on us. I knew a little about firearms now. It wasn't wise for any but the most trusted slaves to show an interest in them, but then I had been trusted before I ran away. Rufus's gun was a flintlock, a long slender Kentucky rifle. He had even let me fire it a couple of times . . . before. And I had looked down the barrel of one like it for his sake. This one, however, was aimed more at Kevin. I stared at it, then at the young man holding it. I kept thinking I knew him, and he kept proving to me that I didn't.

"Rufe, what are you doing!" I demanded.

"Inviting Kevin to dinner," he said. And to Kevin, "Get down. I think Daddy might want to talk to you."

People kept warning me about him, dropping hints that he was meaner than he seemed to be. Sarah had warned me and most of the time, she loved him like one of the sons she had lost. And I had seen the marks he occasionally left on Alice. But he had never been that way with me—not even when he was angry enough to be. I had never feared him as I'd feared his father. Even now, I wasn't as frightened as I probably should have been. I wasn't frightened for myself. That was why I challenged him.

"Rufe, if you shoot anybody, it better be me."

"Dana, shut up!" said Kevin.

"You think I won't?" said Rufus.

"I think if you don't, I'll kill you."

Kevin got down quickly and hauled me down. He didn't understand the kind of relationship Rufus and I had—how dependent we were on each other. Rufus understood though.

"No need for any talk of killing," he said gently—as though he was quieting an angry child. And then to Kevin in a more normal tone, "I just think Daddy might have something to say to you."

"About what?" Kevin asked.

"Well . . . about her keep, maybe."

"My keep!" I exploded, pulling away from Kevin. "My keep! I've worked, worked hard every day I've been here until your father beat me so badly I couldn't work! You people owe me! And you, Goddamnit, owe me more than you could ever pay!"

He swung the rifle to where I wanted it. Straight at me. Now I would either goad him into shooting me or shame him into letting us go—or possibly, I would go home. I might go home wounded, or even dead, but one way or another, I would be away from this time, this place. And if I went home, Kevin would go with me. I caught his hand and held it.

"What are you going to do, Rufe? Keep us here at gun point so you can rob Kevin?"

"Get back to the house," he said. His voice had gone hard.

Kevin and I looked at each other, and I spoke softly.

"I already know all I ever want to find out about being a slave," I told him. "I'd rather be shot than go back in there."

"I won't let them keep you," Kevin promised. "Come on."

"No!" I glared at him. "You stay or go as you please. I'm not going back in that house!"

Rufus cursed in disgust. "Kevin, put her over your shoulder and bring her in."

Kevin didn't move. I would have been amazed if he had.

"Still trying to get other people to do your dirty work for you, aren't you, Rufe?" I said bitterly. "First your father, now Kevin. To think I wasted my time saving your worthless life!" I stepped toward the mare and caught her reins as though to remount. At that moment, Rufus's composure broke.

"You're not leaving!" he shouted. He sort of crouched around the gun, clearly on the verge of firing. "Damn you, you're not leaving me!"

He was going to shoot. I had pushed him too far. I was Alice all over again, rejecting him. Terrified in spite of myself, I dove past the mare's head, not caring how I fell as long as I put something between myself and the rifle.

I hit the ground—not too hard—tried to scramble up, and found that I couldn't. My balance was gone. I heard shouting —Kevin's voice, Rufus's voice . . . Suddenly, I saw the gun, blurred, but seemingly only inches from my head. I hit at it and missed. It wasn't quite where it appeared to be. Everything was distorted, blurred.

"Kevin!" I screamed. I couldn't leave him behind again—not even if my scream made Rufus fire.

Something landed heavily on my back and I screamed again, this time in pain. Everything went dark.

The Storm

H OME.
   I couldn't have been unconscious for more than a minute. I came to on the living room floor to find Kevin bending over me. There was no one for me to mistake him for this time. It was him, and he was home. We were home. My back felt as though I'd taken another beating, but it didn't matter. I'd gotten us home without either of us being shot.

"I'm sorry," said Kevin.

I focused on him clearly. "Sorry about what?"

"Doesn't your back hurt?"

I lowered my head, rested it on my hand. "It hurts."

"I fell on you. Between Rufus and the horse and you screaming, I don't know how it happened, but . . ."

"Thank God it did happen. Don't be sorry, Kevin, you're here. You'd be stranded again if you hadn't fallen on me."

He sighed, nodded. "Can you get up? I think I'd hurt you more by lifting you than you'd hurt yourself by walking."

I got up slowly, cautiously, found that it didn't hurt any more to stand than it did to lie down. My head was clear now, and I could walk without trouble.

"Go to bed," said Kevin. "Get some rest."

"Come with me."

Something of the expression he'd had when we met in the laundry yard came back to him and he took my hands.

"Come with me," I repeated softly.

"Dana, you're hurt. Your back . . ."

"Hey."

He stopped, pulled me closer.

"Five years?" I whispered.

"That long. Yes."

"They hurt you." I fingered the scar on his forehead.

"That's nothing. It healed years ago. But you . . ."

"Please come with me."

He did. He was so careful, so fearful of hurting me. He did hurt me, of course. I had known he would, but it didn't matter.

We were safe. He was home. I'd brought him back. That was enough.

Eventually, we slept.

He wasn't in the room when I awoke. I lay still listening until I heard him opening and closing doors in the kitchen. And I heard him cursing. He had a slight accent, I realized. Nothing really noticeable, but he did sound a little like Rufus and Tom Weylin. Just a little.

I shook my head and tried to put the comparison out of my mind. He sounded as though he were looking for something, and after five years didn't know where to find it. I got up and went to help.

I found him fiddling with the stove, turning the burners on, staring into the blue flame, turning them off, opening the oven, peering in. He had his back to me and didn't see or hear me. Before I could say anything, he slammed the oven door and stalked away shaking his head. "Christ," he muttered. "If I'm not home yet, maybe I don't have a home."

He went into the dining room without noticing me. I stayed where I was, thinking, remembering.

I could recall walking along the narrow dirt road that ran past the Weylin house and seeing the house, shadowy in twilight, boxy and familiar, yellow light showing from some of the windows—Weylin was surprisingly extravagant with his candles and oil. I had heard that other people were not. I could recall feeling relief at seeing the house, feeling that I had come home. And having to stop and correct myself, remind myself that I was in an alien, dangerous place. I could recall being surprised that I would come to think of such a place as home.

That was more than two months ago when I went to get help for Rufus. I had been home to 1976, to this house, and it hadn't felt that homelike. It didn't now. For one thing, Kevin and I had lived here together for only two days. The fact that I'd had eight extra days here alone didn't really help. The time, the year, was right, but the house just wasn't familiar enough. I felt as though I were losing my place here in my own time. Rufus's time was a sharper, stronger reality. The work was harder, the smells and tastes were stronger, the danger was greater, the pain was worse . . . Rufus's time demanded things of me that had never been demanded before, and it could easily kill me if I did not meet its demands. That was a stark, powerful reality that the gentle conveniences and luxuries of this house, of *now*, could not touch.

And if I felt that way after spending only short periods in the past, what must Kevin be feeling after five years. His white skin had saved him from much of the trouble I had faced, but still, he couldn't have had an easy time.

I found him in the living room trying knobs on the television set. It was new to us, that television, like the house. The on/off switch was under the screen out of sight, and Kevin clearly didn't remember.

I went to it, reached under, and switched the set on. There was a public service announcement on advising women to see their doctors and take care of themselves while they were pregnant.

"Turn it off," said Kevin.

I obeyed.

"I saw a woman die in childbirth once," he said.

I nodded. "I never saw it, but I kept hearing about it happening. It was pretty common back then, I guess. Poor medical care or none at all."

"No, medical care had nothing to do with the case I saw. This woman's master strung her up by her wrists and beat her until the baby came out of her—dropped onto the ground."

I swallowed, looked away rubbing my wrists. "I see." Would Weylin have done such a thing to one of his pregnant slave women, I wondered. Probably not. He had more business sense than that. Dead mother, dead baby—dead loss. I'd heard stories, though, about other slaveholders who didn't care what they did. There was a woman on Weylin's plantation whose former master had cut three fingers from her right hand when he caught her writing. She had a baby nearly every year, that woman. Nine so far, seven surviving. Weylin called her a good breeder, and he never whipped her. He was selling off her children, though, one by one.

Kevin stared at the blank TV screen, then turned away with a bitter laugh. "I feel like this is just another stopover," he said. "A little less real than the others, maybe."

"Stopover?"

"Like Philadelphia. Like New York and Boston. Like that farm in Maine . . ."

"You did get to Maine, then?"

"Yes. Almost bought a farm there. Would have been a stupid mistake. Then a friend in Boston forwarded me Weylin's letter. Home at last, I thought, and you . . ." He looked at me. "Well. I got half of what I wanted. You're still you."

I went to him with relief that surprised me. I hadn't realized how much I'd worried, even now, that I might not be "still me" as far as he was concerned.

"Everything is so soft here," he said, "so easy . . ."

"I know."

"It's good. Hell, I wouldn't go back to some of the pestholes I've lived in for pay. But still . . ."

We were walking through the dining room, through the hall. We stopped at my office and he went in to look at the map of the United States that I had on the wall. "I kept going farther and farther up the east coast," he said. "I guess I would have wound up in Canada next. But in all my traveling, do you know the only time I ever felt relieved and eager to be going to a place?"

"I think so," I said quietly.

"It was when . . ." He stopped, realizing what I had said, and frowned at me.

"It was when you went back to Maryland," I said. "When you visited the Weylins to see whether I was there."

He looked surprised, but strangely pleased. "How could you know that?"

"It's true, isn't it?"

"It's true."

"I felt it the last time Rufus called me. I've got no love at all for that place, but so help me, when I saw it again, it was so much like coming home that it scared me."

Kevin stroked his beard. "I grew this to come back."

"Why?"

"To disguise myself. You ever hear of a man named Denmark Vesey?"

"The freedman who plotted rebellion down in South Carolina."

"Yes. Well, Vesey never got beyond the planning stage, but

he scared the hell out of a lot of white people. And a lot of black people suffered for it. Around that time, I was accused of helping slaves to escape. I barely got out ahead of the mob."

"Were you at the Weylins' then?"

"No, I had a job teaching school." He rubbed the scar on his forehead. "I'll tell you all about it, Dana, but some other time. Now, somehow, I've got to fit myself back into nineteen seventy-six. If I can."

"You can."

He shrugged.

"One more thing. Just one."

He looked at me questioningly.

"Were you helping slaves to escape?"

"Of course I was! I fed them, hid them during the day, and when night came, I pointed them toward a free black family who would feed and hide them the next day."

I smiled and said nothing. He sounded angry, almost defensive about what he had done.

"I guess I'm not used to saying things like that to people who understand them," he said.

"I know. It's enough that you did what you did."

He rubbed his head again. "Five years is longer than it sounds. So much longer."

We went on to his office. Both our offices were ex-bedrooms in the solidly built old frame house we had bought. They were big comfortable rooms that reminded me a little of the rooms in the Weylin house.

No. I shook my head, denying the impression. This house was nothing like the Weylin house. I watched Kevin look around his office. He circled the room, stopping at his desk, at the file cabinets, at the book cases. He stood for a moment looking at the shelf filled with copies of *The Water of Meribah*, his most successful novel—the novel that had bought us this house. He touched a copy as though to take it down, then left it and drifted back to his typewriter. He fumbled with that for a moment, remembered how to turn it on, then looked at the stack of blank paper beside it and turned it off again. Abruptly, he brought his fist down hard on it.

I jumped at the sudden sound. "You'll break it, Kevin."

"What difference would that make?"

I winced, remembered my own attempts to write when I'd been home last. I had tried and tried and only managed to fill my wastebasket.

"What am I going to do?" said Kevin, turning his back on the typewriter. "Christ, if I can't feel anything even in here . . ."

"You will. Give yourself time."

He picked up his electric pencil sharpener, examined it as though he did not know what it was, then seemed to remember. He put it down, took a pencil from a china cup on the desk, and put it in the sharpener. The little machine obligingly ground the pencil to a fine point. Kevin stared at the point for a moment, then at the sharpener.

"A toy," he said. "Nothing but a damned toy."

"That's what I said when you bought it," I told him. I tried to smile and make it a joke, but there was something in his voice that scared me.

With a sudden slash of his hand, he knocked both the sharpener and the cup of pencils from his desk. The pencils scattered and the cup broke. The sharpener bounced hard on the bare floor, just missing the rug. I unplugged it quickly.

"Kevin . . ." He stalked out of the room before I could finish. I ran after him, caught his arm. "Kevin!"

He stopped, glared at me as though I was some stranger who had dared to lay hands on him.

"Kevin, you can't come back all at once any more than you can leave all at once. It takes time. After a while, though, things will fall into place."

His expression did not change.

I took his face between my hands and looked into his eyes, now truly cold. "I don't know what it was like for you," I said, "being gone so long, having so little control over whether you'd ever get back. I can't really know, I guess. But I do know . . . that I almost didn't want to be alive when I thought I'd left you behind for good. But now that you're back . . ."

He pulled away from me and walked out of the room. The expression on his face was like something I'd seen, something I was used to seeing on Tom Weylin. Something closed and ugly.

I didn't go after him when I left his office. I didn't know what to do to help him, and I didn't want to look at him and see things that reminded me of Weylin. But because I went to the bedroom, I found him.

He was standing beside the dresser looking at a picture of himself—himself as he had been. He had always hated having his picture taken, but I had talked him into this one, a close-up of the young face under a cap of thick gray hair, dark brows, pale eyes . . .

I was afraid he would throw the picture down, smash it as he had tried to smash the pencil sharpener. I took it from his hand. He let it go easily and turned to look at himself in the dresser mirror. He ran a hand through his hair, still thick and gray. He would probably never be bald. But he looked old now; the young face had changed more than could be accounted for by the new lines in his face or the beard.

"Kevin?"

He closed his eyes. "Leave me alone for a while, Dana," he said softly. "I just need to be by myself and get used to . . . to things again."

There was suddenly a loud, house-shaking sonic boom and Kevin jumped back against the dresser looking around wildly.

"Just a jet passing overhead," I told him.

He gave me what almost seemed to be a look of hatred, then brushed past me, went to his office and shut the door.

I left him alone. I didn't know what else to do—or even whether there was anything I could do. Maybe this was something he had to work out for himself. Maybe it was something that only time could help. Maybe anything. But I felt so damned helpless as I looked down the hall at his closed door. Finally, I went to bathe, and that hurt enough to hold my attention for a while. Then I checked my denim bag, put in a bottle of antiseptic, Kevin's large bottle of Excedrin, and an old pocket knife to replace the switchblade. The knife was large and easily as deadly as the switchblade I had lost, but I wouldn't be able to use it as quickly, and I would have a harder time surprising an opponent with it. I considered taking a kitchen knife of some kind instead, but I thought one big enough to be effective would be too hard to hide. Not that any kind of knife had been very effective for me so far. Having one just made me feel safer.

I dropped the knife into the bag and replaced soap, tooth

paste, some clothing, a few other things. My thoughts went
back to Kevin. Did he blame me for the five years he had lost,
I wondered. Or if he didn't now, would he when he tried to
write again? He would try. Writing was his profession. I wondered whether he had been able to write during the five years,
or rather, whether he had been able to publish. I was sure he
had been writing. I couldn't imagine either of us going for five
years without writing. Maybe he'd kept a journal or something.
He had changed—in five years he couldn't help changing. But
the markets he wrote for hadn't changed. He might have a
frustrating time for a while. And he might blame me.

It had been so good seeing him again, loving him, knowing
his exile was ended. I had thought everything would be all
right. Now I wondered if anything would be all right.

I put on a loose dress and went to the kitchen to see what we
could make a meal of—if I could get Kevin to eat. The chops I
had put out to defrost over two months ago were still icy. How
long had we been away, then? What day was it? Somehow, neither of us had bothered to find out.

I turned on the radio and found a news station—tuned in
right in the middle of a story about the war in Lebanon. The
war there was worse. The President was ordering an evacuation
of nonofficial Americans. That sounded like what he had been
ordering on the day Rufus called me. A moment later, the an-
nouncer mentioned the day, confirming what I had thought. I
had been away for only a few hours. Kevin had been away for
eight days. Nineteen seventy-six had not gone on without us.

The news switched to a story about South Africa—blacks
rioting there and dying wholesale in battles with police over
the policies of the white supremacist government.

I turned off the radio and tried to cook the meal in peace.
South African whites had always struck me as people who
would have been happier living in the nineteenth century, or
the eighteenth. In fact, they were living in the past as far as
their race relations went. They lived in ease and comfort sup-
ported by huge numbers of blacks whom they kept in poverty
and held in contempt. Tom Weylin would have felt right at
home.

After a while, the smell of food brought Kevin out of his
office, but he ate in silence.

"Can't I help?" I asked finally.

"Help with what?"

There was an edge to his voice that made me wary. I didn't answer.

"I'm all right," he said grudgingly.

"No you're not."

He put his fork down. "How long were you away this time?"

"A few hours. Or just over two months. Take your pick."

"There was a newspaper in my office. I was reading it. I don't know how old it is, but . . ."

"It's today's paper. It came the morning Rufus called me last. That's this morning if you want to believe the calendar. June eighteenth."

"It doesn't matter. I wasted my time reading that paper. I didn't know what the hell it was talking about most of the time."

"It's like I said. The confusion doesn't go away all at once. It doesn't for me either."

"It was so good coming home at first."

"It was good. It still is."

"I don't know. I don't know anything."

"You're in too much of a hurry. You . . ." I stopped, realized I was swaying a little on my chair. "Oh God, no!" I whispered.

"I suppose I am," said Kevin. "I wonder how people just out of prison manage to readjust."

"Kevin, go get my bag. I left it in the bedroom."

"What? Why . . . ?"

"Go, Kevin!"

He went, understanding finally. I sat still, praying that he would come back in time. I could feel tears streaming down my face. So soon, so soon . . . Why couldn't I have had just a few days with him—a few days of peace at home?

I felt something pressed into my hands and I grasped it. My bag. I opened my eyes to the dark blur of it, and the larger blur of Kevin standing near me. I was suddenly afraid of what he might do.

"Get away, Kevin!"

He said something, but suddenly, there was too much noise for me to hear him—even if he had still been there.

2

There was water, rain pouring down on me. I was sitting in mud clutching my bag.

I got up sheltering my bag as much as I could so that eventually, I'd have something dry to change into. I looked around grimly for Rufus.

I couldn't find him. I peered through the dim gray light, looked around until I realized where I was. I could see the familiar boxy Weylin house in the distance, yellow light at one window. At least there would be no long walk for me this time. In this storm, that was something to be grateful for. But where was Rufus? If he was in trouble inside the house, why had I arrived outside?

I shrugged and started toward the house. If he was there, it would be stupid for me to waste time out here. Not that I could get any wetter.

I tripped over him.

He was lying face down in a puddle so deep the water almost covered his head. Face down.

I grabbed him and pulled him out of the water and over to a tree that would shelter us a little from the rain. A moment later, there was thunder and a flash of lightning, and I dragged him away from the tree again. With his ability to draw bad luck I didn't want to take chances.

He was alive. As I moved him, he threw up on himself and partly on me. I almost joined him. He began to cough and mutter and I realized that he was either drunk or sick. More probably drunk. He was also heavy. He didn't look any bigger than he had when I saw him last, but he was soaking wet now, and he was beginning to struggle feebly.

I had been dragging him toward the house while he was still. Now, I dropped him in disgust and went to the house alone. Some stronger, more tolerant person could drag or carry him the rest of the way.

Nigel answered the door, stood peering down at me. "Who the devil . . . ?"

"It's Dana, Nigel."

"Dana?" He was suddenly alert. "What happened? Where's Marse Rufe?"

"Out there. He was too heavy for me."

"Where?"

I looked back the way I had come and could not see Rufus. If he had flipped himself over again . . .

"Damn!" I muttered. "Come on." I led him back to the gray lump—still face up—that was Rufus. "Watch it," I said. "He threw up on me."

Nigel picked Rufus up like a sack of grain, threw him over his shoulder, and strode back to the house in such quick long strides that I had to run to keep up. Rufus threw up again down Nigel's back, but Nigel paid no attention. The rain washed them both fairly clean before we reached the house.

Inside, we met Weylin who was coming down the stairs. He stopped short as he saw us. "You!" he said, staring at me.

"Hello, Mr. Weylin," I said wearily. He looked bent and old —thinner than ever. He walked with a cane.

"Is Rufus all right? Is he . . . ?"

"He's alive," I said. "I found him unconscious, face down in a ditch. A little more and he would have drowned."

"If you're here, I suppose he would have." The old man looked at Nigel. "Take him up to his room and put him to bed. Dana, you . . ." He stopped, looked at my dripping, clinging —to him—immodestly short dress. It was the kind of loose smocklike garment that little children of both sexes wore before they were old enough to work. It clearly offended Weylin more than my pants ever had. "Haven't you got something decent to put on?" he asked.

I looked at my wet bag. "Decent, maybe, but probably not dry."

"Go put on what you've got, then come back down to the library."

He wanted to talk to me, I thought. Just what I needed at the end of a long jumbled day. Weylin didn't talk to me normally except to give orders. When he did, it was always harrowing. There was so much that I couldn't say; he took offense so easily.

I followed Nigel up the stairs, then went on to the narrow, ladderlike attic stairs. My old corner was empty so I went there to put my bag down and search through it. I found a nearly dry shirt and a pair of Levi's that were wet only at the ankles. I dried myself, changed, combed my hair, and spread out some of my wettest clothing to dry. Then I went down to Weylin. I had learned not to worry about leaving my things in the attic. Other house servants examined them. I knew that because I had caught them at it now and then. But nothing was ever missing.

Apprehensively, I went through the library door.

"You look as young as you ever did," Weylin complained sourly when he saw me.

"Yes, sir." I'd agree with anything he said if it would get me away from him sooner.

"What happened to you there? Your face."

I touched the scab. "That's where you kicked me, Mr. Weylin."

He had been sitting in a worn old arm chair, but now he surged out of it like a young man, his cane a blunt wooden sword before him. "What are you talking about! It's been six years since I've seen you."

"Yes, sir."

"Well!"

"For me, it's only been a few hours." I thought Rufus and Kevin had probably told him enough to enable him to understand, whether he believed or not. And perhaps he did understand. He seemed to get angrier.

"Who in hell ever said you were an educated nigger? You can't even tell a decent lie. Six years for me is six years for you!"

"Yes, sir." Why did he bother to ask me questions? Why did I bother to answer them?

He sat down again and leaned forward, one hand resting on his cane. His voice was softer, though, when he spoke. "That Franklin get back home all right?"

"Yes, sir." What would happen if I asked him where he thought that home was? But no, he had done at least one decent thing for Kevin and me, no matter what he was. I met his eyes for a moment. "Thank you."

"I didn't do it for you."

My temper flared suddenly. "I don't give a damn why you did it! I'm just telling you, one human being to another, that I'm grateful. Why can't you leave it at that!"

The old man's face went pale. "You want a good whipping!" he said. "You must not have had one for a while."

I said nothing. I realized then, though, that if he ever hit me again, I would break his scrawny neck. I would not endure it again.

Weylin leaned back in his chair. "Rufus always said you didn't know your place any better than a wild animal," he muttered. "I always said you were just another crazy nigger."

I stood watching him.

"Why'd you help my son again?" he asked.

I settled down a little, shrugged. "Nobody ought to die the way he would have—lying in a ditch, drowning in mud and whiskey and his own vomit."

"Stop it!" Weylin shouted. "I'll take the cowhide to you myself! I'll . . ." He fell silent, gasped for breath. His face was still dead white. He'd make himself really sick if he didn't regain some of his old control.

I dropped back into indifference. "Yes, sir."

After a moment he had control of himself. In fact, he sounded perfectly calm again. "You and Rufus had some trouble when you saw him last."

"Yes, sir." Having Rufus try to shoot me had been troublesome.

"I hoped you would go on helping him. You know there's always a home for you here if you do."

I smiled a little in spite of myself. "Bad nigger that I am, eh?"

"Is that the way you think of yourself?"

I laughed bitterly. "No. I don't kid myself much. Your son is still alive, isn't he?"

"You're bad enough. I don't know any other white man who would put up with you."

"If you can manage to put up with me a little more humanely, I'll go on doing what I can for Mister Rufus."

He frowned. "Now what are you talking about?"

"I'm saying the day I'm beaten just once more, your son is on his own."

His eyes widened, perhaps in surprise. Then be began to tremble. I had never before seen a man literally trembling with anger. "You're threatening him!" he stammered. "By God, you are crazy!"

"Crazy or sane, I mean what I say." My back and side ached as though to warn me, but for the moment, I wasn't afraid. He loved his son no matter how he behaved toward him, and he knew I could do as I threatened. "At the rate Mister Rufus has accidents," I said, "he might live another six or seven years without me. I wouldn't count on more than that."

"You damned black bitch!" He shook his cane at me like an extended forefinger. "If you think you can get away with making threats . . . giving orders . . ." He ran out of breath and began gasping again. I watched without sympathy, wondering whether he was already sick. "Get out!" he gasped. "Go to Rufus. Take care of him. If anything happens to him, I'll flay you alive!"

My aunt used to say things like that to me when I was little and did something to annoy her—"Girl, I'm going to skin you alive!" And she'd get my uncle's belt and use it on me. But it had never occurred to me that anyone could make such a threat and mean it literally as Weylin meant it now. I turned and left him before he could see that my courage had vanished. He could get help from his neighbors, from the patrollers, probably even from whatever police officials the area had. He could do anything he wanted to to me, and I had no enforceable rights. None at all.

3

Rufus was sick again. When I reached his room I found him lying in bed shaking violently while Nigel tried to keep him wrapped in blankets.

"What's wrong with him?" I asked.

"Nothing," said Nigel. "Got the ague again, I guess."

"Ague?"

"Yeah, he's had it before. He'll be all right."

He didn't look all right to me. "Has anyone gone for the doctor?"

"Marse Tom don't hardly get Doc West for ague. He says all the doc knows is bleeding and blistering and purging and puking and making folks sicker than they was to start."

I swallowed, remembered the pompous little man I had disliked so. "Is the doctor really that bad, Nigel?"

"He gave me some stuff once, nearly killed me. From then on, I just let Sarah doctor me when I'm sick. 'Least she don't dose niggers like they was horses or mules."

I shook my head and went close to Rufus's bed. He looked miserable, seemed to be in pain. I tried to think what the ague might be; the word was familiar, but I couldn't remember what I'd heard or read about it.

Rufus looked up at me, red-eyed, and tried to smile, though the grimace he managed was far from pleasant. To my surprise, his attempt touched me. I hadn't expected to still care about him except for my own and my family's sake. I didn't want to care.

"Idiot," I muttered down at him.

He managed to look hurt.

I looked at Nigel, wondered whether the disease could be as unimportant as he thought. Would he think it was important if he had been the one on his back shaking?

Nigel was busy plucking his wet shirt away from his skin. No one had given him a chance to change his clothes, I realized.

"Nigel, I'll stay here if you want to go dry off," I said.

He looked up, smiled at me. "You go away for six years," he said, "then come back and fit right in. It's like you never left."

"Every time I go I keep hoping I'll never come back."

He nodded. "But at least you get some time of freedom."

I looked away, feeling strangely guilty that, yes, I did get some time of freedom. Not enough, but probably more than Nigel would ever know. I didn't like feeling guilty about it. Then something bit me on my ear and I forgot my guilt. As I slapped at my ear, I remembered, finally, what the ague was.

Malaria.

I wondered dully whether the mosquito that had just bitten me was carrying the disease. In my reading I'd come across a lot of information on malaria and none of it led me to believe the disease was as harmless as Nigel seemed to think. It might not kill, but it weakened and it recurred and it could lower one's resistance to other diseases. Also, with Rufus lying exposed as he was to new mosquito attacks, the disease could be spread over the plantation and beyond.

"Nigel, is there anything we can hang up to keep the mosquitoes off him?"

"Mosquitoes! He wouldn't feel it if twenty mosquitoes bit him now."

"No, but the rest of us would be feeling it eventually."

"What do you mean?"

"Does anyone else have it now?"

"Don't think so. Some of the children are sick, but I think they have something wrong with their faces—one side all swollen up."

Mumps? Never mind. "Well, let's see if we can keep this from spreading. Is there any kind of mosquito netting—or whatever people use here?"

"Sure, for white folks. But . . ."

"Would you get some? With the help of the canopy, we should be able to enclose him completely."

"Dana, listen!"

I looked at him.

"What do mosquitoes have to do with the ague?"

I blinked, stared at him in surprise. He didn't know. Of course he didn't. Doctors of the day didn't know. Which probably meant that Nigel wouldn't believe me when I told him. After all, how could a thing as tiny as a mosquito make anybody sick? "Nigel, you know where I'm from, don't you?"

He gave me something that wasn't quite a smile. "Not New York."

"No."

"I know where Marse Rufe said you was from."

"It shouldn't be that hard for you to believe him. You've seen me go home at least once."

"Twice."

"Well?"

He shrugged. "I can't say. If I hadn't seen . . . the way you go home, I'd just figure you were one crazy nigger. But I haven't ever seen anybody do what you did. I don't want to believe you, but I guess I do."

"Good." I took a deep breath. "Where I'm from, people have learned that mosquitoes carry ague. They bite someone who's sick with it, then later they bite healthy people and give them the disease."

"How?"

"They suck blood from the sick and . . . pass on some of that blood when they bite a healthy person. Like a mad dog that bites a man and drives the man mad." No talk about microorganisms. Nigel not only wouldn't believe me, he might decide I really was crazy.

"Doc says it's something in the air that spreads ague—something off bad water and garbage. A miasma, he called it."

"He's wrong. He's wrong about the bleeding and purging and the rest, he was wrong when he dosed you, and he's wrong now. It's a wonder any of his patients survive."

"I heard he was good and quick when it comes to cutting off legs or arms."

I had to look at Nigel to see whether he was making a grisly joke. He wasn't. "Get the mosquito net," I said wearily. "Let's do what we can to keep that butcher away from here."

He nodded and went away. I wondered whether or not he believed me, but it didn't really matter. It wouldn't cost anyone anything to take this small precaution.

I looked down at Rufus to see that he had stopped trembling and closed his eyes. His breathing was regular and I thought he was asleep.

"Why do you keep trying to kill yourself?" I said softly.

I hadn't expected an answer so I was surprised when he spoke quietly. "Most of the time, living just isn't worth the trouble."

I sat down next to his bed. "It never occurred to me that you might really want to die."

"I don't." He opened his eyes, looked at me, then shut them again and covered them with his hands. "But if your eyes and your head and your leg hurt the way mine do, dying might start to look good."

"Your eyes hurt?"

"When I look around."

"Did they hurt before when you had ague?"

"No. This isn't ague. Ague is bad enough. My leg feels like it's coming off, and my head . . . !"

He scared me. His pain seemed to increase and he twisted his body as though to move away from it, then untwisted quickly and lay panting.

"Rufe, I'm going to get your father. If he sees how sick you are, he'll send for the doctor."

He seemed to be too involved with his own pain to answer.

I didn't want to leave him until Nigel came back, though I had no idea what I could do for him. My problem was solved when Weylin came in with Nigel.

"What is all this about mosquitoes giving people ague?" he demanded.

"We may be able to forget about that," I said. "This doesn't look like malaria. Ague. He's in a lot of pain. I think someone should go for the doctor."

"You're doctor enough for him."

"But . . ." I stopped, took a deep breath, made myself calm down. Rufus was groaning behind me. "Mr. Weylin, I'm no doctor. I don't have any idea what's wrong with him. Whatever professional help is available, you should get it for him."

"Should I now?"

"His life may be at stake."

Weylin's mouth was set in a straight hard line. "If he dies, you die, and you won't die easy."

"You already said that. But no matter what you do to me, your son will still be dead. Is that what you want?"

"You do your job," he said stubbornly, "and he'll live. You're something different. I don't know what—witch, devil, I don't care. Whatever you are, you just about brought a girl back to life when you came here last, and she wasn't even the one you came to help. You come out of nowhere and go back into nowhere. Years ago, I would have sworn there couldn't even be anybody like you. You're not natural! But you can feel pain —and you can die. Remember that and do your job. Take care of your master."

"But, I tell you . . ."

He walked out of the room and shut the door behind him.

4

We got the mosquito netting and used it, just in case. Nigel said Weylin didn't really mind letting us have it. He just didn't want to hear any more damned nonsense about mosquitoes. He didn't like to be taken for a fool.

"He's as close to being scared of you as he's ever been of anything," said Nigel. "I think he'd rather try to kill you than admit it though."

"I don't see any sign of fear in him."

"You don't know him the way I do." Nigel paused. "Could he kill you, Dana?"

"I don't know. It's possible."

"We better get Marse Rufe well then. Sarah has a kind of tea she makes that kind of helps the ague. Maybe it will help whatever Marse Rufe has now."

"Would you ask her to brew up a pot?"

He nodded and went out.

Sarah came upstairs with Nigel to bring Rufus the tea and to see me. She looked old now. Her hair was streaked with gray and her face lined. She walked with a limp.

"Dropped a kettle on my foot," she said. "Couldn't walk at all for a while." She gave me the feeling that everyone was getting older, passing me by. She brought me roast beef and bread to eat.

Rufus had a fever now. He didn't want the tea, but I coaxed and bullied until he swallowed it. Then we all waited, but all that happened was that Rufus's other leg began to hurt. His eyes bothered him most because moving them hurt him, and he couldn't help following my movements or Nigel's around the room. Finally, I put a cool damp cloth over them. That seemed to help. He still had a lot of pain in his joints—his arms, his legs, everywhere. I thought I could ease that, so I took his candle and went up to the attic for my bag. I was just in time to catch a little girl trying to get the top off my Excedrin bottle. It scared me. She could just as easily have chosen the sleeping pills. The attic wasn't as safe a place as I had thought.

"No, honey, give those to me."

"They yours?"

"Yes."

"They candy?"

Good Lord. "No, they're medicine. Nasty medicine."

"Ugh!" she said, and handed them back to me. She went back to her pallet next to another child. They were new children. I wondered whether the two little boys who had preceded them had been sold or sent to the fields.

I took the Excedrin, what was left of the aspirin, and the sleeping pills back down with me. I would have to keep them somewhere in Rufus's room or eventually one of the kids would figure out how to get the safety caps off.

Rufus had thrown off the damp cloth and was knotted on his side in pain when I got back to him. Nigel had lain down on the floor before the fireplace and gone to sleep. He could have gone back to his cabin, but he had asked me if I wanted him to stay since this was my first night back, and I'd said yes.

I dissolved three aspirins in water and tried to get Rufus to drink it. He wouldn't even open his mouth. So I woke Nigel, and Nigel held him down while I held his nose and poured the bad-tasting solution into his mouth as he gasped for air. He cursed us both, but after a while he began to feel a little better. Temporarily.

It was a bad night. I didn't get much sleep. Nor was I to get much for six days and nights following. Whatever Rufus had, it was terrible. He was in constant pain, he had fever—once I had to call Nigel to hold him while I tied him down to keep him from hurting himself. I gave him aspirins—too many, but not as many as he wanted. I made him take broth and soup and fruit and vegetable juices. He didn't want them. He never wanted to eat, but he didn't want Nigel holding him down either. He ate.

Alice came in now and then to relieve me. Like Sarah, she looked older. She also looked harder. She was a cool, bitter older sister to the girl I had known.

"Folks treat her bad because of Marse Rufe," Nigel told me. "They figure if she's been with him this long, she must like it."

And Alice said contemptuously, "Who cares what a bunch of niggers think!"

"She lost two babies," Nigel told me. "And the one she's got left is sickly."

"White babies," Alice said. "Look more like him than me. Joe is even red-headed." Joe was the single survivor. I almost cried when I heard that. No Hagar yet. I was so tired of this going back and forth; I wanted so much for it to be over. I couldn't even feel sorry for the friend who had fought for me and taken care of me when I was hurt. I was too busy feeling sorry for myself.

On the third day of his illness, Rufus's fever left him. He was weak and several pounds lighter, but so relieved to be rid of the fever and the pain that nothing else mattered. He thought he was getting well. He wasn't.

The fever and the pain returned for three more days and he got a rash that itched and eventually peeled . . .

At last, he got well and stayed well. I prayed that whatever his disease had been, I wouldn't get it, wouldn't ever have to care for anyone else who had it. A few days after the worst of his symptoms had disappeared, I was allowed to sleep in the attic. I collapsed gratefully onto the pallet Sarah had made me there, and it felt like the world's softest bed. I didn't awaken until late the next morning after long hours of deep, unbroken sleep. I was still a little groggy when Alice came running up the steps and into the attic to get me.

"Marse Tom is sick," she said. "Marse Rufe wants you to come."

"Oh no," I muttered. "Tell him to send for the doctor."

"Already sent for. But Marse Tom is having bad pains in his chest."

The significance of that filtered through to me slowly. "Pains in his chest?"

"Yeah. Come on. They in the parlor."

"God, that sounds like a heart attack. There's nothing I can do."

"Just come. They want you."

I pulled on a pair of pants and threw on a shirt as I ran. What did these people want from me? Magic? If Weylin was having a heart attack, he was going to either recover or die without my help.

I ran down the stairs and into the parlor where Weylin lay on a sofa, ominously still and silent.

"Do something!" Rufus pleaded. "Help him!" His voice sounded as thin and weak as he looked. His sickness had left its marks on him. I wondered how he had gotten downstairs.

Weylin wasn't breathing, and I couldn't find a pulse. For a moment, I stared at him, undecided, repelled, not wanting to touch him again, let alone breathe into him. Then quelling disgust, I began mouth to mouth resuscitation and external heart massage—what did they call it? Cardiopulmonary resuscitation. I knew the name, and I'd seen someone doing it on television. Beyond that, I was completely ignorant. I didn't even know why I was trying to save Weylin. He wasn't worth it. And I didn't know if CPR could do any good in an era when there was no ambulance to call, no one to take over for me even if I somehow got Weylin's heart going—which I didn't expect to do.

Which I didn't do.

Finally, I gave up. I looked around to see Rufus on the floor near me. I didn't know whether he had sat down or fallen, but I was glad he was sitting now.

"I'm sorry, Rufe. He's dead."

"You let him die?"

"He was dead when I got here. I tried to bring him back the way I brought you back when you were drowning. I failed."

"You let him die."

He sounded like a child about to cry. His illness had weakened him so, I thought he might cry. Even healthy people cried and said irrational things when their parents died.

"I did what I could, Rufe. I'm sorry."

"Damn you to hell, you let him die!" He tried to lunge at me, succeeded only in falling over. I moved to help him up, but stopped when he tried to push me away.

"Send Nigel to me," he whispered. "Get Nigel."

I got up and went to find Nigel. Behind me, I heard Rufus say once more, "You just let him die."

5

Things were happening too fast for me. I was almost glad to find myself put back to work with Sarah and Carrie, ignored by Rufus. I needed time to catch up with myself—and catch up with life on the plantation. Carrie and Nigel had three sons now, and Nigel had never mentioned it to me because the youngest was two years old. He had forgotten that I didn't know. I was with him once, as he watched them playing. "It's good to have children," he said softly. "Good to have sons. But it's so hard to see them be slaves."

I met Alice's thin pale little boy and saw with relief that in spite of the way she talked, she obviously loved the child.

"I keep thinking I might wake up and find him cold like the others," she said one day in the cookhouse.

"What did they die of?" I asked.

"Fevers. The doctor came and bled them and purged them, but they still died."

"He bled and purged babies?"

"They were two and three. He said it would break the fever. And it did. But they . . . they died anyway."

"Alice, if I were you, I wouldn't ever let that man near Joe."

She looked at her son sitting on the floor of the cookhouse eating mush and milk. He was five years old and he looked almost white in spite of Alice's dark skin. "I never wanted no doctor near the other two," said Alice. "Marse Rufe sent for him—sent for him and made me let him kill my babies."

Rufus's intentions had been good. Even the doctor's intentions had probably been good. But all Alice knew was that her children were dead and she blamed Rufus. Rufus himself was to teach me about that attitude.

On the day after Weylin was buried, Rufus decided to punish me for letting the old man die. I didn't know whether he honestly believed I had done such a thing. Maybe he just needed to hurt someone. He did lash out at others when he was hurt; I had already seen that.

So on the morning after the funeral, he sent the current overseer, a burly man named Evan Fowler, to get me from the cookhouse. Jake Edwards had either quit or been fired sometime during my six-year absence. Fowler came to tell me I was to work in the fields.

I didn't believe it, even when the man pushed me out of the cookhouse. I thought he was just another Jake Edwards throwing his weight around. But outside, Rufus stood waiting, watching. I looked at him, then back at Fowler.

"This the one?" Fowler asked Rufus.

"That's her," said Rufus. And he turned and went back into the main house.

Stunned, I took the sicklelike corn knife Fowler thrust into my hands and let myself be herded out toward the cornfield. Herded. Fowler got his horse and rode a little behind me as I walked. It was a long walk. The cornfield wasn't where I'd left it. Apparently, even in this time, planters practiced some form of crop rotation. Not that that mattered to me. What in the world could I do in a cornfield?

I glanced back at Fowler. "I've never done field work before," I told him. "I don't know how."

"You'll learn," he said. He used the handle of his whip to scratch his shoulder.

I began to realize that I should have resisted, should have refused to let Fowler bring me out here where only other slaves could see what happened to me. Now it was too late. It was going to be a grim day.

Slaves were walking down rows of corn, chopping the stalks down with golf-swing strokes of their knives. Two slaves worked a row, moving toward each other. Then they gathered the stalks they had cut and stood them in bunches at opposite ends of the row. It looked easy, but I suspected that a day of it could be backbreaking.

Fowler dismounted and pointed toward a row.

"You chop like the others," he said. "Just do what they do. Now get to work." He shoved me toward the row. There was already someone at the other end of it working toward me. Someone quick and strong, I hoped, because I doubted that I would be quick or strong for a while. I hoped that the washing and the scrubbing at the house and the factory and warehouse work back in my own time had made me strong enough just to survive.

I raised the knife and chopped at the first stalk. It bent over, partially cut.

At almost the same moment, Fowler lashed me hard across the back.

I screamed, stumbled, and spun around to face him, still holding my knife. Unimpressed, he hit me across the breasts.

I fell to my knees and doubled over in a blaze of pain. Tears ran down my face. Even Tom Weylin hadn't hit slave women that way—any more than he'd kicked slave men in the groin. Fowler was an animal. I glared up at him in pain and hatred.

"Get up!" he said.

I couldn't. I didn't think anything could make me get up just then—until I saw Fowler raising his whip again.

Somehow, I got up.

"Now do what the others do," he said. "Chop close to the ground. Chop hard!"

I gripped the knife, felt myself much more eager to chop him.

"All right," he said. "Try it and get it over with. I thought you was supposed to be smart."

He was a big man. He hadn't impressed me as being very quick, but he was strong. I was afraid that even if I managed to hurt him, I wouldn't hurt him enough to keep him from killing me. Maybe I should make him try to kill me. Maybe it would get me out of this Godawful place where people punished you for helping them. Maybe it would get me home. But in how many pieces? Fowler would take the knife away from me and give it back edge first.

I turned and slashed furiously at the corn stalk, then at the next. Behind me, Fowler laughed.

"Maybe you got some sense after all," he said.

He watched me for a while, urging me on, literally cracking the whip. By the time he left, I was sweating, shaking, humiliated. I met the woman who had been working toward me and she whispered, "Slow down! Take a lick or two if you have to. You kill yourself today, he'll push you to kill yourself every day."

There was sense in that. Hell, if I went on the way I had been, I wouldn't even last through today. My shoulders were already beginning to ache.

Fowler came back as I was gathering the cut stalks. "What the devil do you think you're doing!" he demanded. "You ought to be halfway down the next row by now." He hit me across the back as I bent down. "Move! You're not in the cookhouse getting fat and lazy now. Move!"

He did that all day. Coming up suddenly, shouting at me, ordering me to go faster no matter how fast I went, cursing me, threatening me. He didn't hit me that often, but he kept me on edge because I never knew when a blow would fall. It got so just the sound of his coming terrified me. I caught myself cringing, jumping at the sound of his voice.

The woman in my row explained, "He's always hard on a new nigger. Make 'em go fast so he can see how fast they can work. Then later on if they slow down, he whip 'em for gettin' lazy."

I made myself slow down. It wasn't hard. I didn't think my shoulders could have hurt much worse if they'd been broken. Sweat ran down into my eyes and my hands were beginning to blister. My back hurt from the blows I'd taken as well as from sore muscles. After a while, it was more painful for me to push myself than it was for me to let Fowler hit me. After a while, I was so tired, I didn't care either way. Pain was pain. After a while, I just wanted to lie down between the rows and not get up again.

I stumbled and fell, got up and fell again. Finally, I lay face-down in the dirt, unable to get up. Then came a welcome blackness. I could have been going home or dying or passing out; it made no difference to me. I was going away from the pain. That was all.

6

I was on my back when I came to and there was a white face floating just above me. For a wild moment, I thought it was Kevin, thought I was home. I said his name eagerly.

"It's me, Dana."

Rufus's voice. I was still in hell. I closed my eyes, not caring what would happen next.

"Dana, get up. You'll be hurt more if I carry you than if you walk."

The words echoed strangely in my head. Kevin had said something like that to me once. I opened my eyes again to be sure it was Rufus.

It was. I was still in the cornfield, still lying in the dirt.

"I came to get you," said Rufus. "Not soon enough, I guess."

I struggled to my feet. He offered a hand to help me, but I ignored it. I brushed myself off a little and followed him down the row toward his horse. From there, we rode together back to the house without a word passing between us. At the house, I went straight to the well, got a bucket of water, carried it up the stairs somehow, then washed, spread antiseptic on my new cuts, and put on clean clothes. I had a headache that eventually drove me down to Rufus's room for some Excedrin. Rufus had used all the aspirins.

Unfortunately, he was in his room.

"Well, you're no good in the fields," he said when he saw me. "That's clear."

I stopped, turned, and stared at him. Just stared. He had been sitting on his bed, leaning back against the headboard, but now he straightened, faced me.

"Don't do anything stupid, Dana."

"Right," I said softly. "I've done enough stupid things. How many times have I saved your life so far?" My aching head sent me to his desk where I had left the Excedrin. I shook three of them into my hand. I had never taken so many before. I had never needed so many before. My hands were trembling.

"Fowler would have given you a good whipping if I hadn't stopped him," said Rufus. "That's not the first beating I've saved you from."

I had my Excedrin. I turned to leave the room.

"Dana!"

I stopped, looked at him. He was thin and weak and hollow-eyed; his illness had left its marks on him. He probably couldn't have carried me to his horse if he'd tried. And he couldn't stop me from leaving now—I thought.

"You walk away from me, Dana, you'll be back in the fields in an hour!"

The threat stunned me. He meant it. He'd send me back out. I stood staring at him, not with anger now, but with surprise—and fear. He could do it. Maybe later, I would have a chance to make him pay, but for now, he could do as he pleased. He sounded more like his father than himself. In that moment, he even looked like his father.

"Don't you ever walk away from me again!" he said. Strangely, he began to sound a little afraid. He repeated the words, spacing them, emphasizing each one. "*Don't you ever walk away from me again!*"

I stood where I was, my head throbbing, my expression as neutral as I could make it. I still had some pride left.

"Get back in here!" he said.

I stood there for a moment longer, then went back to his desk and sat down. And he wilted. The look I associated with his father vanished. He was himself again—whoever that was.

"Dana, don't make me talk to you like that," he said wearily. "Just do what I tell you."

I shook my head, unable to think of anything safe to say. And I guess I wilted. To my shame, I realized I was almost crying. I needed desperately to be alone. Somehow, I kept back the tears.

If he noticed, he didn't say anything. I remembered I still had the Excedrin tablets in my hand, and I took them, swallowed them without water, hoping they'd work quickly, steady me a little. Then I looked at Rufus, saw that he'd lain back again. Was I supposed to stay and watch him sleep?

"I don't see how you can swallow those things like that," he said, rubbing his throat. There was a long silence, then another command. "Say something! Talk to me!"

"Or what?" I asked. "Are you going to have me beaten for not talking to you?"

He muttered something I didn't quite hear.

"What?"

Silence. Then a rush of bitterness from me.

"I saved your life, Rufus! Over and over again." I stopped for a moment, caught my breath. "And I tried to save your father's life. You know I did. You know I didn't kill him or let him die."

He moved uncomfortably, wincing a little. "Give me some of your medicine," he said.

Somehow, I didn't throw the bottle at him. I got up and handed it to him.

"Open it," he said. "I don't want to be bothered with that damn top."

I opened it, shook one tablet into his hand, and snapped the top back on.

He looked at the tablet. "Only one?"

"These are stronger than the others," I said. And also, I wanted to hang on to them for as long as I could. Who knew how many more times he would make me need them. The ones I had taken were beginning to help me already.

"You took three," he said petulantly.

"I needed three. No one has been beating you."

He looked away from me, put the one into his mouth. He still had to chew tablets before he could swallow them. "This tastes worse than the others," he complained.

I ignored him, put the bottle away in the desk.

"Dana?"

"What?"

"I know you tried to help Daddy. I know."

"Then why did you send me to the field? Why did I have to go through all that, Rufe?"

He shrugged, winced, rubbed his shoulders. He still had plenty of sore muscles, apparently. "I guess I just had to make somebody pay. And it seemed that . . . well, people don't die when you're taking care of them."

"I'm not a miracle worker."

"No. Daddy thought you were, though. He didn't like you, but he thought you could heal better than a doctor."

"Well I can't. Sometimes I'm less likely to kill than the doctor, that's all."

"Kill?"

"I don't bleed or purge away people's strength when they need it most. And I know enough to try to keep a wound clean."

"Is that all?"

"That's enough to save a few lives around here, but no, it's not all. I know a little about some diseases. Only a little."

"What do you know about . . . about a woman who's been hurt in childbearing?"

"Been hurt how?" I wondered whether he meant Alice.

"I don't know. The doctor said she wasn't to have any more and she did. The babies died and she almost died. She hasn't been well since."

Now I knew who he was talking about. "Your mother?"

"Yes. She's coming home. I want you to take care of her."

"My God! Rufe, I don't know anything about problems like that! Believe me, nothing at all." What if the woman died in my care. He'd have me beaten to death!

"She wants to come home, now that . . . She wants to come home."

"I can't care for her. I don't know how." I hesitated. "Your mother doesn't like me anyway, Rufe. You know that as well as I do." She hated me. She'd make my life hell out of pure spite.

"There's no one else I'd trust," he said. "Carrie's got her own family now. I'd have to take her out of her cabin away from Nigel and the boys . . ."

"Why?"

"Mama has to have someone with her through the night. What if she needed something?"

"You mean I'd have to sleep in her room?"

"Yes. She'd never have a servant sleep in her room before. Now, though, she's gotten used to it."

"She won't get used to me. I'm telling you, she won't have me." Please heaven!

"I think she will. She's older now, not so full of fire. You give her her laudanum when she needs it and she won't give you much trouble."

"Laudanum?"

"Her medicine. She doesn't need it so much for pain anymore, Aunt May says. But she still needs it."

Since laudanum was an opium extract, I didn't doubt that she still needed it. I was going to have a drug addict on my hands. A drug addict who hated me. "Rufe, couldn't Alice . . ."

"No!" A very sharp no. It occurred to me that Margaret Weylin had more reason to hate Alice than she did to hate me.

"Alice will be having another baby in a few months anyway," said Rufus.

"She will? Then maybe . . ." I shut my mouth, but the thought went on. Maybe this one would be Hagar. Maybe for once, I had something to gain by staying here. If only . . .

"Maybe what?"

"Nothing. It doesn't matter. Rufe, I'm asking you not to put your mother in my care, for her sake and for mine."

He rubbed his forehead. "I'll think about it, Dana, and talk to her. Maybe she remembers someone she'd like. Let me sleep now. I'm still so damn weak."

I started out of the room.

"Dana."

"Yes?" What now?

"Go read a book or something. Don't do any more work today."

"Read a book?"

"Do whatever you want to."

In other words, he was sorry. He was always sorry. He would have been amazed, uncomprehending if I refused to forgive him. I remembered suddenly the way he used to talk to his mother. If he couldn't get what he wanted from her gently, he stopped being gentle. Why not? She always forgave him.

7

Margaret Weylin wanted me. She was thin and pale and weak and older than her years. Her beauty had gone to a kind of fragile gauntness. As I was reintroduced to her, she sipped at her little bottle of dark brownish-red liquid and smiled beneficently.

Nigel carried her up to her room. She could walk a little, but she couldn't manage the stairs. Sometime later, she wanted to see Nigel's children. She was sugary sweet with them. I couldn't remember her being that way with anyone but Rufus before. Slave children hadn't interested her unless her husband had fathered them. Then her interest had been negative. But she gave Nigel's sons candy and they loved her.

She asked to see another slave—one I didn't know—and then wept a little when she heard that one had been sold. She was full of sweetness and charity. It scared me a little. I couldn't quite believe she'd changed that much.

"Dana, can you still read the way you used to?" she asked me.

"Yes, ma'am."

"I wanted you because I remembered how well you read."

I kept my expression neutral. If she didn't remember what she had thought of my reading, I did.

"Read the Bible to me," she said.

"Now?" She had just had her breakfast. I hadn't had anything yet, and I was hungry.

"Now, yes. Read the Sermon on the Mount."

That was the beginning of my first full day with her. When she was tired of hearing me read, she thought of other things for me to do. Her laundry, for instance. She wouldn't trust anyone else to do it. I wondered whether she had already found out that Alice generally did the laundry. And there was cleaning. She didn't believe her room had been swept and dusted until she saw me do it. She didn't believe Sarah understood how she wanted dinner prepared until I went down, got Sarah, and brought her back with me to receive instructions. She had to talk to Carrie and Nigel about the cleaning. She had to inspect the boy and girl who served at the table. In short, she had to prove that she was running her own house again. It had gone along without her for years, but she was back now.

She decided to teach me to sew. I had an old Singer at home and I could sew well enough with it to take care of my needs and Kevin's. But I thought sewing by hand, especially sewing for "pleasure," was slow torture. Margaret Weylin never asked me whether I wanted to learn though. She had time to fill, and it was my job to help her fill it. So I spent long tedious hours trying to imitate her tiny, straight, even stitches, and she spent minutes ripping out my work and lecturing me none too gently on how bad it was.

As the days passed, I learned to take longer than necessary when she sent me on errands. I learned to tell lies to get away from her when I thought I was about to explode. I learned to listen silently while she talked and talked and talked . . . mostly about how much better things were in Baltimore than here. I never learned to like sleeping on the floor of her room, but she wouldn't permit the trundle bed to be brought in. She honestly didn't see that it was any hardship for me to sleep on the floor. Niggers always slept on the floor.

Troublesome as she was, though, Margaret Weylin had mellowed. She didn't have the old bursts of temper any more. Maybe it was the laudanum.

"You're a good girl," she said to me once as I sat near her bed stitching at a slip cover. "Much better than you used to be. Someone must have taught you to behave."

"Yes, ma'am." I didn't even look up.

"Good. You were impudent before. There's nothing worse than an impudent nigger."

"Yes, ma'am."

She depressed me, bored me, angered me, drove me crazy. But my back healed completely while I was with her. The work wasn't hard and she never complained about anything but my sewing. She never threatened me or tried to have me whipped. Rufus said she was pleased with me. That seemed to surprise even him. So I endured her quietly. By now, I knew enough to realize when I was well off. Or I thought I did.

"You ought to see yourself," Alice told me one day as I was hiding out in her cabin—the cabin Rufus had had Nigel build her just before the birth of her first child.

"What do you mean?" I asked.

"Marse Rufe really put the fear of God in you, didn't he?"

"Fear of . . . What are you talking about?"

"You run around fetching and carrying for that woman like you love her. And half a day in the fields was all it took."

"Hell, Alice, leave me alone. I've been listening to nonsense all morning. I don't need yours."

"You don't want to hear me, get out of here. The way you always suckin' up to that woman is enough to make anybody sick."

I got up and went to the cookhouse. There were times when it was stupid to expect reason from Alice, times when it did no good to point out the obvious.

There were two field hands in the cookhouse. One young man who had a broken leg splinted and obviously healing crooked, and one old man who didn't do much work any more. I could hear them before I went in.

"I know Marse Rufe'll get rid of me if he can," said the young man. "I ain't no good to him. His daddy would have got rid of me."

"Won't nobody buy me," said the old man. "I was burnt out long time ago. It's you young ones got to worry."

I went into the cookhouse and the young man who had his mouth open to speak closed it quickly, looking at me with open hostility. The old man simply turned his back. I'd seen slaves do that to Alice. I hadn't noticed them doing it to me before. Suddenly, the cookhouse was no more comfortable than Alice's cabin had been. It might have been different if Sarah or Carrie had been there, but they weren't. I left the cookhouse and went back toward the main house, feeling lonely.

Once I was inside, though, I wondered why I had crept away like that. Why hadn't I fought back? Alice accusing me was ridiculous, and she knew it. But the field hands . . . They just didn't know me, didn't know how loyal I might be to Rufus or Margaret, didn't know what I might report.

And if I told them, how likely would they be to believe me? But still . . .

I went down the hall and toward the stairs slowly, wondering why I hadn't tried to defend myself—at least tried. Was I getting so used to being submissive?

Upstairs, I could hear Margaret Weylin thumping on the

floor with her cane. She didn't use the cane much for walking because she hardly ever walked. She used it to call me.

I turned and went back out of the house, out toward the woods. I had to think. I wasn't getting enough time to myself. Once—God knows how long ago—I had worried that I was keeping too much distance between myself and this alien time. Now, there was no distance at all. When had I stopped acting? Why had I stopped?

There were people coming toward me through the woods. Several people. They were on the road, and I was several feet off it. I crouched in the trees to wait for them to pass. I was in no mood to answer some white man's stupid inevitable questions: "What are you doing here? Who's your master?"

I could have answered without trouble. I was nowhere near the edge of Weylin land. But just for a while, I wanted to be my own master. Before I forgot what it felt like.

A white man went by on horseback leading two dozen black men chained two by two. Chained. They wore handcuffs and iron collars with chains connecting the collars to a central chain that ran between the two lines. Behind the men walked several women roped together neck to neck. A coffle—slaves for sale.

At the end of the procession rode a second white man with a gun in his belt. They were all headed for the Weylin house.

I realized suddenly that the slaves in the cookhouse had not been speculating idly about the possibility of being sold. They had known that there was a sale coming. Field hands who never set foot in the main house, and they had known. I hadn't heard a thing.

Lately, Rufus spent his time either straightening out his father's affairs, or sleeping. The weakness left over from his illness was still with him, and he had no time for me. He barely had time for his mother. But he had time to sell slaves. He had time to make himself that much more like his father.

I let the coffle reach the house far ahead of me. By the time I got there, three slaves were already being added to the line. Two men, one grim-faced, one openly weeping; and one woman who moved as though she were sleepwalking. As I got closer, the woman began to look familiar to me. I stopped, almost not wanting to know who it was. A tall, strongly built, handsome woman.

Tess.

I'd seen her only two or three times this trip. She was still working in the fields, still serving the overseer at night. She'd had no children, and that may have been why she was being sold. Or maybe this was something Margaret Weylin had arranged. She might be that vindictive if she knew of her husband's temporary interest in Tess.

I started toward Tess and the white man who had just tied a rope around her neck, fastening her into the line, saw me. He turned to face me, gun drawn.

I stopped, alarmed, confused . . . I had made no threatening move. "I just wanted to say good-bye to my friend," I told him. I was whispering for some reason.

"Say it from there. She can hear you."

"Tess?"

She stood, head down, shoulders rounded, a little red bundle hanging from one hand. She should have heard me, but I didn't think she had.

"Tess, it's Dana."

She never looked up.

"Dana!" Rufus's voice from near the steps where he was talking with the other white man. "You get away from here. Go inside."

"Tess?" I called once more, willing her to answer. She knew my voice, surely. Why wouldn't she look up? Why wouldn't she speak? Why wouldn't she even move? It was as though I didn't exist for her, as though I wasn't real.

I stepped toward her. I think I would have gone to her, taken the rope from her neck or gotten shot trying. But at that moment, Rufus reached me. He grabbed me, hustled me into the house, into the library.

"Stay here!" he ordered. "Just stay . . ." He stopped, suddenly stumbled against me, clutching at me now, not to hold me where I was, but to keep himself upright. "Damn!"

"How could you do it!" I hissed as he straightened. "Tess . . . those others . . ."

"They're my property!"

I stared at him in disbelief. "Oh my God . . . !"

He passed a hand over his face, turned away. "Look, this sale is something my father arranged before he died. You can't do anything about it, so just stay out of the way!"

"Or what? You going to sell me too? You might as well!"

He went back outside without answering. After a while, I sat down in Tom Weylin's worn arm chair and put my head down on his desk.

8

Carrie covered for me with Margaret Weylin. She wanted me to know that when she caught me heading back upstairs. Actually, I don't know why I was heading upstairs, except that I didn't want to see Rufus again for a while, and there was nowhere else to go.

Carrie stopped me on the stairs, looked at me critically, then took my arm and led me back down and out to her cabin. I didn't know or care what she had in mind, but I did understand when she told me through gestures that she had told Margaret Weylin I was sick. Then she circled her neck with the thumbs and forefingers of both hands and looked at me.

"I saw," I said. "Tess and two others." I drew a ragged breath. "I thought that was over on this plantation. I thought it died with Tom Weylin."

Carrie shrugged.

"I wish I had left Rufus lying in the mud," I said. "To think I saved him so he could do something like this . . . !"

Carrie caught my wrist and shook her head vigorously.

"What do you mean, no? He's no good. He's all grown up now, and part of the system. He could feel for us a little when his father was running things—when he wasn't entirely free himself. But now, he's in charge. And I guess he had to do something right away, to prove it."

Carrie clasped her hands around her neck again. Then she drew closer to me and clasped them around my neck. Finally, she went over to the crib that her youngest child had recently outgrown and there, symbolically, clasped her hands again, leaving enough of an open circle for a small neck.

She straightened and looked at me.

"Everybody?" I asked.

She nodded, gestured widely with her arms as though gathering a group around her. Then, once again, her hands around her neck.

I nodded. She was almost surely right. Margaret Weylin could not run the plantation. Both the land and the people would be sold. And if Tom Weylin was any example, the people would be sold without regard for family ties.

Carrie stood looking down at the crib as though she had read my thought.

"I was beginning to feel like a traitor," I said. "Guilty for saving him. Now . . . I don't know what to feel. Somehow, I always seem to forgive him for what he does to me. I can't hate him the way I should until I see him doing things to other people." I shook my head. "I guess I can see why there are those here who think I'm more white than black."

Carrie made quick waving-aside gestures, her expression annoyed. She came over to me and wiped one side of my face with her fingers—wiped hard. I drew back, and she held her fingers in front of me, showed me both sides. But for once, I didn't understand.

Frustrated, she took me by the hand and led me out to where Nigel was chopping firewood. There, before him, she repeated the face-rubbing gesture, and he nodded.

"She means it doesn't come off, Dana," he said quietly. "The black. She means the devil with people who say you're anything but what you are."

I hugged her and got away from her quickly so that she wouldn't see that I was close to tears. I went up to Margaret Weylin and she'd just had her laudanum. Being with her at such times was like being alone. And being alone was just what I needed.

9

I avoided Rufus for three days after the sale. He made it easy for me. He avoided me too. Then on the fourth day he came looking for me. He found me in his mother's room yes-ma'aming her and changing her bed while she sat looking thin and frail beside the window. She barely ate. I had actually caught myself coaxing her to eat. Then I realized that she enjoyed being coaxed. She could forget to be superior sometimes, and just be someone's old mother. Rufus's mother. Unfortunately.

He came in and said, "Let Carrie finish that, Dana. I have something else for you to do."

"Oh, do you have to take her now?" said Margaret. "She was just . . ."

"I'll send her back later, Mama. And Carrie'll be up to finish your bed in a minute."

I left the room silently, not looking forward to whatever he had in mind.

"Down to the library," he said right behind me.

I glanced back at him, trying to gauge his mood, but he only looked tired. He ate well and got twice the rest he should have needed, but he always looked tired.

"Wait a minute," he said.

I stopped.

"Did you bring another of those pens with the ink inside?"

"Yes."

"Get it."

I went up to the attic where I still kept most of my things. I'd brought a packet of three pens this time, but I only took one back down with me—in case he still took as much pleasure as he had last trip in wasting ink.

"You ever hear of dengue fever?" he asked as he went down the stairs.

"No."

"Well, according to the doc in town, that's what I had. I told him about it." He had been going back and forth to town often since his father's death. "Doc said he didn't see how I'd made it without bleeding and a good emetic. Says I'm still weak because I didn't get all the poisons out of my body."

"Put yourself in his hands," I said quietly. "And with a little luck, that will solve both our problems."

He frowned uncertainly. "What do you mean by that?"

"Not a thing."

He turned and caught me by the shoulders in a grip that he probably meant to be painful. It wasn't. "Are you trying to say you want me to die?"

I sighed. "If I did, you would, wouldn't you?"

Silence. He let go of me and we went into the library. He sat down in his father's old arm chair and motioned me into a hard Windsor chair nearby. Which was one step up from his father who had always made me stand before him like a school kid sent to the principal's office.

"If you think that little sale was bad—and Daddy really had already arranged it—you better make sure nothing happens to me." Rufus leaned back and looked at me wearily. "Do you know what would happen to the people here if I died?"

I nodded. "What bothers me," I said, "is what's going to happen to them if you live."

"You don't think I'm going to do anything to them, do you?"

"Of course you are. And I'll have to watch and remember and decide when you've gone too far. Believe me, I'm not looking forward to the job."

"You take a lot on yourself."

"None of it was my idea."

He muttered something inaudible, and probably obscene. "You ought to be in the fields," he added. "God knows why I didn't leave you out there. You would have learned a few things."

"I would have been killed. You would have had to start taking very good care of yourself." I shrugged. "I don't think you have the knack."

"Damnit, Dana . . . What's the good of sitting here trading threats? I don't believe you want to hurt me any more than I want to hurt you."

I said nothing.

"I brought you down here to write a few letters for me, not fight with me."

"Letters?"

He nodded. "I'll tell you, I hate to write. Don't mind reading so much, but I hate to write."

"You didn't hate it six years ago."

"I didn't have to do it then. I didn't have eight or nine people all wanting answers, and wanting them now."

I twisted the pen in my hands. "You'll never know how hard I worked in my own time to avoid doing jobs like this."

He grinned suddenly. "Yes I do. Kevin told me. He told me about the books you wrote too. Your own books."

"That's how he and I earn our living."

"Yeah. Well, I thought you might miss it—writing your own things, I mean. So I got enough paper for you to write for both of us."

I looked at him, not quite sure I'd heard right. I had read that paper in this time was expensive, and I had seen that Weylin had never had very much of it. But here was Rufus offering . . . Offering what? A bribe? Another apology?

"What's the matter?" he said. "Seems to me, this is better than any offer I've made you so far."

"No doubt."

He got paper, made room for me at the desk.

"Rufe, are you going to sell anyone else?"

He hesitated. "I hope not. I don't like it."

"What's to hope? Why can't you just not do it?"

Another hesitation. "Daddy left debts, Dana. He was the most careful man I know with money, but he still left debts."

"But won't your crops pay them?"

"Some of them."

"Oh. What are you going to do?"

"Get somebody who makes her living by writing to write some very persuasive letters."

10

I wrote his letters. I had to read several of the letters he'd received first to pick up the stilted formal style of the day. I didn't want Rufus having to face some creditor that I had angered with my twentieth-century brevity—which could come across as nineteenth-century abruptness, even discourtesy. Rufus gave me a general idea of what he wanted me to say and then approved or disapproved of the way I said it. Usually, he approved. Then we started to go over his father's books together. I never did get back to Margaret Weylin.

And I wasn't ever to get back to her full time. Rufus brought a young girl named Beth in from the fields to help with the housework. That eventually freed Carrie to spend more time with Margaret. I continued to sleep in Margaret's room because I agreed with Rufus that Carrie belonged with her family, at least at night. That meant I had to put up with Margaret waking me up when she couldn't sleep and complaining bitterly that Rufus had taken me away just when she and I were beginning to get on so well . . .

"What does he have you doing?" she asked me several times —suspiciously.

I told her.

"Seems as though he could do that himself. Tom always did it himself."

Rufus could have done it himself too, I thought, though I never said it aloud. He just didn't like working alone. Actually, he didn't like working at all. But if he had to do it, he wanted company. I didn't realize how much he preferred my company in particular until he came in one night a little drunk and found Alice and me eating together in her cabin. He had been away eating with a family in town—"Some people with daughters they want to get rid of," Alice had told me. She had said it with no concern at all even though she knew her life could become much harder if Rufus married. Rufus had property and slaves and was apparently quite eligible.

He came home, and not finding either of us in the house, came out to Alice's cabin. He opened the door and saw us both looking up at him from the table, and he smiled happily.

"Behold the woman," he said. And he looked from one to the other of us. "You really are only one woman. Did you know that?"

He tottered away.

Alice and I looked at each other. I thought she would laugh because she took any opportunity she could find to laugh at him—though not to his face because he would beat her when he decided she needed it.

She didn't laugh. She shuddered, then got up, not too gracefully—her pregnancy was showing now—and looked out the door after him.

After a while, she asked, "Does he ever take you to bed, Dana?"

I jumped. Her bluntness could still startle me. "No. He doesn't want me and I don't want him."

She glanced back at me over one shoulder. "What you think your wants got to do with it?"

I said nothing because I liked her. And no answer I could give could help sounding like criticism of her.

"You know," she said, "you gentle him for me. He hardly hits me at all when you're here. And he never hits you."

"He arranges for other people to hit me."

"But still . . . I know what he means. He likes me in bed, and you out of bed, and you and I look alike if you can believe what people say."

"We look alike if we can believe our own eyes!"

"I guess so. Anyway, all that means we're two halves of the same woman—at least in his crazy head."

11

The time passed slowly, uneventfully, as I waited for the birth of the child I hoped would be Hagar. I went on helping Rufus and his mother. I kept a journal in shorthand. ("What the devil are these chicken marks?" Rufus asked me when he looked over my shoulder one day.) It was such a relief to be able to say what I felt, even in writing, without worrying that I might get myself or someone else into trouble. One of my secretarial classes had finally come in handy.

I tried husking corn and blistered my slow clumsy hands while experienced field hands sped through the work effortlessly, enjoying themselves. There was no reason for me to join them, but they seemed to be making a party of the husking —Rufus gave them a little whiskey to help them along—and I needed a party, needed anything that would relieve my boredom, take my mind off myself.

It was a party, all right. A wild rough kind of party that nobody modified because "the master's women"—Alice and I —were there. People working near me around the small mountain of corn laughed at my blisters and told me I was being initiated. A jug went around and I tasted it, choked, and drew more laughter. Surprisingly companionable laughter. A man with huge muscles told me it was too bad I was already spoken for, and that earned me hostile looks from three women. After the work, there were great quantities of food— chicken, pork, vegetables, corn bread, fruit—better food than the herring and corn meal field hands usually saw so much of. Rufus came out to play hero for providing such a good meal, and the people gave him the praise he wanted. Then they made gross jokes about him behind his back. Strangely, they seemed to like him, hold him in contempt, and fear him all at the same time. This confused me because I felt just about the same mixture of emotions for him myself. I had thought my feelings were complicated because he and I had such a strange relationship. But then, slavery of any kind fostered strange relationships. Only the overseer drew simple, unconflicting emotions of hatred and fear when he appeared briefly. But then, it was part of the overseer's job to be hated and feared while the master kept his hands clean.

Young people began disappearing in pairs after a while, and some of the older ones stopped their eating or drinking or singing or talking long enough to give them looks of disapproval —or more understanding wistful looks. I thought about Kevin and missed him and knew I wasn't going to sleep well that night.

At Christmas, there was another party—dancing, singing, three marriages.

"Daddy used to make them wait until corn shucking or Christmas to marry," Rufus told me. "They like parties when they marry, and he made a few parties do."

"Anything to pinch a few pennies," I said tactlessly.

He glanced at me. "You'd better be glad he didn't waste money. You're the one who gets upset when some quick money has to be raised."

My mind had caught up with my mouth by then, and I kept quiet. He hadn't sold anyone else. The harvest had been good and the creditors patient.

"Found anybody you want to jump the broom with?" he asked me.

I looked at him startled and saw that he wasn't serious. He was smiling and watching the slaves do a bowing, partner-changing dance to the music of a banjo.

"What would you do if I had found someone?" I asked.

"Sell him," he said. His smile was still in place, but there was no longer any humor in it. I noticed, now, that he was watching the big muscular man who had tried to get me to dance —the same man who had spoken to me at the corn husking. I would have to ask Sarah to tell him not to speak to me again. He didn't mean anything, but that wouldn't save him if Rufus got angry.

"One husband is enough for me," I said.

"Kevin?"

"Of course, Kevin."

"He's a long way off."

There was something in his tone that shouldn't have been there. I turned to face him. "Don't talk stupid."

He jumped and looked around quickly to see whether anyone had heard.

"You watch your mouth," he said.

"Watch yours."

He stalked away angrily. We'd been working together too much lately, especially now that Alice was so advanced in her pregnancy. I was grateful when Alice herself created another job for me—a job that got me away from him regularly. Sometime during the week-long Christmas holiday, Alice persuaded him to let me teach their son Joe to read and write.

"It was my Christmas present," she told me. "He asked me what I wanted, and I told him I wanted my son not to be ignorant. You know, I had to fight with him all week to get him to say yes!"

But he had said it, finally, and the boy came to me every day to learn to draw big clumsy letters on the slate Rufus bought him and read simple words and rhymes from the books Rufus himself had used. But unlike Rufus, Joe wasn't bored with what he was learning. He fastened onto the lessons as though they were puzzles arranged for his entertainment—puzzles he loved solving. He could get so intense—throw screaming kicking tantrums when something seemed to be eluding him. But not all that much eluded him.

"You've got a damn bright little kid there," I told Rufus. "You ought to be proud."

Rufus looked surprised—as though it had never occurred to him that there might be anything special about the undersized runny-nosed child. He had spent his life watching his father ignore, even sell, the children he had had with black women. Apparently, it had never occurred to Rufus to break that tradition. Until now.

Now, he began to take an interest in his son. Perhaps he was only curious at first, but the boy captured him. I caught them together once in the library, the boy sitting on one of Rufus's knees and studying a map that Rufus had just brought home. The map was spread on Rufus's desk.

"Is this our river?" the boy was asking.

"No, that's the Miles River, northeast of here. This map doesn't show our river."

"Why not?"

"It's too small."

"What is?" The boy peered up at him. "Our river or this map?"

"Both, I suspect."

"Let's draw it in, then. Where does it go?"

Rufus hesitated. "Just about here. But we don't have to draw it in."

"Why? Don't you want the map to be right?"

I made a noise and Rufus looked up at me. I thought he looked almost ashamed for a moment. He put the boy down quickly and shooed him away.

"Nothing but questions," Rufus complained to me.

"Enjoy it, Rufe. At least he's not out setting fire to the stable or trying to drown himself."

He couldn't quite keep from laughing. "Alice said something like that." He frowned a little. "She wants me to free him."

I nodded. Alice had already told me she meant to ask for the boy's freedom.

"You put her up to it, I guess."

I stared at him. "Rufe, if there's a woman on the place who makes up her own mind, it's Alice. I didn't put her up to a thing."

"Well . . . now she's got something else to make up her mind about."

"What?"

"Nothing. Nothing to you. I just mean to make her earn what she wants for a change," he said.

I couldn't get any more out of him than that. Eventually, though, Alice told me what he wanted.

"He wants me to like him," she said with heavy contempt. "Or maybe even love him. I think he wants me to be more like you!"

"I guarantee you he doesn't."

She closed her eyes. "I don't care what he wants. If I thought it would make him free my children, I'd try to do it. But he lies! And he won't put it down on no paper."

"He likes Joe," I said. "He ought to. Joe looks like a slightly darker version of him at that age. Anyway, he might decide on his own to free the boy."

"And this one?" She patted her stomach. "And the others? He'll make sure there're others."

"I don't know. I'll push him whenever I can."

"I should have took Joe and tried to run before I got pregnant again."

"You're still thinking about running?"

"Wouldn't you be if you didn't have another way to get free?" I nodded.

"I don't mean to spend my life here watching my children grow up as slaves and maybe get sold."

"He wouldn't . . ."

"You don't know what he would do! He don't treat you the way he treats me. When I'm strong again after I have this baby, I'm going."

"With the baby?"

"You don't think I'm going to leave it here, do you?"

"But . . . I don't see how you can make it."

"I know more now than I did when Isaac and me left. I can make it."

I drew a deep breath. "When the time comes, if I can help you, I will."

"Get me a bottle of laudanum," she said.

"Laudanum!"

"I'll have the baby to keep quiet. Old Mama won't let me near her, but she likes you. Get it."

"All right." I didn't like it. Didn't like the idea of her trying to run with a baby and a small child, didn't like the idea of her trying to run at all. But she was right. In her place, I would have tried. I would have tried sooner and gotten killed sooner, but I would have done it alone.

"You think about this a while longer," I said. "You'll get the laudanum and anything else I can supply, but you think."

"I've already thought."

"Not enough. I shouldn't say this, but think what's going to happen if the dogs catch Joe, or if they pull you down and get the baby."

12

The baby was a girl, born in the second month of the new year. She was her mother's daughter, born darker skinned than Joe would probably ever be.

"'Bout time I had a baby to look like me," said Alice when she saw her.

"You could have at least tried for red hair," said Rufus. He was there too, peering at the baby's wrinkled little face, peering with even more concern at Alice's face, sweat-streaked and weary.

For the first and only time, I saw her smile at him—a real smile. No sarcasm, no ridicule. It silenced him for several seconds.

Carrie and I had helped with the birth. Now, we left quietly, both of us probably thinking the same thing. That if Alice and Rufus were going to make peace, finally, neither of us wanted to break their mood.

They called the baby Hagar. Rufus said that was the ugliest name he had ever heard, but it was Alice's choice, and he let it stand. I thought it was the most beautiful name I had ever heard. I felt almost free, half-free if such a thing was possible, half-way home. I was gleeful at first—secretly elated. I even kidded Alice about the names she chose for her children. Joseph and Hagar. And the two others whose names I thought silently—Miriam and Aaron. I said, "Someday Rufus is going to get religion and read enough of the Bible to wonder about those children's names."

Alice shrugged. "If Hagar had been a boy, I would have called her Ishmael. In the Bible, people might be slaves for a while, but they didn't have to stay slaves."

My mood was so good, I almost laughed. But she wouldn't have understood that, and I couldn't have explained. I kept it all in somehow, and congratulated myself that the Bible wasn't the only place where slaves broke free. Her names were only symbolic, but I had more than symbols to remind me that freedom was possible—probable—and for me, very near.

Or was it?

Slowly, I began to calm down. The danger to my family was

past, yes. Hagar had been born. But the danger to me personally . . . the danger to me personally still walked and talked and sometimes sat with Alice in her cabin in the evening as she nursed Hagar. I was there with them a couple of times, and I felt like an intruder.

I was not free. Not any more than Alice was, or her children with their names. In fact, it looked as though Alice might get free before I did. She caught me alone one evening and pulled me into her cabin. It was empty except for the sleeping Hagar. Joe was out collecting cuts and bruises from sturdier children.

"Did you get the laudanum?" she demanded.

I peered at her through the semidarkness. Rufus kept her well supplied with candles, but at the moment, the only light in the room came from the window and from a low fire over which two pots simmered. "Alice, are you sure you still want it?"

I saw her frown. "Sure I want it! 'Course I want it! What's the matter with you?"

I hedged a little. "It's so soon . . . The baby's only a few weeks old."

"You get me that stuff so I can leave when I want to!"

"I've got it."

"Give it to me!"

"Goddamnit, Alice, will you slow down! Look, you keep working on him the way you have been, and you can get whatever you want and live to enjoy it."

To my surprise, her stony expression crumbled, and she began to cry. "He'll never let any of us go," she said. "The more you give him, the more he wants." She paused, wiped her eyes, then added softly, "I got to go while I still can—before I turn into just what people call me." She looked at me and did the thing that made her so much like Rufus, though neither of them recognized it. "I got to go before I turn into what you are!" she said bitterly.

Sarah had cornered me once and said, "What you let her talk to you like that for? She can't get away with it with nobody else."

I didn't know. Guilt, maybe. In spite of everything, my life was easier than hers. Maybe I tried to make up for that by taking her abuse. Everything had its limits, though.

"You want my help, Alice, you watch your mouth!"

"Watch yours," she mocked.

I stared at her in astonishment, remembering, knowing exactly what she had overheard.

"If I talked to him the way you do, he'd have me hangin' in the barn," she said.

"If you go on talking to me the way you do, I won't care what he does to you."

She looked at me for a long time without saying anything. Finally, she smiled. "You'll care. And you'll help me. Else, you'd have to see yourself for the white nigger you are, and you couldn't stand that."

Rufus never called my bluff. Alice did it automatically—and because I was bluffing, she got away with it. I got up and walked away from her. Behind me, I thought I heard her laugh.

Some days later, I gave her the laudanum. Later that same day, Rufus began talking about sending Joe to school up North when he was a little older.

"Do you mean to free the boy, Rufe?"

He nodded.

"Good. Tell Alice."

"When I get around to it."

I didn't argue with him; I told her myself.

"It don't matter what he says," she told me. "Did he show you any free papers?"

"No."

"When he does, and you read them to me, maybe I'll believe him. I'm tellin' you, he uses those children just the way you use a bit on a horse. I'm tired of havin' a bit in my mouth."

I didn't blame her. But still, I didn't want her to go, didn't want her to risk Joe and Hagar. Hell, I didn't even want her to risk herself. Elsewhere, under other circumstances, I would probably have disliked her. But here, we had a common enemy to unite us.

13

I planned to stay on the Weylin plantation long enough to see Alice leave, to find out whether she would be able to keep her freedom this time. I managed to talk her into waiting until early summer to go. And I was prepared to wait that long myself before I tried some dangerous trick that might get me home. I was homesick and Kevinsick and damned sick of Margaret Weylin's floor and Alice's mouth, but I could wait a few more months. I thought.

I talked Rufus into letting me teach Nigel's two older sons and the two children who served at the table along with Joe. Surprisingly, the children liked it. I couldn't recall having liked school much when I was their ages. Rufus liked it because Joe was as bright as I had said—bright and competitive. He had a head start on the others, and he didn't intend to lose it.

"Why weren't you like that about learning?" I asked Rufus.

"Don't bother me," he muttered.

Some of his neighbors found out what I was doing and offered him fatherly advice. It was dangerous to educate slaves, they warned. Education made blacks dissatisfied with slavery. It spoiled them for field work. The Methodist minister said it made them disobedient, made them want more than the Lord intended them to have. Another man said educating slaves was illegal. When Rufus replied that he had checked and that it wasn't illegal in Maryland, the man said it should have been. Talk. Rufus shrugged it off without ever saying how much of it he believed. It was enough that he sided with me, and my school continued. I got the feeling that Alice was keeping him happy—and maybe finally enjoying herself a little in the process. I guessed from what she had told me that this was what was frightening her so, driving her away from the plantation, causing her to lash out at me. She was trying to deal with guilt of her own.

But she was waiting and using some discretion. I relaxed, spent my spare moments trying to think of a way to get home. I didn't want to depend on someone else's chance violence again—violence that, if it came, could be more effective than I wanted.

Then Sam James stopped me out by the cookhouse and my complacency was brought to an end.

I saw him waiting for me beside the cookhouse door—a big young man. I mistook him for Nigel at first. Then I recognized him. Sarah had told me his name. He had spoken to me at the corn husking, and again at Christmas. Then Sarah had spoken to him for me and he had said nothing else. Until now.

"I'm Sam," he said. "Remember at Christmas?"

"Yes. But I thought Sarah told you . . ."

"She did. Look, it ain't that. I just wanted to see if maybe you'd teach my brother and sister to read."

"Your . . . Oh. How old are they?"

"Sister was born the year you came here last . . . brother, the year before that."

"I'll have to get permission. Ask Sarah about it in a few days but don't come to me again." I thought of the expression I had seen on Rufus's face as he looked at this man. "Maybe I'm too cautious, but I don't want you getting in trouble because of me."

He gave me a long searching look. "You want to be with that white man, girl?"

"If I were anywhere else, no black child on the place would be learning anything."

"That ain't what I mean."

"Yes it is. It's all part of the same thing."

"Some folks say . . ."

"Hold on." I was suddenly angry. "I don't want to hear what 'some folks' say. 'Some folks' let Fowler drive them into the fields every day and work them like mules."

"*Let* him . . . ?"

"Let him! They do it to keep the skin on their backs and breath in their bodies. Well, they're not the only ones who have to do things they don't like to stay alive and whole. Now you tell me why that should be so hard for 'some folks' to understand?"

He sighed. "That's what I told them. But you better off than they are, so they get jealous." He gave me another of his long searching looks. "I still say it's too bad you already spoke for."

I grinned. "Get out of here, Sam. Field hands aren't the only ones who can be jealous."

He went. That was all. Innocent—completely innocent. But three days later, a trader led Sam away in chains.

Rufus never said a word to me. He didn't accuse me of anything. I wouldn't have known Sam had been sold if I hadn't glanced out the window of Margaret Weylin's room and seen the coffle.

I told Margaret some hasty lie, then ran out of her room,

down the stairs, and out the door. I ran headlong into Rufus, and felt him steady me, hold me. The weakness that his dengue fever had left was finally gone. His grip was formidable.

"Get back in the house!" he hissed.

I saw Sam beyond him being chained into line. There were people a few feet away from him crying loudly. Two women, a boy and a girl. His family.

"Rufe," I pleaded desperately, "don't do this. There's no need!"

He pushed me back toward the door and I struggled against him.

"Rufe, please! Listen, he came to ask me to teach his brother and sister to read. That's all!"

It was like talking to the wall of the house. I managed to break away from him for a moment just as the younger of the two weeping women spotted me.

"You whore!" she screamed. She had not been permitted to approach the coffle, but she approached me. "You no-'count nigger whore, why couldn't you leave my brother alone!"

She would have attacked me. And field hand that she was, strengthened by hard work, she would probably have given me the beating she thought I deserved. But Rufus stepped between us.

"Get back to work, Sally!"

She didn't move, stood glaring at him until the older woman, probably her mother, reached her and pulled her away.

I caught Rufus by the hand and spoke low to him. "Please, Rufe. If you do this, you'll destroy what you mean to preserve. Please don't . . ."

He hit me.

It was a first, and so unexpected that I stumbled backward and fell.

And it was a mistake. It was the breaking of an unspoken agreement between us—a very basic agreement—and he knew it.

I got up slowly, watching him with anger and betrayal.

"Get in the house and stay there," he said.

I turned my back and went to the cookhouse, deliberately disobeying. I could hear one of the traders say, "You ought to sell that one too. Troublemaker!"

At the cookhouse, I heated water, got it warm, not hot. Then I took a basin of it up to the attic. It was hot there, and empty except for the pallets and my bag in its corner. I went over to it, washed my knife in antiseptic, and hooked the drawstring of my bag over my shoulder.

And in the warm water I cut my wrists.

The Rope

I AWOKE IN darkness and lay still for several seconds trying to think where I was and when I had gone to sleep.

I was lying on something unbelievably soft and comfortable . . .

My bed. Home. Kevin?

I could hear regular breathing beside me now. I sat up and reached out to turn on the lamp—or I tried to. Sitting up made me faint and dizzy. For a moment, I thought Rufus was pulling me back to him before I could even see home. Then I became aware that my wrists were bandaged and throbbing —and I remembered what I had done.

The lamp on Kevin's side of the bed went on and I could see him beardless now, but with his thatch of gray hair uncut.

I lay flat and looked up at him happily. "You're beautiful," I said. "You look a little like a heroic portrait I saw once of Andrew Jackson."

"No way," he said. "Man was skinny as hell. I've seen him."

"But you haven't seen my heroic portrait."

"Why the hell did you cut your wrists? You could have bled to death! Or did you cut them yourself?"

"Yes. It got me home."

"There must be a safer way."

I rubbed my wrists gingerly. "There isn't any safe way to almost kill yourself. I was afraid of the sleeping pills. I took them with me because I wanted to be able to die if . . . if I wanted to die. But I was afraid that if I used them to get home, I might die before you or some doctor figured out what was wrong with me. Or that if I didn't die, I'd have some grisly side-effect—like gangrene."

"I see," he said after a while.

"Did you bandage me?"

"Me? No, I thought this was too serious for me to handle alone. I stopped the bleeding as best I could and called Lou George. He bandaged you." Louis George was a doctor friend Kevin had met through his writing. Kevin had

246

interviewed George for an article once, and the two had taken a liking to each other. They wound up doing a nonfiction book together.

"Lou said you managed to miss the main arteries in both arms," Kevin told me. "Said you didn't do much more than scratch yourself."

"With all that blood!"

"It wasn't that much. You were probably too frightened to cut as deeply as you could have."

I sighed. "Well . . . I guess I'm glad I didn't do much damage—as long as I got home."

"How would you feel about seeing a psychiatrist?"

"Seeing a . . . Are you kidding?"

"I am, but Lou wasn't. He says if you're doing things like this, you need help."

"Oh God. Do I have to? The lies I'd have to invent!"

"No, this time you probably won't have to. Lou is a friend. You do it again, though, and . . . well, you could be locked up for psychiatric treatment whether you like it or not. The law tries to protect people like you from themselves."

I found myself laughing, almost crying. I put my head on his shoulder and wondered whether a little time in some sort of mental institution would be worse than several months of slavery. I doubted it.

"How long was I gone this time?" I asked.

"About three hours. How long was it for you?"

"Eight months."

"Eight . . ." He put his arm over me, holding me. "No wonder you cut your wrists."

"Hagar has been born."

"Has she?" There was silence for a moment, then, "What's that going to mean?"

I twisted uncomfortably and, by accident, put pressure on one of my wrists. The sudden pain made me gasp.

"Be careful," he said. "Treat yourself gently for a change."

"Where's my bag?"

"Here." He pulled the blanket aside and let me see that I was securely tied to my denim bag. "What are you going to do, Dana?"

"I don't know."

"What's he like now?"

He. Rufus. He had become such a fixture in my life that it wasn't even necessary to say his name. "His father died," I said. "He's running things now."

"Well?"

"I don't know. How do you do well at owning and trading in slaves?"

"Not well," Kevin decided. He got up and went to the kitchen, came back with a glass of water. "Did you want anything to eat? I can get you something."

"I'm not hungry."

"What did he do to you, finally, to make you cut your wrists?"

"Nothing to me. Nothing important. He sold a man away from his family when there was no need for him to. He hit me when I objected. Maybe he'll never be as hard as his father was, but he's a man of his time."

"Then . . . it doesn't seem to me that you have such a difficult decision ahead of you."

"But I do. I talked to Carrie about it once, and she said . . ."

"Carrie?" He looked at me strangely.

"Yes. She said . . . Oh. She gets her meaning across, Kevin. Weren't you around the place long enough to find that out?"

"She never tried to get much across to me. I used to wonder whether she was a little retarded."

"God, no! Far from it. If you had gotten to know her, you wouldn't even suspect."

He managed to shrug. "Well, anyway, what did she tell you?"

"That if I had let Rufus die, everyone would have been sold. More families would have been separated. She has three children now."

He was silent for several seconds. Then, "She might be sold with her children if they're young. But I doubt that anyone would bother to keep her and her husband together. Someone would buy her and breed her to a new man. It is breeding, you know."

"Yes. So you see, my decision isn't as easy as you thought."

"But . . . they're being sold anyway."

"Not all of them. Good Lord, Kevin, their lives are hard enough."

"What about your life?"

"It's better than anything most of them will ever know."

"It may not be as he gets older."

I sat up, trying to ignore my own weakness. "Kevin, tell me what you want me to do."

He looked away, said nothing. I gave him several seconds, but he kept silent.

"It's real now, isn't it," I said softly. "We talked about it before—God knows how long ago—but somehow, it was abstract then. Now . . . Kevin, if you can't even say it, how can you expect me to do it?"

2

We had fifteen full days together this time. I marked them off on the calendar—June 19 through July 3. With some kind of reverse symbolism, Rufus called me back on July 4. But at least Kevin and I had a chance to grow back into the twentieth century. We didn't seem to have to grow back into each other. The separations hadn't been good for us, but they hadn't hurt us that much either. It was easy for us to be together, knowing we shared experiences no one else would believe. It wasn't as easy, though, for us to be with other people.

My cousin came over, and when Kevin answered the door, she didn't recognize him.

"What's the matter with him?" she whispered later when she and I were alone.

"He's been sick," I lied.

"With what?"

"The doctor isn't sure what it was. Kevin is much better now, though."

"He looks just like my girl friend's father did, and he had cancer."

"Julie, for Godsake!"

"I'm sorry, but . . . never mind. He hasn't hit you again, has he?"

"No."

"Well, that's something. You'd better take care of yourself. You don't look so good either."

Kevin tried driving—his first time after five years of horses and buggies. He said the traffic confused him, made him more nervous than he could see any reason for. He said he'd almost killed a couple of people. Then he put the car in the garage and left it there.

Of course, I wouldn't drive, wouldn't even ride with someone else while there was still a chance of Rufus snatching me away. After the first week, though, Kevin began to doubt that I would be called again.

I didn't doubt it. For the sake of the people whose lives Rufus controlled, I didn't wish him dead, but I wouldn't rest easy until I knew he was. As things stood now, sooner or later, he would get himself into trouble again and call me. I kept my denim bag nearby.

"You know, someday, you're going to have to stop dragging that thing around with you and come back to life," Kevin said after two weeks. He had just tried driving again, and when he came in, his hands were shaking. "Hell, half the time I wonder if you're not eager to go back to Maryland anyway."

I had been watching television—or at least, the television was on. Actually, I was looking over some journal pages I had managed to bring home in my bag, wondering whether I could weave them into a story. Now, I looked up at Kevin. "Me?"

"Why not? Eight months, after all."

I put my journal pages down and got up to turn off the television.

"Leave it on," said Kevin.

I turned it off. "I think you've got something to say to me," I said. "And I think I should hear it clearly."

"You don't want to hear anything."

"No, I don't. But I'm going to, aren't I?"

"My God, Dana, after two weeks . . ."

"It was eight days, time before last. And about three hours last time. The intervals between trips don't mean anything."

"How old was he last time?"

"He turned twenty-five when I was there last. And, though I'll never be able to prove it, I turned twenty-seven."

"He's grown up."

I shrugged.

"Do you remember what he said just before he tried to shoot you?"

"No. I had other things on my mind."

"I had forgotten it myself, but it's come back to me. He said, 'You're not going to leave me!'"

I thought for a moment. "Yes, that sounds about right."

"It doesn't sound right to me."

"I mean it sounds like what he said! I don't have any control over what he says."

"But still . . ." He paused, looked at me as though he expected me to say something. I didn't. "It sounded more like what I might say to you if you were leaving."

"Would you?"

"You know what I mean."

"Say what you mean. I can't answer you unless you say it."

He drew a deep breath. "All right. You've said he was a man of his time, and you've told me what he's done to Alice. What's he done to you?"

"Sent me to the field, had me beaten, made me spend nearly eight months sleeping on the floor of his mother's room, sold people . . . He's done plenty, but the worst of it was to other people. He hasn't raped me, Kevin. He understands, though you don't seem to, that for him that would be a form of suicide."

"You mean there's something he could do to make you kill him, after all?"

I sighed, went over to him, and sat down on the arm of his chair. I looked down at him. "Tell me you believe I'm lying to you."

He looked at me uncertainly. "Look, if anything did happen, I could understand it. I know how it was back then."

"You mean you could forgive me for having been raped?"

"Dana, I lived there. I know what those people were like. And Rufus's attitude toward you . . ."

"Was sensible most of the time. He knew I could kill him just by turning my back at the right moment. And he believed that I wouldn't have him because I loved you. He said something like that once. He was wrong, but I never told him so."

"Wrong?"

"At least partly. Of course I love you, and I don't want anyone else. But there's another reason, and when I'm back there it's the most important reason. I don't think Rufus would have understood it. Maybe you won't either."

"Tell me."

I thought for a moment, tried to find the right words. If I could make him understand, then surely he would believe me. He had to believe. He was my anchor here in my own time. The only person who had any idea what I was going through.

"You know what I thought," I said, "when I saw Tess tied into that coffle?" I had told him about Tess and about Sam— that I had known them, that Rufus had sold them. I hadn't told him the details though—especially not the details of Sam's sale. I had been trying for two weeks to avoid sending his thoughts in the direction they had taken now.

"What does Tess have to do with . . . ?"

"I thought, that could be me—standing there with a rope around my neck waiting to be led away like someone's dog!" I stopped, looked down at him, then went on softly. "I'm not property, Kevin. I'm not a horse or a sack of wheat. If I have to seem to be property, if I have to accept limits on my freedom for Rufus's sake, then he also has to accept limits—on his behavior toward me. He has to leave me enough control of my own life to make living look better to me than killing and dying."

"If your black ancestors had felt that way, you wouldn't be here," said Kevin.

"I told you when all this started that I didn't have their endurance. I still don't. Some of them will go on struggling to survive, no matter what. I'm not like that."

He smiled a little. "I suspect that you are."

I shook my head. He thought I was being modest or something. He didn't understand.

Then I realized that he had smiled. I looked down at him questioningly.

He sobered. "I had to know."

"And do you, now?"

"Yes."

That felt like truth. It felt enough like truth for me not to mind that he had only half understood me.

"Have you decided what you're going to do about Rufus?" he asked.

I shook my head. "You know, it's not only what will happen

to the slaves that worries me . . . if I turn my back on him. It's what might happen to me."

"You'll be finished with him."

"I might be finished period. I might not be able to get home."

"Your coming home has never had anything to do with him. You come home when your life is in danger."

"But how do I come home? Is the power mine, or do I tap some power in him? All this started with him, after all. I don't know whether I need him or not. And I won't know until he's not around."

3

A couple of Kevin's friends came over on the Fourth of July and tried to get us to go to the Rose Bowl with them for the fireworks. Kevin wanted to go—more to get out of the house than for any other reason, I suspected. I told him to go ahead, but he wouldn't go without me. As it turned out, there was no chance for me to go, anyway. As Kevin's friends left the house, I began to feel dizzy.

I stumbled toward my bag, fell before I reached it, crawled toward it, grabbed it just as Kevin came in from saying good-bye to his friends.

"Dana," he was saying, "we can't stay cooped up in this house any longer waiting for something that isn't . . ."

He was gone.

Instead of lying on the floor of my living room, I was lying on the ground in the sun, almost directly over a hill of large black ants.

Before I could get up, someone kicked me, fell on me heavily. I had the breath knocked out of me for a moment.

"Dana!" said Rufus's voice. "What the hell are you doing here?"

I looked up, saw him sprawled across me where he had fallen. We got up just as something began to bite me—the ants, probably. I brushed myself off quickly.

"I said what are you doing here!" He sounded angry. He looked no older than he had been when I'd last seen him, but something was wrong with him. He looked haggard and weary —looked as though it had been too long since he'd slept last, looked as though it would be even longer before he was able to sleep again.

"I don't know what I'm doing here, Rufe. I never do until I find out what's wrong with you."

He stared at me for a long moment. His eyes were red and under them were dark smudges. Finally, he grabbed me by the arm and led me back the way he had come. We were on the plantation not far from the house. Nothing looked changed. I saw two of Nigel's sons wrestling, rolling around on the ground. They were the two I had been teaching, and they were no bigger than they had been when I saw them last.

"Rufe, how long have I been gone?"

He didn't answer. He was leading me toward the barn, I saw, and apparently I wasn't going to learn anything until I got there.

He stopped at the barn door and pushed me through it. He didn't follow me in.

I looked around, seeing very little at first as my eyes became accustomed to the dimmer light. I turned to the place where I had been strung up and whipped—and jumped back in surprise when I saw that someone was hanging there. Hanging by the neck. A woman.

Alice.

I stared at her not believing, not wanting to believe . . . I touched her and her flesh was cold and hard. The dead gray face was ugly in death as it had never been in life. The mouth was open. The eyes were open and staring. Her head was bare and her hair loose and short like mine. She had never liked to tie it up the way other women did. It was one of the things that had made us look even more alike—the only two consistently bareheaded women on the place. Her dress was dark red and her apron clean and white. She wore shoes that Rufus had had made specifically for her, not the rough heavy shoes or boots other slaves wore. It was as though she had dressed up and combed her hair and then . . .

I wanted her down.

I looked around, saw that the rope had been tied to a wall peg, thrown over a beam. I broke my fingernails, trying to untie it until I remembered my knife. I got it from my bag and cut Alice down.

She fell stiffly like something that would break when it hit the floor. But she landed without breaking and I took the rope from her neck and closed her eyes. For a time, I just sat with her, holding her head and crying silently.

Eventually, Rufus came in. I looked up at him and he looked away.

"Did she do this to herself?" I asked.

"Yes. To herself."

"Why?"

He didn't answer.

"Rufe?"

He shook his head slowly from side to side.

"Where are her children?"

He turned and walked out of the barn.

I straightened Alice's body and her dress and looked around for something to cover her with. There was nothing.

I left the barn and went across an expanse of grass to the cookhouse. Sarah was there chopping meat with that frightening speed and co-ordination of hers. I had told her once that it always looked as though she was about to cut off a finger or two, and she had laughed. She still had all ten.

"Sarah?" There was such a difference in our ages now that everyone else my age called her "Aunt Sarah." I knew it was a title of respect in this culture, and I respected her. But I couldn't quite manage "Aunt" any more than I could have managed "Mammy." She didn't seem to mind.

She looked up. "Dana! Girl, what are you doing back here? What Marse Rufe done now?"

"I'm not sure. But, Sarah, Alice is dead."

Sarah put down her cleaver and sat on the bench next to the table. "Oh Lord. Poor child. He finally killed her."

"I don't know," I said. I went over and sat beside her. "I think she did it to herself. Hung herself. I just took her down."

"He did it!" she hissed. "Even if he didn't put the rope on her, he drove her to it. He sold her babies!"

I frowned. Sarah had spoken clearly enough, loudly enough, but for a moment, I didn't understand. "Joe and Hagar? His children?"

"What he care 'bout that?"

"But . . . he did care. He was going to . . . Why would he do such a thing?"

"She run off." Sarah faced me. "You must have known she was goin'. You and her was like sisters."

I didn't need the reminder. I got up, feeling that I had to move around, distract myself, or I would cry again.

"You sure fought like sisters," said Sarah. "Always fussin' at each other, stompin' away from each other, comin' back. Right after you left, she knocked the devil out of a field hand who was runnin' you down."

Had she? She would. Insulting me was her prerogative. No trespassing. I paced from the table to the hearth to a small work table. Back to Sarah.

"Dana, where is she?"

"In the barn."

"He'll give her a big funeral." Sarah shook her head. "It's funny. I thought she was finally settlin' down with him—getting not to mind so much."

"If she was, I don't think she could have forgiven herself for it."

Sarah shrugged.

"When she ran . . . did he beat her?"

"Not much. 'Bout much as old Marse Tom whipped you that time."

That gentle spanking, yes.

"The whipping didn't matter much. But when he took away her children, I thought she was go' die right there. She was screaming and crying and carrying on. Then she got sick and I had to take care of her." Sarah was silent for a moment. "I didn't want to even be close to her. When Marse Tom sold my babies, I just wanted to lay down and die. Seeing her like she was brought all that back."

Carrie came in then, her face wet with tears. She came up to me without surprise, and hugged me.

"You know?" I asked.

She nodded, then made her sign for white people and pushed me toward the door. I went.

I found Rufus at his desk in the library fondling a hand gun. He looked up and saw me just as I was about to withdraw. It had occurred to me suddenly, certainly, that this was where he had been heading when he called me. What had his call been, then? A subconscious desire for me to stop him from shooting himself?

"Come in, Dana." His voice sounded empty and dead.

I pulled my old Windsor chair up to his desk and sat down. "How could you do it, Rufe?"

He didn't answer.

"Your son and your daughter . . . How could you sell them?"

"I didn't."

That stopped me. I had been prepared for almost any other answer—or no answer. But a denial . . . "But . . . but . . ."

"She ran away."

"I know."

"We were getting along. You know. You were here. It was good. Once, when you were gone, she came to my room. She came on her own."

"Rufe . . . ?"

"Everything was all right. I even went on with Joe's lessons. Me! I told her I would free both of them."

"She didn't believe you. You wouldn't put anything into writing."

"I would have."

I shrugged. "Where are the children, Rufe?"

"In Baltimore with my mother's sister."

"But . . . why?"

"To punish her, scare her. To make her see what could happen if she didn't . . . if she tried to leave me."

"Oh God! But you could have at least brought them back when she got sick."

"I wish I had."

"Why didn't you?"

"I don't know."

I turned away from him in disgust. "You killed her. Just as though you had put that gun to her head and fired."

He looked at the gun, put it down quickly.

"What are you going to do now?"

"Nigel's gone to get a coffin. A decent one, not just

a homemade box. And he'll hire a minister to come out tomorrow."

"I mean what are you going to do for your son and your daughter?"

He looked at me helplessly.

"Two certificates of freedom," I said. "You owe them that, at least. You've deprived them of their mother."

"Damn you, Dana! Stop saying that! Stop saying I killed her."

I just looked at him.

"Why did you leave me! If you hadn't gone, she might not have run away!"

I rubbed my face where he had hit me when I begged him not to sell Sam.

"You didn't have to go!"

"You were turning into something I didn't want to stay near."

Silence.

"Two certificates of freedom, Rufe, all legal. Raise them free. That's the least you can do."

4

There was an outdoor funeral the next day. Everyone attended—field hands, house servants, even the indifferent Evan Fowler.

The minister was a tall coal-black deep-voiced freedman with a face that reminded me of a picture I had of my father who had died before I was old enough to know him. The minister was literate. He held a Bible in his huge hands and read from Job and Ecclesiastes until I could hardly stand to listen. I had shrugged off my aunt and uncle's strict Baptist teachings years before. But even now, especially now, the bitter melancholy words of Job could still reach me. "Man that is born of a woman is of few days, and full of trouble. He cometh forth like a flower, and is cut down: he fleeth also as a shadow, and continueth not . . ."

I kept quiet somehow, wiped away silent tears, beat away flies and mosquitoes, heard the whispers.

"She gone to hell! Don't you know folks kills theyself goes to hell!"

"Shut your mouth! Marse Rufe'll make you think you down there with her!"

Silence.

They buried her.

There was a big dinner afterward. My relatives at home had dinners after funerals too. I had never thought about how far back the custom might go.

I ate a little, then went away to the library where I could be alone, where I would write. Sometimes I wrote things because I couldn't say them, couldn't sort out my feelings about them, couldn't keep them bottled up inside me. It was a kind of writing I always destroyed afterward. It was for no one else. Not even Kevin.

Rufus came in later when I was nearly written out. He came to the desk, sat down in my old Windsor—I was in his chair—and put his head down. We didn't say anything, but we sat together for a while.

The next day, he took me to town with him, took me to the old brick Court House, and let me watch while he had certificates of freedom drawn up for his children.

"If I bring them back," he said on the ride home, "will you take care of them?"

I shook my head. "It wouldn't be good for them, Rufe. This isn't my home. They'd get used to me, then I'd be gone."

"Who, then?"

"Carrie. Sarah will help her."

He nodded listlessly.

Early one morning a few days later, he left for Easton Point where he could catch a steamboat to Baltimore. I offered to go with him to help with the children, but all that got me was a look of suspicion—a look I couldn't help understanding.

"Rufe, I don't have to go to Baltimore to escape from you. I really want to help."

"Just stay here," he said. And he went out to talk to Evan Fowler before he left. He knew how I had gone home last. He had asked me, and I had told him.

"But why?" he had demanded. "You could have killed yourself."

"There're worse things than being dead," I had said.

He had turned and walked away from me.

Now he watched more than he had before. He couldn't

watch me all the time, of course, and unless he wanted to keep me chained, he couldn't prevent me from taking one route or another out of his world if that was what I wanted to do. He couldn't control me. That clearly bothered him.

Evan Fowler was in the house more than he had to be while Rufus was gone. He said little to me, gave me no orders. But he was there. I took refuge in Margaret Weylin's room, and she was so pleased she talked endlessly. I found myself laughing and actually holding conversations with her as though we were just a couple of lonely people talking without the extra burden of stupid barriers.

Rufus came back, came to the house carrying the dark little girl and leading the boy who seemed to look even more like him. Joe saw me in the hall and ran to me.

"Aunt Dana, Aunt Dana!" And a hug later, "I can read better now. Daddy's been teaching me. Wanna hear?"

"Sure I do." I looked up at Rufus. *Daddy?*

He glared at me tight-lipped as though daring me to speak. All I had wanted to say, though, was, "What took you so long?" The boy had spent his short life calling his father "Master." Well, now that he no longer had a mother, I supposed Rufus thought it was time he had a father. I managed to smile at Rufus—a real smile. I didn't want him feeling embarrassed or defensive for finally acknowledging his son.

He smiled back, seemed to relax.

"How about my getting classes going again?"

He nodded. "I guess the others haven't had time to forget much."

They hadn't. As it turned out, I had only been away for three months. The children had had a kind of early summer vacation. Now they went back to school. And I, slowly, delicately, went to work on Rufus, began to push him toward freeing a few more of them, perhaps several more of them—perhaps in his will, all of them. I had heard of slaveholders doing such things. The Civil War was still thirty years away. I might be able to get some of the adult slaves freed while they were still young enough to build new lives. I might be able to do some good for everyone, finally. At least, I felt secure enough to try, now that my own freedom was within reach.

Rufus had been keeping me with him more than he needed

me now. He called me to share his meals openly, and he seemed to listen when I talked to him about freeing the slaves. But he made no promises. I wondered whether he thought making a will was foolish at his age—or maybe it was freeing more slaves that he thought was foolish. He didn't say anything, so I couldn't tell.

Finally, though, he did answer me, told me much more than I wanted to know. None of it should have surprised me at all.

"Dana," he said one afternoon in the library, "I'd have to be crazy to make a will freeing these people and then tell you about it. I could die damn young for that kind of craziness."

I had to look at him to see whether he was serious. But looking at him confused me even more. He was smiling, but I got the feeling he was completely serious. He believed I would kill him to free his slaves. Strangely, the idea had not occurred to me. My suggestion had been innocent. But he might have a point. Eventually, it would have occurred to me.

"I used to have nightmares about you," he said. "They started when I was little—right after I set fire to the draperies. Remember the fire?"

"Of course."

"I'd dream about you and wake up in a cold sweat."

"Dream . . . about me killing you?"

"Not exactly." He paused, gave me a long unreadable look. "I'd dream about you leaving me."

I frowned. That was close to the thing Kevin had heard him say—the thing that had awakened Kevin's suspicions. "I leave," I said carefully. "I have to. I don't belong here."

"Yes you do! As far as I'm concerned, you do. But that's not what I mean. You leave, and sooner or later you come back. But in my nightmares, you leave without helping me. You walk away and leave me in trouble, hurting, maybe dying."

"Oh. Are you sure those dreams started when you were little? They sound more like something you would have come up with after your fight with Isaac."

"They got worse then," he admitted. "But they started way back at the fire—as soon as I realized you could help me or not, just as you chose. I had those nightmares for years. Then when Alice had been here awhile, they went away. Now they've come back."

He stopped, looked at me as though he expected me to say something—to reassure him, perhaps, to promise him that I would never do such a thing. But I couldn't quite bring myself to say the words.

"You see?" he said quietly.

I moved uncomfortably in my chair. "Rufe, do you know how many people live to ripe old ages without ever getting into the kind of trouble that causes you to need me? If you don't trust me, then you have more reason than ever to be careful."

"Tell me I can trust you."

More discomfort. "You keep doing things that make it impossible for me to trust you—even though you know it has to work both ways."

He shook his head. "I don't know. I never know how to treat you. You confuse everybody. You sound too white to the field hands—like some kind of traitor, I guess."

"I know what they think."

"Daddy always thought you were dangerous because you knew too many white ways, but you were black. Too black, he said. The kind of black who watches and thinks and makes trouble. I told that to Alice and she laughed. She said sometimes Daddy showed more sense than I did. She said he was right about you, and that I'd find out some day."

I jumped. Had Alice really said such a thing?

"And my mother," continued Rufus calmly, "says if she closes her eyes while you and her are talking, she can forget you're black without even trying."

"I'm black," I said. "And when you sell a black man away from his family just because he talked to me, you can't expect me to have any good feelings toward you."

He looked away. We hadn't really discussed Sam before. We had talked around him, alluded to him without quite mentioning him.

"He wanted you," said Rufus bluntly.

I stared at him, knowing now why we hadn't spoken of Sam. It was too dangerous. It could lead to speaking of other things. We needed safe subjects now, Rufus and I—the price of corn, supplies for the slaves, that sort of thing.

"Sam didn't do anything," I said. "You sold him for what you thought he was thinking."

"He wanted you," Rufus repeated.

So do you, I thought. No Alice to take the pressure off any more. It was time for me to go home. I started to get up.

"Don't leave, Dana."

I stopped. I didn't want to hurry away—run away—from him. I didn't want to give him any indication that I was going to the attic to reopen the tender new scar tissue at my wrists. I sat down again. And he leaned back in his chair and looked at me until I wished I had taken the chance of hurrying away.

"What am I going to do when you go home this time?" he whispered.

"You'll survive."

"I wonder . . . why I should bother."

"For your children, at least," I said. "Her children. They're all you have left of her."

He closed his eyes, rubbed one hand over them. "They should be your children now," he said. "If you had any feelings for them, you'd stay."

For them? "You know I can't."

"You could if you wanted to. I wouldn't hurt you, and you wouldn't have to hurt yourself . . . again."

"You wouldn't hurt me until something frustrated you, made you angry or jealous. You wouldn't hurt me until someone hurt you. Rufe, I know you. I couldn't stay here even if I didn't have a home to go back to—and someone waiting for me there."

"That Kevin!"

"Yes."

"I wish I had shot him."

"If you had, you'd be dead yourself by now."

He turned his body so that he faced me squarely. "You say that as though it means something."

I got up to leave. There was nothing more to be said. He had asked for what he knew I could not give, and I had refused.

"You know, Dana," he said softly, "when you sent Alice to me that first time, and I saw how much she hated me, I thought, I'll fall asleep beside her and she'll kill me. She'll hit me with a candlestick. She'll set fire to the bed. She'll bring a knife up from the cookhouse . . .

"I thought all that, but I wasn't afraid. Because if she killed me, that would be that. Nothing else would matter. But if I lived, I would have her. And, by God, I had to have her."

He stood up and came over to me. I stepped back, but he caught my arms anyway. "You're so much like her, I can hardly stand it," he said.

"Let go of me, Rufe!"

"You were one woman," he said. "You and her. One woman. Two halves of a whole."

I had to get away from him. "Let me go, or I'll make your dream real!" Abandonment. The one weapon Alice hadn't had. Rufus didn't seem to be afraid of dying. Now, in his grief, he seemed almost to want death. But he was afraid of dying alone, afraid of being deserted by the person he had depended on for so long.

He stood holding my arms, perhaps trying to decide what he should do. After a moment, I felt his grip loosen, and I pulled away. I knew I had to go now before he submerged his fear. He could do it. He could talk himself into anything.

I left the library, went up the main stairs, then the attic stairs. Over to my bag, my knife . . .

Footsteps on the stairs.

The knife!

I opened it, hesitated, then slipped the knife, blade still open, back into my bag.

He opened the door, came in, looked around the big hot empty room. He saw me at once, but still, he looked around —to see whether we were alone?

We were.

He came over and sat next to me on my pallet. "I'm sorry, Dana," he said.

Sorry? For what he had nearly done, or for what he was about to do? Sorry. He had apologized to me many times in many ways before, but his apologies had always been oblique, "Eat with me, Dana. Sarah is cooking up something special." Or, "Here, Dana, here's a new book I bought for you in town." Or, "Here's some cloth, Dana. Maybe you can make yourself something from it."

Things. Gifts given when he knew he had hurt or offended me. But he had never before said, "I'm sorry, Dana." I looked at him uncertainly.

"I've never felt so lonesome in my life," he said.

The words touched me as no others could have. I knew about loneliness. I found my thoughts going back to the time I had gone home without Kevin—the loneliness, the fear, sometimes the hopelessness I had felt then. Hopelessness wouldn't be a sometime thing to Rufus, though. Alice was dead and buried. He had only his children left. But at least one of them had also loved Alice. Joe.

"Where'd my mama go?" he demanded on his first day home.

"Away," Rufus had said. "She went away."

"When is she coming back?"

"I don't know."

The boy came to me. "Aunt Dana, where'd my mama go?"

"Honey . . . she died."

"Died?"

"Yes. Like old Aunt Mary." Who at last had drifted the final distance to her reward. She had lived over eighty years—had come over from Africa, people said. Nigel had made a box and Mary had been laid to rest near where Alice lay now.

"But Mama wasn't old."

"No, she was sick, Joe."

"Daddy said she went away."

"Well . . . to heaven."

"No!"

He had cried and I had tried to comfort him. I remembered the pain of my own mother's death—grief, loneliness, uncertainty in my aunt and uncle's house . . .

I had held the boy and told him he still had his daddy—please God. And that Sarah and Carrie and Nigel loved him. They wouldn't let anything happen to him—as though they had the power to protect him, or even themselves.

I let Joe go to his mother's cabin to be alone for a while. He wanted to. Then I told Rufus what I had done. And Rufus hadn't known whether to hit me or thank me. He had glared at me, the skin of his face drawn tight, intense. Then, finally, he had relaxed and nodded and gone out to find his son.

Now, he sat with me—being sorry and lonely and wanting me to take the place of the dead.

"You never hated me, did you?" he asked.

"Never for long. I don't know why. You worked hard to earn my hatred, Rufe."

"She hated me. From the first time I forced her."

"I don't blame her."

"Until just before she ran. She had stopped hating me. I wonder how long it will take you."

"What?"

"To stop hating."

Oh God. Almost against my will, I closed my fingers around the handle of the knife still concealed in my bag. He took my other hand, held it between his own in a grip that I knew would only be gentle until I tried to pull away.

"Rufe," I said, "your children . . ."

"They're free."

"But they're young. They need you to protect their freedom."

"Then it's up to you, isn't it?"

I twisted my hand, tried to get it away from him in sudden anger. At once, his hold went from caressing to imprisoning. My right hand had become wet and slippery on the knife.

"It's up to you," he repeated.

"No, Goddamnit, it isn't! Keeping you alive has been up to me for too long! Why didn't you shoot yourself when you started to? I wouldn't have stopped you!"

"I know."

The softness of his voice made me look up at him.

"So what else do I have to lose?" he asked. He pushed me back on the pallet, and for a few moments, we lay there, still. What was he waiting for? What was I waiting for?

He lay with his head on my shoulder, his left arm around me, his right hand still holding my hand, and slowly, I realized how easy it would be for me to continue to be still and forgive him even this. So easy, in spite of all my talk. But it would be so hard to raise the knife, drive it into the flesh I had saved so many times. So hard to kill . . .

He was not hurting me, would not hurt me if I remained as I was. He was not his father, old and ugly, brutal and disgusting. He smelled of soap, as though he had bathed recently—for me? The red hair was neatly combed and a little damp. I would never be to him what Tess had been to his father—a thing passed around like the whiskey jug at a husking. He wouldn't do that to me or sell me or . . .

No.

I could feel the knife in my hand, still slippery with perspiration. A slave was a slave. Anything could be done to her. And Rufus was Rufus—erratic, alternately generous and vicious. I could accept him as my ancestor, my younger brother, my friend, but not as my master, and not as my lover. He had understood that once.

I twisted sharply, broke away from him. He caught me, trying not to hurt me. I was aware of him trying not to hurt me even as I raised the knife, even as I sank it into his side.

He screamed. I had never heard anyone scream that way —an animal sound. He screamed again, a lower ugly gurgle.

He lost his hold on my hand for a moment, but caught my arm before I could get away. Then he brought up the fist of his free hand to punch me once, and again as the patroller had done so long ago.

I pulled the knife free of him somehow, raised it, and brought it down again into his back.

This time he only grunted. He collapsed across me, somehow still alive, still holding my arm.

I lay beneath him, half conscious from the blows, and sick. My stomach seemed to twist, and I vomited on both of us.

"Dana?"

A voice. A man's voice.

I managed to turn my head and see Nigel standing in the doorway.

"Dana, what . . . ? Oh no. God, no!"

"Nigel . . ." moaned Rufus, and he gave a long shuddering sigh. His body went limp and leaden across me. I pushed him away somehow—everything but his hand still on my arm. Then I convulsed with terrible, wrenching sickness.

Something harder and stronger than Rufus's hand clamped down on my arm, squeezing it, stiffening it, pressing into it— painlessly, at first—melting into it, meshing with it as though somehow my arm were being absorbed into something. Something cold and nonliving.

Something . . . paint, plaster, wood—a wall. The wall of my living room. I was back at home—in my own house, in my own time. But I was still caught somehow, joined to the wall as though my arm were growing out of it—or growing into it. From the elbow to the ends of the fingers, my left arm had become a part of the wall. I looked at the spot where flesh joined with plaster, stared at it uncomprehending. It was the exact spot Rufus's fingers had grasped.

I pulled my arm toward me, pulled hard.

And suddenly, there was an avalanche of pain, red impossible agony! And I screamed and screamed.

Epilogue

W E FLEW to Maryland as soon as my arm was well enough. There, we rented a car—Kevin was driving again, finally —and wandered around Baltimore and over to Easton. There was a bridge now, not the steamship Rufus had used. And at last I got a good look at the town I had lived so near and seen so little of. We found the courthouse and an old church, a few other buildings time had not worn away. And we found Burger King and Holiday Inn and Texaco and schools with black kids and white kids together and older people who looked at Kevin and me, then looked again.

We went into the countryside, into what was still woods and farmland, and found a few of the old houses. A couple of them could have been the Weylin house. They were well-kept and handsomer, but basically, they were the same red-brick Georgian Colonials.

But Rufus's house was gone. As nearly as we could tell, its site was now covered by a broad field of corn. The house was dust, like Rufus.

I was the one who insisted on trying to find his grave, questioning the farmer about it because Rufus, like his father, like old Mary and Alice, had probably been buried on the plantation.

But the farmer knew nothing—or at least, said nothing. The only clue we found—more than a clue, really—was an old newspaper article—a notice that Mr. Rufus Weylin had been killed when his house caught fire and was partially destroyed. And in later papers, notice of the sale of the slaves from Mr. Rufus Weylin's estate. These slaves were listed by their first names with their approximate ages and their skills given. All three of Nigel's sons were listed, but Nigel and Carrie were not. Sarah was listed, but Joe and Hagar were not. Everyone else was listed. Everyone.

I thought about that, put together as many pieces as I could. The fire, for instance. Nigel had probably set it to cover what I had done—and he had covered. Rufus was assumed to have burned to death. I could find nothing in the incomplete newspaper records to suggest that he had been murdered, or even that the fire had been arson. Nigel must have done a good job. He must also have managed to get Margaret Weylin out of the house alive. There was no mention of her dying. And Margaret had relatives in Baltimore. Also, Hagar's home had been in Baltimore.

Kevin and I went back to Baltimore to skim newspapers, legal records, anything we could find that might tie Margaret and Hagar together or mention them at all. Margaret might have taken both children. Perhaps with Alice dead she had accepted them. They were her grandchildren, after all, the son and daughter of her only child. She might have cared for them. She might also have held them as slaves. But even if she had, Hagar, at least, lived long enough for the Fourteenth Amendment to free her.

"He could have left a will," Kevin told me outside one of our haunts, the Maryland Historical Society. "He could have freed those people at least when he had no more use for them."

"But there was his mother to consider," I said. "And he was only twenty-five. He probably thought he had plenty of time to make a will."

"Stop defending him," muttered Kevin.

I hesitated, then shook my head. "I wasn't. I guess in a way, I was defending myself. You see, I know why he wouldn't make that kind of will. I asked him, and he told me."

"Why?"

"Because of me. He was afraid I'd kill him afterwards."

"You wouldn't even have had to know about it!"

"Yes, but I guess he wasn't taking any chances."

"Was he right . . . to be afraid?"

"I don't know."

"I doubt it, considering what you took from him. I don't think you were really capable of killing him until he attacked you."

And barely then, I thought. Kevin would never know what those last moments had been like. I had outlined them for him, and he'd asked few questions. For that I was grateful. Now I said simply, "Self-defense."

"Yes," he said.

"But the cost . . . Nigel's children, Sarah, all the others
. . ."

"It's over," he said. "There's nothing you can do to change
any of it now."

"I know." I drew a deep breath. "I wonder whether the children were allowed to stay together—maybe stay with Sarah."

"You've looked," he said. "And you've found no records.
You'll probably never know."

I touched the scar Tom Weylin's boot had left on my face,
touched my empty left sleeve. "I know," I repeated. "Why
did I even want to come here. You'd think I would have had
enough of the past."

"You probably needed to come for the same reason I did."
He shrugged. "To try to understand. To touch solid evidence
that those people existed. To reassure yourself that you're
sane."

I looked back at the brick building of the Historical Society,
itself a converted early mansion. "If we told anyone else about
this, anyone at all, they wouldn't think we were so sane."

"We are," he said. "And now that the boy is dead, we have
some chance of staying that way."

FLEDGLING

To Frances Louis
for listening

One

I AWOKE TO darkness.

I was hungry—starving!—and I was in pain. There was nothing in my world but hunger and pain, no other people, no other time, no other feelings.

I was lying on something hard and uneven, and it hurt me. One side of me was hot, burning. I tried to drag myself away from the heat source, whatever it was, moving slowly, feeling my way until I found coolness, smoothness, less pain.

It hurt to move. It hurt even to breathe. My head pounded and throbbed, and I held it between my hands, whimpering. The sound of my voice, even the touch of my hands seemed to make the pain worse. In two places my head felt crusty and lumpy and . . . almost soft.

And I was so *hungry*.

The hunger was a violent twisting inside me. I curled my empty, wounded body tightly, knees against chest, and whimpered in pain. I clutched at whatever I was lying on. After a time, I came to understand, to remember, that what I was lying on should have been a *bed*. I remembered little by little what a bed was. My hands were grasping not at a mattress, not at pillows, sheets, or blankets, but at things that I didn't recognize, at first. Hardness, powder, something light and brittle. Gradually, I understood that I must be lying on the ground—on stone, earth, and perhaps dry leaves.

The worst was, no matter where I looked, there was no hint of light. I couldn't see my own hands as I held them up in front of me. Was it so dark, then? Or was there something wrong with my eyes? Was I blind?

I lay in the dark, trembling. What if I were blind?

Then I heard something coming toward me, something large and noisy, some animal. I couldn't see it, but after a moment, I could smell it. It smelled . . . not exactly good, but at least edible. Starved as I was, I was in no condition to hunt. I lay trembling and whimpering as the pain of my hunger grew and eclipsed everything.

It seemed that I should be able to locate the creature by the noise it was making. Then, if it wasn't frightened off by the noise I was making, maybe I could catch it and kill it and eat it.

Or maybe not. I tried to get up, fell back, groaning, discovering all over again how badly every part of my body hurt. I lay still, trying to keep quiet, trying to relax my body and not tremble. And the creature wandered closer.

I waited. I knew I couldn't chase it, but if it came close enough, I might really be able to get my hands on it.

After what seemed a long time, it found me. It came to me like a tame thing, and I lay almost out of control, trembling and gasping, and thinking only, *food!* So much food. It touched my face, my wrist, my throat, causing me pain somehow each time it touched me and making noises of its own.

The pain of my hunger won over all my other pain. I discovered that I was strong in spite of all the things that were wrong with me. I seized the animal. It fought me, tore at me, struggled to escape, but I had it. I clung to it, rode it, found its throat, tasted its blood, smelled its terror. I tore at its throat with my teeth until it collapsed. Then, at last, I fed, gorged myself on the fresh meat that I needed.

I ate as much meat as I could. Then, my hunger sated and my pain dulled, I slept alongside what remained of my prey.

When I awoke, my darkness had begun to give way. I could see light again, and I could see blurred shadowy shapes that blocked the light. I didn't know what the shapes were, but I could see them. I began to believe then that my eyes had been injured somehow, but that they were healing. After a while there was too much light. It burned not only my eyes, but my skin.

I turned away from the light, dragged myself and my prey farther into the cool dimness that seemed to be so close to me, but took so much effort to reach. When I had gone far enough to escape the light, I fed again, slept again, awoke, and fed. I lost count of the number of times I did this. But after a while, something went wrong with the meat. It began to smell so bad that, even though I was still hungry, I couldn't make myself touch it again. In fact, the smell of it was making me sick. I needed to get away from it. I remembered enough to understand that it was rotting. Meat rotted after a while, it stank and the insects got into it.

I needed fresh meat.

My injuries seemed to be healing, and it was easier for me to move around. I could see much better, especially when there wasn't so much light. I had come to remember sometime during one of my meals that the time of less light was called night and that I preferred it to the day. I wasn't only healing, I was remembering things. And now, at least during the night, I could hunt.

My head still hurt, throbbed dully most of the time, but the pain was bearable. It was not the agony it had been.

I got wet as soon as I crawled out of my shelter where the remains of my prey lay rotting. I sat still for a while, feeling the wetness—water falling on my head, my back, and into my lap. After a while, I understood that it was raining—raining very hard. I could not recall feeling rain on my skin before—water falling from the sky, gently pounding my skin.

I decided I liked it. I climbed to my feet slowly, my knees protesting the movement with individual outbursts of pain. Once I was up, I stood still for a while, trying to get used to balancing on my legs. I held on to the rocks that happened to be next to me and stood looking around, trying to understand where I was. I was standing on the side of a hill, from which rose a solid, vertical mass of rock. I had to look at these things, let the sight of them remind me what they were called—the hillside, the rock face, the trees—pine?—that grew on the hill as far as the sheer wall of rock. I saw all this, but still, I had no idea where I was or where I should be or how I had come to be there or even why I was there—there was so much that I didn't know.

The rain came down harder. It still seemed good to me. I let it wash away my prey's blood and my own, let it clean off the crust of dirt that I had picked up from where I had lain. When I was a little cleaner, I cupped my hands together, caught water in them, and drank it. That was so good that I spent a long time just catching rain and drinking it.

After a while, the rain lessened, and I decided that it was time for me to go. I began to walk down the hill. It wasn't an easy walk at first. My knees still hurt, and it was hard for me to keep my balance. I stopped once and looked back. I could see then that I had come from a shallow hillside cave. It was almost invisible to me now, concealed behind a screen of trees. It had been a good place to hide and heal. It had kept me safe, that small hidden place. But how had I come to be in it? Where had I come from? How had I been hurt and left alone, starving? And now that I was better, where should I go?

I wandered, not aware of going anywhere in particular, except down the hill. I knew no other people, could remember no other people. I frowned, picking my way among the trees, bushes, and rocks over the wet ground. I was recognizing things now, at least by category—bushes, rocks, mud . . . I tried to remember something more about myself—anything that had happened to me before I awoke in the cave. Nothing at all occurred to me.

As I walked, it suddenly occurred to me that my feet were bare. I was walking carefully, not stepping on anything that would hurt me, but I could see and understand now that my feet and legs were bare. I knew I should have shoes on. In fact, I knew I should be dressed. But I was bare all over. I was naked.

I stopped and looked at myself. My skin was scarred, badly scarred over every part of my body that I could see. The scars were broad, creased, shiny patches of mottled red-brown skin. Had I always been scarred? Was my face scarred? I touched one of the broad scars across my abdomen, then touched my face. It felt the same. My face might be scarred. I wondered how I looked. I felt my head and discovered that I had almost no hair. I had touched my head, expecting hair. There should have been hair. But I was bald except for a small patch of hair on the back of my head. And higher up on my head there was a misshapen place, an indentation that hurt when I touched it and seemed even more wrong than my hairlessness or my scars. I remembered discovering, as I lay in the cave, that my head felt lumpy and soft in two places, as though the flesh had been damaged and the skull broken. There was no softness now. My head, like the rest of me, was healing.

Somehow, I had been hurt very badly, and yet I couldn't remember how.

I needed to remember and I needed to cover myself. Being naked had seemed completely normal until I became aware of it. Then it seemed intolerable. But most important, I needed to eat again.

I resumed my downhill walk. Eventually I came to flatter, open land—farmland with something growing in some of the fields and other fields, already harvested or empty for some other reason. Again, I was remembering things—fragments —understanding a little of what I saw, perhaps just because I saw it.

Off to one side there was a collection of what I gradually recognized as the burned remains of several houses and out-buildings. All of these had been burned so thoroughly that as far as I could see, they offered no real shelter. This had been a little village surrounded by farmland and woods. There were animal pens and the good smells of animals that could be eaten, but the pens were empty. I thought the place must once have provided comfortable homes for several people. That felt right. It felt like something I would want—living together with other people instead of wandering alone. The idea was a little frightening, though. I didn't know any other people. I knew they existed, but thinking about them, wondering about them scared me almost as much as it interested me.

People had lived in these houses sometime not long ago. Now plants had begun to grow and to cover the burned spaces. Where were the people who had lived here? Had I lived here?

It occurred to me that I had come to this place hoping to kill an animal and eat it. Somehow, I had expected to find food here. And yet I remembered nothing about this place. I recognized nothing except in the most general way—animal pens, fields, burned remnants of buildings. So why would I expect to find food here? How had I known to come here? Either I had visited here before or this place had been my home. If it was my home, why didn't I recognize it as home? Had my injuries come from the fire that destroyed this place? I had an endless stream of questions and no answers.

I turned away, meaning to go back into the trees and hunt an animal—a deer, I thought suddenly. The word came into my thoughts, and at once, I knew what a deer was. It was a large animal. It would provide meat for several meals.

Then I stopped. As hungry as I was, I wanted to go down

and take a closer look at the burned houses. They must have something to do with me or they would not hold my interest the way they did.

I walked down toward the burned buildings. I might at least be able to find something to wear. I was not cold. Even walking in the rain had not made me cold, but I wanted clothing badly. I felt very vulnerable without it. I did not want to be naked when I found other people, and I thought I must, sooner or later, find other people.

Eight of the buildings had been large houses. Their fireplaces, sinks, and bathtubs told me that much. I walked through each of them, hoping to see something familiar, something that triggered a memory, a memory about people. In one, at the bottom of a pile of charred rubble, I found a pair of jeans that were only burned a little at the bottoms of the legs, and I found three slightly burned shirts that were wearable. All of it was too large in every way—too broad, too long . . . Another person my size would have fit easily into the shirts with me. And there were no wearable underwear, no wearable shoes. And, of course, there was nothing to eat.

Feeding my hunger suddenly became more important than anything. I put on the pants and two of the shirts. I used the third shirt to keep the pants up, tying it around my waist and turning the top of the pants down over it. I rolled up the legs of the pants, then I went back into the trees. After a time I scented a doe. I stalked her, killed her, ate as much of her flesh as I could. I took part of the carcass up a tree with me to keep it safe from scavenging animals. I slept in the tree for a while.

Then the sun rose, and it burned my skin and my eyes. I climbed down and used a tree branch and my hands to dig a shallow trench. When I finished it, I lay down in it and covered myself with leaf litter and earth. That and my clothing— I folded one of my shirts over my face—proved to be enough of a shield to protect me from sunlight.

I lived that way for the next three days and nights, eating, hunting, examining the ruin during the night, and hiding myself in the earth during the day. Sometimes I slept. Sometimes I lay awake, listening to the sounds around me. I couldn't identify most of them, but I listened.

On the fourth night curiosity and restlessness got the better of me. I had begun to feel dissatisfied, hungry for something other than deer flesh. I didn't know what I wanted, but I went exploring. That was how, for the first time in my memory, I met another person.

Two

I<small>T WAS</small> raining again—a steady, gentle rain that had been coming down for some time.

I had discovered a paved road that led away from the burned houses. I had walked on it for some time before I remembered the word "road," and that led to my remembering cars and trucks, although I hadn't yet seen either. The road I was on led to a metal gate, which I climbed over, then to another, slightly wider road, and I had to choose a direction. I chose the downslope direction and walked along for a while in contentment until I came to a third still wider road. Again, I chose to go downhill. It was easier to walk along the road than to pick my way through the rocks, trees, underbrush, and creeks, although the pavement was hard against my bare feet.

A blue car came along the road behind me, and I walked well to one side so that I could look at it, and it would pass me without hitting me. It couldn't have been the first car I had ever seen. I knew that because I recognized it as a car and found nothing surprising about it. But it was the first car I could remember seeing.

I was surprised when the car stopped alongside me.

The person inside was, at first, just a face, shoulders, a pair of hands. Then I understood that I was seeing a young man, pale-skinned, brown-haired, broad, and tall. His hair brushed against the top of the inside of his car. His shoulders were so broad that even alone in the car, he looked crowded. His car seemed to fit him almost as badly as my clothing fitted me. He lowered his window, looked out at me, and asked, "Are you all right?"

I heard the words, but at first, they meant nothing at all. They were noise. After a moment, though, they seemed to click into place as language. I understood them. It took me a moment longer before I realized that I should answer. I couldn't remember ever speaking to another person, and at first, I wasn't sure I could do it.

I opened my mouth, cleared my throat, coughed, then finally managed to say, "I . . . am. Yes, I am all right." My voice sounded strange and hoarse to my own ears. It wasn't only that I couldn't recall speaking to anyone else. I couldn't remember ever speaking at all. Yet it seemed that I knew how.

"No, you're not," the man said. "You're soaking wet and filthy, and . . . God, how old are you?"

I opened my mouth, then closed it again. I didn't have any idea how old I was or why my age should matter.

"Is that blood on your shirt?" he asked.

I looked down. "I killed a deer," I said. In all, I had killed two deer. And I did have their blood on my clothing. The rain hadn't washed it away.

He stared at me for several seconds. "Look, is there someplace I can take you? Do you have family or friends somewhere around here?"

I shook my head. "I don't know. I don't think so."

"You shouldn't be out here in the middle of the night in the rain!" he said. "You can't be any more than ten or eleven. Where are you going?"

"Just walking," I said, because I didn't know what else to say. Where was I going? Where would he think I should be going? Home, perhaps. "Home," I lied. "I'm going home." Then I wondered why I had lied. Was it important for this stranger to think that I had a home and was going there? Or was it only that I didn't want him to realize how little I knew about myself, about anything?

"I'll take you home," he said. "Get in."

I surprised myself completely by instantly wanting to go with him. I went around to the passenger side of his car and opened the door. Then I stopped, confused. "I don't really have a home," I said. I closed the door and stepped back.

He leaned over and opened the door. "Look," he said, "I can't leave you out here. You're a kid, for Godsake. Come on, I'll at least take you someplace dry." He reached into the backseat and picked up a big piece of thick cloth. "Here's a blanket. Get in and wrap up."

I wasn't uncomfortable. Being wet didn't bother me, and I wasn't cold. Yet I wanted to get into the car with him. I didn't want him to drive away without me. Now that I'd had a few more moments to absorb his scent I realized he smelled . . . really interesting. Also, I didn't want to stop talking to him. I felt almost as hungry for conversation as I was for food. A taste of it had only whetted my appetite.

I wrapped the blanket around me and got into the car.

"Did someone hurt you?" he asked when he had gotten the car moving again. "Were you in someone's car?"

"I was hurt," I said. "I'm all right now."

He glanced at me. "Are you sure? I can take you to a hospital."

"I don't need a hospital," I said quickly, even though, at first, I wasn't sure what a hospital was. Then I knew that it was a place where the sick and injured were taken for care. There would be a lot of people all around me at a hospital. That was enough to make it frightening. "No hospital."

Another glance. "Okay," he said. "What's your name?"

I opened my mouth to answer, then closed it. After a while, I admitted, "I don't know what my name is. I don't remember."

He glanced at me several times before saying anything about that. After a while he said, "Okay, you don't want to tell me, then. Did you run away? Get tired of home and strike out on your own?"

"I don't think so," I frowned. "I don't think I would do that. I don't remember, really, but that doesn't feel like something I would do."

There was another long silence. "You really don't remember? You're not kidding?"

"I'm not. My . . . my injuries are healed now, but I still don't remember things."

He didn't say anything for a while. Then, "You really don't know what your own name is?"

"That's right."

"Then you do need a hospital."

"No, I don't. No!"

"Why? The doctors there might be able to help you."

Might they? Then why did the idea of going among them scare me so? I knew absolutely that I didn't want to put myself into the hands of strangers. I didn't want to be even near large numbers of strangers. "No hospital," I repeated.

Again, he didn't say anything, but this time, there was something different about his silence. I looked at him and suddenly believed that he meant to deliver me to a hospital anyway, and

I panicked. I unfastened the seat belt that he had insisted I buckle and pushed aside the blanket. I turned to open the car door. He grabbed my arm before I could figure out how to get it open. He had huge hands that wrapped completely around my arm. He pulled me back, pulled me hard against the little low wall that divided his legs from mine.

He scared me. I was less than half his size, and he meant to force me to go where I didn't want to go. I pulled away from him, dodged his hand as he grasped at me, tried again to open the door, only to be caught again.

I caught his wrist, squeezed it, and yanked it away from my arm. He yelped, said "Shit!" and managed to rub his wrist with the hand still holding the steering wheel. "What the hell's wrong with you?" he demanded.

I put my back against the door that I had been trying to open. "Are you going to take me to the hospital even though I don't want to go?" I asked.

He nodded, still rubbing his wrist. "The hospital or the police station. Your choice."

"Neither!" Being turned over to the police scared me even more than the idea of going to the hospital did. I turned to try again to get the door open.

And again, he grasped my left upper arm, pulling me back from the door. His fingers wrapped all the way around my upper arm and held me tightly, pulling me away from the door. I understood him a little better now that I'd had my hands on him. I thought I could break his wrist if I wanted to. He was big but not that strong. Or, at least, I was stronger. But I didn't want to break his bones. He seemed to want to help me, although he didn't know how. And he did smell good. I didn't have the words to say how good he smelled. Breaking his bones would be wrong.

I bit him—just a quick bite and release on the meaty part of his hand where his thumb was.

"Goddamnit!" he shouted, jerking his hand away. Then he made another grab for me before I could get the door open. There were several buttons on the door, and I didn't know which of them would make it open. None of them seemed to work. That gave him a chance to get his hand on me a third time.

"Be still!" he ordered and gave me a hard shake. "You'll kill yourself! If you're crazy enough to try to jump out of a moving car, you should be in a mental hospital."

I stared down at the bleeding marks I'd made on his hand, and suddenly I was unable to think about anything else. I ducked my head and licked away the blood, licked the wound I had made. He tensed, almost pulling his hand away. Then he stopped, seemed to relax. He let me take his hand between my own. I looked at him, saw him glancing at me, felt the car zigzag a little on the road.

He frowned and pulled away from me, all the while, looking uncertain, unhappy. I caught his hand again between mine and held it. I felt him try to pull away. He shook me, actually lifting me into the air a little, trying to get away from me, but I didn't let go. I licked at the blood welling up where my teeth had cut him.

He made a noise, a kind of gasp. Abruptly, he drove completely across the road to a spot where there was room to stop the car without blocking other cars—the few other cars that came along. He made a huge fist of the hand that was no longer needed to steer the car. I watched him draw it back to hit me. I thought I should be afraid, should try to stop him, but I was calm. Somehow, I couldn't believe he would hit me.

He frowned, shook his head. After a while he dropped his hand to his lap and glared at me. "What are you doing?" he demanded, watching me, not pulling away at all now, but looking as though he wanted to—or as though he thought he should want to.

I didn't answer. I wasn't getting enough blood from his hand. I wanted to bite him again, but I didn't want him afraid or angry. I didn't know why I cared about that, but it seemed important. Also, I knew hands weren't as good for getting blood as wrists and throats were. I looked at him and saw that he was looking intently at me.

"It doesn't hurt anymore," he said. "It feels good. Which is weird. How do you do that?"

"I don't know," I told him. "You taste good."

"Do I?" He lifted me, squeezed past the division between the seats to my side of the car, and put me on his lap.

"Let me bite you again," I whispered.

He smiled. "If I do, what will you let me do?"

I heard consent in his voice, and I hauled myself up and kissed the side of his neck, searching with my tongue and my nose for the largest blood source there. A moment later, I bit hard into the side of his neck. He convulsed and I held on to him. He writhed under me, not struggling, but holding me as I took more of his blood. I took enough blood to satisfy a hunger I hadn't realized I had until a few moments before. I could have taken more, but I didn't want to hurt him. He tasted wonderful, and he had fed me without trying to escape or to hurt me. I licked the bite until it stopped bleeding. I wished I could make it heal, wished I could repay him by healing him.

He sighed and held me, leaning back in his seat and letting me lean against him. "So what was that?" he asked after a while. "How did you do that? And why the hell did it feel so fantastic?"

He had enjoyed it—maybe as much as I had. I felt pleased, felt myself smile. That was right somehow. I'd done it right. That meant I'd done it before, even though I couldn't remember.

"Keep me with you," I said, and I knew I meant it the moment I said it. He would have a place to live. If I could go there with him, maybe the things I saw there would help me begin to get my memory back—and I would have a home.

"Do you really not have anywhere to go or anyone looking for you?" he asked.

"I don't think I have anyone," I said. "I don't remember. I need to find out who I am and what happened to me and . . . and everything."

"Do you always bite?"

I leaned back against him. "I don't know."

"You're a vampire, you know."

I thought about that. The word stirred no memories. "What's a vampire?"

He laughed. "You. You bite. You drink blood. He grimaced and shook his head. "My God, you drink blood."

"I guess I do." I licked at his neck.

"And you're way too young," he said. "Jailbait. Super jailbait."

Since I didn't know what "jailbait" was and I had no idea how old I was, I didn't say anything.

"Do you remember how you got that blood on your clothes? Who else have you been chewing on?"

"I killed a deer. In fact, I killed two deer."

"Sure you did."

"Keep me with you."

I was watching his face as I said it. He looked confused again, worried, but he held me against his body and nodded. "Yeah," he said. "I'm not sure how I'm going to do that, but yeah. I want you with me. I don't think I should keep you. Hell, I know I shouldn't. But I'll do it anyway."

"I don't think I'm supposed to be alone," I said. "I don't know who I should be with, though, because I can't remember ever having been with anyone."

"So you'll be with me." He smiled and his confusion seemed to be gone. "I'll need to call you something. What do you want to be called?"

"I don't know."

"Do you want me to give you a name?"

I smiled, liking him, feeling completely at ease with him. "Give me a name," I said. I licked at his neck a little more.

"Renee," he said. "A friend of mine told me it meant 're-born.' That's sort of what's happened to you. You've been re-born into a new life. You'll probably remember your old life pretty soon, but for now, you're Renee." He shivered against me as I licked his neck. "Damn that feels good," he said. Then, "I rent a cabin from my uncle. If I take you there, you'll have to stay inside during the day. If he and my aunt see you, they'll probably throw us both out."

"I can sleep during the day. I won't go out until dark."

"Just right for a vampire," he said. "How did you kill those deer?"

I shrugged. "Ran them down and broke their necks."

"Uh-huh. Then what?"

"Ate some of their meat. Hid the rest in a tree until I was hungry again. Ate it until the parts I wanted were gone."

"How did you cook it? It's been raining like hell for the past few days. How did you find dry wood for your fire?"

"No fire. I didn't need a fire."

"You ate the deer raw?"

"Yes."

"Oh God, no you didn't." Something seemed to occur to him suddenly. "Show me your knife."

I hesitated. "Knife?"

"To clean and skin the deer."

"A thing? A tool?"

"A tool for cutting, yes."

"I don't have a knife."

He held me away from him and stared at me. "Show me your teeth," he said.

I bared my teeth for him.

"Good God," he said. "Are those what you bit me with?" He put his hand to his neck. "You *are* a damned vampire."

"Didn't hurt you," I said. He looked afraid. He started to push me away, then got that confused look again and pulled me back to him. "Do vampires eat deer?" I asked. I licked at his neck again.

He raised a hand to stop me, then dropped the hand to his side. "What are you, then?" he whispered.

And I said the only thing I could: "I don't know." I drew back, held his face between my hands, liking him, glad that I had found him. "Help me find out."

Three

O N THE drive to his cabin, the man told me that his name was Wright Hamlin and that he was a construction worker. He had been a student in a nearby place called Seattle at something called the University of Washington for two years. Then he had dropped out because he didn't know where he was heading or even where he wanted to be heading. His father had been disgusted with him and had sent him to work for his uncle who owned a construction company. He'd worked for his uncle for three years now, and his current job was helping to build houses in a new community to the south of where he'd picked me up.

"I like the work," he told me as he drove. "I still don't know where I'm headed, but the work I'm doing is worth something. People will live in those houses someday."

I understood only that he liked the work he was doing. As he told me a little about it, though, I realized I would have to be careful about taking blood from him. I understood— or perhaps remembered—that people could be weakened by blood loss. If I made Wright weak, he might get hurt. When I thought about it, I knew I would want more blood—want it as badly as I had previously wanted meat. And as I thought about meat, I realized that I didn't want it anymore. The idea of eating it disgusted me. Taking Wright's blood had been the most satisfying thing I could remember doing. I didn't know what that meant—whether it made me what Wright thought of as a vampire or not. I realized that to avoid hurting Wright, to avoid hurting anyone, I would have to find several people to take blood from. I wasn't sure how to do that, but it had to be done.

Wright told me what he remembered about vampires—that they're immortal unless someone stabs them in the heart with a wooden stake, and yet even without being stabbed they're dead, or undead. Whatever that means. They drink blood, they have no reflection in mirrors, they can become bats or wolves, they turn other people into vampires either by drinking their blood or by making the convert drink the vampire's blood. This last detail seemed to depend on which story you were reading or which movie you were watching. That was the other thing about vampires. They were fictional beings. Folklore. There were no vampires.

So what was I?

It bothered Wright that all he wanted to do now was keep me with him, that he was taking me to his home and not to the police or to a hospital. "I'm going to get into trouble," he said. "It's just a matter of when."

"What will happen to you?" I asked.

He shrugged. "I don't know. Jail, maybe. You're so young. I should care about that. It should be scaring the hell out of me. It is scaring me, but not enough to make me dump you."

I thought about that for a while. He had let me bite him. I knew from the way he touched me and looked at me that he would let me bite him again when I wanted to. And he would do what he could to help me find out who I was and what had happened to me.

"How can I keep you from getting into trouble?" I asked.

He shook his head. "In the long run, you probably can't. For now, though, get down on the floor."

I looked at him.

"Get down, now. I can't let my uncle and aunt or the neighbors see you."

I slid from the seat and curled myself up on the floor of his car. If I had been a little bigger, it wouldn't have been possible. As it was, it wasn't comfortable. But it didn't matter. He threw the blanket over me. After that, I could feel the car making several turns, slowing, turning once more, then stopping.

"Okay," he said. "We're at the carport behind my cabin. No one can see us."

I unfolded myself, got back up onto the seat, and looked around. There was a scattering of trees, lights from distant houses, and next to us, a small house. Wright got out of the car, and I looked quickly to see which button or lever he used to open the door. It was one I had tried when he was threatening to take me to a hospital or the police. It hadn't worked then, but it worked now. The door opened.

I got out and asked, "Why wouldn't it open before?"

"I locked it," he said. "I didn't want you smearing yourself all over the pavement."

". . . what?"

"I locked the door to keep you safe. You were trying to jump from a moving car, for Godsake. You would have been badly hurt or killed if you had succeeded."

"Oh."

He took me by the arm and led me into his house.

Once I was inside, I looked around and immediately recognized that I was in a kitchen. Even though I could not recall ever having been in an intact kitchen before, I recognized it and the things in it—the refrigerator, the stove, the sink, a counter where a few dishes sat on a dish towel, a dish cabinet above the counter, and beside it, a second cabinet where my nose told me food was sometimes stored. I remembered the blackened refrigerators and sinks at the burned ruin. But this was what a kitchen should look like when everything worked.

The kitchen was small—just a corner of the cabin, really. Beyond it was a wooden table with four chairs. Alongside the kitchen on the opposite side of the cabin was a small room— a bathroom, I saw when I looked in. Beyond the bathroom was the rest of the cabin—a combination living room-bedroom containing a bed, a chest of drawers, a soft chair facing a stone fireplace, and a small television on top of a black bookcase filled with books. I recognized all these things as soon as I saw them.

I went through the cabin, touching things, wondering about the few that I did not recognize. Wright would tell me and show me. He was exactly what I needed right now. I turned to face him again. "Tell me what else to do to keep you out of trouble."

"Just don't let anyone see you," he said. "Don't go out until after dark and don't . . ." He looked at me silently for a while. "Don't hurt anyone."

That surprised me. I had no intention of hurting anyone. "All right," I said.

He smiled. "You look so innocent and so young. But you're dangerous, aren't you? I felt how strong you are. And look what you've done to me."

"What have I done?"

"You bit me. Now you're all I can think about. You're going to do it again, aren't you?"

"I am."

He drew an uneven breath. "Yeah. I thought so. I probably shouldn't let you."

I looked up at him.

He took another breath. "Shit, you can do it right now if you want to."

I rested my head against his arm and sighed. "It might hurt you to lose more blood so soon. I don't want to hurt you."

"Don't you? Why not? You don't even know me."

"You're helping me, and you don't know me. You let me into your car and now into your house."

"Yeah. I wonder how much that's going to cost me." He put his hand on my shoulder and walked me over to the table. There he sat down and drew me close so that he could open one of my filthy shirts, then the other. Having reached skin, he stroked my chest. "No breasts," he said. "Pity. I guess you really are a kid. Or maybe . . . Are you sure you're female?"

"I'm female," I said. "Of course I am."

He peeled off my two shirts and threw them into the trash can. "I'll give you a T-shirt to sleep in," he said. "One of my T-shirts should be about the size of a nightgown for you. To-morrow I'll buy you a few things."

He seemed to think of something suddenly. He took my arm and led me into the bathroom. There, over the sink, was a large mirror. He stood me in front of it and seemed relieved to see that the mirror reflected two people instead of only one.

I touched my face and the short fuzz of black hair on my head, and I tried to see someone I recognized. I was a lean, sharp-faced, large-eyed, brown-skinned person—a complete stranger. Did I look like a child of about ten or eleven? Was I? How could I know? I examined my teeth and saw nothing startling about them until I asked Wright to show me his.

Mine looked sharper, but smaller. My canine teeth—Wright told me they were called that—were longer and sharper than his. Would people notice the difference? It wasn't a big differ-ence. Would it frighten people? I hoped not. And how was it that I could recognize a refrigerator, a sink, even a mirror, but fail to recognize my own face in the mirror?

"I don't know this person," I said. "It's as though I've never seen her before." Then I had another thought. "My scars are gone."

"What?" he asked. "What scars?"

"I was all scarred. A few nights ago . . . three nights before this one, I was scarred. I remember thinking that I must have been burned—all over. And I couldn't see for a while when I first woke up, so maybe my eyes were scarred, too." I sighed. "That's why I hurt so much and why I was so hungry and so tired. All I've done is eat and sleep. My body had so much healing to do."

"Scars don't vanish just because wounds heal," he said. "Especially not burn scars." He pushed up the sleeve of his right arm to display a shiny, creased patch of skin bigger than my hand. "I got this when I was ten, fooling around our barbecue pit. Caught my sleeve on fire."

I took his arm and looked at the scar, touched it. I didn't like it. It felt the way my own skin had when I examined my scars. I had the feeling I should be able to make his scars go away too, but I didn't know how. I turned his hand to look at the bite mark I'd made, and he gasped. The wound seemed to me to be healing as it should, but he snatched his arm from me and examined the hand.

"It's already healing!" he said.

"It should be healing," I said. "Are you hungry?"

"Now that you mention it, I am. I had a big meal at a café not far from the job site, but I'm hungry again."

"You should eat."

"Yeah, but I'm not into raw meat."

"Eat what's right for you. Eat what your body wants."

"But you ate raw meat to heal?" he asked.

His words triggered something in me—a memory. It felt real, true. I spoke it aloud: "All I need is fresh human blood when I'm healthy and everything's normal. I need fresh meat for healing injuries and illnesses, for sustaining growth spurts, and for carrying a child."

He put his hands on my shoulders. "You know that? You remember it?"

"I think so. It sounds right. It feels right."

"So, then," he said, "what are you?"

I looked up at him, saw that I had scared him, and took one of his huge hands between mine. "I don't know what I am. I don't know why I remembered just now about flesh and blood. But you helped me do it. You asked me questions and you made me look into the mirror. Maybe now, with you to help me, I'll remember more and more."

"If you're right about what you've remembered so far, you're not human," he said.

"What if I'm not?" I asked. "What would that mean?"

"I don't know." He reached down and tugged at my jeans. "Take these off," he said.

I undid the shirt that I had twisted and tied around me to keep the jeans up, then I took them off.

He first seemed frozen with surprise that I had done as he said. Then, slowly, he walked around me, looking. "Well, you're a girl, all right," he whispered. At last, he took me by the hand and led me back to the main room of the cabin.

He led me to the chest of drawers next to the bed. There, in the top drawer, he found a white T-shirt. "Put this on," he said, handing it to me.

I put it on. It fell past my knees, and I looked up at him.

"You tired?" he asked. "You want to go to sleep?"

"Not sleepy," I said. "Can I wash?" I hadn't minded being dirty until the clean shirt made me think about just how dirty I was.

"Sure," he said. "Go take a shower. Then come keep me company while I eat."

I went into the bathroom, recognized the shower head over the bathtub, and figured out how to turn the shower on. Then I took off the T-shirt and stepped in. It was a hot, controlled rain, wonderful for getting clean and feeling better. I stayed under the shower longer than necessary just because it felt so good. Then, finally, I dried myself on the big blue towel that was there and that smelled of Wright.

I put the T-shirt back on and went out to Wright who was sitting at his table, eating things that I recognized first by scent then by sight. He was eating scrambled eggs and chunks of ham together between thick slices of bread.

"Can you eat any of this?" Wright asked as he enjoyed the food and drank from a brown bottle of beer.

I smiled. "No, but I think I must have known people who ate things like that because I recognize them. Right now, I'll get some water. That's all I want."

"Until you want to chew on me again, eh?"

I got up to get the water and touched his shoulder as I passed him. It was good to see him eat, to know that he was well. It made me feel relieved. I hadn't hurt him. That was more important to me than I'd realized.

I sat down with a glass of water and sipped it.

"Why'd you do that?" he asked after a long silence. "Why'd you let me undress you like that?"

"You wanted to," I said.

"You would let anyone who wanted to, do that?"

I frowned, then shook my head. "I bit you—twice."

"So?"

"Taking my clothes off with you is all right."

"Is it?"

I frowned, remembering how badly I had wanted to cover myself when I was naked in the woods. I must have been used to wearing clothes in my life before the cave. I had wanted to be dressed as soon as I knew I was naked. Yet when Wright had taken my shirts, I hadn't minded. And I hadn't minded taking off the jeans when he asked me to. It had felt like what I should do.

"I don't think I'm as young as you believe," I said. "I mean, I may be, but I don't think so."

"You don't have any body hair at all," he told me.

"Should I?" I asked.

"Most people over eleven or twelve do."

I thought about that. "I don't know," I said finally. "I don't know enough about myself to say what my age might be or even whether I'm human. But I'm old enough to have sex with you if you want to."

He choked on his sandwich and spent time coughing and taking swallows of beer.

"I think you're supposed to," I continued, then frowned. "No, that's not right. I mean, I think you're supposed to be free to, if you want to."

"Because I let you bite me?"

"I don't know. Maybe."

"A reward for my suffering."

I leaned back, looking at him. "Does it hurt?"

"You know damn well it doesn't."

He drank a couple of swallows more, then stood up, took my hand, and led me to his bed. I sat on the bed, and he started to pull the T-shirt over my head.

"No," I said, and he stopped and stood looking at me, waiting. "Let me see you." I pulled at his shirt and unbuttoned one of the buttons. "You've seen me."

He nodded, finished unbuttoning his shirt, and pulled his undershirt over his head.

His broad chest was covered with a mat of brown hair so thick that it was almost like fur, and I stroked it and felt him shiver.

He kicked off his shoes and stripped off his pants and underwear. There was a great deal more fur on him everywhere, and he was already erect and eager.

I had seen a man this way before. I could not remember who he had been, could not recall a specific face or body. But all this was familiar and good to me, and I felt my own eagerness and growing excitement. I pulled the T-shirt over my head and let him push me back onto the bed, let him touch me while I petted and played with his fur and explored his body until, gasping, he caught my hands and held them. He covered me with his huge, furry blanket of a body. He was so tall that he took care to hold himself up on his elbows so that my face was not crushed into his chest.

He was very careful at first, afraid of hurting me, still afraid that I might be too young for this, too small. Then, when it was clear that I was not being hurt at all, when I had wrapped my arms and legs around him, he forgot his fears, forgot everything.

I forgot myself, too. I bit him again just beneath his left nipple and took a little more blood. He shouted and squeezed the breath from me. Then he collapsed on me, empty, spent.

It bothered me later, as he lay sleeping beside me, that I had taken more blood. If I didn't find another source of blood soon, I would weaken him too much.

I got up quietly, washed, and put on his T-shirt. I would not let myself be seen, but I had to go out and look around. I had to see who and what else might be nearby.

Four

WRIGHT LIVED in an area where houses were widely scattered along a road. They sat well back from the road, and sometimes they were surrounded by trees. It was as though the people in each of these houses were pretending they lived alone in the woods. Most of the other houses were much larger than Wright's cabin. His closest neighbor was one of these larger houses—a two-story house made of wood, painted white, and now full of light. This must be where Wright's aunt and uncle lived. I could hear people talking downstairs and music coming from upstairs. Best to let these people alone, at least until they slept.

Three houses away there were no lights, and the people were already asleep. I could hear the soft, even breathing of two of them upstairs in a front bedroom.

I went around the house looking for a quiet way in. The house had plenty of windows, but the ones on the lower floor were closed and locked. On one side, though, where the trees screened the house from the road and the neighbors, I found a little platform next to a second-floor window, and the window was partly open. I stared up at the platform, recognizing it, remembering that it was called a "balcony," but knowing nothing about it beyond that. Things kept coming to me in this frustrating, almost useless way.

I shook my head in annoyance and decided that I could leap the distance from the ground to the balcony. I'd made longer leaps on my two deer hunts, and the balcony, at least, wasn't moving. But I was concerned that I might make too much noise.

Well, if I awoke more than one person, I would run. If I were quick enough, maybe no one would catch me.

That's when I remembered that more might happen to me than just capture. I might be shot. I recalled being shot once before—perhaps more than once. This, like the balcony, proved to be another of my limited, nearly useless slivers of memory. I remembered the hammering impact of the bullet. I remembered that it hurt me more than anything had ever hurt

298

me. But who had shot me? Why? Where had I been when it happened? Did it have something to do with my winding up in the cave?

Nothing.

No answers.

Just slivers of memory, tormenting me.

I stood slightly back from the balcony, seeing and understanding how far up it was, how I must grasp the somehow familiar wrought iron, hold it, and haul myself up. It was like watching a deer and figuring out where to leap so that I could seize it, or at least run it down with the least effort.

I stooped, looked up at the place on the balcony where I intended to land, jumped, landed there, caught the wrought-iron railing, pulled myself up and over it. Then I froze. Had anyone heard me?

I didn't move for several seconds—not until I was sure no one was moving nearby. The breathing I could hear was the even, undisturbed breathing of sleeping people. The room I slipped into was occupied by one person—a woman, sleeping alone. I crept closer to her bed and took a deep breath.

This woman didn't smell as enticing as Wright had. She was older, no longer able to have children, but not yet truly old. For her age, though, she was healthy and strong, and from what I could see of her body stretched out on the bed, she was almost as tall as Wright, but slender. I didn't like her age, and I thought she was too thin, but her height and her good health beckoned to me. And her aloneness was good, somehow. There were other people in the house, but none of them had been in her room for a long time. She didn't smell of other people. Perhaps it was only because she had bathed, but I got the impression that no one had touched her in a long while.

Most important, though, she could feed me without harm to herself. Wright was larger and could give more blood, but this woman had possibilities. I needed to know several more people like her.

I moved closer to the bed and the sleeping woman—and knew suddenly that there was a gun in the room. I smelled it. It was a terrifyingly familiar smell.

I almost turned and ran out. Being shot had apparently done me more harm than I realized. It had left me an irrational fear to deal with. The pain had been very bad, but I was not in danger of being shot now. No one was holding this gun. It was out of sight somewhere, perhaps in one of the drawers of the little table that sat next to the head of the woman's bed.

I stood still until my fear quieted. I would not be shot tonight.

When I was calm, I lay down beside the woman and covered her mouth with my hand as she woke. I held on to her with my other arm and both my legs as she began to struggle. Once I was sure of my hold on her, I bit into her neck. She struggled wildly at first, tried to bite me, tried to scream. But after I had fed for a few seconds, she stopped struggling. I held her a little longer, to be sure she was subdued; then, when she gave no more trouble, I let her go. She lay still, eyes closed.

I fed slowly, licking rather than sucking. I wasn't hungry. Perhaps tomorrow I would come back and take a full meal from her. Now I was only making certain of her, seeing to it that she would be here, available to me when I needed her. After a while, I whispered to her, "Is it good?"

She moaned—a satisfied little sound.

"Leave your balcony door unlocked from now on, and don't tell anyone about me."

"You'll come back?"

"Shall I?"

"Come back tomorrow."

"Maybe. Soon."

She started to turn to face me.

"No," I said. "No, stay as you are."

She obeyed.

I licked at her neck for a while, then asked, "What's your name?"

"Theodora Harden."

"I'll see you again, Theodora."

"Don't go. Not yet."

I left her, content that she would welcome me when I came back. I wandered up and down both sides of the road until I had found four more—two men and two women—who were young enough, healthy, and big enough. One by one, I collected them. I would stay with Wright but go to these others when I needed them. Were they enough? I didn't know.

I went back to Wright's cabin, still wide awake, and sat at his table. I wanted to think about what I had done. It bothered me somehow that it had all been so easy, that I had had no trouble taking blood from six people including Wright. Once I had tasted them, they enjoyed the way I made them feel. Instead of being afraid or angry, they were first confused, then trusting and welcoming, eager for more of the pleasure that I could give them. It happened that way each time. I didn't understand it, but I had done it in a comfortable, knowing way. I had done it as though it was what I was supposed to do.

Was there something in my saliva that pacified people and pleasured them? What else could it be? It must also help them heal. Wright had been surprised with how quickly his hand was healing. That meant healing must normally take longer for him. And that meant I could at least help the people who helped me. That felt important.

On the other hand, it felt wrong to me that I was blundering around, knowing almost nothing, yet involving other people in my life. And yet it seemed I had to involve them. I hadn't hurt anyone so far, but I could have. And I probably would unless I could remember something useful.

I thought back as far as I could remember, closed my eyes and thought myself back to the blindness and pain of the little cave. I had emerged from it almost like a child being born. Should I go back there? Could I even find the place now? Yes, I thought I could find it. But why go back? Could there be anything there that would help me remember how I'd gotten there?

I had gone from the cave down to the site of the burned houses. I had found nothing that looked familiar at the houses, but maybe it would help me to know when the houses burned and why and who had done it. Also, it might help to know who had lived at the houses. I had found no burned bodies, although there had been places that smelled of burned flesh. So maybe the people who lived there had been hurt but had gotten away, or maybe they had been killed and were taken away. If I had lived there, I had certainly gotten away. Maybe in the confusion of the fire, we'd gotten separated. But why hadn't the others—whoever they were—looked for me, searched the forest and the hillside? Why had I been left to fend for myself after being so badly injured? Maybe they were all dead.

I went back again, to my memory of the cave. I had awakened in terrible pain—blind, lost, naked. And then some animal had come to me, had come right up to me, making me a gift of its flesh. And I had killed it and eaten it.

I thought about the animal and its odd behavior. Then, in memory, I saw the remains of the animal, scattered around the cave. I had seen it briefly, just before I left the cave. I had been able to see then, but I had not been aware enough to understand what I was seeing. What I had killed . . . and eaten . . . in the cave had not been an animal. It had been a man.

I had not seen his face, but I had seen his short, straight black hair. I had seen his feet, his genitals, one of his hands . . .

A man.

He had come up through the trees and spotted me in the shallow cave. He came to me. He touched my face, sought a pulse in my wrist, then my throat. It hurt when he touched me because my burns were still raw. He had whispered something. I hadn't understood the words at the time, hadn't even understood that they were words. He bent over me. I could feel him there, warm—a large, edible-smelling patch of warmth—so tempting to my starving, damaged body and to my damaged mind. Close enough to touch. And I grabbed him and I tore out his throat and I ate him.

I was capable of that. I had done that.

I sat for a long time, stunned, not knowing what to think. The words that the man had whispered when he found me were, "Oh my God, it's her. Please let her be alive." That was what he said just before I killed him.

I put my head down on the table. The man had known me. He had cared about me. Perhaps I had had a relationship with him like the one I was developing with Wright. I must have had such relationships with someone—several someones.

How could I have killed such a person?

I couldn't kill Wright. Could I? I'd been with him for only one night, and yet there was a bond between us. But I had not recognized the other man. I couldn't see his face—had no memory of ever seeing his face—but his scent should have told me what he was. How was it that he had smelled only like food to me and not like a person at all?

I heard Wright wake up. Heard his breathing change. After a moment, he got up and came over to me. The room was dim but not dark. There was a window in the kitchen area where the moonlight shone in.

"What's going on?" he asked. He put his hands on my shoulders and rubbed me pleasantly.

I sat up. "I've been trying to remember things," I said.

"Any luck?"

"Pain, hunger, bad things. Nothing from before I woke up hurt and blind in the cave." I couldn't tell him about the man I'd killed. How could I ever tell him about a thing like that?

"Give it time," he said. "You'll get it back. If you'd see a doctor—"

"No! No hospital. No doctor."

"Why?"

"Why?" I stood up, turning to face him. He stepped back, startled, and I realized I had moved too quickly—faster than he expected me to move. No matter. It helped me make my point. "Wright, I don't know what I am, but I'm not like you. I think maybe . . . maybe I look a lot more human than I am. I don't want to draw attention to myself, maybe have people try to lock me up because they're afraid of me."

"For Godsake, girl, no one's going to lock you up."

"No? I look like a child. I might be locked up for my own safety even if they weren't afraid of my differences. You thought I was a child."

He grinned. "I don't any more." Then he hugged himself, hands rubbing his furry forearms a little.

I realized that he had gotten cold standing naked in the un-heated room while he talked with me. "Come back to bed and get warm," I said.

He got back into bed, pulling me against him as I slid in beside him.

"Can you get information for me?" I asked.

"Information?"

"About memory and not being able to remember things."

"Amnesia," he said, and just like that, the word was familiar to me.

"Amnesia, yes. And about vampires," I said. "Most of what

you told me . . . I don't think it has anything to do with me. But I do need blood. Maybe there are bits of truth mixed into the movies and folktales."

"I'd like to know how old you are," he said.

"When I know, I'll tell you. But, Wright, don't tell anyone about me. Don't tell your friends or your family or anyone."

"You know I wouldn't. I'm more likely to get into trouble than you are if anyone found out about you."

"I think your trouble would be shorter-lived than mine," I said.

"I won't say a word."

After a while, I thought of something else. "There was a fire, Wright. Some houses surrounded by farmland and woods. Eight houses not far from where you picked me up. Do you remember hearing about it?"

He shook his head. "Sounds big, but no, I don't remember hearing anything about it. Do you know when the fire happened?"

"No. I found the ruin when I was able to get up and walk around. There weren't any bodies or bones or anything. It was just a burned-out ruin."

"How close is it to where I picked you up?"

"I don't know. I had been wandering away from it since just after sundown when I met you. I wasn't going anywhere in particular. I was feeling frustrated. I'd been hunting, eating, sleeping, and going over the ruin for three days, not even knowing what I was looking for." I shook my head against the pillow. "I believe I could find the place because I've been there. It seems that I have a very good memory for the little I've done and sensed in the past few days."

"Maybe this weekend you could show me the ruin."

"All right."

"Meanwhile, it's almost time for me to get up and get ready for work."

"It's not dawn yet."

"Yeah, how about that? But before I go, I'm going to show you how to use my computer. Do you remember computers?"

I frowned, then nodded. "I remember what they are. Like refrigerators. But I don't think I know how to use one."

"Like refrigerators?"

"I mean, sometimes when you say something or I see something—like when I saw your refrigerator—I know what it is, what it's for, but I don't remember how I know or if I've ever had one."

"Okay. Let's get you online, and you can gather some information yourself." We got up again, and he put on a white terry-cloth robe and put one of his vast plaid shirts on me. I wasn't cold, but I didn't mind. His computer was a slender laptop that he took from the back of the black bookcase where I had not noticed it. He opened it on his kitchen counter where there was an electrical outlet and a phone jack. He turned it on, making sure I saw everything he did and what he typed in to get online. Then he shut everything down and made me do it. It all felt vaguely familiar to me. I was comfortable with it. When I'd gone through the process, he was happy.

"I don't use the thing much anymore," he said. "I thought for a moment I'd forgotten my password."

It occurred to me just then that his memory would improve. I managed not to say it, but, yes, his memory should improve because I was with him, because now and then, I would bite him, injecting whatever I injected into people when I bit them. I didn't say anything about it because I didn't want him to ask me questions I couldn't answer—like what other changes might be in store for him.

"I'm going to stop by the library on my way home," he said. "I'll see what I can find for you about vampires and amnesia. Maybe I can even scare up something on your fire."

"Thank you."

He grinned. "We aim to please." He went off to take a shower and get dressed.

By the time he came out, clean and shaved, dressed in blue jeans and a red plaid shirt like the one I had on, I had already looked through a huge amount of nonsense about vampires. Apparently they were in fashion with some people. There were television shows, movies, plays, and novels about them. There were groups devoted to talking about them endlessly in online chat groups. There were even people who tried to look the way they thought a vampire should look—a cloaked figure with long, sharp teeth, and long, dark hair . . .

"Anything useful?" Wright asked me.

"Nothing," I said. "Worthless stuff."

He nodded. "Stay away from the TV stuff and movies. Go with folklore and mythology, maybe anthropology. And there are some medical conditions I've heard of. There's one that makes people so allergic to sunlight that they only go out at night, and maybe superstitious people of the past thought they were vampires. There's also a disease or a psychological condition that makes people think they're vampires."

"You mean they're insane?"

"I don't know. If a psychiatrist found out what you eat and drink, he might think you're insane."

"Even if I bit him?"

He looked away. "I don't know. I think that might convince him whether he liked it or not. Renee, are you going to go unconscious during the day?"

"I'll probably sleep for a while."

"But will it be normal sleep? I mean, would you be able to wake up if the house were on fire or if someone broke in—not that either of those things is likely?"

"I just sleep," I said. "Normal sleep. The sun hurts my eyes and my skin, and I seem to prefer to sleep during the day— the way you prefer to sleep at night. I don't catch fire or turn to ash or dust or anything like what I've read about so far on your computer. Anything that would wake you up would wake me up."

"Okay, good. Lock the door when I leave. Nobody should be coming in here when I'm not home. If someone knocks, ignore them. If the phone rings, don't answer it." He started to leave, then turned back, frowning. "Ordinary sun exposure burns your skin even though you're black?"

"I'm . . ." I stopped. I had been about to protest that I was brown, not black, but before I could speak, I understood what he meant. Then his question triggered another memory. I looked at him. "I think I'm an experiment. I think I can withstand the sun better than . . . others of my kind. I burn, but I don't burn as fast as they do. It's like an allergy we all have to the sun. I don't know who the experimenters are, though, the ones who made me black."

He became intensely interested. "Do you know if the

experimenters were like you—sort of vampires—or were they like me?"

"Don't know." I looked at him. "But keep asking me things. Whenever you think of a question, ask me. Sometimes it helps."

He nodded, then kissed me. "I've got to go."

"Breakfast?" I said.

"I ate it last night. I'll pick something up on the way to work. I've got to go grocery shopping this evening. It's a good thing you don't eat."

And he went out the door and was gone.

Five

I SPENT MOST of the day at the computer making no real progress. There were diseases that people might once have mistaken for vampirism. One of them was called porphyria. It was probably what Wright thought of as a sun-allergy disease. In fact, it was a group of diseases caused by pigments that settled in peoples' teeth, bones, and skin. The worst of the porphyriac diseases made people so vulnerable to light that they developed huge sores as parts of their flesh eroded away. They might lose their noses or their lips or patches of their cheeks. They would look grotesque.

That was interesting, but it awakened no memories in me. After all, I had already proved that if I were badly burned or wounded, I would heal.

There were river-borne microorganisms that caused people to develop problems with their memories just as there were microorganisms that could cause people to look hideous and, in the past perhaps, be mistaken for vampires. But that had nothing to do with me either. Whoever and whatever I was, no one seemed to be writing about my kind. Perhaps my kind did not want to be written about.

I wandered from site to site, picking up more bits of interesting, but useless, information. Finally, I switched to hunting through information about recent fires. I found a couple of articles that probably referred to what I was coming to think of as "my fire."

They said the houses had been abandoned. The fire had happened three weeks ago and had definitely been arson. Gasoline had been splashed about liberally, then set alight. Fortunately, the fire had not spread to the surrounding forest—as it probably would have if the houses had truly been abandoned. There would have been plenty of bushes, vines, grasses, and young trees to carry the fire straight into the woods. Instead, there had been a broad clearing around the houses, and there had been farm fields, stubbly and bare.

The houses had not been abandoned. I was not wrong about the scents of burned flesh that I had found here and there in them. Those houses were close to the cave where I had awakened. I had gone straight to them from the cave as though my body knew where it was going even though my memory was gone. I must have either been living in one of those houses or visiting one. And there had definitely been other people around at the time of the fire. Why would the articles deny this?

Wright had said we could go back to the ruin on the weekend. According to the computer, today was Thursday. The weekend was only a day away.

I wanted to go back now, on foot, and comb through the ruin again. I was more alert and aware now. My body had finished healing. Maybe I could find something.

But it was daytime, almost noon. I felt tired from all my running around the night before and stiff from sitting for hours at the computer. I turned it off, got up, and decided to soak for a while in the tub before I went to bed. That may have been a mistake. Someone knocked on the door while I was filling the tub. I turned the water off, afraid they'd already heard it, afraid they would know someone was in the cabin when it was supposed to be empty.

The knock came again, and a woman's voice called out, "Wright? Are you home?"

I kept quiet. After a while, I heard her go away. I soaked nervously in the water I had already drawn and went to bed.

When Wright got home—long after sunset—he brought groceries, an "everything" pizza, a library book about vampires written by an anthropologist, and some clothing for me. There were two pairs of jeans, four T-shirts, socks, underwear, a pair of Reebok athletic shoes, and a jacket with a hood. Everything except the shoes was a little big. Somehow he'd gotten shoes that were just the right size. He'd held each of my feet in his hands, and that must have helped. And he'd bought a belt. That would keep the jeans up. The rest of it worked fine even though it was a little large.

"You're even smaller than I thought," he said. "I'm usually pretty good at estimating the size of things I've seen and handled."

"I'm lean," I said. "I feed on blood most of the time. I don't think I could get fat."

"Probably not." He stowed the groceries in his refrigerator, then turned and looked at me. "My neck is completely healed."

"I thought it would be."

"I mean, no scar. Nothing. No scar on my hand, either."

I went to him and looked for myself. "Good," I said when I had seen. "I don't want to leave you all scarred. How do you feel?"

"Fine. I thought I might feel a little weak, like I did when I donated blood, but I'm fine. I don't think you took very much."

"I think I probably took more than I should have from you yesterday. Who did you donate blood to?"

"Friend of mine was in a car wreck. They saved him, but he lost a lot of blood."

"He took blood from you?"

"No, nothing like that. He . . . do you know what a transfusion is?"

I thought about it and then realized that I did know. "In the hospital, blood was sent from a container directly into your friend's veins."

"That's right, but it wasn't my blood. He and I aren't even the same blood type. I just gave to offset a little of what he had used." He bent, picked me up, and kissed me. "It isn't nearly as much fun as what you do."

I had already found that I enjoyed any skin-to-skin contact with him. For a few moments, I gave myself up to that enjoyment. Then, reluctantly, I drew back. "Someone was here today," I said. "A woman came to the door while I was filling the tub for a bath. I think she heard the water running. She knocked and called your name."

"Older woman?" he asked.

"I couldn't see her."

"My aunt, maybe. My aunt and uncle live in the big house out front." He gestured toward the front of the cabin with the arm that wasn't holding me. Then he put me down. "You probably saw it last night. They had company so it was all lit up."

"Can she get in here? Does she have a key?"

"Yeah. My uncle does anyway. But they don't snoop. I think you'll be okay in here."

I wasn't so sure, but I let it go. If the woman ever came into the cabin while Wright was at work, I would bite her. Then she would accept my being here, keep it secret, feed me, and then maybe help me find some of the answers I was looking for.

"I'm glad we're going back to the site of the fire this weekend," I said. "I found articles that said the place was abandoned and that vandals set it afire."

"Good work," he said. "I thought you'd find something online."

"But why would it say that?" I demanded. "I'm sure it wasn't abandoned. In fact, I'm pretty sure I was there. It was close to the cave where I woke up and not really close to anything else."

He thought about that, then shook his head. "I found articles at the library that said the same thing," he said. "They were from two small newspapers in the area. The reporters wouldn't have any reason to lie."

I shook my head. "If I can find them, I can get them to tell me why they lied. But first I want to go to the ruin. I'm connected with that place somehow. I'm sure I am. And Wright, the clothing I was wearing when you found me, I got it at one of the burned houses. It had been folded and put away . . . maybe in a drawer or on a shelf. When I found it, it was at the bottom of a big pile of half-charred clothing, and it had only been burned a little. Why should an abandoned house have piles of clean, folded clothing in it?"

Wright nodded. "I'll take you back there then," he said. "Saturday?"

"Friday night." I stood on tiptoe and still could not reach him. I was annoyed for once that he was so tall, but he picked me up again and held me against him. I bit him a little at the base of his throat, drew a few drops of blood. It wasn't necessary, but we both enjoyed it. He stood still, holding me, letting me lick at the wound.

After a while, he sighed. "Okay, Friday. Are you going to let me eat my pizza while it's hot?"

I licked once more, then pulled away from him reluctantly and slid down his body. "Eat," I said, and picked up the vampire book. "I'll read and wait for you."

The book was interesting but not that helpful. Many cultures seemed to have folklore about vampires of one kind or another.

Some could hypnotize people by staring at them. Some read and controlled people's thoughts. It would be handy to be able to do things like that. Easier than biting them and waiting for the chemicals in my saliva to do their work.

Not all vampires drank blood according to the book. Some ate flesh either from the living or from the dead. Some took in a kind of spiritual essence or energy—whatever that meant. All took something from their subjects, usually not caring how they injured the subject. Many killed their subjects. Many were dead themselves, but magically reanimated by the blood, flesh, or energy they took. One feeding usually meant the taking of one life. And that made no sense, at least for those who took blood. Who could need that much blood? Why kill a person who would willingly feed you again and again if you handled them carefully? No wonder vampires in folklore were feared, hated, and hunted.

Then my thoughts drifted back to the man I had killed at the cave. I killed and fed as viciously as any fictional vampire. I ate a man without ever recognizing him as a man. I'd not yet read of a vampire doing that, but I had done it.

Did others of my kind do such things? Had I done such a thing before? Had someone found out about us and tried to kill us back at the ruin? That would seem almost . . . just. But what about the other people who had been at the ruin? Had they been like Wright or like me? Had the ruin been a nest of vampires? I could still remember the scents I had found here and there around the ruin where flesh had been burned. Now I tried to sort through them, understand who was who.

After a while, I understood that some of them had been like me and some like Wright—vampires and other people living and dying together. What did that mean?

Wright got up, came to stand beside me, and took the book out of my hands. He laid it open, its pages facedown on the table. "I think I'm strong enough to take you on now," he said.

Perhaps he was, but I took only a few drops more of his blood while I enjoyed sex with him. It seemed necessary to take small amounts of his blood often. I felt a need for it that was something beyond hunger. It was a need for his blood specifically. No one else's. I took it slowly and gave him as much pleasure as I could. In fact, I took delight in leaving him pleasurably exhausted.

I went out later when Wright was asleep and took a full meal from Theodora. She was smaller and older than Wright, and she would probably feel a little weak tomorrow, tired perhaps.

"What work do you do?" I asked her when she looked ready to drift off to sleep.

"I work for the county library," she said. Then she laughed. "It doesn't pay very well, but I enjoy it." And then, as though my question had opened the door for her to talk to me, she said, "I didn't think you were real. I thought I'd dreamed you."

"I could be just a dream," I said. I stroked her shoulder and licked the bite. I wondered what work was done in libraries, then knew. I had been in libraries. I had memories of rooms filled with books. Theodora worked with books and with people who used books.

"You're a vampire," she said, breaking into my thoughts.

"Am I?" I went on licking her bite.

"Are you going to kill me?" she asked as though she didn't care what the answer might be. And there was no tension in her.

"Of course not. But you shouldn't go to work tomorrow. You might be a little weak."

"I'll be all right. I don't like to take time off."

"Yes, you will be all right. Stay home tomorrow."

She said nothing for a moment. She moved restlessly against me, moved away, then came back, accepting again, at ease. "All right. Will you come back to me again? Please come back."

"In a week, maybe."

"That long?"

"I want you healthy."

She kissed me. After a moment of surprise, I kissed her back. I held her, and she seemed very comfortable in my arms.

"Be real," she said. "Please be real."

"I'm real," I told her. "Sleep now. I'm real, and I'll come to you again. Sleep."

She went to sleep, happily fitted against me, one arm over and around me. I lay with her a few moments, then slipped free and went home to Wright's cabin.

On Friday evening after dark, Wright drove me back along the road where he had found me. The road was almost as empty on Friday as it had been when I walked it, barefoot and soaking wet. One or two cars every now and then. At least it wasn't raining tonight.

"I picked you up near here," Wright said.

I looked around and couldn't make out much beyond his headlights. "Pull off the road when you can and turn your lights off," I said.

"You can see in the dark like a cat, can't you?" he asked.

"I can see in the dark," I said. "I don't know anything about cats so I can't compare myself to them."

He found a spot where there was room to pull completely off the road and park. There, he stopped and turned off his headlights. Across the road from us there was a hillside and, on our side of the road, a steep slope downward toward a little creek. This was a heavily wooded area, although there was a clear-cut area not far behind us.

"We're not far from the national forest," he said. "We're running parallel to it. Does anything look familiar?"

"Nothing yet," I said. I got out of the car and looked down into the trees, letting my eyes adjust to the darkness.

I had walked this road. I began to walk it now, backtracking. After a while, Wright began to follow me in the car. He didn't turn his lights on but seemed to have no trouble seeing me. I began to jog, always looking around, knowing that at some point it would be time for me to turn off onto a side road and go down into the woods.

I jogged for several minutes, then, on impulse, began to run. Wright followed until finally I spotted the side road that led to the ruin. I turned but he didn't.

When he didn't follow, I stopped and waited for him to realize he'd lost me. It seemed to take a surprisingly long time. Finally, the car came back, lights on now, driving slowly. Then he spotted me, and I beckoned to him to turn. Once he had turned, I went to the car and got in.

"I didn't even see this road," he said. "I had no idea where you'd gone. Do you know you were running about fifteen miles an hour?"

"I don't know what that means," I said.

"I suspect it means you should try out for the Olympic Games. Are you tired?"

"I'm not. It was a good run, though. What are the Olympic Games?"

"Never mind. Probably too public for you. For someone your size, though, that was a fantastic run."

"It was easier than running down a deer."

"Where are we going? Don't let me pass the place."

"I won't." I not only watched, I opened my window and smelled the air. "Here," I said. "This little road coming up."

"Private road," Wright said. "Open the gate for me, would you?"

I did, but the gate made me think for a moment. I had not opened a gate going out. I had climbed over it. It wasn't a real barrier. Anyone could climb it or walk around it or open it and drive through.

Wright drove through, and I closed the gate and got back into the car. Just a few moments later, we were as close to the ruin as it was safe to drive. There were places where rubble from the houses lay in the road, and Wright said he wanted to be careful with his tires.

"This was a whole community," he said. "Plus a lot of land."

I led him around, showing him the place, choosing the easiest paths I could find, but I discovered that he couldn't see very well. The moon wasn't up yet, and it was too dark for him. He kept stumbling over the rubble, over stones, over the unevenness of the ground. He would have fallen several times had I not steadied him. He wasn't happy with my doing that.

"You're a hell of a lot stronger than you have any right to be," he said.

"I couldn't carry you," I said. "You're too big. So I need to keep you from getting hurt."

He looked down at me and smiled. "Somehow, I suspect you would find a way to carry me if you had to."

I laughed in spite of myself.

"You're pretty sure this was your home, then?"

I looked around. "I'm not sure, but I think it was. I don't remember. It's just a feeling." Then I stopped. I'd caught a scent that I hadn't noticed before, one that I didn't understand.

"Someone's been here," I said. "Someone . . ." I took a deep breath, then several small, sampling breaths. Then I looked up at Wright. "I don't know for sure, but I think it may have been someone like me."

"How can you tell?"

"I smell him. It's a different scent—more like me than like you even though he's male."

"You know he's male? You can tell that from a smell?"

"Yes. Males smell male. It isn't something I could miss. You smell male."

He looked uncomfortable. "Is that good or bad?"

I smiled. "I enjoy your scent. It reminds me of all sorts of good feelings."

He gave me a long, hungry look. "Go have the rest of your look-around on your own. You'll finish faster without me. Suddenly I want to get out of here. I'm eager to get back home."

"All right," I said. "We can go as soon as I find out about our visitor."

"This other guy, yeah." Suddenly, he sounded less happy.

"He may be able to tell me about myself, Wright. He may be my relative."

He nodded slowly. "Okay. When was he here?"

"Not that long ago. Last night I think. I need to know where he came from and where he went. Stay here. I won't go far, but I need to follow the scent."

"I think I'll come with you after all."

I put my hand on his arm. "You said you'd wait. Stay here, Wright."

He stared at me, clearly unhappy, but after a moment he nodded. "Watch yourself," he said.

I turned away from him and began to zigzag through the rubble until I felt I had the direction of the scent—the direction from which the man had come and in which he had gone. It was like a thread that drew me.

I followed it as quickly as I could to the opposite end of the ruin and beyond, through a stand of trees and on to a broad, open meadow. It ended there. I walked through the trees and into the meadow, confused, no longer understanding what I was looking for. I found marks on the ground, marks that were wrong for a car or a truck. There were two of them—long, narrow indentations too narrow and far apart to be tire marks. The word helicopter occurred to me suddenly, and I found that I knew what a helicopter was. I had a picture of one in my mind—clear bubble, rotor blades on top, metal structure sweeping back to the tail rotor, and two long runners instead of wheels. When had I ever seen such a thing?

Had a helicopter landed here, then? Had a man of my people gotten out and looked around the ruin, then gotten back into the copter and flown away?

That had probably happened. I couldn't think of any reason why it would be impossible.

Would he come back, then? Was he my relative? Had he been looking for me? Or had he had something to do with setting the fire?

If I had stayed in the area instead of wandering out to the highway and getting into Wright's car, I might have already been in contact with people who knew who I was, knew much more about me than I did. Or I might have been hurt again or killed.

I walked around where the copter had landed, looking to see whether anything had been dropped or thrown away. But there was nothing except that faint ghostly scent.

Then I caught another scent, fresh this time. Two scents. Another person—a male like Wright, but not Wright. And there was a gun of some kind. Where had the man come from? The wind—what there was of it—came to me from beyond where the helicopter had landed. That was how I had come to notice the scent of the first stranger. This new man must have passed me on his way to the ruin. If he had passed far enough away, I wouldn't have noticed, focused as I was on the helicopter and its occupant. But now I thought he must be somewhere near Wright. He and his gun must be somewhere near Wright.

I turned, ran back through the trees toward Wright. I spotted the man with the gun before I got near him. He was moving closer to Wright, not making himself known, watching Wright from hiding.

I meant to confront the man with the gun and perhaps take his gun away. I was intensely uncomfortable with his having it and being able to see Wright while Wright could not see him.

I saw him as I emerged from the trees. I saw him raise the gun —a rifle, long and deadly looking. He pointed it at Wright, and I was too far away to stop him. I ran flat out, as fast as I could.

I headed toward Wright and tried to put myself between him and the gun. I expected to be shot at any moment, but I had time to hit Wright in his midsection and knock him down, knock the air out of him just as the rifle went off. Then, with Wright safely on the ground, I went after the shooter.

He fired once more before I reached him, and this time, in spite of my speed, he hit me. An instant later, I hit him with my whole body. And while I could still think, while I was aware enough to be careful, I sank my teeth into his throat and took his blood—only his blood.

Six

I DIDN'T CARE whether I hurt or killed the gunman. I had knocked him unconscious when I hit him. Now I took his blood because he'd spilled mine, and because suddenly, I was in pain. Suddenly, I needed to heal. He was lucky I was aware enough not to take his flesh.

Moments later, I heard Wright's uneven steps coming toward me, and I was afraid. I went on taking the gunman's blood because it seemed to be the least harmful thing I could do at the moment.

I let the man go when Wright stood over us. I looked up at him then and, to my relief, did not in the slightest want to eat him. He stared at me, eyes wide.

"Are you shot?" he asked.

"My right leg," I said.

He was on his knees, lifting me, pulling my jeans down to examine my bloody leg. It hurt almost too much. I screamed, but I didn't harm him.

"I'm sorry," he said. "I'm so sorry. I thought you might be bleeding—losing too much blood." He hesitated. "Why aren't you bleeding more?"

"I don't ever bleed much."

"Oh." He stared at the wound. "That makes sense, I guess. Your body would know how to conserve blood if anyone's did. The bullet went all the way through. You have to go to a doctor now."

I shook my head. "I'll heal. I just need meat. Fresh meat."

He looked at the gunman. "It's a shame you can't eat him."

I stared down at him. "I can," I said. The gunman didn't wash himself often enough, but he was young and strong. His bite wound was already beginning to close. He wasn't going to die, even though I'd taken quite a bit more blood from him than I would from Wright or Theodora. If he had managed to shoot Wright, I would have made sure he died. "I can," I repeated. "But I really don't want to."

Wright smiled a little as though he thought I was joking. Then, still looking at the wound, he said, "Renee, you'll get an infection. There are probably all kinds of germs already crawling around in that wound and maybe pieces of your jeans, too. Look, I'll get you fresh meat if you'll just see a doctor."

"No doctor. I've been shot before. Some of the wounds I woke up with in the cave were bullet wounds. I need fresh meat and sleep, that's all. My body will heal itself."

There was a long silence. I lay where I was, feeling leaden, wanting to sleep. I had taken perhaps twice as much blood from the gunman as I would have dared to take from Wright or Theodora, and I still wasn't satisfied. I needed to sleep for a while, though, and let my body heal a little before I ate flesh.

The gunman would awaken thirsty and weak, maybe feeling sick.

And how did I know that?

It was one more sliver of memory, incomplete, but at least, this time, not useless.

"Shall I take you home?" Wright asked finally. "I can stop at the store for a couple of steaks."

I shook my head. "I don't want to be with you when I wake up. I'll be too hungry. I might hurt you."

"I don't think there's much chance of that," he said with just a hint of a smile.

He didn't understand. "I'm serious, Wright, I could hurt you. I . . . I might not be thinking clearly when I wake up."

"What do you want me to do?"

"Look around for a sheltered place here in the ruins. I'll need to be out of the sun when it comes up. You might have to heap some of the rubble up around me to make enough shade."

"You want me to leave you here? You want to spend . . . what, tonight and tomorrow out here?"

"I will spend tonight and tomorrow out here. Come back for me Sunday morning before sunrise."

"But there's no need—"

"Don't buy steaks unless you want them for yourself. I'll hunt. There are plenty of deer in the woods."

"Renee—!"

"Build a shelter," I said. "Put me in it. Then go home. Come back Sunday morning before sunrise."

There were several seconds of silence. Finally, he said, "What about this guy?" He nudged the gunman with his foot. "What do we do with him? Why did he want to shoot you anyway? Was it just because you scared him?"

"Me?" I said surprised. "He was aiming at you when I hit you. I couldn't reach him in time to stop him from shooting you. That's why I knocked you down—so he'd miss. Then I went after him."

He took a moment to absorb this. "God, I didn't know what the hell happened. What if he'd killed you?"

"He could have, I guess, but I didn't think he'd be fast enough. And he wasn't."

"He shot you!"

"Annoying," I said. "It really hurts. You'd better take his gun and keep it."

"Good idea." He picked it up.

"Find me a place that will be out of the sun. Otherwise, I'll have to heal a burn as well as a bullet wound."

He nodded. "Okay, but you haven't answered. What about him?" He nodded toward the gunman.

"I'll talk to him. I want to know why he tried to shoot you."

"You aren't afraid to have him here?"

"I don't want him here, but he's here. I'll try not to hurt him, but if I do, I do."

"When you're asleep, he might decide to finish what he started."

"He won't. As long as you've got his rifle, he can't."

"You bit him. That's why you aren't afraid of him, isn't it?"

"I'm afraid *for* him. I'm afraid I might not be able to stop myself from killing him."

"You know what I mean."

I did know what he meant. He was beginning to understand his relationship with me—as I had already begun to under-stand it. "Because I bit him, he'll obey me," I said. "He won't hurt me if I tell him not to."

He fingered the place where I'd last bitten him and stared down at me.

I took a deep breath. "I think you can still walk away from me, Wright, if you want to," I said. I wet my lips. "If you do it now, you can still go."

"Be free of you?" he asked.

"If you want to be free of me, yes. I'll even help you."

"Why? You want to get rid of me?"

"You know I don't."

"But you want to help me leave you?" He made it a flat statement, not a question.

"If that's what you want."

"Why?"

I took a deep breath, trying to stay alert. "Because I think . . . I think it would be wrong for me to keep you with me against your will."

"You think that, do you?" Again, it wasn't a real question. So I didn't bother to answer it.

"How?" he asked.

"What?"

"How can you help me leave you?"

"I can tell you to go. I think I can make it . . . maybe not comfortable, but at least possible for you to go and have your life back and just . . . forget about me."

"I didn't know what it would be like with you. I didn't know I would feel . . . almost as though I can't make it without you."

"I know." I closed my eyes in pain. "I didn't know what I was starting when I bit you the first couple of times. I didn't remember. I still don't remember much, but I know the bites tie you to me. That comforted me—that you were with me. But now, maybe you don't want to be with me. If that's what you've decided, tell me. Tell me now, and I'll try to help you go."

There was nothing from him for a long time. I felt as though I were drifting. My body wanted to go to sleep, demanded sleep, and somehow, I did doze a little. When he put his palm against my face, I jerked awake.

"I'm going to take you to one of the chimneys," he said. "I'll make a shelter for you there."

"If you want to go," I said, "you should tell me now." I paused. "I won't be able to stay awake long. And . . . Wright, if you don't take this chance, I don't think you'll be able to leave me. Ever. I won't be able to let you, and you couldn't stand separation from me. I know that much. Even now, it's probably hard for you to make the decision, but you should go if you want to go. It's all right."

"It's not all right," he said.

"Wright, it is. You should—"

"No!" He shook his head. "Don't tell me that. Do not tell me that!" He grasped my face between his hands, made me look at him.

"What shall I do?" I asked.

"I don't know. I don't want to lose you."

"Freedom, Wright. Now or never."

"I don't want to lose you. I truly don't. I've only known you for a few days, but I know I want you with me."

I kissed his hand, glad of his decision. It would have been hard to let him go—perhaps the hardest thing I could recall doing. I would have done it, but it would have been terrible. All I could do now was make things as safe as possible for both of us.

"Okay, then. Choose a good spot and build a shelter around me—something that won't let the sun in."

He walked around the ruin, stumbling and cursing now and then, but not falling. Eventually he found a reasonably intact little corner with two wall fragments still standing. That was better than a chimney because it was less of a potential trap. There was no part of it that I couldn't break through if I had to. It might once have been part of a closet. I drifted off to sleep while he was cleaning the debris out of it. I awoke again when he lifted me and put me in the corner.

Once I had found a comfortable position, he walled me in with stones, pieces of charred wood, tree branches, and pipe. After a while the little shelter he was building was perfect for keeping the sun out. When he finished, he reached in through the small opening he'd left and woke me up again.

"Go home," I told him, and before he could protest, I added, "Come back Sunday morning. I'll have found something to eat by then. Deer, rabbits, something."

"Just in case, I'll bring you a steak or two."

"All right." I wouldn't be wanting the steaks, but it had finally occurred to me that getting them and bringing them would make him feel better.

"What can we do to make you safer from this idiot?" he asked about the still-unconscious shooter.

"Take the gun. That will be enough."

"He could knock this shelter down at high noon while you're asleep."

"If he does that, I'll kill him. I'll have no choice. I'll get a nasty sunburn, and it will take me a little longer to heal, but that's the worst. Let me sleep, Wright."

I listened and heard him leave. He didn't want to, but he left.

Two or three hours later, the man who'd shot me finally woke up. He coughed several times and cursed. That's what woke me—the noise he made. Because I didn't dare confront him yet, I kept quiet. He got up, stumbled fell, then staggered away, his uneven steps fading as he moved away from me. He didn't seem to notice that his rifle was gone. And he didn't come near my little enclosure at all.

I slept through the rest of the night and the day. By the time the sun went down, I was starving—literally. My body had been hard at work repairing itself, and now it had to have food. I pushed away the wall of rubble that Wright had built and stood up. I was trembling with hunger as I fastened the jeans that Wright had pulled up after he examined my leg but had left loose for comfort. I took a few deep breaths, then first limped, then walked, then jogged off in the one direction I didn't smell human beings.

Hunting steadied me, focused me. And hunting was good because it meant I would eat soon.

I wound up eating most of someone's little nanny goat. I didn't mean to take a domestic animal, but it was all I found after hours of searching. It must have escaped from some farm. Better the goat than its owner.

Relieved and sated, I began hiking back toward the ruin to wait for Wright. Then I caught the scent of other people nearby. Farms. I had avoided them while I was hunting, but now I let myself take in the scents and sort them out, see whether I recognized any of them.

And I found the gunman.

It wasn't midnight yet—too early for Wright to have arrived. I had time to talk to the man who had caused me so much pain and nearly cost Wright his life. I turned toward the farm and began to jog.

I came out of the woods and ran through the farm fields toward the scent. It came from a one-story, gray farmhouse with a red roof. That meant I might be able to go straight into the room where the gunman was snoring. There were three other people in the house, so I would have to be careful. At least everyone was asleep.

I found a window to the gunman's bedroom, but it was closed and locked. I could think of no way to open it quietly. The doors were also locked. I went around the house and found no open door or window. I could get into the house easily, but not quietly.

I went back to the gunman's bedroom window—a big window. I pulled my jacket sleeve down over my hand and closed my hand around the sleeve opening so that my fist was completely covered. This was made easier by the fact that the jacket, like the rest of my clothing, was a little too big. With one quick blow, I broke the window near where I saw the latch. Then I ducked below the windowsill and froze, listening. If people were alerted by the noise, I wanted to know at once.

There was no change in anyone's breathing except the gunman's. His snoring stopped, then began again. I waited, not wanting there to be too many alien sounds too close together. Then I reached in, turned the window latch, and raised the window. The window opened easily, silently. I stepped in and closed it after me.

At that point, the man in the bed stopped snoring again. The colder air from outside had probably roused him.

As quickly as I could, I crossed the room to the bed, turned his face to the pillow, grabbed his hands, dropped my weight onto him, and bit him.

He bucked and struggled, and I worried that if he kept it up, he would either buck me off or force me to break his bones. But I had already bitten him once. He should be ready to listen to me.

"Be still," I whispered, "and be quiet."

And he obeyed. He lay still and silent while I took a little more of his blood. Then I sat up and looked around. His door was closed, but there were people in the room next to his. I had heard their breathing when I was outside—two people. On the other hand, because his closet and theirs separated the two rooms, I could barely hear them now. Maybe they wouldn't hear us.

"Sit up and keep your voice low," I said to the gunman. "What's your name?"

He put his hand to his neck. "What did you do?" he whispered.

"What's your name?" I repeated.

"Raleigh Curtis."

"Who else is in this house?"

"My brother. My sister-in-law. Their kid."

"So is this their house?"

"Yeah. I got laid off my job, so they let me stay here."

"All right. Why did you shoot me, Raleigh?"

He squinted, trying to see me in the dark, then reached for his bedside lamp.

"No," I said. "No light. Just talk to me."

"I didn't know what you were," he said. "You just shot out of nowhere. I thought you were some kind of wild cat." He paused. "Hey, do that thing again on my neck."

I shrugged. Why not? He would definitely be sick the next day, but I didn't care. I took a little more of his blood while he lay back trembling and writhing and whispering over and over, "Oh my God, oh my God, oh my God."

When I stopped, he begged, "Do it some more. Jesus, that's the best feeling I've ever had in my life."

"No more now," I said. "Talk to me. You said you shot me because I scared you."

"Yeah. Where'd you come from like that?"

"Why were you aiming your rifle at the man? He didn't scare you."

"Had to."

"Why?"

He frowned and rubbed his head. "Had to."

"Tell me why."

He hesitated, still frowning. "He was there. He shouldn't have been there. It wasn't his property."

"It wasn't yours either." This was only a guess, but it seemed reasonable.

"He shouldn't have been there."

"Why was it your job to drive him off or kill him?"

Silence.

"Tell me why." After three bites, he should have been eager to tell me. Instead, he almost seemed to be in pain.

He held his head between his hands and whimpered. "I can't tell you," he said. "I want to, but I can't. My head hurts."

Something occurred to me suddenly. "Did you see the man in the helicopter?"

He put his face into the pillow, whimpering. "I saw him," he said, his voice muffled, barely understandable.

"When did he come? Thursday night?"

He looked up at me, gray-faced, and rubbed his neck, not where I had bitten him, but on the opposite side. "Yeah. Thursday."

"Did he see you, talk to you?"

He moaned, face twisted in pain. He seemed to be about to cry. "Please don't ask me. I can't say. I can't say."

The man, the male of my kind, had found him, bitten him, and ordered him to guard the ruin and not tell anyone why he was doing it. But what was there to guard? What was there to shoot a person over?

In spite of myself, I began to feel sorry for Raleigh. His head probably did hurt. He was torn between obeying me and obeying the man from the helicopter. That kind of thing wasn't supposed to happen. Just thinking about it made me intensely uncomfortable, and, of course, I didn't know why. I waited, hoping to remember more. But there was no more, except that I began to feel ashamed of myself, began to feel as though I owed Raleigh an apology.

"Raleigh."

"Yeah?"

"It's all right. I won't ask you about the man in the helicopter any more. It's all right."

"Okay." He looked as though he hadn't taken a breath for too long, and now, suddenly, he could breathe again. He also looked like he was no longer in pain.

"I want to meet the man in the helicopter," I said. "If he comes to you again, I want you to tell him about me."

"Tell him what?"

"Tell him I bit you. Tell him I want to meet him. Tell him I'll come back to the burned houses next Friday night. And tell him I didn't know that you . . . that you knew him. If he asks you any questions about me, it's okay to answer. All right?"

"Yeah. What's your name?"

Good question. "Don't bother about a name. Describe me to him. I think he'll know. And don't tell anyone else about either of us. Make up lies if you have to."

"Okay."

I started to get up, but he caught my hand. Then he let it go. "That thing you did," he said, touching the spot I'd bitten. "That was really good."

"It will probably make you feel weak and sick for a while," I said. "I'm sorry for that. You'll be all right in a couple of days."

"Worth it," he said.

And I left feeling better, feeling as though he'd forgiven me. Whoever I was before, it seemed I had had strong beliefs about what was right and what wasn't. It wasn't right to bite someone who had already been claimed by another of my kind. Certainly it hadn't been all right to drain Raleigh to the point of sickness when he wasn't truly responsible for shooting me. Why on earth would one of my own people take the chance of being responsible for a pointless shooting, perhaps even a death?

I jogged back toward the ruin. Eight chimneys, much burned rubble, a few standing timbers and remnant walls. That's what was left. Why did it need guarding? The guarding should have come before the fire when it might have done some good.

Finally, I jogged over to the unblocked part of the private road, coming out where Wright and I had parked the night before. I heard him coming—heard him stop down at the gate, then start again. I waited, making sure it was his car and not some stranger's. The moment I recognized the car and caught his scent, I could hardly wait to see him. The instant he stopped the car, I pulled the passenger door open and slid inside.

He was there, smelling worried and nervous. And somehow he didn't see me until I was sitting next to him, closing the door.

He jumped, then grabbed me and yanked me into a huge hug.

I found myself laughing as he examined me, checked my leg, then the rest of me. "I'm fine," I said, and kissed him and felt alarmingly glad to see him. "Let's go home," I said at last. "I want a hot bath, and then I want you."

He held me in his lap, and I was surprised that he had managed to move me there without my realizing it. "Anytime," he said. "Now, if you like."

I kissed his throat. "Not now. Let's go home."

Seven

A WEEK LATER, we went back to the ruin.
I wanted Wright to park the car beside the gate to the private road. I thought it would be safest for him to stay with the car while I went in alone. But I had told him the little that Raleigh Curtis had told me, and Wright was adamant. He was going with me.

"You don't know what this guy will do," he said. "What if he just grabs you and takes you away with him? Hell, what if he's the one who torched those houses to begin with?"

"He's of my kind," I said. "Even if he doesn't know anything about me, he'll probably know someone who does. Or at least he can tell me about my people. I have to know who I am, Wright, and what I am."

"Then I have to go with you," he said. "And I think I'd better take my nice new rifle along."

I had not made any effort to get Raleigh Curtis's rifle back to him. If he didn't have it, he couldn't shoot some exploring stranger with it. Wright had kept the gun and had gone out and bought bullets for it.

"This guy is a man of your kind," he told me. "An adult male who is probably a lot bigger and stronger than you. I'm telling you, Renee, he might just decide to do what he wants with you no matter what you want."

He was afraid of losing me, afraid this other man would take me from him. He might be right. And he was probably right in thinking that the man would be bigger and stronger than I was.

That last possibility was enough to make me want Wright to stay with me and keep the gun handy. We left his cabin well before sunset because he wanted to get a look at the ruin in something more than starlight. To be sure he would be able to see well, he took along a flashlight zipped in his jacket pocket —the pocket that wasn't full of bullets.

With my jeans, my shirt, and my hooded jacket, I was reasonably well covered up so I didn't mind the daylight. It was a gray day anyway, with rain threatening but not yet falling. That kind of light was much easier on my eyes than direct sunlight.

"He won't be there yet," I told Wright as he drove. "If he's coming, he'll show up after sundown."

"If?" Wright asked.

"Maybe Raleigh didn't see him and couldn't pass along my message. Maybe he's not interested in meeting me. Maybe he had something else to do."

"Maybe you're getting nervous about meeting him," Wright said.

I was, so I didn't answer.

"You should have gotten Raleigh's phone number. Then you could have called and asked him if he'd passed on your message."

"He might not tell me," I said. "I'm not sure I'd trust him to tell me the truth on the phone." I stopped suddenly and turned to face him. "Wright . . . listen, if this guy bites you, you tell him whatever he wants to know. Do that, okay?"

He shook his head. "I don't think I'll be letting him bite me."

"But if he does. If he does."

"Okay." And after a moment, "You don't want me to suffer like Raleigh did, is that it?"

"I don't want you to suffer."

He gave me a strange little smile. "That's good to know."

We went on for a few minutes, then turned down the side road. By the time we reached the gate, we should have been close enough to the ruin for me to get a good scent picture of it, if only the wind had been blowing toward us.

"Wait here," I said when we reached the gate. "I'm going to make sure Raleigh or someone else isn't waiting for us with another gun."

He grabbed me around the waist. "Whoa," he said. "You don't need to be shot again."

I was half out of the car, but I stopped and turned back toward him into his arms. "I'll circle around and get whatever scents there are," I said. "Stay here. Don't make noise unless you need help." And I slipped away from him.

I ran around the area, stopping now and then, trying to hear, see, and scent everything. As I expected, there was no helicopter yet. Raleigh had not been near the place recently. Someone else had, but I didn't recognize his scent. It was a young man, not of my kind, not carrying a gun. But he wasn't there now. No one was there now.

I went back to the gate where I'd left Wright and managed to surprise him again. He'd gotten out of the car and was leaning against the gate.

"Good God, woman!" he said when I caught his arm. "Make some noise when you walk."

I laughed. "No one's there. This whole night might turn out to be a waste of time, but let's go in anyway."

We got back into the car and drove in. At the ruin, we spent our time looking through the rubble and finding a few unburned or partially burned things: a pen, forks and spoons, a pair of scissors, a small jar of buttons . . . I recognized everything I found until I discovered a small silver-colored thing on the ground near where Wright had piled burned wood to wall me into my shelter. It must have been under the wood that I had pushed aside when I broke out.

"It's a crucifix," Wright told me when I showed it to him. "It must have been worn by one of the people who lived here. Or maybe the arsonist lost it." He gave a humorless smile. "You never know who's liable to turn out to be religious."

"But what is it?" I asked. "What's a crucifix? I kept running across that word when I was reading about vampires, but none of the writers ever explained what it was except to say that it scared off vampires."

He put it back into my hand. "This one's real silver, I think. Does it bother you to hold it?"

"It doesn't. It's a tiny man stuck to a tiny "†"-shaped thing. And there's a loop at the top. I think it used to be attached to something."

"Probably a chain," he said. "Another perfectly good vampire superstition down the drain."

"What?"

"This is a religious symbol, Renee—an important one. It's supposed to hurt vampires because vampires are supposed to be evil. According to every vampire movie I've ever seen, you should not only be afraid of it but it should burn your skin if it touches you."

"It isn't hot."

"I know, I know. Don't worry about it. It's just movie bullshit." He went to look around the chimneys and examine broken, discolored remains of water heaters, sinks, bathtubs, and refrigerators. As I looked around, I realized that some of the houses were missing sinks and tubs, and I wondered. Perhaps people had come here when Raleigh wasn't on guard and taken them away. Or perhaps Raleigh and his relatives had taken them. But why? Who would want such things?

Then Wright found something outside the houses more than half buried in the ground near one of the chimneys: a gleaming gold chain with a little gold bird attached to it—a crested bird with wings spread as though it were flying.

"I'm surprised something like this is still here," he said. "I'll bet plenty of people have been through here, picking up souvenirs." He wiped the thing on his shirt, then let it slide like liquid into my hand.

"Pretty," I said, examining it.

"Let me put it on you."

I thought about whether I wanted the property of a person who was probably dead around my neck, but then shrugged, handed it back to him, and let him put it on me. He wanted to. And he seemed to like the effect once it was on.

"Your hair is growing out," he said. "This is just what you need to decorate yourself a little."

My hair was growing out, crinkly and black and about an inch long, and my head was no longer disfigured by broken places. I'd had Wright trim the one patch of hair that hadn't been burned off so that now it was all growing out fairly evenly. I thought I almost looked female again.

"Did you ever think I was a boy?" I asked him. "I mean when you stopped for me on the road that first time?"

"No, I never did," he said. "I should have, I guess. You were almost bald and wearing filthy, ill-fitting clothes that could have been a man's. But when I first saw you in the headlights, I thought, 'What a lovely, elfin little girl. What in hell is she doing out here by herself?'"

"Elfin?"

"Like an elf. According to some stories, an elf is a short, slender, magical being—another mythical creature. Maybe I'll run into one of them on a dark road someday."

I laughed. Then I heard the helicopter. "He's coming," I said. "It's early for him to be awake and out. He must be eager to meet me."

"I don't hear a thing," Wright said, "but I'll take your word for it. Shall I get out of sight?"

"No. You couldn't hide your scent from him. Let's wait over by that largest chimney." It was a big brick chimney that rose from a massive double fireplace. It might shelter us if our visitor decided to try to shoot us.

The copter didn't bother about landing in the meadow this time. I wondered why he had landed there before. Habit? Or was this stranger someone who would have come to visit the eight houses when they were intact and occupied?

The copter, looking like a large, misshapen bug, landed in what Wright said must have once been a big vegetable garden. He had been able to identify several of the scorched, mostly dead plants. The copter crushed a number of the survivors—cabbages and potatoes mostly.

The pilot jumped out, ducked under the rotors, and looked around. Once he spotted us, he came straight toward us. Wright, who had been checking the rifle, now stood straight, watching the stranger intently. I watched him, too. He was a tall, spidery man, empty-handed, and visibly my kind except that he was blond and very pale-skinned—not just light-skinned like Wright, but as white as the pages of Wright's books. Even so, apart from color, if I ever grew tall, I would look much like him—tall and lean, probably not elfin at all.

"Shori?" the man asked. I liked his voice at once, and he smelled . . . safe somehow. I mean his scent made me feel safe, although I couldn't say why. Then I realized that he was looking at me, had spoken to me. And what had he meant by that one word?

I stood away from the chimney.

"How did you survive, Shori? Where have you been?"

He was calling me "Shori." I let out a breath. "You know me, then," I said.

"Of course I do! What's the matter with you?"

I breathed a little more, trying to decide what to say. The truth seemed humiliating, somehow, admitting such a significant weakness to this stranger, telling him that I knew nothing at all about myself. But what else could I do? I said, "I woke up weeks ago in a cave not far from here. I have no memory of anything that happened before then. And . . . I don't know you."

He reached out to me, but I stepped back out of his reach.

"I don't know you," I repeated.

Off to one side, I saw Wright come to attention. He didn't point the rifle at the stranger, he pointed it downward. He held it across his body in both hands, his right forefinger near the trigger, so that aiming it at the man would only be a matter of moving it slightly.

The man dropped his hand to his side. He glanced at Wright, then seemed to dismiss him. "My name is Iosif Petrescu," he said. "I'm your father."

I stood staring at him, feeling nothing for him. I didn't know him. And yet he might be telling the truth. How could I know? Would he lie about such a thing? Why?

"And I'm . . . Shori?"

"The name your human mother gave you is Shori. Your surname is Matthews. Your Ina mothers were distant relatives of mine named Mateescu, but in the 1950s, when there was a great deal of suspicion about foreign-sounding names, they decided to Anglicize the name to Matthews."

"My mothers . . . ?"

He looked around at the rubble. "Listen," he said. "We don't have to talk here in the midst of all this. Come to my home."

"I lived . . . here?"

"You did, yes. You were born here. Doesn't this setting stir any memories?"

"No memories. Only a feeling that I'm somehow connected to this place. I came here when I was able to leave the cave where I woke up, but I didn't know why. It was as though my feet just brought me here."

"Home," he said. "For you, this was home."

I nodded. "But you don't live here?"

He looked surprised. "No. We don't live males and females together as humans do."

I swallowed, then asked the question I had to ask: "What are we?"

"Vampires, of course—not that we call ourselves by that name." He smiled, showing his very human-looking teeth, except for the canines, which looked a little longer and sharper than the other people's, as my own did. If his teeth were like mine, they were all sharper than other people's. They had to be. He said, "We have very little in common with the vampire creatures Bram Stoker described in *Dracula*, but we are long-lived blood drinkers." He looked at Wright. "You knew what she was, didn't you?"

Wright nodded. "I knew she needed blood to live."

Iosif sighed, then spoke wearily as though he were saying something he had to say too many times before. "We live alongside, yet apart from, human beings, except for those humans who become our symbionts. We have much longer lives than humans. Most of us must sleep during the day and, yes, we need blood to live. Human blood is most satisfying to us, and fortunately, we don't have to injure the humans we take it from. But we are born as we are. We can't magically convert humans into our kind. We do keep those who join with us healthier, stronger, and harder to kill than they would be without us. In that way, we lengthen their lives by several decades."

That got Wright's attention. "How long?" he asked.

"How long will you live?"

"Yes."

Iosif took a deep breath, then said, "Barring accident or homicide, chances are you'll live to be between 170 and 200 years old."

"Two hundred . . . I will? Healthy years?"

"Yes. Your immune system will be greatly strengthened by Shori's venom, and it will be less likely to turn on you and give you one of humanity's many autoimmune diseases. And her venom will help keep your heart and circulatory system healthy. Your health is important to her."

"Sounds too good to be true."

"It is mutualistic symbiosis. You know you're joined with her."

Wright nodded. "It scares me a little. I want to be with her, need to be with her, even though I don't really understand what I'm getting into." After a moment, he asked, "How long do your kind live?"

"Long," Iosif said. "Although we're not immortal any more than you are. How old do you think your Shori is?"

"I've been calling her Renee," he said. "I'm Wright Hamlin, by the way."

"How old is she?"

"I thought she was maybe ten or eleven when I met her. Later, I knew she had to be older, even though she didn't look it. Maybe eighteen or nineteen?"

Iosif smiled without humor. "That would make things legal at least."

Wright's face went red, and I looked from him to Iosif, not understanding.

"Don't worry, Wright," Iosif said after a moment. "In fact, Shori is a child. She has at least one more important growth stage to go through before she's old enough to bear children. Her child-bearing years will begin when she's about seventy. In all, she should live about five hundred years. Right now, she's fifty-three."

Wright opened his mouth, but didn't say anything. He just stared, first at Iosif, then at me. I knew that Wright was twenty-three, sexually mature, and aware of much that went on in the world. If Iosif was telling the truth, I was almost twice Wright's age, and yet I knew almost nothing. Someone had taken away most of my fifty-three years of life.

"Who did this?" I asked, gesturing at the ruin. "Who set the fire? Did anyone else survive?"

"I wasn't here," Iosif said. "I don't know who did it. And I haven't found . . . any other survivors. I've arranged for the other people who live in this area to keep their eyes open."

That got my attention. "You were careless. Raleigh Curtis wasn't just keeping his eyes open. He was going to shoot Wright. He did shoot me."

"Accident. He didn't know you were one of us. If he'd seen you clearly, he wouldn't have fired."

"Why would he want to shoot Wright?"

"He didn't know Wright was with you."

"Iosif, why shoot anyone over this rubble? Only the people who did this should be punished."

He stared at me. "Someone burned your mothers and your sisters as well as all of the human members of your family to death here. They shot the ones who tried to get out, shot them and threw most of them back into the fire. How you escaped, I have no idea, but we found the others, burned, broken . . . My people and I found them. We were coming for a visit, and we actually arrived before the firemen, which meant we were able to get control of them and see to it that they recalled this place as abandoned. When the fire was out, we cleaned up and covered up because we didn't want the remains examined by the coroner. We searched the area for several nights, hunting for survivors and questioning the local humans, finding out what they knew and seeing to it that they only remembered things that wouldn't expose or damage us. In fact, the neighbors didn't know anything. So we didn't catch the killers. We thought, though, that some of them might come back to enjoy remembering what they'd done. Criminals have done that in the past."

"To enjoy the memory of killing . . . How many people?" I demanded.

"Seventy-eight. Everyone except you."

I wet my lips, looked away from him, remembering the cave. "Maybe only seventy-seven," I said. I wanted badly not to say it, but somehow, not saying it would have made me feel even worse.

Iosif touched me, put his hand on my chin and turned my head so that I faced him. He or someone else had done that before. It felt familiar and steadying. He had straight, collar-length white-blond hair framing his sharp, narrow face and large gray eyes with their huge dark-adapted pupils. He still didn't look familiar. I didn't know him. But his touch no longer alarmed me.

I said, "Someone found me as I was waking up in the cave. I don't know how long I'd been there. Several days, at least. But finally, I was regaining consciousness, and someone found me. I didn't know at the time that it was . . . a person, a man. I didn't know anything except . . . I killed him." I couldn't bring myself to say the rest—that I'd not only killed the man, but eaten him. It shamed me so much that I moved my face away from his fingers, took a step back from him. "I still don't know who he was, but I remember the sounds he made. I heard them clearly, although at the time I didn't even recognize what he said as speech. Later, when I was safe with Wright, I was able to sort through the memories and understand what he said. I think he knew me. I think he'd been looking for me."

"What did he say?" Wright asked. He had moved closer to me.

It was terrible that he was hearing this. I shut my eyes for a moment, then answered his question. "He said, 'Oh my God, it's her. Please let her be alive.'"

There was silence.

Iosif sighed, then nodded. "He wasn't from here, Shori, he was from my community."

I looked at him and saw his sorrow. He knew who the man was, and he mourned him. I shook my head. "I'm sorry."

To my surprise, Wright pulled me against him. I leaned on him gratefully.

"I sent my people out to hunt," Iosif said. "We thought you would have survived, if anyone did. Only one of my men didn't come back from the search. We never found him. Where is your cave?"

I turned to look around, then described as best I could where the cave was. "I can take you there," I said.

Iosif nodded. "If his remains are still there, I'll have them collected and buried."

"I'm sorry," I repeated, my voice not much more than a whisper.

He stared at me, first with anger and grief, then, it seemed, only with sorrow. "You are, aren't you? I'm glad of that. You've forgotten who and what you are, but you still have at least some of the morality you were taught."

After a while, Wright asked, "Why did you think she had a better chance of surviving?"

"Her dark skin," Iosif said. "The sun wouldn't disable her at once. She's a faster runner than most of us, in spite of her small size. And she would have come awake faster when everything started. She's a light sleeper, compared to most of us, and she doesn't absolutely have to sleep during the day."

"She said she thought she was an experiment of some kind," Wright said.

"Yes. Some of us have tried for centuries to find ways to be less vulnerable during the day. Shori is our latest and most successful effort in that direction. She's also, through genetic engineering, part human. We were experimenting with genetic engineering well before humanity learned to do it—before they even learned that it was possible."

"We, who?" I asked.

"Our kind. We are Ina. We are probably responsible for much of the world's vampire mythology, but among ourselves, we are Ina."

The name meant no more to me than his face did. It was so hard to know nothing—absolutely nothing all the time. "I hate this," I said. "You tell me things, and I still don't feel as though I know them. They aren't real to me. What are we? Why are we different from human beings? Are we human beings? Are we just another race?"

"No. We're not another race, we're another species. We can't interbreed with them. We've never been able to do that. Sex, but no children."

"Are we related to them? Where do we come from?"

"I think we must be related to them," he said. "We're too genetically similar to them for any other explanation to be likely. Not all of us believe that, though. We have our own traditions—our own folklore, our own religions. You can read my books if you want to."

I nodded. "I'll read them. I wonder if they'll mean anything to me."

"You've probably suffered a severe head injury," Iosif said. "I've heard of this happening to us before. Our tissue regenerates, even our brain tissue. But memories . . . well, sometimes they return."

"And sometimes they don't."

"Yes."

"I know I had a head wound—more than one. The bones of my skull were broken, but they healed. How can we survive such things?"

He smiled. "There's a recently developed belief among some of our younger people that the Ina landed here from another world thousands of years ago. I think it's nonsense, but who knows. I suppose that idea's no worse than one of our oldest legends. It says we were placed here by a great mother goddess who created us and gave us Earth to live on until we became wise enough to come home to live in paradise with her. Actually, I think we evolved right here on Earth alongside humanity as a cousin species like the chimpanzee. Perhaps we're the more gifted cousin."

I didn't know what to think—or say—about any of that. "All right," I said. "You said the Ina people live in single-sex groups —men with men and women with women."

"Adults do, yes. Young males leave their mothers when they're a little older than you are now. They live the last years of their childhood and all of their adult years with their fathers. I'm the only surviving son of my father's family so my sons have only one father. Our human symbionts may be of either sex, but among us, sons live with brothers and fathers. Daughters live with their mothers and sisters. In a case like this, though, since you're not fully adult, you would be welcome to join my community for a while—until you get your memories back or relearn the things you need to know and until you come of age."

"I live with Wright."

"Bring him with you, of course, and any others you've come to need. I'll have a house built for you and yours."

I looked at Wright and was not surprised to see that he was shaking his head. "I have a job," he said. "Hell, I have a life. Renee . . . Shori will be all right with me."

Iosif stared at him with an expression I couldn't read. "And you will teach her about her people and their ways?" he said. "You'll teach her her history, and help her into the adulthood she is approaching? You'll help her find mates and negotiate with their family when the time comes?" He stood straight and gazed down at Wright. He wasn't that much taller than Wright, but he gave the impression of looking down from a great height. "Tell me how you will do these things," he said.

Wright glared at him, his expression flickering between anger and uncertainty. Finally, he looked away. After a moment, he shook his head. "Where?" he asked.

"A few miles north of Darrington."

"I'd want to keep my job."

"Of course. Why not?"

"It's a long way. We'd . . . have a house?"

"You'd be guests in my house until your house is finished. We're interested in keeping Shori safe and teaching her what she needs to know to get on with her life. You're already a greater part of her life than you realize."

"I want to be with her."

"I want you with her. But tell me, what's your life been like with her? What do your friends and neighbors think about your relationship with her?"

Wright opened his mouth, then closed it again. He stared at Iosif angrily.

Iosif nodded. "You've been hiding her. Of course you have —lest someone think you were having an improper relationship with a child. Once you're living with us, there will be no need to hide. And to us, there is nothing improper about your relationship."

Eight

THAT SAME night, Iosif flew Wright and me up to see the community that was to become our new home. As we arrived, we could see from the air five large, well-lit, two-story houses built along what was probably another private road. There were also two barns, several sheds and garages, animal pens, and fields and gardens, all a few miles north of the lights of a small town—Darrington, I assumed.

Iosif promised to fly Wright and me back to the ruin later that night so that we could pick up Wright's car and go back to his cabin. If things went as Iosif intended, we would move in a week. He gave us each a card that showed his address and phone numbers and that gave directions for driving to his community. He said he would send a truck and two people to help load Wright's things onto it. Anything that didn't fit in our temporary quarters could be stored in one of the barns until our house was ready.

"You live in such out-of-the-way places," Wright complained. "This is even more isolated than the other one. I'm going to have a hell of a commute. I don't know whether it's going to be possible."

Iosif ignored him. When we landed on a large paved area not far from the largest of the houses, he said, "You need to know that it's best to avoid cities. Cities overload our senses —the noise, the smells, the lights . . . They overload us in every possible way. Some of us get used to it, but others just get sick."

"That's a surprise," Wright said. "The movies I've seen and the books I've read say vampires like cities—that their large populations make it easy for vampires to be anonymous."

Iosif nodded. "Vampires in books and movies usually seem to be trying to kill people or trying to turn them into vampires. Since we don't do either of those things, we don't need cities. Fortunately." Iosif turned and jumped out of his side of the helicopter, while Wright slid out the other side, then reached in and lifted me out. Then Wright quickly caught up with Iosif and stood in his path like a human wall.

"I want to know what's going to happen to me," he said. "I need to know that."

Iosif nodded. "Of course you do." He glanced at me. "How long have you two been together?"

"Eleven days," I said.

"My God," Wright said. "Eleven days? Is that all? I feel as though I've had her with me for so much longer than that."

"And yet you're healthy and strong," Iosif said. "And you obviously want to keep her with you."

"I do. I'm not entirely sure that it's my idea, but I do. What will I become, though? What have I become? You said she'll . . . find a mate. What happens to me then?"

"You are her first symbiont, the first member of her new family. Her mating can't change that. She'll visit her mates and they'll visit her, but you'll live with her. No one could separate the two of you now without killing you, and no one would try."

"Killing me . . . ? Why would I die? What would I die of?"

"Of the lack of what she provides."

"But what—?"

"Come into the house, Wright. I'll see that you get all the answers you need. You might not like them all, but you have a right to hear them."

We walked from the side to the front of the large house. Iosif's community was clearly nocturnal. The Ina were naturally nocturnal, and their symbionts had apparently adjusted to being awake at night. There were lights on in all the houses, and people—human symbionts and their children, I guessed —moved around, living their lives. A red-haired woman was backing a car out of a garage. She had a small, red-blond baby strapped into a special seat in the back. Two little boys were raking leaves, and pausing now and then to throw them at one another. They were my size, and I wondered how old they were. A little girl was sweeping leaves from a porch with a broom that was almost too big for her to manage. A man was on a ladder, doing something to the rain gutter of one of the houses. Several adults stood talking together in one of the broad yards.

Wright and I followed Iosif into the biggest house and found ourselves in a room that stretched from the front to the back of the house. Wright's whole cabin might have filled a third of it. There were several couches, several chairs large and small, and several little tables scattered around the room.

Iosif said, "We meet here on Sunday evenings or when there's something that needs community-wide discussion."

There was a broad picture window on the backyard side of the great room; it ran across the top half of the wall from one end of the room to the other. At one of the end walls, there was a huge fireplace where a log burned with much snapping and sparking. Books filled built-in bookcases on the two re-maining walls.

In a corner near the fireplace, two men and a woman—all human—sat at a small table, their heads together, talking qui-etly. There were steaming cups of coffee on the table. There was no light in the room except the fire. Iosif walked us over to the three people.

"Brook, Yale, Nicholas."

They looked up, saw me, and were on their feet at once, staring. "Shori!" the woman said. She came around her chair and hugged me. She was a stranger as far as I was concerned, and I would have drawn away from any possibility of a hug, but she smelled of Iosif. Something in me seemed to accept her. She smelled of someone I had decided was all right. "My God, girl," she said, "where have you been? Iosif, where did you find her?"

Both men looked at me, then at Wright. One of them smiled. "Welcome," he said to Wright. "Looks like Shori was able to take care of herself."

Iosif put his hand on my shoulder as the woman let me go. "Is any of this familiar to you? Do you know these people, this house?"

I shook my head. "I like the room, but I don't remember it." I looked at the three people. "And I'm sorry, but I don't remember any of you either."

All three of them stared at Iosif.

"She was very badly injured," he said. "Head injuries. As a result, she's lost her memory. And she was alone until she found Wright Hamlin here. I'm hoping her memory will return."

"Don't you have your own medical people?" Wright asked. "People who know how to help your kind?"

"We do," Iosif said. "But for Ina, that tends to mean someone to fix badly broken bones so that they heal straight or binding serious wounds so that they'll heal faster."

"You don't want to see what they mean by 'a serious wound,'" one of the men said. "Intestines spilling out, legs gone, that sort of thing."

"I don't," Wright agreed. "Shori told me she had been badly burned as well as shot. But she healed on her own. Not a scar."

"Except for not knowing herself or her people," Iosif said. "I would call that a large scar. Unfortunately, it's not one we know how to fix."

"Did I have friends here?" I asked. "People who might know me especially well?"

"Your four brothers are here," he said. He looked at the three humans. "Look after Wright for a while," he said. "Answer fully any questions he asks. He's with Shori now. He's her first, but he knows almost nothing." He took my arm and began to lead me away.

"Renee?" Wright said to me, and I stopped. It eased something in me to hear him call me by the name he had given me. "You okay?" he asked.

I nodded. "Yell if you need me. I'll hear."

He nodded. He looked as though my words eased something in him.

I followed Iosif down a long hallway.

"These bedrooms belong to me and my human family," he told me. "They're the three you just met and five others who aren't here right now. They've all been with me for years. Eight is a good number for me, although at other times in my life I've had seven or even ten. I'm wealthy enough to care for all of them if I have to, and they feed me. They're free to hold jobs away from the community, even live elsewhere part time, and sometimes they do. But at least three of them are always here. They work out a schedule among themselves."

We went through a door at the end of the hallway and out onto a broad lawn. I stopped in the middle of the lawn. "Do they mind?" I asked.

"Mind?"

"That you need eight. That none of them can be your only one." I paused. "Because I think Wright is going to mind."

"When he understands that you have to have others?"

"Yes."

"He'll mind. I can see that he's very possessive of you—and very protective." He paused, then said, "Let him mind, Shori. Talk to him. Help him. Reassure him. Stop violence. But let him feel what he feels and settle his feelings his own way."

"All right."

"I suspect this kind of thing needs to be said more to my sons than to you, but you should hear it, at least once: treat your people well, Shori. Let them see that you trust them and let them solve their own problems, make their own decisions. Do that and they will willingly commit their lives to you. Bully them, control them out of fear or malice or just for your own convenience, and after a while, you'll have to spend all your time thinking for them, controlling them, and stifling their resentment. Do you understand?"

"I do, yes. I've made him do things but only to keep him safe—mostly to keep him safe from me—especially when Raleigh Curtis shot me."

He nodded. "That sort of thing is necessary whether they understand or not. How many do you have other than Wright?"

"I've drunk from five others, but Wright doesn't know about any of them." I paused, then looked at him. "I don't know whether they've come to need me. How will I be able to tell about the others? Will you look at them and tell me?"

"It isn't sight," he said, "it's scent. Did you notice Brook's scent?"

"She smelled of you."

"And Wright smells of you—unmistakably. The scent won't wash away or wear away. It's part of them now. That should give you some idea of how we hold them."

"Something, some chemical, in our saliva?"

"Exactly. We addict them to a substance in our saliva—in our venom—that floods our mouths when we feed. I've heard it called a powerful hypnotic drug. It makes them highly suggestible and deeply attached to the source of the substance. They come to need it. Brook and Wright both need it. Brook knows, and by now, Wright probably knows, too."

"And they die if they can't have it?"

"They die if they're taken from us or if we die, but their

death is caused by another component of the venom. They die of strokes or heart attacks because we aren't there to take the extra red blood cells that our venom encourages their bodies to make. Their doctors can help them if they understand the problem quickly enough. But their psychological addiction tends to prevent them from going to a doctor. They hunt for their Ina—or any Ina until it's too late."

"Until they die or until they're badly disabled."

"Yes. And even if they find an Ina not their own, they might not survive. They die unless another of us is able to take them over. That doesn't always work. Their bodies detect individual differences in our venom, and those differences make them sick when they have to adapt to a new Ina. They're addicted to their particular Ina and no other. And yet we always try to save their lives if their Ina symbiont has died. When I realized what had happened to your mothers' community, I told my people to look for wounded human symbionts as well as for you. I knew my mates were dead. I . . . found the places where they died, found their scents and small fragments of charred flesh . . ."

I gave him a moment to remember the dead and to deal with his obvious pain. I found that I almost envied his pain. He hurt because he remembered. After a while, I said, "You didn't find anyone?"

"We didn't find anyone alive. Hugh Tang, the man you killed, found you, but we didn't know that."

"All dead," I whispered. "And for me, it's as though they never existed."

"I'm sorry," he said. "I can't even pretend to understand what it's like for you to be missing so much of your memory. I want to help you recover as much of it as possible. That's why we need to get you moved into my house and dealing with people who know you." He hesitated. "To do that, we need to clear away the remnants of the life you've been living with Wright. So think. Which of the humans you've been feeding from has begun to smell as much like you as Wright does?"

I carefully reviewed my last contact with each of the humans who had fed me. "None of them," I said. "But there's one . . . she's older—too old to have children—but I like her. I want her."

He gave me a long sad look. "Your attentions will keep her

healthy and help her live longer than she would otherwise, but with such a late start, she won't live much past one hundred, and it's going to be really painful for you when she dies. It's always hard to lose them."

"Can she stay here?"

"Of course. There's a large guest wing on the side of the great room opposite my family rooms. You and yours can live there in comfort and privacy until we get your house built."

"Thank you."

"You'll need more than two humans."

"I don't like the others that I've been using. I needed them, but I don't want to keep them."

He nodded. "It goes that way sometimes. I'll introduce you to others. I know adult children of our symbionts who have been waiting and hoping to join an Ina child. Some of them can't wait to join us; others can't wait to leave us. But before you meet them, you'll have to spend the next week going once more to each of the ones you don't want. You'll have to talk to them, tell them to forget you, and become just a romantic dream to them. Otherwise, chances are they'll look for you. They don't need you, but they'll want you. They might waste their lives looking for you."

"All right."

We began to walk again. He said, "I'm taking you to see your youngest brother, Stefan, because you were close to him. You spent the first twenty-five years of your life with him at your mothers' community. The two of you were always phoning each other after Stefan moved here. While you're with him, though, don't mention Hugh Tang."

"All right."

"Did you kill Hugh because you'd gone mad with hunger? Did you eat him?"

". . . yes."

"I thought so. He was Stefan's symbiont. He had met you several times, and Stefan chose him to be part of the search party because he knew Hugh would recognize you. I'll tell your brother what happened later."

We entered one of the smaller houses through the back door. In the kitchen, we found three women working. One was stirring and seasoning something in a pot on the stove, one was searching through a huge, double-doored refrigerator, and one was mixing things in a large bowl.

"Esther, Celia, Daryl," Iosif said, gesturing toward each of them as he said their names so that I would know who was who. Two of them, Esther and Celia, had skin as dark as mine, and I looked at them with interest. They were the first black people I remembered meeting. And yet the genes for my dark skin had to have come from someone like these women. The women turned to look at us, saw me, and Esther whispered my name.

"Shori! Oh my goodness."

But they were all strangers to me. Iosif told them what had happened to me, while I examined each face. I could see that they knew me, but I didn't know them. I felt tired all of a sudden, hopeless. I followed Iosif into the living room where he introduced me to my youngest brother, Stefan, and to more of his human symbionts—two men and two women. The symbionts left us as soon as they'd greeted me and heard about my memory loss. I did not know them, didn't know the house, didn't know anything.

Then I did know one small thing—something I deduced rather than remembered. I could see that Stefan was darker than Iosif, darker than Wright. He was a light brown to my darker brown, and that meant . . .

"You're an experiment, too," I said to him when we'd talked for a while.

"Of course I am," he said. "I should have been you, so to speak. We have the same black human mother."

I smiled, comforted that I had been right to believe that one of my mothers had been a black human. "Did I know her?"

"You were her favorite. Whenever I did something wrong, she'd shake her head and say I wasn't really what she had in mind anyway." He smiled sadly, remembering. "She said I was too much like Iosif."

"And someone murdered her," I said. "Someone murdered them all."

"Someone did."

"Why? Why would anyone do that?"

He shook his head. "If we knew why, we might already have found out who. I don't understand how this person was able to kill everyone—except you. Our Ina mothers were powerful. They should have been . . . much harder to kill."

"Could it have happened because humans thought we were vampires?" I asked. "I mean, if they thought we were killing people, they might have—"

"No," Stefan and Iosif said together. Then Iosif said, "We live in rural areas. People around us know one another. They know us—or they think they do. No one had died mysteriously in my mates' home territory except my mates themselves and their community."

"I don't mean that we have been killing people," I said. "I mean . . . what if someone saw one of us feeding and . . . drew the wrong conclusions?"

Iosif and Stefan looked at one another. Finally Iosif said, "I don't believe that could have happened. Your mothers and sisters were even more careful than we are."

"I don't believe humans could have done it," Stefan said.

"I was burned and shot," I said. "Anyone can use fire and guns."

Iosif shook his head. "I questioned several of the people who live near your mothers' community. There was nothing wrong, no trouble, no suspicions, no grudges."

"When I went to the ruin today," I said, "someone had been there. He was human, young, unarmed, and he'd walked all around the ruin. Did you notice?"

"Yes. He prowls. He lives in your general area but down toward the town of Gold Bar. He's sixteen, and I suspect he prowls without his parents' knowledge." He shook his head. "We combed the area very thoroughly. He was one of the people we checked. He didn't know anything. No one knows anything."

I sighed. "They don't and I don't." I looked from one lean, sharp face to the other, realizing that they had drawn away from me a little, and now they looked oddly uncomfortable. They fidgeted and glanced at one another now and then.

I said, "Tell me about my family, my mothers. How many mothers did I have anyway? Were they all sisters except for the human one? How many sisters did I have?"

"Our mothers were three sisters," Stefan said, "and one human woman who donated DNA. Also, there were two

eldermothers—our mothers' surviving mothers. The two
eldermothers were the ones who made it possible for us—you
in particular—to be born with better-than-usual protection
from the sun and more daytime alertness."

"They integrated the human DNA with our own somehow?"

"They did, yes. They were both over 350 years old, and biology fascinated them. Once their children were mated, they
studied with humans from several universities and with other
Ina who were working on the problem. They understood more
about the uses of viruses in genetic engineering than anyone
I've ever heard of, and they understood it well before humans
did. They were fantastic people to work with and talk to." He
paused, shaking his head. "I still can't believe that they're dead
—that someone would murder them that way."

"Could their work be the reason they were murdered?" I
asked. "Did anyone object to it or try to stop it?"

Stefan looked at Iosif and Iosif shook his head. "I don't believe so. Shori, our people have been trying to do this for generations. If you could remember, you'd know what a celebrity
you are. People traveled from South America, Europe, Asia,
and Africa to see you and to understand what our mothers had
done."

"There are Ina in Africa, and they haven't done this?"

"Not yet."

"Was anyone visiting just before the fire?"

"Don't know," Iosif said. "I hadn't spoken to your mothers for a week and a half. When I phoned them in the early
morning and told them I wanted to visit the next night, they
said they would be expecting me. They said if I came, I had to
stay a few days." He smiled, apparently taking pleasure in his
memories, then his expression sagged into sadness. "They told
me to bring at least five symbionts. I took them at their word.
The next night, I gathered five of my people and drove down
there. Vasile had wanted to use the helicopter for something
so I took one of the bigger cars. When I got there, I found
smoke and ashes and death." He paused, staring out into nothing. "Once I'd seen it and understood it, I called home to get
Stefan and Radu to come down with some of their symbionts
to help clean things up, to hunt for survivors, and to keep our
secrets secret."

So that was how Hugh Tang had wound up at the cave look-ing for me. "What have you learned since then?" I asked.

He turned away from me, paced a few steps away, then the same few back. "Nothing!" The word was a harsh whisper. "Not one goddamned thing."

I sighed. Suddenly, I'd had enough. "I think I need to go home," I said. "Let's go get Wright, and you can take us back to the ruin."

"You are home." He stood in front of me and looked down at me with an expression I couldn't read, except that it wasn't an altogether friendly expression. "You must think of this place as your home."

"I will," I said. "I'll be glad to come back here and learn more about my life, my family. But I'm tired now. I feel . . . I need to go back to things that feel familiar."

"I was hoping to convince you to stay here until tomorrow night," he said.

I shook my head. "Take me back."

"Shori, it would be best for you to stay here. Wright has hid-den you successfully for this long, but if anything went wrong, if even one person spotted you with him and decided to make trouble—"

"You promised to give us a week," I said. "That was the first promise you made me."

He stared down at me. I stared back.

After a while, he sighed and turned away. "Child, I've lost everyone but you."

Stefan said, "All of our female family is dead, Shori. You're the last."

I wanted more than ever to go home, to be away from them and alone with Wright. And yet they pulled at me somehow—my father and my brother. They were strangers, but they were my father and my brother. "I'm sorry," I said. "I need to go."

"We Ina are sexually territorial," Iosif said. "And you're a little too old to be sharing territory with the adult males of your family—with any adult Ina male since you're too young to mate. That's what's bothering you."

"You mean I feel uncomfortable with you and Stefan just because you're male?"

"Yes."

"Then how can I live here?"

"Let's go back to Wright. I think you'll feel better when you're with him." He led me away from Stefan toward a side door. I looked back once, but Stefan had already turned away.

"Is he feeling territorial, too?" I asked.

"No. He's willing for you to be here because he fears for you—and for himself. And you're not mature yet, so there's no real danger . . ."

"Danger?"

He led me through the door, and we headed back across the lawn.

"Danger, Iosif?"

"We are not human, child. Male and female Ina adults don't live together. We can't. Mates visit, but that's all."

"What is the danger?"

"As your body changes, and especially as your scent changes, you will be perceived more and more as an available adult female."

"By my brothers?"

He nodded, looking away from me.

"By you?"

Another nod. "We won't hurt you, Shori. Truly, we won't. By the time you come of age, I'll have found mates for you. I was already talking to the Gordon family about you and your sisters . . . Now . . . now I intend to sell your mothers' land. That money should be enough to give you a start at a different location when you're a little older."

"I don't think I want to live here."

"I know, but it will be all right. It will only be until you look more adult. Your brothers and I have our genetic predispositions—our instincts—but we are also intelligent. We are aware of our urges. We can stand still even when the instinct to move is powerful."

"You said I'm a child."

"You are, now more than ever with your memory loss. You can play sexually with your symbionts, but you're too young to mate. You can't yet conceive a child, and you're not yet as large or as strong as you will be. Your scent right now is interesting, but for us, it's more irritating than enticing."

We went back into his house. "You'll take us back to the ruin tonight," I told him. "You said you would. Were you speaking the truth?"

"I was, but I shouldn't have said it. I'm afraid for you, Shori."

"But you'll do it."

There was a long silence. Finally he agreed. "I will."

We went down the long hallway again and into the great room. There, Wright sat alone in one of the large chairs. The other three humans had left him. I went up to him, wanting to touch him from behind, wanting to lay my hands on his shoulders, but not doing it. I wondered what Iosif's symbionts had said to him, what they had made him feel about being with me. I walked around and stood in front of him, looking down, trying to sense his mood.

He looked up at me, his face telling me only that he was not happy. "What happens now?" he asked.

"We go home," I said.

He looked at Iosif, then back at me. "Yeah? Okay." He got up, then spoke to Iosif. "You're letting her go? I didn't really believe you would do that."

"You thought I was lying to you?" Iosif said.

"I thought your . . . paternal feelings might kick in and make you keep her in spite of your promise."

"She's tough and resilient, but I fear for her. I'm desperate to keep her."

"So . . . ?"

"She wants to go . . . and . . . I understand why. Keep her hidden, Wright. Except for my people and hers, I don't believe anyone knows she's alive. I even got that boy, Raleigh Curtis, to forget about her. Keep her hidden and bring her back to me on Friday."

Wright licked his lips. "I don't understand, but I'll bring her back."

"Even though you don't want to?"

". . . yes."

They looked at each other, each wearing a similar expression of weariness, misery, and resignation.

I took Wright's hand, and the three of us went out to the copter. Wright said nothing more. He let me hold his hand, but he did not hold mine.

Nine

WRIGHT AND I didn't talk until we reached the car. We had flown all the way back to the ruin in silence, had said goodbye to Iosif and watched him fly away. When we got into the car and began our drive home, Wright finally said, "You have others already, don't you? Other . . . symbionts."

"Not yet," I said. "I've gone to others for nourishment. I can't take all that I need from you every night. But I haven't . . . I mean none of the others . . ."

"None of the others are bound to you yet."

"Yes."

"Why am I?"

"I wanted you." I touched his shoulder, rested my hand on his upper arm. "I think you wanted me, too. From the night you found me, we wanted each other."

He glanced at me. "I don't know. I never really had a chance to figure that out."

"You did. When I was shot, I gave you a chance. It was . . . very hard for me to do that, but I did it. I would have let you go—helped you go."

"And you think I could have just gone away and not come back? I had to leave you lying on the ground bleeding. You insisted on it. How could I not come back to make sure you were all right?"

"You knew I would heal. I told you you weren't bound to me then. I offered you freedom. I told you I wouldn't be able to offer it again."

"I remember," he said. He sounded angry. "But I didn't know then that I was agreeing to be part of a harem. You left that little bit out."

I knew what a harem was. One of the books I'd read had referred to Dracula's three wives as his harem, and I'd looked the word up. "You're not part of a harem," I said. "You and I have a symbiotic relationship, and it's a relationship that I want and need. But didn't you see all those children? I'll have mates someday, and you can have yours. You can have a family if you want one."

356

He turned to glare at me, and the car swerved, forcing him to pay attention to his driving. "What am I supposed to do? Help produce the next generation of symbionts?"

I kept quiet for a moment, wondering at the rage in his voice. "What would be the point of that?" I asked finally.

"Just as easy to snatch them off the street, eh?"

I sighed and rubbed my forehead. "Iosif said the children of some symbionts stay in the hope of finding an Ina child to bond with. Others choose to make lives for themselves outside."

He made a sound—almost a moan. For a while, he said nothing.

Finally, I asked, "Do you want to leave me?"

"Why bother to ask me that?" he demanded. "I can't leave you. I can't even really want to leave you."

"Then what do you want?"

He sighed and shook his head. "I don't know. I know I wish I had driven past you on the road eleven nights ago and not stopped. And yet, I know that if I could have you all to myself, I'd stop for you again, even knowing what I know about you."

"That would kill you. Quickly."

"I know."

But he didn't care—or he didn't think he would have cared. "What did those three people tell you?" I asked. "What did they say that's made you so angry and so miserable? Was it only that I take blood from several symbionts instead of draining one person until I kill him?"

"That probably would have been enough."

I rested my head against his arm so that I could touch him without looking at him. I needed to touch him. And yet, he had to understand. "I've fed from you and from five other people —three women and two men. I'll keep one of the women if she wants to stay with me. I think she will. The others will forget me or remember me as just a dream."

"Did you sleep with any of them?"

"Did I have sex with them, you mean? No. Except for the one woman, I fed and came back to you. I stayed longer with her because something in her comforts and pleases me. Her name is Theodora Harden. I don't know why I like her so much, but I do."

"Swing both ways, do you?"

I frowned, startled and confused by the terrible bitterness in his voice. "What?"

"Sex with men and with women?"

"With my symbionts if both they and I want it. For the moment, that's you."

"For the moment."

I reached up to slip my hand under his jacket and shirt to touch the bare flesh of his neck. It was unmarked. I had only nipped him a little for pleasure the night before, then I went to one of the others while he slept. He had healed by morning. Tonight, I had intended to do something that wouldn't heal nearly as fast.

And yet when we reached his cabin, we went in and went to bed without saying or doing anything at all. I didn't bite him because he clearly didn't want me to. I fell asleep fitted against his furry back, taking comfort in his presence even though he was angry and confused. At least he didn't push me away.

Finally, some time later, he shook me awake, shook me hard, saying, "Do it! Do it, damnit! I should get some pleasure out of all this if I don't get anything else."

I put my fingers over his lips gently. When he fell silent, I kissed first his mouth, then his throat. He was so angry—so filled with rage and confusion.

He rolled onto me, pushing my legs apart, pushing them out of his way, then thrust hard into me. I bit him more deeply than I had intended and wrapped my arms and legs around him as I took his blood. He groaned, writhing against me, holding me, thrusting harder until I had taken all I needed of his blood, until he had all he needed of me.

After a long while, he rolled off me, sated for the moment in body if not in mind.

"Did I hurt you?" he asked very softly.

I pulled myself onto his chest and lapped at the ragged edges of the bite. "You didn't hurt me," I said. "Were you trying to hurt me?"

"I think I was," he said.

I went on lapping. There was more bleeding than usual. "Did I hurt you?" I asked.

"No, of course not. What you do ought to hurt, but except for that first instant when you break the skin, it never does."

He slipped his arms around me, and it was more the way he usually held me.

"It's good to know we don't hurt each other even when we're upset."

"I don't know how to deal with all this, Renee . . . Shori. It's like being told that extraterrestrials have arrived, and I'm sleeping with one of them."

I laughed. "That may be true, except that if we arrived, it must have happened thousands of years ago."

"Do you believe that—that your people come from another planet? I remember your father said something about a theory like that."

"According to Iosif, some younger Ina believe it. Some don't. He doesn't. I don't know what to think about it. If I could get my memory back, then maybe I'd have an opinion that was worth bothering about."

"Do you believe Iosif is your father?"

I nodded against his chest. Then the sweet smell of his blood made me go on licking at the bite.

"Why? If he's a stranger to you, why do you believe him?"

"I don't know. Maybe it's something about his manner, his body language. But more likely it's his scent. I kept hoping to remember something while I was with him, any little thing. But there was nothing. He introduced me to my brother Stefan, and still, there was nothing. But I never doubted that they were who they said they were. And all their human symbionts recognized me."

"Yeah," Wright said.

"You talked to three symbionts. Do you think they were lying?"

"No, I don't think they were lying." He ran his hand over my head and down my back. "They said I was lucky to have you—lucky to be your first. That was when I realized that . . . of course you'd have to already have others, even though I didn't know about them. Then the woman, Brook, told me all Ina have several symbionts."

"How much blood do you think you could provide?"

"You . . . you taste me just about every day."

"Just a little. I crave you. I do. And I enjoy pleasuring you."

"That's the right attitude," he said. He rolled over, trapping me beneath him and thrust into me again. This time I was the one who could not help but let out a groan of pleasure. He laughed, delighted.

Later, as we lay together, more satisfied, more at ease, he said, "They'll be coming for us next Friday."

"Yes," I said. "I don't want to go live with them, but I think we have to."

"I was going to say that."

"I need to learn how to set up my own household—how to make it work. When I can do that, when I've learned the things I need to know to do that, we'll go out on our own."

"How big a household?" he asked.

"You, me, five or six others. We don't all have to live in the same house the way my brothers do with their symbionts, but we need to be near one another."

"It'll be rough to live together in your father's house."

"He says he'll sell my mothers' property, and when I'm older, the money will give me a start somewhere else."

"And he'll hook you up with a male Ina, or rather, with a group of Ina brothers. My God, a group of brothers . . ."

I said nothing. My mothers had lived together in the same community, shared a mate, and worked things out somehow. It could be done. It was the Ina way. "That will all happen in the future," I said. "Next week, we'll be in rooms at Iosif's house, you and I and Theodora. She's one of our neighbors, a few doors down. You might know her."

There was a long silence. Finally he asked, "Is she pretty?"

I smiled. "Not pretty. Not young either. But I like her."

"Are you going to tell her to join us . . . or ask her?"

"Ask her. But she'll come."

"Because she's already fallen so far under your influence that she won't be able to help herself?"

"She'll want to come. She doesn't have to, but she'll want to."

He sighed. "I think the scariest thing about all this so far is that all three of those symbionts seem genuinely happy. What do you figure? Old Iosif told them they were living in the best of all possible worlds, and they bought it because as far as they're concerned, he's God?"

"He didn't," I said.

"You asked?"

"He told me that it was wrong, shortsighted, and harmful to symbionts to do such things. I didn't ask. I had already figured that out."

"So you believe that's what he believes?"

"I do, at least on this subject."

"Shit."

I kissed him and turned over and went to sleep.

During the next week, I visited each of my people, fed from them, and said good-bye. I became a dream to them, as Iosif had suggested, and I left them. Finally, on Thursday, I visited Theodora.

I paid attention to her house and waited until shortly after sunset when she was alone. Then I visited her.

I hadn't seen her for a while, but as I looked at her large, handsome house, it occurred to me that in spite of what I had said to Wright, perhaps I should not ask Theodora to join me until I had a home, something more than rooms in Iosif's house to offer her. The thought surprised me. It occurred to me after I reached her front door and rang the doorbell.

I heard her come to the door. Then there was a long pause while, I suppose, she looked out through the peephole and tried to figure out who I might be. She had never seen me before. I had visited her in darkness three times and had not allowed her to turn on a light. She must have gotten an idea of my general size, but she had never seen my face, my coloring, or the fact that I looked so young.

Finally, she opened the door, looked down at me questioningly, and said, "Hello there."

"Hello," I said, and as she recognized my voice, as her expression began to change to one of shock, I said, "Invite me in."

At once, she stood aside and said, "Come in."

This was a bit of vampire theater. I knew it, and I was fairly sure she knew it, too. She had probably been brushing up on vampires recently. Of course, I didn't need permission to enter her home or anyone else's. I did find it interesting, though, that human beings made up these fantasy safeguards, little magics, like garlic and crucifixes, that would somehow keep them safe from my kind—or from what they imagined my kind to be.

I walked past her into the house. There was, near the front door, a broad staircase on one side and a living room almost as large as Iosif's on the other. The walls were a very pale green, and the woodwork was white. All the furniture was, somehow, exactly where it should be and exactly what it should be. Iosif's living room was more lived-in, more imperfect, more comfortable to be in. I began to feel even more uneasy about asking Theodora to come with me.

She came up behind me, and when I turned to face her, she stopped, staring at me with a kind of horror.

"Is it my skin color or my apparent age that's upsetting you so?" I asked.

"Why are you here?" she demanded.

"To talk with you," I said. "To have you see me."

"I didn't want to see you!"

I nodded. "It will make a difference," I said, "but not as great a difference as you think." I went to her, took her arm, tried to lead her into the perfect living room.

She pulled back and said, "Not here." She took my hand and led me up the stairs into a room whose walls were covered with books. There was a sofa and two chairs also piled high with books and papers. In the middle of the room was a large, messy desk covered with open books, papers, a computer and monitor, a radio, a telephone, a box of pencils and pens, a stack of notebooks and crossword puzzle magazines, a long decorative wooden box of compact discs, bottles of aspirin, hand lotion, antacid, correction fluid, and who knew what else.

I stared at it and burst out laughing. It was the most disorderly mass of stuff I had run across, and yet it all looked—felt —familiar. Had I once had an equally messy desk? Had one of my mothers or sisters? I would ask Iosif. Anyway, it was the opposite of the living room downstairs, and that was a relief.

Theodora had been clearing books off a chair so that I could sit down. She stopped when I laughed, followed my gaze, and said, "Oh. I forget how awful that must look to strangers. No one ever sees it but me."

I laughed again. "No, this is who you are. This is what I wanted to see." I drew a deep breath, assuring myself that she was still free of me, still unaddicted. She was, and that was a good thing, although it felt like a flaw I should fix at once.

"I write poetry," she said. She almost seemed embarrassed about it. "I've published three books. Poetry doesn't really pay, but I enjoy writing it."

I took some of the books off the sofa and piled them on the chair she had been clearing for me, then took her hand and drew her to the sofa. She sat with me even though she didn't want to—or she didn't want to want to. I felt that she was teaching me about herself every moment. I turned her to face me and just enjoyed looking at her. She had waist-length, dark-brown hair with many strands of gray. Her eyes were the same dark brown as her hair, and the flesh at the corners of them was indented with arrays of fine lines—the only lines on her face. She was a little heavier than was good for her. Plump might have been the best word to describe her. It made her face full and round. She wore no makeup at all—not even lipstick. She had been at home, relaxing without her family around her.

After a moment, I leaned against her, put my head on her shoulder, and she put her arm around me, then took it away, then put it back. She smelled remarkably enticing.

"I don't understand," she said.

"I don't either," I said. "But the things I don't understand are probably not the same ones giving you trouble. How long do we have before your family comes home?"

"They're visiting my son-in-law's family in Portland. They won't be home until tomorrow." The moment she said this, she began to look nervous, as though she was afraid of what I might make of her solitude, her vulnerability.

"Good," I said. "I need to talk to you, tell you my story, hear yours. Then I have something to ask of you."

"Who are you?" she demanded. "What's your name? What . . . What . . . ?"

"What am I?"

". . . yes." She looked away, embarrassed.

I pulled her down to a comfortable level and bit her gently, then hard enough to start blood flowing on its own so that I could be lazy and just take it as it came. After a while, I said, "You told me I was a vampire."

She had not objected to anything I'd done even when I climbed onto her lap, straddled her, and rested against her, lapping occasionally at the blood. She put her arms around me and held me against her as though I might try to escape.

"You are a vampire," she said. "Although according to what I've read, you're supposed to be a tall, handsome, fully grown white man. Just my luck. But you must be a vampire. How could you do this if you weren't? How could I let you do it? How could it feel so good when it should be disgusting and painful? And how could the wound heal so quickly and without scars?"

"You don't believe in vampires."

"I didn't use to. And I never thought they would be so small and . . . like you."

"I've been called an elfin little girl."

"That's exactly right."

"In a way, it is. I'm a child according to the standards of my people, but my people age more slowly than yours, and I have an extra problem. I may be older than you are in years. As far as my memory is concerned, though, I was born just a few weeks ago."

"But how can that—?"

"Shh." I started to get off her lap, and she tried to hold me where I was. "No," I said. "Let me go." She released me, and I sat beside her and leaned against her.

"Three, maybe four weeks ago," I began, "I woke up in a shallow cave a few miles from here. I'm being vague about when and where because I don't know enough to be exact. During my first days in the cave I was blind and in and out of consciousness. I was in a lot of pain, and I had no memory of anything that had happened before the cave."

"Amnesia."

"Yes." I told her the rest of it, told her about killing Hugh Tang, but not about eating him, told her about hunting deer and eating them. I told her about Wright finding me and taking me in, and about finding my father and brothers. I told her the little I knew about the Ina and about what an Ina community was like. I told her I wasn't human, and she believed me. She wasn't even surprised.

"You want me to be part of such a community?" she asked.

"I do, but not yet."

"Not . . . yet?"

"My father is having a house built for me. Come to me when the house is ready. I'll see to it that there's space for your books and other things—a place where you can write your poetry."

"How long?"

"I don't know. No more than a year."

She shook her head. "I don't want to wait that long."

I was surprised. I had been careful to let her make up her own mind, and I had believed she would come with me, but not so quickly. "I have nothing to offer you now," I said. I'll be living in rooms in my father's house. He says you can come, but when I saw what you have here, I thought you'd want to wait until you could have something similar with me."

"I have no patience," she said. "I want to be with you now."

I liked that more than I could have said, and yet I wondered about it. "Why?" I asked her. I had no idea what she would say.

She blinked at me, looked surprised, hurt. "Why do you want me?"

I thought about that, about how to say it in a way she might understand. "You have a particularly good scent," I said. "I mean, not only do you smell healthy, you smell . . . open, wanting, alone. When I came to you the first time, you were afraid at first, then glad and welcoming, excited, but you didn't smell of other people."

She frowned. "Do you mean that I smelled lonely?"

"I think so, yes, longing, needing . . ."

"I didn't imagine that loneliness had a scent."

"Why do you want me?" I repeated.

She hugged me against her. "I am lonely," she said. "Or I was until you came to me that first time. You've made me feel more than I have since I was a girl. I hoped you would go on wanting me—or at least that's what I hoped when I wasn't worrying that I was losing my mind, imagining things." She hesitated. "You need me," she said. "No one else does, but you do."

"Your family?"

"Not really, no. This is my home, and I'm glad to be able to help my daughter and her husband by having them come live here, but since my husband died, all I've really cared about—all I've been able to care about—is my poetry."

"You would be able to bring only some of your things to my father's house," I said.

"A few boxes of books, some clothing, and I'll be fine."

I looked around the room doubtfully. "Wright and I will be moving tomorrow. I'll need your telephone number so I can reach you. If you don't change your mind, we'll come back for you and your things the Friday after next."

"Promise me."

"I have."

"Will you stay with me tonight?"

"For a while. Have you eaten?"

"Eaten?" She looked at me. "I haven't even thought of eating, although I suppose I'd better. Do you eat regular food at all, ever?"

"No."

"All right. Come keep me company in the kitchen while I microwave something to eat. I don't think I should miss very many meals if I'm going to be with you."

"Exactly right," I said, and enjoyed every moment of the flesh-to-flesh contact when she bent and kissed me.

Ten

NO ONE came for us on Friday.

When the night was half gone, Wright tried to phone Iosif—tried each of the numbers he had given us. At first, there was no answer, then there was a computerized voice saying that the number he was calling was out of service. He made several fruitless attempts.

"We need to go there," I said.

He looked at me for a moment, then nodded. "Let's go," he said.

I grabbed a blanket from the bed, thinking that we might have to spend part of the coming day in the car. I didn't want to think about why that might happen, but I wanted to be ready for it. Thoughts of the burned-out ruin that had been my mothers' community jumped into my mind, and I couldn't ignore them.

Wright was not certain how to reach Iosif's community. His maps didn't show the tiny community, of course. Iosif's card contained a sketch of a map that turned out to be hard to follow. We got onto what seemed to be the right side-road, but found no turn-off where Wright had expected one. We tried another side road, then another, but still did not find the community.

Finally, I did what I hadn't wanted to do.

"This is no good," I said. "We're in the right general area. Find a place to park, and I'll go out and find the community. I can find it by scent if not by sight."

He didn't want me to go. He wanted to keep driving around or, if necessary, go home and try again during the day.

I shook my head. "Find a safe place and park. I need to go to them and see that they're all right. And if . . . if they're not all right, if this is anything like what happened to my mothers, you can't be there. If my father or my brothers are injured, they'll be dangerous. They might not be able to stop themselves from killing you."

"And eating me," he said. He didn't even make it a question.

I said nothing for a moment, stared at him. Had the human symbionts told him or had he guessed? I hated that he knew but clearly, he did know. "Yes," I admitted finally. "That's probably what would happen. Park and wait for me."

He parked on the highway at a place where the road's shoulder was wide. "This will do as well as anywhere," he said. "If anyone wants to know what I'm up to, I got sleepy and decided to play it safe and catch a nap."

"If you have to move," I said, "wait for me somewhere south of here along the road. I'll find you. If you have to leave the area—"

"I won't leave you!"

"Wright, hear me. Do this. If you're in danger from the police, from an Ina, from anyone at all, leave me, go home. I'll get there when I can. Don't look for me. Go home."

He shook his head, but he would do it. After a moment, he said, "You honestly believe you could find your way to my cabin from here?"

"I could," I said. "If I have to, I will." I took his hand from where it was still resting on the steering wheel. Such a huge hand. I kissed it then turned to go.

"Shori!" he said.

I had opened the door to get out of the car, but his tone stopped me.

"Feed," he said.

He was right. I was probably going to have to cover a few miles and face I-didn't-know-what. Best to be at full strength. I shut the door and kneeled on the seat to reach him. He lifted me over onto his lap, kissed me, and waited.

I bit him deeply and felt him spasm and go hard under me. I hadn't bitten him this way for a week, hadn't taken a full meal from him. I had hoped we would share this night in our new quarters. I liked to take my time when I truly fed from him, tear sounds from him, exhaust him with pleasure, enjoy his body as well as his blood. But not now. I took his blood quickly, rocking against him, then stayed for just a few minutes more, licking the wound to begin its healing, comforting him, comforting myself. Finally I hugged him and got out of the car. "Stay safe," I said.

He nodded. "You too."

I left him and began to run. We were in the right general area but were, I thought, south of our target. Wright had turned off too soon. I ran along the road, alert for cars and for a telltale wisp of scent. I was moving in a generally northerly direction through woods, alongside a river that sometimes veered away from the road and sometimes came close to it. I passed the occasional house, cluster of houses, or farm, but these were strictly human places.

After a while I did catch a scent. I didn't bother about finding the side-road. I followed the scent cross-country through the woods, past a house that had been almost completely hidden by trees. I didn't care about private property or rugged terrain. All I cared about were the scents drifting in the air and what they could tell me. I stopped every now and then to take a few deep breaths, turning into the wind, sorting through the various scents. Running, I might miss something. Standing still, eyes closed, breathing deeply, I could sort through far more scents—plant, animal, human, mineral—than I wanted to bother with.

There was a gradual change. After a while, what I smelled most was smoke—old smoke, days old, and ash clinging to the trees, stirred up by my feet, by the feet of animals, by cars on the narrow little roads I crossed.

Smoke and burned flesh. Human flesh and Ina flesh.

When I found my father's and brothers' homes, they looked much like the ruin of my mothers' community. The buildings had been completely destroyed, burned to rubble, and then trampled by many feet. My father and my brothers had been there, but they were gone now. I could smell death, but I could not see it. I did not know yet who had died and who had survived. Someone had come for my male family, and whoever it was had been as thorough as they had when they came for my mothers and my sisters.

The place that had been Iosif's community was full of strange, bad smells—the scents of people who should not have been there, who had nothing to do with Iosif or his people. Whose scent was I finding? The arsonists? Firemen? The police? Neighbors? All of these, probably.

I stood amid the rubble and looked around, trying to understand. Was Iosif dead? And Stefan? I hadn't even met my other three brothers and their symbionts. All dead? None wounded and surviving in hiding?

Then I remembered that some of Iosif's symbionts worked away from the community, even lived away from it part of the time. Did they know what had happened? If they didn't, they would be coming back here soon. They would come, needing Iosif or one of my brothers. When they found out what had happened, they would have to find another Ina to bond with just to survive. Could I help? Was I too young? I was definitely too ignorant. Surely they would know of other Ina communities. If they had come home and found only rubble, they might already have taken refuge in some other community.

When had the fire happened? Days ago, surely. The place was cold. Even the freshest human smells I found were all at least a day or two old.

Who had done this and why? First my mothers' community, now my father's. Even Iosif had had no idea who attacked my mothers. He had been deeply angry and frustrated at his own ignorance. If he didn't know, how could I find out?

Someone had targeted my family. Someone had succeeded in killing all of my relatives. And if this had to do with the experiments that had given me my useful human characteristics —what else could it be?—then it was likely that I was the main target.

I began to run again, to circle the community, stopping often to sample scents more thoroughly and hunting for fresh scents, any hint that some member of my family might be alive, hiding, healing. I found the narrow private road that led to where the houses had been, and I followed it out to a two-lane public road. There, I closed my eyes and turned toward where Wright was waiting. I could get back to him in half an hour.

But I didn't want to go back to him yet. I wanted to learn all I could, all that my eyes and my nose could tell me.

I went back to the rubble—charred planks, blackened jagged sections of wall, broken glass, standing chimneys, burned and partially burned furniture, appliances, broken ceramic tile in what had been the kitchens and the bathrooms, unrecognizable lumps of blackened plastic, a spot where an Ina had died . . .

I stood still at that place, trying to recognize the scent, realizing that I couldn't because it was the wrong scent, that of a dead male whom I had not met, burned to ash and bone, definitely dead.

I had not known him. He must have been one of my brothers but one I had not met. He had died in one of the three houses I had not entered.

I stared at the spot for a long time and caught myself wondering what the Ina did with their dead. What were their ceremonies? I knew something about human funeral services from my vampire research. I had read through a great deal of material about death, burial, and what could go wrong to cause the dead to become undead. It was all nonsense as far as I was concerned, but it had taught me that proper respect for the dead was important to humans. Was it important to Ina as well?

What had been done with the remains of both my male and my female families? Had the police taken them? Where would they take them? I would have to talk to Wright about that and perhaps to Theodora. She worked at a library. If she didn't know, she would know how to find out.

But if I somehow got the remains, what could I do but bury them or scatter their ashes after, perhaps, a more thorough cremation? I didn't know any Ina rituals, any Ina religion, any living Ina people.

I found another place where someone had died—a symbiont this time, a female. I had not met her. I was grateful for that. After a while, I made myself go to the house that had been my father's. I walked through it slowly, found two spots where symbionts I did not know had died. Then I found two that I did know—the two men I had met in Iosif's huge front room, Nicholas and Yale. I stood for a long time, staring at the spots where the two men had died. I had not known them, but they had been healthy and alive only a week before. They had welcomed me, had been friendly to Wright. It did not seem possible that they were dead now, reduced to two smudges of burned flesh that smelled of Iosif and of their own individual human scents.

Then, in the remains of what must have been a large bedroom, I found a place that smelled so strongly of Iosif that it had to be the spot where he died. Had he tried to get out? He was not near a window or a door. I got the impression that he was lying flat on his back when he died. Had he been shot? I found no bullets, but perhaps the police had taken them away. And if there had ever been a smell of gunpowder, it had been overwhelmed by all the other smells of burning and death. Iosif had certainly burned. A small quantity of his ashes were still here, mixed with the ashes of the house and its contents.

He was definitely dead.

I stood over the spot, eyes closed, hugging myself.

Iosif was dead. I'd hardly begun to know him, and he was dead. I had begun to like him, and he was dead.

I folded to the ground in anguish, knowing that I could do nothing to help him, nothing to change the situation. Nothing at all. My family was destroyed, and I couldn't even grieve for them properly because I remembered so little.

"Shori?"

I jumped up and back several steps. I had been so involved with my thoughts and feelings that I had let someone walk right up to me. I had heard nothing, smelled nothing.

At least I could see that I had startled the person who had surprised me. I had moved fast, and it was dark. She was looking around as though her eyes had not followed my movement, as though she did not know where I had gone. Then she spotted me. By then I understood that she was human and that she didn't see very well in the dark, that she smelled of my father and that I knew who she was.

"Brook," I said.

She looked around at the devastation, then looked at me, tears streaming down her face.

I went to her and hugged her, as she had hugged me when we met. She hugged back, crying even harder.

"Were you here when this happened?" she asked finally.

"No. We were supposed to move in tonight."

"Do you know if . . . ? I mean, did you see Iosif?"

I looked back at the place where Iosif had died, where a very small quantity of his ashes still remained. "He didn't survive," I said.

She stared at me silently, frowning as though I had said words she could not understand. Then she began to make a noise. It began as a moan and went on to become an impossibly long, ragged scream. She fell to the ground, gasping and moaning. "Oh God," she cried. "Oh God, Iosif, Iosif."

Someone else was coming.

Brook had come in a car, I realized. I had been so focused on my own distress that I had missed not only the sound and smell of a person walking up to me, but the noise of a car as well. Now someone else was coming from the car—another human female. This one had a handgun, and she was aiming it at me.

I jumped away from Brook, ran wide around her, leaping through the rubble as fast as I could. I reached the woman with the gun before she could track me and shoot me, and I knocked the gun from her hand before she could fire and grabbed her. I absolutely did not want to spend another day and night recovering from a bullet wound.

This woman was also someone I'd met—Celia, one of Stefan's symbionts. She had been in his kitchen with two other women whose scents I was glad not to have found.

"Celia, it's Shori," I said into her ear as she struggled against me. "Celia!" She lifted me completely off the ground, but she couldn't break my hold on her. "It's Shori," I repeated in her ear. "Stop struggling. I don't want to hurt you."

After a moment, she stopped struggling. "Shori?"

"Yes."

"Did you do this?"

That surprised me into silence. Celia was one of the two black women in the kitchen. She had seemed friendly and interesting. Now there was nothing but grief and anger in her expression.

Brook came up at that moment and said, "Celia, it's Shori. You know she didn't do this."

"I know what she did to Hugh!" Celia said.

I let go of her. Hugh Tang was symbiont with her to Stefan. They were family.

Celia jabbed her fist up, clearly meaning to hit me. I dodged the first jab, then grabbed one fist, then the other. She tried to kick me, so I tripped her and took her to the ground.

She lay stunned for a moment, breathless and gasping since I fell on top of her. She glared up at me. I couldn't think of anything helpful to say so I kept quiet. She and I lay on the ground. After a moment, she looked away from me and her muscles relaxed.

"Let me up," she said.

I didn't move or loosen my hold on her.

"What do you want me to do, say 'please'?"

"I truly don't want to hurt you," I said, "but if you attack me again, I will."

After a moment, she nodded. "Let me go. I won't bother you."

I took her at her word and let her up.

"She says Iosif's dead," Brook said.

Immediately, Celia confronted me. "How do you know he's dead? Were you here when all this happened? Did you see?"

I took both their hands, although Celia tried to snatch hers away, and led them over to the place where Iosif had burned. "He died here," I told them. "I can smell that much. I don't know whether it was only the fire or whether he was shot, too. I couldn't find any bullets. But he died here. A few of his ashes are still here."

I looked at one woman, then the other. Both now had tears streaming down their faces. They believed me. "I don't remember anything about Ina funerals or beliefs about death," I said. "Do either of you know other Ina families—Iosif's mothers perhaps—who would be able to do what should be done?"

"His mothers were killed in Russia during World War II," Brook said. She and Celia looked at one another. "We went to Seattle to shop and visit our relatives. That's why we weren't here. The only Ina phone numbers I know from memory are the numbers of several of the people who lived here and some of your mothers' phone numbers." She looked at Celia.

"I knew some of our community's numbers and Shori's mothers' numbers too," Celia said. "That's all."

It occurred to me then for no reason I could put my finger on that Celia was much younger than Brook—young enough to be Brook's daughter. Brook was only a few years younger than Theodora but except for very small signs, she appeared to be the same age as Celia. That, I realized, was what happened when a human became an Ina symbiont while she was still young. Wright would age slowly the way Brook had.

I pulled my thoughts back to the rubble we stood in. "When did you go into Seattle?" I asked.

Celia answered, "Five nights ago."

"I won't be able to visit my relatives many more times," Brook said. "My sister and my mother are aging a lot faster than I am, and they keep staring at me and asking me what my secret is."

Celia and I both raised an eyebrow and looked at her in the same way. She noticed it, glanced at the spot where Iosif had died, and whispered, "Oh God."

I took a deep breath, glanced at Celia, then left them and walked toward Stefan's house. They followed, saying nothing. Then they stood outside the site of the house while I walked through the rooms, finding five symbionts, including the two I'd met when I met Celia. And I found a misshapen bullet inside a charred plank. I had to break apart what was left of the plank to get at it, but once I had it, I found a faint blood scent. One of the symbionts. The bullet had passed through the man's body and gone into the wood.

Finally, I found the place where Stefan's body had fallen and burned in one of the bedrooms near part of the window frame. Had he been trying to get out or . . . might he have been firing a gun at his attackers? I couldn't be certain, but it seemed likely to me that he died fighting against whomever had done this.

I went back to Celia and shook my head. "I'm sorry. He didn't survive either."

She glared at me as though I'd killed him—a look filled with grief and rage.

"Where," she demanded. "Where did he die?"

"Over here."

They both followed me to the place where Stefan had died curled on his side, limbs drawn tight against his body.

"Here," I said.

Celia looked down, then knelt and put her hands flat in the ashes, taking up some of what remained of Stefan. For a long time, she said nothing. I glanced to the east where the sky was growing a little more light.

After a while, Celia looked up at Brook. "He was shooting back at them," she said. "He could have made himself do it, even if they came during the day. Days were hard on him, but he could wake up enough to shoot back."

Brook nodded. "He could have."

"That's what I thought," I said.

Celia glared at me, then closed her eyes, tears spilling down her face. "You can't tell for sure?"

"No. But I know there was shooting. I found a bullet that smelled of one of the other members of his household. And Stefan's position . . . somehow it seemed that he might have been shooting back. I hope he hit some of them."

"He had guns," Celia said. "Iosif didn't like guns, but Stefan did."

It hadn't helped him survive.

"It's almost dawn," I said. "Will you drive me back to where Wright is waiting? I can direct you."

They looked at each other, then at me.

"Drive me to Wright, then follow us to his cabin," I said. "Although we'll have to find another place soon. The cabin is almost too small for two people."

"Iosif owns—owned—a house outside Arlington," Brook said. "Some of us used it to commute to jobs or to entertain visiting family members. There are three bedrooms, three baths. It's a nice place, and it's ours. We have a right to be there."

I nodded, relieved. "That would be better. Could other symbionts be there already?"

Brook looked at Celia.

"I don't use it," Celia said. "I haven't kept up with the schedule."

"I don't think anyone's there," Brook said. "If there is . . . if some of us are there, Shori, they need you, too."

I nodded. "Take me back to Wright. Then we'll go there."

During the sad, silent trip back to Wright's car, I had time to be afraid. These two women's lives were in my hands, and yet I had no idea how to save them. Of course I would take their blood. I didn't want to, but I would. They smelled like my father and my brother. They smelled almost Ina, and that was enough to make them unappetizing. And yet I would make myself take their blood. Would that be enough? Iosif had told me almost nothing. What else should I do? I could talk to them. What I told them to do, they would try to do, once I'd taken their blood. Would that be enough?

If it wasn't, they were dead.

Eleven

To GET to the house that my father had bought for his symbionts and my brothers', we followed the highway through
dense woods, past the occasional lonely house or farm, past
side roads and alongside the river. I asked Wright whether the
river had a name.

"That's the north fork of the Stillaguamish," he told me.
"Don't ask me what 'Stillaguamish' means because I have no
idea. But it's the name of a local Native American tribe."

Eventually we reached more populated areas where houses
and farms were more visible, scattered along the highway.
There were still many trees, but now there were more smells
of people and domestic animals nearby. In particular, there was
the scent of horses. I recognized it from the time I'd spent
prowling around Wright's neighborhood. Horses made noises
and moved around restlessly when I got close enough to them
to be noticed. My scent apparently disturbed them. Yet their
scent had become one of the many that meant "home" to me.

Wright and I followed the women's car talking quietly. I told
him what had happened to my father's community and that
Celia and Brook had survived because they were in Seattle.

He shook his head. "I don't know what to make of this," he
said. "Your kind have some serious enemies. What we need to
do is find some place safe where we can hunker down, pool
information, and figure out what to do. There's probably a
way to tip the police to these people if we can just figure out
who they are."

As he spoke, I realized that I was willing to go further than
that. If we found the people who had murdered both my male
and my female families, I wanted to kill them, had to kill them.
How else could I keep my new family safe?

My new family . . .

"Wright," I said softly and saw him glance at me. "Celia and
Brook will be with us now. They have to be."

There was a moment of silence. Then he said, "They're not
going to die?"

"Not if I can take them over. I'm going to try."

377

"You'll feed from them."

"Yes." I hesitated. "And I don't know what's going to happen. I don't remember anything about this. Iosif told me it had to be done when an Ina died and left symbionts, but he didn't tell me much. He couldn't know . . . how soon I would need the information."

"Maybe Brook and Celia know."

I turned away from him, looked out the window. The sun was well up now, and in spite of the threatening rain clouds, it was getting bright enough to bother me. I reached into the backseat, grabbed the blanket I had brought, and wrapped myself in it. Once I'd done that, except for my eyes, I was almost comfortable.

"Look in the glove compartment there," Wright said gesturing. "There should be a pair of sunglasses."

I looked at the glove compartment, decided how it must open, opened it, and found the glasses. They were too big for my face, and I had to keep pushing them up my nose, but they were very dark, and I immediately felt better. "Thank you," I said and touched his face. He needed to shave. I rubbed the brown stubble and found even that good to touch.

He took my hand and kissed it, then said, "Why don't you want to ask Brook and Celia what they know?"

I sighed. Of course he had not forgotten the question. "Embarrassment," I said. "Pride. Imagine a doctor who has to ask her patient how to perform a life-saving operation."

"Not a confidence builder," he said. "I can see that. But if they know anything, you need to find out."

"I do." I drew a deep breath. "Brook is older. Maybe I'll feed from her first and find out what she knows."

"She can't be much older. They look about the same age."

"Do they? Brook is older by about twenty years."

"That much?" He looked skeptical. "How can you tell?"

I thought about it. "Her skin shows it a little. I guess it's as much the way she smells as the way she looks. She smells . . . much more Ina than Celia does. She's been with my father longer than Celia's been with my brother. I think Celia is about your age."

He shook his head. "Brook doesn't have any wrinkles, not even those little lines around the eyes."

"I know."

"No gray either. Is her hair dyed?"

"It isn't, no."

"Jesus, am I still going to look that young in twenty years?"

I smiled. "You should."

He glanced at me and grinned, delighted.

"I think we're here," I said.

The car ahead of us had turned and pulled into the driveway of a long, low ranch house. There were no other houses in sight. We turned down the same driveway, and when Brook stopped, Wright said, "Hang on a moment." He jumped out and went to speak to the two women. I listened curiously. He wanted them to pull into the garage that I could see farther back on the property. It bothered him that this house was connected with Iosif's family. He thought the killers might know about it.

"You heard that didn't you?" he asked me when he came back.

I nodded. "You may be right. I hoped we could settle here for a while, but maybe we shouldn't. Even the police might come here to look for information about Iosif."

He pulled the car into the garage alongside Brook's. The garage had room enough for three cars, but there was no other car in it. "True," he said. "But we won't be able to use my cabin for long either. I already told my aunt and uncle that I was leaving." He hesitated. "Actually, they sort of told me I had to go. They know . . . well they think that I've been sneaking girls in."

I laughed in spite of everything.

"My aunt listened at the door a few nights ago. She told my uncle she heard 'sex noises.' My uncle told me he understands, said he was young once. But he says I've got to go because my aunt doesn't understand."

I shook my head. "You're an adult. What do they expect?"

He pulled me against him for a moment. "Just be glad they haven't seen you."

I was. I got out of the car and stood waiting, wrapped in my blanket, in the shadow of the garage until Brook had opened the back door, then I hurried inside. There was, even from the back, not another house in sight. There were other people around. I could smell them. But they were a comfortable distance away, and the many trees probably helped make their houses less visible.

Inside, the rooms were clean, and there were dishes in the cupboard. There were canned and frozen foods, towels, and clean bedding.

"The rule," Brook said, "is to leave the place clean and well-stocked. People tend to do that. Tended to do that."

"Let's settle somewhere," I said to Celia and Brook. "I need to talk with you both."

Wright had walked down the hallway to look out the side door. Now he was wandering back, looking into each of the bedrooms. He looked up at me when I spoke.

I shrugged. "I changed my mind," I told him.

"About what?" Celia demanded. I looked at her and noticed that she was beginning to sweat. The house was cool. As soon as we got in, Brook had complained that it was cold. She had reset the thermostat from fifty-five to seventy, but the house had not even begun to warm up. Yet Celia was hot. And she was afraid.

I waited until we'd all found chairs in the living room. "About our becoming a family," I said.

Both women looked uncomfortable.

"If you know any other Ina, and you would prefer to go to them, you should do it now, while you can," I said. "If not, if you're going to join with me, then I need your help."

"We're here," Celia said. She wiped her forehead with a hand that trembled a little. "You know we don't know anyone else."

"And you know I have amnesia. I have no memory of seeing or hearing about the handling of symbionts whose Ina has died. Iosif told me a little, but anything either of you know—anything at all—you should tell me, for your own sakes."

Brook nodded. "I wondered what you knew." She took a deep breath. "It scares me that you're a child, but at least you're female. That might save us."

"Why?" I asked.

She looked surprised. "You don't know that either?" She shook her head and sighed deeply. "Venom from Ina females is more potent than venom from males. That's what Iosif told me. It has something to do with the way prehistoric Ina females used to get and keep mates." She smiled a little. "Now females find mates for their sons, and males for their daughters, and it's all very civilized. But long ago, groups of sisters competed to capture groups of brothers, and the competition was chemical. If a group of sisters had the venom to hold a group of brothers, they were more likely to have several healthy children, and their sons would have a safe haven with their fathers when they came of age. And their daughters were more likely to have even more potent venom."

"The sons would have more potent venom, too," Wright said.

"Yes, but among the Ina, the females competed. It's like the way males have competed among humans. There was a time when a big, strong man might push other men aside and marry a lot of wives, pass on his genes to a lot of children. His size and strength might be passed to his daughters as well as his sons, but his daughters were still likely to be smaller and weaker than his sons.

"Ina children, male and female, wind up with more potent venom, but the female's is still more potent than the male's. In that sense, the Ina are kind of a matriarchy. And a little thing like Shori might be a real power." She took a deep breath and glanced at Celia. "Ina men are sort of like us, like symbionts. They become addicted to the venom of one group of sisters. That's what it means to be mated. Once they're addicted, they aren't fertile with other females, and from time to time, they need their females. Need . . . like I need Iosif."

She knew more about Ina reproduction and Ina history than I did. She should, of course, after so many years with Iosif. But still, hearing it from her made me uncomfortable. I tried to ignore my discomfort. "You were with Iosif a long time," I said.

"Yeah." She blinked and looked off into the distance at nothing. "Twenty-two years," she said. She covered her face with her hands, curled her body away from me on the chair, crying. Like Celia, she was a lot bigger than I was, but for a moment, she seemed to be a small, helpless person in deep distress. Yet I didn't want to touch her. I would have to soon enough.

She said through her tears, "I always *knew* that I would die before him and that was good. I was so willing to accept him when he asked me. God, I loved him. And I thought it meant

I would never be alone. My father died when I was eight. I had a brother who drowned when he was seven. And my sister's husband died of cancer when they'd been married for only two years. I thought I had finally found a way to avoid all that pain —a way never to be alone again." She was crying again.

"I'm Iosif's daughter," I said. "I hope that my venom is strong and that you'll come to me. It won't be the same, I know, but you won't be alone. I want you with me."

"Why should you?" Celia demanded. "You don't know us."

"With my amnesia, I don't know anyone," I said. "I'm getting to know Wright. And there's a woman named Theodora. I'm getting to know her. And, Celia, I'm only beginning to know myself."

She looked at me for several seconds, then shuddered and turned away. "I hate this," she said. "Damn, I hate this!"

And this was the way a symbiont behaved when she was missing her Ina. Or at least this was the way Celia behaved— suspicious, short-tempered, afraid. Brook and Celia were both grieving, but Celia must have been longer without Stefan than Brook had been without Iosif.

I got up and went to Celia, trying to ignore the fact that she clearly didn't want me to touch her. She was sensible enough not to protest when I took her hand, drew her to her feet, and led her away into one of the bedrooms.

"I hate this," she said again and turned her face away from me as I encouraged her to lie down on the huge bed. She smelled more of Stefan than she had before, and I truly didn't want to touch her. Where I would have enjoyed tasting Theodora or Wright, I had to force myself to touch Celia.

She turned back to face me and caught my expression. "You don't want to do it," she said. She was crying again, her body stiff with anger.

"Of course I don't," I said, and I slid into bed next to her. "Stefan has posted olfactory keep-out signs all over you. Didn't you ever wonder why Ina can live together without going after one another's symbionts?"

"It happens sometimes."

"But only with new symbionts, right?"

"You have amnesia, and yet you know that?"

"I'm alive, Celia. My senses work. I can't help but know." I unbuttoned her shirt to bare her neck. "What I don't know is how this will be for you. Not good, maybe."

"Scares me," she admitted.

I nodded. "Bear it. Bear it and keep still. Later, when I can, I'll make it up to you."

She nodded. "You remind me of Stefan a little. He told me I reminded him of you."

I bit her. I was more abrupt than I should have been, but her scent was repelling me more and more. I had to do it quickly if I were going to be able to do it at all.

She gave a little scream, then frantically tried to push me away, tried to struggle free, tried to hit me . . . I had to use both my arms and my legs to hold her still, had to wrap myself all around her. If she'd been any bigger, I would have had to knock her unconscious. In fact, that might have been kinder. I kept waiting for her to accept me, the way strangers did when I climbed through their windows and bit them. But she couldn't. And strangely, it never occurred to me to detach for a moment and order her to be still. I would have done that with a stranger, but I never thought to do it with her.

She managed not to scream anymore after that first strangled sound, but she struggled wildly, frantically until I stopped taking her blood. I had only tasted her, taking much less than a full meal. It was as much as I could stand. I hoped it was enough.

I gave her a moment to understand that I had stopped, and when she stopped struggling, I let her go. "Did I hurt you?" I asked.

She was crying silently. She cringed as I leaned over to lick the bite and take the blood that was still coming. She put her hands on my shoulders and pushed but managed not to push hard. I went on licking the bite. She needed that to help with healing.

"I always liked that so much when Stefan did it," she said.

"It should be enjoyable," I said, although I wasn't enjoying myself at all. I was doing what seemed to be my duty. "And it helps your wounds heal quickly and cleanly. It will be enjoyable again someday soon."

She relaxed a little, and I thought I might be reaching her. "Maybe," she said. "Maybe you've got some kind of keep-out

sign on you, too—as far as I'm concerned, I mean. I panicked.
I couldn't control myself. Your bite didn't hurt, but it was . . .
it was horrible." She drew away from me with a shudder.

"But do you feel better?" I asked.

"Better?"

"You've stopped shaking."

"Oh. Yeah. Thanks . . . I guess."

"I don't know exactly how long it will be before we can take
pleasure in one another, but I think it's important that you do
feel better now. Next time will be easier and more comfortable." Now that I'd bitten her, it would. It seemed best to tell
her that.

"Hope so."

I left her alone in the huge bed. She wouldn't have been able
to sleep if I'd stayed. I wouldn't have been able to sleep if I'd
stayed.

I went to the bathroom, washed, and then just stayed there.
I knew I had to go to Brook soon. The longer I waited, the
harder it would be. Maybe Brook would have an easier time
since she hadn't seemed so needy. Or perhaps it would be
worse because she'd been with Iosif for so long. Was twenty-
two years a long time when she would live to be maybe two
hundred? If only I knew what I was doing.

I sat on the side of the bathtub for a long time, hearing
Celia cry until she fell asleep, hearing Wright moving around
the kitchen, hearing Brook breathing softly in one of the bedrooms. She was not asleep, but she was not moving around either. She was sitting or lying down—probably waiting for me.

I got up and went to her.

"I thought you could wait," she said when she saw me. "If
you wanted to, you could wait until tomorrow. I mean, I'm all
right now. I'm not getting the shakes or anything."

I didn't sigh. I didn't say anything. I only went to the bed
where she lay atop the bedspread and lay down beside her. Her
scent was so much like my father's that if I closed my eyes, it
was almost as though I were lying in bed beside Iosif, and even
though I had begun to trust Iosif and even to like him, I had
not found him appetizing in any way at all.

"We will get through this," I said. "What you feel now will
end."

She sighed and closed her eyes. "I hope so," she said. "Do it."

I did it. And when I was finished, I left her crying into a pillow. She was no more able to take comfort from me than Celia had been, and there was no comfort for me in either of them. I went out, hoping to find the comfort I needed with Wright. He was in the living room, eating a ham sandwich and a bag of microwave popcorn and watching a television that I had not noticed before. He aimed the remote and stopped the program as I came in.

"No cable," he said, "but movies and old TV shows galore." He gestured toward the shelves of tapes and DVDs in the cabinet. Then, after a moment, he asked, "How are things?"

I shook my head and went to sit next to him on the arm of his chair. I had worried that he would draw away from me, resent my bringing two strangers into our family, but he reached up, lifted me with a hand under one of my arms, and put me on his lap. I made myself comfortable there, his arms around me. I sighed with contentment.

"Things were horrible," I said. "But they're better now."

That was when I heard the people outside, first two of them, then, as I sat up and away from Wright's chest and the beat of his heart, I heard more. I couldn't tell how many.

Then I smelled the gasoline.

Twelve

I TURNED TO speak very softly into Wright's ear. "The killers are here." I covered his mouth with my hand. "They're
here now. They have guns and gasoline. Go wake Brook and
Celia—quietly!—and look after them. Keep them safe. Watch
the side door. When I clear a way, get them out of here. Don't
worry about me. Don't try to help me. Go. Now."

I slid off his lap, avoided his grasping hands, grabbed my
blanket and glasses, and ran for the side door. There were men
—human males—at the front and back doors, and at least one
was heading for the side door at the end of the hall, but no
one reached it before I slipped out of it and down the three
concrete steps to the ground.

The men were spreading gasoline all around the house, quietly splashing it on the wood siding so that it puddled on the
ground. I threw my blanket on the ground alongside an oak
tree that was losing its leaves. It was probably overhanging the
house too much to survive what was to come. It gave me shade,
though, and kept me from burning. I put the glasses on, then
turned toward the sounds of a man who was approaching from
the front yard, spreading his gasoline as quietly as he could.

He was like the deer I had killed—just prey. He was my first
deer that day. Before he realized I was there, I was on his back,
one hand over his nose and mouth, my legs around him, riding
him, my other arm around his head under his chin. I broke his
neck, and an instant later, as he collapsed, I tore out his throat.
I wanted no noise from him.

He'd had a gun—a big strange-looking one. I picked it up by
the barrel, thrust it into the house through the door I'd come
out of. Then I moved the dead man's gasoline can to the oak
tree.

Another man was coming around from the backyard, and he
was my second deer, as quickly dispatched as the first. It was
almost a relief to use my speed and strength without worrying
about hurting someone. And it was good to kill these men who
had surely taken part in killing my families.

Someone in the house opened the side door a crack, and I

beckoned with both hands, calling them out. That same instant, someone threw something through two or three of the windows, smashing them. Someone in the backyard lit the gasoline, and flames roared around the house on every side but the one I had cleared. Through a window, I could see that there was fire inside the house, too.

Wright, Celia, and Brook spilled noisily out of the house, but the roar of the fire probably drowned out the noise they made at least as far as the gunmen were concerned. Wright had the gun I had left for him. I snatched up the second man's gun and thrust it into Celia's hand. Of the two women, I thought she would be more likely to know how to use it. She started to say something, but I put a hand over her mouth.

She nodded and positioned herself so that she and Wright had Brook and me between them. She watched the front while Wright watched the back.

I went to Wright who was edging away from the heat of the fire, but still looking toward the backyard. He glanced back at me.

I touched his mouth briefly with my fingers to keep him silent, then stepped ahead of him, acting on what I had heard and he had not. For the second time that day, I had to evade his hands. One more gunman was coming around the house, around the fire at a run, perhaps to see what had happened to his friends. He was my third deer. Best not to make noise until we had to.

How many gunmen were left? How many had there been? There hadn't been time for me to listen and estimate, but I tried to think back to what I had heard. Then my concentration was shattered by the sudden, deep, quick spitting of Celia's gun. She had shot a man who had come around the house from the front.

The man fell, and even if no one had heard the strange spitting sound of Celia's gun, someone must have seen him go down. The element of surprise was gone.

I snatched the gun of the man I'd just killed, shouted to the others, and all of us sprinted for the shelter of trees. They would give us cover when the other gunmen came to see what the shooting was about.

We all reached the trees in time. I was with Brook behind the oak, which, high above, was already catching fire where it over-hung the house. I gave her the gun and she frowned, studying it. Meanwhile, Wright and Celia were already firing. I could see men firing back from both the front and the backyards, but they could not aim very well because they lacked cover where they were. We had trees, but they had only the burning house. If they had tried to reach trees that might have shielded them, Wright or Celia would have gotten a clear shot at them. If we survived, I would get Wright and Celia to teach me to shoot.

Then there was the sound of sirens in the distance. I heard it and froze, wondering how we could avoid being caught either by the gunmen or by the police. Then Brook looked up from her gun, and I realized she was beginning to hear the sirens, too.

And the gunmen heard them. The shooting from the other side dribbled away to silence. Wright and Celia stopped their very careful firing because suddenly they had no targets.

I could hear the remaining gunmen running, their footsteps going away from us, toward the street. I showed myself, walking out away from the tree, providing a target for anyone who had stayed behind.

No one shot me.

I ran to the garage, lifted one of the doors, and glanced toward the side of the house, where I hoped Wright, Celia, and Brook were paying attention.

They were coming, all three of them, at a run.

I opened the other garage door and waited until they were all in the cars. Then I got in and we fled.

We fled slowly. Wright said we shouldn't speed, shouldn't do anything that might make us memorable to anyone who saw us or bring us to the attention of the police. He was leading this time so his judgment kept Brook's speed down. There were no neighbors near enough to see the house or report that we'd left it (and left several corpses) just after the fire began. In fact, the guns had made so little noise that I wondered whether human ears had heard them with the houses so far apart. It was almost certainly the smoke that had caught someone's attention. That meant the emergency call probably went to the fire depart-ment. Firemen would arrive, begin to put out the fire, find the bodies, and then call the police. They would also find the gas cans. We had to avoid getting involved in the investigation that would surely follow. I had seen too many police programs on Wright's television to believe there was any story we could tell the police about this that would keep us out of jail.

"Where are we going?" I asked Wright.

"God," he said. "I don't know. Back to the cabin for now, I guess."

"No," I said. "Your relatives are there in the front house. Let's not lead anyone to them."

"Do you think that's likely? Whoever these people are, they don't know anything about me." He shook his head. What he had been through seemed to be too much for him suddenly. "Whoever they are . . . Who the hell are they? Why did they try to kill us? I've never shot at anyone before—never even wanted to."

"We're all alive," I said.

He glanced at me. "Yeah."

"We should find a place to stop when we've gotten a few miles farther away. We need to talk with the others, find out if they know of another place where we can stay for a while."

"Any place they know is probably as dangerous as the place we just left."

I sighed and nodded. "We need to be far away from all this," I said. "I can't believe that Brook was with Iosif for twenty-two years, and yet she knows of no relatives but my mothers, no friends or business associates."

"I was wondering about that," he said. "Do you think she's lying?"

I thought about that for a moment, then said, "I don't think so. I just think she knows more than she realizes she knows. Maybe Iosif told her not to remember or not to share what she knows with anyone outside his family. I mean, as things are, I don't know where to begin a search for more of my kind. I don't even know whether I should be looking for them. I don't want to get people killed, but I have to do something. I have to find out who these murderers are and why they want to kill us. And I have to find a way to stop them." I paused, then fidgeted uncomfortably. I already had the beginnings of a burn on my face and arms, and had left my jacket in the house. "Wright, would you be cold if I used your jacket?"

"What?" He glanced at me, then said, "Oh." I helped him struggle out of his jacket, pulling it off of him while he drove. Once I had it, I covered myself with it as though it were the blanket that I had lost, probably leaving it beside the oak tree. The jacket was warm and smelled of Wright and was a very comfortable thing to be wrapped in.

"You and I are conspicuous together," he said. "But you could go into a clothing store with Celia and pass as her daughter. You could get yourself some clothes that fit and another jacket with a hood, maybe a pair of gloves and some sunglasses that fit your face."

"All right. We should get food, too, for the three of you. It should be things you can open and eat right here in the car. I'm not sure when we'll dare to settle somewhere."

"I should be back at work on Monday."

I looked at him, then looked away. "I know. I'm sorry. I don't have any idea when this will be over."

He drove silently for a few minutes. We were, I realized, still headed southwest toward Arlington. Once we arrived in Arlington, he seemed to know his way around. He took us straight to a supermarket where we could buy the food we needed. Once we were parked, we moved over to the larger car to talk with Celia and Brook.

"Don't you need to sleep?" Brook asked me as soon as we got into the backseat. "Doesn't the fact that it's day bother you at all?"

"I'm tired," I admitted. "You're probably all tired."

"But don't you sleep during the day?" Celia asked. It occurred to me that they had been discussing me. Better that than terrifying themselves over the fact that several men had just tried to murder us.

"I prefer to sleep during the day," I said, "but I don't have to. I can sleep whenever I'm tired."

Brook looked at Celia. "That's why we're not dead," she said. "They came during the day, thinking that any Ina in the house would be asleep, completely unconscious."

"Why didn't it help her save her mothers?" Celia asked.

Brook looked at me.

"I don't know," I said. "Have either of you ever heard of a community being destroyed the way my parents' communities were? I mean, has it happened before anywhere else?"

Both women shook their heads. Brook said, "Not that I know of."

"Maybe that's it then." I thought for a moment. "If no one was expecting trouble, probably no one was keeping watch. Why would they? I don't know whether I usually slept during the day. My mothers did, so I probably did, too, just because it was more convenient to be up when they were. I'll bet the symbionts had adapted to a nocturnal way of life just as symbionts had in Iosif's community. But I don't know. That's the trouble; I don't know anything." I looked at Brook. "You must have spent time at my mothers' community. Wasn't everyone nocturnal?"

"Pretty much," she answered. "Your eldermothers had three or four symbionts who did research for them. They were often awake during the day. I guess it didn't help."

I looked at Celia. "Did Stefan always sleep during the day?"

"He said he got stupid if he didn't sleep," she answered. "He got sluggish and clumsy."

"Iosif had to sleep," Brook said. "He would go completely unconscious wherever he happened to be when the sun came up. And once he got to sleep, it was impossible to wake him up until after sundown."

Wright put his arm around me. "You're definitely the new, improved model," he said.

I nodded. "I think maybe someone's decided there shouldn't be a new, improved model."

"We were talking about that," Brook said. "About how maybe this is all because someone doesn't like the experimenting that your family was doing. Or someone envied your family for producing you and Stefan. I don't know."

"How could it be about her?" Wright wanted to know. "Those guys were human, not Ina."

"They may be symbionts," Celia said.

"Or one of them might be a symbiont and the rest hirelings," Brook added.

Wright frowned. "Maybe. But it seems to me they could just as easily be ordinary human beings who imagine they're fighting vampires."

"And who have focused only on my family," I said.

"We don't know that. Hell, we're in the same boat you are, Shori. We don't really know anything."

I nodded and yawned. "We probably know more than we realize. I think we'll be able to come up with at least a few answers after we've gotten some rest."

"Why are we in this parking lot?" Brook asked.

"To get food for you," I said. "After that, we'll find a place to park in the woods. We can get some sleep in the cars. Later, when we're rested, we'll see what we can figure out."

"I thought we would go to your house," Celia said to Wright.

"His relatives' home is too close by," I said. "I don't want them to get hurt or killed because someone's after us—or after me. I don't want that to happen to anyone. So no hotel for now."

The two women exchanged another look, and this time I had no idea what they were thinking.

"Let's go buy what we need," Wright said. "Celia, while Brook and I shop for food, can you be Shori's mother or her big sister? There's a clothing store . . ." He opened the glove compartment, found a pencil and a small wire-bound notebook. "Here's the address," he said, writing. "And here's how to get there. I did some work here in Arlington last year. I remember the place. This clothing store is only a few blocks from here, and it's a good place for buying cheap casual clothes. She needs a couple of pairs of jeans, shirts, a good hooded jacket, gloves, and sunglasses that will fit her face. Okay?"

Celia nodded. "No problem if you have money. I spent most of what Stefan gave me in Seattle. He's going to—" She stopped, frowned, and looked away from us across the parking lot. She wiped at her eyes with her fingers but said nothing more.

After a moment, Wright got his wallet out of his pocket and put several twenties into her hand. "I see an ATM over there," he said. "I'll get more—enough for a few days."

"We need gas, too," Brook said. She looked at me, then looked past me. "I have my checkbook and a credit card, but they're both Iosif's accounts. I don't know whether using them will attract the attention of the police—or of our enemies. I have enough money to fill our tank, but if this lasts, if we're on the run for more than a few days, money is likely to become a problem." There was an oddly false note in her voice, as though she were lying somehow. She smelled nervous, and I didn't like the way she looked past me rather than at me. I thought about it, and after a moment, I understood.

"Money will not be a problem," I said, "and you know it."

Brook looked a little embarrassed. After a moment, she nodded. "I wasn't sure you knew . . . what to do," she said.

And Wright said, "What do you expect her to do?"

"Steal," I said. "She expects me to be a very good thief. I will be. People will be happy to give me money once I've bitten them."

He looked at me doubtfully, and I reached up to touch his stubbly chin.

"You should get a razor, too," I said.

"I don't want you getting in trouble for stealing," he said.

"I won't." I shrugged. "I don't want to do it. I don't feel good about doing it, but I'll do what's necessary to sustain us." I glanced at Brook, feeling almost angry with her. "Ask me questions when you want to know things. Tell me whatever you believe I should know. Complain whenever you want to complain. But don't talk to other people when you mean your words for me, and speak the truth."

She shrugged. "All right."

My anger ebbed away. "Let's go buy what we need," I said.

"Hang on a minute," Wright said. He wrote something else in the wire-bound notebook. Then he tore out the page and handed it to Celia. "Those are my sizes. If you can, get me a pair of jeans and a sweatshirt."

She looked at the sizes, smiled, and said, "Okay."

We left them. Celia and I took her car—one of Iosif's cars, she said—and drove to the clothing store. She found it easily, following Wright's directions, and that seemed to surprise her.

"I usually get lost at least once and have to stop and ask somebody for directions," she said. And then, "Listen, you're my sister, okay? I refuse to believe I look old enough to be your mother."

I laughed. "How old are you?"

"Twenty-three. Stefan found me when I was nineteen, right after I'd moved out of my mother's house."

"Twenty-three, same as Wright."

"Yeah. And he's your first. You did very well for yourself. He's a decent-looking big bear of a guy, and he's nice. That jacket of his looks like a way-too-big coat on you."

"When he found me, when he stopped to pick me up, I couldn't believe how good he smelled. My memory was so destroyed that I didn't even know what I wanted from him, but his scent pulled me into the car with him."

Celia laughed, then looked sad and stared at nothing for a moment. "Stefan would say things like that. I've always wondered what it would be like to be one of you, so tuned in to smells and sounds, living so long and being so strong. It doesn't seem fair that you can't convert us like all the stories say."

"That would be very strange," I said. "If a dog bit a man, no one would expect the man to become a dog. He might get an infection and die, but that's the worst."

"You haven't found out about werewolves yet, then."

"I've read about them on Wright's computer. A lot of the people who write about vampires seem to be interested in werewolves, too." I shook my head. "Ina are probably responsible for most vampire legends. I wonder what started the werewolf legends."

"I've thought about that," Celia said. "It was probably rabies. People get bitten, go crazy, froth at the mouth, run around like animals, attacking other people who then come down with the same problems . . . That would probably be enough to make ancient people come up with the idea of werewolves. Shori, what did you get mad at Brook about a few minutes ago?"

I looked at her and, after a moment, decided that she had asked a real question. "She touched my pride, I think. She worries that I can't take care of the three of you. I worry that I won't always know how to take care of you. I hate my ignorance. I need to learn from you since there is no adult Ina to ask."

"Before I saw what you did today, I figured we'd be the ones taking care of you."

"You will. Iosif called it 'mutualistic symbiosis.' I think it's also called just 'mutualism.'"

"Yeah, those were his words for it. Before Stefan brought me to meet him, I'd never even heard those words used that way before. I thought he had made them up until I found them in a science dictionary. So you want us to be straight with you even if you don't always like what we say?"

"Yes."

"Works for me. Let's get you some clothes."

I wound up with two pairs of boy's blue jeans that actually fit, two long-sleeved shirts, one red and one black, a pair of gloves, a jacket with a hood, sunglasses, and some underwear. Then Celia used the last of her own money as well as the last of what Wright had given her to get him a pair of jeans and a hooded sweatshirt. Then we headed back to the supermarket to meet Wright and Brook.

"Brook and I are lucky we left our suitcases in the back of the car," Celia said. "A Laundromat would be a good idea for us, but otherwise, we're okay. Did you hear that saleswoman? She said you were the cutest thing she'd seen all day. She figured you were about ten."

I shook my head. I'd said almost nothing to the woman. I had no idea how to act like a ten-year-old human child. "Does it bother you that I'm so small?"

She grinned. "It did at first. Now I kind of like it. After seeing you in action today, I think you'd be goddamn scary if you were bigger."

"I will grow."

"Yeah, but before you do, I'll have time to get used to you." She paused. "How about you? Are you okay with me?"

"You mean do I want you?"

". . . yeah. You didn't exactly choose us."

"I inherited you, both of you, from my father's family. You're mine."

"You want us?"

I smiled up at her. "Oh, yes."

Thirteen

WE TURNED northeast again and drove until we found a place where we could go off a side road and camp in the woods, far enough away from the road and the highway to be invisible. I took a look around before I went to sleep, made sure there was no one near us, no one watching us.

After I got back, I asked Celia to stay awake and keep one of the guns handy until dark. She was a good shot, she'd had some rest, and she said she wasn't very tired. We had the three guns I had taken from the gunmen and Celia's handgun—a semiautomatic Beretta. She told me the gunmen had used silenced Heckler & Koch submachine guns. She said she'd never seen one before, but she'd read about them.

"The gunmen meant to kill us all, but to do it quietly," she said. "I don't think anyone heard the shooting over the noise of the fire and the distance between houses. We need to avoid these people, at least until we find a few more friends."

I agreed with her. But at that moment, I just wanted to sleep. I went to sleep in the backseat of Wright's car and woke briefly as Wright lifted me out and put me down in Brook's car, where someone had folded the back seats down and spread clothing on them to make them less uncomfortable.

"What are you doing?" I whispered.

He climbed in, lay down beside me, and pulled me against him. "Go back to sleep," he said into my ear. I did. The makeshift bed turned out to be not so uncomfortable after all.

Then Brook lay down on the other side of me, and her scent disturbed me, made me want to get up and go sleep somewhere else. I tried to ignore it. Her scent would change, was already beginning to change. I slept.

Sometime later, after dark, I bit her.

She struggled. I had to hold her to keep her still and silent at first. Then, after a minute, she gave a long sigh and lay as I'd positioned her, accepting me as much as she could. She didn't enjoy herself, but after that first panic, she at least did not seem to be suffering.

I had only tasted her before. Now I took a full meal from her—not an emotionally satisfying meal, but a physically sustaining one. Afterward, I spent time lapping at the wound until she truly relaxed against me. She eased back into sleep and never noticed when I got up, stepped over her, and got out of the car.

I closed the door as quietly as I could and stood beside it. Not being fully satisfied made me restless. I paced away from the car, then back toward it. I found myself wondering whether Brook, Celia, and Theodora would be better able to sustain me when they were as fully mine as Wright was. Would they be enough? I was much smaller than my father who had preferred to have eight symbionts. My demands must be smaller.

Mustn't they?

I shook my head in disgust. My ignorance wasn't just annoying. It was dangerous. How could I take care of my symbionts when I didn't even know how to protect them from me?

I stopped beside the car and looked through its back window at Brook and Wright, now lying next to each other, both still asleep. Both had been touching me. Now that I had moved, they were almost touching one another.

My feelings shifted at once from fear for them to confusion. I wanted to crawl between them again and feel them both lying comfortably, reassuringly against me. They were both mine. And yet there was something deeply right about seeing them together as they were.

Celia came up behind me, looked at me, glanced into the car, then drew me away from it. We went to the other car and sat there. "I long for a shower," I said.

"Me too," Celia said. "You mind if I go to sleep now?"

"Go ahead." She had already climbed into the backseat of Wright's car. She put her handgun on the floor and lay on her back on the seat.

"I think I need to say something you won't like hearing," she said.

"All right."

She closed her eyes for several seconds, then said, "Stefan told me what happened to Hugh Tang. He told me and he told Oriana Bernardi because he knew we both loved Hugh."

Loved? I listened to her with growing confusion. I didn't know what to say so I said nothing.

"The relationship among an Ina and several symbionts is about the closest thing I've seen to a workable group marriage," she said. "With us, sometimes people got jealous and started to pull the family apart, and . . . well . . . Stefan would have to talk to them. He said the first time that happened, he was still living with his mothers and one of them had to tell him what to do, and even then he could hardly do it because he was feeling so confused himself. He didn't say 'jealous.' He said 'confused.'"

I nodded. "Confused."

"I don't really understand that, but then, we are different species."

"How did you wind up with Hugh?"

She smiled. "Hugh had been with Stefan for a few years when Stefan asked me to join him. When I'd been there for a while, Hugh asked for me. Stefan said that was up to me, so Hugh asked me. It scared me because I didn't understand at first how an Ina household works, that everyone went to Stefan, fed him, loved him, but that we could have relationships with one another, too, or with other nearby symbionts. Well, I didn't go to Hugh when he first asked, but after a while, I did. He was a good man."

"I'm sorry," I said. "I wish he hadn't found me when he did."

"I know."

I looked at her lying there, not looking at me. "Thank you for telling me," I said.

She nodded and looked at me finally. "You're welcome. I didn't just say it for your benefit, though. I figure I might want to have a kid someday."

I wanted that—a home in which my symbionts enjoyed being with me and enjoyed one another and raised their children as I raised mine. That felt right, felt good.

I left Celia alone so she could sleep, and I checked the area again to make sure we were still as alone as we seemed to be. Once I was sure of that, I set out at a jog, then a run to find out who our nearest neighbors were. I followed my nose and found a farm where two adults and four children lived, along with horses, chickens, geese, and goats. I found three other houses, widely separated along the side road, but without farm fields around them. I found no real community on the territory I covered.

It seemed we had privacy and a little more time to recover and decide what to do. I could question Celia and, in particular, Brook.

I went back to the cars and used some of the disposable wipes that Wright and Brook had bought to clean up as best I could. Then I put on clean clothes. As I got my jeans on, I heard Brook wake up and slip out of the car behind me. She made slightly different noises breathing and moving around than Wright or Celia did.

"God, it's dark out here," she said. "If I weren't a symbiont, I don't think I could see at all. Aren't you cold?"

I wasn't really, but I pulled on an undershirt, then put my long-sleeved shirt on, buttoned it, and pulled on my new jacket. "I'm all right," I said. "I'm glad you're awake. I need to talk to you."

"Sure."

"Eat first. Do whatever you need to do. This will probably take a while."

"That doesn't sound good."

"I hope it won't be too bad. Your neck okay?"

She pulled her collar aside and showed me the half-healed wound. "It . . . wasn't so bad this time."

"It will get better."

"I know."

She pulled open the white Styrofoam cooler they had bought and filled with ice and food. She took out a plastic packet of four strips of pepper-smoked salmon and a bottle of water. She made a sandwich with the salmon and some bread from one of the grocery bags. When she'd eaten that and drunk the water, she got more water from the chest and dug out a blueberry muffin and two bananas from one of the bags. It didn't seem to bother her that I sat in the car watching her—that I enjoyed watching her.

Finally she took the plastic can of wipes and went away into the trees to make her own effort to clean up. While she did that, Wright awoke and stumbled off in a different direction.

A few moments later he came back and got another plastic can of wipes, scrubbed his face and hands, then got into the food.

"You okay?" he asked me.

"I'm fine. I'm going to see what I can learn from Brook. I need some idea where to find adult Ina. Now that I know what my parents' communities faced—humans with gasoline and guns—I think I can ask for help without endangering other Ina or their symbionts."

"You didn't think so yesterday."

"I do now. I still don't want to stay at the cabin near your relatives. Anyone I go to will have to post guards, stop shutting down during the day, be willing to fight and kill, be able to plant false stories in the memories of any witnesses, and be able to deal with the police. Ina families with symbionts can do that if they know they should. They can survive and help remove a threat."

He shook his head. "I just can't figure out why human beings would be killing your kind plus a hell of a lot of their own kind unless it's some kind of misguided vampire hunting."

"It may be," I said. "I don't know. But I'm pretty sure it's something to do with my family's genetic experiments. Will you sit with us and speak up whenever you think of anything useful?"

"Sure. Not that I'm going to know what's useful."

"Unless something she says shakes loose some part of my memory, you'll know as much as I do."

"Scary thought," he said. Then, "Here's Brook."

"I'm cold," she said, rubbing her hands together. "Let's get back into the car." Once we had moved the clothing we'd slept on and put the back seats up, we all climbed in, Brook in front and Wright and I in the back. "Okay," she said, "what do you want to talk about?"

"We need help," I told her. "I need to find adult Ina who will help me get rid of these assassins and then help me learn what I need to know to do right by the family I seem to be building. So I need you to tell me whatever you can about Iosif's Ina friends and relatives."

"I told you, I don't know how to contact any of them. Outside of our community, the only ones I had phone numbers for were your mothers."

"But you would have heard of others," I said. "Whether or not you know how to reach them, you would have heard their names, maybe met them."

She shook her head. "Iosif was unusual because he was so alone. He was too young to take part in the various Ina council meetings, and he had no elderfathers to represent his family. His brothers and his fathers, like his mothers and sisters, are all dead. Most of his relatives used to be scattered around Romania and Russia and Hungary. They died during the twentieth century—most of them during and after World War II when a lot of European Ina were killed. His sisters died with his mothers during the war. The Nazis got them. And his brothers and fathers were killed later by the Communists. They were some kind of nobility—had a lot of land taken from them before the war. Afterward, with all the destruction, I guess there was nothing left to take but their lives. Iosif was barely able to get out. They all should have left well before the war, but they were stubborn. They said no one would drive them from their homes."

"Were all Ina originally based in Romania—Transylvania?"

"No, they've been scattered all over Europe and the Middle East for millennia, or so their records say. They claim to have written records that go back more than ten thousand years. Iosif told me about them. I think he believed what he was saying, but I never quite believed him. Ten thousand years!" She shook her head. "Written history just doesn't go back that far. Anyway, now Ina are scattered all over the world. You just happen to be descended from people who lived in what Iosif used to call 'vampire country.' I think some of your ancestors there were outed and executed as vampires a few centuries ago. Iosif used to joke about it in a bitter way. He said that, physically, he and most Ina fit in badly wherever they go—tall, ultrapale, lean, wiry people. They usually looked like foreigners, and when times got bad, they were treated like foreigners—suspected, disliked, driven out, or killed."

"He told Wright and me that there is an Ina theory that claims the Ina were sent here from another world."

"Yes, that's something young Ina have come up with. They read and go to movies and pick up and adapt whatever's current. For a while, there was an idea that Ina were angels of some kind. And there's the old standby legend of the Ina being sent here by a great mother goddess. You're all supposed to be stuck here until you prove yourselves," she said. "Did Iosif tell you that one?"

"He did," Wright said. "It's a little like Christianity."

"It isn't, really," Brook said. "They're not supposed to go home in some spiritual way after they die. Some future generation of them is supposed to leave this world en masse and go to paradise—or back to the homeworld. It might be mythology or it might be that you and I have finally found—and joined —those extraterrestrial aliens that people keep claiming to spot on lonely back roads."

Wright laughed. Then he stopped laughing and shook his head. "There's another intelligent species here on Earth, and they're vampires. What am I laughing at?"

I took his hand and held it, looking at him. He looked at me, put his head back against the seat, and curled his fingers around my hand.

"Didn't other Ina visit Iosif?" I asked. "Did you ever meet others?"

She nodded. "That was scary sometimes."

"Why?"

"Because not everyone treats symbionts as people. I didn't realize that until I'd been with Iosif for a few years, but it's true. I remember one guest—actually, he came back recently to negotiate with Iosif for an introduction to you and your sisters. You weren't old enough yet, but he hoped to win all three of you for himself and his brothers when you came of age. That was never going to happen because your father was smart enough to see what he was."

"There were three of us?" I said, my mind latching on to this new bit of information about my past, about my family. "I didn't know that. I asked Iosif, but I was asking him so many questions . . . he never got around to answering that one."

"There were three of you. This was not a man Iosif would ever have introduced to you or your sisters. This man liked to . . . amuse himself with other Ina's symbionts. He was very careful and protective of his own, but he liked sending them among us with instructions to start trouble, raise suspicions and jealousies, start fights. He liked to watch arguments and fights.

His symbionts were so good, so subtle that we didn't realize what was happening at first. It excited the hell out of him when two of Radu's symbionts almost killed one another. He got something sexual out of watching. The symbionts would have died if they hadn't been symbionts—but then, they never would have been endangered if they hadn't been symbionts."

"Radu," I said, remembering that Iosif had mentioned the name.

"Your brothers were Stefan, Vasile, Mihai, and Radu. It was your father's right to name them, and he named them for the dead—his two brothers and two of his fathers who died in Romania. Your mothers liked plainer, American-sounding names. Your sisters were Barbara and Helen. You were lucky. Your human mother claimed the right to name you." She smiled. "'Shori' is the name of a kind of bird—an East African crested nightingale. It's a nice name."

"Oh," Wright said. We looked at each other, then I reached into my shirt and pulled out the gold chain with the crested bird.

"Was this mine before?" I asked, showing it to her. "Wright found it in the rubble of my mothers' houses."

She turned the car's interior light on and looked at the bird, then looked at me. "Your human mother gave you this. I think she loved you as though she had given birth to you herself. Her name was Jessica Margaret Grant."

Jessica Margaret Grant. I shut my eyes and tried to find something of this woman in my memory—something. But there was nothing. All of my life had been erased, and I could not bring it back. Each time I was confronted with the reality of this, it was like turning to go into what should have been a familiar, welcoming place and finding absolutely nothing, emptiness, space.

After a moment, I said, "I wouldn't want to meet the Ina you described. What about others? Who's visited Iosif or one of my brothers recently?"

Brook frowned. "There was one a few months ago. He and Vasile owned some sort of business together. He was interested in joining with you and your sisters, and Vasile thought it might be a good match. Iosif was willing to be convinced so this man—what was his name? One of the Gordon family . . .

Daniel Gordon! He had his brothers come to see us. Their ancestors were English, I think. They immigrated first to Canada, then to the United States. All the symbionts of Iosif's community were told to notice them, notice their behavior, talk to their symbionts, and listen to them. We did, and no one spotted anything bad. They seemed to be good, normal people. Shori, you met them yourself and liked them, even though it was way too soon for you to mate. They had heard about you and they wanted to meet you. Iosif went down, collected you, and brought you to stay with us for a few days."

"All because of my dark skin?" I said.

"That's the most obvious reason. You're not only able to stay completely awake and alert during the day, but you don't burn."

"I burn."

"You didn't yesterday."

"I blistered a little. I tried to keep covered up, and it was cloudy yesterday. Did the brothers like me?"

"Have you healed?" Wright asked, interrupting. "I meant to buy you some sunscreen, but I forgot."

"I healed," I said and wondered what all this talk of my mating was doing to him. I looked at him but couldn't read anything more than mild concern in his expression as he examined my face—probably for burns.

"The Gordon brothers were delighted with you," Brook said. "They wished you were a little older, but they were willing to wait. They planned to go down to meet your sisters and your mothers. I don't know whether or not that had happened, but it would have been necessary. Your mothers would have to meet the whole Gordon family and then give or refuse their consent."

"Where do the Gordons live?" I asked.

She hesitated, frowned. "Somewhere on the coast of northern California."

"You don't know exactly where?"

She shook her head. "Their community has a name—Punta Nublada—but it's not a real town. It's only the four brothers and their three fathers and a couple of elderfathers who were born in the sixteen hundreds. It's amazing to meet people like that."

"You met them?" Wright asked.

"I went with Iosif and one of Shori's mothers and some other symbionts to visit them. I loved the trip, but I didn't know where I was most of the time. I know we flew into San Francisco Airport—at night, of course—and a couple of symbionts from Punta Nublada met us in vans and drove us up. It was more than two hours north of San Francisco Airport and on the coast. That's all I know. They have a lot of land. Inland, away from their community, they own vineyards. They have a wine-making business, which is kind of funny when you think about it."

Wright laughed. "Yeah. I'll bet they still don't drink it."

"What?" I demanded.

"Old joke from a vampire movie," Wright said. "From the Bela Lugosi version of *Dracula*. Someone offers the Count a glass, and he says, 'I do not drink . . . wine.'"

I shrugged. Maybe I'd watch the movie someday and see why that was funny. "We'll go to Punta Nublada," I said. "You'll find it for us, Brook."

She looked distressed. "I don't know where it is, I swear."

"Did you sleep while you were being driven?"

"No, but it was dark."

"You can see in this darkness—here, under the trees. Your night vision is good."

"It is. But most of what I saw was headlights and taillights."

I nodded. "They can be a problem. But I think you saw more than you realize."

"I didn't," she said. "I really didn't."

"We need help, Brook," I said. "Can you think of anyone else—anyone other than the Gordons—who might help us?"

She faced me and shook her head. "But these people may not help us, even if we find them. I don't know whether there was a confirmed agreement between your family and theirs. And even if there was, they . . . I'm sorry, Shori. They might not want you without your sisters. It's hard for only children to find mates. Iosif said it would have been hard for him, but he was already mated when his brothers were killed. His mates were just smart enough to get out before he did."

I shrugged. "All right, even if the Gordons don't still want to mate with me, they should be willing to help find and stop the assassins. That's what I really need help with, after all. Human gangs wiping out two whole communities of Ina. Any Ina should be willing to do something about that—out of self-preservation if nothing else."

"They should."

"Then you find them, and I'll put it to them in just that way. Self-preservation. Iosif must have seen some good in them." I looked at her, and she looked away. "I feel as though I know humans better than I know my own kind—not that that's saying much. Am I missing something here? Is there some reason these people might not help us?"

She shook her head. "I think they will help, even if they don't want you as a mate. I'm just scared I won't be able to find them for you."

"Yes you will," I said. "You'll find them. Then once we get some peace, we can begin to assemble a household. The Gordons should be able to give us phone numbers and addresses of other Ina—my mothers' brothers, perhaps. Are they alive?"

"Your mothers' brothers? Yes. I've never met them, but you have." Suddenly she put her hands to her face. She didn't cry, but she looked as though she wanted to. "How can I do this?" she demanded. "You can't depend on me. I don't really know anything."

"You can," I said. "You will. Don't worry about it. Just know that you will."

Wright said, "We can drive down—all the way to San Francisco Airport if we have to. From there, we can turn north again, and maybe Brook can find the way."

"We'll start tonight," I said.

He nodded. "What about Celia? She might know something."

"She needed to sleep. We'll tell her when she wakes up, and I'll find out what she knows."

"We need maps," Wright said. "I don't know the way, except that we'll be going south, probably on I-5. We'll make San Francisco Airport our destination, so when we reach California, we should stick to a coastal route—probably U.S. 101—until we reach the airport or until Brook recognizes something."

"We should go back to your cabin first," I said, "or if you don't want to do that, you can let me out a few blocks from there. I need to talk to Theodora and see whether or not she should come with us."

He nodded. "I need to talk to my uncle anyway, to let him know that I haven't just disappeared on him and that I want my job. I want him to be willing to hire me again when this is over. I want to get some of my stuff, too. Hell, I was all packed to leave anyway."

"Let's go now," I said. "We've got hours of darkness left. By daybreak, we should be well on our way."

Fourteen

ONCE WE got back to Wright's cabin, I went to visit Theodora. I slipped into her bedroom by way of her balcony, woke her, and told her what had happened and what we were going to do. Her scent was still mostly her own so I knew I could leave her, lonely but safe.

"I want to go with you!" she protested.

"I know," I told her. "But it will be better if you wait. I can't protect you now. I don't even have the prospect of a home now, and I have no Ina allies. It was only luck that none of us was hurt or killed at the Arlington house."

"You protected them."

"Luck," I said. "They could so easily have been burned or shot. Wright could have left the television on, and I might not have heard the intruders until it was too late. I want you with me, and you will be. But not yet."

She cried and wanted me to at least stay the rest of the night with her. I bit her a little—only to taste her—then held her and lapped at the wound until she was focused on the pleasure. She was like Wright. She had some hold on me beyond the blood. At last, I knew I had to go so I told her to sleep. She resisted briefly, took something from the very back and bottom of the middle drawer in her night table, and put it in my hand. "You might need this," she whispered. "Take it. I've got more." Then she kissed me and let herself drift off to sleep.

She had put money into my hand, a thick roll of twenty-dollar bills with a rubber band around it. I took it back to Wright's cabin. He was in the main house, talking to his uncle. He and the two women had each had a shower. By the time Wright came back, I was having one, and the women were eating the meal they had prepared. We were all wasting time, and I knew it, but I enjoyed my shower and let them enjoy their microwaved mugs of vegetable soup, slabs of canned ham, and dinner rolls heated in the convection oven—simple, quickly prepared food.

They finished, cleaned up, took out the trash, and made sandwiches of the last of the ham and some cheddar cheese

Wright had had in his refrigerator. Meanwhile, I put Wright's two suitcases and the canvas travel bag he had given me for my things into his car. Wright already had a book of maps called *The Thomas Guide: King and Snohomish Counties*—we were in Snohomish—and a map of Pierce County. We would get whatever else we needed as we traveled, although, according to Wright, all we really had to do was get on I-5 and stay on it until we got to California, then switch over to U.S. 101. None of that meant anything to me. I meant to look at the relevant maps in *The Thomas Guide* while we traveled. I needed, for my own comfort, to have some idea of where we were going.

Wright came out ahead of the two women, and I put the money Theodora had given me into his hand. "Take this," I said. "If I get separated from the rest of you, you take care of Brook and Celia. All of you would have to find other Ina as quickly as possible."

His hand closed around the money, then he looked at it in the light from the back door of the cabin. His mouth dropped open. "Where did you get this?"

"From Theodora. She said we might need it, and we might."

He put the money in an inside pocket of his jacket and zipped the pocket. "I'll use it to keep us all as safe as I can," he said. "But don't imagine I would just drive off and leave you, Shori. I wouldn't. I couldn't."

"I hope it won't be necessary. But if it is necessary to keep you safe, to keep Celia and Brook safe, you'll do it. You will do it!"

He drew back from me, angry, wanting to dispute, yet knowing he would obey. "Sometimes I forget that you can do that to me," he said.

"I do it to save your life," I said.

After a while he sighed. "You're a scary little person," he said.

I had no idea what to say to that so I ignored it. "Theodora wanted to come, too," I said. "I couldn't let her, even though I wanted her to. The only person I want more is you. I need you to be safe, and I need you to keep Brook and Celia safe."

He shook his head, then put his arm around my shoulders, his expression going from angry to bemused. "That is the most unromantic declaration of love I've ever heard. Or is that what you're saying? Do you love me, Shori, or do I just taste good?"

"You don't taste good," I said, smiling. "You taste wonderful." I grew more serious. "I would rather be shot again than lose you."

"More and more romantic," he said and shook his head. He bent, lifted me off my feet, and kissed me. I nipped him, tasted him, and heard him draw a quick breath. He held me hard against him, and I closed my eyes for a moment, submerged in the scent, the feel, and taste of him.

Then Brook came out with her own suitcase. She had taken it from the back of her car to get at her toiletries. "We'd better get going," she said, noticing the way Wright and I held each other, then looking away.

We sighed. Wright put me down, and we let each other go.

Celia came out carrying the sandwiches, each bagged with the apples and bananas that Wright had had in the cabin. She handed a bag to Wright and one to Brook, then said, "You guys got everything?"

We nodded, and Wright went to turn off the lights and lock the door.

We drove, Wright with me in one car and Celia with Brook in the other. We drove through what was left of the night and into the day. By daybreak we had reached Salem, Oregon. We were still, according to the maps, hundreds of miles north of San Francisco Airport. We got two motel rooms at a place that did not force us to park our cars where they could be seen from the street—just in case someone was hunting us. We picked up a map of the area, the others ate the food they had brought, and we all went to bed.

I lay awake for a while next to Wright, wondering whether I should even be in bed. Perhaps I should stay awake, keep watch. But I couldn't quite believe that humans would have been able to follow us without my noticing them. And I couldn't believe they would be willing to kill a motel full of humans unrelated to Ina if they did find us. Also, the motel was filled with windows—eyes—and perhaps with curiosity. Our enemies liked concealment and quiet. I could sleep. In fact, this was an excellent place to sleep. I let myself drift off.

Once Wright had slept off some of his weariness, he woke me up and told me to try biting him now and see what happened.

I laughed and bit him. I didn't take much blood because I had taken a full meal from him only two days before. Still, I was eager to see what happened, and he didn't disappoint me.

After a few hours, we got up and got on the road again. We didn't hurry. We stopped for meals, stayed within the speed limit, and, as a result, spent one more night in a motel. This time I was hungry enough to leave the room while Wright was asleep and wait until I spotted a stranger letting himself into his room. I slipped in with him before he realized I was there. I bit him and had a nourishing, but unsatisfying, meal. Afterward, I told him to keep the bite mark hidden until it healed and to remember only that he'd had an odd dream.

Sometime later, after we got underway on our third night, I realized that I should be riding with Brook to do what I could to encourage her memory. I didn't really know whether she would remember more clearly or focus her attention more narrowly if I were there to prod her, but I meant to find out. When we stopped for gas, I switched cars.

"Do you want me to send Celia to keep you company?" I asked Wright. "Or would you rather have some time to yourself?"

He hesitated, then said, "Send her. I'll ask her questions and find out more about this symbiont business."

I looked at him and saw that he wasn't asking me to send Celia to him, he was daring me. And he was smiling a little as he did it.

"Ask," I said. "I'm afraid for you to talk to them and learn what they know—because I know so little. But you should talk to them. We're a family, or the beginnings of one. We'll be together for a very long time."

"It's all right," he said, immediately contrite. "A little solitude might be good for me."

"No," I said. "Talk to her. Get to know her. Ask your questions. It isn't all right, but it will be." I walked away to where Brook was putting gas into her car.

"What?" she asked.

"I'm switching cars," I said. "I want to do what I can to prod your memory."

She sighed. "I'm still afraid I won't remember."

"I'll drive, then," Celia said through her open window. "We're more likely to survive the trip if the driver isn't looking all around trying to remember stuff."

She was right. Brook hadn't been driving when she visited these people before. Best for her not to be driving now. I went back and told Wright he would be driving alone after all and told him why.

He grinned. "Decided you didn't want me to know everything, then," he said.

I grinned back at him. "That must be it."

They went into the store that was attached to the gas station and bought more maps, food, bottled water, and ice. Then Wright and Celia consulted over the new maps. Somewhere in Sonoma or Mendocino County in California we decided to use State Route 1 instead of U.S. 101 as we'd planned because Brook said State Route 1 "felt" like the right road. This apparently had to be discussed again. Then, finally, we were on our way. Celia led off.

Brook and I sat in the backseat, and she studied a huge, sheetlike map. Finally she put the map down and looked at me. "We're close enough," she said, "but I don't recognize anything yet."

"Are you still worried about your memory?" I asked.

She nodded. "Of course I am."

"You will remember," I said. "When you see things you've seen before, you're going to recognize them. You've been to this place before. You've seen the way, going and coming. Now you'll see the way a third time, and you'll get us there. Look out the windows. Don't worry about the map."

She took a deep breath and nodded.

And yet we drove all the way to the Golden Gate Bridge before she began to see things that looked familiar to her. By then we had to cross the bridge, then find a place to turn back. On our way back, though, she kept seeing familiar landmarks, businesses, signs.

"I think I paid more attention when we were traveling to Punta Nublada from the airport," she said. "We were headed north, the way we are now, and I know this place now. It all seemed so new to me when I came this way with Iosif. I hadn't been anywhere far from home for a long time. I was so excited."

Just over two hours later, a newly confident Brook had us turn down a narrow paved road that took us to a gravel road that led, finally, to Punta Nublada, a community of eleven large houses with garages and several other buildings scattered along either side of the road. It was almost a village. Behind some of the houses, I could see the remains of large gardens, most of them finished for the year, stark and empty. The community was dark and still, as though it were a humans-only place and everyone were asleep. I wondered why. I could smell Ina males nearby.

"Which house belongs to the oldest son, or perhaps we should see one of the elderfathers?" I asked, then had another thought. "Wait, which is the home of Daniel Gordon, the one you said first approached Iosif."

"Daniel?" Brook asked. "He is the oldest son."

"Show me which home is his."

"Third house on the right."

We stopped there. I got out and understood something interesting and frightening at once. There were people—human and Ina—watching us with guns. I smelled the guns, I saw some of the people hiding in the darkness. I smelled them and knew they were all strangers to me, but I sorted through them anyway. The scents of the Ina were very disturbing. These people were nervous. Some of the humans were frightened. At least none of the humans present had been among those who attacked Wright, Celia, Brook, and me. That possibility had not occurred to me until I smelled all the guns.

"Don't get out yet," I said to Celia and Brook. But behind us, Wright had already gotten out and come to stand beside me. It frightened me how vulnerable he was, how vulnerable we all were, but if these people wanted to shoot us, surely they would already have done it.

I took Wright's hand, or rather, I touched one of his huge hands and allowed it to swallow mine, and we walked to the front porch of Daniel Gordon's house.

"This the guy who wants to be your mate?" he asked in a soft voice that I thought he tried hard to keep neutral.

"Things have changed," I said, knowing that he was not my only listener. "I don't know what they want now. But for the sake of the past, I hope they will speak with me and not just point guns at me."

Wright froze, drew me closer to him, and I realized he had known nothing of those who watched us. He saw no one until the tall, male Ina stepped into view on the broad front porch.

"Shori," he said, making a greeting of my name.

Of course, he was a stranger to me. "You're Daniel Gordon?" I asked.

He frowned.

"If you and your people are this alert," I said, "you must know what's happened to my family—to my mothers, my sisters, my brothers, and my father. It almost happened to me, too. I had a serious head injury. Because of it, I don't remember you at all. I don't remember any part of my life before getting hurt. So I have to ask: Are you Daniel Gordon?"

After what seemed to be a long while, he answered, "Yes, I'm Daniel."

"Then I need to talk with you about what's happened to my family and, very nearly, to me and my symbionts."

Daniel looked at Wright, at our joined hands, at the two women in the car. Finally, he nodded. "You and your people are welcome here," he said.

There was an almost-silent withdrawal of armed watchers. I saw a few of the humans around Daniel's house and the houses of his nearest neighbors lower their guns and turn away. I turned to the car and beckoned to Brook and Celia.

They came out of the car and up to us, and Daniel looked at them, lifted his head and sampled their scent, then looked at me again. He recognized them. I could see that in his expression —realization and surprise.

"Those two . . ." He frowned. "They aren't yours, Shori."

"They were my father's and my brother Stefan's. They're with me now." I knew they smelled wrong, but if he knew what had happened to my family, he must know why they smelled the way they did—of both the dead and the living.

"We must question them," he said. "We've heard what happened on the radio, read about it in the newspaper, seen it on television. Two of my fathers even went up to look around.

And yet even they don't understand any of this. Who did these things?"

"We'll share everything we know," I said, "although that isn't much. We came here because we need help against the assassins."

"Who are they? Do you have any idea?"

"We don't know who they are, but we killed some of them when they attacked us." And I repeated, "We'll tell you all we can."

"How did you survive?"

I sighed. "Call your brothers and your fathers from the shadows, and let's go into your house and talk."

His fathers and brothers had gathered around us in near silence and just far enough away to prevent my symbionts from seeing them. They were listening and sampling our scents and looking us over. I didn't see that it would do them any harm to examine us in comfort and with courtesy.

Perhaps Daniel thought so, too. He turned, opened his door, switched on a light, and stood aside. "Come in, Shori," he said. "Be welcome."

We went up the steps into the house, into a large room of dark wood and deep green wallpaper. A large flat-screen television set covered much of one end wall. Beneath it on shelves was a large collection of tapes and DVDs. At the opposite end of the room was a massive stone fireplace. Along one side wall there were three windows, each as big as the front door, and between them and alongside them, there were tall bookcases filled with books. On the other side wall there were photographs, dozens of them, some in black and white, some in color, most of them of outdoor scenes—woods, rivers, huge trees, rock cliffs, waterfalls. They would have been beautiful if they had not been so crowded together.

There were a great many chairs and little tables around the room. We and the brothers and fathers who came in after us found places to sit. Wright, Celia, Brook, and I sat together on a pair of two-person seats at the fireplace end of the room. The fathers and brothers of Gordon sat around us, surrounding us on three sides, crowding us. Our world was suddenly filled with tall, pale, vaguely menacing, spidery men, and I was annoyed with them for being even vaguely menacing and scaring my symbionts. I watched them, wondering why I was not afraid. They seemed to want me to be afraid. They stared at the four of us in silence that was as close to hostile as silence could be. Or maybe they only wanted my symbionts to be afraid.

My symbionts *were* afraid. Even Wright was afraid, although he tried to hide it. He couldn't hide his scent, though. Celia and Brook didn't try to hide their fear at all.

I looked at Daniel who sat nearest to me. "Do you believe that I or my people murdered my families?"

He stared back at me. "We don't know what happened."

"I didn't ask you what you knew. I asked whether you believe that I or my people murdered my families?"

He glanced back at his fathers and brothers. "I don't. I don't even believe you could have."

"Then stop scaring my symbionts. If you have questions, ask them."

"You're a child," one of the older men said. "And the two women with you are not your symbionts."

I looked at him with disgust. He had already heard me answer this. I repeated the answer exactly: "They were my father's and my brother Stefan's. They're with me now."

"You don't have to keep them," he said. "They can have a home here . . . if you took them only out of duty."

"They're with me now," I repeated.

The older man took a deep breath. "All right," he said. "Tell us what you know, Shori." And the pressure on us eased somehow, as it had when the guns were lowered outside. I felt it, even though I hadn't been afraid. I looked at my symbionts and saw that they felt it, too. They were relaxing a little.

I turned back to face the Gordons and sighed. After a moment of gathering my thoughts, I summarized the things that had happened to me. I talked about awakening amnesiac in the cave, about Hugh Tang, finding the ruin, finding Wright, and later finding my father, who told me that the ruin had been the community of my mothers, then losing my father and all of his community and except Celia and Brook, going to the Arlington house and almost dying there, discovering that our attackers were all human . . .

One of the Gordons interrupted to ask, "Were you able to question any of them?"

I shook my head. "We killed several of them. The rest escaped. We only just escaped ourselves. The fire had attracted attention, and I didn't want to have to deal with firemen or the police."

"You weren't seen," Daniel said. "Or if you were, it's being kept very secret. There's been nothing in the media about cars escaping the scene, and none of the sources my fathers created have phoned to tell us about anyone escaping. The police seem very frustrated."

"Good," I said. "I mean I didn't know whether or not we were seen. We spent the next night in our cars in the woods. Then, because Brook had been here once, I thought I could get her to bring us back here."

A Gordon who looked about fifty and who was, almost certainly, one of the two oldest people present spoke with quiet courtesy: "May we question your symbionts?" He had a British accent. I had heard BBC reporters on Wright's radio back at the cabin talking the way this man did.

I looked at Celia and Brook, then at Wright. "It's all right," I said. "Tell them whatever they want to know." They looked alert but not afraid or even uncomfortable. I nodded to the older man. "All right," I said. "By the way, what's your name?"

"I'm Preston Gordon," he said. "I'm sorry. We should all introduce ourselves." And they did. Preston and Hayden were the two oldest. They were brothers and looked almost enough alike to be twins, except that Hayden was taller and Preston had a thicker mop of white-blond hair. Their sons were Wells, Manning, Henry, and Edward. And they in turn were the fathers of Daniel, Wayne, Philip, and William. William was, I suspected, only fifteen or twenty years older than I was. Although no one said so, I got the impression that I'd met most of them, perhaps all of them, before. What did it say to them that I couldn't remember any of them now? It embarrassed me, but there was nothing I could do about it.

Preston directed his first question to Brook. "Did you recognize anyone among those your group killed? Had you seen any of them before?"

"No," Brook told him. "I didn't get to see all their faces, but the ones I saw, I had never seen before."

William asked, "How many did you kill, Shori, you personally, I mean."

"Three," I said surprised. "Why?"

"Three men," he said and grinned. "You must be stronger than you look."

I frowned because that was a foolish thing to say. Of course I was stronger than I looked, just as he was stronger than he looked.

Daniel said, "Shori, we didn't know about your mothers. There was apparently no news coverage. Do you know why that was?"

"Iosif and two of my brothers covered it up. He said they did. And even so, there was some local coverage. He convinced local reporters and apparently the police that my mothers' community had been abandoned, that someone burned a cluster of abandoned houses. That's news, but it's not important news. And he saw to it that some of my mothers' neighbors kept an eye on the place. He thought the killers might come back to gloat."

Preston shook his head. "I see. Iosif must have worked very hard to keep things quiet. Brook, did he say anything to you about his effort to cover up and, perhaps, about his effort to investigate?"

"He told me what happened," she said. "He didn't understand how it could have happened, who could have been powerful enough to do it. He said it must have happened during the day—that that was the only way Shori's mothers could have been surprised. And he thought Shori might have survived if anyone did. But . . . I don't believe he thought of it as something that would happen again. I never got the impression that he was worried about it happening to our community."

Celia nodded. "Stefan flew down with him to help with the neighbors. They took Hugh Tang and some other symbionts with them to search for survivors. They really did think it was just a single terrible crime. I mean, you hear about people committing mass murder—shooting up their schools or their workplaces all of a sudden—or you hear about serial murders where someone kills people one by one over a period of months or years, but serial mass murder . . . I don't think I've ever heard of that except in war."

"Iosif didn't know anything," I said. "I talked to him about it. He was frustrated, grieving, angry . . . He hated not knowing at least as much as I hate it."

There was a brief silence, then Daniel spoke to Wright. "What about you? You're the outsider brought into all this almost by accident. What are your impressions?"

Wright thought for a moment, frowning a little. Then he said, "Chances are, this is all happening for one of three reasons. It's happening because some human group has spotted your kind and decided you're all dangerous, evil vampires. Or it's happening because some Ina group or Ina individual is jealous of the success Shori's family had with blending human and Ina DNA and having children who can stay awake through the day and not burn so easily in the sun. Or it's happening because Shori is black, and racists—probably Ina racists—don't like the idea that a good part of the answer to your daytime problems is melanin. Those are the most obvious possibilities. I wondered at first whether it could be someone or some family who just hated Shori's family—an old fashioned Hatfields and McCoys family feud—but Iosif and his sons would have known about anyone who hated them that much."

Philip Gordon, younger than Daniel, older than William, said, "You're assuming that if Ina did it, they used humans as their daytime weapons."

"I am assuming that," Wright said.

"We don't do that!" Preston said, his mouth turned down with disgust.

"I'm glad to hear it," Wright told him. "Of course I didn't think that anyone Iosif would introduce to his female family would do that. But there are other Ina. And your species seems to be as much made up of individuals as mine is. Some people are ethical, some aren't."

I watched the Gordons as he spoke. The younger ones listened, indifferent, but the older ones didn't much like what he was saying. It seemed to make them uncomfortable, embarrassed. I wondered why. At least no one tried to shut Wright up. That was important. I wouldn't have wanted to stay in a community that was contemptuous of my symbionts.

I also liked the fact that Wright wasn't afraid to say what he thought.

The Gordons talked among themselves about the possibilities Wright had offered, and they didn't seem to like any of them, but I suspected that their objections came more from wounded pride than from logic. Ina didn't use humans as daytime weapons against other Ina. They hadn't done anything like that for centuries.

And Ina were careful, both Preston and Hayden insisted. No Ina would leave evidence of vampiric behavior for humans to find. And according to Daniel, Ina families all over the world were happy about my family's success with genetic engineering. They hoped to use the same methods to enable their own future generations to function during the day.

And the Ina weren't racists, Wells insisted. Human racism meant nothing to the Ina because human races meant nothing to them. They looked for congenial human symbionts wherever they happened to be, without regard for anything but personal appeal.

And of course, there was no feud. According to Preston, nothing of that kind had happened for more than a thousand years. Nothing of the kind could happen without a great many people knowing about it. Iosif certainly would have known, and he and his mates would have been on guard.

"Speaking of being on guard," I said loudly.

The Gordons stopped and one by one turned to look at me.

"Speaking of being on guard," I repeated, "it's good that you have people guarding this place now, but are you also keeping watch during the day?"

Silence.

"We haven't been," Edward said at last. He was probably the youngest of the fathers. "We'll have to now." He paused. "And, Shori, you'll have to stay with us until this business is over, until we've found these killers and dealt with them."

"Thank you," I said. "I came here hoping for help and refuge. If I stay, I might be most useful as part of your day watch."

That seemed to interest them. "You can stay awake all day, every day and sleep at night?" William asked me.

I nodded. "I can as long as I get enough sleep," I said. "If I'm allowed to sleep most of the night, I should be all right during the day. And . . . it will keep me out of your way."

There was an uncomfortable silence. I had noticed that a

couple of the unmated sons were already beginning to fidget as my scent worked on them. And Daniel tended to stare at me in a way that made me want to touch him. I liked his looks as well as his scent. I wondered whether I had liked him before, when my memory was intact.

"I'll need you to tell your day-watch symbionts to listen to me. When the killers attacked the Arlington house, they were fast and coordinated. If I'd been just a little slower or if Wright had been slower to wake up Celia and Brook and get them out, we might have died."

"We'll talk to our symbionts," Preston said. "We'll introduce them to you and tell them to obey you in any action against attackers, but Shori . . ." He stopped talking and just looked at me.

"I'll do all I can to keep them safe," I said.

Fifteen

THE GORDONS had a guest house at Punta Nublada.
It was a comfortable two-story, five-bedroom house,
smaller than the sprawling family houses but easily large
enough for us and as ready to be lived in as Iosif's guest house
had been. It was usually used by visiting Ina and their symbionts or visiting members of the Gordon symbionts' families.
Daniel said such people imagined that their relatives lived in a
commune that had somehow survived from the 1960s. Then
he had to tell me something about the 1960s. I might not have
asked, but I found I enjoyed hearing his voice.

My symbionts and I moved our things from the cars into the
house and relaxed for the rest of the night. There was canned
and frozen food, as there had been in the Arlington house, and
Wright, Celia, and Brook put together a meal. A short time
later we were all asleep.

Just before dawn, though, I left the bed I was sharing with
Wright and went to the room Celia had chosen. I was hungry but didn't want to be in too much of a hurry with her. I
slipped into her bed, turned her toward me, and kissed her as
she woke. Once the surprise and stiffness had gone out of her,
I found the place on her neck where I could feel her pulse most
strongly. I licked the dark, salt-and-bitter skin where I would
bite her. She didn't struggle. Her body jerked once when I bit
her, then it was still. Afterward, she dozed off easily, resting
against me while I licked the wound I had made. Like Brook,
she still wasn't enjoying herself, but at least she was no longer
suffering.

When she was asleep, I got up, showered, dressed, and went
outside while it was still comfortably dim. I meant to wander
around, take a look at the place. But I found Preston sitting
on a seat that swung from chains attached to the ceiling on the
front porch of the guest house. He looked up at me, smiled,
and said, "I hoped you would get up before I got too drowsy.
I'm here to speak with you on behalf of the son of one of my
symbionts."

I sat down next to him. "All right," I said.

He smiled. "We love our mates," he said. "Their venom never lets us go. We would be lost if it did. But our symbionts . . . they never truly understand how deeply we treasure them. This boy . . . I still miss his mother."

I waited, very curious. I liked him. That was interesting. I didn't know him, but I liked him. He smelled good somehow, not in the slightest edible, not even sexually interesting, but good, comfortable to be with.

"One of my symbionts had a son," he said. "Then about ten years ago, she was killed in a traffic accident in San Francisco. She had gone there to visit her sister. I might have been able to help, but I wasn't notified until she was dead. Her husband is still alive, still here. He's one of William's symbionts. But in this matter . . . Well, I promised father and son I would speak to you. The son is twenty-two and just out of college. He's heard about you and seen your picture. Last night when you arrived, he saw you for the first time. He says he would like to join with you if you'll have him. He has a degree in business administration, and I think you'll eventually need someone like him to help you manage the business affairs of your families."

I drew a deep breath and smiled sadly. "I don't know about that, but I think I need more symbionts soon. I don't believe three is enough, and I'm worried about hurting the ones I have."

"I wondered whether you were aware of the danger," he said. "You do need more people quickly. In fact, you need three or four more symbionts."

"I left one back in Washington. We have an emotional connection, but that's all so far. I refused to bring her because I didn't know what I would find here, and I didn't know whether I could protect her."

"With our help, you should be able to do that."

"And I have no home," I said. "I'll have to start from nothing. I'll do that, but with my memory gone, I'll need a lot of information from you. I don't really know how to be Ina."

"You do, I believe, even though you don't realize that you do. Your manner is very much that of an intelligent, somewhat arrogant, young Ina female. I think you learned long before you lost your memory that you could have things pretty much your own way." He smiled.

"You see that in my behavior?" I asked, surprised.

"Yes, I do. Don't worry about it. A little self-confidence may be just what you need right now."

"I have nothing to be confident about," I said. "I really do need to learn all I can from you and your family."

"Of course you do. Ask us any questions you like. Best to ask only the fathers. You won't torment us quite so much."

I nodded. "I'm sorry about that. I know my scent bothers you."

"Do you remember?"

"No. Iosif told me."

"I see. Will you have my symbiont's son?"

"Of course I will, if it turns out he and I like each other. What's his name?"

"Joel Harrison. I think you'll like him, and as I've said, he's seen you and he wants to be with you. And as a bonus, his father saw you last night, too. They were both on guard. He got a look at you and liked the way you stood up for your symbionts. He said you would take care of Joel."

"As best I can," I said. "But—"

"You're with us now. You aren't alone. And what you said earlier about having nothing . . . that probably isn't true. Your mothers and your father owned large tracts of land, several apartment buildings in Seattle run by a management company, and interests in several businesses. They had substantial incomes. Daniel was involved in some sort of business venture with one of your brothers. He knows something about their affairs, and we can find out more. Eventually, what they owned will be yours."

"Thank you," I said. "I knew they owned the land they lived on, but I didn't have any idea what else there was or how to find out about it." I frowned, remembering something I had read about on Wright's computer. "Would they have left wills?"

He frowned. "Well, yes, but they would never have foreseen being so completely wiped out. We'll find out. Somewhere along the line, there will be a lawyer or two who's been bitten and who, as a result, will be very helpful and very honorable about seeing that your rights are respected."

I nodded and repeated, "Thank you."

He stood up, and it was as though he suddenly unfolded,

tall and lean. "You're welcome, Shori. Now, I think I'd better introduce you to Joel so that I can get to bed." He raised his arm and beckoned. A young man emerged from one of the houses across the road. The man was as tall as Wright, but not as heavily muscled. And this man was as dark skinned as I was and had hair like mine. He walked toward me with a little smile on his face. I got the impression he was excited—both happy and very nervous.

I liked the way he looked—strong and wiry and healthy and brown, striding as though there were springs in his legs.

"You will have to talk to your first," Preston said.

I glanced up at him, startled.

"You don't want them fighting or competing with one another in ways that make the rest of you miserable. Each must find a way to accept the other. Each must find a way to accept the other's relationship with you. You must help them do this."

I sighed.

The young man came up to me, towering over me, smiling down.

"Shori Matthews, this is Joel Harrison," Preston said. "I believe the two of you will be very good for one another."

"Thank you," I said to him. And to Joel, "Welcome."

"I've been looking forward to meeting you," Joel said. Slowly, deliberately, he extended his arm, wrist up, clearly not so that we could shake hands.

I laughed, took the hand, kissed his wrist, and said to him, "Later."

"Date," he said. "Is there room for me over here?"

"There's room."

"I'll get my stuff."

I watched him walk away, then said to Preston, "He smells wonderful."

Preston crooked his mouth in something less than a smile. "Yes. He's been told that, I'm afraid. Be good to each other."

He had started to walk away from me when I stopped him. "Preston, do you know whether I had my own family of symbionts before . . . before the fire?"

He looked back. "Of course you did. You can't remember them at all?"

"Not at all."

"Good."

I stared at him.

"Child . . . you have no idea how much it hurts when they die. And you've lost all of yours. All seven. If you remembered them, the pain would be overwhelming . . . unbearable."

"But they were mine, and I don't recall their scents or their tastes or the sounds of their voices or even their names."

"Good," Preston repeated softly. "Let them rest in peace, Shori. Actually, that's all you can do." He walked slowly away to the house Joel had gone into. I watched him go, wondering how many symbionts he had lost over the years, over the centuries.

The sun was rising now and growing bright enough to be uncomfortable even through the low clouds. I went back inside and found Celia frying frozen sausages from the refrigerator.

"How are you?" I asked.

"I'm good," she said. "How about you? You didn't hurt me, but you filled up on me, didn't you?"

"I did." I looked at the sausages. "Do you need more food? You can get things from one of the other houses." That felt right. No one here would wonder why a symbiont needed to eat well.

"Some butter?" she asked. "There are frozen waffles in the refrigerator, and there's syrup in the cupboard—good maple syrup—but no butter."

"Go to the house next door and tell whoever answers that you're with me. If they don't have what you want, they'll tell you who does."

She nodded. "Okay. Don't let my sausages burn." And she ran off to the nearest house, introduced herself, and asked not only for butter, but for fresh fruit and milk as well. I listened while turning her sausages. Wright hadn't managed to teach me to cook, but he had cooked food around me often enough for me to be able to keep pork sausage from burning. The symbiont who answered Celia just said sure, introduced herself as Jill Renner, put the things Celia wanted into a bag, and told her to have a good breakfast. Celia thanked her and brought them back to the guest-house kitchen. Brook came in just then, and she dove right into the bag, took out a banana, and began to peel and eat it.

"A new symbiont will be coming in sometime soon," I told her. "Offer him breakfast, would you?"

"Ooh," Brook said. "*Him?*"

"Damn," Celia said and sighed. "See, now here's where I don't envy you guys. You're going to go upstairs and kick that nice hairy man of yours right in his balls, aren't you? A new man already! Damn."

"Keep the new guy down here until I come back," I said.

I left them and went up to talk to Wright.

Wright had showered and was shaving. There was another sink in the bathroom—one that had a chair in front of it and a large low mirror with lights around it. I sat down in the chair and watched him shave before a similar, higher mirror. He had collected his electric razor from his cabin when we stopped there and was using it now to sweep his whiskers away quickly and easily.

Then he looked at me. "Something wrong?" he asked.

"Not wrong," I said. "But perhaps something that will be hard for you." I frowned. "Hard on you. And I don't want it to be."

"Tell me."

I thought about how to do that and decided that directness was best. "Preston has offered me another symbiont, one whose mother, when she was alive, was one of Preston's symbionts. The new one's name is Joel Harrison."

He turned his shaver off and put it on the sink. "I see. Is Preston the father?"

I stared at him in surprise. "Wright, that's not possible."

"I didn't think it was, but I thought I'd ask, since you didn't mention the father."

"I don't know who Joel's father is, but he's here. He's one of William's symbionts. Joel's mother was killed in a traffic accident ten years ago."

"What does the father think about his son coming to you?"

"He wanted his son to come to me. He asked Preston to introduce us."

"So he's pimping his own son."

I hesitated. "I don't know what that means, but your voice says it's something disgusting. Joel's father hasn't done anything disgusting, Wright. He and Joel both looked at me and decided I would be good for Joel. He's been away at school. He could have stayed away, could have come back now and then to visit his father. But he chose a life with the Ina, with us. I'm glad of it. I need him."

"For what? You need him for what?"

I looked at him, wanting to touch him, knowing that at that moment he did not want to be touched. "Three of you aren't enough to sustain me for long without harm to you. I'm going to try to have Theodora brought here, too."

He shook his head angrily. "I don't mind the women so much I guess. I kind of like the two downstairs. I was hoping you'd get all women—except me. I think I could deal with that." He turned around, filled with energy and violence, and punched the wall, breaking it, leaving a fist-sized hole. And he had hurt his hand. I could smell the blood. But he did not seem to notice. "Hell," he said, "you don't even know Harrison. Maybe you'll hate him."

I shrugged. "If I don't like him, I'll have to find someone else and soon."

He looked at me sadly. "My little vampire."

"Still," I said.

He stepped over to me, picked me up with a hand under one arm, sat down, and sat me on his lap. I took his injured hand and looked at it, licked away the blood, saw that he hadn't done himself much damage. It would heal overnight like a shallow bite.

"I could get a lot more pissed with you if you were bigger," he said softly.

"I hope not," I said.

He wrapped both arms around me, held me against him. "I don't think I can do this, Shori. I can't share you."

I leaned back against him. "You can," I said softly. "You will. It will be all right. Not now, perhaps, but eventually, it *will* be all right."

"Just like that." The bitterness and sorrow in his voice was terrible.

I turned on his lap, straddled him, and looked up at him.

After a moment, he said, "I want you for myself. It scares me how much I love you, Shori."

I pulled his head down and kissed him, then rested my

forehead against his chest, savoring his scent, his wonderful furry body, the beat of his heart. "Preston says our symbionts never know how much we treasure them," I said.

"You treasure me?"

"You know I do."

He held me away from him and looked at me. "You've taken over my life," he said. "And now you want me to share you with another man."

"I do," I said. "Share me. Don't fight with him. Don't hurt the family by fighting with him. Accept him."

He shook his head. "I can't."

"You can," I repeated. "You will. He's part of the family that we must form. He's one of us."

When I left him and went down to the kitchen, I found Joel sitting at the table drinking coffee with Brook and Celia.

"Hey," he said when I came in. He had two large rolling suitcases parked near his chair.

"Hey," I said reflexively. "Come talk to me." I took his hand and led him to the other end of the house to what I had been told was the "family room."

"Don't you mean that *you're* going to talk to *me*?" Joel asked as he sat down in one of the large leather-covered chairs. I sat on the arm of his chair.

"First things first," I said and took the wrist he had offered earlier. He watched me raise it to my mouth and kiss it a second time, and he smiled. I bit him.

He was delicious. I had intended only to taste him and get a little of my venom into him, but he was such a treat that I took a little more than a taste. And I lingered over his wrist longer than was necessary.

Finally, I looked up at him and found him leaning back bonelessly in the chair. "God," he said. "I hit the jackpot."

"How have you managed to stay unattached?" I asked. "Didn't anyone here want you?"

He smiled. "Everyone wanted me. Everyone except Preston and Hayden. They said I was too young to join with them. The others . . . they left me alone when I asked them to, but before that, they were all after me. And I didn't want to join with a man. There's too much sexual feeling involved when you guys feed. I wanted that from a woman. Preston said he would check with nearby female families after I finished college, and he's taken me to see a couple of them, but I wasn't interested. You are the only Ina I've ever been attracted to."

"After seeing me only once?"

"Yeah. I didn't even see you when you were here before . . . before your parents died. I had gone to San Francisco to spend time with some friends from college." He shook his head. "I liked your looks when I saw the pictures the Gordons had of you and your sisters. When I saw you last night, I didn't have a chance."

I didn't know what to make of that. "I'm only beginning to form my family," I said. "You would probably have an easier life with anyone here or any of the female families you've seen. You know my memory only goes back a few weeks."

"I heard."

"And when I leave the Gordons, I'll be alone."

He nodded. "Then let me help you make a new family."

I looked at him and saw that his expression had changed, had become more serious. Good. "I want you to be part of my new family," I said. "More than that, I need you. But you and my first will have to accept each other. You will accept him. There will be peace between you. No fighting. No endangering the rest of us with destructive competitions."

"All right. I doubt that your first and I will ever be anything like friends, but I know how it is. I suppose you told him the same thing."

"Of course." I paused. "He helped me, Joel. When I had no one else, when I had no idea who or what I was, he helped me."

"I wish I had had the chance to do such a thing." He reached up and touched my face. "Like I said, let me help you make a new family."

A little later that morning, I put on my hooded jacket, sunglasses, and gloves and walked around to each of the houses of the community. I spotted the guards from outside, then went into the houses to do what I could to help them be less easily spotted. Being easily spotted by the kind of attackers my symbionts and I had faced would mean easily shot.

The Gordon symbionts greeted me by touching me—my

shoulders, arms, hands. I found that I was comfortable with that, although I had not expected it. It was as though they had to touch me to believe that I could be Ina and yet be awake.

"You aren't drowsy at all?" a woman named Linda Higuera asked. She was a nervous, muscular brown woman, at least six feet tall and leaning on a rifle. We were on the third floor of William's house, and she was one of his symbionts. From what I had seen, William preferred big, powerful-looking symbionts, male and female. Wise of him.

"I'm not drowsy," I said. "As long as I don't get too much sun, I'm fine."

She shook her head. "I wish William could do that. I would feel safer if he could at least wake up if we need him."

I shrugged. "Your turn to keep him safe."

She thought about that, then nodded. "You're right. Damn. He's so strong, I've just gotten used to depending on him. Guess it ought to work both ways." She stopped and thought for a moment. "Do you have a phone?"

"There are phones in the guest house."

"I mean a cell phone."

"No, I don't." I wasn't entirely sure what a cell phone was.

"You should have one so we can talk to each other if something happens. The house phones are too easy to disable."

That made sense. "Is there one I can borrow?"

She sent me down to wake up a huge man named Martin, a man so brown he was almost black. Martin not only supplied me with a charged cell phone, but saved several numbers on it and made me repeat the names that went with them and whose house each person was in. Then he showed me how to make a call, and I made a practice call to the guard at Daniel's house. Finally, he dug out a charger and showed me how to use that.

"Here's your number," he said, making it flash across the phone's small screen, "just in case you have to give it to somebody."

"Thank you," I said, and he grinned.

"No problem. How's Linda doing up there?"

"Doing well," I said. "Alert and thoughtful."

"And how about my son?" he asked in a different tone. "How's he?"

I looked at him, startled. "You're Joel's father?"

"Yep. Martin Harrison. Joel move into the guest house yet?"

"He has, yes. I like him."

"Good. You're what he wants. If you take care of him, he'll take care of you."

I nodded and left him feeling much better about the safety of the Gordon community. With or without me, these people would not be caught by surprise and murdered, and now I could communicate with them in a quiet, effective way.

I walked around the community once more, stopping now and then to listen to the activity around me. There were symbionts eating meals, making love, discussing children who were away at boarding schools, discussing the vineyards and the winery, pruning nearby trees, washing dishes, ordering audiobooks by phone, typing on computers . . . There were little children playing games and singing songs in a room at Hayden's house. It seemed that here some symbionts still carried on most of their activities during the day while others had switched to a nocturnal schedule to spend more time with their Ina.

As I wandered back toward the guest house, I found myself paying attention to a conversation that Wright and Brook were having there.

"They take over our lives," Brook said. "They don't even think about it, they just do it as though it were their right. And we let them because they give us so much satisfaction and . . . just pure pleasure."

Wright grunted. "We let them because we have no choice. By the time we realize what's happened to us, it's too late."

There was a long pause. "It's not usually that way," Brook said. "Iosif told me what would happen if I accepted him, that I would become addicted and need him. That I would have to obey. That if he died, I might die. Not that I could imagine him dying. That seemed so impossible . . . But he told me all that. Then he asked me to come to him anyway, to accept him and stay with him because I could live for maybe two hundred years and be healthy and look and feel young, and because he wanted me and needed me. I wasn't hooked when he asked. He'd only bitten me a couple of times. I could have walked away—or run like hell. He told me later that he thought I might run. He said people did run sometimes out of superstitious fear or out of the puritanical belief that anything that feels that good must have a huge downside somewhere along the line. Then he had to find them and talk them into believing he was a dream or an ordinary boyfriend."

Wright said, "By the time Shori asked me—or rather, by the time she offered to let me go—I was very thoroughly hooked, psychologically if not physically."

"That was probably because of her memory loss."

Wright made an "mmmm" sound of agreement. "I suppose. She's shown herself to be a weirdly ethical little thing most of the time. It still bothers me, though, and now there's this new guy she told me about . . ."

"Joel," Brook said. "You haven't met him yet?"

"She didn't hang around to introduce us. I met him in the upstairs hall. He had the nerve to ask me which bedrooms were empty. You know she never even told me he was black."

"They're not human, Wright. They don't care about white or black."

"I know. I even know she needs the guy—or at least, she needs a few more people. But I hate the bastard. I'm not going to do anything to him. I'll deal with this somehow, but Jesus God, I hate him!"

"You're jealous."

"Of course I am!"

"You aren't sure you want her, but you don't want anyone else to have her."

"Well, it's not like I can leave. Hell, I can feel the hold she's got on me. I can't even think of leaving her without getting scared."

"Would you change that?" Brook asked. "If you could escape her, would you?"

". . . I don't know."

"I think you do. I've seen you with her."

"I can't imagine being without her, but I'm not sure I would have begun if I'd known what I was getting into." There was a silence, then he asked, "What about you? How do you feel about the way she claimed you?"

"Better," Brook admitted.

"Better?"

"She got us out of the Arlington house alive, and she

shouldn't have been able to do that. And she stood her ground last night. The Gordons were pushing her, trying to intimidate her a little just to see what she would do, what she was like. Well, she's strong, and it matters to her how other Ina treat us. We can trust her. Celia said we could, but I wasn't sure."

"You're saying you want to be her symbiont, not some man's? I mean, I thought that after choosing to be with Iosif . . ."

There was another short silence, then Brook said, "I would probably have chosen a man if I'd had a choice initially. But I'm okay with Shori. I can find myself a human man if I need one. I can't believe what she's done for Celia and me. I've seen symbionts who've lost their Ina. An old Ina who was visiting died while he was with us. I saw his symbionts in withdrawal, and I heard them screaming when other Ina tried to save their lives by taking them over. It was bad. Convulsions, pain, help-less fear and revulsion for the Ina who is only trying to help. It went on for days, weeks. It was really horrible. One of the symbionts died. But with Shori . . . she's fed from me twice, and already it doesn't hurt anymore. It's not fun, but it's not bad. I can't wait to know what it will be like when I'm fully her symbiont."

"So . . . they don't all feel the same when they bite?"

"No more than we all look the same. Their venom is different —very individual. I suspect her bite is spectacular. That's why she was able to get you the way she did."

"And she's only a kid," he said.

They said nothing more. I listened for a few moments for more conversation, then for outsiders, intruders. When I knew that the community was safe, for the moment, I thought about what Brook and Wright had said. What they had said, over-all, was that, except for Wright's problem with Joel, they were content with me. It felt remarkably good to know this. I was relieved, even though I had not realized I needed relief. Wright would have to find his own way to accept Joel, and Joel would have to do the same with Wright. There would be a period of unease that I would have to pay attention to, but we would get through it. Other families of Ina and symbionts proved that it could be done.

That day, there were no intruders. The symbionts kept watch, with fresh guards arriving every three hours so that no one got too tired or drowsy. I met a few more of them and liked their variety—a dentist, an oceanographer, a potter, a writer who also worked as a translator (Mandarin Chinese), a plumber, an internist, two nurses, a beautician who was also a barber, and, of course, farmers and winegrowers. And those were just the ones I met. Some no longer did the work they had trained to do except on behalf of the people of Punta Nublada. Some worked in nearby towns or in the Bay Area two or three days out of the week. Some worked in the vineyards and the winery that the Gordons owned. Some, who were self employed, worked in Punta Nublada. Three of the buildings I had mistaken for barns or storage buildings proved to be full of offices, studios, and workshops.

"We fill our time as we please," Jill Renner told me during her watch at Wayne Gordon's house, next to the guest house. "We help support the community whether we have jobs away from it or stay here, whether we bring in money or not." She was the daughter and granddaughter of symbionts and had been much relieved when Wayne Gordon took an interest in her and asked her to accept him. She had a half-healed bite just visible on the side of her neck. I realized that she wanted it to be seen. She was proud of Wayne's obvious attentions to her. Interesting.

That night Wayne and Manning, one of Wayne's fathers, drove to a local airfield where they kept a private plane. Each took two symbionts with him, so I assumed they expected to be gone for two full nights—not that they couldn't graze on strangers if they had to. The Gordons called it grazing. It was what I'd done when I lived with Wright at his cabin, except for Theodora. Ina often found new symbionts when they grazed.

Wayne and Manning came to the guest house before they left to tell me that they were going up to Washington to begin to work out the legal affairs of my male and female families and to look at the ruins of their former communities in the hope that they would see something that we had missed. I had Brook tell them the exact address of Iosif's guest house near Arlington. Let them look at that, too.

"Shall I go?" I asked them. "Won't you need me as daughter and only survivor? Anyway, I think I'd like to collect Theodora."

"We won't need you yet," Wayne said. He was tall even for

an Ina, the tallest in his family. He towered over even his tallest symbionts. "We'll have to produce you eventually, but for now, we just want to find out who handled Iosif's and your mothers' legal affairs. Then we'll bite them and see how quickly all this can be sorted out. The land should be yours whether or not you want to live on any of it. If you like, you can sell one parcel and use the money to get a couple of houses started on the other. And your parents owned apartment houses in Seattle and quite a bit more than just the land their communities stood on. We need to learn all we can about their business affairs before you can even begin to decide what to do."

I nodded. "Can you collect Theodora?"

"Give us her address."

I called Wright, described Theodora's location three doors east of his uncle's house, and he told Wayne how to find her.

"Theodora Harden," I said. "I'll phone her and tell her you'll be there . . . when?"

They worked that out. They would pick up Theodora on their way home on the third night.

"Thank you," I said. "Be careful. Someone should always be awake and on guard."

They nodded and went out to their huge, boxy car. Joel told me it was called a Hummer and that it cost more money than some houses.

Then they were gone.

The next day, Punta Nublada was attacked.

Sixteen

THE ATTACKERS arrived just after ten the next morning. Except for me, all Ina were asleep. I had spent nearly an hour on the phone with Theodora and was thinking about her, wanting her, looking forward to seeing her. Then I heard the cars.

They drove into the community in three large, quiet cars, each almost as big as the Gordons' Hummer, and I heard them before I was able to see them from my perch at one of the dormer windows in the guest-house bedroom that Wright and I shared. I didn't know who the newcomers were. They weren't talking among themselves. They weren't making much noise of any kind, but the moment I heard their approach, I was suspicious. I phoned two other houses and told the symbionts there to alert everyone else.

"Wake everyone," I said. "Wrap your Ina in blankets and be ready to get them out of the house. These people like to set fires. Watch. If they carry large containers, if they try to spread any liquid, shoot them."

I was worried about innocent visitors being killed by frightened symbionts, but I was even more worried about the Gordons and their symbionts being killed in their sleep, perhaps because of me or something to do with my family.

I pulled on my hooded jacket and put on my sunglasses and gloves. The sun was shining outside. There were no clouds. Finally I ran downstairs and found Wright in the kitchen. He hadn't spoken to me at all today because I had spent part of the night with Joel. I grasped his arms. "This may be an attack," I said. "Get Brook, Celia, and Joel. Get guns. Watch! Don't show yourselves and don't fire unless you see gas containers or guns."

I needed to be outside so that I could keep an eye on things and take whatever action was needed. I went out the back door. I had my phone in my pocket—set to vibrate, not ring —but no gun. I would kill quietly if I had to kill.

The cars came down the private road that led to the Gordon houses. They stopped before they reached the first house

—the guest house—and men spilled out of the doors. Each carried some burden in his hand, and at once I could smell the gasoline.

I phoned the nearest house—Wayne's house—and said, "Shoot them. Now!"

There was a moment when I thought they would not obey me. Then the shooting started. The symbionts had a wild mixture of rifles, handguns, and shotguns. The sound was an uneven mix of pops, thunderous roars, and intermediate bangs. Somehow, most of the invaders went down in that first barrage. They were used to taking their victims completely by surprise, setting their fires, and shooting the desperate who awoke and tried to run. Now it was the raiders who were running—at least those still able to run.

I heard someone running my way, around the side of the guest house toward the back, away from the road. The runner was human and smelled strongly of gasoline. He was spilling gasoline as he ran. He never saw me.

I let him come around the house to me, let him get completely out of sight of his friends, and then hit him with my whole body. As he went down, I broke his neck. He was too slow to understand fully what was happening. He made no noise beyond the rush of air from his lungs when I hit him.

I left his gun and his gasoline can out of sight behind a garage, then I ran along the backs of the houses, hoping that if anyone saw me, I would be moving too fast for them to aim and shoot. I ran around the community, killing three more men as the symbionts went on shooting and as someone set fire to Henry's house, then to Wayne's.

I saw that Henry was being looked after—three of his symbionts were carrying him from his house thickly wrapped from head to toe in blankets. They took him into William's house. The rest of Henry's symbionts poured out of his house, too, and three of them found hoses and began to fight the fire. The other two guarded them with rifles.

I felt a particular duty toward Wayne's symbionts because he had gone up to Washington to help me. I made sure everyone was out of his house, checked with the symbionts flowing out the doors, and told them to count themselves. All were present and healthy, three of them carrying young children whom they took to William's house. The rest got hoses and shovels and began to fight the fire. They needed no help from me.

I went through the community, looking everywhere. There was no more shooting. All the intruders seemed to be dead or wounded. Then I heard footsteps and caught an unfamiliar scent. I realized there was at least one intruder still alive and trying to get back to one of their cars. I spotted him moving behind the houses. He took off his shirt as he slipped past Preston's house. He wanted to blend in, look, at least from a distance, like one of the male symbionts who had been awakened unexpectedly and were now fighting the fires or tending the wounded, shirtless.

Shirtless or not, this man smelled of gasoline and alienness. He was an outsider. There was nothing of the Gordon community about him.

I ran after him as he sprinted from the back of Preston's house toward one of the buildings that housed offices and studios. This did not take him closer to any of his group's cars. He couldn't have reached them without running across a broad open space. But the building was unlocked, and it would have given him a place to hide and bide his time. It was his bad luck that I had seen him.

I caught up with him, tripped him, and dragged him down just as he reached the building. He fell hard and knocked himself out on the concrete steps in front of the building. I was glad of that. I wanted him unconscious, not dead. I had questions to ask him. I took a full meal from him while he lay there. I didn't need it yet in spite of the running around and fighting I'd done, but I needed him cooperative.

He came to as I finished and tried to buck me off him.

"Be still," I said. "Relax."

He stopped struggling and lay still as I lapped at the bite just enough to stop the bleeding and begin the healing.

"All right," I said. "Let's go see how things stand between your people and mine." I stood up and waited for him to get up. He was a short, stocky, black-haired man, clean shaven but disfigured by the beginnings of a big lump over his left eye and a lower lip rapidly swelling from a blow that had probably loosened some of his teeth.

He stumbled to his feet. "They'll kill me," he said, mumbling a little because of the swelling lip and looking toward the clusters of people putting out the fires, gathering weapons, moving cans of gasoline away from the houses, checking dead or wounded raiders, keeping children away from the bodies.

"Stay close to me and do as I say," I told him. "If you're with me and if you don't hurt anyone, they won't kill you."

"They will!"

"Obey me, and I won't let anyone hurt you."

He looked at me, dazed. After a moment he nodded. "Okay."

"How many of you were there in those three cars?" I asked, glancing back at the cars. None of this group should escape. Not one.

"Eighteen," he said. "Six in each car."

"That many and your gear. You must have really been packed in."

I walked him back toward the houses, made him pick up his shirt and put it on again. Then I spotted Wright. He came toward me, looking past me at the raider.

"Don't worry about him," I said. "Are Celia, Brook, and Joel all right?"

"They're fine."

I nodded, relieved, and told him where to find the men I'd killed and their guns and their gasoline. "Get other symbionts to help you collect them," I said. "There should be a total of eighteen raiders, living and dead, including this one."

"Okay," he said. "Why is this one still alive?"

"I've got questions for him," I said. "Are any of the rest of them alive?"

"Two. They're shot, and they've been kicked around a little. The symbionts were pissed as hell at them."

"Good. Make sure the dead, their cars, and the rest of their possessions are gathered and shut up out of sight in case the noise or the smoke attracts outside attention." The Gordons had no neighbors who could be seen from the houses, but the noise might have reached some not-too-distant farm. And the smoke might be seen, although there was much less of it now. The fires were almost out. Two houses had been damaged, but none of them had been destroyed. That was amazing. "Where are the survivors?" I asked.

He pointed them out in the yard where they had been laid,

then he said with concern, "Shori, your face is beginning to blister. You should get inside. If it gets any worse, you might have scars."

I touched his throat just at the spot I had so often bitten. "I won't scar anymore than you do when I bite you. Thank you for worrying about me, though." I left him. My raider followed me as though I were leading him with a rope.

The two surviving raiders were battered and unconscious. They lay on the grass in front of Edward's house. "Don't hurt them any more," I told the symbionts who were guarding them. "When they can talk, your Ina will want to question them. I will, too."

"Our doctor will look at them when she gets around to them," a man named Christian Brownlee said. He stared at my raider, then ignored him. My raider inched closer to me.

"Are all the symbionts alive?" I asked.

He nodded. "Five hurt. They're in Hayden's house."

I knew the Gordons had a doctor and two nurses among the ninety or so adult humans in the community, and I went to Hayden's house, expecting to find her at work there. She was.

The doctor was one of Hayden's symbionts. She was an internist named Carmen Tanaka, and she was assisted not only by the two nurses, a man and a woman, but by three other symbionts. She was busy but not too busy to lecture me.

"You stay out of the sun," she said. "You're blistering."

"I came to see whether I could be of use," I told her. "I don't know whether there is anything I can do to help heal symbionts not my own, but I want to help if I can."

Carmen looked up from the leg wound that she was cleaning. The bullet had apparently gone straight through the man's calf. "If any of them were in danger or likely to be in danger before their Ina awake, I'd ask for your help," she said. "But as things are, you'd just cause them unnecessary pain and create problems between them and their Ina."

I nodded. "Let me know if anything changes," I said. "I'm going to do what I can for the raiders who survived. We're going to want to talk to them later."

"Is this one?" she looked at my companion.

"Yes."

She looked at the bite wound on the man's neck and nodded.

"If you bite the others, you'll help them avoid infection and they'll heal faster and be more manageable."

I nodded and went out to tend to the raiders. Once I finished with them, I took my raider back to the guest house, gave him a cold bottle of beer from the stock we'd found in the pantry, and sat down with him at the kitchen table.

"What's your name?" I asked him.

"Victor Colon."

"All right, Victor. Tell me why you attacked this place."

He frowned. "We had to."

"Tell me why you had to."

He frowned, looking confused. It was a kind of confusion that worried me since it seemed to me that it could mean only one thing.

Celia and Brook came into the kitchen, saw us, and stopped.

"Come in," I said. "Did you come to get food?"

"We missed lunch," Brook said. "We probably shouldn't be hungry after all this, but we are."

"It's all right," I said. "Eat something. Fix some for Victor here, too. And sit and talk with us."

They didn't understand, but they obeyed. They cooked hamburger sandwiches for themselves and one for Victor Colon. They had found loaves of multigrain bread, hamburger meat, and bags of French fries in the freezer, and had put the meat and bread in the lower part of the refrigerator to thaw. Now, they fried the meat and the potatoes in cast-iron pans on the stove. There was salt and pepper, mustard and catsup, and a pickle relish in the cupboard but, of course, no fresh vegetables. At some point we were going to have to find a supermarket.

Once they all had food and bottles of beer from the refrigerator, and I had a glass of water, the confused man seemed more at ease. As he ate, he watched Celia and Brook with interest. He was seeing them, I thought, simply as attractive women. He stared at Celia's breasts, at Brook's legs. They knew what he was doing, of course. It seemed to amuse them. After a few glances at me, they relaxed and behaved as though Victor were one of us or, at least, as though he belonged at our table.

Celia asked, "Where do you come from?"

Victor answered easily, "L.A. I still live there."

Brook nodded. "I went down to Los Angeles a few years ago to visit my aunt—my mother's sister. It's too hot there."

"Yeah, it's hot," Victor said. "But I wish I were there now. This thing didn't go down the way it was supposed to."

"If it had, we'd be dead," Celia said. "What the hell did we ever do to you? Why do you want to kill us?" Oddly, at that moment she handed him another bottle of beer. He'd already finished two.

Victor frowned. "We had to," he said. He shook his head, reverting to that blank confusion that so worried me.

"Oh my God," Brook said. She looked at me, and I knew she had seen what I had seen.

Celia said, "What? What?"

"Victor," Brook said, "who told you and your friends to kill us?"

"Nobody," he responded, and he began to get angry. "We're not kids! Nobody tells us what to do." He drank several swallows of his beer.

"You know what you want to do?" Brook said.

"Yeah, I do."

"Do you want to kill us?"

He thought about that for several seconds. "I don't know. No. No, I'm okay here with you pretty ladies."

I decided he was getting too relaxed. "Victor," I began, "do you know me? Who am I?"

He surprised me. "Dirty little nigger bitch," he said reflexively. "Goddamn mongrel cub." Then he gasped and clutched his head between his hands. After a moment, he put his head down on the table and groaned.

It was clear that he was in pain. His face had suddenly gone a deep red.

"Didn't mean to say that," he whispered. "Didn't mean to call you that." He looked at me. "Sorry. Didn't mean it."

"They call me those things, don't they?"

He nodded.

"Because I'm dark-skinned?"

"And human," he said. "Ina mixed with some human or maybe human mixed with a little Ina. That's not supposed to happen. Not ever. Couldn't let you and you . . . your kind . . . your family . . . breed."

So much death just to keep us from breeding. "Do you think I should die, Victor?" I asked.

"I . . . No!"

"Then why try to kill me?"

Confusion crept back into his eyes. "I just want to go home."

"Victor." I waited until he sat up and faced me. "If you leave here, do you think they'll send you after me again?"

"No," he said. He swallowed a little more beer. "I won't do it. I don't want to hurt you."

"Then you'll have to stay here, at least for a while."

"I . . . can I stay here with you?"

"For a while." If I bit him a time or two more and then questioned him, I might get the name of our attackers from him—the name of whoever had bitten him before me, then sent him out to kill. And if I got that name, the Gordons would probably recognize it.

"Okay," he said. He finished his beer. Celia looked at me, but I shook my head. No more beer for now.

"You're tired, Victor," I said. "You should get some sleep."

"I am tired," he said agreeably. "We drove all night. You got a spare bed?"

"I'll show you," I said and took him upstairs to our last empty bedroom. I had intended to give it to Theodora. We would have to get rid of Victor soon. Maybe one of the other houses would have room for him. "You'll sleep until I awaken you," I told him.

"Will you bite me again?" he asked.

"Shall I?" I didn't really want to, but of course I would.

"Yeah."

"All right. When I awaken you, I will."

"Listen," he said when I turned to leave. "I didn't mean to call you . . . what I called you. My sister, she married a Dominican guy. Her kids are darker than you, and they're my blood, too. I would kick the crap out of anyone who called them what I called you."

"You only answered my question," I said. "But I need more answers. I need to know all that you can tell me."

He froze. "Can't," he said. "I can't. My head hurts." He held it between his hands as though to press the pain out of it somehow.

"I know. Don't worry about it right now. Just get some sleep."

He nodded, eyelids drooping, and went off to bed. I felt like going off to bed myself, but I went back down to the kitchen where Celia and Brook were waiting for me. Wright and Joel had joined them. Wright spoke first.

"All eighteen attackers are accounted for," he said. "No one got away."

I nodded. That was one good thing. None of them would be running home to tell the Ina who had sent them that they had failed, although that would no doubt be obvious before long. And what would happen then? I sighed.

Joel seemed to respond to my thought. "So some Ina is sicking these guys on us," he said. "When he sees it didn't work this time, he'll send more."

"It seems that way," I said wearily. I sat down. "I don't know my own people well enough to understand this. I feel comfortable with the Gordons, but I don't really know them. I don't know how many Ina might be offended by the part of me that's human." I wanted to put my head down on the table and close my eyes.

"The Gordons will help you," Joel said. "Preston and Hayden are decent old guys. They can be trusted."

I nodded. "I know." But of course I didn't know. I hoped. "Tonight we'll talk to the prisoners. Maybe we'll all learn something."

"Like which Ina have been trying to kill you," Celia said.

I nodded. "Maybe. I don't know whether we can find that out yet. It may be too soon. But Victor isn't really injured, so we can begin questioning him tonight. The others, though, they might need time to recover, and they might know things that Victor doesn't. Or we might just use them to verify what Victor says."

"You're sure you can make Victor tell you what he knows?" Wright asked.

"I can. So could the Gordons. It will hurt him, though, stress him a lot. It might kill him. I don't believe any of this is his fault, so I don't want to push him that far."

"You remember that," he asked, "that your questioning him could kill him?"

I nodded. "I saw his face when I asked him who I was, and he answered. It hurt him. In that moment, I knew I could kill him with a few words. But he's only a tool—one of eighteen tools used today."

"What makes you so sure he's not a willing tool?" Celia asked.

"His manner," I said. "He's confused, sometimes afraid, but not really angry or hateful." I shrugged. "I could be wrong about him. If I am, we'll find out over the next few days."

"You're sure it's all right to leave him alone upstairs?" Wright said.

"He'll sleep until I wake him," I said. "And when he wakes, I won't be the only one wanting to question him."

Seventeen

I WENT UPSTAIRS feeling tired and a little depressed. I didn't know why I should feel that way. I was close to finding out who was threatening me, and I had taken a full meal from Victor, which should have restored my energy after all my running around in the sun and blistering my face until it hurt. Somehow, it hadn't.

I had taken off my shoes and was lying down on the bed Wright and I usually shared when Brook looked in and said, "Come to my room and lie down with me for a little while."

The moment she suggested it, it was all I wanted to do. I slid from the bed and went down the hall to her room.

I lay down beside her, and she turned me on one side and lay against me so that I could feel her all along my back.

"Better?" she asked against my neck. "Or is this hurting your face?"

I sighed. "Much better." I pulled one of her arms around me. "My face is healing. Why do I feel better?"

"You need to touch your symbionts more," she said. "Temporaries like Victor don't matter in the same way, and Joel isn't yours yet. You need to touch us and know that we're here for you, ready to help you if you need us." She brought her hand up to my hair and stroked gently. "And we need to be touched. It pleases us just as it pleases you. We protect and feed you, and you protect and feed us. That's the way an Ina-and-symbiont household works, or that's the way it *should* work. I think it will work that way with you."

I brought her hand to my mouth and kissed it. "Thank you," I said.

"Sleep a little," she said. "It isn't likely that there will be any more danger today. Take a nap."

I drifted off to sleep in utter contentment.

"Shori?"

I awoke sometime after dark and disentangled myself from Brook as gently as I could. I got up, listening. Someone had called my name. Daniel's voice, not speaking loudly, not in the room with me, not even in the house, but clearly speaking my name to me.

I didn't want to wake Brook so I went to the bathroom down the hall. The window there faced the road and the other houses.

"Yes," I said aloud, eyes closed, listening.

"Bring your captive to my house for questioning," he said. "You can act as his protector, as some of us will scare him."

"Other Ina ordered him to kill us," I said. "He's their tool, not a willing volunteer."

Silence. Then, "All right. Bring him anyway. We won't hurt him any more than we have to."

"We'll be over in a few minutes."

I went to Wright's and my bedroom and got my shoes from beneath the bed. Wright was there, snoring softly. I didn't disturb him. I went back to the bathroom, put my shoes on, and washed my face, all the while thinking about how easily Daniel and I had spoken. I had heard him even though he had not left his house, and he had known that I would hear him. I stood for a moment in the bathroom and listened, focusing my listening first on the guest house where Victor and my four symbionts were all asleep, breathing softly, evenly. Then I focused on Preston's house and heard a female symbiont tell a male named Hiram that he should telephone his sister in Pittsburgh because she had phoned him while he was out helping with the wounded. A male was trying to repair something. He was cursing it steadily, making metallic clattering noises, and insisting, apparently to no one at all, "It's not supposed to do that!" And a woman was reading a story about a wild horse to a little girl.

Of course I had been focusing my listening almost since I awoke in the cave, but I had not been around other Ina enough to know how sensitive our hearing could be. It had never occurred to me that someone could awaken me and get my full attention just by calling my name in a normal voice from another house across and down the road. Had I heard because on some level I was listening for my name? No, this couldn't have been the first time people talked about me when I wasn't present or wasn't awake.

But it probably was the first time someone so far away had spoken *to* me as I slept. And perhaps that small thing, the tone of Daniel's voice alone, had been enough to catch my attention.

I went to Victor's room and woke him. Then, because I had promised and because it would help me get information out of him later, I bit him again, tasting him, taking only a little blood. He lay writhing against me, holding me to him, accepting the pleasure I gave him as willingly as I accepted his blood. I found myself wondering whether anyone had ever investigated the workings of Ina salivary glands or tried to synthesize our saliva. It was no wonder that Ina like my father worked so hard to conceal our existence.

When the bite wound had ceased to bleed, we got up, and I took him over to Daniel's house where all of the Gordons, except those who had flown up to Washington, waited.

"What's going to happen to me?" he asked as we went. He seemed frightened but resigned. He had been in Ina hands long enough to know that there was no escape, no way of refusing his fate, whatever it turned out to be.

"I don't know," I said. "You do your best for us, and I'll do my best for you. Relax and answer all questions truthfully."

When we reached Daniel's house, I saw that the Gordons had gathered in the living room. There were no symbionts present. That was interesting. I had not even thought of awakening my symbionts to bring them along. If Victor died tonight, I didn't want them to see it happen. I didn't want to confront them with the reality of what could happen to them if some Ina who hated me got hold of them. But they knew, of course. They were all intelligent people. They even had some idea of what I could do to them if I were to lose my mind and turn against them. But they trusted me, and I wanted—needed —their trust. They didn't have to see the worst.

I sat with Victor. He was alone and afraid, actually shaking. He needed someone to at least seem to be on his side. He was the alien among us, the human being among nonhumans, and he knew it.

"His name is Victor Colon," I told the Gordons when we were settled. "Victor," I said and waited until he looked at me. "Who are they?"

He responded in that quick, automatic way that said he wasn't thinking. He was just responding obediently, answering the question with information he had been given. "They're the Gordon family. Most of it." He looked them over. "Two are missing. We were told there would be ten. Ten Gordons and you." He glanced at me.

I nodded. "Good. Relax now, listen to their questions and answer them all. Tell the truth." I looked at the Gordons. They must know more than I did about questioning humans who had been misused by Ina. I would leave it to them as much as possible.

Preston said, "What else are we, Victor? What else do you know about us?"

"That you're sick. That you're doing medical experiments on people like the Nazis did. That you are prostituting women and kids. I believed it. Now, I don't know if it's true." He was trembling more than ever. He jumped when I put my hand on his arm, then he settled down a little. "They said we all had to work together to stop you."

"How many of you were there?" This was from Hayden, the other elder of the group. They were centuries old, Hayden and Preston, although they looked like tall, lean, middle-aged men in their late forties or early fifties, perhaps. Their symbionts had told me they were the ones who had emigrated here from England, arriving at the colony of Virginia in the late eighteenth century.

"There were twenty-three of us at first," Victor said. "Some got killed. Jesus, first five guys dead and now just about everyone else . . . Today there were eighteen of us."

"Eighteen," Hayden said nodding. "And were they your friends, the other men? Did you know them well?"

"I didn't know them at all until we all got together."

"They were strangers?"

"Yeah."

"But you joined with them to come to kill us?"

Victor shook his head. "They said you were doing all this stuff . . ."

"Where were you?" Preston asked quietly. "Where did you get together?"

"L.A." Victor frowned. "I live in L.A."

"And how were you recruited? How were you made part of the group that was to come for us?"

Victor frowned. He didn't appear to be in pain. It was as though he were trying hard to remember and understand. He said, "It almost feels like I've always been working with them. I mean, I know I wasn't, but it really feels like that, like nothing really matters but the work we did together. I remember I had been watching TV with my brother and two of my cousins. The Lakers were on. Basketball, you know? I needed some cigarettes. I went down to the liquor store to buy some, and this tall, skinny, pale guy pulled me into an alley. He was goddamn strong. I couldn't get away from him. He . . . he bit me." Victor looked down at me. "I thought he was crazy. I fought. I'm strong. But then he told me to stop fighting. And I did." He stopped talking, looked at me, suddenly grabbed me by the shoulders. "What do you people do to us when you bite us? What is it? You're goddamn vampires!"

He shook me. I think he meant to hurt me, but he wasn't really strong enough to do that. I took his hands, first one, then the other, from my arms. I held them between my hands and looked into his frightened eyes.

"Answer us honestly, Victor, and you'll be all right. Relax. You'll be all right."

"I don't want you to bite me again," he said.

I shrugged. "All right."

"No!" he shouted. And then more softly, "No, I'm lying. I do want it again, tomorrow, now, anytime. I need it!" His voice dropped to a whisper. "But I don't want to need it. It's like coke or something."

I suddenly felt like hugging him, comforting him, but I didn't move. "Relax, Victor," I said. "Just relax and answer our questions."

The Gordons watched both of us with obvious interest. Daniel, in particular, never looked away from me. I supposed that I was as much on trial as Victor was but in a different way. What did I remember? How well did I compensate for what I didn't remember?

Did they still want me? I thought Daniel did. His scent pulled at me. His brothers smelled interesting, but his scent was disturbing. Compelling.

I sighed and dragged my attention back to Victor. I looked from Preston to Hayden. The others had left the questioning to them so far.

"Victor," Preston said, "where were you taken after you were bitten for the first time?"

"The guy had a big Toyota Sequoia. He told me to get in and just sit there. I did, and he just drove around. He was spotting other guys and picking them up. I guess I was his first catch of the night. He caught five more guys, then he took us all out to some houses up above Altadena, up in the San Gabriel Mountains, kind of all by themselves on a dead-end road. His family was there. They all looked like him—tall, lean, pale guys. And there were a lot of other just ordinary people."

There was a stir among the Gordons. They didn't say anything, but I could see that they knew something. Most likely, they knew which Ina family lived above Altadena in the San Gabriel Mountains. I had no idea how far away these places might be, but they did.

"Victor," Hayden said, "when did all this happen? When were you taken and bitten for the first time?"

He frowned. "More than a month ago? Yeah, it was that long. Maybe six weeks."

I could see what was coming. I stared at the rug, needing to hear more, needing to hear everything, but not quite wanting to hear it. It was only reasonable that Victor had been one of those used to kill both my families.

"So you've done other jobs, then, haven't you?" Hayden continued.

"Up in Washington State, yeah," Victor agreed. "We did three jobs up there."

"How did you get there?"

"They flew us up in private planes with all our gear. Then we rented cars. Followed the maps we were given."

"So they gave you new identities? Credit cards?"

"Not me. Five of the other guys. And they gave them plenty of cash. They had cell phones, too. They'd call in when we were ready to do a job and tell us to go ahead. Then they'd call in afterward and we'd be told what to do next, which was mostly to get motel rooms and wait for the call to get into position for the next job. The five guys they chose, they were all ex-military. One used to be Special Forces. They told the rest of us what to do."

So by now, with no phone call, their bosses must have realized that something was wrong. I wondered how long it would take these enemy Ina to collect new human tools and send them out to try again.

"You said you did three jobs," Preston said. "Where in Washington did you do those . . . jobs?"

"One a few miles outside a little town called Gold Bar. Another not too far from a town called . . . Darlington? No, Darrington. That's it. And one at a house near the town of Arlington. That's all up in western Washington. Pretty country. Trees, mountains, rivers, waterfalls, little towns. Nothing like L.A."

"You were successful in Washington?"

"Yeah, mostly. We hit the first two, and everything went the way it was supposed to. Something went wrong at the third. People got killed. The cops almost got us."

"Weren't people supposed to get killed?"

"I mean . . . our people got killed. We didn't know what happened at first. Later we heard on the radio that two got shot and three had their throats ripped out. The rest of us never saw what did that—a dog, maybe. A big dog. Anyway, the cops were coming, and we had to run."

I thought about telling him exactly what had killed his friends, then decided not to. None of it was his doing, really. Even so, I didn't want to be sitting next to him any longer. I didn't want to know him or ever see him again. But he was not the one who would pay for what had been done to my families. He was not the one I had to stop if I were going to survive.

I took a deep breath and spoke to Preston. "Do you know who's doing this?"

He looked at Victor. "Who are they, Victor? What's the name of the family who recruited you and sent you to kill us?"

Victor's body jerked as though someone had kicked him. He looked at me desperately, confusion and pain in his eyes.

Hayden picked up the question. "Do you know them, Victor? What is their family name?"

Victor nodded quickly, eager to please. "I know, but I can't say . . . please, I can't."

"Is the name 'Silk'?"

Victor grabbed his head with both hands and screamed— a long, ragged, tearing shriek. Then he passed out.

I didn't want to care. It was clear from the Gordons' expressions that they didn't care. But I had bitten him twice. I didn't want him, wouldn't have kept him as my symbiont, but I did care what happened to him. I couldn't ignore him. It seemed that the bites made me feel connected to him and at least a little responsible for him.

I listened to his heartbeat, first racing, then slowing to a strong, regular beat. His breathing stuttered to a regular sleeping rhythm. "What can we do with him?" I asked Preston. "I can talk him into forgetting all this and send him home, but what if the Silk family picks him up again?"

"You feel that you need to help him, in spite of everything?" he asked.

I nodded. "I don't want him. I don't like him. But none of this really has anything to do with him."

He looked around at his brother and his sons. Most of them shrugged.

Daniel said, "I don't think the Silks will bother about him. They won't know he survived. They probably don't even know exactly where he lived before they picked him up. He's just a tool. They might have rewarded him if he survived, but if they think he's dead, that will be the end of it. We need to check what he's said with what the other prisoners say. If their stories agree, they can all go home. You can send them back to their families."

I nodded. "I'll fix Victor. Do you want me to fix the others, too?"

"Once we've questioned them, you might as well. You've already bitten them." He didn't sound entirely happy about this. I wondered why.

"Is there transportation back to L.A. from somewhere around here?" I asked.

"We'll get them back." Daniel looked uncomfortable. "Shori, I think your venom is the reason this man is still alive, the reason he was able to answer as many questions as he did."

This was obvious so I looked at him and waited for him to say something that wasn't obvious.

"I mean, *your* venom. If one of us had bitten him instead of you, I think he'd be dead now."

I nodded, interested. That was something I hadn't known.

"And that means that if the Silks do get him again somehow and question him, he won't survive. There may be female relatives of the Silks—sisters or daughters—with venom that's as strong as yours. They could question him, but chances are, they won't. And he wouldn't survive being questioned by males. Their venom would make it necessary for him to answer but not really possible. The dilemma would kill him. He'd probably die of a stroke or a heart attack as soon as they began."

I looked at Victor and sighed. "Is there anything we can do to keep him safe?"

"No," Preston said. "It really isn't likely that the Silks will pick him up again. He'll probably be all right. But unless one of us wants to adopt him as a symbiont, we can't keep him safe. Daniel only wanted you to know . . . everything." I heard disapproval in his voice, and I didn't understand it. I decided to ignore it, at least for now.

I looked at Daniel and thought he looked a little embarrassed, that he was staring past me rather than at me. "Thank you," I said. "So much of my memory is gone that I'm grateful for any knowledge. I need to know the consequences of what I do."

Daniel got up and left the room.

I looked after him, surprised, then looked at Preston. "When should Victor be ready to go?"

"A couple of nights from now. After we've questioned the others."

"All right," I paused. "Can one of you take him? I don't want him back at the guest house."

Preston glanced at the doorway Daniel had gone through. "Don't worry," he said. "We'll take care of him."

"Thank you," I said with relief. Then I changed the subject and asked a question I had been wanting to ask since I arrived. "Are there . . . do you have Ina books, histories I could read to learn more about our people? I hate my ignorance. As things stand now, I don't even know what questions to ask to begin to understand things."

It was Hayden who answered, smiling. "I'll bring you a few books. I should have thought of it before. Do you read Ina?"

I sighed and shrugged. "I honestly don't know. We'll find out."

Eighteen

To my surprise, I did read and speak Ina.

Hayden brought me three books and sat with me while I read aloud from the first in a language that I could not recall having heard or seen. And yet as soon as I opened the book, the language seemed to click into place with an oddly comfortable shifting of mental gears. I suppose I had spoken English from the time I met Wright because he and everyone else had spoken English to me. If I had heard only Ina since leaving the cave, I might not know yet that I spoke English.

I shook my head and switched back to English. "I wonder what else I'll remember if someone prods me."

"Do you understand what you've read, Shori?" Hayden asked.

I glanced at the symbols—clusters of straight lines of different lengths, inclined in every possible direction, and often crossed at some point by one or more S-shaped lines. They told the Ina creation myth. "Iosif told me a little about this," I said. "It's an Ina myth or legend. The goddess who made us sent us here so that we could grow strong and wise, then prove ourselves by finding our way back home to her."

"Back to paradise or back to another planet," Hayden said. "There was a time when Ina believed that paradise was elsewhere in this world, on some hidden island or lost continent. Now that this world has been so thoroughly explored, believers look outward either to the supernatural or to rather questionable science."

"People truly believe this?" I frowned. "I thought the story was like one of the Greek or Norse myths." I had run across these in Wright's books.

"There was a time when those were believed, too. A great many of us still believe in the old stories, interpreted one way or another. What you're holding could be called the first volume of our bible. Your parents believed the stories were metaphors and mythologized history. We do, too. None of us are much interested in things mystical. I don't believe you were either before, but now I suppose you'll have to read the books, talk

457

to believers as well as nonbelievers, and make up your mind all over again."

"How old is this book?" I asked.

"We believe that its oldest chapters were originally written on clay tablets about ten thousand years ago. Before that, they had been part of our oral tradition. How long before that had they been told among us? I don't know. No one knows."

"So old? Are there human things ten thousand years old?"

"Writings, you mean? No. There were wandering family bands, villages of human farmers, and there were nomadic human herders. They left behind remnants of their lives—stone tools, carved stone figurines, pottery, woven matting, stone and wood dwellings, some carving on bone and stone, painting on cave or cliff walls, that sort of thing."

I nodded, interested. "What signs did we leave?"

"We had already joined with humans ten thousand years ago, taking their blood and safeguarding the ones who accepted us from most physical harm. I suspect that by then we had already been around for a very long time. Whenever we evolved or arrived, it was much longer ago than ten thousand years. Ten thousand years ago, we were already thinly spread among human tribes and family bands. Even then, that was the most comfortable way for us to live.

"Our earliest writings say that we joined humans around the rivers that would eventually be called Tigris and Euphrates and that we had scattered north and west into what's now Russia, Ukraine, Romania, Hungary, and those regions. Some of us wandered as nomads with our human families. Some blended into stationary farming communities. Either way, we were not then as we are now. We were weak and sick. I don't know why. The stories say we displeased the goddess and were suffering her punishment. The group that believes in an outer-space origin says that our bodies needed time to adjust to living on Earth.

"For a while, it seemed that we might not survive. I think that's when some of us began to find a new use for the writing we had developed for secret directional signs, territorial declarations, warnings of danger, and mating needs. I think some of us were writing to leave behind some sign that we had lived, because it seemed we would all die. We weren't reproducing well. Our children, when they were conceived, often did not survive their births. Those who did survive were not strong. Few mated families managed to have more than one or two children of their own. Everyone took in orphans and tried to weave new families from remnants of the old. We suffered long periods of an Ina-specific epidemic illness that made it difficult or impossible for our bodies to use the blood or meat that we consumed, so that we ate well and yet starved. We believe now that the disease was spread among us by Ina nomads and by families traveling to be near mates.

"Our bodies were no better at dealing with this illness than our human contemporaries were at dealing with their illnesses. But while our attentions helped them deal with their infections, defects, and injuries, they could not help us deal with ours. We died in greater numbers than we could afford. It got harder and harder for us to find mates. Then, gradually, we began to heal. Perhaps we had simply undergone a kind of microbial winnowing. The illness killed most of us. Those left were resistant to it, as were their children.

"Even when we were fit, though, we had to be careful. Non-symbiont humans might attack us and murder us to steal our possessions or because we were careless and lived too long in one place without seeming to age." He shrugged. "Some humans wanted to know how we could live so long. What secret magic did we possess to avoid growing old? What could be done to us to force us to share our magic with them?

"Suspicions about us grew out of control now and then down through the ages, and we had to run or fight, or we were tortured and murdered as demons or as possessors of valuable secrets. Sometimes they hacked at us until they thought we were dead, then buried us. When we healed, we came out of our graves confused, mad with hunger . . . perhaps simply mad. Well, that's how in some cultures we became the 'walking dead' or the 'undead.' That's why they learned to burn or behead us."

"What about the wooden stake through the heart?" I asked.

"That might work or it might not. There's nothing magical about wood. If the stake leaves enough of the heart intact, we heal. One of my fathers was buried with a stake in his heart. He lived and . . . killed six or seven people when he came out of his grave. As a result, my families had to leave Romania and

change their names. That's how my brothers and I happened
to grow up in England."

He sighed. "Even in the most savage of times, when there
were Ina family feuds that were like small wars, it almost never
happened that we wiped out whole families. What is happening now, what happened to your families, Shori, is rare and
terrible."

"And by coming here, I've brought it to your family," I said.
"I'm sorry for that. I just . . . didn't know what to do or
where else to go. And I was afraid for my symbionts."

Hayden nodded, watching me. "I don't believe my sons'
sons would have wanted you to go to anyone else, although
you're already making Daniel's life uncomfortable."

I wasn't surprised, but I didn't know what to say.

He smiled. "You didn't know, did you?"

"I thought I might be. I'm sorry."

"You needn't be. It's normal. Daniel apologizes for his behavior. He knows you're much too young to make the kind of
commitment he's thinking of. And your efforts and warnings
have kept us safe so far. No one is seriously hurt. What we do
next, though . . . well . . ." He sighed. "I suppose we will
do what we must. These murders must be stopped."

He wouldn't talk about what he and his family meant to do
next. He only told me to keep the books as long as I needed
them and to come to him when I wanted more or if I wanted
to talk about what I'd read.

When he was gone, instead of reading more, I went up to
where Wright lay sleeping. I undressed and climbed into bed
beside him. He awoke enough to curl his body around mine.

"You okay?" he asked, his chin against the top of my head.

"Better," I said. "Better now."

"Do they know who killed your family or, rather, whose idea
it was?"

"They know one family name, and where they live. The two
injured captives can't be questioned yet."

"Is Victor alive, Shori?"

"He is." I swallowed. "Even though he remembers helping
to murder both of my families. He even remembers attacking
the house at Arlington where you and I and Celia and Brook
could have died."

"But it wasn't his idea."

"It wasn't. So far, the Silk family seems to be guilty of all three attacks."

"Silk," he said. "Interesting name. I wonder if you knew them before."

"I don't think so. None of the Gordons mentioned any connection between them and me, and I think at least one of them would have."

"What will be done to them?"

"I don't know. Hayden wouldn't tell me. But I don't think anything will be done until the other two prisoners are questioned."

"You bit them."

"I did. It will help them heal quickly."

He moved me so that we lay eye-to-eye and took my face between his hands. "It will help you question them."

"Of course it will."

"What will happen to them after that, to Victor and the other two captives?"

"When we've finished questioning them, I'll help them forget us because I'm the one who bit them. Then they'll be sent back to their families." I rubbed his shoulders. "They're not anyone's symbionts, Wright. They're only someone's tools. People who never wanted them, never cared about them, kidnapped them and used them to kill my families."

He nodded. "I understand that, but . . . they did what they did."

"The Silks are responsible, not Victor and the others."

He nodded again. "Okay."

He didn't sound happy. "What?" I asked.

"I don't know exactly. I guess I'm just learning more about what I've stumbled into and become part of."

I was silent for several seconds, then asked, "Shall I let you alone tonight? I can go sleep with one of the others."

"Not with Victor?"

I drew back, staring at him.

"Where is he?" he asked.

"At Daniel's house. Daniel had room for him, and Theodora will be here soon. And . . . I didn't want him here."

After a while, he nodded.

"Shall I go?"

"Of course not." He pulled me against him. He caressed my face, my throat. Then, as he kissed me, he slipped his free hand between my thighs. "Are you hungry?" he asked.

I shook my head against him. "No, but I want to be close to you anyway."

"Do you? Good. If you taste me, I want you to do it from my thigh."

I laughed, surprised. "I've heard of doing it that way, although I don't know whether I ever have. You've been talking to someone!"

"What if I have?"

I found myself grinning at him. An instant later, I threw the blankets off him and dove for his thigh. He had nothing on, and I had him by the right thigh before he realized I had moved. Then I looked up at him. He looked startled, almost afraid. Then he seemed to catch my mood. He laughed— a deep, good, sweet sound. By touch and scent I found the large, tempting artery. I bit him, took his blood, and rode his leg as he convulsed and shouted.

The next night, the Gordons and I questioned the other two prisoners. Hayden and Preston questioned them while I prodded and reassured them. I had bitten each of them twice. They trusted me, needed to please me.

They, too, told us about what sounded like members of the Silk family abducting them at night. One had been in downtown Los Angeles, looking for one of his girls—one of the prostitutes who worked for him. He was angry with her. He didn't think she was working hard enough, and he meant to teach her a lesson. Hayden had to explain this to me, and at last I found out what a pimp was. The explanation made me wonder what other unsavory things I didn't remember about human habits.

The other captive had been on his way to the Huntington Memorial Hospital in Pasadena to pick up his mother who was a nurse there and whose shift was ending. Her car had stopped running the day before, and he had promised to meet her and give her a lift home.

One prisoner was a pimp. The other was a college student

keeping a promise to his mother. Both had been collected by members of the Silk family and sent north to kill my family and me. Neither had any information beyond what Victor had already told us.

When both captives were unconscious, much stressed by being made to talk about things that they had been ordered not to talk about, the Gordons and I looked at one another. Again, except for the captives, the company was all Ina.

"What can we do?" I took a deep breath and looked at the younger Gordon males—men who might someday be the fathers of my children. "These people have killed my family. Now they've come after you. They'll probably come after you again."

"I believe they will unless we stop them," Hayden said.

Daniel nodded once. "So we stop them."

"Oh my," Preston said, his head down, one hand rubbing his forehead.

"What else can we do?" Hayden demanded.

"I know." Preston glanced at him sadly. "I'm not disagreeing. I'm just thinking about what it will mean, now and in the long run."

Hayden made a growling sound low in his throat. "They should have thought about what it would mean."

Wells, one of Daniel's fathers, said, "I've been thinking about it since yesterday. We need to start by talking to the Fotopoulos and Braithwaite families, and perhaps the Svoboda and the Dahlman families as well. The Dahlmans are related to the Silks through Milo, aren't they? All these people are related in one way or another to the Silks and to Shori."

And I thought, *I still have relatives.* I didn't know them, didn't know whether they knew me. But they were alive. What would that mean?

"Don't phone the Dahlmans yet," Preston said. "Make them your eighth or ninth call. Try the Leontyevs and the Akhmatovas, and perhaps the Marcu and Nagy families."

"You believe we'll have time to bring together a Council of Judgment before they try again to kill us?" Daniel demanded.

Hayden and Preston looked at one another—the two elder-fathers of the Gordons. Apparently they would decide.

"As soon as we get agreement from seven of the thirteen

families, I'll call the Silks," Preston said. "I know Milo Silk, or I thought I did. How he and his sons have gotten involved in all this, I can't imagine. Anyway, once they've been notified that we're calling a Council of Judgment, that we have the first seven families, they won't instigate another attack. They won't dare."

"Why not?" I asked.

Everyone looked at me as though I'd said something very stupid.

I stared back at them. "My memory goes back a few weeks and no further," I said. "I ask because I don't know, and I don't want to make assumptions about anything this important." And because I was annoyed. I let my tone of voice say, *You should all realize this. I've explained it before.*

Hayden said, "If they attack us after we've called for a Council, the judgment will automatically go against them. Our legal system is ancient and very strong. That part of it in particular is absolute. It's kept feuds from getting out of control for centuries."

"And what does that mean?" I asked. "What would happen to them if they attacked you again?"

"The adults would be killed, and their children dispersed among us to become members of other families." He stared down at me. "We would bring the adults to you. You are the person most wronged in all this and the only surviving daughter. I think you could manage it."

"Manage . . . I would be their executioner?"

"You would be, yes. You would bite them and speak to them, command them to take their lives. I suspect that you would grant them a gentler death than they deserve."

For a moment, I was shocked speechless. Of course I knew I could kill humans directly by destroying their bodies or indirectly by biting them and then telling them to do things that were harmful to them, but kill Ina just by biting them and ordering them to die?

"I was almost tempted not to tell you," Hayden said. "Your youth and your amnesia make you both very attractive and very frightening."

"I can really do that? Bite another Ina and just . . . tell him to kill himself?"

They all looked at one another. Preston said, "Hayden, damnit—"

Hayden held up both hands, palms outward. "She needs to know. We've had a chance to see what sort of person she is. And let's face it, it's too dangerous for her not to know. If not for the crime that took her memory, she would know." He looked at me. "When you're physically mature, you'll take blood from your mates, and they'll take blood from you. That's the way you'll bond. The only other reason for you to take blood from an Ina male would be to kill him."

I thought about that for several seconds, then asked an uncomfortable, but necessary, question: "It wouldn't work on an Ina female?"

"It might. Your handling of the human captives says you're strong. But if you go against another Ina female, you might die. Even if you manage to kill her, you might die, too."

I thought about this. It dovetailed with what Brook had told me. "Do you know," I said, "I have no memory of ever having seen or spoken to an Ina female. I've only seen my father, one of my brothers, and you. I try to picture a female, and I can't."

"They learn early to be careful of what they say," Hayden told me. "It's one of their first and most important lessons. I believe that's a lesson you've remembered in spite of your amnesia."

I nodded. "I was always careful with my symbionts, even before I understood fully why I should be. But now . . . I might have to kill the Silks?"

"Probably not," Hayden said. "That kind of thing hasn't happened in living memory. The Silks will respect the call for a Council of Judgment."

"I hope so," I said. "What can I do now to help?" They were beginning to get up. Some of them took phones from their pockets. Daniel went to the kitchen and brought back a cordless phone for Hayden.

"Nothing yet," Hayden told me. "You'll have to speak at the Council."

"All right. But shouldn't we keep the three captives? Shouldn't they speak, too?"

He shook his head. "Who would believe them? By now you

could have taken them over completely and taught them to say
—and to believe—anything at all."

"All right. But why should the Council believe me—or you
for that matter?"

He smiled. "I don't think they would believe me. I'm 372
years old. I think they might feel that someone my age might
be able to lie to them successfully. You're a child. They'll assume that they'll be able to read your body language well
enough to know whether or not you're lying."

"Will they be your age?"

"Some will be older."

I sighed. "They're probably right then. It doesn't matter. I
haven't felt inclined to tell lies. So far, my problem is ignorance,
not dishonesty."

Nineteen

THERE WAS a great deal of telephoning, conference calling, faxing, and e-mailing.

First, what Hayden called "the rule of seven" had to be satisfied. Seven families with whom both the Silks and I share a common ancestor within seven generations of the oldest living Silk or Matthews had to agree to send representatives to Punta Nublada for a Council of Judgment that would judge the accusations that I and the Gordon family were making against the Silk family. Once that was done, Preston phoned the Silk family. First Russell Silk, one of the elderfathers, denied all responsibility for wiping out my families, denied any knowledge of it. Then Milo Silk, the oldest living family member, came on and he denied everything, too. They had both heard of a mass murder in Washington State but had not realized that it involved two Ina communities. They were very sorry for me, of course, but none of it had anything to do with them.

Preston put the call on speaker phone and let all of us hear it.

"Nevertheless," he told Milo Silk, "we've heard evidence that your family is responsible, and we've called for a Council of Judgment. We've met the rule of seven."

"This is madness," Milo argued. "We didn't do it, Preston. I swear to you. Look, we don't care for the genetic engineering experiments that the Matthews and Petrescu families have been carrying out, and we've made no secret of it, but—"

"Milo," Preston said, "this is the required notification. The first seven families are Braithwaite, Fotopoulos, Akhmatova, Leontyev, Rappaport, Nagy, and Svoboda. We will also be asking the Dahlmans, the Silvesters, the Vines, the Westfalls, the Nicolaus, and the Kalands. Do you object to any of these?"

"I object to all of them," Milo said angrily. "This is insanity!"

"The rule of seven has been met," Preston repeated.

After a moment of absolute silence, Russell's voice replaced Milo's. "I object to the Vines," he said. "They are not friends of the Silk family, even though they are related to us. During the ninth century, their family fought ours in a long feud."

Preston stared at the floor, thinking. "Will you accept the Marcus?"

There was another silence, longer this time. Then finally, "Yes. We accept the Marcus. We also object to the Silvesters. Three of my sons had a financial dispute with two of them five years ago. It was not settled amicably."

Preston looked at Hayden. Hayden asked, "Will you accept the Wymans?"

"No!" a third voice said. "Not that pack of wolves. Do you realize—" Then the voice was cut off, and there was a long silence. Finally Milo came on again.

"We will not accept the Wymans," he said. And after a pause, he said, "Individual animus." He had a deep, quiet voice that somehow made everything he said sound important.

"The Andreis?" Preston asked, looking at his own family as though he were asking them. His family offered no objection.

There was a silent pause from the Silks. Finally, Milo said, "Fine."

"Are you content with the list now?" Preston asked.

More silence.

"The Kalands," Russell said. "We would prefer the Morarius."

Preston stretched out a long forefinger and pressed the button on the phone marked "hold." "Objections to the Morarius?" he said.

The Gordons looked at one another.

"I don't like them," Daniel said. "They're proud people with not that much to be proud of. But I don't suppose that's reason enough to object to them."

The others shrugged.

Preston touched the hold button again and said, "We accept the Morariu family, Milo. Ten nights from tonight, we will all meet here at Punta Nublada for a Council of Judgment. You should begin to prepare for your family's journey. And maybe you should talk to your sons, especially the younger ones. You may not know everything." He switched the phone off.

Just before dawn, Manning and Wayne drove in with their symbionts and Theodora.

She got out of the Hummer and looked around at the houses. All of them were still lit from within in the early-morning darkness. There were people moving around both inside and out, and although she could not know it, there were people watching. I had been asleep, but I awoke at the sound of the car coming in. I looked out, saw her climb out of the car and look. Quickly, I put on jeans, pulled a T-shirt over my head, and ran out shoeless to meet her. She didn't see me until I reached her and took her hand.

She jumped, turned, saw me, and to my surprise, grabbed me, lifted me off the ground, and hugged me hard against her.

I found myself laughing with joy and hugging her back. When my feet were on the ground again, I took her into the guest house. "Have you eaten?" I asked. "Brook and Celia went shopping yesterday so we have plenty of food." Joel had taken them to a distant mall where they could get groceries, some more clothes, and whatever else they might need. Wright and I had each provided them with a list so we were all taken care of for a while.

"I had a late dinner," Theodora said. "The other people, the symbionts—is that what they're called?"

"It is, yes. It's what you'll be called, too, if you stay with me."

She gave me a shy smile and looked downward. "They said I should have a hearty meal before I reached you."

I laughed again, hungry for her, suddenly eager. "Come on upstairs. How are you? Is everything all right with your family?"

She got ahead of me and stopped me, hands on my shoulders. "I'm going to have to phone my daughter in a few hours. She's worried about me. She tried to stop me from leaving. Sometime soon, she's going to want to visit."

"Phone her whenever you like," I said. "I have to tell you more of what's going on here so you'll understand why she won't be able to visit you for a while. But you can go see her."

"Sounds like bad news."

"Difficult, I think, but not bad. This is a time to be careful. We've found out who has been attacking us, and we're going to have something called a Council of Judgment to deal with them."

She looked at me as though she were trying to read my expression. "Is there danger right now?"

In the early-morning darkness with all the Gordon men

awake and alert? With the Council of Judgment already being organized? "No, not now."

"Good," she said. "Then tell me about it in the morning."

I smiled. "It is morning. But you're right. First things first."

I took her to the spare room. I had changed the bedding myself and made certain that the room was clean and ready for her. "I know I promised you more than this," I said as she looked around. "I will keep my promise. It's just going to take longer than I thought."

"I want to be with you," she said. "It's all I've wanted since you first came to me. I don't truly understand my feelings for you, but they're stronger than anything I've ever felt, stronger than anything I ever expected to feel. We'll find a way."

I shut the door, went to her, and began to undo her blouse. "We will," I said.

The next night I met with Wayne and Manning to find out what I could about my families' land and business affairs.

"Your mothers and father understood how to live by human rules," Manning said. "Their affairs are very much in order. You will have to work through the lawyers, but everything your families owned will be yours, and there's cash enough for you to be able to pay your taxes without selling anything you don't want to sell."

"I don't know what I want to do, really," I said. "I mean, I don't know anything." I looked at Manning—one of the fathers of Daniel, Wayne, William and Philip. He was a quiet, kindly man, and there was something about his expression that looked uncomfortably close to pity.

"Tell me about the lawyers," I said quickly. "Are there one or two who would make good symbionts?"

Manning shrugged. "I'm not sure what a good symbiont might be for you. Your Theodora is too old, but she loves you absolutely. She's exactly the kind of person I would expect to be able to resist one of us—older, educated, well-off—but she couldn't wait to get to you."

"She was lonely," I said. "Tell me about the lawyers."

"One of the ones I bit might be good for you," Wayne said. I liked Wayne's long, quiet face. He was the only one of the four sons who towered over me even when he was sitting down. "Tell me about that one," I said.

He nodded. "She's thirty-five. She has a good reputation among the others at her firm. She's a good attorney even though she hates her work. She feels that she made a mistake going to law school, but now, she doesn't know what else she might do. She's an orphan with a brother who died six years ago. She's divorced and has no children."

"You investigated her. You planned to suggest that I go after her."

"Yes. You'll need a lawyer. She'll help you, she'll teach you, she'll be your connection to the rest of the legal world, and once you have her—if you're as right for each other as I think —she'll be completely loyal to you." He took a folded paper from his pants pocket and handed it to me. "Her name, home address, and work address."

"Thank you," I said and put the paper in my own pocket. "I don't think I'll be able to go see her until after the Council of Judgment."

"I think that would be best," Manning said. "The lawyers Wayne and I bit will look after your interests until then. But you should find her as soon as the Council ends. You need more than five symbionts."

I continued to keep watch every day. I didn't believe there would be another attack, but why take chances?

I saw the bodies of the attackers buried with a great deal of a powder called quicklime in a long, deep trench dug by a small tractor around one of the gardens well away from the houses. I saw the attackers' cars driven away by gloved symbionts, followed by a Punta Nublada car. And, of course, only the Punta Nublada car returned.

I saw the three living attackers taken away to San Francisco where they would be three ordinary men catching three different Greyhound buses back to southern California where they lived. They wouldn't attract attention. No one would be likely to remember them. The Gordons had supplied them with money, and I had supplied them with the outline of a memory of going north to do some work driving trucks, hauling cargo up and down the coast. They could each fill in the details according to their own past work experience. As it happened, they had all driven trucks of one kind or another professionally, so they would be able, as Hayden put it, to confabulate to their hearts' content. But they would not remember one another, Punta Nublada, my families' communities, or the house near Arlington. I told them to forget those things completely and to remember only the truck-driving job. It was unnerving to see that I could do such a thing, but clearly, I could. I did. I even helped the pimp decide that he was sick of abusing women for a living. His cousin had a landscaping company. He would work for his cousin for a while or for someone else and then go back to school. He was only twenty-one. I made him tell me what he believed he should and could do. Then I told him to go do it.

Meanwhile, the Gordons and their symbionts worked hard to prepare for the fact that they were soon going to have a great deal of company. The Silk family—all their Ina and most of their symbionts—would be coming. Two representatives from each of thirteen other families would be coming, each bringing three or four symbionts. A Council of Judgment traditionally lasted three days.

Most of the Gordon symbionts were excited and looking forward to meeting friends and relatives they hadn't seen for months or even years. Would Judith Cho sym Ion Andrei be there? Or Loren Hanson sym Elizabeth Akhmatova? Did anyone know? What about Carl Schwarcz sym Peter Marcu? No one bothered asking me since it was clear that I knew nothing, but they chattered among themselves around me, happily ignoring me except to say that it was a shame I wouldn't get to enjoy any of the parties.

Only a few of them were apprehensive. To most, the Council of Judgment was an Ina thing that had little to do with them. Their Ina had disputes to settle. The symbionts planned to have parties. I enjoyed watching and listening to them. It was comforting somehow.

Several went out to buy the huge amounts of food and other supplies that would be needed to keep well over a hundred extra symbionts comfortable. Others prepared the guest quarters in each of the houses and transformed offices, studios, storage space, and even space in the two barns into places fit for human and Ina habitation. Every house had guest quarters—three or four bedrooms and a couple of bathrooms. These would be enough for a couple of traveling Ina and a few symbionts. And then there was the guest house itself, intended especially for human guests. My symbionts and I had arrived at a time when the Gordons' symbionts had no guests visiting, so we had had the whole guest house to ourselves. Now we would have to share the kitchen and the dining room and give up the downstairs bathroom, as well as the living room and family room.

The Council meetings would be held in one of the metal storage buildings. Martin Harrison, Joel's father and William's symbiont, the man who had given me a cell phone and taught me to use it, now seemed to be in charge of preparations for the visitors. Once I understood that, I found him and asked if I could follow him around for a while to see what he did and to ask him questions.

"I really want you to tell me if I'm in the way or if I'm being too irritating, because I can't always tell," I said, and he laughed. It was a loud, deep, joyful-sounding laugh that was a pleasure to hear even though I knew he was laughing at me.

"All right, Shori, I'll do that," he said. "I was a high-school history teacher when Hayden found me. It will be good to have a student again."

"Hayden found you? Not William?"

"Hayden found me *for* William." He shook his head. "William hadn't yet come of age, and Hayden thought the boy could stand to learn more of human history. Hayden thought I'd make a good bodyguard, too, since William goes completely unconscious during the day. He said I smelled right, for godsake. I understand that now, but I didn't then. I wanted to believe he was crazy, but he'd bitten me by then, and I couldn't just ignore what he told me."

"Did you mind that you would be symbiont to another man?" I asked, remembering the question that Wright had asked Brook.

He gave me an odd look. "You don't care what you pry into, do you?"

I didn't answer—since I didn't know what to say.

"There are plenty of women here," he said. "I married one

of them shortly after I decided to stay." He lifted an eyebrow. "How's your new symbiont—the one who came in last night?"

"Theodora?" I smiled, seeing the connection. "She says she doesn't understand her feelings for me but that they are important to her."

"I'll bet. I saw you two. You were all over each other. That's the way it goes. It doesn't seem to matter to most humans what our lives were before we meet you. You bite us, and that's all it takes. I didn't understand at all. Hayden ambushed me as I got home from work one day. He bit me, and after that I never really had a chance. I didn't have any idea what I was getting into."

"Are you ever sorry you got into it?"

He gave me another strange look, this broad, tall black man. Joel had his coloring but would never have his size. Martin just stood, looking down at me as though trying to decide something. After a while, he said, "The Gordons are decent people. Hayden brought me here, showed me around, introduced me to William, who was tall and spindly but looked almost as young as you do now. Hayden let me know what was going to happen if I stayed. He let me know while I could still leave, and I did leave. They didn't stop me. William asked me to stay, but that made me run faster. The whole thing was too weird for me. Worse, I thought it sounded more like slavery than symbiosis. It scared the hell out of me. I stayed away for about ten months. I'd only been bitten three times in all, so I wasn't physically addicted. No pain, no sickness. But psychologically . . . Well, I couldn't forget it. I wanted it like crazy. Hell, I thought I was crazy. All of a sudden, I lived in a world where vampires were real. I couldn't tell anyone about them. Hayden had seen to that. But I knew they were real. And I wanted to be with them. After a while, I quit my job, packed my things, put what I could in my car, gave the rest away, and drove here. God, it was a relief." He stopped and smiled down at me. "Your first doesn't want any other life, girl, no more than Joel does. The only difference is Joel knows it. Wright is still finding out."

"You've talked to him?"

"Yeah. He'll be all right. How's he getting along with Joel?"

"When he can, he pretends Joel isn't there. When he can't do that, he's civil."

"It's rough on him. Rough on both of them, really. Ease their way as best you can. This Council of Judgment should help a little—distraction, excitement, new people, plenty to do."

"It scares me a little."

"The Council? Sensory overload for you and the other Ina. That's why Councils are only three days long."

"No, I mean . . . having Wright and Joel as well as Brook, Celia, and Theodora. It scares me. I need them. I care about them more than I thought I could care about anyone. But having them scares me."

"Good," he said. "It ought to. Pay attention. Help them when they need help." He paused. "Only when they need help."

I nodded. "I will." I looked into his broad dark face, uncertainly. "Do you want your son to be with me?"

"It's what he wants."

"Is it all right with you?"

"If you treat him right." He looked past me at nothing for several seconds. "I wanted him to live in the human world for a few years, get more education than we could give him here. He did that. But to tell the truth, I wanted him to stay out there, make a life for himself, forget about vampires. Then he comes back, and all he wants to do is find himself a nice vampire girl." He smiled, and it wasn't an altogether happy smile. "I think he'll want to do more once he's been with you for a while. He'll want to write or teach or something. Too much energy in that boy for him to be just some kind of house-husband."

"Theodora wants more, too. Once this Council of Judgment is finished, I'll have to decide what to do, how best to build a home for us all. When that's done, my symbionts will be able to do what they want to do."

"Good girl." He took a deep breath and started toward the nearest building of offices and studios. "Now let's go figure out how many people can be jammed into these studios. Thank God the weather hasn't gotten cold yet."

Twenty

THE NIGHT before the Council was to begin, members of the Leontyev family arrived. I didn't know them, of course, and until they arrived and Martin mentioned it, no one had bothered to tell me that Leontyev was the name of my mothers' male family—the family of their fathers, elderfathers, brothers, and brothers' sons.

The Leontyevs and their symbionts arrived in two cars—a pair of Jeep Cherokees—while I was coming back from showing the very cool and distant Zoë and Helena Fotopoulos and their symbionts to their rooms in one of the office complexes. Martin had given me a list of who was coming and where they were to sleep. He said, "If you want to learn, you might as well help. This will give you a chance to meet people." He was, I had noticed, good at putting people to work.

The Leontyevs were older males, Konstantin and Vladimir, each with three symbionts. Martin intended them to stay with Henry Gordon. I came to get them, introduced myself, and realized from their expressions that something was wrong.

"I've had a serious head injury," I told them. "As a result of it, I have amnesia. If I knew you before, I'm sorry. I don't remember you now."

"You don't remember . . . anything?" the one Martin had pointed out to me as Konstantin asked.

"Not people or events. I remember language. I recognize many objects. Sometimes I recall disconnected bits about myself or about the Ina in general. But I've lost my past, my memory of my families, symbionts, friends . . . The people of my families who are dead are so completely gone from me that I can't truly miss them or mourn them because, for me, it's as though they never existed."

Konstantin gazed down at me with almost too much sympathy. A human who looked that way would surely cry. After a moment, he said, "Shori, we're your mothers' fathers. You've known us all of your life."

I looked at them, took in their tall leanness, trying to find in

476

them something I recognized. They looked more like relatives of Hayden and Preston Gordon—just two more pale blond men who appeared to be in their mid-to-late forties but who were actually closer to their mid–four hundreds.

And suddenly, I found myself wondering what that meant. What had their lives been like so long ago? What had the world been like? I should ask Martin who had once been a history teacher.

The faces and the ages of these two elderfathers—my elderfathers, my mothers' fathers—triggered no memories. They were strangers.

"I'm sorry," I told them. "I'll have to get to know you all over again. And you'll have to get to know me. I can't even pretend to be the person I was before the injury."

"I'm grateful the Gordons were able to take you in and care for you," the one called Vladimir said. "How did they find you?"

I stared at him, surprised, suddenly angry. "I found them. I've survived three attacks, and twice helped fight the attackers off. I helped to question the surviving attackers who came here a few days ago. Only my memory of my life before I was hurt is impaired."

They looked at each other, then at me. "My apologies," Vladimir said. He lifted his head a little and smiled down his long nose at me. He managed to look more amused than condescending. "Whether you remember or not, you still have my Shori's temper."

I took them to the rooms that Henry Gordon had set aside for them in his house. Before I left, I showed them Martin's list and asked one more question. "Are any of these people close female relatives of mine?"

They looked at the list, then looked at one another, each of them frowning. In that moment, they looked almost identical. Then Vladimir said, "I believe your closest surviving female blood relatives are too young to be involved in this. They're children or young women busy with children. For instance, your brothers were mated and had two girls and a boy, all of whom are still very young children. Your mothers' brothers have adult female children, but those children are too young for Council duty."

"Wouldn't they be around my age or older? Some of them must be adults."

"Yes. They're mated so the youngest of them is years older than you. But, unless they're directly involved, people aren't usually called to Councils of Judgment unless their children are adult and mated."

That explained why everyone I'd seen so far seemed to be around the ages of Hayden and Preston.

"All right," I said. "I've been told that all Council members are related to me in one way or another. Who among the women members are my closest relatives? And did any of them know me before?" I asked.

Again the two paused to think. At last, Konstantin said, "The Braithwaites. The Braithwaite eldermothers are Joan, Irene, Amy, and Margaret. Two of them will be coming. They're the daughters of your second elderfathers."

I frowned trying to understand that.

"They are the daughters of your father's father's father," Vladimir clarified. "They know you, knew you before. You can talk to them. But, Shori, you can talk to us, too. We are your family. We've come here to see that your interests are protected and that the people responsible for what happened to you and to so many of our relatives pay for what they've done."

I remembered hearing from Hayden that Joan and Margaret Braithwaite would be coming. In fact, they were arriving tonight. "Thank you," I said. "I . . . I just need to see and talk to an Ina female. I have no memory of ever doing that before today. I've met several males since my injury, but until I met Zoë and Helena Fotopoulos this morning, no females. It's very strange to be an Ina female and yet have no clear idea of what Ina females are like."

Konstantin smiled. "Talk to the Braithwaites then. Elizabeth I was on the throne of England when Joan and Irene were born, so I'm not sure you'll learn much from them about being a young Ina woman now. But all four sisters have met you, Shori, and I think they like you. Go ahead and talk with them when they come."

I kept watch for the Braithwaite women, pestering Martin to look whenever female Ina drove in. The Braithwaites arrived just after midnight. Before I could ask Martin about them,

Daniel came out to welcome them. I heard him call them by name. I watched as he stood talking with them.

Joan and Margaret Braithwaite were a head shorter than Daniel, but still taller than Celia or Brook. They were very straight, very pale women in white shirts and long black skirts. Their hair was twisted and pinned up neatly on their heads. One was brown-haired—the first brown-haired Ina I'd seen —and one was blond. Their chests, beneath their clean, handsome, long-sleeved shirts, were as flat as mine. I suspected that that meant I would not be growing the breasts Wright liked on women. Yet as ignorant as I was, even I wouldn't have mistaken these two for men. There was something undeniably feminine and interestingly seductive about them, even to me. Was it their scents? Did my scent make me seem interesting to other people?

I realized that I wanted Joan and Margaret to think well of me, to like me. That was important somehow. Their scent was definitely influencing me. Was it something they were doing deliberately, I wondered. Could they control it? Could I? I would ask them if I could manage to be alone with one of them.

"Shori?" the brown-haired one said to me as I stood off to one side, almost hiding in the shadows, watching them. Daniel had called the blond woman Joan, so this one must be Margaret.

I was immediately ashamed of myself for hiding and staring. "I'm sorry," I said, stepping forward. "I have no memory of seeing Ina females before today. I've been waiting for you because I was told you are my closest female relatives on the Council."

Daniel looked at me with that strange, strained look of his that ranged between hostility and hunger. I had come to see that look more and more as my stay with the Gordons lengthened. I had seen it on Daniel, William, Philip, and Wayne. Without saying a word, Daniel turned and walked away. I was fairly sure his longing made him seem even more ill-mannered than my ignorance made me. We would have to talk, Daniel and I. If my presence was disturbing him so much, we should at least take a few moments to speak privately together, to get to know each other a little.

"That was interesting," Joan Braithwaite said. She looked at Daniel's retreating back.

"When this is over, I'm hoping I can leave here for a while and stop irritating Daniel and his brothers," I said.

Margaret said, as though we'd known one another for a long time, "Will you mate with them?"

"I think so. I was afraid at first that they might not want me, now that I have to get to know everything all over again . . . and now that I'm alone."

"You truly don't remember anything about your mothers, your sisters?" Margaret asked. "You don't remember any other women?"

"I don't remember anyone," I said. "As I said, I haven't seen an Ina woman since my injury until today. I've only seen males."

The two Braithwaite sisters looked at one another. After a moment, Margaret said, "Take us to our quarters, then I'll talk with you."

I hesitated, remembering the list. "Your quarters are in the offices. This way." I took them and their six symbionts, each carrying a suitcase or a garment bag or both, to the offices and the studio that were to be their living quarters. The symbionts were four men and two women. All four of the men were large and strong looking. They must have smelled very interesting before the Braithwaites claimed them. Two of the men were brown with very straight, very black hair. They were enough alike to be brothers. The other two were pale, muscular men. One of the women—the smallest of them—was startlingly beautiful. She was smaller than Celia, my smallest symbiont, and I'm not sure I would have chosen her as a symbiont out of fear that I would take too much blood from her. The other woman was tall and strong looking and deeply interested in one of the brown men.

"Those two got married last week," Margaret told me when we had left the symbionts in their rooms and Joan in hers. I was alone with Margaret in the office she had chosen as her bedroom. Her arrangement seemed to be to have a room of her own and have her symbionts come to her when she needed them. "Eden, the young woman, is mine and Arun is Joan's," she said. I realized she had noticed me noticing the affectionate pair.

"Do they mind sharing each other with you and Joan?" I asked. "I mean, are they still content to be symbionts?"

"Oh yes." She smiled. "Symbionts usually choose to mate with one another because, as symbionts, they share a life that other humans not only couldn't understand or accept, but . . . well, think about it, Shori. Symbionts age much more slowly than other humans, depending on how young they are when they accept us. How could they have a long-term relationship with someone who ages according to the human norm? People have tried it, but it doesn't work."

I nodded. "I have no coherent idea of what does work. I'm still finding out how Ina families live. I know I should leave here as soon as I can, but then what? I can provide for myself and my symbionts, but I don't know how to be part of the web of Ina society that obviously exists. How can I offer my symbionts the contacts they'll need with other symbionts?" I sighed. "I've forgotten almost everything I spent fifty-three years learning."

"But you're still a child," Margaret Braithwaite said. "You could be adopted into one of your secondary families. Once this business with the Silks is attended to, you'll be welcome in a number of communities."

"If I did that, what would happen to my connection with the Gordons?"

She thought about that, then shook her head. "If you're adopted into another community, you mate where they mate unless you could convince them to accept the Gordons. And you'd have to find a community with unmated daughters so that you can join them before the group of you mated. First adoption, then mating."

"My family was negotiating with the Gordon sons to mate with my sisters and me, and the Gordons have helped me, taken risks for me."

"You want to mate with them, then? It isn't just that at the moment, they're all you've got?"

"I think I do. I like them. But it's true that right now, I don't know any other eligible mates."

"Then you'll have to do what your father did. He lost his family in the European wars. Your mothers lost a few people, too. You had five eldermothers. Three were killed. At that point, your mothers left eastern Europe. Did you know that you were the only one of your sisters to be born here in the United States?"

"I didn't know. The others were born in Romania?"

"Two in Romania and one in England. I met your mothers in England. They had young children, and two of them were pregnant when they reached England. They made themselves over, became English women, and begged your fathers to join them. But your fathers had once owned a great estate in Romania until it was taken from them after World War I and broken up and sold to small farmers. Your fathers' family had lived there for at least two thousand years under several different names, and they truly didn't want to leave. My own family lived there long enough for my mothers to mate with the fathers of your elderfathers. Eventually, though, we went to Greece, then to Italy, then to England. We were always willing to move to avoid trouble or to take advantage of opportunity. From England, we moved to the United States just after World War I. My mothers said there would be another war soon, and they wanted to avoid it as much as possible. No place on Earth was safe, of course, and we lost people, but we were never winnowed down to one person as your father's family was. He had absolutely no primary relatives left who were of his age or older."

"He said my mothers were his distant relatives," I said.

"You remember him?" Margaret asked.

"I met him after my injury." I told her about finding my father, my brothers, then almost at once losing them again.

When I'd finished, she shook her head. "You'll tell of that several more times during the nights of the Council." She drew a deep breath. "Your father fled Romania just before the Communists took over. Most Ina had already left or died. I don't believe any stayed after the war, and I don't think any family has gone back.

"Anyway, your father went to your mothers. He and his four remaining symbionts had little more than their clothing and a few pieces of jewelry that had belonged to his mothers, who were dead. He and your mothers and their symbionts left England for the United States shortly after he joined them. When your mothers settled in the state of Washington, they invited him to live with them for a while, until his oldest son came of age, but your father chose to follow our ways and live apart from his mates. Until his sons grew up, he was alone with his symbionts, acquiring property and money, building his first houses, and acquiring a few more symbionts—people who could help him establish a community and help prepare his sons for adult life."

"So that when his sons were men and went to him, he was able to help them begin their adult lives," I said.

"Yes. He must have been very lonely, but he was a proud man. He did what he believed he should do."

I watched her as she spoke. "It's not the same for me," I said at last. "When my father's kinsmen were killed, he was an adult, already mated, and most of his children already born. I'll be alone with my symbionts, growing up, then bearing and raising my children. I'll have no one to help me, no one to teach them how to be an adult Ina."

She nodded. "That will happen if you permit it. It would be wiser, though, to make friends with several communities of your female secondary families and work for them. Learn from them. I've been told that you can stay awake during the day and go out in the sun like humans. Is this true?"

"I can stay awake," I said, "but when I go outside, I need to cover as much skin as possible and wear dark glasses. Otherwise, I burn, and I can't see very well except with very dark glasses. The sun hurts my eyes."

"But you've walked in it?"

"I have. I think it makes me hungrier to walk in it, though. I burn a little—my face mostly—then I have to heal. My first wants me to wear sunblock, and one of the Gordon symbionts told me I should get something called a ski mask to cover my face. With that and with dark glasses and gloves, I would be completely covered, but I think I would look very strange."

"That's . . . Child, do you understand your uniqueness, your great value?"

"The Silks don't see me as valuable."

She closed her eyes and shook her head. "Stupid, stupid

people," she whispered almost to herself. Then to me, "Are you sleepy during the day? Is it hard to stay awake? Hard to think?"

"No, I'm alert," I said. "I tire faster during the day than I do at night, but it isn't important. I mean, it doesn't stop me from doing anything. And I can sleep as comfortably at night as during the day."

"You are a treasure. You would be an asset to any community since most of humanity works during the day. Most human troublemakers cause trouble during the day. We've evolved methods for dealing with this, but there isn't a community that wouldn't be happy to have an Ina guardian who could be awake and alert during the day. I know of several cases where it would have saved lives."

"It didn't save my families," I said. "It did save the Gordons, although I'm pretty sure that it was my being here that put them in danger to begin with."

"Only because some of us are fools." She looked at me for several seconds, then said, "When this business is over, spend a year or two with each of your secondary families if they'll permit it. They can teach you and you can guard them. Later, when you come of age, you might even adopt a sister from among their more adventurous young daughters before you mate. Find a young girl who feels lost among too many sisters and eager to go out on her own." She paused. "Do you remember how to read?"

"I read English and Ina," I said. "Those are the only two languages I've seen in written form since my injury."

"You read Ina? Excellent! I hope you'll teach your children that skill. Some of our people don't bother to teach their children to read Ina any longer. Some day our native language will be forgotten."

I frowned. "Why should it be forgotten? It's part of our history."

"Shori," she said sadly, wearily, "what do you know of our history?"

"Almost nothing," I said, echoing her tone. "I've been reading it, though. Hayden loaned me some of his books. That's how we found out that I could read Ina."

"I see," she said, and she seemed happier. "What are you reading?"

"*The Book of the Goddess*," I said. "I don't know yet how much of it is truly history. It seems to be some combination of religion, metaphor, and history."

"Perhaps. But that's a very long conversation in itself. Someday, when you've had time to relearn more of what you've lost, I would love to discuss it with you."

She gave me a card that contained her name and address, her phone number, her fax number, and her e-mail address. She laughed as I looked it over. "We used to be so isolated from one another," she said. "We sent messages by travelers or hired humans to carry messages or packages. We rarely traveled because it was so uncomfortable and so dangerous. Not only were there highwaymen, but local authorities who had to be bribed, and there was always, always the sun. Now travel and communication are so easy. If you need to talk, call me."

I thanked her and turned to go but then stopped at the door for a last question. "I wanted to ask you something that is probably very personal, but I think I need to know."

She nodded, waiting.

"Your scent . . . do you deliberately use it to influence people? I mean, can you control the way it affects people or who it affects?"

She laughed aloud, laughed for several seconds, stopped, then laughed again. Finally, she said, "Shori, child, I'm an old woman! My scent is barely interesting compared to yours. I don't want to imagine what you'll be like by the time you come of age."

Twenty-One

I RAN INTO Daniel on my way out of the building where the Braithwaites were staying. I got the impression he was waiting for me. "Leave the greeting of guests for a little while," he said. "You and I should talk."

I agreed with him, so I followed him back to his house, enjoying the dark, smoky scent of him. It contrasted oddly with his pale, almost translucent skin and his white-blond hair. There were more people than ever milling around the grounds. Peter and Thomas Marcu and their several symbionts were hauling suitcases into Daniel's guest quarters. Daniel led me past them back toward his own rooms. He kept almost taking my hand. He would reach a little, then catch himself, and drop his hand to his side.

His quarters were two large wood-paneled rooms, a room-sized closet, and a big bathroom. He sat down in a tall chair and said nothing while I explored. In the bathroom was a huge tub—large enough for two, perhaps three people. There was also a huge walk-in shower with a built-in seat and two shower heads. One shower head was fixed to the tile-covered wall, and the other could be held like a hair dryer and directed anywhere. I had no memory of ever having seen such an opulent bathroom, but there was nothing in it that confused me.

The bedroom contained a huge bed in the middle of the floor surrounded by bookcases, a stereo system, and a large television.

I went back to the first room where Daniel waited, looking impatient but not complaining. There was a desk there, a computer, more bookcases, a telephone, file cabinets—like Theodora's office but much tidier. There were other tall chairs. I pulled one of them close to him, placing it in front of him, and I sat down.

"Is there any way for me to be here without tormenting you?" I asked.

"No," he said. "But it doesn't matter. I want you here. I've wanted you here since I first saw you before you lost your memory. You will mate with us."

486

"I will if you and your brothers still want me."

He seemed to relax a little, to let his body sag in the chair. "Of course we do."

"Hayden says I'm too young to make such a commitment," I said.

He shook his head. "Hayden says a great many things. He says you're too great a risk because you're all alone. He says we should look around, find a family with several unmated females. He says you might leave us with only one son or none. He says he would welcome you in a moment if you had even one sister, but you alone . . . He says it's too dangerous for our family."

I drew a deep breath, and I think I sagged a little, too. "I thought he liked me, that he wanted me as your mate."

"Did he say he did?"

"He didn't. But he seemed . . . I don't know."

"Preston wants you. He thinks you're worth the risk. He says your mothers made genetic alterations directly to the germ line, so that you'll be able to pass on your strengths to your children. At least some of them will be able to be awake and alert during the day, able to walk in sunlight. Preston says you have the scent of a female who will have no trouble producing children. His sense of smell is legendary among Ina. I believe him." He paused, leaned forward, took my hands. "My brothers and I will mate with you."

I smiled and answered, "I will mate with you and your brothers." It felt like the thing I should say. It felt formal and right.

Daniel closed his eyes and took a deep breath. Then he opened them and without warning came to his feet, pulling me up with him, lifting me off the floor to wrap me in a rough, hard embrace. Nothing more. It didn't frighten me, didn't even startle me. On some level, I had expected it. I accepted it. I touched my closed lips to his face, his throat, but not his mouth. I gave him small, chaste kisses. I didn't bite him. I was surprised that I wanted to. He was Ina, not human, not a potential symbiont, not a temporary food source. And yet, I wanted very much to bite into the tender flesh of his throat, to taste him, to let the sweet, smoky scent of him become a flavor as well.

I rubbed my face against him, caught up in his scent and

my unexpected longing. Then I drew back. He didn't put me down, but held me comfortably against him. "Why do I want to bite you?" I asked.

He grinned. "Do you? Good. I thought you might actually do it."

"Shall I?"

"No, little mate, not yet. Not for a few more years. I admit, though, that I half-hoped you would, that maybe with your memory gone, you would simply give in to my scent, my nearness. If you had, well . . . If you had, no one could prevent our union. No one would even try."

"You would be tied to me, wouldn't you? You would be infertile with other Ina."

"I'm already tied to you."

"You're not. I haven't tied you to me. I won't until I'm fully adult. I'll come to you then, if you and your brothers are still unmated and if you still want me. If I live to become adult, then I'll tie you to me."

"Of course you'll live!"

I kissed his neck again. This time I licked his throat. He shuddered and let me slide down his body to the floor. "I'll live if this Council of Judgment is able to stop the attempts on my life," I said. "Can we just sit and talk about the Council for a few minutes, or would it be easier on you if I went to Preston?"

"Stay here," he said. "I'd rather have you with me for a little longer. Here, I can touch you without people thinking that I'm a selfish monster who doesn't care about his family."

I smiled, thinking about the feel of his hands. "You can touch me. You can trust me." He smelled even more enticing than Joel, but I would not taste him.

He sat down, reached out with his long wiry arms, caught me around the waist, and lifted me onto his lap. Wright did the same thing whenever he could, and Joel had begun to do it. I decided I liked it and wondered whether I would someday grow too big for them to be able to do it. I hoped not. I leaned against him, content, listening to the deep, steady beat of his heart. "What will happen?" I asked. "Tell me about the Council."

"I've witnessed seven Councils of Judgment," he said. "Hayden and Preston take me or one of my brothers along whenever they're invited to one. They want us to experience them. We won't be called to serve until we're around their age, but at least we can begin to understand how things work. We can see that our Councils aren't games like the trials humans have. The work of a Council of Judgment is to learn the truth and then decide what to do about it within our law. It isn't about following laws so strictly that the guilty go unpunished or the innocent are made to suffer. It isn't about protecting everyone's rights. It's about finding the truth, period, and then deciding what to do about it." He hesitated. "Have you seen or read about the trials that go on in this country?"

I thought for a moment, hoping some memory would come to the surface, but none did. "I don't remember any," I said. "Except on a fictional show I saw on Wright's TV."

"Good and bad," he said. "Human trials are often games to see which lawyer is best able to use the law, the jury's beliefs and prejudices, and his own theatrical ability to win. There's talk about justice, of course, but if a murderer has a good lawyer, he might go unpunished even though his guilt is obvious. If an innocent person has a bad lawyer, he might lose and pay with his life or his freedom even though people can see that he's innocent. Our judges are our elders, people who have lived three, four, five centuries. They sense truth more effectively than people my age, although I can sense it, too."

He settled me more comfortably against him. At least I was more comfortable.

"The problems arise when friendship or family connections get in the way of honest judgment. That can happen to humans and to us. That's why there are so many on a Council. And that's why everyone on the Council is related to both sides."

"Is a Council ever wrong?" I asked.

"It's happened." He drew a deep breath. "And when it happens, everyone knows it. It's usually a result of friendship or loyalty causing dishonesty. Or the problem might be fear and intimidation. That kind of injustice hasn't happened for over a thousand years, but I've read about it. It dishonors everyone involved, and everyone remembers. Members of the families that profit from it have difficulty getting mates for their young. Sometimes they don't survive as families."

"They are punished?" I asked.

"They are ostracized," he said. "They might survive, but only if they move to some distant part of the world and manage to find mates. Today, with communication so improved, even moving might not work.

"But you need to know procedure and propriety for this trial. Will you remember what I say? Do you have any trouble remembering new things?"

"None at all," I said.

He looked at me for a moment, then nodded. "You will speak after everyone is welcomed and the proceedings are blessed. Preston will welcome them as host and moderator. Then the oldest person present will offer blessing. Then you'll speak. You're making the accusations, so you'll need to tell your story. You must be tired of doing that, but you'll do it one more time, very thoroughly and accurately. No one will interrupt you, and most will remember exactly what you say. The Council will listen. Some of them will just want to learn enough to make a decision based on the truth or falsity of what you say. Others will want to find reason to doubt you so that they can better attack you and defend the Silks. And then there are those who will want to defend you against attack."

"Why should I need to be defended? The Silks need to be defended."

"They will be. And their advocate will probably—"

"Wait a moment. Their advocate? Who's that?"

"You and the Silks will both be asked to choose an advocate from among the Council members. You should think about who you'll want. I suggest you consider Joan Braithwaite, Elizabeth Akhmatova, or either of the Leontyev brothers. We won't know for sure which member of each family will be on the Council until the first session."

"I haven't met Elizabeth Akhmatova at all."

"She's smart, and she was a good friend of your elder-mothers'. She or one of the others will help you if anyone on the Silks' side tries to show that because of your memory loss, you may be lying or confused or perhaps not even sane."

I frowned, feeling pulled toward several questions. "Even if I were all those things, it would not make the Silks less responsible."

"But it could, Shori. It could mean that you might not know the difference between lies and truth. You might be delusional, for instance, and able to tell lies that you actually believe. If you're delusional, if you could be shown to be delusional, then anything you say becomes suspect. Anything you've sensed or done may not be as it seems. Tell the complete truth, and remember what you've said."

"Of course. I would have done that anyway. But what about the Silks' lies? If they say they didn't do it, even though they did, how could my being delusional matter?"

"It might not. But you're one small person, one child, and the Silks are a large and respected family. There may be people on the Council who are sorry that your two families are dead and who see the guilt of the Silks, but who don't want to see a third Ina family destroyed. You can count on us—my whole family—to back you up on what almost happened here at Punta Nublada and on what we learned from the prisoners, but you must represent your mothers and your father. You must bring them into the room with you and stand them beside you whenever you can. Do you understand?"

I frowned. "I think so. I wonder, though, if the Ina way is so much better than the one you say the humans have."

"It's our way," he said. "It's the system you must work within if you're to be safe, if you're to keep your symbionts safe, and if, someday, you're to keep our children safe."

I took one of his long hands and held it in my lap. "All right," I said.

"And don't lose your temper. There will be a lot of questions. Tomorrow, after you've told your story, you'll be questioned by whomever the Silks choose as their family representative, you'll be questioned by the advocate of the Silks, and you'll be questioned by any other member of the Council who chooses to question you. It won't be easy. You shouldn't make it easy on them either. You get to ask questions, too. And you can —should, in fact—call on us to support your memory of what happened here. On the first night, you and the Silk representative will be the ones asking and answering questions. On the second, both of you can call others to support what you've said, and they will be questioned. On the third, the Council will ask any final questions it has, and a decision will be made.

This can be flexible. If you or the Silks need to ask more questions on the third day, you can. But that's the way it will go in general." He hesitated, thinking. "It will probably provoke the hell out of you. The Council members can question you or the Silks' representative or anyone either of you call for questioning. So if you get asked the same question ten times or twenty or fifty, give the same answer, briefly and accurately, and don't let it bother you."

"I won't."

"And never answer an accusation that hasn't been made. Even if you believe someone is hinting that you're delusional or otherwise mentally damaged, don't deny what they say unless they make the accusation outright."

"All right."

"Someone might offer you pity and sympathy for your disability. Make them state the disability. Make them say what they mean. Make them support it with evidence. If they say that you're delusional or mentally deficient or too grief stricken to know what you're saying—which, I believe, you definitely would be if your memory were intact—make them explain how they've come to that conclusion. Then, by your questions and your behavior, prove them wrong. If, on the other hand, they can't say what it is they're pitying you for, they must be the ones who are confused. You see?"

"I see."

"Someone might pretend to misunderstand you, might misstate what you've said, then ask you to agree with them. Don't let them get away with it. Pay attention."

"I will."

"Everything will be recorded. Every Ina family gets to see and hear Council proceedings these days. It didn't used to be that way, of course, but now that we can keep an accurate audio-visual record, we do. That means you can ask for a replay if anyone tries to insist on a misstatement of anything you've said."

"How likely is that?"

"I don't know. Most of us have excellent memories. That's why your amnesia will cause some Council members to distrust you at first. Just be yourself. They'll know your intellect is all right as soon as they've heard your story. Anyway, it's dangerous for anyone to lie about someone else's questions or answers. I've seen it happen, though. People feel that things are going against them. They're afraid. We have no prisons, after all."

I thought about that and found that I knew what prisons were. Humans often locked up their lawbreakers in cages—prisons. "No Ina prisons? Why?"

"None of us are willing to spend our lives in prison with the lawbreakers. Maintaining a prison isn't quite as unpleasant as being a prisoner in one, but it's bad enough. And levying fines would be meaningless. It's too easy for us to get money from the human population. For lesser crimes, most likely we amputate something. An arm, a leg, both arms, both legs . . . If the sentence is death, we decapitate the lawbreakers and burn their bodies."

"Decapitate?" I stared up at him. "Amputate . . . ? Cut off people's heads, arms, or legs?"

"That's right. Amputations and executions are also recorded. Amputations are punishments of pain, humiliation, and inconvenience. Limbs grow back completely in a few months, maybe a year or two for legs taken off at the hip. Of course, when it's done, people are given nothing for the pain, and the pain is terrible. It hurts for a long time, although once people are returned to their families, the families can help them with the pain. They're permitted to, not required to."

"You're sure that arms and legs cut off . . . grow back?"

He held his left hand in front of me. "I was in a traffic accident ten years ago. I lost three fingers and part of my hand. In about a month and a half, I had a whole hand again."

"That long?" I hesitated, then asked, "Did you eat raw meat?"

"At first. I don't digest it well, though. If I had been able to eat more of it, I probably would have healed faster."

"You probably would have," I said. And I wondered if he would heal more quickly once he was mated with me. I thought I would like to give him that.

He continued: "The Silks won't be having anything amputated, though. What they've done is too serious for that. If the

Council condemns them, they'll either be killed—the adults will be killed, I mean—or they will be broken up as a family. Their youngest members will be scattered to any families that will have them, and the older ones will be left to wither alone. They might try anything they can think of to avoid those possibilities."

"They . . . they would lose their children?"

"Yes. They would not be seen as fit to raise them."

"That seems cruel to the children. And . . . what if they have more children?"

"It might happen. Or their mates might shun them, blame them for the loss of young sons who have been separated and sent to live thousands of miles apart, probably on different continents. Adoption is not cruel, by the way. There are blood exchanges to ease it and seal it. People miss one another, of course, but by letter, phone, and computer, they can keep contact. I hear they tend not to, but they can. Adoptees are truly accepted and accepting once they're in their new circumstances. But for the adults, it's the end. What adult wouldn't fear such a thing and do almost anything to avoid it?"

"If they had let my families alone, they wouldn't be facing it."

"They must have felt very strongly compelled to do what they did. And . . . Shori, if you had been anyone else, they would have succeeded. You not only survived twice, but you came to us with what you knew, and you led the fight to destroy most of the assassins and to question the survivors. They thought mixing human genes with ours would weaken us. You proved them very wrong."

We sat together for a while longer in warm, easy silence. I felt that I had known him much longer than the few days that I'd been living at Punta Nublada.

I turned toward him and opened his shirt.

"What are you doing?" He was shocked, but he did nothing to stop me.

"Looking at you. I wanted to see whether you had hair on your chest." He didn't.

"We tend not to have much body hair."

He had very smooth skin. I kissed it and ran my hands over it, loving the feel of him. Then I stopped and slipped down off his lap because I wanted so badly to taste him, drink him, to lie beneath that tall, lean body and feel him inside me.

He watched me, left the decision to me. If I tried to bite him, even now, he would let me do it. And then what? If I died, he, at least, might age and die childless. His brothers might mate elsewhere, but he could not. "How can you risk yourself this way?" I whispered.

"I know what I want," he said.

I decided that I had better protect him from his wants. He wouldn't send me away, and he should have. I took his hands, his broad hands with long, long fingers that were almost unlined, that were like, but unlike, the hands of my symbionts, larger versions of my own. I took his hands and I kissed them. Then I left him.

On the first night of the Council of Judgment, proceedings were to begin at nine.

They would be held in a large storage building a few dozen yards beyond the last house—Henry's—along the private road. The building had been emptied, and the equipment usually stored in it was sitting outside in the cold, rainy weather—two pickup trucks, two small tractors, a small crane that I'd heard called a cherry picker. Lesser tools had been stored in other buildings. Stacks of metal folding chairs and tables had been rented and trucked in. All this had been done quickly and efficiently by the Gordons and their symbionts with my symbionts and me helping where we could.

Attending were all thirteen of the Silks, all ten of the Gordons, of course, and two representatives each from the thirteen other families, all strangers to me, or near strangers like the Leontyevs and the Braithwaites. They would judge the Silks . . . and me and perhaps make it possible for me to get to know myself again and get on with my life without having to be on guard every day against another attack.

Could a Council of Judgment really do that? What if it couldn't?

The thirteen families were Fotopoulos, Marcu, Morariu, Dahlman, Rappaport, Westfall, Nicolau, Andrei, Svoboda, Akhmatova, Nagy, and of course, Leontyev and Braithwaite. One representative would act as a Council member and the other as a substitute. There were six male families and seven female. I asked Preston whether the balance of sexes meant anything.

"Nothing at all," he told me. I was working with my symbionts to set up rows of metal chairs, and he was doing something to one of the video cameras that would be recording the Council sessions. "You heard how the decisions were made. The Silks traded names with us until we had a group that both would accept. We have acted as your representative in this because you no longer know these people."

"Did I know them all before?" I asked.

"You knew them. Some you knew well. Others you knew only by family and reputation."

"If you tell me about them now, I'll remember what you say."

"I don't doubt it. But for now, you shouldn't know them. They must see that you don't know them, see how much has been taken from you. Just be yourself. They should see that you have been seriously wounded, but that it hasn't destroyed you."

"It has destroyed who I was."

"Not as thoroughly as you think, child." He gave me a long, quiet look. "Did you taste Daniel's blood?"

The question surprised me. "I will taste it," I said. "I will when I've survived all this," I said. "When I believe I can join with someone and not have it be a death sentence for either of us. And when I've grown a little more."

"He said he offered himself to you."

"And I promised that I would mate with him and his brothers. But not now."

He smiled. "Good. Even alone, you're the best mate my sons' sons could hope for. They all want you."

"Daniel said that Hayden—"

"Don't worry about Hayden. He likes you, Shori. He's just afraid for the family, afraid for so much to depend on one tiny female. Once we get through this Council, I'll convince him."

I believed him.

He left us—Wright, Joel, Theodora, Celia, Brook, and me—to finish making neat rows of a hundred and fifty chairs. There was room for more, and there were more chairs if it turned out that more symbionts wanted to observe, but most of them had intended to be outside roasting meat over contained fires —barbeque pits—and eating and drinking too much. With the rain, many were partying inside the houses. There was even a small party for the children of the Gordon symbionts.

Wright had decided to stay with me through the proceedings, although I had told him he could go enjoy himself if he wanted to. After the chairs and the folding tables had been set up as Preston had instructed, I told Celia, Brook, Joel, and Theodora that they could go or stay as they chose. Joel stayed, probably because he knew Wright was staying. Brook and Celia went off to renew old friendships, and Theodora went with them. Theodora seemed cheerful and excited.

"I've moved to Mars," she told me. "Now I've got to go learn how to be a good Martian. Who better to teach me than the other immigrants?"

It surprised me that I understood what she meant. And it pleased me that she was so happy. There was no feeling of stress or falseness about her; she was truly happy.

"She's exactly where she wants to be," Wright said when she was gone. "She's with you, and you're going to keep her with you. As far as she's concerned, she's died and gone to heaven. People keep falling in love with you, Shori—men, women, old, young—it doesn't seem to matter."

I looked up at him, surprised that I understood him, too. "Why don't you want to learn from the other immigrants?" I asked.

"Oh, I do," he said and grinned at me. "Of course I do. But right now, I want to learn from the Martians themselves."

"You want to see how the Council works."

"Exactly."

"So do I, although I wish I were doing it as just an interested spectator." We finished our part of the preparation—bringing trays with covered pitchers of water and plastic cups to the storage building. We distributed them among the front tables for the Council members and put some on the tables next to the wall in the back for everyone else. Then we chose seats in the first row. I thought I should be in the front so that I could stand and speak when necessary, and I wanted Joel and Wright beside me since they'd chosen to stay.

"Have you ever been to one of these Council meetings?" Wright asked Joel, surprising me. With me encouraging them, giving them small commands, they had recently begun to speak to one another beyond what was absolutely necessary.

"I never have," Joel said. "There's never been one here during my lifetime, not while I was at home, anyway."

There was something comforting about having them on either side of me. They eased the stress I had been feeling without their doing anything at all.

Ina and some symbionts had begun to come in and choose seats. This first night of the Council was to begin at nine and run until five the next morning.

There was no special clothing worn by members of the Council or by audience members except for the many jackets and coats. The building was unheated, and the symbionts seemed to need extra clothing over their jeans and sweatshirts, their casual dresses, or their party clothing. Several symbionts came in from their parties, apparently deciding that they preferred to watch the proceedings of the Council to eating, drinking, and dancing. Earlier that evening, just after it was fully dark, Joel and I had wandered into the noisiest party—the one at William's house—for a few moments to see, as Joel said, what was going on. It was the first time I could remember seeing people dance to music that was being played on a stereo.

"It looks like fun," I said.

Joel smiled. "It is fun. Want to learn?"

"I do," I said. "But not now. Not tonight." And we had gone back to help with the preparations. I looked back, though, liking the joy and the sweat and the easy sexiness of it all, wishing I could have stayed and let him teach me.

Twenty-Two

IRONICALLY, THE oldest person present was Milo Silk. He was 541 years old—ancient even for an Ina. According to the world history I had been reading, when he was born, there were no Europeans in the Americas or Australia. Ferdinand and Isabella, who would someday send Christopher Columbus out exploring, were not yet even married. All Ina were in Europe and the Middle East, traveling with Gypsies, blending as best they could into more stationary populations or even finding their ways into this or that aristocracy or royal court. That world was Mars to me, and if Milo Silk were anyone else, I would have wanted very much to spend time with him and hear any stories he would tell about the worlds of his childhood and youth.

As things were, though, I had avoided him and his family until now. And yet, he was asked to bless the opening of Council proceedings. I thought they should have changed the custom and invited an elder who was less involved in causing suffering and death to speak what Preston had told me should be words of unity and peace. But everyone seemed to expect Milo to do it. After all, he hadn't been judged guilty of anything—yet.

Milo Silk stood up in his place directly across from where I had eventually been told to sit. He and I were at opposite ends of a broad arc of cloth-draped, metal-framed tables. Twelve members of the Council sat two to a table. The odd Council member, Peter Marcu, had a table to himself, as did Milo Silk and I and Preston Gordon, who sat at the center of the arc and who was moderating and representing the host family.

The Gordon symbionts had set up a sound system. They'd scattered speakers along the length of the big room and put on each of the tables a slender, flexible microphone for each person. There was also a stand-alone microphone centered between the two prongs of the arc of tables.

Martin Harrison had shown me how to use my microphone —how to turn it on or off, how to take it from its stand and hold it if I wanted to, how close to it I should be when I spoke into it. Wright and Joel had watched all this, looking around

499

as the other Council members and Milo were seated. Then
Wright kissed me on the forehead and said, confusingly, "Break
a leg." Then he'd gone back to his seat in the front row where
he had left his jacket holding his chair and sat there alone.

Joel had stayed with me a little longer, holding my hands
between his. "Are you afraid?" he asked.

I shook my head. "Nervous, but not afraid. I wish it were
over."

He grinned. "You'll impress the hell out of them." He kissed
the palms of my hands—each of them—then went back to sit
one seat from Wright, my former seat empty between them.

No one had told them they couldn't sit at the table with me,
and I would have been happy to have them there. Even before
I sat down at the table, it had looked like a lonely place. But
both men had seen, as I had, that there were only Ina at the
tables, and they had drawn their own conclusions. They were
probably right. Moments later, Brook came in and sat down
between them.

Then Preston stood up, introduced himself, welcomed everyone, and asked Milo to bless the meeting.

Milo stood up and, microphone in hand, began to speak.

"May we remember always that we are Ina," he said in his
deep, quiet voice. "We are an ancient and honorable people
with more than ten thousand years of recorded history. We
are a proud and powerful people, well aware of our duty to
our families, to our kind, and to the truths that make us who
we are. May we look after our human symbionts with kindness
and firmness. May we care for them and keep them from harm.
May we be loving, loyal, and generous to our mates. May the
proceedings of this Council of Judgment be carried on with
honor, justice, and truth. May we remember and honor the
Goddess as we strive to do and to be all that she expects of
us. May we put aside those things that do not honor her. May
we put them aside and take care never again to be touched by
them, never seduced by them, never soiled by them. May we
remember always that our strength flows from our uniqueness
and our unity. We are Ina! That is what this Council must protect. Now, then! Let us begin." He closed his straight line of a
mouth and sat down.

Milo had looked directly at me as he spoke his last few sentences. He was straight bodied and white haired, six and a half feet tall, and even leaner than most Ina. He was sharp featured and fierce looking somehow. If he were human, I wouldn't have been surprised to hear that he was sixty, perhaps sixty-five years old. He had, I thought, spoken condescendingly of human symbionts and contemptuously of me, and yet in his deep voice, his words had had a majestic sound to them.

Preston Gordon straightened in his seat at the center of the arc. I got the impression Preston was actually enjoying his position. He repeated his welcome to the members of the Council, their deputies, and their symbionts. He assured them that if they needed or wanted anything at all, they had only to speak to a member of the Gordon family. Then he introduced each Council member, although probably everyone knew them except me, some of the newer symbionts, and, ironically, some of the younger Silks. I listened carefully and remembered. Preston had already told me a little about each of the visiting families. Now I was getting a chance to put faces to the names.

There was Zoë Fotopoulos, whose family had once lived in Greece, but who, for a century now, lived on a cattle ranch in Montana.

There was Joan Braithwaite, who I was glad to see again and whose family lived in western Oregon where they raised, among other things, Christmas trees.

There was Alexander Svoboda, whose family had come from what was, at the time, Czechoslovakia a few years before World War II to establish a community in the northern Sierra Nevada Mountains where they now owned a vacation resort.

Peter Marcu had come down from British Columbia where his family owned several tourist-oriented businesses, including one that helicoptered tourists to isolated areas and guided them on memorable mountain hikes.

Vladimir Leontyev and his family had lived in Alaska since Alaska was still Russian territory. They owned a fleet of fishing boats and interests in a cannery and a plant that processed frozen food.

Ana Morariu's family were neighbors of the Gordons, living only about two hundred miles away in Humboldt County where several of her people were teachers, writers, and artists and owned two hotels that served people visiting the national and state parks.

Katharine Dahlman's family ran a ranch that was a tourist resort in Arizona, but they were planning to move to Canada, away from the sun and toward the longer nights of northern winters. Katharine and her sister Sophia were noticeably short for Ina women. In fact, that was the first thing I noticed about them. Other Ina females who had come to the Council were at least six feet tall. But the Dahlmans were only Celia's height, and Celia had told me she was five feet seven inches tall. She'd said she liked being around me since other Ina females made her feel short. She had measured me gleefully and discovered I was an inch under five feet tall. But I still had some growing to do. I wondered how Katharine and Sophia Dahlman felt about their height.

Alice Rappaport's family had a ranch in Texas where she was, for legal reasons, actually married to her first. He had taken her name legally and was enjoying himself, doing what he had always wanted to do: run a ranch and run it profitably. Alice, her sister, and the six symbionts they had brought with them were using the living, dining, and family rooms of the guest house as their quarters so I'd had a chance to talk to them. According to Alice, female Ina families had passed for human for thousands of years by marrying male symbionts and organizing their communities to look like human villages.

Harold Westfall was also married to his first for legal as well as social reasons. He lived in South Carolina and felt that anything he could do to seem normal and unworthy of notice was a good thing. He and his family had been in South Carolina for 160 years, and yet I got the impression that he still was not comfortable there. I wondered why he stayed.

Kira Nicolau and her family had left Romania for Russia, then left Russia just before the Communist Revolution in 1917, and had eventually settled in Idaho in a valley so isolated that they felt they had no reason to put on a show of human normality. They'd dug wells, cut their own logs, built their own cabins. They used the wind and sun to make their electricity, planted their crops and kept enough chickens, hogs, goats, and milk cows to supply their symbionts with food and make a small profit. They shopped maybe twice a year to buy the things they either couldn't make or didn't want to bother making. If they hadn't had to visit their mates and attend the occasional Council of Judgment, they might have vanished completely from the awareness of other Ina.

Ion Andrei, on the other hand, lived in a suburb of Chicago. His family, too, were planning to move to Canada. They owned interests in several Chicago businesses. They had been in the Chicago area for over a century, but now they were beginning to feel swallowed by the growing population.

During the northern hemisphere's winter, Walter Nagy and his family lived on a farm on Washington's Olympic Peninsula. During the southern hemisphere's winter, the whole family moved to a ranch in Argentina. In fact, they had just gotten back from Argentina. "We could get even more hours of darkness if we moved farther north and farther south," he had told me when I met him. "But we like comfort, too. We don't mind a little cold weather, but do mind snow and ice." His family also owned income property in New York City and in Palo Alto and San Francisco. The few among them who bothered to work were artists, writers, and musicians.

Finally, there was Elizabeth Akhmatova, whose family lived in Colorado in a Rocky Mountain community. They had gradually developed the land surrounding their community, building houses, stores, shops, and a nearby resort area until a fair-sized town had grown around them. They had held on to the property until it became popular and highly valued, and now, they were gradually selling it off at very high prices. She and her family had come to North America in 1875, and they were about to make their third major move, this time to Canada. They liked to find areas with potential, acquire vast stretches of land, and develop it.

Preston introduced them all, then introduced me and welcomed me. Finally, he asked me to stand and tell my story.

I stood, holding my microphone the way Milo had. I began my story with my first memory of awakening in the cave, confused, in pain, without my memory, and racked with intense hunger. I told them about Hugh Tang—all of it—about the ruin that I had not recognized as my home, about Wright and my father and the destruction of my father's community—the whole story up to and including the raid on the Gordons and the capturing and questioning of Victor and his two friends. The telling took more than an hour.

At last, I finished and sat down. There were several seconds of absolute silence. Then Milo Silk stood up. "Does this child have an advocate?" he demanded. He spoke the word "child" as though he wanted to say a much nastier word but restrained himself.

Before I could say that I didn't yet have an advocate, Vladimir Leontyev spoke up.

"I am one of the fathers of Shori Matthews's mothers," he said. "I believe I'm her nearest living relative on the Council. My brothers and I may be her nearest living relatives period. If Shori wishes it, I will be her advocate."

I leaned forward so that I could see him and said, "I must ask questions because of my memory loss. I mean no offense, Vladimir, but if you become my advocate, will it be a problem that you and I don't really know each other anymore?"

"It won't be a problem," he said. "Family is what matters here. You are of great importance to me because you are one of my descendants."

"Will you speak for me or will you help me understand rules and customs so that I can speak for myself?"

"Both, probably," he said, "but I would prefer the latter."

I nodded. "So would I. I understand that the Silks will also have to have an advocate."

Vladimir gave me a small smile, then looked at Milo Silk. "Who on the Council will be your family's advocate, Milo?"

"I speak for my family," he said.

Preston Gordon said, "Milo, in our negotiations with your family, one of your sons mentioned that a member of the Dahlman family might be persuaded to be your advocate."

"When have you known me to need someone to speak for me?" he demanded.

Preston looked at him, looked down at his own spidery hands resting on the table, then faced Milo again. "Let me advise you, just this once. Your family needs more protection than you can give it. Don't let your pride destroy your family."

Milo looked away from him, kept quiet for several seconds. After a while, he said, "Katharine Dahlman is the oldest daughter of my sisters," Milo said. "I ask that she be my advocate."

Katharine Dahlman managed, by sitting very straight, to look not only important, but a little taller. She lowered her head in a slow nod. "Of course," she said in a deep, quiet contralto—a female version of Milo's voice. It was the voice of a larger woman, somehow. "Will you question the child, Milo, or shall I?"

Milo looked down at the table, and I remembered that he had been writing while I spoke. Perhaps he had not trusted the two video cameras that were being used to record the session. Perhaps he had made notes of the questions he wanted to ask me. Or perhaps he had his own memory problems. I faced him across the arc, ready to be questioned, but he turned his body and tried to face Preston.

"I have my doubts, Preston, whether this child should even be here," he said. "She has suffered terrible losses, and she admits that she hasn't recovered from her injuries."

I resisted an impulse to say that I had recovered, or had recovered as much as I was likely to. Instead, I waited to see what Preston would say. He looked at me, then at Vladimir.

Vladimir said, "Shori, have you recovered from your injuries?"

"I am recovered," I said. "My memory may or may not return. I'm beginning to relearn what I've lost, and I remember clearly all that has happened to me since I awoke in the cave." I looked across at Milo and decided that he would speak directly to me in a minute or two. He didn't want to, but he would.

"Has the child been examined by a physician?" Milo asked. "I understand there is a human physician among the symbionts here. If not, one of my family's symbionts is a physician."

That was too much. I had been at Punta Nublada long enough to recognize that Milo was being openly insulting. He was saying that my body was not Ina enough to heal itself, that the human part of me had somehow crippled me.

"Milo!" I said, not loudly, but sharply. He looked at me before he could stop himself and then looked away smoothly, as though he had only glanced at me by accident. I leaned forward, facing him across the arc. "I am Ina, Milo."

He stared at me, then turned again to Preston. "For the child's own sake, I request that she be examined by a physician."

I said, "What are those notes you're making there, Milo? No one else is taking notes. Are you having difficulties with your memory, too?"

He glared at me. Katharine Dahlman glared at me.

"I am Ina, Milo, and if the doctor must examine me, then for your own sake, I request that she also examine you."

"You're not Ina!" he shouted. He slammed his palm down on the table, making a sound like a gunshot. "You're not! And you have no more business at this Council than would a clever dog!"

People jumped. Katharine Dahlman said, "Preston, could we break for a few minutes?" She didn't wait but stood up and went around to Milo who had risen to his feet and was leaning forward, fists on the table, glaring at me.

"Fifteen minutes," Preston said and glanced at his watch.

People poured themselves glasses of water, got up to stretch their legs, or turned to talk to one another. At first no one on the Council spoke to me. Most didn't even look at me.

Some went to speak to audience members, and Wright, Joel, and Brook took this to mean that they could come talk to me. They reached me at the same moment as Vladimir Leontyev and Joan Braithwaite.

The two Ina and the three humans stared at one another for a moment, then Joan leaned on the table, clicked off my microphone, and said, "Shori, there are people in this room who have loved that old man for centuries."

I focused on her and bit back all the things I could have said. She knew them as well as I did. That old man either ordered my families killed or sat by and watched while his sons did it. That old man had just told me I was no better than a dog because I had human as well as Ina genes. That old man is not sane. All true, all obvious.

"What should I have done?" I asked her.

She looked surprised. "Nothing," she said. "Nothing at all."

"You should have let me do it," Vladimir said. "I'm only about ninety years younger than he is. A rebuke from me would have been more easily accepted."

"Would you have done it?" Wright asked him.

Vladimir took a deep breath. "Eventually."

"It's done," I said. "What happens now?"

"You didn't think of that question before you humiliated him?" Joan asked. "You didn't wonder what would happen afterward?"

"I didn't humiliate him," I said, finally stating the obvious. "I would not have humiliated him. I just stood back and let him humiliate himself."

"Others won't see it that way."

"Are we rid of him?" I asked. "Will he step aside and let one of his sons represent the family?"

She looked at me as though she didn't particularly like me. "He might," she said. "What good do you imagine that will do you?"

"Perhaps the new representative will at least dislike me as one-individual-to-another, and not as man-to-animal."

"And no doubt that will make you feel better," she said. "But it won't help you. You've shown your teeth, Shori. They're sharp and set in strong female jaws. You are now less the victim and more the potentially dangerous opponent. You begin to overshadow your dead."

I thought about that, although I didn't want to think about it. I wanted to go on feeling angry and justified. But finally I sighed. "You're right. What shall I do?"

She nodded. Apparently I had asked the right question. "Remember your dead," she said. "Keep them around you. And remember what you want. What do you want?"

"To punish them for what they've done," I said. "To stop them from hunting me. To stop them from killing anyone else."

She nodded once, then turned and walked across the arc toward where people were very gently arguing with Milo.

"She's right," Wright said to me, "but she's cold."

"She's just female," Joel said.

"And oldest sister," Brook added. "I'll bet the younger one, Margaret, is gentler."

"She is," I said.

"Nevertheless, Joan's advice is good," Vladimir told me.

"I know," I said.

"The truth is your best weapon," he said. "Put aside that

temper of yours. Use the truth intelligently." He turned and went back to his place in the arc.

Brook watched him go. Then she stepped behind me and put her hands on my shoulders. She massaged my neck and shoulders so that I began to relax before I realized I needed to. I looked up at her.

"Good?" she asked.

"Good," I said.

Joel laughed. "Ina need to be touched, especially young Ina. I don't think you always realize how much you need it, Shori."

"We'll have to see that she gets what she needs," Wright said, looking at me. The look made me smile and shake my head.

"You should all go back to your seats," I said. "They're about to start the Council again."

They went back to their seats, and on the other side of the arc, another of the Silks—Russell, I had heard him called—sat down in Milo's place.

Twenty-Three

Russell Silk had no story to tell. He denied all involvement in the death of my families and in the attacks on the Arlington house and on the Gordons. He denied that his family was involved in any of it. He suggested that I was confused or mistaken or that the humans who had been used as weapons had been given false information intended to incriminate the Silk family—which happened to be the only male Ina family in Los Angeles County. Who would create such a fiction? He did not know. He and his family were victims . . . just as I was.

That was a sickening enough lie to make me wonder if I would have been able to keep my temper had I not lost my memory. If I could remember my mothers, my sisters, and my symbionts, if I could recall my father and my brothers as anything more than kindly strangers, I might not have been able to bear it. I thought Russell might have said it hoping to make me angry, hoping to pay me back for what I said to Milo.

Vladimir Leontyev spoke up. "Russell, are you saying that you know as a matter of fact that neither your father, your brothers, your sons, or their sons were involved in collecting a group of human males, making them your tools, and then sending them to kill the Petrescu, Matthews, and Gordon families?"

Russell looked offended. "I don't believe any member of my family would do such a thing," he said.

Vladimir shook his head. "That isn't what I asked. Do you know for a fact that no member of your family did this?"

"I haven't investigated my family," he said. "I'm not a human police detective."

"So you don't know for certain whether or not members of your family did this?"

"I don't believe they did!" He paused and looked away from Vladimir. "But I don't know with absolute certainty."

I didn't believe him. I don't think I would have believed him even if I hadn't helped to question Victor and his friends. Russell knew what his relatives had been up to, and now he was lying about it. By his silence or by his active participation, he had helped to murder my families.

"I have a question for Shori," Katharine Dahlman said.

I looked at her with interest. I hadn't made up my mind about her yet. How close was she to the Silks and what they had done?

"I'm sorry to ask you about things that may be painful to you," she said, "but what do you remember about your mothers and your sisters?"

"Nothing," I said. "Nothing at all."

"Their names?"

"I've been told that my sisters were named Barbara and Helen."

"And your mothers? Your eldermothers?"

"I don't know."

"Your symbionts . . . how many symbionts did you have?"

"I'm told I had seven. I don't remember any of them."

"You recall no names? Nothing?"

"Nothing."

"So you feel nothing for these people who were once closer to you than any others?"

I looked downward. "It's as though they're strangers. It's terrible to me that I can't recall them even enough to mourn them. I hate that they are dead—my families—but for me, it's as though they never lived."

"Thank you for your honesty," she said. I still didn't know what to think of her. She didn't like me, but she was polite. Did she dislike me because what I said endangered the Silks? Or did she dislike me because I was part human?

"Do you know how old you are, Shori?" Russell asked.

"My father told me I am fifty-three."

"And . . . do you know how tall you are, how much you weigh?"

"I'm 4 feet 11 inches tall. I don't know what I weigh."

"Do you know what the average height is for an Ina female your age?"

"I have no idea."

"The average is 5 feet 6 inches. What does that say to you?"

I stared at him, then gave the 5 foot 7 inch Katharine Dahlman a long look. Finally, I faced him again. At least I wasn't the only person who asked questions without fully considering the effects of the answers. "I'm not sure what you want me to say," I told him.

He glared at me for a moment, then said, "Apart from what you say the three human captives told you, do you have any evidence at all that the Silk family has done anything to harm your families?"

"Three humans questioned separately and all telling the same story? Yes, that's all I have, Russell."

We questioned each other repeatedly, Russell Silk and I and our advocates. Factual questions only. Were you told . . . ? Did you see . . . ? Did you hear . . . ? Did you scent . . . ? Did you taste . . . ?

No speeches were permitted, no arguments except through questions, no interrupting each other. Preston Gordon could and did cut us off, though, whenever he heard us stray from these guidelines. He did this with a fairness that infuriated both Russell and me, and he paid no attention when we glared at him.

The Council members could ask us questions and question our answers. The purpose of accused and accuser questioning one another was to give the Council the opportunity to make use of their formidable senses. They watched, listened, and breathed the air as we spoke. Together, they had thousands of years of experience reading body language.

When our questions to one another waned, we began the second night's work early. By mutual agreement, we began to question others, first Russell, then me. Any of the Silks or the Gordons could be asked to speak. If asked, they could not refuse. I intended to work my way through the two youngest of the four generations of Silks—four fathers and five unmated young sons—and have them come to the free-standing microphone one by one to answer my questions and any that Russell or the Council members might want to put to them. The unmated young ones were of the greatest interest to me. They were the ones I most wanted to be heard and seen by the Council. I thought my own scent would reach them and trouble them, and perhaps they would have a harder time keeping their minds on any lies they meant to tell. But now it was Russell Silk's turn. The first person he called was Daniel Gordon.

"Did you actually see the attack on your community that the child Shori Matthews says she defeated?" Russell demanded.

"She did not say she defeated it," Daniel answered. "She and several Gordon symbionts worked together to defeat it."

"Did you see this!"

"It happened during the day," Daniel said. "No Ina other than Shori could have seen it. Over half of our symbionts saw it, though. They not only helped fight off the attack, but captured two of the attackers alive so that they could be questioned. Shori captured the third. She prepared the captives for interrogation but did not touch any of our symbionts."

Russell stared at him, frowned as though he did not believe him, and changed the subject. "Have you ever known Shori to seem confused or uncertain of her surroundings, her intentions, her perceptions?" he asked.

Daniel shook his head. "Never."

"Have you ever heard Shori show disregard for the welfare of other Ina?"

"No, never."

Russell shook his head, as though in disgust. "And yet, isn't it true, Daniel, that Shori Matthews has bound you to her as her mate?"

"She has not," Daniel said.

Russell looked at the Council members. "I believe this to be untrue," he said. "He was seen taking the child into his quarters."

There was a moment of silence. Council members looked carefully at Daniel, breathing deeply to examine his scent. Finally two of them spoke.

"He is not bound," Alexander Svoboda said.

Elizabeth Akhmatova echoed, "He is not bound."

They were, according to what I'd heard, the oldest male and female Council members. One by one, the other members of the Council nodded, either accepting their elders' perceptions and judgment or coming to the same conclusion by way of their own senses. Alice Rappaport took several deep breaths, making a show of taking in Daniel's scent and judging it. She was the last to nod.

I wondered who had seen Daniel and me together, come to their own conclusions about what we were up to, and then run to tell the Silks all about it. Had it been the Marcu family who was staying in Daniel's house? Or perhaps it had been someone outside who saw him approach me and take me into his house. Or was it a Silk symbiont? If symbionts could be used as weapons, they could also be used as spies.

Russell looked surprised by the Council's conclusion. "You have no connection with Shori then?" he asked Daniel.

"We are promised to one another," Daniel said. "When this is over, when she's older and physically mature, my brothers and I will mate with her." He looked at me and smiled. I couldn't help smiling back at him.

Council member Ana Morariu said, "Do you believe the things Shori has told us tonight?"

"I do," Daniel said. "I've seen some of it for myself. I was present when the captives were questioned. Shori and my fathers and elderfathers questioned them. I saw, I heard, I breathed their scent. Because of that, I believe her."

"Are you sure that's why you believe her?" Russell demanded. "Would you believe her if Shori were already mated with other people or if you were?"

He repeated, "I was present when the captives were questioned. I know what I saw and heard."

They didn't make him say it a third time. I think they saw that they could not move him, and their senses told them that he believed that he was speaking the truth. Martin Harrison, of all people, had explained this to me days before. "Of course, the Ina can't sense absolute truth," he'd said. "At best, they can be fairly certain when someone fully believes what he's saying. They sense stress, changing degrees of stress. You do that yourself, don't you? You smell sweat, adrenaline, you see any hint of trembling, hear any difference in the voice or breathing or even the heartbeat."

"I do," I said. "I notice those things and others that I don't always have names for, but I don't always know how to interpret what I sense."

"Experience will take care of that," he said. "That's why the older Ina are so good at spotting truth and untangling lies. They use their senses, their intelligence, and their long experience."

"How can you know all that?" I asked him.

"It's what we all do, Ina and human," he said. "The Ina are just a lot better at it. They do it consciously and with more acute senses. They usually have better memories, and they can pile up more years of practice than humans can. We humans do a little of it and give it names like 'intuition' or 'instinct' or even 'ESP.' In fact, it's just good old conscious and unconscious use of your senses, your experience, and your intelligence."

I asked Preston about it later, and he grinned. "Been talking to Martin?"

"I have," I said. "Is he right?"

"Oh, yes. The man loves to teach. You're a blessing to him."

"How can he know what very old Ina are doing? Did you tell him?"

"No, he just keeps his eyes and ears open. His nose is no better than most other humans', but his intelligence is first-rate. His son is a lot like him."

That left me thinking again of Joel and wondering how like his father he would turn out to be.

The first day of the Council of Judgment ended with an effort on the part of the Silks to make me look irresponsible (at best) and make Daniel and, by extension, the Gordons look as though they were lying. They failed in both efforts. They would have one more day to try to undermine us. On the third day, judgment would be argued, truth acknowledged, and the Council would say, according to Ina law, what must be done.

That was all. It seemed almost . . . easy. Would the Silks simply give themselves up to be killed or allow their unmated young sons to be sent away to other communities? Could anyone do that?

As the Council ended its session just an hour before dawn, I felt the need to talk to someone. Then Brook, Wright, and Joel came to collect me, and I realized I was almost weak with hunger. Joel and Brook both recognized the signs, though I don't think Wright did yet.

"Let's go home," Brook said.

I nodded. I wanted to go find Martin Harrison and ask him questions, but I thought that might be better done during the day when other Ina could not listen.

I let my symbionts walk me home, then kissed each of them, and went to find Celia. I had not touched her for four nights.

Tonight she would be expecting me. She was not entirely mine yet, not bound to me, as Daniel would say. Not quite. Tonight would be her turning point. Her scent told me she was almost there. Tonight, she would be mine.

She was asleep, warm and smelling of the soap she had used when she bathed earlier that night. In spite of her bath, she also smelled of the man she had had sex with before washing. I took in the scent and, after a moment, was able to picture the man—a symbiont of Peter Marcu's. He was a short, muscular man with very smooth skin—skin so dark it looked truly black. Someone had said he was from Ghana and that his name was Kwasi Tuntum. He had tired her out, made her sleepy. Eventually I would wake her up. I didn't think she would mind.

But when I slipped into bed beside her, she opened her eyes. I didn't think she could see me, but she said, "Hey, Shori, I thought you forgot about me."

"You didn't think that," I said. "You were enjoying yourself too much with Kwasi to worry about me forgetting you."

She froze next to me. I could feel her body go rigid.

I kissed her face, then her mouth. "Do you really care that I know?" I asked. "I can't help knowing."

"You . . . don't mind?"

"Should I mind?"

She shrugged against me. "Stefan didn't mind. He said I had the right to have human partners and have kids if I wanted them. After all, he couldn't give me kids." She frowned.

I said, "Why did it bother you that he didn't mind?"

She was silent for a long time. I used the time to explore what Kwasi had done with her. He had kissed her mouth and her neck and her breasts. He had kissed her between her breasts and taken her nipples into his mouth . . . I tried that, and she giggled. I'd never heard her giggle before. Then her scent changed, and she made a different sort of noise in her throat.

"What are you doing?" she asked.

"Learning," I said after a moment. "Why did it bother you that Stefan didn't mind your having sex with other people?"

"I think I wanted him to love me more—love me so much that he couldn't not care that I went with another guy."

"He cared. I'm female and I care. But if you're mine, I can accept the rest. And you do have the right to have your own human mate, your own children, or just have pleasure with a man when that's what you want." I lay on my back and moved her so that her body rested against mine. "I know how to take my pleasure with you," I said. "Will you teach me to pleasure you?"

"You will pleasure me this time, I think. I want you to feed. I love the feel of you against me. I almost feel the way I did when I knew Stefan wanted me, when I wanted him."

I smiled, hungry for her, starved for her, but taking my time enjoying the anticipation as much as I would soon enjoy feeding.

She looked up at me, perhaps able to see me a little now. "I'll teach you more when this Council thing is over. And you can teach me what else I can do to make you feel good. But for now, you're hungry. You have that scary, gaunt look." She rubbed the back of my neck. "You'd think I'd be afraid of you when you look like that, wouldn't you? Come here to me." She rolled us over onto our sides, facing one another, holding me against her, so welcoming that I couldn't wait any longer. I bit her deeply, hurt her a little, but also pleased her. She held me as though she thought I might leave her too soon. She held me as though laying claim to me.

That afternoon, right after Celia and I got up, Martin Harrison came to see me. I had intended to find him eventually. I was surprised that with all the work he had to do satisfying the Gordons' guests, he had time to come looking for me. And I was surprised at the way he looked—tired, angry, sad, but struggling to keep his expression under control.

"You and I have gotten to know each other a little," he said. "I've come to you now because I believe it's better for you to hear what you have to hear from someone who isn't a stranger."

I stared back at him suddenly afraid, although I didn't know what I was afraid of. His expression made me not want to know.

"Hear what?" Celia asked. She spoke to Martin, but she was looking at me. She got up and came over to stand beside me. I had been keeping her company while she cooked and ate a huge meal and took vitamins and an iron supplement that she'd had in her luggage. She said Stefan had always made her take vitamins and an iron supplement because she had been his smallest symbiont, and he worried about her health. She had stopped taking them when he died. Now she had dug them out of her suitcase and begun using them again.

She was wearing a pullover sweater that fully displayed her half-healed bite. As it happened, Martin also had a half-healed bite on his neck. It showed just above the collar of his shirt. "What do you want her to hear?" Celia asked again. Wright, Joel, and Brook came in just then, flanked by two Gordon symbionts. I realized suddenly that the Gordon symbionts had gone out and found my symbionts and brought them to me, and I could see by their faces that they didn't know why any more than I did.

Martin glanced at them, then looked at Celia—a kind look. A frighteningly kind look. "Stay close to her today and to-night," he said to Celia. "All of you, stay close. She'll need you."

"What do you mean?" Celia demanded.

Suddenly, it occurred to me that someone was missing. "Theodora!" I said. "What's happened to Theodora?"

Martin sighed and turned to face me. "Carmen was going into San Francisco today," he said. "She needed some medical supplies, and she wanted to see her youngest sister who's just had twins. Carmen found Theodora lying on the ground be-tween Hayden's house and his garage. Theodora's dead, Shori."

Twenty-Four

S EVERAL GORDON symbionts had gathered around Theodora's body, but they had not touched it. Only Carmen had done that, checking to see whether Theodora was alive, whether she could be helped . . .

Martin told me that when Carmen told him Theodora was dead, he asked her to stay with the body and keep everyone else away while he went to find me and send others to find the rest of my symbionts.

I was not fully in control of myself as I approached Theodora. I had demanded that Martin take me to her, but I was not truly seeing or understanding what was happening around me. I could not believe my Theodora was dead. It made no sense that she would be dead. None. Then I touched her cold flesh.

"She's been dead since early this morning," Carmen said behind me.

My own eyes and nose had already told me that much. Hours dead. Dead well before sunrise. Dead while Russell Silk and I tore at one another. Dead while I lay making Celia my own. Dead.

I found myself on my knees beside Theodora making sounds I could not recall ever having made before. She had come to me because she trusted me, loved me. She had been so happy when I asked her to join me here at Punta Nublada where she should have been safe. I had promised her a good life, had had every intention of keeping my promise. I would have kept her with me for the rest of her life. How could she be dead?

I wanted the people around me gone. I wanted to be let alone to examine Theodora, to understand her death. I must have made some gesture because the watching symbionts all took a few steps back. I knelt on the ground alongside Theodora, selecting out scents that were not her own, separating them into odors and groups of odors that I recognized. Theodora had gone to at least one of the parties, and that made for a confusion of scents—sweat, blood, aftershave, cologne, food and drink of several kinds, sexual arousal, many personal scents. There were fourteen distinct, personal human scents.

The odor that screamed loudest at me was the strong blood-scent in Theodora's hair—her blood. I looked and found the wound there. Her hair was stiff and matted with dried blood. Dead blood. I touched her head, ran my fingers over it, and found the place where there was a softness, an indentation. Someone had hit her so hard that they broke her skull.

Someone had murdered her.

Who had done it? Why? No one knew her here. No one had reason to harm her. No one would have harmed her . . . except, perhaps, to harm me. Would someone do that? Murder one person in the hope of causing pain to another? Why not? Someone—the Silks, surely—had murdered nearly two hundred people, human and Ina, in the hope of killing me, killing all that my eldermothers had created.

I closed my eyes, tried to quiet my thoughts and focus on Theodora. After a moment, I breathed deeply again and continued sorting through the scents. She had been in contact with fourteen different humans—Gordon symbionts and visitors. I didn't recognize all of them, but six I could picture. These were people I had met or had had pointed out to me. The others . . . the other scents I would remember. When I found the people they belonged to, I would know them. Any of them could have killed her, or perhaps they had only brushed against her at one of the parties. Perhaps they had danced with her or touched her in some other casual way. She had not had sex with anyone recently.

There seemed no way to tell which of the fourteen might have hit her, but . . . Had her blood splashed on the killer? Had the killer kept the weapon used to kill her? Had the killer touched her at all beyond battering her to death, perhaps to examine her to be certain she was dead?

I put my face down closer to her broken, bloody head. But then the scent of dead blood, of Theodora's beloved body, ten or more hours dead, became all that I could smell, and I had to turn away from it after a moment. I stood up and stepped a short distance away, gasping, sick, desperate for clean air.

Someone spoke to me, came near, and I shouted, "Let me alone! Get away from me!" A moment later, I realized that I had shouted at Wright, my first. I had told him to go away. Stupid of me. Stupid!

I looked up at him, saw that he was already backing away, not wanting to go but going.

"I'm sorry," I said. "Stay here, Wright. Stay near me while I finish this."

I breathed deeply for a moment, then turned back to Theodora and tried again. I rolled her from her back onto her side so that I could see and smell whatever had been trapped under her. The significant odors were more blood, of course, and the scents of five more people. Again, I recognized some of them—three of the five. Through the night, then, nineteen people had had enough contact with Theodora to leave their scents on her—nineteen people, any one of whom might be her murderer. I would have to find each of them and speak to them or to their Ina.

I stood up, finally, and went on looking at my dead Theodora. I would have to go to her daughter and son-in-law and tell them that she was dead. They couldn't know everything, but they had a right to know that. After I found her killer, I would go to her family.

I looked around for Martin. He was still there. The onlookers had gone away, but Martin and my four symbionts still waited.

"Has anyone left the community today?" I asked.

He shook his head. "Not that I know of."

"Could someone have left without your knowing?"

"Of course. I have to sleep, too, girl."

And William Gordon had bitten him early this morning. I looked back at Theodora. "I don't know what should be done with the dead, Martin."

"She should be cleaned up, given a funeral, and . . . well, buried. We have our own cemetery here."

I still didn't know what to do. Theodora should be prepared for burial. A memorial service of some kind should be arranged. Her killer should be caught, should be killed. And yet in a few hours the Council of Judgment would begin its second night, and I would have to be there.

"Shori, girl," Martin said. He spoke with such gentleness that I wanted to run away from him. I could not dissolve emotionally and lose myself in grief. I did not dare. There was no time.

"Shori, we'll take care of her body. We'll prepare her for burial. We can have services for her after the Council is over. You go find out who did this. That's what you want to do, isn't it?"

I looked at him, and all I could do was nod.

"Leave her to us." He almost turned away, then stopped and drew a deep breath. "Two things, Shori. They're important."

"All right," I said.

He looked down and met my gaze with a different expression —harder, unhappy, but determined.

"Tell me, Martin," I said. "You've been a friend. Go ahead and say whatever it is that you don't want to say."

He nodded. "Don't kill anyone. No matter how certain you are that you've found the right person, don't kill. Not yet. Chances are, the murderer is one of the visitors—one of the Gordon family's guests. You are more than a guest. You'll be mated to the sons of the family in a few years. But still . . . Tell Preston or Hayden what's happened before you take a life."

I stared at him, unable to answer at first. Until that moment, if I had learned that Martin himself had killed Theodora, I'm not sure I could have stopped myself from killing him. And yet, I understood on some murky emotional level and from slivers of recovered memory that it would be a serious offense against the Gordons to kill one of their guests. I couldn't remember anyone ever doing such a thing, but I felt enough horror and disgust at the thought of doing it to know that I must not.

"I won't kill anyone," I said finally.

Another nod.

"And don't bite anyone."

That one was even harder. But I could see the reason for it. If I found the killer, he or she would be the symbiont of someone here. Again, I knew—again without understanding fully how I knew—that it would be wrong to interfere with someone else's symbiont.

"The Ina might be the guilty one," I said. "Probably would be."

"All the more reason not to abuse the symbiont."

"I won't bite unless someone attacks me," I said. "I would rather bite than break bones or tear flesh." And I walked away from him. My symbionts followed me.

When we were alone, Wright pulled me to him and hugged me and held me for a while. I felt as though I wanted to stay that way, safe with him, breathing his good, familiar scent. It mattered more than I would have thought possible that he was alive, that he loved me and wanted somehow to comfort me. I knew that if I let him, he would take me home and put me to bed and stay with me until I fell asleep. I knew he would do that because I had come to know him that well. I longed to let him do that.

But there was no time. If possible, by the time tonight's Council session began, I wanted to know who had killed Theodora. I wanted to prevent the murderer from leaving or killing anyone else, and I wanted to put this new crime before the Council to see whether they would deal with it. If they didn't, I would.

I pushed back from Wright and realized that he had lifted me off the ground and was holding me so that I could look at him almost at eye level. I kissed the side of his mouth, then kissed his mouth and said, "Put me down."

He set me on my feet. "What do you want us to do?" he asked.

And I almost disintegrated again. He understood. Of course he did. "I need you to stay together," I said. "Protect one another." I looked at each of them, missing immediately the face that was not there. "I don't know whether Theodora's murder has anything to do with the other attempts on us or with Council of Judgment, but it seems likely." I paused. It hurt to say her name. I took a breath and went on. "Go talk to Jill Renner sym Wayne. She spent some time with Theodora last night and left her scent for me to find. She wouldn't have hurt Theodora, but she might have seen her having trouble with someone or leaving a party with someone. Was there a party at Wayne's house last night?"

"Sym Wayne?" Wright said, frowning. "Is that how you say it, then, when someone is a symbiont? That's what happens to our names? We're sym Shori?"

"You are," I said.

"Something you remembered?"

"No. Something I learned from hearing people talk. What about Wayne's house? Was there a party?"

"Not at Wayne's," Celia said. "But there was a party at Edward's and a big party at Philip's. Jill, Theodora, and I were at both of them. Theodora was a little shy at first, and she kind of hung out with me at Edward's. We ate there and talked with a lot of people. But at Philip's she met a couple of guys. They got her dancing, and the three of them just sort of stayed together, dancing and flirting and enjoying themselves."

Wright frowned at Celia as though she had said something wrong, but Celia ignored him.

"Who were the two men?" I asked.

"A couple of older guys. I don't know their names or who their Ina is. They were both graying, maybe five-ten, well built. They could have been brothers. They looked a lot alike."

"Did you touch them?" I asked. "Shake hands or squeeze past them?"

She shook her head.

"Tell me what you can about them. See them in your memory, and tell me what you see." We were walking toward Wayne's house where Jill Renner was probably still asleep.

Celia frowned and looked desperate for a moment, as though she were grasping for something that she couldn't quite reach but had to reach. She glanced at me, then closed her eyes, focusing, remembering. Finally she said, "They both had the same salt-and-pepper hair—black with a lot of white. One of them had a mustache. It was salt-and-pepper, too. They aren't with the Gordons. I'm sure of that. Westfall! I think they're the two male Westfall symbionts. The rest of the Westfall syms are women. These guys talk like they've been here for a long time, but every now and then you could hear a little English accent . . ." She let her voice trail away. Then she said, "The one with the mustache, he has a scar on his forehead, or maybe it's a birthmark. I'm not sure which. I don't know how big it is. It starts just below the hairline and goes back into the hair. It's a red oval, or I think it would have been oval if I could have seen all of it."

"All right," I said. "Relax. I know who you mean. I've never spoken to them, but I saw them and got their scent when the Westfalls arrived. Their scents were on Theodora. You're right. They probably are brothers. I'll find them. The rest of you go talk to Jill Renner."

"Let me stay with you," Joel said. "I know a lot of the visitors, and they know me. I might be able to help."

I glanced up at him and nodded. "You three, watch out for one another."

Brook, Celia, and Wright went off to knock on Wayne's door, and Joel and I went down the road to Wells Gordon's house where the Westfalls—Harold and John—were staying with their eight symbionts, including the two who may have been among the last people to see Theodora alive.

I didn't suspect them of killing Theodora. The Westfalls, from what Preston had told me, were not closely related to me or to the Silks, but they were very interested in the success my eldermothers had had mixing human and Ina DNA and giving me the day. They were not offended by it as the Silks were.

I thought about Milo, about his contempt for me and his less lethal, but no less real, contempt for symbionts—probably for all humans. Ina could not survive without humans, and yet Milo seemed to consider them little more than useful domestic animals. What must life be like for his symbionts?

And how did families who thought like the Silks get along with other Ina? Joan Braithwaite had said that there were many who loved Milo. They must have loved him in spite of his arrogance. Or perhaps they loved him for what he had been when he was younger. He was far from lovable now.

I had read in one of the books I'd borrowed from Hayden about the periods of feuding between Ina families during which Ina fought mainly by doing what the Silks had done to my families—using humans as weapons—using them to kill members of one another's families. Hayden said that hadn't happened anywhere in the world for centuries. It was considered as barbaric among Ina as boiling people in oil was among humans.

And yet, somehow it had come back into fashion.

"I need to see the two male Westfall symbionts," I told Dulce Ramos, the Wells Gordon's symbiont who happened to be awake.

She nodded and said, "Okay." Then, "Hey, Joel," and took Joel and me upstairs and into the house's guest quarters. "Those two are brothers—twins, I think—Gerald and Eric

Cooper. Eric's the one with the mustache." She paused. "I heard what happened. I'm sorry."

I nodded. "Thank you."

"Do you think the Westfall syms did it?"

"No. But they might have seen something."

The Westfall symbionts were asleep, keeping the same hours as their Ina. Awakened, the Cooper brothers came out together, short salt-and-pepper hair standing up in spikes all over their heads. They wore handsome robes made of very smooth, deep red material. They were just as Celia had described them, now sleepy but interested.

"I had heard you could stay awake during the day," Eric said. "But I didn't believe it until now."

I shrugged. "I can," I said, "but while I was asleep this morning someone killed one of my symbionts."

Both men went very still. "Theodora?" Gerald asked.

"Theodora," I said.

"Oh my God, I'm so sorry. Killed? Someone killed her? My God."

"Early this morning. She's been dead now for about ten hours."

He nodded. "And you're talking to us because we spent some time talking to her last night."

"I'm talking to you because both your scents are on her," I said.

"We both danced with her," Eric said. "She was so happy, having such a good time. She was a delight."

"She talked mainly about you," Gerald said. "She made us remember what it was like to be in a brand-new symbiosis. She was very much in love with you, said she thought her life was pretty much over until you broke into her house one night, swept her off her feet, and confused the hell out of her."

I wanted to laugh about that. Then I wanted to run away from these strangers, find a dark corner, and huddle there rocking my body back and forth, moaning and mourning. They were speaking honestly about Theodora as far as I could sense, and yet I hated them. They had been with her talking to her, listening to her, touching her during her last hours. They were strangers, and they had been there with her. I had not.

Beside me, Joel took my hand and held it. That helped a little, steadied me a little.

I struggled to keep my voice and my expression neutral because frightening these men would not get me the information I wanted. And I couldn't just stir their memories by telling them to remember. They weren't mine. The best I could do would be to ask their Ina to nudge their memories when he awoke. For now, I could only try to persuade them. "Do you remember what time it was when you left her?" I asked.

"She left us," Gerald said. "She said she was tired and wanted to go to bed. Said she wasn't used to having a social life again. I think it was around two this morning." He looked at his brother. "Two?"

"Closer to three," Eric said. "We offered to walk her home, but she just smiled and kissed us both and went on her way. I saw her go out the front door. That's the last time I saw her."

"Did you see anyone paying attention to her?" I asked.

Both men frowned, then Eric shook his head. "I was looking at her. I might have missed what someone else was doing." He glanced at me. "No offense, but I would have taken her to bed if I could have."

I nodded. I had understood that. "I don't think she was ready for that yet."

"She wasn't." He paused. "As soon as she was gone, though, two men left. I don't know them or which families they're with. Hell, I don't even know if they were together. They did leave at the same time, though."

"Tell me what you remember about them," I said. "Did you see their faces?"

"Only for a moment," Eric said. "Young-looking men. Brown hair. Medium brown. Both of them."

"Another pair of brothers?" I asked.

They looked at one another, then back at me. "No, I don't believe so," Gerald said. "They were a Mutt-and-Jeff pair."

I frowned.

"A tall fellow and a short one," Gerald explained. "And they didn't look alike at all except for the hair. Just two guys."

"How short was the short guy?" Joel asked.

Gerald frowned. "Too short to be a symbiont, really. I think most Ina would worry about taking on such a small man."

Mentally, I went through the list of people who had left their scents on Theodora's body. Of the ones I could identify, three of them were brown-haired men. Only one might be called short by everyone except me. Gerald was right. The man I was thinking of was slender and short, actually too small to be a symbiont. Most Ina worried about hurting smaller humans. In great need, even I might take more blood than a small human could survive losing. "Estimate the height of the shorter man," I said, just to be sure.

"He was maybe five-three or four," Eric said.

Joel whistled. "That might mean his Ina was female," he said.

"Jack Roan," I said. "His scent was on Theodora. Jack Roan sym Katharine Dahlman. And Katharine Dahlman and her sister are the shortest adult Ina I've ever seen. Did Jack dance with Theodora at all?"

"If he did, it was before we arrived," Eric said. "We were at another party at Manning's house. She would have had plenty of time to dance with other people before we arrived."

But she probably hadn't. Theodora had not left Celia until Eric and Gerald took an interest. I needed to talk with Jack Roan as soon as possible.

But Jack Roan had gone—had left Punta Nublada. I went to the office complex where the Dahlmans were staying and he wasn't there.

The complex was also where the Braithwaites were staying, and one of Margaret Braithwaite's symbionts, a man named Zane Carter, told me he had seen Roan go—had seen him take one of the Dahlman cars and leave that morning. Carter assumed Roan had been sent out on some errand for Katharine or her sister Sophia.

Also, the other brown-haired man from the party turned up—the one who had left the party at the same time as Roan. He turned out to be someone that I knew or, at least, that I was aware of. He was Hiram Majors sym Preston, and his scent had not been on Theodora. I was relieved to know that once I knew he was with the Gordons. He came to me on his own when he heard that I was looking for Roan . . . and heard why I was looking for him.

"I was talking to Jack last night," he told me when he caught up with me as Joel and I were leaving the office complex. "Turns out he and my sister both went to Carnegie Mellon in Pittsburgh at the same time. He knew her. Saw her in some play—she was a drama major—and then ran into her the next day and invited her to have coffee with him." Hiram shrugged. "I'm cut off from my family out here. It was good to talk to someone from home."

"Did he leave abruptly last night?" I asked.

"Yes," Hiram admitted. "I think he had been watching your . . . Theodora?"

"That was her name."

"I hadn't really noticed her until she walked past us and out the door, and Jack looked at her and said he had to go do something for Katharine. Said he'd forgotten until that minute." Hiram shook his head. "That's why I remember him so clearly."

"God," Joel said. "What a stupid thing for one symbiont to say to another."

"Why?" I asked, not thinking.

They both stared at me. Joel answered, "You don't forget something your Ina tells you to do. You can't. That's one of the first things you learn as a symbiont. Jack Roan was—I guess —so eager to go after Theodora that he told a really stupid lie."

Twenty-Five

I ASKED LAYLA CORY, Preston's first, to let me know when he was awake.

Then I went back to the guest house to talk with Wright, Brook, and Celia.

"Jill Renner saw Jack talking to Theodora," Brook said when I told them about Jack Roan.

"She recognized him because he's so short," Wright said. "She'd noticed him before."

"Where were they talking?" I asked.

"Outside," he said. "Near Hayden's house. It was around two thirty or three this morning. She was on her way home."

"Jill said she couldn't hear what they were saying," Celia said. "But it didn't look like anything bad was happening. I mean, Jill said he wasn't touching her or anything."

As soon as Layla Cory phoned me, I left my symbionts at the guest house, went to Preston, and told him what had happened and what I had learned. We talked in his den, next to his bedroom. The den was a windowless, wood-paneled room with leather-covered chairs, oriental rugs on the floor, and many shelves of old, leather-covered books. It felt, somehow, like a cave—the cave Preston was born from each day.

"Katharine Dahlman," he said, and he shook his head. "I've known Katharine for three centuries. Her family and mine . . . well, I can't say we've been friends, but we've usually gotten along. Are you sure?" We sat facing one another in the vast leather chairs. I had slipped off my shoes and curled up in the chair because it was easier than sitting with my legs sticking straight out or sitting forward on the edge with my feet dangling well above the floor. It was a comfortable chair to curl up in. Under different circumstances, I would have been completely content there.

"I'm sure my Theodora is dead," I said, "murdered by being hit so hard that part of her skull was broken. I'm sure Jack Roan sym Katharine Dahlman followed her from the party at Philip's house after lying about why he was leaving the party. Jill Renner went to the same parties as Theodora, and she said

early this morning she saw Roan talking to Theodora near
Hayden's house. Sometime after that, Zane Carter saw Roan
leaving Punta Nublada. I can't claim to know more than that,
but that should be enough."

Preston looked at me for a moment, then shook his head.

"I loved Theodora, and she was mine," I said. "She came
to me willingly, eagerly. And now, because she loved me, she's
dead."

"You don't know that," he said.

"I can't prove it," I said. "But I know it. So do you." I took a
deep breath. "I promised Martin Harrison I wouldn't kill anyone before I talked to you or Hayden. And because the Council goes on tonight, I can't try to track Roan." I took another
breath. "Preston, what can I do? She trusted herself to me. I
want a life for her life. I will have a life for her life."

Preston turned his face away. "Roan's life?"

"Katharine's life!"

"No."

I said nothing more. I would have Katharine Dahlman's life.
We would not play the game of killing off one another's symbionts as though they weren't even people, as though they were
nothing.

I jumped down from the chair, grabbed my shoes, and
started to walk away from him.

"Who will protect the rest of your symbionts if you kill
Katharine?" Preston demanded. "Her family will come after
you. You'll have stepped outside the law, and they will be free
to protect themselves. They'll kill you, and they'll kill your
symbionts, too, if they try to help you. And of course they will
try. Do you want the rest of your people dead?"

"The Dahlmans are the ones who stepped outside the law!"

"I agree with you; they almost certainly have. But that isn't
yet proved."

"My family is gone!" I said, turning to face him again. "My
memory of them is gone. I can't even mourn them properly
because for me, they never really lived. Now I have begun to
relearn who I am, to rebuild my life, and my enemies are still
killing my people. Where is there safety for my symbionts or
for me?"

"Go on with the Council of Judgment."

If he had been anyone other than Preston, I would have walked away without bothering to comment. But Preston had become important to me. It wasn't only that I liked him. He was Daniel's elderfather. And he favored a mating between his sons and me. "Why?" I demanded. "Why should I wait?"

"Think about why this was done, Shori. Think. You were very much in control of yourself last night. If your memory were intact, you wouldn't have been, you couldn't have been so calm as you sat in the same room with the people who probably had your families killed. I don't think you were expected to be calm. I think the Silks and perhaps the Dahlmans expected you not only to look unusual with your dark skin, but to be out of your mind with pain, grief, and anger, to be a pitiable, dangerous, crazed thing. We Ina don't handle loss as well as most humans do. It's a much rarer thing with us, and when it happens, the grief is . . . almost unbearable."

I looked away from him. "I know what the grief is like!"

"Of course you do. You stand there hugging yourself as though you were trying to hold yourself together. They did this to you, Shori. They want you this way!"

I found myself leaning against the wall, wanting to slide down it, wanting to dissolve to the floor. "What can I do?" I said. "How can Katharine be punished when the Silks are the only ones everyone is paying attention to?"

"The facts are what the Council is supposed to pay attention to."

"But Katharine Dahlman is a member of the Council."

"Challenge her tonight. Tell the Council what has happened just as you told me. Facts only. Let them draw their own conclusions. Let them question you. Then ask that Katharine be removed from the Council."

"And they'll do it? All I have to do is ask, and they'll do it?"

"Yes. They'll question her. Then they'll do it because they'll know you're telling the truth, and they'll decide her guilt or innocence as well as her punishment—if there is to be punishment—tomorrow night, when they decide what to do about the Silks. But once she leaves the Council, someone else will have to go, too. Chances are it will be Vlad."

If there was to be punishment? If? If they didn't punish her, I would. I would kill her. I would find a way to do it, a way that would not leave my symbionts unprotected. Perhaps I could find a human criminal—a murderer—and have him kill her and then die himself before he could be made to say who had sent him. Katharine's people would know as I knew, but if she could get away with it, so could I. I had to do something. What I wanted to do was tear her apart with my teeth and hands. Maybe it would come to that.

Then my mind registered the other thing that Preston had said. Vladimir Leontyev, my advocate, one of my mothers' fathers, off the Council. "Why?" I demanded.

"Numerical balance. All Councils of Judgment must have an odd number of members. If Katharine were to leave the Council because of an injury or an emergency at home, her sister Sophia would take her place. Under the circumstances, I don't think you or your advocate would find Sophia any more acceptable than Katharine."

"I agree," I said. Who knew whether this was something both sisters had agreed to do or something Katharine had thought of on her own.

"Also," Preston said, "it will strike people as reasonable that both you and the Silks lose your advocates."

"It's as though they're playing a game. After all, I'm not trying to get at her because she's the Silks' advocate."

"It's not a game, Shori. The Council will know why Katharine must go. But it will be best for you if you do this according to custom." He frowned, looked at me, then looked away. "You, more than anyone, must show that you can follow our ways. You must not give the people who have decided to be your enemies any advantage. You must seem more Ina than they."

"I don't know how to do that."

"You know enough. When you don't know, ask."

"Who shall I ask? Who will be my advocate now?"

He thought for a moment. "Joan Braithwaite?"

I had to think about that, too. "If Margaret were the Council member, I'd say yes, but Joan . . . Just how friendly is she with the Silks?"

"Because of the way she spoke to you last night?"

"That and . . . when she finished with me, she went over to talk with the Silks."

"You should have listened to what she said to them, to Milo in particular."

I waited.

"She told him to give his place to one of his sons or she would, before the Council, question his mental stability."

"As he questioned mine."

"Yes. Stupid of him. But as I've told you, you were not what the Silks expected you to be. You should have been, by all reckoning, only a husk of a person, mad with grief and rage or simply mad." He paused. "I wonder if that's part of why your memory is gone, not just because you suffered blows to the head, but because of the emotional blow of the death of all your symbionts, your sisters, and your mothers—everyone. You must have seen it happen. Maybe that's what destroyed the person you were."

I thought about that. I tried to let his words touch off some feeling, some grief or pain, some memory. But those people were strangers. Right now, there was only Theodora and the pain of just thinking her name. "I don't know," I said. "Maybe I'll never know."

"Go talk to Joan, Shori. See her before tonight's session begins."

I looked into his kindly face, and it scared me how much I liked him and depended on him, even though I didn't really know him very well. But then, I didn't know anyone very well. "What would Joan have done differently if she had been my advocate from the beginning?" I asked.

He gave me a faint, unhappy smile. "From what I know of her, I think she would have spoken to you just as harshly as she did speak, perhaps even more so. But she wouldn't have spoken to the Silks at all, and perhaps Milo would have gone on representing his family and eventually offending almost everyone. Go talk to her, Shori. Do it now."

I went, stopping at the guest house to check on Wright, Joel, Brook, and Celia. I needed to see them to be certain they were all right, I needed to touch each of them. They were sharing a meal of roast beef, a mixture of brown-and-wild rice, gravy, and green beans with the six Rappaport symbionts.

"I need all of you to come to the Council tonight," I said. I didn't think I could stand it if they stayed away, if I couldn't see them and know that they were all right for so many hours.

"We figured," Celia said.

"Don't worry," Wright said. "We were going to go to the Council hall as soon as we finished dinner." The storage building had become "the Council hall" overnight.

"Stay together," I said. "Take care of one another."

They nodded, and I left them. I went to the offices that the Braithwaites were using as living space. I would have given a lot just to sit with my symbionts, watch them eat, hear their voices, walk them over to the Council hall where I would make sure they got seats in the front so that I could always see them. Instead, I went to find Joan Braithwaite.

I tripped and almost fell on the steps that lead up into the offices. I hurt my foot enough to stand still for a moment and wait for it to stop throbbing. It occurred to me as I stood there that I could not recall stumbling like that since the day I left the cave and had healed enough to hunt. This was what Preston had meant. Theodora had been murdered so that I would begin to stumble in all sorts of ways.

I stood still for a minute more, breathing, regaining my balance as best I could. Then I went in and found Joan.

She was in the office that was her bedroom, sitting at the desk, writing in a wire-bound notebook. She closed the notebook as I came in. The folding bed that had been moved in for her was heaped with blankets that she had thrown aside. Her clothing, books, and other things were scattered around the room. She kept a messy room the way Theodora had. Somehow, that made me like her a little.

"I suppose you've come to ask me to be your advocate," she said in her quick, no-nonsense way.

"I have," I said, relieved that she already knew. Zane Carter, who had told me about seeing Jack Roan drive away, had probably told both Joan and Margaret everything.

"You haven't hurt anyone?" Joan demanded.

I shook my head. "I promised Martin Harrison that I wouldn't. I said I'd wait until I talked with Preston or Hayden. When I talked with Preston, he sent me to you."

She turned her chair so that she faced me, hands resting on the arms of the chair. "So you're pretty much in control of yourself, then? You're over the shock?"

I just stared at her.

After a while, she nodded. "When your rage is choking you, it is best to say nothing. How are your remaining symbionts?"

"Fine." Yes. Fine. Putting up with me and my need to hover over them.

"There are people on the Council who are going to ask you much more painful questions than I have so far, Shori. Someone will surely ask you whether you killed your Theodora yourself."

My mouth fell open. "What? I . . . what?"

"And someone will want to know whether she had accepted you fully, whether she was bound to you."

I couldn't say anything for several seconds. On some level, I understood what Joan was doing. I didn't love her for it, but I understood. Still, it took me a while to be able to respond coherently.

"She had accepted me," I said at last. I cleared my throat. "Theodora loved me. I bound her to me here at Punta Nublada. She was mine when she died. Before she arrived several days ago, we hadn't been together often enough to be fully bound, but she wanted to be. She wanted to be with me, and I wanted her. I loved her."

"Do you understand why I ask that?"

"I don't."

She looked downward, licked her lips. "Symbionts—fully bound symbionts—give up a great deal of freedom to be with us. Sometimes, after a while, they resent us even though they don't truly want to leave, even though they love us. As a result, they behave badly. I don't blame them, but—"

"She didn't resent me. She didn't really know what she was giving up yet. And . . . she trusted me."

"Let me finish. Our senses are so much more acute than theirs, we're so much faster and stronger than they are that it's a good thing they have some protection against us. In fact, it's extremely difficult for us to kill or injure our bound symbionts. It's hard, very hard, even to want to do such a thing.

"Even Milo hasn't been able to do it. He resents his need of them, sees it as a weakness, and yet he loves them. He would stand between his symbionts and any danger. He might shout at them, but even then, he would be careful. He would not order them to harm themselves or one another. And he would never harm one of them. I think it's an instinct for self-preservation on our part. We need our symbionts more than most of them know. We need not only their blood, but physical contact with them and emotional reassurance from them. Companionship. I've never known even one of us to survive without symbionts. We should be able to do it—survive through casual hunting. But the truth is that that only works for short periods. Then we sicken. We either weave ourselves a family of symbionts, or we die. Our bodies need theirs. But human beings who are not bound to us, who are bound to other Ina, or not bound at all . . . they have no protection against us except whatever decency, whatever morality we choose to live up to. You see?"

I did. And she had just told me more about the basics of being Ina than anyone else ever had. I wondered what other necessary things I didn't know. I took a deep breath. "I see," I said. "Theodora was bound to me. And I never hurt her. I never would have hurt her."

She watched me as I spoke, no doubt judging me, deciding whether I was telling the truth, whether I was worth her time. "All right," she said. "All right, I'll be your advocate when the time comes." She glanced at her watch. "Let's go to the hall."

Twenty-Six

WHEN KATHARINE DAHLMAN heard what I had to say, she denied everything. Neither she nor her symbiont Jack Roan had anything at all to do with the death of "the person Shori Matthews is attempting to claim as her symbiont."

"They had chosen one another," Vladimir Leontyev said. "We all saw that they had."

"Where is Jack Roan?" Joan Braithwaite asked.

"I don't know," Katharine said. "My other symbionts have told me he had to go—some family emergency. He has family in Los Angeles, in Phoenix, Arizona, and in Austin, Texas." She said all this with an odd, sly, smiling expression that I had not seen before. And, of course, she was lying. Everything she'd said was a lie. I got the impression she didn't care that we knew.

Vladimir looked disgusted. "You're telling us Roan is yours, but you have no idea which of those three large cities in three different states he's gone to visit?"

Katharine gave a small shrug. "It was an emergency," she said. "He couldn't wait until I awoke. I trust my people."

"You should," I said. "Your people are clearly very competent, especially when it comes to murdering an unsuspecting symbiont who's never done them any harm." I looked along the arc at the other Council members. "I request that she be removed from this Council."

"You request!" Katharine seemed to choke on the words. "I request that you be removed from this room! You're a child, clearly too young to know how to behave. And I challenge your right to represent the interests of families who are unfortunately dead. You are their descendant, but because of their error, because of their great error, you are not Ina! No one can be certain of the truth of anything you say because you are neither Ina nor human. Your scent, your reactions, your facial expressions, your body language—none of it is right. You say your symbiont has just died. If that were so, you would be prostrate. You would not be able to sit here telling lies and arguing. True Ina know the pain of losing a symbiont. We are Ina. You are nothing!"

There was a swell of voices from the audience—much denial, but some agreement. All the visiting and local Ina were present in the audience or on the Council. The rest of the seats were filled by symbionts who also had opinions about me. Not surprisingly, the symbionts who spoke were on my side. It was the Ina who were divided.

Preston stood up. "Listen to me!" he roared in a voice Milo Silk would have been proud of, and the room went utterly silent. After a few seconds, he repeated more quietly, "Listen to me. Shori Matthews is as Ina as the rest of us. In addition, she carries the potentially life-saving human DNA that has darkened her skin and given her something we've sought for generations: the ability to walk in sunlight, to stay awake and alert during the day." He paused, then raised his voice again. "Her mothers, her sisters, her father, and her brothers were Ina, and they have been murdered along with all but two of their symbionts. All of Shori's own first symbionts have been murdered. This Council has met to determine who's responsible for those murders, and now it must also consider the murder of Theodora Harden, one of Shori's new symbionts. We are here to discover the guilt or innocence of those accused of these murders and, if they are found guilty, to decide what is to be done with the murderers. Based on what we've heard so far, I don't believe Katharine Dahlman should be a member of this Council."

Katharine Dahlman sat very straight and stared angrily at Preston. "You want your sons to mate with this person. You want them to get black, human children from her. Here in the United States, even most humans will look down on them. When I came to this country, such people were kept as property, as slaves. You are biased in Shori's favor and not a voting member of this Council. I won't give up my place because you say so."

Preston stared at her, expressionless, still. "Council members, count yourselves for or against Katharine remaining one of you." He paused until all of them had turned to look at him. "Zoë Fotopoulos?" he said, turning to look at Zoë. She sat farthest from me, next to Russell Silk's table.

Zoë looked from Katharine to Preston, then shook her head. "Katharine should go," she said. "And we need to consider what to do about her directing her symbiont to kill Shori's symbiont. Like the Silks, she must be judged."

"She must be judged," Preston echoed. "Joan Braithwaite?"

"Katharine should go," Joan said stiffly. "Her fears have made her stupid. We cannot afford to have stupid Council members. The decisions we make here are important. They should be made with a clear head." She did not look at Katharine as she spoke, but Katharine stared at her with obvious hatred.

"Alexander Svoboda?" Preston continued.

"Katharine should go," he said, "but we'd better decide now who will go with her to keep our numbers right."

"Peter Marcu?"

"She should go," he said. "But she's the Silk advocate. Maybe Vlad should be the other member to go."

"Vladimir Leontyev?"

My elderfather looked angrier than the rest of them. It had taken me a moment and a look from him to realize that he was angry on my behalf. Something more had been done to me, and he was furious about it. "Katharine must go!" he said. "If that means I go, too, then so be it. How could she have imagined that this would be overlooked? Our symbionts are not tools to be used to kill other people's symbionts. Those days are long past and nothing should be permitted to revive them."

"Ana Morariu?"

Ana hesitated and stared down at the table. "Katharine should stay," she said. "Let's take care of one question at a time. After all, Katharine may be telling the truth about her symbiont. We shouldn't judge her so quickly." Several people frowned at her or looked away. Others nodded. Vladimir was right. Katharine had made little effort to make her lies believable—as though she expected at least some of the people present to go along with her because using her symbiont to murder the symbiont of someone as insignificant as I was such a small thing. It was a little sin that could be overlooked among friends. Friends like Ana Morariu.

"Alice Rappaport?"

"She should go." Alice looked at Katharine, then looked away and shook her head. "Over the centuries, I've seen too much racial prejudice among humans. It isn't a weed we need growing among us."

"Harold Westfall?"

"She should go. I, too, have seen more than enough racism."

"Kira Nicolau?"

"Katharine should go. She may be right in what she says about Shori, but she did send her symbiont to kill a human whom Shori called her symbiont. No member of a Council of Judgment should have done such a thing, and no Council of Judgment should tolerate such a thing."

"Ion Andrei?"

"I believe Katharine should stay. If she's made a mistake—*if* she's made a mistake—well, we can look into it another time."

"Walter Nagy?"

"She should go. None of us want to go back to the days of feuds carried on by murdering one another's symbionts."

"Elizabeth Akhmatova?"

"She should go. How can she murder another Ina's symbiont and not think anything of it? What sort of person could do such a thing?"

That was a very good question.

Katharine seemed surprised that the vote went against her. She had truly expected to benefit from what she had done. She had gotten her symbiont out of my reach so that I couldn't track him and kill him before she awoke. In fact, I wouldn't have killed him. His life did not interest me. Hers did. But she didn't know me, and she wasn't willing to take chances with Jack Roan's precious skin. She had imagined that her fellow Council members—all Ina, all around her age —would accept what she had done, even if they didn't like it. She believed I would either lose control and disgrace myself before the Council—possibly by attacking her—or if I didn't, she could use my apparent lack of feeling to point out how un-Ina I was. She won either way. What did the life of my Theodora matter?

Katharine left the table, glaring at me as though I had somehow done her an injury. I hadn't. But I would. I surely would.

After a little more discussion, Vladimir left, too. I was sorry to see him go. Wright called him my granddad. Ina, for some reason, didn't use the words humans used to described kinship —"grandfather," "aunt," "cousin"—but I liked the idea of Vladimir and Konstantin as my elderfathers. It comforted me that I still had elderfathers, that I was a youngerdaughter to someone.

Both Vladimir and Katharine went to sit in the audience. Wayne and Philip Gordon brought them chairs. Once that was done, the Council could return to the question of whether the Silks had killed my families.

The Silks first questioned several of the Gordons, including Preston, who stood up like the others at the free-standing microphone and quietly answered the same offensive questions. He answered them without protest.

No, he was not concerned about allowing his sons to mate with someone who was, among other things, a genetic experiment.

"I've had a chance to get to know her," he said. "She's an intelligent, healthy, likable young female. When she's older, she'll bear strong children, and some of them will walk in sunlight."

Then Russell called Hayden and asked the same question of him.

"I am concerned because she is alone," Hayden said. "I hope that she will adopt a sister before she mates with my youngersons. My brother is right about Shori. She is bright, healthy, and likable. When her sisters were alive, I saw a mating between them and my youngersons as a perfect match—or as near perfect as any joining can be."

I felt better about Hayden after that. He seemed to be telling the truth. I hoped he was. He was old enough to slip a lie past me and perhaps past everyone else in the room. But why should he?

The Silks had brought along a doctor who was one of their symbionts, poor man. Russell asked the Council to allow the doctor to question me about my injuries. It was intended to be offensive, another effort, like Milo's, to treat me as human rather than Ina and, of course, to humiliate me.

"He may be able to give us some insight into Shori's amnesia," Russell said innocently. "Humans are more familiar with memory problems."

Ion Andrei, Russell's new advocate, said, "Russell has the right to stand aside and let someone with specialized knowledge speak for him."

Joan Braithwaite sighed. "We could waste a lot of time

arguing whether or not to permit the doctor's questions. Let's not do that. Shori, are you willing to be questioned by this man?"

"I'm not," I said.

She nodded, looked at me for a moment. "The implications of the request are offensive," she said. "They're intended to be. Nevertheless, I advise you to let the doctor question you. He means no harm. He's only one more symbiont being used to cause you pain. Ironic and nasty, isn't it? No matter. I advise you to bear the pain so that anyone on the Council who has doubts about you can see a little more of who and what you are."

I did not like Joan Braithwaite. But I thought I might eventually love her. She was one of the few fairly close relatives I had left. "All right," I said. "I'll answer the doctor's questions."

The doctor was called to the free-standing microphone. He was a tall red-haired man with freckles, the first redhead I could recall seeing. "Do you have any pain, Shori?" he asked. "Have any of the injuries you suffered caused you any difficulties?"

"I have no pain now," I said. "I did before my injuries healed, of course, but they've healed completely except for my memory."

"Do you remember your injuries? Can you describe them?"

I thought back unhappily. "I was burned over most of my body, my face, my head. My head was not only burned, but . . . the bones of my skull were broken so that in two places my head felt . . . felt almost soft when I touched it. I was blind. It hurt to breathe. Well, it hurt to do anything at all. I could move, but my coordination was bad at first. That's all."

The doctor stared at me, and his expression went from disbelieving to a look that I could only describe as hungry. Odd to see a human being look that way. Just for an instant, he looked the way Ina do when we're very, very hungry. He got himself under control after a moment and managed to look only mildly interested. "How long did it take these injuries to heal?" he asked.

"I'm not sure," I said. "I slept a lot at first, when the pain let me sleep. I was mostly aware of the pain. I remember all that happened once I was able to leave the cave, but I'm not sure about some of what went on before that."

"But you remember killing and eating Hugh Tang?"

I drew back and stared at the man, wondering how much of what he asked was what he had been told to ask. Were Joan and I wrong? Was the doctor having fun? "I've said that I remember killing and eating Hugh Tang," I said.

He looked uncomfortable. "Could you tell us," he said, "about anything at all that you've been able to remember of your life before you were injured?"

"I recall nothing of my past before the cave," I said, as though I hadn't said it a dozen times the night before.

"Does this trouble you?" he asked.

"Of course it does."

"What is your answer to it, then? Do you simply accept your memory loss?"

"I have no choice. I am relearning the things that I should know about myself and my people."

"Do you feel yourself to be a different person because of your loss?"

I had an almost overwhelming impulse to scream at him. Instead, I kept silent until I could manage my voice. Then I spoke carefully into the microphone. "My childhood is gone. My families are gone. My first symbionts are gone. Most of my education is gone. The first fifty-three years of my life are gone. Is that what you mean by 'a different person'?"

He hesitated.

Russell Silk said, "It isn't yet your time to question. Answer the symbiont's question."

I ignored him and spoke to the doctor. "Have I answered your question?"

He did not move, but now he looked very uncomfortable. He did not meet my gaze. "Yes," he said. "Yes, you have."

The doctor went on to ask several more questions that I had already answered in one way or another. By the time he ran out of questions, I thought he looked more than a little ashamed of himself. His manner seemed mildly apologetic, and I was feeling sorry for him again. How had he happened to wind up in one of the Silk households?

"Is the doctor boring you, Shori?" Russell asked, surprising me. He didn't like addressing me directly. It was a family trait.

I said, "I'm sure he's doing exactly what you've instructed him to do."

"I have no more questions," the doctor said. He was a

neurologist, Carmen told me later, a doctor who specializes in diseases and disorders of the central nervous system. No wonder he had been so interested in my injuries. I wondered whether he hated the Silks.

Finally, it was my turn to ask questions. I used my turn to call Russell's sons and their unmated young-adult sons to the microphone for questioning. I asked each of them whether they had known that anyone in their family was arranging to kill the Petrescu and Matthews families.

Alan Silk, one of the younger sons of Russell and his brothers, was my best subject—a good-looking, 180-year-old male who hadn't learned much so far about lying successfully but who insisted on lying.

"I know nothing about the killing of those families," he said in response to my question. "My family had nothing to do with any of that. We would never take part in such things."

I ignored this. "Did you help other members of your family collect humans in Los Angeles or in Pasadena, humans who were later used to kill the Matthews and the Petrescus?"

"I did not! None of us did. In fact, I wouldn't be surprised to learn that your male and female families destroyed each other."

Russell winced, but Alan didn't see it because he was glaring at me.

"Is that what you believe?" I asked. "Do you believe that my mothers and sisters and my father and brothers killed one another?"

He began to look uncomfortable. "Maybe," he muttered. "I don't know."

"You don't know what you believe?"

He glared at me. "I believe my family had nothing to do with what happened, that's what I believe. My family is honorable and it's Ina!"

"Do you believe that my families killed each other?"

He looked around angrily, glancing at his new advocate, Ion Andrei, who had apparently decided not to get into this particular foolish argument. "I don't know what they did," he muttered angrily. He held his hands in front of him, one clutching the other.

I sighed. "All right," I said. "Let's see what you believe about something else. Several humans were used to kill my families.

How do you feel about that? Are humans just tools for us to use whenever we find a use for them?"

"No!" he said. "Of course not." He looked at me with contempt. "No true Ina could even ask such a question." He suddenly swung his arms at his sides, then held them in front of him again, as though he didn't know what to do with them.

"What are humans, then? What are they to you?"

He stopped glaring at me and looked uncertainly at Russell.

Russell said, "What do his opinions of humans have to do with the deaths of your families?"

"Humans were used as the killer's surrogates," I said. "What do you think of using them that way?"

"Me?" Russell asked.

"You," I said.

"Have you finished questioning Alan, then?"

"I haven't. But you did jump in and it's my time to ask questions. You've had yours. If you would like, though, I will question you as soon as I finish with Alan."

He looked both confused and annoyed. Since he didn't seem to know what to say, I returned my attention to Alan.

"Are humans tools, then? Should we be free to use them according to our needs?"

"Of course not!"

"Is it wrong to send humans out to kill Ina and their symbionts?"

"Of course it's wrong!"

"Do you know anyone who has ever done that?"

"No!" He almost shouted the word. The sound of his own voice magnified by the microphone seemed to startle him, and he was silent for a moment. Then he repeated, "No. Of course not. No."

Every one of his responses to my questions about humans was a lie. I suspected that his brothers lied when I questioned them. I wanted to believe they were lying. But my senses told me that Alan, with his little twitches and his false outrage . . . Alan was definitely lying.

If I could see it, anyone on the Council could see it.

Twenty-Seven

WHEN THE second night of the Council ended, I was exhausted and yet restless. I wasn't hungry, and I couldn't have slept. I needed to run. I thought if I circled the community, running as fast as I could, I might burn off some of my tension.

I got up from my table and joined my symbionts. I walked outside with them, and we headed back toward the guest house.

"What's to stop Katharine Dahlman from escaping?" Wright asked. "She could decide to join her symbiont in Texas or wherever he is."

"She won't run," Joel said. "She's got too much pride. She won't shame herself or her family by running. Besides . . ." He paused. I glanced back at him. "Besides," he said to me, "she might believe that she has a better chance of surviving if she stays here and takes her punishment."

I said nothing. I only looked at him.

He shrugged.

At the guest house, the four of them went straight to the kitchen. While they were preparing themselves a meal, I went out to run. I didn't begin to feel right until I'd done not one, but three laps around the community. I was the only one running. Everyone else, Ina and human, had trudged back to their meals and their beds.

When I came in, I avoided the kitchen and dining room where I could hear all four of my symbionts and the six Rappaport symbionts moving around, talking, eating. I went upstairs and took a shower. I was planning to spend the night with Joel. My custom was that I could taste anyone anytime—a small delight for me and for my symbionts, a pleasure greater than a kiss, but not as intense as feeding or making love. I made sure, though, that I took a complete meal from each of them only every fifth night.

Now it would have to be every fourth. I would soon have to get more symbionts, but how could I think about doing that now?

Dry and dressed in one of Wright's T-shirts, I somehow wound up in Theodora's room. I wasn't thinking. Her scent drew me. I sat down on her bed, then stretched out on it, surrounded by her scent. I closed my eyes, and it was as though she would come through the door any minute and see me there and look at me in her sidelong way and come onto the bed with me, laughing.

A couple of nights after she arrived, she had found me reading one of Hayden's books written in Ina, and I'd read parts of it to her, first in Ina, then in English. She had been fascinated and wanted me to teach her to read and speak Ina. She said that if she was going to have a longer life span than she had expected, she might as well do something with it. I liked the idea of teaching her because it would force me to go back to the basics of the language, and I hoped that might help me remember a little about the person I had been when I learned it.

I lay there and got lost in Theodora's scent and in grief.

I must have stayed lost for some time, lying on the bed, twisted in the bedding.

Then Joel was there with me, taking the bedding from around me, raising me to my feet, taking me to his room. I looked around the room, then at Joel. He put me on the bed, then got in beside me.

After a while, it occurred to me to say, "Thank you."

"Sleep," he said. "Or feed now if you like."

"Later."

"I'll be here."

I turned and leaned up on my elbow to look down at his face.

"What?" he asked.

I shook my head. "Why did you want me?" I asked.

"What?"

"You know what I am, what I can do. Why didn't you escape us when you could have? You could have stayed in school or gotten a job. The Gordons would have let you go."

He slipped his arms around me and pulled me down against him. "I like who you are," he said. "And I can deal with what you can do." He hesitated. "Or are you thinking about Theodora? Are you feeling responsible for what happened to her?

Do you believe that she was killed because she was with you, and so why the hell would I want to be with you?"

I nodded. "She *was* killed because she was with me. She trusted me. Her death is not my doing directly, but I should have left her in Washington, where she was safe, until all this was over. I knew that. I missed her so much, though, and I had to have more symbionts here with me."

"If she hadn't been here, one of the rest of us would have died," he said. "Theodora was probably the weakest of us, the easiest to kill, but I'll bet if she hadn't been here, Katharine would have sent her man after Brook or Celia."

I nodded. "I know."

"Katharine's guilty. Not you."

I nodded against his shoulder and repeated, "I know." After a while, I said, "You knew much more than most would-be symbionts. You really should have stayed away, made a life for yourself in the human world."

"I might have gone away if you hadn't turned up. You're not only a lovely little thing, but you're willing to ask me questions."

Instead of just ordering him around, yes. That would be important to a symbiont, to anyone. "I won't always ask," I admitted.

"I know," he said. He kissed me. "I want this life, Shori. I've never wanted any other. I want to live to be two hundred years old, and I want all the pleasure I know you can give me. I want to live disease free and strong, and never get feeble or senile. And I want you. You know I want you."

In fact, he wanted me right then. At once. His hunger ignited mine, and in spite of everything, I did still need to feed. I wanted him.

I lost myself in his wonderful scent. Blindly, I found his neck and bit him deeply before I fully realized what I was doing. I hadn't been so confused and disoriented since I awoke in the cave. I needed more blood than I usually did. He held me even though I took no care with him. Afterward, when I was fully aware, I was both ashamed and concerned.

I raised myself above him and looked down at him. He gave me a sideways smile—a real smile, not just patient suffering. But still . . . I put my face down against his chest. "I'm sorry," I said.

He laughed. "You know you don't have anything to apologize for." He pulled the blanket up around us, rolled us over, and slipped into me.

I kissed his throat and licked his neck where it was still bleeding.

Sometime later, as we lay together, sated, but still taking pleasure in the feel of skin against skin, I said, "You're mine. Did you know that? Your scent is so enticing, and I've nibbled on you so often. You're mine."

He laughed softly—a contented, gentle sound. "I thought I might be," he said.

That afternoon, we were all awake and restless, so Celia suggested we get away from Punta Nublada for a while and take a drive, have a picnic—a meal to be eaten outside and away from so many strangers. I liked the idea. It was a chance for us to get to know one another a little better and a chance to think beyond the last Council night.

While I added my hooded jacket, gloves, and sunglasses to my usual jeans and T-shirt, the four of them prepared a meal from the refrigerator. Celia told me I looked as though I were about to go out into the dead of winter.

"Aren't you hot?" she asked.

"I'm not," I said. "The weather is cool. I'll be fine." They felt changes in the weather more than I did.

They took me at my word and packed their food and some cold soda and beer in the Styrofoam cooler that we had bought for our night in the woods in Washington. They had made sandwiches from leftover turkey, roast beef, and cheddar cheese, and took along a few bananas, some red seedless grapes, and the remains of a German chocolate cake. We all fit comfortably in Celia and Brook's car, and Brook drove us out to the highway and then northward toward a place Joel knew about.

We chose a space on the bluffs overlooking the ocean where there was a flat patch of grass and bare rock to sit on and from where we could watch the waves pounding the beach and the rocks below. Brook had thought ahead enough to bring along a blanket and a pair of large towels from the guest house linen closet. Now she spread them on the ground for us, sat down on one of the towels, and began eating a thick turkey-and-cheddar sandwich. The others took food from the cooler and sat around eating and drinking and speculating about whether the Silk symbionts hated their Ina.

"I think they do," Celia said. "They must. I would if I had to put up with those people."

"They don't," Brook said. "I met one of them when they first arrived. She's a historian. She writes books—novels under one name and popular history under another. She says she couldn't have found a better place to wind up. She says Russell's generation and even Milo help her get the little details right, especially in the fiction. She says she likes working with them. Maybe she's unusual, but I didn't get the feeling that she resented them."

Joel said, "I think that doctor who questioned Shori yesterday joined them so he could learn more about what they are and what makes them tick. I wonder what questions he would have asked if he'd had a choice."

"He's definitely hungry to know more," I said. "He wants to understand how we survive terrible injuries, how we heal."

Joel nodded and took a second roast-beef sandwich. "I wonder what he'd do if he discovered something, some combination of genes, say, that produced substances that caused rapid healing. Who would he tell?"

"No one," I said. "The Silks would never let him tell anyone."

"Maybe he just wants it for himself," Wright said. "Maybe he just wants to be able to heal the way Shori did."

I shook my head. "I don't believe anyone would want to go through a healing like that. I can't begin to tell you what the pain was like."

They all looked at me, and I realized that the doctor wasn't the only one who wanted to heal the way I did.

I spread my hands. "I'm sharing the ability with you in the only way I can," I said. "You're already better at healing than you were."

They nodded and opened more food, soda, and tall brown bottles of beer.

After a while I said, "I have to ask you something, and I need you to think about the question and be honest." I paused and looked at each of them. "Have any of you had a problem with either of the Braithwaites or their symbionts?" I asked.

There was silence. Brook had lain down on her back on her towel and closed her eyes, but she was not dozing. Celia was sitting next to Joel, glancing at him now and then. Her scent let me know that she was very much attracted to him. He, on the other hand, was glancing at Wright who had sat down next to me, taken my gloved hand, kissed it, bit it a little as he looked at me, then held it between his own hands. He was showing off. And for the moment, I was letting him get away with it.

"The Braithwaites," Celia said. "Joan could cut glass with that tongue of hers, but I think she's really okay. She just says what she means."

"Are you thinking about moving in with the Braithwaites?" Joel asked.

"I am, yes, for a while . . . if they'll have me. That's why I'm asking all of you whether you've seen anything or know anything against them. If you have reason to want to avoid them, tell me now."

"I like them," Joel said. "They're strong, decent people, not bigots like the Silks and the Dahlmans and a couple of the other Council members."

"I barely know the Braithwaites," Brook said. "I danced with one of their symbionts at a party." She smiled. "He was okay, and I got the impression he was happy, that he liked being their symbiont. That's usually a good sign."

I got the impression she thought the Braithwaite symbiont was more than just "okay." Brook might wind up enjoying our stay with the Braithwaites more than the rest of us—if the Braithwaites agreed to let me visit them for a while.

"So you're not thinking of trying to get them to adopt you?" Joel asked.

"I don't believe I want to be adopted," I said. "I can't remember my female family at all, but I'm part of them. I can learn about them and see that their memory is continued by continuing their family. If I'm adopted, my female family vanishes into history just like my male family did. And I've promised to mate with the Gordons." I thought of Daniel and almost smiled. "I don't know whether that will happen, but I hope it will, and I'm not going to do anything to prevent it."

"So you'll wind up having six or eight children all by your-self," Wright said. "Is that the way it will be?"

"Eventually," I said. "But I'm thinking about doing what Hayden said last night—adopting a relative, a young girl from a family with too many girls. That way there will be two of us. Preston says I can't do that until I'm an adult myself, although I can look around. I hope to be able to live with several differ-ent families and learn what they can teach me. I'll read their books, listen to their elders."

"You're trying to get yourself an education," Joel said.

I nodded. "I have to re-educate myself. Right now, you probably know more about Ina history and about being Ina than I do. I have to learn. Problem is, I don't know what my re-education will cost."

He smiled. "Better ask," he said. "Although, actually, I think Joan will tell you whether you ask or not. Learning is good, though. My father made sure I picked up as much education as I could even before I went off to college. From what Hayden has told me, I'm one of maybe a few hundred humans in the world who can speak and read Ina."

And Theodora would have been another, I thought.

"It will be a while before we have a home," I said. "But as my families' affairs are sorted out, and we begin to have more money, you'll be able to have the things you want and do what you want to do. Maybe one of you wants to write books or learn another language or learn woodworking or real estate." I smiled. "Whatever you like. And there will be more of you. At least three more, eventually."

"Seven people," Wright said. "I understand the need, but I don't like it."

"I like the idea of moving around for a while," Brook said. "When I was with Iosif, we didn't travel much at all. Except for elders going to Councils of one kind or another, most adult Ina do very little traveling, probably because traveling is such a production, with so many people needing to travel together. I'm definitely ready to do some traveling."

"Once you've traveled for a while, you'll probably be ready to settle down again pretty fast," Celia said. "My father was in the army while I was growing up. We moved all the time. As soon as I made friends or began to like a school, we were gone again. This sounds as though it will be like that. Meet a friend, spot a nice guy, start a project, then you're on your way somewhere else."

"We'll be staying mostly with female families, won't we?" Wright asked.

"We will," I said. "If it doesn't cause trouble, we'll pay short visits to the Gordons and the Leontyevs, but as I understand it, my pheromones are going to give males more and more trouble as I approach adulthood."

"Bound to be true," Wright growled into my ear. The growl made my whole body tingle.

"Stop that," I said, laughing, and he laughed, too.

"So all we have to do," Celia said, "is get through tonight. Then we can get on with our lives."

I talked with Margaret Braithwaite that evening. I went to her office-bedroom before the third night of the Council could begin.

"Shori, you shouldn't ask me about this now," she said. "You should have waited until judgment was passed and the Council had concluded its business."

I had found her looking through a book she'd borrowed from Hayden. I hadn't seen her borrow it, but the book smelled deeply of him and only a little of her. One of his older Ina histories.

"Why should I have waited?" I asked. "Have I broken some rule?"

"Oh, no. No rule. It's just that . . . It's just that you might not want to come to us once you hear the judgment."

I thought about that. It seemed impossible that anyone had failed to hear the lies that the Silks and Katharine Dahlman had told. The elders were much more experienced than I was in reading the signs.

"Is it possible that the Council members will fail to see what the Silks have done?" I asked.

"It is not possible," she said. "The problem isn't their guilt and Katharine's. The problem is what to do about it. What punishment to impose?"

"They killed twelve Ina—all of my male and female families —and nearly a hundred symbionts. From what I've heard, none of the people they killed had ever harmed them. How can they be allowed to get away with what they've done?"

"You want them to die."

"I want them to die."

"Would you help kill them?"

I stared back at her. "I would."

She sighed. "They'll die, Shori, but not in the quick satisfying way you probably hope for. That won't happen—except, perhaps, in Katharine's case. She and her family haven't been good about maintaining friendships and alliances. Very stupid of them. But the Silk family will not be killed today."

"Why?"

"Because as terrible as their crimes are, I don't believe the Council vote will be unanimous. Understand, I'm telling you what I believe, not what I know. I might be wrong, although I doubt it. The Council won't want to wipe out an ancient and once-respected family. They'll want to give them a chance to survive."

I didn't say anything for a while. I hated Katharine Dahlman. I would see her dead sooner or later, no matter what anyone said. I hated the Silks, too, but it was a different, less immediate hate. They had killed people I no longer knew, and they had killed without knowing me. I wanted to see the Silks dead, but I didn't *need* to see them dead in the way that I needed to see Katharine dead. That wasn't the way I should have felt, but it was the way I did feel.

I said, "Daniel told me that the Silks' unmated sons might be taken from them and adopted by other families."

Joan nodded. "I think that will happen. If it does, the word will be spread tonight by mail, by phone, and by e-mail to all the world's Ina communities. I'm glad Daniel let you know what could happen."

"What if the Silks decide to come after me again? I was their main target all along because I was the one in whom the human genetic mix worked best. They killed so many just to get to me."

"They have the possibility of rebuilding their family if Russell's sons' generation can convince their mates to try to have more children. They will lose that opportunity if they make another attempt on your life or on the lives of your people—even if they fail. If they try again, they will be killed."

I looked at her for several seconds. "You truly believe this will stop them from secretly trying to kill me or perhaps trying to kill my children in the future?"

"Ina are linked worldwide, Shori. If the Silks give their word —and they must give it if they are to leave here alive—and then break it, they will all be killed and any new sons adopted away. Their family will vanish. They know this."

"Then . . . will you permit me to come to you with my symbionts, learn from you for a while, work for you to pay our way?"

She sighed. "For how long?"

I hesitated. "One year. Perhaps two."

"Come back to me when the Council has finished with its business. I believe that we will welcome you, but I can't answer until I've spoken with my sister."

There was a formal feel to all this—as though we had spoken ritual words. Had we? I would find out eventually.

"What about Katharine?" I asked.

She shook her head. "I don't know."

"I don't believe I could let her go."

"Wait and see."

"Theodora wasn't even a person to Katharine. She was just something Katharine could snatch away from me to make me weaker."

"I know. Don't give her what she wants. Wait, Shori. Wait and see."

Twenty-Eight

THERE WERE no parties on the night of the third Council session. The hall was so full that there was not enough seating for everyone. People stood or brought chairs from the houses. No one seemed to want to sit on the concrete floor. Seats had been roped off for my symbionts in front, as had seats on the opposite side of the hall for the Silks and their symbionts.

The members of the Council seated themselves as usual, in the same order, and when they were all settled, Preston stood up. This was everyone's signal to be quiet and pay attention. Preston waited until silence had worked its way from the front to the back of the room. Then he said, "Russell Silk, do you have anything further to say or any more questions to ask of Shori Matthews or of anyone that you or she has asked to speak to this Council?"

This was Russell's last chance to speak, to defend his family, and to make me look bad. Of course, anyone he called, I could question, too.

Russell stood up. "I have no one else to call," he said, holding his microphone, looking out toward the audience. Then he turned and faced the Council. "I suppose in a sense, I call on all of you to remember that my family has maintained good and honorable friendships with many of you. Remember that the Silk family helped some of you immigrate to this country in times of war or political chaos in your former homes. Remember that in all the time you've known us, we have not lied to you or cheated you.

"What matters most to us, to every member of the Silk family, is the welfare of the Ina people. We Ina are vastly outnumbered by the human beings of this world. And how many of us have been butchered in their wars? They destroy one another by the millions, and it makes no difference to their numbers. They breed and breed and breed, while we live long and breed slowly. Their lives are brief and, without us, riddled with disease and violence. And yet, we need them. We take them into our families, and with our help, they are able to live longer, stay free of disease, and get along with one another. We could not live without them.

"But we are not them!

"We are not them!

"Children of the great Goddess, we are not them!"

He shook with the intensity of his feeling. He had to take several breaths before he could continue. "We are not them," he whispered. "Nor should we try to be them. Ever. Not for any reason. Not even to gain the day; the cost is too great."

He stood for a second longer in silence, then sat down and put his microphone back on its stand. The room had gone completely silent.

Once he sat down, Preston broke the silence. "Shori, is there anyone you would like to question or anything you would like to say?"

"I have questions," I said, standing up with my microphone. I had thought of something as Russell spoke—something prompted by what he had said and by my having seen Joan Braithwaite reading a history book just a short while ago. It seemed to me that Russell had just admitted that his family had killed my families. He wanted us to believe that he had done it for a good reason. I said to Preston, "I want to ask you a few questions, if that's all right."

Preston looked surprised. "All right. Russell questioned me so I do qualify as someone you can question now."

I nodded. "I ask this because of my limited knowledge of Ina law. Preston, is there a legal, nonlethal way of questioning someone's behavior? I mean, if I believed that you were doing something that could be harmful to other Ina, would I be able to bring it to the attention of a council of some kind or some other group?"

Preston did not smile, did not change expression at all, but I got the impression he was pleased with me. "There is," he said. "If you believed I were doing something to the detriment of the Ina, something that was not exactly against law, but that you seriously believed was harmful, you could ask for a Council of the Goddess."

Russell snatched up his microphone and protested. "Council of the . . . That hasn't been done for at least twenty-five hundred years."

"You are aware of it, then?" I asked him.

"It wouldn't have been taken seriously. No one's done it for two thousand—"

"Did you try?"

"Your families made no secret of the fact that they didn't even believe in the Goddess!"

From the hypothetical to the real. Careless of him. "Would that have mattered?" I asked. "Could my family have ignored a call to take part in a Council of the Goddess?"

Russell said nothing. Perhaps he had remembered where he was and exactly what was being argued.

"Preston, would it have mattered?"

"The rule of seven would apply," Preston answered. "If the rule of seven is satisfied and the accused family refuses to attend, the Council would be carried on regardless of its absence. The family would be bound by any vote of the Council, as though it had been present. If the family were ordered to stop whatever they were doing, and they refused to stop, they would be punished."

I stared across at Russell. "Preston, has the Silk family ever tried to assemble a Council of the Goddess to discuss or warn against the genetic work of my eldermothers?"

"Not to my knowledge," Preston said. "Russell?"

Again, Russell said nothing. It didn't matter. Surely he had already said enough. I sat down and put my microphone back in its place.

"Does any Council member have questions?" Preston asked.

No one spoke.

"All right," he said. "Council members, I ask you now to count yourselves. Is the Silk family guilty of having made human beings their tools and sent those human tools to kill the Petrescu and the Matthews families? Are the Silks also guilty of sending their tools to burn the Petrescu guest house where Shori Matthews and her symbionts were staying? Are the Silks guilty of sending their tools to attack the Gordon family here at Punta Nublada? And also, was Katharine Dahlman, the Silks' first advocate, guilty of sending one of her symbionts, Jack Roan, to kill one of Shori Matthews's symbionts, Theodora Harden?" He paused, then said, "Zoë Fotopoulos?"

I had decided that Zoë was the most beautiful Ina I had ever seen. Her age—over three hundred—didn't seem to matter. She was tall, lean, and blond like most Ina but was a striking, memorable woman. When she arrived, I had asked Wright what he thought of her. He said, "Sculpted. Perfect, like one of those Greek statues. If she had boobs, I'd say she was the best-looking woman I've ever seen."

Poor Wright. Maybe one of the Braithwaite symbionts would have large breasts.

"Shori Matthews has told us the truth," Zoë said. "I have not once caught her in a lie. Either she has been very careful or she is exactly what she seems to be. My impression is that she is exactly what she appears to be—a child, deeply wronged by both the Silk family and Katharine Dahlman. Members of the Silk family, on the other hand, have lied again and again. And Katharine Dahlman has lied. It seems that all this killing was done because Shori's families were experimenting with ways of using human DNA to enable us to walk in daylight. And it seems that no legal methods of questioning or stopping the experiments were even attempted." She took a deep breath. "I stand with Shori against both the Silks and Katharine Dahlman."

"Joan Braithwaite?" Preston said.

"Shori told the truth, and Katharine and the Silks lied," Joan said. "That's all that matters. I must stand with Shori against both."

"Alexander Svoboda?"

"I stand with Shori against Katharine Dahlman," he said. "But I must stand with the Silks against Shori. Shori has told the truth, as far as she knows, as far as she is able to understand with her damaged memory, but I can't condemn the Silks as a family because of what one child, one seriously impaired child, believes."

And yet, every Silk who had spoken to the Council had lied about what he had done, about what he knew, or both. How could Katharine Dahlman be punished for killing one symbiont and the Silks let off for killing twelve Ina and nearly a hundred symbionts? But that was Alexander's less than courageous decision.

"Peter Marcu?" Preston said.

"I stand with Shori," Peter Marcu said. "I don't want to. My family has been friends with the Silks for four generations. There was even a time when we got along well with the Dahlmans. But Shori has been telling the truth all along, and the others have been lying. Whatever their reasons are for what they've done, they did do it, and for the sake of the rest of our people and all our symbionts, we cannot allow this to go unpunished."

"Ana Morariu?"

"I stand with the Silks and with Katharine Dahlman," Ana said. "Shori Matthews is much too impaired to be permitted to speak against other Ina. How can we destroy people's lives, even kill them on the word of a child whose mind has been all but destroyed and who, even if she were healthy, is barely Ina at all? It is a tragedy that the Petrescu and Matthews families are dead. We shouldn't deepen the tragedy by killing or disrupting other families."

She was the one who had said Katharine Dahlman might be telling the truth. Now she seemed to be saying that my families had simply been unlucky and had, for some unknown reason, died, and that it would be wrong to punish anyone for that. Nothing wrong, she seemed to think, with letting your friends get away with mass murder.

"Alice Rappaport?"

"I stand with Shori," Alice said. "Katharine and the Silks are liars, people who use murder but never think to use the law. They know better than anyone here that we can't let them go unpunished. And what about the rest of you? Do you want to return to a world of lawless family feuds and mass killing?"

"Harold Westfall?"

"I stand with Shori," Harold said. "To let this go would be to endanger us all in the long run. Both the Silks and Katharine must be punished for what we all know they've done."

He glanced at me unhappily. I got the impression he didn't want to be here. He didn't want to stand with me. I suspected he didn't even like me much. But he was doing his duty and trying to do it as honestly as he could. I respected that and was grateful for it.

"Kira Nicolau."

"I stand with Shori as far as Katharine is concerned," Kira said. "What Katharine did was completely wrong, and I have no doubt that she did it. I don't believe she even meant to convince us otherwise; it just didn't seem very important to her. But as to the other problem, I must stand with the Silks. I don't believe Shori's memories and accusations should be trusted. I'm not convinced that Shori understands the situation as well as she believes she does. She believes what she says, that's clear. In that sense, she is telling the truth. But like Alexander, I'm not willing to disrupt or destroy the Silk family on the word of someone as disabled as Shori Matthews clearly is."

Nothing about the lies the Silks had told. Nothing about my dead families. And yet, Kira herself was telling the truth as far as I could see. She really seemed to believe that I was so impaired that I didn't know what I was talking about. She had somehow convinced herself of that.

"Ion Andrei?"

There was a moment of silence. Finally Ion said, "I stand with the Silks and with Katharine. I don't want to. I believe the Silks may have murdered Shori's families. It's certainly possible. And Katharine may have sent her symbiont after Shori's symbiont. But, like Kira, I cannot in good conscience base such a judgment on the words of someone as disabled as Shori is."

It was painful to listen to them. I wanted to scream at them. How could they blind all their senses so selectively? And how could they see me as so impaired? Maybe they needed to see me that way. Maybe it helped them deal with their conscience.

"Walter Nagy?"

"I stand with Shori," Walter said. "And I would stand with her even if she were out of her mind because it is so painfully obvious that the Silks and Katharine Dahlman were lying almost every time they answered a question. They have committed murder and, in the case of the Silks, mass murder. If we excuse that in those we like, we open a door that we tried to lock tight centuries ago. Make no mistake. If we ignore these murders, we invite people to settle disputes themselves, and we risk exposure in the human world. We are, every one of us, vulnerable to the fires that consumed Shori's families."

There was a moment of silence. Finally, Preston said, "Elizabeth Akhmatova?"

"I stand with Shori," Elizabeth said. "For all the reasons Walter's just given, I stand with her. And I stand with her because I've watched her. She *is* impaired. I can't imagine what it would be like to lose the memory of nearly all of the years of one's life. Her memory was stolen from her. But her ability to reason wasn't stolen. The questions she's asked—questions that were answered again and again with lies and misdirection —were good, sensible questions. The questions she answered, she answered honestly. The murderers who killed her families and her symbiont, the thieves who stole her past from her— should these people be rewarded because they did such a savagely thorough job? No, of course not. Shori, on the other hand, should be rewarded for using her intellect to protect herself and to find the murderers."

Twenty-Nine

A ND THAT was that.

There was a moment of silence, then Preston stood up. "The decision is made," he said.

"A majority of seven members of this eleven-member Council of Judgment have stood with Shori Matthews and against both Katharine Dahlman and the Silk family. Therefore, Katharine Dahlman and the Silk family must be punished for the wrongs they have done. But because the decision was not unanimous, their punishment must be other than death.

"For the wrongs the Silk family has done—for their complete destruction of the Petrescu family, for their nearly complete destruction of the Matthews family, and for their attempted destruction of the Gordon family—the penalty, by written law, is the dissolution of the Silk family. The five unmated Silk sons must be adopted by five families in five countries other than the United States of America. Each will mate as the males of his new family mate. They will be Silk no longer."

The room was utterly silent. Even the Silks made no sound. I wondered how they could keep silent. Was it pride? Was it pain? Were they refusing to believe the sentence or only refusing to let others see their pain? I looked across the room at Russell Silk.

He stared back at me with utter hatred. If he could have killed me, I think he would have done it with pleasure. I realized coldly that I felt the same toward him. If he came after me and I could kill him, I would—joyfully.

Preston said, "Russell, you've heard your family's sentence."

Russell managed to turn away from me and direct his hateful stare at Preston.

"Stand," Preston ordered.

Russell made no move to rise. He turned to look at me again. He looked as though he wanted to kill me so badly that it was hurting him.

"Russell Silk," Preston said in that big, deep, clear voice of his. "Stand," he said, "Stand and speak for yourself and your family."

Russell Silk rose slowly, and I watched him. He was at the very edge of his control. If he lost control, he would certainly come for me. He was half again my height and easily twice my weight—an adult Ina male. Not a deer. But he was old. Perhaps not as fast as a deer. Watching him, I decided I could ride him. I could be on him before he could stop me. I could tear out his throat. It wouldn't kill him, although my venom might tame him for me, make him obey. If it didn't, it would surely slow him down, give me a chance to twist his head right off. No one could recover from that. I could do that. I could.

"You must accept the sentence," Preston said. "Then each member of your family must stand and accept it. By your acceptance, you give your word, each of you, that there will be peace between the Silks and the Matthews, peace between the Silks and the Gordons, peace for a period of at least three hundred years from today."

Preston paused, his eyes on Russell as intently as mine were. "The penalty for refusing to accept your sentence or for breaking your word once you've given it is immediate death—death for you, Russell, and for each mated member of your family." He paused and looked at the Silk family waiting in the audience. "Do you accept your sentence?" he demanded.

Russell launched himself toward me.

I stood up and away from the table, ready for him, eager for him. It was like being eager for sex or for feeding.

But before he could reach me, before I could taste his blood, two of his sons and one of his brothers leaped up from the front row, grabbed him, and dragged him down. They held him while he struggled beneath them, screaming. At first, it seemed that he wasn't making words. He was only looking at me and screaming. Then I began to recognize words: "Murdering black mongrel bitch . . ." and "What will she give us all? Fur? Tails?"

He didn't shed tears. I wondered suddenly whether we could cry the way humans did. Russell just lay curled on his side, moaning and choking.

I watched the whole group of Silks, clustered in the first

few rows on Russell's side of the room. Milo glared at me, but the others were focused on Russell, who seemed to be slowly regaining his sanity.

Wright and Joel got up and came toward me, but I waved them back to their seats. They couldn't regrow lost parts. Better for them to stay clear.

Milo looked from me to them—a long, slow look. Then he looked at me again. It was an obvious threat.

Daniel Gordon, his fathers, and his brothers came up to stand behind me. In silence, they looked back at Milo.

The pile of Silks on the floor untangled itself, and all four of them stood up. After a moment, Russell went back to his table and stood by it. The rest of his family watched him, as the three who had restrained him went back to their seats.

At the same time, the Gordons behind me melted away and went back to their seats as silently as they had come. I sat down at my table.

Preston repeated in an oddly gentle voice, "Russell Silk, do you accept your sentence?"

It was as though there had been no interruption. Russell looked down at his table, then stared at me. "What is to be done with the Matthews child?" he demanded.

"Nothing at all," Preston said.

"She should be adopted. She's a child. She's ill. She should be looked after, brought into a family that can teach her how to at least pretend to be Ina."

"You created Shori's problems," Preston said. "But solving them is not your concern. Your only concern now is whether you accept your sentence or reject it. Now, for the last time, do you accept your sentence?"

Russell looked at his family—his father, his brothers, his sons, and his five youngersons who would soon be leaving the Silk family to be adopted by others. Adoption was apparently so permanent a thing that there was no possibility of their sneaking back home or uniting as Silks in another country or another part of the United States. For one thing, they would eventually be mated to different families of females. And their sons would never be Silks.

It took Russell almost a full minute to make himself say the words: "I . . . accept . . . the sentence."

"Milo Silk?" Preston said.

Milo stood up. In an ancient, paper-dry voice that I had not heard from him before, he said, "I accept the sentence." Then he sat down again and sagged forward in his chair, staring at the floor, elbows resting on his knees.

Once he had said it, each of the rest of his sons could say it. Then their sons could say it. Finally the youngest, unmated sons—those who were giving their word that they accepted absolute, permanent banishment—could say it. It still seemed wrong to me that they should be the ones to bear the worst of the punishment. Each might never see his fathers or his brothers again, and three of them were children. They were the only ones truly not responsible for what their elders had done to my families.

It occurred to me suddenly that Russell had asked about my being adopted because if I, like his sons, became a member of a different family, he might not be legally forbidden from attacking me. If I were not Shori Matthews, but Shori Braithwaite, for instance, I might be fair game. The Braithwaites might be fair game. I had no intention of being adopted, but I did intend to ask Preston if my suspicions were true.

The Gordons quietly separated the Silks from their unmated sons. The sons' symbionts joined them quickly, and that was a good thing. It would ease their pain to have these loved and needed people with them, people they had probably known most of their lives. The sons would be taken from their fathers but not from the humans who were closest to them. In fact, someone would have to collect the rest of their symbionts back at the Silk community and reunite them with their Ina. I was glad to see that one of the son's symbionts was the doctor who had questioned me. It was good that he could be away from the ugly contempt of the adults. The Silk son to whom he was bound was taller than I was, but he looked no older.

The youngest Silks and their symbionts were herded out of the room by several adult Ina—the siblings of those who had served on the Council of Judgment. Perhaps these were the people who would have had to carry out the death sentence if there had been one. Was that the arrangement? One brother or sister passed judgment and the other helped to carry out the sentence?

The adult Silks watched, distraught. Their obvious pain was so much at odds with their utter stillness that it was hard to look at them. They stared at their children, their family's future, walking away, and in that vast room, no one spoke a word.

Then the youngest Silks were gone, and we all sat looking at one another.

Preston coughed—an odd sound from him since he did it to get our attention rather than to clear his throat. "We must also attend to the matter of Katharine Dahlman," he said. He looked at her where she sat near the Silks. "Stand, please, Katharine, and come forward."

Very slowly, she stood up and came to the microphone that stood alone in the arc.

Preston, also standing, faced her. "For the wrong that you've done, Katharine Dahlman—for using your own symbiont, Jack Roan, as a murderous tool, for having him kill Theodora Harden, the symbiont of Shori Matthews—you must, according to written law, have both your legs severed at mid-thigh." He took a breath. "Katharine, do you accept your sentence?"

She leaned forward to speak into the microphone, then had to lower it to her height. "I do not," she said when she had finished. "The punishment is too extreme. It does not fit the minor crime that I committed."

"Minor crime!" I said loudly. "How can murdering a woman who never harmed you, who never even threatened you be a minor crime?"

She didn't even glance at me. "I ask that the members of the Council consider my punishment and count themselves for or against it."

I looked at Preston. I found it intolerable that Katharine would be permitted to live. Now she was whining about having to suffer at all. If she accepted her punishment, in a year or two, she would have legs again and be fine, but Theodora would still be dead. Minor crime?

"I will give up my left hand to pay for my . . . crime," Katharine said. "That's more than justice."

"Or perhaps only a finger!" I said. "Maybe a fingernail would do. But if the penalty is so small, then I should be able to do to you what you did to me. Which of your symbionts shall I take?"

She looked at me with more hatred and contempt than I would have thought she could manage, then she turned away and spoke to Preston. "I demand a count of the Council. I have a right to that."

"There has been a count as to your guilt. Once that vote went against you, your guilt and punishment were decided. You have no right to negotiate, and you know it. You knew the law long before you decided to break it."

She looked away from him, stared past him, and said nothing for several seconds. Finally, she shook her head. "I can't accept it. It's unjust. That human was not a symbiont because Shori is not Ina! And . . . and at my age, the punishment would probably kill me."

What did that mean? Was she saying she thought it was all right to kill innocent human beings who were not symbionts?

Preston hesitated, then spoke gently. "Katharine, this isn't a death sentence. It will be bad. It's supposed to be bad. Consider what you did to earn it. But your family will look after you, and in a year or two, you'll have healed. But refusing the sentence, Katharine . . . that would be death."

She shook her head. "Then kill me! Go ahead. Kill me! I cannot accept the punishment you've ordered."

The two of them, not far apart in age, stared at one another. "We'll take a short break," he said. "Katharine, go talk with your sister and your symbionts. Think about what you're doing. He stepped away from his place at the table and glanced at his silent audience. "We'll resume in one hour."

My symbionts hesitated, then came up to me. I didn't know why they hesitated until they stayed back and let Wright be the first to touch me. He took my hand, and when I took his huge hand between both of mine, the others came up to me.

I realized that they were afraid of me. What had I said or done? How had I looked or acted to make these people whom I loved and needed most afraid of me? I stood and hugged each of them, holding Brook for a little longer than the others because she was trembling so.

"The tension in this place is like a bad smell," I said. "Let's go back to the house for a little while."

We left the hall and headed toward the guest house. We

weren't talking. I think we all wanted what I had said—a little time away from the anger and hatred and pain in the hall. Joel had put his arm around me and was, I think, deliberately distracting me with his scent. I needed to be distracted. Both he and Brook knew enough about the Ina to do something like that.

I sat with them in the kitchen while they had coffee and cinnamon-apple muffins. Wright was talking about building our first house himself, and the others didn't believe he could do it. I did. I kind of liked the idea.

They dared me to taste the coffee, and I tasted it. It was less appealing than plain water, but not disgusting. I wondered what other human food or drink I could tolerate. When I had more time, I might find out.

We talked for a while longer, then got up and headed back. Suddenly there was confusion and shouting. Not too far ahead of us, people came spilling out of Henry's house. Before I could understand what was going on, Katharine Dahlman was there in front of us. She had run from Henry's house, run faster than a human could, but not that fast for an Ina. She was holding something in front of her, clutched in both hands.

It took a moment for me to understand that she was holding a rifle. She ran ahead of the crowd, then stopped suddenly and leveled the gun at my symbionts and me.

I charged her. I was terrified that she would kill another of my symbionts before I could stop her.

Again, I had not kept them safe.

She fired.

And I felt as though I'd been punched hard, hammered in the stomach by something impossibly strong.

It was as though I hung in midair for an instant, not going forward, not dropping. It didn't happen that way, of course, but I felt as though it did. In fact, my momentum carried me into her. I hit her with my feet, and she started to fall. I hit the rifle with my hand, shoved it upward, and made her next shot go wild. Her weapon was an old bolt-action rifle, perhaps one of those kept handy while the Gordons were worried about being attacked. If it had been automatic like the ones our attackers had used against us, or if Katharine had been quick with it, she might have shot me again before I reached her. She might have battered me down with bullets, then while I was helpless, she could have finished killing me.

Instead, I reached her. As we struggled on the ground I tore the gun from her hands and threw it away. I was surprised that I could. She was an adult and larger than I was, even though she was small for an Ina. I could feel her in my hands as she twisted and tried to push me away, tried to tear herself free of me, tried to bite me.

My own strength was bleeding away. She was winning, holding on to me, pulling me close so that she could bite and tear. With the last of my strength, I rammed my hand upward, hit her hard under the chin, pulled myself up, and bit down hard into the flesh of her throat.

She screamed. Either she was terrified of my getting control of her or her pain overwhelmed her. I had not bitten her for nourishment or out of affection. I meant to destroy her throat, tear it to pieces. She let go of my shoulders to grab my head and push my face away, and in the instant of opportunity that gave me, I went for a better grip on her with my teeth. I bit through her larynx. She would do no more screaming for a while. And I broke her neck—or tried to. I wasn't sure whether I managed it or not because I lost consciousness before the worst of my own pain could catch up with me.

And then it was over.

Epilogue

I REGAINED CONSCIOUSNESS slowly. It was like struggling up through mud.

I was naked except for one of Wright's big T-shirts. Someone had undressed me and put me to bed. The room was very dark, and I lay alone in bed. I couldn't see well at first. I wasn't in pain from my wound, but I felt weak—weak on a whole different scale from anything I'd felt since the cave. In fact, this felt like awakening in the cave. This time, though, I thought I'd only lost a night or two.

Then I smelled meat somewhere just beyond the bed. I turned toward it, literally starving. My body had used up its resources healing itself and had reached the point of beginning to consume its own muscle tissue as fuel.

I scuttled toward the meat, desperate for it.

Someone said, "Stop, Shori!"

And I stopped. It was Wright. My first.

I pulled back, seeing him now, tall, broad, and shadowy, sitting in a chair next to the bed. I hadn't touched him, wouldn't touch him. I pulled back, away from him, clutching the mattress, whimpering. The hunger was a massive twisting hurt inside me, but I would not touch him. I heard him moving around, then I caught a different scent. Beef. Food.

"Here," he said. "Take it. Eat." He gave me a big dish filled with lean pieces of raw meat. It wasn't as freshly killed as I would have preferred, but it was good enough. I gulped the meat, bit the pieces into smaller chunks, and swallowed them barely chewed, then gulped more. I finished the platter and grabbed the new one that Wright offered me, gulping much of it, then, with growing contentment, finishing the rest more slowly, actually chewing before I swallowed, feeling almost content, finally content.

I put the platter down, leaned back against the headboard, and sighed. "Thank you," I said. "But next time—if this ever happens again—don't stay with me. Just leave the meat."

"I don't see where you put it all," he said. "You're so small.

571

If you were human, I'd expect you to be sick after eating like that."

"I was sick—from the need to eat."

"I know but . . . oh, it doesn't matter. I'm just grateful you're all right."

"You shouldn't have been here," I told him again. I shook my head, tried to shake off the memory of Hugh Tang. "How could the Gordons let you stay here with me?"

"They didn't," he said. "They said we should put the meat in a cooler and leave it in here with you. They said none of us should go in, that we should wait until you came out."

"You should have."

He put something in my hands. It turned out to be several disposable wipes. I used them to clean my hands and face. Then he poured water from a pitcher into a glass and handed me the glass. I had seen neither the pitcher nor the glass until he picked them up from the night table. I was focused on him —his scent, the sound of his heartbeat, his breathing, his voice. It was so good to have him nearby even though he shouldn't have been.

I took the glass and drank. "Thank you," I said. "Why did you disobey the Gordons? You know what I could have done."

"I'm not Hugh Tang," he said. "And you didn't have a head wound this time. I knew you wouldn't hurt me."

I stared at him, amazed and angry. "You don't understand. The hunger is so terrible . . . Even without a head wound, I might have killed you."

"You stopped the instant I spoke. I don't believe you would have touched me. In fact, without the head injury, I don't think you would have touched anyone else who had the presence of mind to speak to you. I was pretty sure I was safe here."

"You don't know what it's like to be so . . . so hungry."

He put his hand on my arm. "I don't. And I wish you hadn't had to go through it. I know you were afraid Katharine was going to shoot one of us." Very slowly, he gathered me to him. I let him because it felt so good, so completely comfortable to rest against him.

"Are the others all right?" I asked, knowing they were. His manner would have been very different if someone had been badly injured. Or killed.

He smiled. "They're fine. They're worried about you. They've been sitting with you when I had to take breaks. It's been three nights. Preston told us it would be at least three nights. Hayden said it would more likely be five or six nights, but Joel said that for Ina medical problems, you can just about always trust Preston."

I shook my head, amazed, thinking about what could have happened. What if I had awakened and scared Celia or Brook or attacked them because they tried to run away? "I'm glad I woke when you were here."

"Me too."

"And . . . what about Katharine?"

"Dead. Wells and Manning took care of it since executions are the business of the host family. They can do it themselves or bring in other families to help. But this time they didn't need help. They beheaded her, then burned both the head and the body. She might have healed from what you did to her. Her throat was already beginning to. But she refused to accept the judgment against her. She preferred death. She said she was just sorry she couldn't take you with her. Her sister Sophia accepted the judgment on behalf of the Dahlman family. Preston says that means we won't have to worry about them coming after us."

"Good. I hope that promise is as good as the Gordons think it is."

"I asked Hayden about that. He's kind of the Gordons' historian. He said we shouldn't worry, that not many people want to risk sacrificing the lives of their whole adult family to violate a judgment. It's supposed to be a matter of honor, anyway. He said the Dahlmans aren't a likable family, but it seems that they are, by their own standards, an honorable one. Sophia Dahlman is the oldest of them now, and she's given her word. They'll keep it."

I sighed. "I wonder how you can be honorable and still kill the innocent?"

"Don't know," he said. "They're your people."

I looked up at him. "We'll have to learn about them together."

"Well," he said, "Katharine was the guilty one, and now she's dead."

He was right. That's what mattered. Theodora was avenged and the rest of my symbionts were safe. What about my mothers and sisters, my father and brothers? What about my memory?

They were all gone. The person I had been was gone. I couldn't bring anyone back, not even myself. I could only learn what I could about the Ina, about my families. I would restore what could be restored. The Matthews family could begin again. The Petrescu family could not.

"All the Council members have gone home," Wright said. "Joan and Margaret Braithwaite left you a letter and their addresses and phone numbers. They're okay with us spending a year or two with them after you've straightened out your parents' affairs and talked to Theodora's family. Joan says if you're going to survive on your own, you'll need good teachers, and she's willing to be one of them. She also said she thought you'd make a damn good ally someday."

I thought about that and nodded. "She's right. I will."

STORIES

Childfinder

Standardization of psionic ability through large segments of the population must have given different peoples wonderful opportunities to understand each other. Such abilities could bridge age-old divisions of race, religion, nationality, etc. as could nothing else. Psi could have put the human race on the road to utopia.

Away from the organization. As far away as I could get. 835 South Madison. An unfurnished three room house for $60 a month. Rain through the roof in the winter, insects through the walls in the summer. Most of the electrical outlets not working. Most of the faucets working all the time whether they were turned off or not. Tenant pays utilities. My house. And there were seven more just like it. All set in a straggly row and called a court.

Not that I minded the place really. I'd lived in worse. And I killed every damn rat and roach on the premises before I moved in. Besides, there was this kid next door. Young, educable, with the beginnings of a talent she was presently using for shoplifting. A pre-telepath.

Saturday.

She came over at 10 a.m., banging on the door as though she intended to come through it whether I opened it or not. Considering her background and the condition of the door, she might have.

I let her in. Ten years old, dirty, filthy really even at this hour of the morning. Which meant she had probably gone to bed that way. Her mother worked at night and her older sister knew better than to try to make her do anything she didn't want to do. Like bathe. Most of her hair was pulled back in a linty pony tail. The kind that advertised the fact that she had just started "combing" it herself.

"Come on in. What do you want?" I knew what she wanted. I'd been waiting for her all morning. But it made her suspicious when I was too nice or too understanding.

577

"Here's your book." She wasn't comfortable handing it to me.

"What happened to the cover?"

"Larry played with it and tore it off."

"Valerie, what'd you let a two-year-old play with a book for?"

"Mama said share it with him."

I took the book from her, keeping my expression just short of disgust. People don't like you breaking up their things. She knew it and she didn't expect me to be happy. Actually I didn't care. There was only one thing I cared about.

"Did you read it?"

"Yeah."

"Like it?"

"Yeah."

"What did you like about it?"

She shrugged. "I don't know." Beginning of battle. You drag words out of her, one by painful one. You prove to her that she can do a lot more thinking than she's used to . . . if she wants to. Then you make her want to. And all the time you push her, guide her thinking just a little. Partly to get her used to mental communication—like letting a baby hear speech so it can learn to talk. And partly to shock her into thinking along new and not always pleasant lines. That last is ugly. Not something I like to do to kids. The adults I do it to usually can't be reached any other way. Most of the time they're not salvageable anyway. All the kids like Valerie have is a few years of failure conditioning. Not quite enough to be fatal.

Valerie said, "I liked the parts where Harriet helped those slaves get away."

"She could have been killed every time she helped them."

"Yeah."

"Why do you think she kept doing it?"

Again the bored shrug. "I don't know. Wanted them to get free, I guess."

Off-the-top-of-her-head stuff. She had liked the book all right, at least while she was reading it. It was a juvenile bio-graphy of Harriet Tubman, well written, fast moving, and ex-citing. There were a lot of reasons for Valerie to get more than a couple of evenings entertainment out of it. Reasons beyond the ones usually given for making a black kid read that kind of book. Right now, though, her mind had wandered outside, where the rest of the court kids were screaming and chasing each other up and down the driveway.

I hit her with a scene from the book. Herself in Harriet's place. Seven or eight people following her north. Night. North star. White people nearby. Danger. Close call. Fear. One of her followers wanting to turn back, and another, and another. Fear like a barrier you could reach out and touch. Gun in her hand, telling them they would go on with her or be shot.

Push.

Reading it and living it are two different things. Valerie got the whole scene in a few seconds like a really vivid dream. Not the kind of dream someone her age ought to be having, but she was going to have to grow up pretty fast.

She shook herself and muttered something like, "Long-haired motherfucker!" It was one of the kinder names that people in our court called each other from time to time. But at that moment Valerie was applying it to the first of Harriet's would-be deserters.

She looked at me, frowning. "They always got halfway up north and then somebody would get scared and want to go back. How come they were so scared to just go ahead and be free?"

Breakthrough. The kids outside were forgotten for the moment. She had asked a question she wanted the answer to.

I worked with Valerie until her brother—an older one, not Larry—banged on the door and yelled, "Valerie, Mama say come do these dishes."

She left, taking another book with her, a step closer to being ready. I became aware of somebody else as Valerie left.

A woman coming down the driveway to my house. She spoke to Valerie in the kind of first grade language that the ten-year-old had come to know and dislike years ago.

"My, that's a big book you have there. Are you going to read all that?"

Valerie muttered something that might have been either "yes" or "no," leaped the distance between her porch and mine and disappeared into her house. She had left my door open, and the woman walked in like she owned the place. Organization woman. White, of course. White people came to the court to turn off the utilities, evict tenants, sell overpriced junk and take care of other equally savory kinds of business. This would be one of those other kinds. For once, I was glad of Valerie's youth and ignorance. She didn't know anything the organization could lift out of her thoughts and use against me.

I said, "Eve, if you don't know how to talk to kids why don't you just pass by without saying anything?"

"I was only trying to be pleasant to her because she's one of yours." She sat down uninvited and smoothed first her dress, then her hair. Her hair was long and when she was nervous she liked to fool with it. Now she was starting to twist a piece of it around her fingers.

"Did she think you were pleasant?"

Eve changed the subject. "We've missed you. We want you to come to a meeting today . . . if you have time."

"I don't." A lot of things I wouldn't like could happen to me at one of their meetings.

"Barbara, come. Really, if you don't there's going to be trouble."

"There'll be trouble no matter what. But I didn't know it was so close. Thanks for the warning." So they were finally getting worried enough about what I was doing to think about forcing me back to the fold.

She looked around at my so-called house and listened to the kids screaming outside. "What is it you're so willing to fight for? What do you have here that you couldn't have more of with us?"

"Valeries."

"I've told you before, Barbara, bring the children. We want them too."

"Do you? Are you sure? These are the same kids you wouldn't even consider before I left. You took one look into them and you couldn't get out fast enough."

"All right, we were wrong. You're the childfinder and we should have listened. Come back now and we will listen."

"I don't need you any more." The way they hadn't needed me before I started finding pre-psi kids. I know a lot about them, about the way they feel. The kind of things normal people can only guess about each other.

Silence for a moment. As silent as my court gets, anyway.

"So the others are right. You're forming an opposing organization."

"We won't oppose you unless we have to."

"A segregated Black only group. . . . Don't you see, you're setting yourself up for the same troubles that plague the normals."

"No. Until you get another childfinder, I don't think they'll be quite the same. More like reversed." I almost said, "How does it feel to be on the downside for a change." Almost. And to one of the new people—the next step for mankind.

Honest to God, that's the way they talked when I was with them. They had everything they needed then. Somebody to pull them all together—all the ones who had managed to mature on their own. The ones who had been solitary misfits, human trash, until they got together. I was one of them. I know just how low they were before someone with the talent to reach out and call them together matured. That led to the organization and the organization led me to find out that I hadn't been as mature as I thought. Led me to discover that I was the other thing they needed. Somebody who could recognize normal-appearing kids who had psi potential before they got too old and the potential in them died from lack of use. Originally the organization was a group of exceptions. Most pre-psi kids don't mature without help. That's why the organization had stayed the same size since the day I left it.

Eve was saying, "Sooner or later we're bound to get another childfinder."

That was true. Except that I was likely to see their childfinder before they did. I'd seen two white potential ones so far. I hate to hurt kids. I mean it. My specialty is helping them. But I crippled those two for good. The best they can hope for now —if they knew enough to hope—is to be normal with traces of psionic ability.

"Barbara." There was a change in Eve's voice that made me look at her. "I didn't want to say this, but . . . well, you can't watch *all* the kids you've collected *all* the time. Especially since you're still out looking for new ones. We would hate to do anything, but . . ."

They wouldn't hate it. And they wouldn't be careful. Where

I'd cripple a kid painlessly, they would kill him. After all that buildup about the organization wanting them.

"Don't come after my kids, Eve."

"Do you think I'd want to? Do you think it was my idea? You're the one who won't listen to reason. . . ."

"Don't come after my kids! You'll lose a lot more than you bargain for if you do. You'd be surprised how fast some of them are growing up. And they know a lot more about you than you know about them."

She got mad then and tried one of her organization tricks. Swiping at me. Trying to grab what I knew out of my thoughts before I could realize what she was doing and stop her. But who's more likely to know more about that kind of thing? Someone who spends months teaching it to kids, or someone who's had to be polite most of the time and pretend it doesn't exist? She didn't get a thing. Not even the satisfaction of taking me by surprise. So she left. Just like that. She got up and walked out.

I didn't reach after her until she was outside in the driveway. I meant to catch her just as she started to give way to her anger and let her guard down a little. I meant to show her how that little trick worked!

I never got to do it.

There were three organization men waiting in her car. She stood in the driveway and called them to her. Then she started back toward my house with them surrounding her. Her protection.

Three. And they weren't teachers. They were the world's first psionic brawlers. They fought among themselves mostly. Sparring, jockeying for position in the organization, fooling around. It kept them alert and in shape.

I never even thought of running. They were set to have too much fun as it was. Something like this had been bound to happen sooner or later anyway. I had known that for a long time.

The four of them came in and faced me silently. They didn't have to say anything.

I shrugged. "Do you mind if I get my things?"

They took long enough answering to have been doing some silent arguing about it. I wouldn't know for sure because I had shut myself up as tight as I could in my own head. Anything I let slip now, they would grab. I'd been bragging about how much my kids knew about the organization. Now, one slip and the organization would know all about my kids.

Eve. "I'll bring what you need, Barbara." She evidently spoke for all of them.

As they herded me toward the door, one of the men said, "How long did you think we'd let you get away with this shit anyway?"

I was making things too easy for him. He wanted to make me mad enough to do something stupid. Like dropping my guard.

I never had time to get mad. Just as the man finished speaking, one of the other two yelled. It would have taken me a little longer to realize what was going on without that yell. Not that the realization helped me.

The men and Eve fell to the floor unconscious before they could even spot their attackers. It happened so fast they appeared to fall in unison.

I stared down at them for a moment muttering, "Oh God!" Then I started to feel the anger that the organization man's question had not had time to bring. I had to force myself calm before I could come out of my mental shell.

The first thing I got when I did come out was an identity. Not a "my name is." Just a mental impression that I recognized like the sound of a familiar voice. I reached out.

Jordan.

Hey. His thought was easy, like his voice. *Why don't you let somebody know you in trouble? If we hadn't felt you closing yourself off a minute ago they would have had you and gone before we could do anything.*

Confusion. I didn't know what to feel. I was let down rather than relieved. And the fear that I had managed to conceal from my organization captors now had to be concealed from Jordan, because he wouldn't understand it any more than they would have. The only safe emotion was anger, and he didn't deserve that. He'd only been trying to help.

Jordan again. *You better get out of there now. The organization must know what we did to their pigs. They'll be sending twenty people after you instead of four.*

No doubt. He was seventeen. One of the first kids I'd found after leaving the organization. Not too long ago a college student from Kenya had told him he looked like a Watusi man. His head was still pretty big over that.

Jordan, let them come to. I sent the thought, knowing beforehand what his answer would be. He replied true to form.

What? Shit, they almost got you once! What you want to . . . ?

Looks to me like she wanted them to get her. Another identity. Jessie Mae. One of my developing childfinders and a lot better telepath than she ought to be at fifteen.

It had to happen sooner or later. I managed to make it no more than an unemotional statement of fact.

Like hell it did! Both of them and a lot of others besides. All the older ones were in on this. And in a way, that was good. Later nobody would be able to blame anybody else for whatever happened.

They know me, Jordan. I can't hide from them. They can find me wherever I am and they can use me to find you.

Jordan. *You don't have to hide from them. There's enough of us to stop them.*

Softly. *Man, I know there is. But it's not time yet. Because all you can do is stop them. How long do you think you can hold them? Or do you figure they'll all be as easy as these four?*

Silence. Belligerent mutterings. Little "we can take them right now" fantasies beginning to grow in several minds at once.

I shoved all the disgust I could into my next thought. *I thought I had managed to teach one or two of you something.* If you really put your heart in it, you can make a single mildly worded thought like that carry more slap than all the profanity you could use.

They all shut up. A couple of them jerked away from me in surprise as though they were dodging an expected blow.

I continued only a little more gently. *I thought I had taught you to look out for yourselves. To do what you had to to keep yourselves alive and together and hidden until you're too strong for the organization to touch.*

I paused for a moment. *You know you're in danger of being found every time you're with me. We're just lucky they took as long as they did to decide that we're something to worry about. Lucky they gave you time to . . .*

Time to get ready. Time to learn to make it on their own. Yeah. Start out strong like you're going to hit them if they don't behave. And then wind up carrying on worse than they are. Shit.

I was tired. Almost too tired to be afraid any more. *Jordan, bring them to me, please. And Jessie Mae, as soon as I leave, come get Valerie. She doesn't know anything, but I'm afraid of what they might do to her to find that out for sure.*

Jordan answered first. *Barbara, I'd sooner kill them now than let them get up and take you.*

Then Jessie Mae. *We need you! What happens to us if they take you?*

You . . . survive, honey. You don't need me. You already know about all I can teach you.

Abruptly Jessie Mae was projecting so intensely I could almost see her—tall, stronger than a girl was supposed to be, her face perpetually set in a defiant scowl. She hadn't cried since she was seven years old. *You're going to let them kill you. You're going to let them take you away and kill you!*

No I'm not.

You are! I'm not so dumb I can't see that!

You are dumb! Or you could see that they want me alive and well so I can work for them. They think. I can string them along as long as I have to. I could feel her disbelief like a rock in my mind. *Anyway . . . anyway, Jessie Mae, I swear to God I'm not going to let them kill me.*

She wavered slightly, less sure of herself. *Barbara . . .*

Do what I tell you, Jessie Mae, Jordan. Just do it. I closed them out to give them time to consider and to hide my half-lie before they saw it for what it was.

I wasn't exactly going to let the organization kill me. There was too much chance that they might learn something from me as I died. They would definitely try. And no amount of "stringing them along" would work long. Especially after this little show of strength the kids had put on. So in a couple of minutes, as soon as Jordan let Eve and her friends regain consciousness, I was going to forget everything I knew about pre-psi kids and finding them. Thinking about it, about forgetting, about erasing the thing that had become as important to me as breathing, brought my fear back full force. It was like saying I was going to kill myself. I almost envied those white kids I'd crippled. They never knew what they were losing.

But afraid or not, I was going to do it. I had started something that I wasn't going to let the organization stop. Partly because my kids deserved their chance. And partly because they were going to settle a lot of scores for me and a few million other people . . . someday.

On the floor one of the men groaned and opened his eyes.

Historians believe that an atmosphere of tolerance and peace would be a natural outgrowth of a psionic society.

Records of the fate of the psis are sketchy. Legend tells us that they were all victims of a disease to which they were particularly vulnerable. Whatever happened, we may be sure that their civilization is one that was destroyed by purely external forces.

                    Psi: History of a Vanished People

Afterword

"Childfinder" is the product of Harlan Ellison week at the Clarion Science Fiction Writers' Workshop. It is also the product of my generally pessimistic outlook. After a few years of watching the human species make things unnecessarily difficult for itself I have little hope that it will do anything more than survive and continue its cycle of errors. An incident from my own childhood illustrates my point.

When I was little my mother worked and I was often left with one of my aunts or my grandmother. Sometimes when this happened, I would disagree with whichever of my cousins I found myself with. If the disagreement was noisy enough, whoever was in charge of us would come to the door and warn, "Now you all get along out there! No fighting!" We would stop obediently and wait until she went away before we resumed the fight. Aunt or grandmother, she always seemed surprised when one of us came in bloody.

After such an experience, I am surprised to find myself writing the same kind of warning in "Childfinder." "Get along out there! No fighting!" But in at least one way I'm different from my aunts and my grandmother. I know no one's listening.

Crossover

A T WORK that day, they put her to soldering J9 connectors into a harness, and they expected her to do twice as many as everyone else. She did, of course, but her only reward was resentment from the slower girls down the line because she was making them look bad. At lunch a couple of them came to her solitary corner table and told her to ease off. That was how it was. If she did good work, other employees resented her and her lead man ignored her. If her work fell off, other employees ignored her and her lead man wrote "bad attitude" on her work review. She hadn't had a raise in two years. She would have quit long ago had she not been afraid to try to start all over again at a new place where the people might be even worse.

Through the afternoon all she wanted was two or three aspirins and sleep. She had not had a headache for three months and this one scared her.

As usual, though, she managed to finish the day. When she got off she even felt hungry enough to make a side trip to the store for a can of something for dinner. It was her headache that drove her to make the shorter trip to the liquor store instead of going to the grocery store. *It was her headache.*

The liquor store was on a corner only two blocks from where she worked. It was across from a pool hall and a bar and near a cheap hotel. That made it a gathering place for certain kinds of people.

There was a crowd on the corner when she got there. Besides the usual drunks and prostitutes, there was a group of teenage boys who were bored enough not to ignore her. For a moment they whispered to each other, laughing. Then as she passed them, the calls began.

"Hey, Jeffery, there go your old woman!"

"Lady, you sure shouldn't have let that car run over you face!"

"Hey, lady, this boy say he go for you!"

A wino sidled up to her. "Come on, baby, let's you and me go up to my room."

She jerked herself out of the alcoholic cloud that surrounded him and went into the store. The clerk there was rude to her because he was rude to everyone. He did not matter any more than the others. The wino tried to catch her by the arm as she left.

"Come on, you not in too big a hurry to talk to me. . . ." She almost ran from him, barely controlling her disgust. She left him standing, swaying slightly in the middle of the street, staring after her.

As she neared the hotel she noticed someone standing in the narrow doorway. A man who had something wrong with his face. *Something* . . . She almost turned and went back toward the drunk. But the man stepped out and came over to her during her moment of hesitation. She looked around quickly, her eyes wide with fear. No one was paying any particular attention to her. Even the wino had begun to move away.

The man said, "I don't go away if you ignore me." He had a scar that ran the length of his face from eye to chin on the left side. When he talked or smiled or frowned, it moved and she could watch it and ignore everything else. Sometimes she could even avoid listening to him. Now she watched it and thought quickly.

"So you got out." There was nothing but bitterness in her voice.

He laughed and the scar curved, wormlike. "This morning. I expected you to be there to meet me."

"No you didn't. I told you three months ago you could stay locked up forever as far as I was concerned."

"And you didn't mean it then either. Ninety days. That's a long time."

"You should have thought about that before you got into the fight."

"Yeah. Man hits me and pulls a knife. I had all the time in the world to remember you didn't want me fighting." He paused. "You know, you could have come to see me just once while I was in."

"I'm sorry." Toneless. False without any attempt to hide the falseness.

He made a sound of disgust. "The day you're sorry for anything . . ."

"All right, I'm not sorry. I don't give a damn." She narrowed her eyes and threw the words at him. "Why don't you go find a girl who will come to see you next time you get put away?"

The scar hardly moved when he spoke. "Things changed that much in three months?"

"They changed that much."

"You find somebody else to kind of help you forget about me?"

Now she laughed, once, with absolute bitterness. "Not one, baby, dozens! Didn't you see them all back there on the corner? They couldn't wait to get to me!"

Quietly: "All right. All right, be quiet." He put an arm around her and walked with her toward her apartment.

Later, when they had eaten and made love, she sat head in hands trying not to think while he talked at her. She paid no attention until he asked a question that she wanted to answer.

"Don't you ever wish for a decent-looking guy to come and get you out of that factory and out of this dump you live in . . . and away from me?"

"What would a decent-looking guy want with me?"

Instead of answering he said, "You still have that bottle of sleeping pills in your medicine cabinet?"

When she did not answer, he went to look. "Nonprescription now," he said when he came back. "What happened to the others?"

"I poured them down the toilet."

"Why?"

Again she did not answer.

After a moment, he said more gently, "When?"

"When I . . . when they put you in jail."

"And you acted like you didn't expect to see me again."

She shook her head. "I didn't."

"I don't want to die any more than you do."

She jumped and glanced at him. He knew better than to talk like that. He did it to hurt her. That was all.

She said, "I'd rather be dead than here picking up where we left off three months ago."

"Then why'd you throw out the pills?"

"So I would live. Without you."

He smiled. "And when did you decide you couldn't?"

She threw the heavy glass ashtray beside the bed. It flew wide of him, dented the wall behind him, and broke into three pieces.

He looked from the pieces to her. "You would have made your point better if you had tried to hit me."

She began to cry and she was not aware when the crying became screaming. "Get out of here! Leave me alone! *Leave me alone!*"

He didn't move.

Then her neighbor was pounding on the door to find out what all the noise was about. She calmed herself enough to open it, but while she was reassuring the woman that everything was all right, he came up behind her and stood there. She did not have to look around to know he was there. Still, she did not come near losing control until her neighbor said, "You must be lonesome over here by yourself. Why don't you come around to my apartment and talk for a while?"

It was as though her neighbor were playing a stupid childish joke on her. It should have been a joke. Somehow, she got rid of the woman without breaking down.

Then she turned and stared at the man—at the scar marring a face that had never been handsome. She shook her head, crying again but paying no attention to her tears. He seemed to know better than to touch her.

After a while she got her coat and started out the door.

"I'm going with you."

The look she gave him contained all the stored-up viciousness of the day. "Do whatever you want." She saw fear in his eyes for the first time.

"Where are you going?"

She said, "You didn't have to meet me on the street today. Or come to the door just now. You didn't have to talk about . . ."

"Jane, where are you going?"

There were few things she hated more than her own name. In all the time they had been together, he could not have used it more than twice. She slammed the door in his face.

"What am I that I could need you anyway?" She wished she had said the words to him but it didn't matter. It was just another of the things she didn't have the courage to do. Like accepting the loneliness or dying or . . .

She retraced her steps back to the liquor store. The boys had gone, but the wino was still there leaning against a telephone pole and holding a bag shaped by the bottle inside it.

"So you come back, huh?" He couldn't stand at a distance and talk. He had to put his face right up next to hers. It was an act of will for her not to vomit.

He thrust the bag at her. "You can have a little bit if you want. I got some more in my room. . . ."

She stared at the bottle for a moment, then almost snatched it from him. She drank without giving herself time to taste or think or gag. She had lived around drunks most of her life. She knew that if she could get enough down, nothing would matter.

She let the wino guide her toward the hotel. There was a scar-faced man coming toward them from down the block. She sucked another swallow from the bottle and waited for him to vanish.

Afterword

In the terrible little jobs that I used to get at factories, warehouses, food-processing plants, offices, and retail outlets, there always seemed to be at least one or two very odd people. Everyone knew about them. Sometimes they were actually on medication; sometimes not. But with or without medication, they had serious, noticeable problems.

I lived in terror of joining them. Those grindingly dull jobs, I thought, were capable of sending anyone up the wall. I suspect most of my coworkers thought I was already pretty strange. I spent my breaks writing, or I was tired and cranky from getting up early in the morning to write at home.

"Crossover" not only grew out of that time but was written during that time. It was written during the summer of 1970 at Clarion Science Fiction and Fantasy Writers' Workshop. When I went to Clarion I hadn't sold any of my stories. Then Robin Scott Wilson, at the time director of Clarion, bought "Crossover," and Harlan Ellison bought another of my stories. I was overjoyed. I thought I was on my way as a writer. No more failure and scut work. In fact, I had five more years of rejection slips and horrible little jobs ahead of me before I sold another word.

I didn't wind up hallucinating or turning to alcohol as the character in "Crossover" does, but I did keep noticing the company oddities everywhere I worked, and they went right on scaring me back to the typewriter whenever I strayed.

Near of Kin

"SHE WANTED you," my uncle said. "She didn't have to have a child, you know. Not even twenty-two years ago."

"I know." I sat down opposite him in a comfortable wooden rocking chair in the living room of my mother's apartment. At my feet were papers stuffed into a large cardboard lettuce box—papers loose and dog-eared, flat and enveloped, important and trivial, all jumbled together. Here was her marriage certificate, the deed to property she'd owned in Oregon, a handmade card done in green and red crayon on cheap age-darkened paper—"To Mama," it said. "Merry Christmas." I had made it when I was six and given it to my grandmother whom I called mama then. Now I wondered whether my grandmother had passed it on to my mother along with a kindly lie.

"She was widowed just before you were born," my uncle said. "She just couldn't face caring for a child all alone."

"People do it all the time," I said.

"She wasn't 'people,' she was herself. She knew what she could handle and what she couldn't. She saw to it that you had a good home with your grandmother."

I looked at him, wondering why he still bothered to defend her. What difference did it make now what I felt for her—or didn't feel. "I remember when I was about eight," I said. "She came to see me, and I asked if I could stay with her for awhile. She said I couldn't, said she had to work, didn't have room, didn't have enough money, and a lot of other things. The message I got was that she didn't want to be bothered with me. So I asked her if she was really my mother or if maybe I was adopted."

My uncle winced. "What did she say?"

"Nothing. She hit me."

He sighed. "That temper of hers. She was too nervous, too high-strung. That was one of the reasons she left you with your grandmother."

"What were the others?"

"I think you just listed them. Lack of money, space, time . . ."

"Patience, love . . ."

My uncle shrugged. "Is that what you wanted to talk to me about? All your reasons for disliking your mother?"

"No."

"Well?"

I stared at the box on the floor. The bottom of it had broken with the weight of the papers when I took it from my mother's closet. Maybe there was masking tape somewhere in the apartment. I got up to look, thinking my uncle might get tired of my silence and leave. He did that sometimes—his own quiet form of impatience. It used to scare me when I was little. Now, I would have almost welcomed it. If he left, I wouldn't have to tell him what I wanted to talk to him about . . . yet. He had always been a friend as well as a relative—my mother's five-years-older brother, and the only relative other than my grandmother who'd ever paid more than passing attention to me. He used to talk to me sometimes at my grandmother's house. He treated me like a little adult, because in spite of all the children his married brothers and sisters had, no one had ever convinced him that children were not little adults. He put a lot of pressure on me without realizing he was doing it, but still, I preferred him to the other aunts and uncles, to the old ladies who were my grandmother's friends, to anyone who had ever patted me on the head and told me to be a good little girl. I got along better with him than I had with my mother, so even now, especially now, I didn't want to lose him.

He was still there when I found the tape in a kitchen drawer. He hadn't moved except to take a paper out of the box. He sat reading it while I struggled to tape the box. It was awkward, but I didn't expect him to help me unless I asked—any other male relative, perhaps, but not him.

"What is that?" I asked, glancing at the paper.

"One of your report cards. Fifth grade. Bad."

"Oh God. Throw it out."

"Don't you wonder why she kept it?"

"No. She . . . I think I understood her a little. I think she liked having had a child—I don't know, to prove her womanliness or something, and to see what she could produce. But once she had me, she didn't want to waste her time raising me."

"She had had four miscarriages before you, you know."

"She told me."

"And she did pay attention to you."

"Sometimes. Like whenever I got one of those rotten report cards, she would come over and bawl me out."

"Is that why you got them? To make her angry?"

"I got them because I didn't care one way or the other—until the day you came over and bawled me out and scared the hell out of me. Then I started to care."

"Wait a moment, I remember that. I wasn't trying to scare you. I just thought you had a brain and weren't using it, and I told you so."

"You did. You sat there looking angry and disgusted, and I was afraid you'd given up on me altogether." I glanced at him. "You see? Even if I wasn't adopted, you were. I had to make sure I hung on to you."

That got as much of a smile out of him as anything ever did, and the smile took years off him. He was fifty-seven now, slender, fine boned, still handsome. Everyone in my mother's family was that way—small, almost fragile looking. It made the women attractive. I thought it made the men attractive too, but I knew it had caused my male cousins to spend too much of their time fighting and showing off, trying to prove they were men. It had made them touchy and defensive. I don't know what it had done to this particular uncle when he was a boy, but he wasn't defensive now. If you made him angry, he could deliver an icy verbal shredding. If that wasn't enough, he could handle himself in a fight too—or he could when he was younger—but I had never seen him start trouble. My cousins disliked him, claimed he was ice-cold even when he wasn't angry. When I disagreed with them, they told me I was cold too. What difference did it make? My uncle and I got along comfortably together.

"What are you going to do with her things?" he asked.

"Sell them, give them to the Salvation Army, I don't know. Do you see anything you want?"

He got up and went into the bedroom, moving with that smooth, quick grace of his that time didn't seem to touch. He came back with a picture from my mother's dresser—an enlargement of a snapshot he had taken of my mother, grandmother, and me at Knott's Berry Farm when I was about twelve. Somehow, he had gotten us together and taken us all out for a treat. The picture was the only one I knew of that contained the three of us.

"It would have been better if you had gotten into that photo too," I said. "You should have had some stranger take the picture."

"No, you three look right together—three generations. Are you sure you don't want to keep this picture—or a copy of it?"

I shook my head. "It's yours. Don't you want anything else?"

"No. What are you going to do about that Oregon property? And I think she owned some in Arizona, too."

"Everywhere but here," I muttered. "After all, if she'd used her money to buy a house here, I might have moved in on her. Where did all that money come from anyway? She was supposed to be so damn poor!"

"She's dead," said my uncle flatly. "How much more time and energy are you going to waste resenting her?"

"As little as possible," I said. "I can't quite turn it off like a water faucet though."

"Turn it off when I'm around. She was my sister and I loved her if you didn't." He said it very quietly, mildly.

"Okay."

There was a silence until one of my aunts arrived. She hugged me when I let her in and cried all over me. I endured her because my mother had been her sister, too. She was a tiresome woman who used to visit my grandmother to talk about how gifted her own kids were while she patted me on the head and treated me like the family idiot.

"Stephen," she greeted my uncle. He hated his first name. "What do you have there? A picture. Isn't that nice. Barbara was so pretty then. She was always a beauty. So natural at the funeral . . ."

She wandered into the bedroom and began going through my mother's things. At the closet, she sighed. She was at least twenty pounds heavier than my mother, though I could remember when they were the same size.

"What are you going to do with all these lovely things?" she asked me. "You should save some of them as keepsakes."

"Should I?" I said. I was going to get rid of all of them as soon as possible, of course—bundle them off to the Salvation Army. But this aunt, who had disapproved self-righteously of my mother's unmotherly behavior for years, would be outraged now if I seemed unsentimental about my mother's things.

"Stephen, are you helping out?" my aunt asked.

"No," said my uncle softly.

"Just keeping company, hmm? That's nice. Is there anything I can do?"

"Nothing," said my uncle—which was strange because the question had clearly been directed at me. She looked at him a little surprised, and he looked back expressionlessly.

"Well . . . if you need me for anything, you be sure and call me." She had gathered up a few pieces of my mother's jewelry. Now she grabbed the little black-and-white television. "You don't mind if I take this, do you? My younger kids fight so much over the TV. . . ." She left.

My uncle looked after her and shook his head.

"She's your sister, too," I said, smiling.

"If she wasn't . . . Never mind."

"What?"

"Nothing." That soft warning voice again. I ignored it.

"I know. She's a hypocrite—among other things. I think she liked my mother even less than I did."

"Why did you let her take those things?"

I looked at him. "Because I don't care what happens to anything in this apartment. I just don't care."

"Well . . ." He took a deep breath. "You're no hypocrite, at least. Your mother left a will, you know."

"A will?"

"That property is fairly valuable. She left it to you."

"How do you know?"

"I have a copy of the will. She didn't trust anyone to find it in her things." He waved a hand toward the cardboard box. "Her brand of filing wasn't very dependable."

I nodded unhappily. "It sure wasn't. I don't have any idea what she has here. But look, isn't there any way you could take that property? I don't want it."

"She wanted to do something for you. Let her do it."

"But . . ."

"Let her do it."

I drew a deep breath, then let it out. "Did she leave you anything?"

"No."

"That doesn't seem right."

"I'm content—or I will be when you take what she's given you. There's some money, too."

I frowned, unable to imagine my mother saving any money. I hadn't even found out about the property until I began going through her things. The money was a little too much. But, at least, it gave me the opening I needed. "Is this money from her," I asked him, "or from you?"

He hesitated just for a second, then said, "It's in her will." But there was something wrong with the way he said it—as though I'd caught him a little off guard.

I smiled, but stopped when that seemed to make him uncomfortable. I didn't want to make him uncomfortable. I was going to—I had to—but I didn't look forward to it or take any pleasure in it.

"You're not devious," I told him. "You look as though you could be. You look secretive and controlled."

"I can't help the way I look."

"People tell me I look that way, too."

"No, you look like your mother."

"I think not. I think I look like my father."

He said nothing, just stared at me, frowning. I fingered a few of the dog-eared papers in the box. "Shall I still take the money?"

He did not answer. He only watched me in that way of his that people called cold. It wasn't—I knew what he was like when he was really cold. Now, it was more as though he were in pain, as though I were hurting him. I supposed I was, but I couldn't stop. It was too late to stop. I pressed my fingers nervously into the jumble of papers, then looked down at them for a moment, suddenly resenting them. Why hadn't I stayed at college and left them, left everything to other relatives the way she had always left me to other relatives? Or, having come here like a responsible daughter to wind up my mother's affairs, why hadn't I done just that and kept my mouth shut? What would he do now? Leave? Would I lose him, too?

"I don't care," I said not looking at him. "It doesn't matter. I love you." I had said that to him before dozens of times, obscurely. But I had never said it in just those three words. It was as though I were asking permission somehow. *Is it all right for me to love you?*

"What have you got in that box?" he asked softly.

I frowned for a moment, not understanding. Then I realized what he thought—what my nervousness had made him think. "Nothing about this," I said, "at least nothing that I know of. Don't worry, I don't think she would have written anything down."

"Then how did you know?"

"I didn't know, I guessed. I guessed a long time ago."

"How?"

I kicked at the box. "There were a lot of things," I said. "I guess the easiest one to explain is the way we look, you and I. You should compare one of Grandmother's pictures of you as a young man with my face now—we could be twins. My mother was beautiful; her husband, from his pictures, was a big, handsome man—me . . . I just look like you."

"That doesn't have to mean anything."

"I know. But it meant a lot to me, together with some other less tangible things."

"A guess," he said bitterly. He leaned forward. "I'm really not very devious, am I?" He stood up, started toward the door. I got up quickly to block his way. We were the same height, exactly.

"Please don't go," I said. "Please."

He tried to put me aside gently, but I wouldn't move.

"Say it?" I insisted. "I'll never ask you again, nor will I ever repeat it. She's dead; it can't hurt her anymore." I hesitated. "Please don't walk away from me."

He sighed, looked at the floor for a moment, then at me. "Yes," he said softly.

I let him go and found myself almost crying with relief. I had a father, then. I didn't feel as though I'd ever had a mother, but I had a father. "Thank you," I whispered.

"No one knows," he said. "Not your grandmother, not any of the relatives."

"They won't find out from me."

"No. I never worried about your telling others. I never worried about others except for the pain they might cause her and you—and the pain it might cause you . . . to know."

"I'm not in pain."

"No." He looked at me with what seemed to be amazement and I realized that he had been at least as frightened as I had.

"How did she have her husband's name put on my birth certificate?" I asked.

"By lying. It was a believable lie—her husband was alive when you were conceived. He had left her, but the family didn't find out about that until later, never found out about the timing."

"Did he leave because of you?"

"No. He left because he had found someone else—someone who had borne him a live child instead of having a miscarriage. She came to me when he left—came to talk, to cry, to work out some of her feelings. . . ." He shrugged. "She and I were always close—too close." He shrugged again. "We loved each other. If it had been possible, I would have married her. I don't care how that sounds, I would have done it. As it was, we were afraid when she realized she was pregnant, but she wanted you. There was never any question about that."

I didn't believe him, even now. I believed what I had said before—that she had wanted a child to prove she was woman enough to have one. Once she had her proof, she went on to other things. But he had loved her and I loved him. I said nothing.

"She was always afraid you would find out," he said. "That was why she couldn't bring herself to keep you with her."

"She was ashamed of me."

"She was ashamed of herself."

I looked at him, trying to read his unreadable face. "Were you?"

He nodded. "Of myself—never of you."

"But you didn't just drop me the way she did."

"She didn't drop you either; she couldn't. Why do you think she was so upset when you asked her if you were adopted?"

I shook my head. "She should have trusted me. She should have been more like you."

"She did the best she could as herself."

"I would have loved her. I wouldn't have cared."

"Knowing you, I think you might not have. She couldn't quite believe that though. She couldn't take the chance."

"Do you love me?"

"Yes. So did she, though you don't believe it."

"She and I . . . we should have gotten to know each other. We never did, really."

"No." There was silence, and he looked over at the box of papers. "If you find anything in there that you can't handle, bring it to me."

"All right."

"I'll call you about the will. Are you going back to school?"

"Yes."

He gave me one of his small smiles. "Then you'll need the money, won't you? I don't want to hear any more nonsense about your not taking it." He left, closing the door silently behind him.

Afterword

First of all, "Near of Kin" has *nothing* to do with my novel *Kindred*. I said this to the editor who originally accepted the story for his anthology, but all he remembered was that I had two works with similar titles, and therefore, they must be related. Not at all.

"Near of Kin" grew from my Baptist childhood and my habit, even then, of letting my interests lead me wherever they would. As a good Baptist kid, I read the Bible first as a series of instructions as to how I should believe and behave, then as bits of verse that I was required to memorize, then as a series of interesting, interconnected stories.

The stories got me: stories of conflict, betrayal, torture, murder, exile, and incest. I read them avidly. This was, of course, not exactly what my mother had in mind when she encouraged me to read the Bible. Nevertheless, I found these things fascinating, and when I began writing, I explored these themes in my own stories. "Near of Kin" is one of the odder results of this interest. I remember trying to write it when I was in college, and failing. The idea stayed with me, demanding to be written: A sympathetic story of incest. My examples were Lot's daughters, Abraham's sister-wife, and the sons of Adam with the daughters of Eve.

Speech Sounds

THERE WAS trouble aboard the Washington Boulevard bus. Rye had expected trouble sooner or later in her journey. She had put off going until loneliness and hopelessness drove her out. She believed she might have one group of relatives left alive—a brother and his two children twenty miles away in Pasadena. That was a day's journey one-way, if she were lucky. The unexpected arrival of the bus as she left her Virginia Road home had seemed to be a piece of luck—until the trouble began.

Two young men were involved in a disagreement of some kind, or, more likely, a misunderstanding. They stood in the aisle, grunting and gesturing at each other, each in his own uncertain T stance as the bus lurched over the potholes. The driver seemed to be putting some effort into keeping them off balance. Still, their gestures stopped just short of contact—mock punches, hand games of intimidation to replace lost curses.

People watched the pair, then looked at one another and made small anxious sounds. Two children whimpered.

Rye sat a few feet behind the disputants and across from the back door. She watched the two carefully, knowing the fight would begin when someone's nerve broke or someone's hand slipped or someone came to the end of his limited ability to communicate. These things could happen anytime.

One of them happened as the bus hit an especially large pothole and one man, tall, thin, and sneering, was thrown into his shorter opponent.

Instantly, the shorter man drove his left fist into the disintegrating sneer. He hammered his larger opponent as though he neither had nor needed any weapon other than his left fist. He hit quickly enough, hard enough to batter his opponent down before the taller man could regain his balance or hit back even once.

People screamed or squawked in fear. Those nearby scrambled to get out of the way. Three more young men roared in excitement and gestured wildly. Then, somehow, a second dispute broke out between two of these three—probably because one inadvertently touched or hit the other.

As the second fight scattered frightened passengers, a woman shook the driver's shoulder and grunted as she gestured toward the fighting.

The driver grunted back through bared teeth. Frightened, the woman drew away.

Rye, knowing the methods of bus drivers, braced herself and held on to the crossbar of the seat in front of her. When the driver hit the brakes, she was ready and the combatants were not. They fell over seats and onto screaming passengers, creating even more confusion. At least one more fight started.

The instant the bus came to a full stop, Rye was on her feet, pushing the back door. At the second push, it opened and she jumped out, holding her pack in one arm. Several other passengers followed, but some stayed on the bus. Buses were so rare and irregular now, people rode when they could, no matter what. There might not be another bus today—or tomorrow. People started walking, and if they saw a bus they flagged it down. People making intercity trips like Rye's from Los Angeles to Pasadena made plans to camp out, or risked seeking shelter with locals who might rob or murder them.

The bus did not move, but Rye moved away from it. She intended to wait until the trouble was over and get on again, but if there was shooting, she wanted the protection of a tree. Thus, she was near the curb when a battered blue Ford on the other side of the street made a U-turn and pulled up in front of the bus. Cars were rare these days—as rare as a severe shortage of fuel and of relatively unimpaired mechanics could make them. Cars that still ran were as likely to be used as weapons as they were to serve as transportation. Thus, when the driver of the Ford beckoned to Rye, she moved away warily. The driver got out—a big man, young, neatly bearded with dark, thick hair. He wore a long overcoat and a look of wariness that matched Rye's. She stood several feet from him, waiting to see what he would do. He looked at the bus, now rocking with the combat inside, then at the small cluster of passengers who had gotten off. Finally he looked at Rye again.

She returned his gaze, very much aware of the old forty-five automatic her jacket concealed. She watched his hands.

He pointed with his left hand toward the bus. The dark-tinted windows prevented him from seeing what was happening inside.

His use of the left hand interested Rye more than his obvious question. Left-handed people tended to be less impaired, more reasonable and comprehending, less driven by frustration, confusion, and anger.

She imitated his gesture, pointing toward the bus with her own left hand, then punching the air with both fists.

The man took off his coat revealing a Los Angeles Police Department uniform complete with baton and service revolver.

Rye took another step back from him. There was no more LAPD, no more *any* large organization, governmental or private. There were neighborhood patrols and armed individuals. That was all.

The man took something from his coat pocket, then threw the coat into the car. Then he gestured Rye back, back toward the rear of the bus. He had something made of plastic in his hand. Rye did not understand what he wanted until he went to the rear door of the bus and beckoned her to stand there. She obeyed mainly out of curiosity. Cop or not, maybe he could do something to stop the stupid fighting.

He walked around the front of the bus, to the street side where the driver's window was open. There, she thought she saw him throw something into the bus. She was still trying to peer through the tinted glass when people began stumbling out the rear door, choking and weeping. Gas.

Rye caught an old woman who would have fallen, lifted two little children down when they were in danger of being knocked down and trampled. She could see the bearded man helping people at the front door. She caught a thin old man shoved out by one of the combatants. Staggered by the old man's weight, she was barely able to get out of the way as the last of the young men pushed his way out. This one, bleeding from nose and mouth, stumbled into another, and they grappled blindly, still sobbing from the gas.

The bearded man helped the bus driver out through the front door, though the driver did not seem to appreciate his help. For a moment, Rye thought there would be another fight. The bearded man stepped back and watched the driver gesture threateningly, watched him shout in wordless anger.

The bearded man stood still, made no sound, refused to respond to clearly obscene gestures. The least impaired people tended to do this—stand back unless they were physically threatened and let those with less control scream and jump around. It was as though they felt it beneath them to be as touchy as the less comprehending. This was an attitude of superiority, and that was the way people like the bus driver perceived it. Such "superiority" was frequently punished by beatings, even by death. Rye had had close calls of her own. As a result, she never went unarmed. And in this world where the only likely common language was body language, being armed was often enough. She had rarely had to draw her gun or even display it.

The bearded man's revolver was on constant display. Apparently that was enough for the bus driver. The driver spat in disgust, glared at the bearded man for a moment longer, then strode back to his gas-filled bus. He stared at it for a moment, clearly wanting to get in, but the gas was still too strong. Of the windows, only his tiny driver's window actually opened. The front door was open, but the rear door would not stay open unless someone held it. Of course, the air conditioning had failed long ago. The bus would take some time to clear. It was the driver's property, his livelihood. He had pasted old magazine pictures of items he would accept as fare on its sides. Then he would use what he collected to feed his family or to trade. If his bus did not run, he did not eat. On the other hand, if the inside of his bus was torn apart by senseless fighting, he would not eat very well either. He was apparently unable to perceive this. All he could see was that it would be some time before he could use his bus again. He shook his fist at the bearded man and shouted. There seemed to be words in his shout, but Rye could not understand them. She did not know whether this was his fault or hers. She had heard so little coherent human speech for the past three years, she was no longer certain how well she recognized it, no longer certain of the degree of her own impairment.

The bearded man sighed. He glanced toward his car, then beckoned to Rye. He was ready to leave, but he wanted something from her first. No. No, he wanted her to leave with him. Risk getting into his car when, in spite of his uniform, law and order were nothing—not even words any longer.

She shook her head in a universally understood negative, but the man continued to beckon.

She waved him away. He was doing what the less impaired rarely did—drawing potentially negative attention to another of his kind. People from the bus had begun to look at her.

One of the men who had been fighting tapped another on the arm, then pointed from the bearded man to Rye, and finally held up the first two fingers of his right hand as though giving two-thirds of a Boy Scout salute. The gesture was very quick, its meaning obvious even at a distance. She had been grouped with the bearded man. Now what?

The man who had made the gesture started toward her.

She had no idea what he intended, but she stood her ground. The man was half a foot taller than she was and perhaps ten years younger. She did not imagine she could outrun him. Nor did she expect anyone to help her if she needed help. The people around her were all strangers.

She gestured once—a clear indication to the man to stop. She did not intend to repeat the gesture. Fortunately, the man obeyed. He gestured obscenely and several other men laughed. Loss of verbal language had spawned a whole new set of obscene gestures. The man, with stark simplicity, had accused her of sex with the bearded man and had suggested she accommodate the other men present—beginning with him.

Rye watched him wearily. People might very well stand by and watch if he tried to rape her. They would also stand and watch her shoot him. Would he push things that far?

He did not. After a series of obscene gestures that brought him no closer to her, he turned contemptuously and walked away.

And the bearded man still waited. He had removed his service revolver, holster and all. He beckoned again, both hands empty. No doubt his gun was in the car and within easy reach, but his taking it off impressed her. Maybe he was all right. Maybe he was just alone. She had been alone herself for three years. The illness had stripped her, killing her children one by one, killing her husband, her sister, her parents. . . .

The illness, if it was an illness, had cut even the living off from one another. As it swept over the country, people hardly had time to lay blame on the Soviets (though they were falling silent along with the rest of the world), on a new virus, a new pollutant, radiation, divine retribution. . . . The illness was stroke-swift in the way it cut people down and strokelike in some of its effects. But it was highly specific. Language was always lost or severely impaired. It was never regained. Often there was also paralysis, intellectual impairment, death.

Rye walked toward the bearded man, ignoring the whistling and applauding of two of the young men and their thumbs-up signs to the bearded man. If he had smiled at them or acknowledged them in any way, she would almost certainly have changed her mind. If she had let herself think of the possible deadly consequences of getting into a stranger's car, she would have changed her mind. Instead, she thought of the man who lived across the street from her. He rarely washed since his bout with the illness. And he had gotten into the habit of urinating wherever he happened to be. He had two women already—one tending each of his large gardens. They put up with him in exchange for his protection. He had made it clear that he wanted Rye to become his third woman.

She got into the car and the bearded man shut the door. She watched as he walked around to the driver's door—watched for his sake because his gun was on the seat beside her. And the bus driver and a pair of young men had come a few steps closer. They did nothing, though, until the bearded man was in the car. Then one of them threw a rock. Others followed his example, and as the car drove away, several rocks bounced off harmlessly.

When the bus was some distance behind them, Rye wiped sweat from her forehead and longed to relax. The bus would have taken her more than halfway to Pasadena. She would have had only ten miles to walk. She wondered how far she would have to walk now—and wondered if walking a long distance would be her only problem.

At Figueroa and Washington where the bus normally made a left turn, the bearded man stopped, looked at her, and indicated that she should choose a direction. When she directed him left and he actually turned left, she began to relax. If he was willing to go where she directed, perhaps he was safe.

As they passed blocks of burned, abandoned buildings, empty lots, and wrecked or stripped cars, he slipped a gold chain over his head and handed it to her. The pendant attached to it was a smooth, glassy, black rock. Obsidian. His name might be Rock or Peter or Black, but she decided to think of him as Obsidian. Even her sometimes useless memory would retain a name like Obsidian.

She handed him her own name symbol—a pin in the shape of a large golden stalk of wheat. She had bought it long before the illness and the silence began. Now she wore it, thinking it was as close as she was likely to come to Rye. People like Obsidian who had not known her before probably thought of her as Wheat. Not that it mattered. She would never hear her name spoken again.

Obsidian handed her pin back to her. He caught her hand as she reached for it and rubbed his thumb over her calluses.

He stopped at First Street and asked which way again. Then, after turning right as she had indicated, he parked near the Music Center. There, he took a folded paper from the dashboard and unfolded it. Rye recognized it as a street map, though the writing on it meant nothing to her. He flattened the map, took her hand again, and put her index finger on one spot. He touched her, touched himself, pointed toward the floor. In effect, "We are here." She knew he wanted to know where she was going. She wanted to tell him, but she shook her head sadly. She had lost reading and writing. That was her most serious impairment and her most painful. She had taught history at UCLA. She had done freelance writing. Now she could not even read her own manuscripts. She had a houseful of books that she could neither read nor bring herself to use as fuel. And she had a memory that would not bring back to her much of what she had read before.

She stared at the map, trying to calculate. She had been born in Pasadena, had lived for fifteen years in Los Angeles. Now she was near L.A. Civic Center. She knew the relative positions of the two cities, knew streets, directions, even knew to stay away from freeways, which might be blocked by wrecked cars and destroyed overpasses. She ought to know how to point out Pasadena even though she could not recognize the word.

Hesitantly, she placed her hand over a pale orange patch in the upper right corner of the map. That should be right. Pasadena.

Obsidian lifted her hand and looked under it, then folded the map and put it back on the dashboard. He could read, she realized belatedly. He could probably write, too. Abruptly, she hated him—deep, bitter hatred. What did literacy mean to him—a grown man who played cops and robbers? But he was literate and she was not. She never would be. She felt sick to her stomach with hatred, frustration, and jealousy. And only a few inches from her hand was a loaded gun.

She held herself still, staring at him, almost seeing his blood. But her rage crested and ebbed and she did nothing.

Obsidian reached for her hand with hesitant familiarity. She looked at him. Her face had already revealed too much. No person still living in what was left of human society could fail to recognize that expression, that jealousy.

She closed her eyes wearily, drew a deep breath. She had experienced longing for the past, hatred of the present, growing hopelessness, purposelessness, but she had never experienced such a powerful urge to kill another person. She had left her home, finally, because she had come near to killing herself. She had found no reason to stay alive. Perhaps that was why she had gotten into Obsidian's car. She had never before done such a thing.

He touched her mouth and made chatter motions with thumb and fingers. Could she speak?

She nodded and watched his milder envy come and go. Now both had admitted what it was not safe to admit, and there had been no violence. He tapped his mouth and forehead and shook his head. He did not speak or comprehend spoken language. The illness had played with them, taking away, she suspected, what each valued most.

She plucked at his sleeve, wondering why he had decided on his own to keep the LAPD alive with what he had left. He was sane enough otherwise. Why wasn't he at home raising corn, rabbits, and children? But she did not know how to ask. Then he put his hand on her thigh and she had another question to deal with.

She shook her head. Disease, pregnancy, helpless, solitary agony . . . no.

He massaged her thigh gently and smiled in obvious disbelief.

No one had touched her for three years. She had not wanted

anyone to touch her. What kind of world was this to chance bringing a child into even if the father were willing to stay and help raise it? It was too bad, though. Obsidian could not know how attractive he was to her—young, probably younger than she was, clean, asking for what he wanted rather than demanding it. But none of that mattered. What were a few moments of pleasure measured against a lifetime of consequences?

He pulled her closer to him and for a moment she let herself enjoy the closeness. He smelled good—male and good. She pulled away reluctantly.

He sighed, reached toward the glove compartment. She stiffened, not knowing what to expect, but all he took out was a small box. The writing on it meant nothing to her. She did not understand until he broke the seal, opened the box, and took out a condom. He looked at her, and she first looked away in surprise. Then she giggled. She could not remember when she had last giggled.

He grinned, gestured toward the backseat, and she laughed aloud. Even in her teens, she had disliked backseats of cars. But she looked around at the empty streets and ruined buildings, then she got out and into the backseat. He let her put the condom on him, then seemed surprised at her eagerness.

Sometime later, they sat together, covered by his coat, unwilling to become clothed near strangers again just yet. He made rock-the-baby gestures and looked questioningly at her.

She swallowed, shook her head. She did not know how to tell him her children were dead.

He took her hand and drew a cross in it with his index finger, then made his baby-rocking gesture again.

She nodded, held up three fingers, then turned away, trying to shut out a sudden flood of memories. She had told herself that the children growing up now were to be pitied. They would run through the downtown canyons with no real memory of what the buildings had been or even how they had come to be. Today's children gathered books as well as wood to be burned as fuel. They ran through the streets chasing one another and hooting like chimpanzees. They had no future. They were now all they would ever be.

He put his hand on her shoulder, and she turned suddenly, fumbling for his small box, then urging him to make love to her again. He could give her forgetfulness and pleasure. Until now, nothing had been able to do that. Until now, every day had brought her closer to the time when she would do what she had left home to avoid doing: putting her gun in her mouth and pulling the trigger.

She asked Obsidian if he would come home with her, stay with her.

He looked surprised and pleased once he understood. But he did not answer at once. Finally, he shook his head as she had feared he might. He was probably having too much fun playing cops and robbers and picking up women.

She dressed in silent disappointment, unable to feel any anger toward him. Perhaps he already had a wife and a home. That was likely. The illness had been harder on men than on women—had killed more men, had left male survivors more severely impaired. Men like Obsidian were rare. Women either settled for less or stayed alone. If they found an Obsidian, they did what they could to keep him. Rye suspected he had someone younger, prettier keeping him.

He touched her while she was strapping her gun on and asked with a complicated series of gestures whether it was loaded.

She nodded grimly.

He patted her arm.

She asked once more if he would come home with her, this time using a different series of gestures. He had seemed hesitant. Perhaps he could be courted.

He got out and into the front seat without responding.

She took her place in front again, watching him. Now he plucked at his uniform and looked at her. She thought she was being asked something but did not know what it was.

He took off his badge, tapped it with one finger, then tapped his chest. Of course.

She took the badge from his hand and pinned her wheat stalk to it. If playing cops and robbers was his only insanity, let him play. She would take him, uniform and all. It occurred to her that she might eventually lose him to someone he would meet as he had met her. But she would have him for a while.

He took the street map down again, tapped it, pointed vaguely northeast toward Pasadena, then looked at her.

She shrugged, tapped his shoulder, then her own, and held up her index and second fingers tight together, just to be sure.

He grasped the two fingers and nodded. He was with her.

She took the map from him and threw it onto the dashboard. She pointed back southwest—back toward home. Now she did not have to go to Pasadena. Now she could go on having a brother there and two nephews—three right-handed males. Now she did not have to find out for certain whether she was as alone as she feared. Now she was not alone.

Obsidian took Hill Street south, then Washington west, and she leaned back, wondering what it would be like to have someone again. With what she had scavenged, what she had preserved, and what she grew, there was easily enough food for them. There was certainly room enough in a four-bedroom house. He could move his possessions in. Best of all, the animal across the street would pull back and possibly not force her to kill him.

Obsidian had drawn her closer to him, and she had put her head on his shoulder when suddenly he braked hard, almost throwing her off the seat. Out of the corner of her eye, she saw that someone had run across the street in front of the car. One car on the street and someone had to run in front of it.

Straightening up, Rye saw that the runner was a woman, fleeing from an old frame house to a boarded-up storefront. She ran silently, but the man who followed her a moment later shouted what sounded like garbled words as he ran. He had something in his hand. Not a gun. A knife, perhaps.

The woman tried a door, found it locked, looked around desperately, finally snatched up a fragment of glass broken from the storefront window. With this she turned to face her pursuer. Rye thought she would be more likely to cut her own hand than to hurt anyone else with the glass.

Obsidian jumped from the car, shouting. It was the first time Rye had heard his voice—deep and hoarse from disuse. He made the same sound over and over the way some speechless people did, "Da, da, da!"

Rye got out of the car as Obsidian ran toward the couple. He had drawn his gun. Fearful, she drew her own and released the safety. She looked around to see who else might be attracted to the scene. She saw the man glance at Obsidian, then suddenly lunge at the woman. The woman jabbed his face with her glass, but he caught her arm and managed to stab her twice before Obsidian shot him.

The man doubled, then toppled, clutching his abdomen. Obsidian shouted, then gestured Rye over to help the woman.

Rye moved to the woman's side, remembering that she had little more than bandages and antiseptic in her pack. But the woman was beyond help. She had been stabbed with a long, slender boning knife.

She touched Obsidian to let him know the woman was dead. He had bent to check the wounded man who lay still and also seemed dead. But as Obsidian looked around to see what Rye wanted, the man opened his eyes. Face contorted, he seized Obsidian's just-holstered revolver and fired. The bullet caught Obsidian in the temple and he collapsed.

It happened just that simply, just that fast. An instant later, Rye shot the wounded man as he was turning the gun on her.

And Rye was alone—with three corpses.

She knelt beside Obsidian, dry-eyed, frowning, trying to understand why everything had suddenly changed. Obsidian was gone. He had died and left her—like everyone else.

Two very small children came out of the house from which the man and woman had run—a boy and girl perhaps three years old. Holding hands, they crossed the street toward Rye. They stared at her, then edged past her and went to the dead woman. The girl shook the woman's arm as though trying to wake her.

This was too much. Rye got up, feeling sick to her stomach with grief and anger. If the children began to cry, she thought she would vomit.

They were on their own, those two kids. They were old enough to scavenge. She did not need any more grief. She did not need a stranger's children who would grow up to be hairless chimps.

She went back to the car. She could drive home, at least. She remembered how to drive.

The thought that Obsidian should be buried occurred to her before she reached the car, and she did vomit.

She had found and lost the man so quickly. It was as though she had been snatched from comfort and security and given a sudden, inexplicable beating. Her head would not clear. She could not think.

Somehow, she made herself go back to him, look at him. She found herself on her knees beside him with no memory of having knelt. She stroked his face, his beard. One of the children made a noise and she looked at them, at the woman who was probably their mother. The children looked back at her, obviously frightened. Perhaps it was their fear that reached her finally.

She had been about to drive away and leave them. She had almost done it, almost left two toddlers to die. Surely there had been enough dying. She would have to take the children home with her. She would not be able to live with any other decision. She looked around for a place to bury three bodies. Or two. She wondered if the murderer were the children's father. Before the silence, the police had always said some of the most dangerous calls they went out on were domestic disturbance calls. Obsidian should have known that—not that the knowledge would have kept him in the car. It would not have held her back either. She could not have watched the woman murdered and done nothing.

She dragged Obsidian toward the car. She had nothing to dig with her, and no one to guard for her while she dug. Better to take the bodies with her and bury them next to her husband and her children. Obsidian would come home with her after all.

When she had gotten him onto the floor in the back, she returned for the woman. The little girl, thin, dirty, solemn, stood up and unknowingly gave Rye a gift. As Rye began to drag the woman by her arms, the little girl screamed, "No!"

Rye dropped the woman and stared at the girl.

"No!" the girl repeated. She came to stand beside the woman. "Go away!" she told Rye.

"Don't talk," the little boy said to her. There was no blurring or confusing of sounds. Both children had spoken and Rye had understood. The boy looked at the dead murderer and moved further from him. He took the girl's hand. "Be quiet," he whispered.

Fluent speech! Had the woman died because she could talk and had taught her children to talk? Had she been killed by a husband's festering anger or by a stranger's jealous rage? And the children . . . they must have been born after the silence. Had the disease run its course, then? Or were these children simply immune? Certainly they had had time to fall sick and silent. Rye's mind leaped ahead. What if children of three or fewer years were safe and able to learn language? What if all they needed were teachers? Teachers and protectors.

Rye glanced at the dead murderer. To her shame, she thought she could understand some of the passions that must have driven him, whomever he was. Anger, frustration, hopelessness, insane jealousy . . . how many more of him were there—people willing to destroy what they could not have?

Obsidian had been the protector, had chosen that role for who knew what reason. Perhaps putting on an obsolete uniform and patrolling the empty streets had been what he did instead of putting a gun into his mouth. And now that there was something worth protecting, he was gone.

She had been a teacher. A good one. She had been a protector, too, though only of herself. She had kept herself alive when she had no reason to live. If the illness let these children alone, she could keep them alive.

Somehow she lifted the dead woman into her arms and placed her on the backseat of the car. The children began to cry, but she knelt on the broken pavement and whispered to them, fearful of frightening them with the harshness of her long unused voice.

"It's all right," she told them. "You're going with us, too. Come on." She lifted them both, one in each arm. They were so light. Had they been getting enough to eat?

The boy covered her mouth with his hand, but she moved her face away. "It's all right for me to talk," she told him. "As long as no one's around, it's all right." She put the boy down on the front seat of the car and he moved over without being told to, to make room for the girl. When they were both in the car, Rye leaned against the window, looking at them, seeing that they were less afraid now, that they watched her with at least as much curiosity as fear.

"I'm Valerie Rye," she said, savoring the words. "It's all right for you to talk to me."

Afterword

"Speech Sounds" was conceived in weariness, depression, and sorrow. I began the story feeling little hope or liking for the human species, but by the time I reached the end of it, my hope had come back. It always seems to do that. Here's the story behind "Speech Sounds."

In the early 1980s, a good friend of mine discovered that she was dying of multiple myeloma, an especially dangerous, painful form of cancer. I had lost elderly relatives and family friends to death before this, but I had never lost a personal friend. I had never watched a relatively young person die slowly and painfully of disease. It took my friend a year to die, and I got into the habit of visiting her every Saturday and taking along the latest chapter of the novel I was working on. This happened to be *Clay's Ark*. With its story of disease and death, it was thoroughly inappropriate for the situation. But my friend had always read my novels. She insisted that she wanted to read this one as well. I suspect that neither of us believed she would live to read it in its completed form—although, of course, we didn't talk about this.

I hated going to see her. She was a good person, I loved her, and I hated watching her die. Nevertheless, every Saturday I got on a bus—I don't drive—and went to her hospital room or her apartment. She got thinner and frailer and querulous with pain. I got more depressed.

One Saturday, as I sat on a crowded, smelly bus, trying to keep people from stepping on my ingrown toenail and trying not to think of terrible things, I noticed trouble brewing just across from me. One man had decided he didn't like the way another man was looking at him. Didn't like it at all! It's hard to know where to look when you're wedged in place on a crowded bus.

The wedged-in man argued that he hadn't done anything wrong—which he hadn't. He inched toward the exit as though he meant to get himself out of a potentially bad situation. Then he turned and edged back into the argument. Maybe his own pride was involved. Why the hell should he be the one to run away?

This time the other guy decided that it was his girlfriend—sitting next to him—who was being looked at inappropriately. He attacked.

The fight was short and bloody. The rest of us—the other passengers—ducked and yelled and tried to avoid being hit. In the end, the attacker and his girlfriend pushed their way off the bus, fearful that the driver would call the police. And the guy with the pride sagged, dazed and bloody, looking around as though he wasn't sure what had happened.

I sat where I was, more depressed than ever, hating the whole hopeless, stupid business and wondering whether the human species would ever grow up enough to learn to communicate without using fists of one kind or another.

And the first line of a possible story came to me: "There was trouble aboard the Washington Boulevard bus."

Bloodchild

MY LAST night of childhood began with a visit home. T'Gatoi's sister had given us two sterile eggs. T'Gatoi gave one to my mother, brother, and sisters. She insisted that I eat the other one alone. It didn't matter. There was still enough to leave everyone feeling good. Almost everyone. My mother wouldn't take any. She sat, watching everyone drifting and dreaming without her. Most of the time she watched me.

I lay against T'Gatoi's long, velvet underside, sipping from my egg now and then, wondering why my mother denied herself such a harmless pleasure. Less of her hair would be gray if she indulged now and then. The eggs prolonged life, prolonged vigor. My father, who had never refused one in his life, had lived more than twice as long as he should have. And toward the end of his life, when he should have been slowing down, he had married my mother and fathered four children.

But my mother seemed content to age before she had to. I saw her turn away as several of T'Gatoi's limbs secured me closer. T'Gatoi liked our body heat and took advantage of it whenever she could. When I was little and at home more, my mother used to try to tell me how to behave with T'Gatoi—how to be respectful and always obedient because T'Gatoi was the Tlic government official in charge of the Preserve, and thus the most important of her kind to deal directly with Terrans. It was an honor, my mother said, that such a person had chosen to come into the family. My mother was at her most formal and severe when she was lying.

I had no idea why she was lying, or even what she was lying about. It *was* an honor to have T'Gatoi in the family, but it was hardly a novelty. T'Gatoi and my mother had been friends all my mother's life, and T'Gatoi was not interested in being honored in the house she considered her second home. She simply came in, climbed onto one of her special couches, and called me over to keep her warm. It was impossible to be formal with her while lying against her and hearing her complain as usual that I was too skinny.

"You're better," she said this time, probing me with six or seven of her limbs. "You're gaining weight finally. Thinness is dangerous." The probing changed subtly, became a series of caresses.

"He's still too thin," my mother said sharply.

T'Gatoi lifted her head and perhaps a meter of her body off the couch as though she were sitting up. She looked at my mother, and my mother, her face lined and old looking, turned away.

"Lien, I would like you to have what's left of Gan's egg."

"The eggs are for the children," my mother said.

"They are for the family. Please take it."

Unwillingly obedient, my mother took it from me and put it to her mouth. There were only a few drops left in the now-shrunken, elastic shell, but she squeezed them out, swallowed them, and after a few moments some of the lines of tension began to smooth from her face.

"It's good," she whispered. "Sometimes I forget how good it is."

"You should take more," T'Gatoi said. "Why are you in such a hurry to be old?"

My mother said nothing.

"I like being able to come here," T'Gatoi said. "This place is a refuge because of you, yet you won't take care of yourself."

T'Gatoi was hounded on the outside. Her people wanted more of us made available. Only she and her political faction stood between us and the hordes who did not understand why there was a Preserve—why any Terran could not be courted, paid, drafted, in some way made available to them. Or they did understand, but in their desperation, they did not care. She parceled us out to the desperate and sold us to the rich and powerful for their political support. Thus, we were necessities, status symbols, and an independent people. She oversaw the joining of families, putting an end to the final remnants of the earlier system of breaking up Terran families to suit impatient Tlic. I had lived outside with her. I had seen the desperate eagerness in the way some people looked at me. It was a little frightening to know that only she stood between us and that desperation that could so easily swallow us. My mother would look at her sometimes and say to me, "Take care of her." And I would remember that she too had been outside, had seen.

Now T'Gatoi used four of her limbs to push me away from her onto the floor. "Go on, Gan," she said. "Sit down there with your sisters and enjoy not being sober. You had most of the egg. Lien, come warm me."

My mother hesitated for no reason that I could see. One of my earliest memories is of my mother stretched alongside T'Gatoi, talking about things I could not understand, picking me up from the floor and laughing as she sat me on one of T'Gatoi's segments. She ate her share of eggs then. I wondered when she had stopped, and why.

She lay down now against T'Gatoi, and the whole left row of T'Gatoi's limbs closed around her, holding her loosely, but securely. I had always found it comfortable to lie that way, but except for my older sister, no one else in the family liked it. They said it made them feel caged.

T'Gatoi meant to cage my mother. Once she had, she moved her tail slightly, then spoke. "Not enough egg, Lien. You should have taken it when it was passed to you. You need it badly now."

T'Gatoi's tail moved once more, its whip motion so swift I wouldn't have seen it if I hadn't been watching for it. Her sting drew only a single drop of blood from my mother's bare leg.

My mother cried out—probably in surprise. Being stung doesn't hurt. Then she sighed and I could see her body relax. She moved languidly into a more comfortable position within the cage of T'Gatoi's limbs. "Why did you do that?" she asked, sounding half asleep.

"I could not watch you sitting and suffering any longer."

My mother managed to move her shoulders in a small shrug. "Tomorrow," she said.

"Yes. Tomorrow you will resume your suffering—if you must. But just now, just for now, lie here and warm me and let me ease your way a little."

"He's still mine, you know," my mother said suddenly. "Nothing can buy him from me." Sober, she would not have permitted herself to refer to such things.

"Nothing," T'Gatoi agreed, humoring her.

"Did you think I would sell him for eggs? For long life? My son?"

"Not for anything," T'Gatoi said, stroking my mother's shoulders, toying with her long, graying hair.

I would like to have touched my mother, shared that moment with her. She would take my hand if I touched her now. Freed by the egg and the sting, she would smile and perhaps say things long held in. But tomorrow, she would remember all this as a humiliation. I did not want to be part of a remembered humiliation. Best just be still and know she loved me under all the duty and pride and pain.

"Xuan Hoa, take off her shoes," T'Gatoi said. "In a little while I'll sting her again and she can sleep."

My older sister obeyed, swaying drunkenly as she stood up. When she had finished, she sat down beside me and took my hand. We had always been a unit, she and I.

My mother put the back of her head against T'Gatoi's underside and tried from that impossible angle to look up into the broad, round face. "You're going to sting me again?"

"Yes, Lien."

"I'll sleep until tomorrow noon."

"Good. You need it. When did you sleep last?"

My mother made a wordless sound of annoyance. "I should have stepped on you when you were small enough," she muttered.

It was an old joke between them. They had grown up together, sort of, though T'Gatoi had not, in my mother's lifetime, been small enough for any Terran to step on. She was nearly three times my mother's present age, yet would still be young when my mother died of age. But T'Gatoi and my mother had met as T'Gatoi was coming into a period of rapid development—a kind of Tlic adolescence. My mother was only a child, but for a while they developed at the same rate and had no better friends than each other.

T'Gatoi had even introduced my mother to the man who became my father. My parents, pleased with each other in spite of their different ages, married as T'Gatoi was going into her family's business—politics. She and my mother saw each other less. But sometime before my older sister was born, my mother promised T'Gatoi one of her children. She would have to give one of us to someone, and she preferred T'Gatoi to some stranger.

Years passed. T'Gatoi traveled and increased her influence. The Preserve was hers by the time she came back to my mother to collect what she probably saw as her just reward for her hard work. My older sister took an instant liking to her and wanted to be chosen, but my mother was just coming to term with me and T'Gatoi liked the idea of choosing an infant and watching and taking part in all the phases of development. I'm told I was first caged within T'Gatoi's many limbs only three minutes after my birth. A few days later, I was given my first taste of egg. I tell Terrans that when they ask whether I was ever afraid of her. And I tell it to Tlic when T'Gatoi suggests a young Terran child for them and they, anxious and ignorant, demand an adolescent. Even my brother who had somehow grown up to fear and distrust the Tlic could probably have gone smoothly into one of their families if he had been adopted early enough. Sometimes, I think for his sake he should have been. I looked at him, stretched out on the floor across the room, his eyes open, but glazed as he dreamed his egg dream. No matter what he felt toward the Tlic, he always demanded his share of egg.

"Lien, can you stand up?" T'Gatoi asked suddenly.

"Stand?" my mother said. "I thought I was going to sleep."

"Later. Something sounds wrong outside." The cage was abruptly gone.

"What?"

"Up, Lien!"

My mother recognized her tone and got up just in time to avoid being dumped on the floor. T'Gatoi whipped her three meters of body off her couch, toward the door, and out at full speed. She had bones—ribs, a long spine, a skull, four sets of limb bones per segment. But when she moved that way, twisting, hurling herself into controlled falls, landing running, she seemed not only boneless, but aquatic—something swimming through the air as though it were water. I loved watching her move.

I left my sister and started to follow her out the door, though I wasn't very steady on my own feet. It would have been better to sit and dream, better yet to find a girl and share a waking dream with her. Back when the Tlic saw us as not much more than convenient, big, warm-blooded animals, they would pen several of us together, male and female, and feed us only eggs. That way they could be sure of getting another generation of us no matter how we tried to hold out. We were lucky that didn't go on long. A few generations of it and we would have *been* little more than convenient, big animals.

"Hold the door open, Gan," T'Gatoi said. "And tell the family to stay back."

"What is it?" I asked.

"N'Tlic."

I shrank back against the door. "Here? Alone?"

"He was trying to reach a call box, I suppose." She carried the man past me, unconscious, folded like a coat over some of her limbs. He looked young—my brother's age perhaps—and he was thinner than he should have been. What T'Gatoi would have called dangerously thin.

"Gan, go to the call box," she said. She put the man on the floor and began stripping off his clothing.

I did not move.

After a moment, she looked up at me, her sudden stillness a sign of deep impatience.

"Send Qui," I told her. "I'll stay here. Maybe I can help."

She let her limbs begin to move again, lifting the man and pulling his shirt over his head. "You don't want to see this," she said. "It will be hard. I can't help this man the way his Tlic could."

"I know. But send Qui. He won't want to be of any help here. I'm at least willing to try."

She looked at my brother—older, bigger, stronger, certainly more able to help her here. He was sitting up now, braced against the wall, staring at the man on the floor with undisguised fear and revulsion. Even she could see that he would be useless.

"Qui, go!" she said.

He didn't argue. He stood up, swayed briefly, then steadied, frightened sober.

"This man's name is Bram Lomas," she told him, reading from the man's armband. I fingered my own armband in sympathy. "He needs T'Khotgif Teh. Do you hear?"

"Bram Lomas, T'Khotgif Teh," my brother said. "I'm going." He edged around Lomas and ran out the door.

Lomas began to regain consciousness. He only moaned at first and clutched spasmodically at a pair of T'Gatoi's limbs. My younger sister, finally awake from her egg dream, came close to look at him, until my mother pulled her back.

T'Gatoi removed the man's shoes, then his pants, all the while leaving him two of her limbs to grip. Except for the final few, all her limbs were equally dexterous. "I want no argument from you this time, Gan," she said.

I straightened. "What shall I do?"

"Go out and slaughter an animal that is at least half your size."

"Slaughter? But I've never—"

She knocked me across the room. Her tail was an efficient weapon whether she exposed the sting or not.

I got up, feeling stupid for having ignored her warning, and went into the kitchen. Maybe I could kill something with a knife or an ax. My mother raised a few Terran animals for the table and several thousand local ones for their fur. T'Gatoi would probably prefer something local. An achti, perhaps. Some of those were the right size, though they had about three times as many teeth as I did and a real love of using them. My mother, Hoa, and Qui could kill them with knives. I had never killed one at all, had never slaughtered any animal. I had spent most of my time with T'Gatoi while my brother and sisters were learning the family business. T'Gatoi had been right. I should have been the one to go to the call box. At least I could do that.

I went to the corner cabinet where my mother kept her large house and garden tools. At the back of the cabinet there was a pipe that carried off waste water from the kitchen—except that it didn't anymore. My father had rerouted the waste water below before I was born. Now the pipe could be turned so that one half slid around the other and a rifle could be stored inside. This wasn't our only gun, but it was our most easily accessible one. I would have to use it to shoot one of the biggest of the achti. Then T'Gatoi would probably confiscate it. Firearms were illegal in the Preserve. There had been incidents right after the Preserve was established—Terrans shooting Tlic, shooting N'Tlic. This was before the joining of families began, before everyone had a personal stake in keeping the peace. No one had shot a Tlic in my lifetime or my mother's, but the law still stood—for our protection, we were told. There were stories of whole Terran families wiped out in reprisal back during the assassinations.

I went out to the cages and shot the biggest achti I could find. It was a handsome breeding male, and my mother would not be pleased to see me bring it in. But it was the right size, and I was in a hurry.

I put the achti's long, warm body over my shoulder—glad that some of the weight I'd gained was muscle—and took it to the kitchen. There, I put the gun back in its hiding place. If T'Gatoi noticed the achti's wounds and demanded the gun, I would give it to her. Otherwise, let it stay where my father wanted it.

I turned to take the achti to her, then hesitated. For several seconds, I stood in front of the closed door wondering why I was suddenly afraid. I knew what was going to happen. I hadn't seen it before but T'Gatoi had shown me diagrams and drawings. She had made sure I knew the truth as soon as I was old enough to understand it.

Yet I did not want to go into that room. I wasted a little time choosing a knife from the carved, wooden box in which my mother kept them. T'Gatoi might want one, I told myself, for the tough, heavily furred hide of the achti.

"Gan!" T'Gatoi called, her voice harsh with urgency.

I swallowed. I had not imagined a single moving of the feet could be so difficult. I realized I was trembling and that shamed me. Shame impelled me through the door.

I put the achti down near T'Gatoi and saw that Lomas was unconscious again. She, Lomas, and I were alone in the room —my mother and sisters probably sent out so they would not have to watch. I envied them.

But my mother came back into the room as T'Gatoi seized the achti. Ignoring the knife I offered her, she extended claws from several of her limbs and slit the achti from throat to anus. She looked at me, her yellow eyes intent. "Hold this man's shoulders, Gan."

I stared at Lomas in panic, realizing that I did not want to touch him, let alone hold him. This would not be like shooting an animal. Not as quick, not as merciful, and, I hoped, not as final, but there was nothing I wanted less than to be part of it.

My mother came forward. "Gan, you hold his right side," she said. "I'll hold his left." And if he came to, he would throw her off without realizing he had done it. She was a tiny woman. She often wondered aloud how she had produced, as she said, such "huge" children.

"Never mind," I told her, taking the man's shoulders. "I'll do it." She hovered nearby.

"Don't worry," I said. "I won't shame you. You don't have to stay and watch."

She looked at me uncertainly, then touched my face in a rare caress. Finally, she went back to her bedroom.

T'Gatoi lowered her head in relief. "Thank you, Gan," she said with courtesy more Terran than Tlic. "That one . . . she is always finding new ways for me to make her suffer."

Lomas began to groan and make choked sounds. I had hoped he would stay unconscious. T'Gatoi put her face near his so that he focused on her.

"I've stung you as much as I dare for now," she told him. "When this is over, I'll sting you to sleep and you won't hurt anymore."

"Please," the man begged. "Wait . . ."

"There's no more time, Bram. I'll sting you as soon as it's over. When T'Khotgif arrives she'll give you eggs to help you heal. It will be over soon."

"T'Khotgif!" the man shouted, straining against my hands.

"Soon, Bram." T'Gatoi glanced at me, then placed a claw against his abdomen slightly to the right of the middle, just below the left rib. There was movement on the right side—tiny, seemingly random pulsations moving his brown flesh, creating a concavity here, a convexity there, over and over until I could see the rhythm of it and knew where the next pulse would be.

Lomas's entire body stiffened under T'Gatoi's claw, though she merely rested it against him as she wound the rear section of her body around his legs. He might break my grip, but he would not break hers. He wept helplessly as she used his pants to tie his hands, then pushed his hands above his head so that I could kneel on the cloth between them and pin them in place. She rolled up his shirt and gave it to him to bite down on.

And she opened him.

His body convulsed with the first cut. He almost tore himself away from me. The sound he made . . . I had never heard such sounds come from anything human. T'Gatoi seemed to pay no attention as she lengthened and deepened the cut, now and then pausing to lick away blood. His blood vessels contracted, reacting to the chemistry of her saliva, and the bleeding slowed.

I felt as though I were helping her torture him, helping her consume him. I knew I would vomit soon, didn't know why I hadn't already. I couldn't possibly last until she was finished.

She found the first grub. It was fat and deep red with his blood—both inside and out. It had already eaten its own egg case but apparently had not yet begun to eat its host. At this stage, it would eat any flesh except its mother's. Let alone, it would have gone on excreting the poisons that had both sickened and alerted Lomas. Eventually it would have begun to eat. By the time it ate its way out of Lomas's flesh, Lomas would be dead or dying—and unable to take revenge on the thing that was killing him. There was always a grace period between the time the host sickened and the time the grubs began to eat him.

T'Gatoi picked up the writhing grub carefully and looked at it, somehow ignoring the terrible groans of the man.

Abruptly, the man lost consciousness.

"Good," T'Gatoi looked down at him. "I wish you Terrans could do that at will." She felt nothing. And the thing she held . . .

It was limbless and boneless at this stage, perhaps fifteen centimeters long and two thick, blind and slimy with blood. It was like a large worm. T'Gatoi put it into the belly of the achti, and it began at once to burrow. It would stay there and eat as long as there was anything to eat.

Probing through Lomas's flesh, she found two more, one of them smaller and more vigorous. "A male!" she said happily. He would be dead before I would. He would be through his metamorphosis and screwing everything that would hold still before his sisters even had limbs. He was the only one to make a serious effort to bite T'Gatoi as she placed him in the achti.

Paler worms oozed to visibility in Lomas's flesh. I closed my eyes. It was worse than finding something dead, rotting, and filled with tiny animal grubs. And it was far worse than any drawing or diagram.

"Ah, there are more," T'Gatoi said, plucking out two long, thick grubs. You may have to kill another animal, Gan. Everything lives inside you Terrans."

I had been told all my life that this was a good and necessary thing Tlic and Terran did together—a kind of birth. I had believed it until now. I knew birth was painful and bloody, no matter what. But this was something else, something worse. And I wasn't ready to see it. Maybe I never would be. Yet I couldn't not see it. Closing my eyes didn't help.

T'Gatoi found a grub still eating its egg case. The remains of the case were still wired into a blood vessel by their own little tube or hook or whatever. That was the way the grubs were anchored and the way they fed. They took only blood until they were ready to emerge. Then they ate their stretched, elastic egg cases. Then they ate their hosts.

T'Gatoi bit away the egg case, licked away the blood. Did she like the taste? Did childhood habits die hard—or not die at all?

The whole procedure was wrong, alien. I wouldn't have thought anything about her could seem alien to me.

"One more, I think," she said. "Perhaps two. A good family. In a host animal these days, we would be happy to find one or two alive." She glanced at me. "Go outside, Gan, and empty your stomach. Go now while the man is unconscious."

I staggered out, barely made it. Beneath the tree just beyond the front door, I vomited until there was nothing left to bring up. Finally, I stood shaking, tears streaming down my face. I did not know why I was crying, but I could not stop. I went further from the house to avoid being seen. Every time I closed my eyes I saw red worms crawling over redder human flesh.

There was a car coming toward the house. Since Terrans were forbidden motorized vehicles except for certain farm equipment, I knew this must be Lomas's Tlic with Qui and perhaps a Terran doctor. I wiped my face on my shirt, struggled for control.

"Gan," Qui called as the car stopped. "What happened?" He crawled out of the low, round, Tlic-convenient car door. Another Terran crawled out the other side and went into the house without speaking to me. The doctor. With his help and a few eggs, Lomas might make it.

"T'Khotgif Teh?" I said.

The Tlic driver surged out of her car, reared up half her length before me. She was paler and smaller than T'Gatoi—probably born from the body of an animal. Tlic from Terran bodies were always larger as well as more numerous.

"Six young," I told her. "Maybe seven, all alive. At least one male."

"Lomas?" she said harshly. I liked her for the question and the concern in her voice when she asked it. The last coherent thing he had said was her name.

"He's alive," I said.

She surged away to the house without another word.

"She's been sick," my brother said, watching her go. "When I called, I could hear people telling her she wasn't well enough to go out even for this."

I said nothing. I had extended courtesy to the Tlic. Now I didn't want to talk to anyone. I hoped he would go in—out of curiosity if nothing else.

"Finally found out more than you wanted to know, eh?"

I looked at him.

"Don't give me one of *her* looks," he said. "You're not her. You're just her property."

One of her looks. Had I picked up even an ability to imitate her expressions?

"What'd you do, puke?" He sniffed the air. "So now you know what you're in for."

I walked away from him. He and I had been close when we were kids. He would let me follow him around when I was home, and sometimes T'Gatoi would let me bring him along when she took me into the city. But something had happened when he reached adolescence. I never knew what. He began keeping out of T'Gatoi's way. Then he began running away

—until he realized there was no "away." Not in the Preserve. Certainly not outside. After that he concentrated on getting his share of every egg that came into the house and on looking out for me in a way that made me all but hate him—a way that clearly said, as long as I was all right, he was safe from the Tlic.

"How was it, really?" he demanded, following me.

"I killed an achti. The young ate it."

"You didn't run out of the house and puke because they ate an achti."

"I had . . . never seen a person cut open before." That was true, and enough for him to know. I couldn't talk about the other. Not with him.

"Oh," he said. He glanced at me as though he wanted to say more, but he kept quiet.

We walked, not really headed anywhere. Toward the back, toward the cages, toward the fields.

"Did he say anything?" Qui asked. "Lomas, I mean."

Who else would he mean? "He said 'T'Khotgif.'"

Qui shuddered. "If she had done that to me, she'd be the last person I'd call for."

"You'd call for her. Her sting would ease your pain without killing the grubs in you."

"You think I'd care if they died?"

No. Of course he wouldn't. Would I?

"Shit!" He drew a deep breath. "I've seen what they do. You think this thing with Lomas was bad? It was nothing."

I didn't argue. He didn't know what he was talking about.

"I saw them eat a man," he said.

I turned to face him. "You're lying!"

"*I saw them eat a man.*" He paused. "It was when I was little. I had been to the Hartmund house and I was on my way home. Halfway here, I saw a man and a Tlic and the man was N'Tlic. The ground was hilly. I was able to hide from them and watch. The Tlic wouldn't open the man because she had nothing to feed the grubs. The man couldn't go any further and there were no houses around. He was in so much pain, he told her to kill him. He begged her to kill him. Finally, she did. She cut his throat. One swipe of one claw. I saw the grubs eat their way out, then burrow in again, still eating."

His words made me see Lomas's flesh again, parasitized, crawling. "Why didn't you tell me that?" I whispered.

He looked startled as though he'd forgotten I was listening. "I don't know."

"You started to run away not long after that, didn't you?"

"Yeah. Stupid. Running inside the Preserve. Running in a cage."

I shook my head, said what I should have said to him long ago. "She wouldn't take you, Qui. You don't have to worry."

"She would . . . if anything happened to you."

"No. She'd take Xuan Hoa. Hoa . . . wants it." She wouldn't if she had stayed to watch Lomas.

"They don't take women," he said with contempt.

"They do sometimes." I glanced at him. "Actually, they prefer women. You should be around them when they talk among themselves. They say women have more body fat to protect the grubs. But they usually take men to leave the women free to bear their own young."

"To provide the next generation of host animals," he said, switching from contempt to bitterness.

"It's more than that!" I countered. Was it?

"If it were going to happen to me, I'd want to believe it was more, too."

"It *is* more!" I felt like a kid. Stupid argument.

"Did you think so while T'Gatoi was picking worms out of that guy's guts?"

"It's not supposed to happen that way."

"Sure it is. You weren't supposed to see it, that's all. And his Tlic was supposed to do it. She could sting him unconscious and the operation wouldn't have been as painful. But she'd still open him, pick out the grubs, and if she missed even one, it would poison him and eat him from the inside out."

There was actually a time when my mother told me to show respect for Qui because he was my older brother. I walked away, hating him. In his way, he was gloating. He was safe and I wasn't. I could have hit him, but I didn't think I would be able to stand it when he refused to hit back, when he looked at me with contempt and pity.

He wouldn't let me get away. Longer legged, he swung ahead of me and made me feel as though I were following him.

"I'm sorry," he said.

I strode on, sick and furious.

"Look, it probably won't be that bad with you. T'Gatoi likes you. She'll be careful."

I turned back toward the house, almost running from him.

"Has she done it to you yet?" he asked, keeping up easily. "I mean, you're about the right age for implantation. Has she—"

I hit him. I didn't know I was going to do it, but I think I meant to kill him. If he hadn't been bigger and stronger, I think I would have.

He tried to hold me off, but in the end, had to defend himself. He only hit me a couple of times. That was plenty. I don't remember going down, but when I came to, he was gone. It was worth the pain to be rid of him.

I got up and walked slowly toward the house. The back was dark. No one was in the kitchen. My mother and sisters were sleeping in their bedrooms—or pretending to.

Once I was in the kitchen, I could hear voices—Tlic and Terran from the next room. I couldn't make out what they were saying—didn't want to make it out.

I sat down at my mother's table, waiting for quiet. The table was smooth and worn, heavy and well crafted. My father had made it for her just before he died. I remembered hanging around underfoot when he built it. He didn't mind. Now I sat leaning on it, missing him. I could have talked to him. He had done it three times in his long life. Three clutches of eggs, three times being opened up and sewed up. How had he done it? How did anyone do it?

I got up, took the rifle from its hiding place, and sat down again with it. It needed cleaning, oiling.

All I did was load it.

"Gan?"

She made a lot of little clicking sounds when she walked on bare floor, each limb clicking in succession as it touched down. Waves of little clicks.

She came to the table, raised the front half of her body above it, and surged onto it. Sometimes she moved so smoothly she seemed to flow like water itself. She coiled herself into a small hill in the middle of the table and looked at me.

"That was bad," she said softly. "You should not have seen it. It need not be that way."

"I know."

"T'Khotgif—Ch'Khotgif now—she will die of her disease. She will not live to raise her children. But her sister will provide for them, and for Bram Lomas." Sterile sister. One fertile female in every lot. One to keep the family going. That sister owed Lomas more than she could ever repay.

"He'll live then?"

"Yes."

"I wonder if he would do it again."

"No one would ask him to do that again."

I looked into the yellow eyes, wondering how much I saw and understood there, and how much I only imagined. "No one ever asks us," I said. "You never asked me."

She moved her head slightly. "What's the matter with your face?"

"Nothing. Nothing important." Human eyes probably wouldn't have noticed the swelling in the darkness. The only light was from one of the moons, shining through a window across the room.

"Did you use the rifle to shoot the achti?"

"Yes."

"And do you mean to use it to shoot me?"

I stared at her, outlined in the moonlight—coiled, graceful body. "What does Terran blood taste like to you?"

She said nothing.

"What are you?" I whispered. "What are we to you?"

She lay still, rested her head on her topmost coil. "You know me as no other does," she said softly. "You must decide."

"That's what happened to my face," I told her.

"What?"

"Qui goaded me into deciding to do something. It didn't turn out very well." I moved the gun slightly, brought the barrel up diagonally under my own chin. "At least it was a decision I made."

"As this will be."

"Ask me, Gatoi."

"For my children's lives?"

She would say something like that. She knew how to manipulate people, Terran and Tlic. But not this time.

"I don't want to be a host animal," I said. "Not even yours."

It took her a long time to answer. "We use almost no host animals these days," she said. "You know that."

"You use us."

"We do. We wait long years for you and teach you and join our families to yours." She moved restlessly. "You know you aren't animals to us."

I stared at her, saying nothing.

"The animals we once used began killing most of our eggs after implantation long before your ancestors arrived," she said softly. "You know these things, Gan. Because your people arrived, we are relearning what it means to be a healthy, thriving people. And your ancestors, fleeing from their homeworld, from their own kind who would have killed or enslaved them —they survived because of us. We saw them as people and gave them the Preserve when they still tried to kill us as worms."

At the word "worms," I jumped. I couldn't help it, and she couldn't help noticing it.

"I see," she said quietly. "Would you really rather die than bear my young, Gan?"

I didn't answer.

"Shall I go to Xuan Hoa?"

"Yes!" Hoa wanted it. Let her have it. She hadn't had to watch Lomas. She'd be proud. . . . Not terrified.

T'Gatoi flowed off the table onto the floor, startling me almost too much.

"I'll sleep in Hoa's room tonight," she said. "And sometime tonight or in the morning, I'll tell her."

This was going too fast. My sister Hoa had had almost as much to do with raising me as my mother. I was still close to her—not like Qui. She could want T'Gatoi and still love me.

"Wait! Gatoi!"

She looked back, then raised nearly half her length off the floor and turned to face me. "These are adult things, Gan. This is my life, my family!"

"But she's . . . my sister."

"I have done what you demanded. I have asked you!"

"But—"

"It will be easier for Hoa. She has always expected to carry other lives inside her."

Human lives. Human young who should someday drink at her breasts, not at her veins.

I shook my head. "Don't do it to her, Gatoi." I was not Qui. It seemed I could become him, though, with no effort at all. I could make Xuan Hoa my shield. Would it be easier to know that red worms were growing in her flesh instead of mine?

"Don't do it to Hoa," I repeated.

She stared at me, utterly still.

I looked away, then back at her. "Do it to me."

I lowered the gun from my throat and she leaned forward to take it.

"No," I told her.

"It's the law," she said.

"Leave it for the family. One of them might use it to save my life someday."

She grasped the rifle barrel, but I wouldn't let go. I was pulled into a standing position over her.

"Leave it here!" I repeated. "If we're not your animals, if these are adult things, accept the risk. There is risk, Gatoi, in dealing with a partner."

It was clearly hard for her to let go of the rifle. A shudder went through her and she made a hissing sound of distress. It occurred to me that she was afraid. She was old enough to have seen what guns could do to people. Now her young and this gun would be together in the same house. She did not know about the other guns. In this dispute, they did not matter.

"I will implant the first egg tonight," she said as I put the gun away. "Do you hear, Gan?"

Why else had I been given a whole egg to eat while the rest of the family was left to share one? Why else had my mother kept looking at me as though I were going away from her, going where she could not follow? Did T'Gatoi imagine I hadn't known?

"I hear."

"Now!" I let her push me out of the kitchen, then walked ahead of her toward my bedroom. The sudden urgency in her voice sounded real. "You would have done it to Hoa tonight!" I accused.

"I must do it to someone tonight."

I stopped in spite of her urgency and stood in her way. "Don't you care who?"

She flowed around me and into my bedroom. I found her waiting on the couch we shared. There was nothing in Hoa's room that she could have used. She would have done it to Hoa on the floor. The thought of her doing it to Hoa at all disturbed me in a different way now, and I was suddenly angry.

Yet I undressed and lay down beside her. l knew what to do, what to expect. I had been told all my life. I felt the familiar sting, narcotic, mildly pleasant. Then the blind probing of her ovipositor. The puncture was painless, easy. So easy going in. She undulated slowly against me, her muscles forcing the egg from her body into mine. I held on to a pair of her limbs until I remembered Lomas holding her that way. Then I let go, moved inadvertently, and hurt her. She gave a low cry of pain and I expected to be caged at once within her limbs. When I wasn't, I held on to her again, feeling oddly ashamed.

"I'm sorry," I whispered.

She rubbed my shoulders with four of her limbs.

"Do you care?" I asked. "Do you care that it's me?"

She did not answer for some time. Finally, "You were the one making the choices tonight, Gan. I made mine long ago."

"Would you have gone to Hoa?"

"Yes. How could I put my children into the care of one who hates them?"

"It wasn't . . . hate."

"I know what it was."

"I was afraid."

Silence.

"I still am." I could admit it to her here, now.

"But you came to me . . . to save Hoa."

"Yes." I leaned my forehead against her. She was cool velvet, deceptively soft. "And to keep you for myself," I said. It was so. I didn't understand it, but it was so.

She made a soft hum of contentment. "I couldn't believe I had made such a mistake with you," she said. "I chose you. I believed you had grown to choose me."

"I had, but . . ."

"Lomas."

"Yes."

"I had never known a Terran to see a birth and take it well. Qui has seen one, hasn't he?"

"Yes."

"Terrans should be protected from seeing."

I didn't like the sound of that—and I doubted that it was possible. "Not protected," I said. "Shown. Shown when we're young kids, and shown more than once. Gatoi, no Terran ever sees a birth that goes right. All we see is N'Tlic—pain and terror and maybe death."

She looked down at me. "It is a private thing. It has always been a private thing."

Her tone kept me from insisting—that and the knowledge that if she changed her mind, I might be the first public example. But I had planted the thought in her mind. Chances were it would grow, and eventually she would experiment.

"You won't see it again," she said. "I don't want you thinking any more about shooting me."

The small amount of fluid that came into me with her egg relaxed me as completely as a sterile egg would have, so that I could remember the rifle in my hands and my feelings of fear and revulsion, anger and despair. I could remember the feelings without reviving them. I could talk about them.

"I wouldn't have shot you," I said. "Not you." She had been taken from my father's flesh when he was my age.

"You could have," she insisted.

"Not you." She stood between us and her own people, protecting, interweaving.

"Would you have destroyed yourself?"

I moved carefully, uncomfortable. "I could have done that. I nearly did. That's Qui's 'away.' I wonder if he knows."

"What?"

I did not answer.

"You will live now."

"Yes." *Take care of her*, my mother used to say. Yes.

"I'm healthy and young," she said. "I won't leave you as Lomas was left—alone, N'Tlic. I'll take care of you."

Afterword

It amazes me that some people have seen "Bloodchild" as a story of slavery. It isn't. It's a number of other things, though. On one level, it's a love story between two very different beings. On another, it's a coming-of-age story in which a boy must absorb disturbing information and use it to make a decision that will affect the rest of his life.

On a third level, "Bloodchild" is my pregnant man story. I've always wanted to explore what it might be like for a man to be put into that most unlikely of all positions. Could I write a story in which a man chose to become pregnant *not* through some sort of misplaced competitiveness to prove that a man could do anything a woman could do, not because he was forced to, not even out of curiosity? I wanted to see whether I could write a dramatic story of a man becoming pregnant as an act of love—choosing pregnancy in spite of as well as because of surrounding difficulties.

Also, "Bloodchild" was my effort to ease an old fear of mine. I was going to travel to the Peruvian Amazon to do research for my Xenogenesis books (*Dawn, Adulthood Rites,* and *Imago*), and I worried about my possible reactions to some of the insect life of the area. In particular, I worried about the botfly—an insect with, what seemed to me then, horror-movie habits. There was no shortage of botflies in the part of Peru that I intended to visit.

The botfly lays its eggs in wounds left by the bites of other insects. I found the idea of a maggot living and growing under my skin, eating my flesh as it grew, to be so intolerable, so terrifying that I didn't know how I could stand it if it happened to me. To make matters worse, all that I heard and read advised botfly victims not to try to get rid of their maggot passengers until they got back home to the United States and were able to go to a doctor—or until the fly finished the larval part of its growth cycle, crawled out of its host, and flew away.

The problem was to do what would seem to be the normal thing, to squeeze out the maggot and throw it away, was to invite infection. The maggot becomes literally attached to its host and leaves part of itself behind, broken off, if it's squeezed or cut out. Of course, the part left behind dies and rots, causing infection. Lovely.

When I have to deal with something that disturbs me as much as the botfly did, I write about it. I sort out my problems by writing about them. In a high school classroom on November 22, 1963, I remember grabbing a notebook and beginning to write my response to news of John Kennedy's assassination. Whether I write journal pages, an essay, a short story, or weave my problems into a novel, I find the writing helps me get through the trouble and get on with my life. Writing "Bloodchild" didn't make me like botflies, but for a while, it made them seem more interesting than horrifying.

There's one more thing I tried to do in "Bloodchild." I tried to write a story about paying the rent—a story about an isolated colony of human beings on an inhabited, extrasolar world. At best, they would be a lifetime away from reinforcements. It wouldn't be the British Empire in space, and it wouldn't be *Star Trek*. Sooner or later, the humans would have to make some kind of accommodation with their um . . . their hosts. Chances are this would be an unusual accommodation. Who knows what we humans have that others might be willing to take in trade for a livable space on a world not our own?

The Evening and the Morning and the Night

WHEN I was fifteen and trying to show my independence by getting careless with my diet, my parents took me to a Duryea-Gode disease ward. They wanted me to see, they said, where I was headed if I wasn't careful. In fact, it was where I was headed no matter what. It was only a matter of when: now or later. My parents were putting in their vote for later.

I won't describe the ward. It's enough to say that when they brought me home, I cut my wrists. I did a thorough job of it, old Roman style in a bathtub of warm water. Almost made it. My father dislocated his shoulder breaking down the bathroom door. He and I never forgave each other for that day.

The disease got him almost three years later—just before I went off to college. It was sudden. It doesn't happen that way often. Most people notice themselves beginning to drift—or their relatives notice—and they make arrangements with their chosen institution. People who are noticed and who resist going in can be locked up for a week's observation. I don't doubt that that observation period breaks up a few families. Sending someone away for what turns out to be a false alarm. . . . Well, it isn't the sort of thing the victim is likely to forgive or forget. On the other hand, not sending someone away in time—missing the signs or having a person go off suddenly without signs—is inevitably dangerous for the victim. I've never heard of it going as badly, though, as it did in my family. People normally injure only themselves when their time comes—unless someone is stupid enough to try to handle them without the necessary drugs or restraints.

My father had killed my mother, then killed himself. I wasn't home when it happened. I had stayed at school later than usual, rehearsing graduation exercises. By the time I got home, there were cops everywhere. There was an ambulance, and two attendants were wheeling someone out on a stretcher—someone covered. More than covered. Almost . . . bagged.

The cops wouldn't let me in. I didn't find out until later exactly what had happened. I wish I'd never found out. Dad had killed Mom, then skinned her completely. At least that's how I hope it happened. I mean I hope he killed her first. He broke some of her ribs, damaged her heart. Digging.

Then he began tearing at himself, through skin and bone, digging. He had managed to reach his own heart before he died. It was an especially bad example of the kind of thing that makes people afraid of us. It gets some of us into trouble for picking at a pimple or even for daydreaming. It has inspired restrictive laws, created problems with jobs, housing, schools. . . . The Duryea-Gode Disease Foundation has spent millions telling the world that people like my father don't exist.

A long time later, when I had gotten myself together as best I could, I went to college—to the University of Southern California—on a Dilg scholarship. Dilg is the retreat you try to send your out-of-control DGD relatives to. It's run by controlled DGDs like me, like my parents while they lived. God knows how any controlled DGD stands it. Anyway, the place has a waiting list miles long. My parents put me on it after my suicide attempt, but chances were, I'd be dead by the time my name came up.

I can't say why I went to college—except that I had been going to school all my life and didn't know what else to do. I didn't go with any particular hope. Hell, I knew what I was in for eventually. I was just marking time. Whatever I did was just marking time. If people were willing to pay me to go to school and mark time, why not do it?

The weird part was, I worked hard, got top grades. If you work hard enough at something that doesn't matter, you can forget for a while about the things that do.

Sometimes I thought about trying suicide again. How was it I'd had the courage when I was fifteen but didn't have it now? Two DGD parents—both religious, both as opposed to abortion as they were to suicide. So they had trusted God and the promises of modern medicine and had a child. But how could I look at what had happened to them and trust anything?

I majored in biology. Non-DGDs say something about our disease makes us good at the sciences—genetics, molecular biology, biochemistry. . . . That something was terror. Terror and a kind of driving hopelessness. Some of us went bad and became destructive before we had to—yes, we did produce more than our share of criminals. And some of us went good—spectacularly—and made scientific and medical history. These last kept the doors at least partly open for the rest of us. They made discoveries in genetics, found cures for a couple of rare diseases, made advances against other diseases that weren't so rare—including, ironically, some forms of cancer. But they'd found nothing to help themselves. There had been nothing since the latest improvements in the diet, and those came just before I was born. They, like the original diet, gave more DGDs the courage to have children. They were supposed to do for DGDs what insulin had done for diabetics—give us a normal or nearly normal life span. Maybe they had worked for someone somewhere. They hadn't worked for anyone I knew.

Biology school was a pain in the usual ways. I didn't eat in public anymore, didn't like the way people stared at my biscuits—cleverly dubbed "dog biscuits" in every school I'd ever attended. You'd think university students would be more creative. I didn't like the way people edged away from me when they caught sight of my emblem. I'd begun wearing it on a chain around my neck and putting it down inside my blouse, but people managed to notice it anyway. People who don't eat in public, who drink nothing more interesting than water, who smoke nothing at all—people like that are suspicious. Or rather, they make others suspicious. Sooner or later, one of those others, finding my fingers and wrists bare, would fake an interest in my chain. That would be that. I couldn't hide the emblem in my purse. If anything happened to me, medical people had to see it in time to avoid giving me the medications they might use on a normal person. It isn't just ordinary food we have to avoid, but about a quarter of a *Physicians' Desk Reference* of widely used drugs. Every now and then there are news stories about people who stopped carrying their emblems—probably trying to pass as normal. Then they have an accident. By the time anyone realizes there is anything wrong, it's too late. So I wore my emblem. And one way or another, people got a look at it or got the word from someone who had. "She *is*!" Yeah.

At the beginning of my third year, four other DGDs and I decided to rent a house together. We'd all had enough of being lepers twenty-four hours a day. There was an English major. He wanted to be a writer and tell our story from the inside—which had only been done thirty or forty times before. There was a special-education major who hoped the handicapped would accept her more readily than the able-bodied, a premed who planned to go into research, and a chemistry major who didn't really know what she wanted to do.

Two men and three women. All we had in common was our disease, plus a weird combination of stubborn intensity about whatever we happened to be doing and hopeless cynicism about everything else. Healthy people say no one can concentrate like a DGD. Healthy people have all the time in the world for stupid generalizations and short attention spans.

We did our work, came up for air now and then, ate our biscuits, and attended classes. Our only problem was housecleaning. We worked out a schedule of who would clean what when, who would deal with the yard, whatever. We all agreed on it; then, except for me, everyone seemed to forget about it. I found myself going around reminding people to vacuum, clean the bathroom, mow the lawn. . . . I figured they'd all hate me in no time, but I wasn't going to be their maid, and I wasn't going to live in filth. Nobody complained. Nobody even seemed annoyed. They just came up out of their academic daze, cleaned, mopped, mowed, and went back to it. I got into the habit of running around in the evening reminding people. It didn't bother me if it didn't bother them.

"How'd you get to be housemother?" a visiting DGD asked.

I shrugged. "Who cares? The house works." It did. It worked so well that this new guy wanted to move in. He was a friend of one of the others, and another premed. Not bad looking.

"So do I get in or don't I?" he asked.

"As far as I'm concerned, you do," I said. I did what his friend should have done—introduced him around, then, after he left, talked to the others to make sure nobody had any real objections. He seemed to fit right in. He forgot to clean the toilet or mow the lawn, just like the others. His name was Alan Chi. I thought Chi was a Chinese name, and I wondered. But he told me his father was Nigerian and that in Ibo the word meant a kind of guardian angel or personal God. He said his own personal God hadn't been looking out for him very well to let him be born to two DGD parents. Him too.

I don't think it was much more than that similarity that drew us together at first. Sure, I liked the way he looked, but I was used to liking someone's looks and having him run like hell when he found out what I was. It took me a while to get used to the fact that Alan wasn't going anywhere.

I told him about my visit to the DGD ward when I was fifteen—and my suicide attempt afterward. I had never told anyone else. I was surprised at how relieved it made me feel to tell him. And somehow his reaction didn't surprise me.

"Why didn't you try again?" he asked. We were alone in the living room.

"At first, because of my parents," I said. "My father in particular. I couldn't do that to him again."

"And after him?"

"Fear. Inertia."

He nodded. "When I do it, there'll be no half measures. No being rescued, no waking up in a hospital later."

"You mean to do it?"

"The day I realize I've started to drift. Thank God we get some warning."

"Not necessarily."

"Yes, we do. I've done a lot of reading. Even talked to a couple of doctors. Don't believe the rumors non-DGDs invent."

I looked away, stared into the scarred, empty fireplace. I told him exactly how my father had died—something else I'd never voluntarily told anyone.

He sighed. "Jesus!"

We looked at each other.

"What are you going to do?" he asked.

"I don't know."

He extended a dark, square hand, and I took it and moved closer to him. He was a dark, square man—my height, half again my weight, and none of it fat. He was so bitter sometimes, he scared me.

"My mother started to drift when I was three," he said. "My father only lasted a few months longer. I heard he died a couple of years after he went into the hospital. If the two of them had had any sense, they would have had me aborted the minute my mother realized she was pregnant. But she wanted a kid no matter what. And she was Catholic." He shook his head. "Hell, they should pass a law to sterilize the lot of us."

"They?" I said.

"You want kids?"

"No, but—"

"More like us to wind up chewing their fingers off in some DGD ward."

"I don't want kids, but I don't want someone else telling me I can't have any."

He stared at me until I began to feel stupid and defensive. I moved away from him.

"Do you want someone else telling you what to do with your body?" I asked.

"No need," he said. "I had that taken care of as soon as I was old enough."

This left me staring. I'd thought about sterilization. What DGD hasn't? But I didn't know anyone else our age who had actually gone through with it. That would be like killing part of yourself—even though it wasn't a part you intended to use. Killing part of yourself when so much of you was already dead.

"The damned disease could be wiped out in one generation," he said, "but people are still animals when it comes to breeding. Still following mindless urges, like dogs and cats."

My impulse was to get up and go away, leave him to wallow in his bitterness and depression alone. But I stayed. He seemed to want to live even less than I did. I wondered how he'd made it this far.

"Are you looking forward to doing research?" I probed. "Do you believe you'll be able to—"

"No."

I blinked. The word was as cold and dead a sound as I'd ever heard.

"I don't believe in anything," he said.

I took him to bed. He was the only other double DGD I had ever met, and if nobody did anything for him, he wouldn't last much longer. I couldn't just let him slip away. For a while, maybe we could be each other's reasons for staying alive.

He was a good student—for the same reason I was. And he seemed to shed some of his bitterness as time passed. Being around him helped me understand why, against all sanity, two DGDs would lock in on each other and start talking about marriage. Who else would have us?

We probably wouldn't last very long, anyway. These days,

most DGDs make it to forty, at least. But then, most of them
don't have two DGD parents. As bright as Alan was, he might
not get into medical school because of his double inheritance.
No one would tell him his bad genes were keeping him out,
of course, but we both knew what his chances were. Better to
train doctors who were likely to live long enough to put their
training to use.

Alan's mother had been sent to Dilg. He hadn't seen her or
been able to get any information about her from his grandpar-
ents while he was at home. By the time he left for college, he'd
stopped asking questions. Maybe it was hearing about my parents that made him start again. I was with him when he called
Dilg. Until that moment, he hadn't even known whether his
mother was still alive. Surprisingly, she was.

"Dilg must be good," I said when he hung up. "People
don't usually . . . I mean . . ."

"Yeah, I know," he said. "People don't usually live long once
they're out of control. Dilg is different." We had gone to my
room, where he turned a chair backward and sat down. "Dilg is
what the others ought to be, if you can believe the literature."

"Dilg is a giant DGD ward," I said. "It's richer—probably
better at sucking in the donations—and it's run by people who
can expect to become patients eventually. Apart from that,
what's different?"

"I've read about it," he said. "So should you. They've got
some new treatment. They don't just shut people away to die
the way the others do."

"What else is there to do with them? With us."

"I don't know. It sounded like they have some kind of . . .
sheltered workshop. They've got patients doing things."

"A new drug to control the self-destructiveness?"

"I don't think so. We would have heard about that."

"What else could it be?"

"I'm going up to find out. Will you come with me?"

"You're going up to see your mother."

He took a ragged breath. "Yeah. Will you come with me?"

I went to one of my windows and stared out at the weeds.
We let them thrive in the backyard. In the front we mowed
them, along with the few patches of grass.

"I told you my DGD-ward experience."

"You're not fifteen now. And Dilg isn't some zoo of a ward."

"It's got to be, no matter what they tell the public. And I'm not sure I can stand it."

He got up, came to stand next to me. "Will you try?"

I didn't say anything. I focused on our reflections in the window glass—the two of us together. It looked right, felt right. He put his arm around me, and I leaned back against him. Our being together had been as good for me as it seemed to have been for him. It had given me something to go on besides inertia and fear. I knew I would go with him. It felt like the right thing to do.

"I can't say how I'll act when we get there," I said.

"I can't say how I'll act, either," he admitted. "Especially . . . when I see her."

He made the appointment for the next Saturday afternoon. You make appointments to go to Dilg unless you're a government inspector of some kind. That is the custom, and Dilg gets away with it.

We left L.A. in the rain early Saturday morning. Rain followed us off and on up the coast as far as Santa Barbara. Dilg was hidden away in the hills not far from San Jose. We could have reached it faster by driving up I-5, but neither of us were in the mood for all that bleakness. As it was, we arrived at one P.M. to be met by two armed gate guards. One of these phoned the main building and verified our appointment. Then the other took the wheel from Alan.

"Sorry," he said. "But no one is permitted inside without an escort. We'll meet your guide at the garage."

None of this surprised me. Dilg is a place where not only the patients but much of the staff has DGD. A maximum security prison wouldn't have been as potentially dangerous. On the other hand, I'd never heard of anyone getting chewed up here. Hospitals and rest homes had accidents. Dilg didn't. It was beautiful—an old estate. One that didn't make sense in these days of high taxes. It had been owned by the Dilg family. Oil, chemicals, pharmaceuticals. Ironically, they had even owned part of the late, unlamented Hedeon Laboratories. They'd had a briefly profitable interest in Hedeonco: the magic bullet, the cure for a large percentage of the world's cancer and a number of serious viral diseases—and the cause of Duryea-Gode disease. If one of your parents was treated with Hedeonco and you were conceived after the treatments, you had DGD. If you had kids, you passed it on to them. Not everyone was equally affected. They didn't all commit suicide or murder, but they all mutilated themselves to some degree if they could. And they all drifted—went off into a world of their own and stopped responding to their surroundings.

Anyway, the only Dilg son of his generation had had his life saved by Hedeonco. Then he had watched four of his children die before Doctors Kenneth Duryea and Jan Gode came up with a decent understanding of the problem and a partial solution: the diet. They gave Richard Dilg a way of keeping his next two children alive. He gave the big, cumbersome estate over to the care of DGD patients.

So the main building was an elaborate old mansion. There were other, newer buildings, more like guest houses than institutional buildings. And there were wooded hills all around. Nice country. Green. The ocean wasn't far away. There was an old garage and a small parking lot. Waiting in the lot was a tall, old woman. Our guard pulled up near her, let us out, then parked the car in the half-empty garage.

"Hello," the woman said, extending her hand. "I'm Beatrice Alcantara." The hand was cool and dry and startlingly strong. I thought the woman was DGD, but her age threw me. She appeared to be about sixty, and I had never seen a DGD that old. I wasn't sure why I thought she was DGD. If she was, she must have been an experimental model—one of the first to survive.

"Is it Doctor or Ms.?" Alan asked.

"It's Beatrice," she said. "I am a doctor, but we don't use titles much here."

I glanced at Alan, was surprised to see him smiling at her. He tended to go a long time between smiles. I looked at Beatrice and couldn't see anything to smile about. As we introduced ourselves, I realized I didn't like her. I couldn't see any reason for that either, but my feelings were my feelings. I didn't like her.

"I assume neither of you have been here before," she said, smiling down at us. She was at least six feet tall, and straight.

We shook our heads. "Let's go in the front way, then. I want to prepare you for what we do here. I don't want you to believe you've come to a hospital."

I frowned at her, wondering what else there was to believe. Dilg was called a retreat, but what difference did names make?

The house close up looked like one of the old-style public buildings—massive, baroque front with a single domed tower reaching three stories above the three-story house. Wings of the house stretched for some distance to the right and left of the tower, then cornered and stretched back twice as far. The front doors were huge—one set of wrought iron and one of heavy wood. Neither appeared to be locked. Beatrice pulled open the iron door, pushed the wooden one, and gestured us in.

Inside, the house was an art museum—huge, high ceilinged, tile floored. There were marble columns and niches in which sculptures stood or paintings hung. There were other sculptures displayed around the rooms. At one end of the rooms there was a broad staircase leading up to a gallery that went around the rooms. There more art was displayed. "All this was made here," Beatrice said. "Some of it is even sold from here. Most goes to galleries in the Bay Area or down around L.A. Our only problem is turning out too much of it."

"You mean the patients do this?" I asked.

The old woman nodded. "This and much more. Our people work instead of tearing at themselves or staring into space. One of them invented the p.v. locks that protect this place. Though I almost wish he hadn't. It's gotten us more government attention than we like."

"What kind of locks?" I asked.

"Sorry. Palmprint-voiceprint. The first and the best. We have the patent." She looked at Alan. "Would you like to see what your mother does?"

"Wait a minute," he said. "You're telling us out-of-control DGDs create art and invent things?"

"And that lock," I said. "I've never heard of anything like that. I didn't even see a lock."

"The lock is new," she said. "There have been a few news stories about it. It's not the kind of thing most people would buy for their homes. Too expensive. So it's of limited interest. People tend to look at what's done at Dilg in the way they look at the efforts of idiots savants. Interesting, incomprehensible, but not really important. Those likely to be interested in the lock and able to afford it know about it." She took a deep breath, faced Alan again. "Oh, yes, DGDs create things. At least they do here."

"Out-of-control DGDs."

"Yes."

"I expected to find them weaving baskets or something—at best. I know what DGD wards are like."

"So do I," she said. "I know what they're like in hospitals, and I know what it's like here." She waved a hand toward an abstract painting that looked like a photo I had once seen of the Orion Nebula. Darkness broken by a great cloud of light and color. "Here we can help them channel their energies. They can create something beautiful, useful, even something worthless. But they create. They don't destroy."

"Why?" Alan demanded. "It can't be some drug. We would have heard."

"It's not a drug."

"Then what is it? Why haven't other hospitals—?"

"Alan," she said. "Wait."

He stood frowning at her.

"Do you want to see your mother?"

"Of course I want to see her!"

"Good. Come with me. Things will sort themselves out."

She led us to a corridor past offices where people talked to one another, waved to Beatrice, worked with computers. . . . They could have been anywhere. I wondered how many of them were controlled DGDs. I also wondered what kind of game the old woman was playing with her secrets. We passed through rooms so beautiful and perfectly kept it was obvious they were rarely used. Then at a broad, heavy door, she stopped us.

"Look at anything you like as we go on," she said. "But don't touch anything or anyone. And remember that some of the people you'll see injured themselves before they came to us. They still bear the scars of those injuries. Some of those scars may be difficult to look at, but you'll be in no danger. Keep that in mind. No one here will harm you." She pushed the door open and gestured us in.

Scars didn't bother me much. Disability didn't bother me. It was the act of self-mutilation that scared me. It was someone attacking her own arm as though it were a wild animal. It was someone who had torn at himself and been restrained or drugged off and on for so long that he barely had a recognizable human feature left, but he was still trying with what he did have to dig into his own flesh. Those are a couple of the things I saw at the DGD ward when I was fifteen. Even then I could have stood it better if I hadn't felt I was looking into a kind of temporal mirror.

I wasn't aware of walking through that doorway. I wouldn't have thought I could do it. The old woman said something, though, and I found myself on the other side of the door with the door closing behind me. I turned to stare at her.

She put her hand on my arm. "It's all right," she said quietly. "That door looks like a wall to a great many people."

I backed away from her, out of her reach, repelled by her touch. Shaking hands had been enough, for God's sake.

Something in her seemed to come to attention as she watched me. It made her even straighter. Deliberately, but for no apparent reason, she stepped toward Alan, touched him the way people do sometimes when they brush past—a kind of tactile "Excuse me." In that wide, empty corridor, it was totally unnecessary. For some reason, she wanted to touch him and wanted me to see. What did she think she was doing? Flirting at her age? I glared at her, found myself suppressing an irrational urge to shove her away from him. The violence of the urge amazed me.

Beatrice smiled and turned away. "This way," she said. Alan put his arm around me and tried to lead me after her.

"Wait a minute," I said, not moving.

Beatrice glanced around.

"What just happened?" I asked. I was ready for her to lie—to say nothing happened, pretend not to know what I was talking about.

"Are you planning to study medicine?" she asked.

"What? What does that have to do—?"

"Study medicine. You may be able to do a great deal of good." She strode away, taking long steps so that we had to hurry to keep up. She led us through a room in which some people worked at computer terminals and others with pencils and paper. It would have been an ordinary scene except that some people had half their faces ruined or had only one hand

or leg or had other obvious scars. But they were all in control now. They were working. They were intent but not intent
on self-destruction. Not one was digging into or tearing away
flesh. When we had passed through this room and into a small,
ornate sitting room, Alan grasped Beatrice's arm.

"What is it?" he demanded. "What do you do for them?"

She patted his hand, setting my teeth on edge. "I will tell
you," she said. "I want you to know. But I want you to see
your mother first." To my surprise, he nodded, let it go at that.

"Sit a moment," she said to us.

We sat in comfortable, matching upholstered chairs—Alan
looking reasonably relaxed. What was it about the old lady that
relaxed him but put me on edge? Maybe she reminded him
of his grandmother or something. She didn't remind me of
anyone. And what was that nonsense about studying medicine?

"I wanted you to pass through at least one workroom before
we talked about your mother—and about the two of you." She
turned to face me. "You've had a bad experience at a hospital
or a rest home?"

I looked away from her, not wanting to think about it.
Hadn't the people in that mock office been enough of a reminder? Horror film office. Nightmare office.

"It's all right," she said. "You don't have to go into detail.
Just outline it for me."

I obeyed slowly, against my will, all the while wondering
why I was doing it.

She nodded, unsurprised. "Harsh, loving people, your parents. Are they alive?"

"No."

"Were they both DGD?"

"Yes, but . . . yes."

"Of course, aside from the obvious ugliness of your hospital
experience and its implications for the future, what impressed
you about the people in the ward?"

I didn't know what to answer. What did she want? Why did
she want anything from me? She should have been concerned
with Alan and his mother.

"Did you see people unrestrained?"

"Yes," I whispered. "One woman. I don't know how it happened that she was free. She ran up to us and slammed into my

father without moving him. He was a big man. She bounced off, fell, and . . . began tearing at herself. She bit her own arm and . . . swallowed the flesh she'd bitten away. She tore at the wound she'd made with the nails of her other hand. She . . . I screamed at her to stop." I hugged myself, remembering the young woman, bloody, cannibalizing herself as she lay at our feet, digging into her own flesh. Digging. "They try so hard, fight so hard to get out."

"Out of what?" Alan demanded.

I looked at him, hardly seeing him.

"Lynn," he said gently. "Out of what?"

I shook my head. "Their restraints, their disease, the ward, their bodies . . ."

He glanced at Beatrice, then spoke to me again. "Did the girl talk?"

"No. She screamed."

He turned away from me uncomfortably. "Is this important?" he asked Beatrice.

"Very," she said.

"Well . . . can we talk about it after I see my mother?"

"Then and now." She spoke to me. "Did the girl stop what she was doing when you told her to?"

"The nurses had her a moment later. It didn't matter."

"It mattered. Did she stop?"

"Yes."

"According to the literature, they rarely respond to anyone," Alan said.

"True." Beatrice gave him a sad smile. "Your mother will probably respond to you, though."

"Is she? . . ." He glanced back at the nightmare office. "Is she as controlled as those people?"

"Yes, though she hasn't always been. Your mother works with clay now. She loves shapes and textures and—"

"She's blind," Alan said, voicing the suspicion as though it were fact. Beatrice's words had sent my thoughts in the same direction. Beatrice hesitated. "Yes," she said finally. "And for . . . the usual reason. I had intended to prepare you slowly."

"I've done a lot of reading."

I hadn't done much reading, but I knew what the usual reason was. The woman had gouged, ripped, or otherwise destroyed her eyes. She would be badly scarred. I got up, went over to sit on the arm of Alan's chair. I rested my hand on his shoulder, and he reached up and held it there.

"Can we see her now?" he asked.

Beatrice got up. "This way," she said.

We passed through more workrooms. People painted; assembled machinery; sculpted in wood, stone; even composed and played music. Almost no one noticed us. The patients were true to their disease in that respect. They weren't ignoring us. They clearly didn't know we existed. Only the few controlled-DGD guards gave themselves away by waving or speaking to Beatrice. I watched a woman work quickly, knowledgeably, with a power saw. She obviously understood the perimeters of her body, was not so dissociated as to perceive herself as trapped in something she needed to dig her way out of. What had Dilg done for these people that other hospitals did not do? And how could Dilg withhold its treatment from the others?

"Over there we make our own diet foods," Beatrice said, pointing through a window toward one of the guest houses. "We permit more variety and make fewer mistakes than the commercial preparers. No ordinary person can concentrate on work the way our people can."

I turned to face her. "What are you saying? That the bigots are right? That we have some special gift?"

"Yes," she said. "It's hardly a bad characteristic, is it?"

"It's what people say whenever one of us does well at something. It's their way of denying us credit for our work."

"Yes. But people occasionally come to the right conclusions for the wrong reasons." I shrugged, not interested in arguing with her about it.

"Alan?" she said. He looked at her.

"Your mother is in the next room."

He swallowed, nodded. We both followed her into the room.

Naomi Chi was a small woman, hair still dark, fingers long and thin, graceful as they shaped the clay. Her face was a ruin. Not only her eyes but most of her nose and one ear were gone. What was left was badly scarred. "Her parents were poor," Beatrice said. "I don't know how much they told you, Alan, but they went through all the money they had, trying to keep her at a decent place. Her mother felt so guilty, you know. She was the one who had cancer and took the drug. . . . Eventually, they had to put Naomi in one of those state-approved, custodial-care places. You know the kind. For a while, it was all the government would pay for. Places like that . . . well, sometimes if patients were really troublesome—especially the ones who kept breaking free—they'd put them in a bare room and let them finish themselves. The only things those places took good care of were the maggots, the cockroaches, and the rats."

I shuddered. "I've heard there are still places like that."

"There are," Beatrice said, "kept open by greed and indifference." She looked at Alan. "Your mother survived for three months in one of those places. I took her from it myself. Later I was instrumental in having that particular place closed."

"You took her?" I asked.

"Dilg didn't exist then, but I was working with a group of controlled DGDs in L.A. Naomi's parents heard about us and asked us to take her. A lot of people didn't trust us then. Only a few of us were medically trained. All of us were young, idealistic, and ignorant. We began in an old frame house with a leaky roof. Naomi's parents were grabbing at straws. So were we. And by pure luck, we grabbed a good one. We were able to prove ourselves to the Dilg family and take over these quarters."

"Prove what?" I asked.

She turned to look at Alan and his mother. Alan was staring at Naomi's ruined face, at the ropy, discolored scar tissue. Naomi was shaping the image of an old woman and two children. The gaunt, lined face of the old woman was remarkably vivid—detailed in a way that seemed impossible for a blind sculptress.

Naomi seemed unaware of us. Her total attention remained on her work. Alan forgot about what Beatrice had told us and reached out to touch the scarred face.

Beatrice let it happen. Naomi did not seem to notice. "If I get her attention for you," Beatrice said, "we'll be breaking her routine. We'll have to stay with her until she gets back into it without hurting herself. About half an hour."

"You can get her attention?" he asked.

"Yes."

"Can she? . . ." Alan swallowed. "I've never heard of anything like this. Can she talk?"

"Yes. She may not choose to, though. And if she does, she'll do it very slowly."

"Do it. Get her attention."

"She'll want to touch you."

"That's all right. Do it."

Beatrice took Naomi's hands and held them still, away from the wet clay. For several seconds Naomi tugged at her captive hands, as though unable to understand why they did not move as she wished.

Beatrice stepped closer and spoke quietly. "Stop, Naomi." And Naomi was still, blind face turned toward Beatrice in an attitude of attentive waiting. Totally focused waiting.

"Company, Naomi."

After a few seconds, Naomi made a wordless sound.

Beatrice gestured Alan to her side, gave Naomi one of his hands. It didn't bother me this time when she touched him. I was too interested in what was happening. Naomi examined Alan's hand minutely, then followed the arm up to the shoulder, the neck, the face. Holding his face between her hands, she made a sound. It may have been a word, but I couldn't understand it. All I could think of was the danger of those hands. I thought of my father's hands.

"His name is Alan Chi, Naomi. He's your son." Several seconds passed.

"Son?" she said. This time the word was quite distinct, though her lips had split in many places and had healed badly. "Son?" she repeated anxiously. "Here?"

"He's all right, Naomi. He's come to visit."

"Mother?" he said.

She reexamined his face. He had been three when she started to drift. It didn't seem possible that she could find anything in his face that she would remember. I wondered whether she remembered she had a son.

"Alan?" she said. She found his tears and paused at them. She touched her own face where there should have been an eye, then she reached back toward his eyes. An instant before I would have grabbed her hand, Beatrice did it.

"No!" Beatrice said firmly.

The hand fell limply to Naomi's side. Her face turned toward Beatrice like an antique weather vane swinging around. Beatrice stroked her hair, and Naomi said something I almost understood. Beatrice looked at Alan, who was frowning and wiping away tears.

"Hug your son," Beatrice said softly.

Naomi turned, groping, and Alan seized her in a tight, long hug. Her arms went around him slowly. She spoke words blurred by her ruined mouth but just understandable.

"Parents?" she said. "Did my parents . . . care for you?" Alan looked at her, clearly not understanding.

"She wants to know whether her parents took care of you," I said.

He glanced at me doubtfully, then looked at Beatrice.

"Yes," Beatrice said. "She just wants to know that they cared for you."

"They did," he said. "They kept their promise to you, Mother."

Several seconds passed. Naomi made sounds that even Alan took to be weeping, and he tried to comfort her.

"Who else is here?" she said finally.

This time Alan looked at me. I repeated what she had said.

"Her name is Lynn Mortimer," he said. "I'm . . ." He paused awkwardly. "She and I are going to be married."

After a time, she moved back from him and said my name. My first impulse was to go to her. I wasn't afraid or repelled by her now, but for no reason I could explain, I looked at Beatrice.

"Go," she said. "But you and I will have to talk later."

I went to Naomi, took her hand.

"Bea?" she said.

"I'm Lynn," I said softly.

She drew a quick breath. "No," she said. "No, you're . . ."

"I'm Lynn. Do you want Bea? She's here."

She said nothing. She put her hand to my face, explored it slowly. I let her do it, confident that I could stop her if she turned violent. But first one hand, then both, went over me very gently.

"You'll marry my son?" she said finally.

"Yes."

"Good. You'll keep him safe."

As much as possible, we'll keep each other safe. "Yes," I said.

"Good. No one will close him away from himself. No one will tie him or cage him." Her hand wandered to her own face again, nails biting in slightly.

"No," I said softly, catching the hand. "I want you to be safe, too."

The mouth moved. I think it smiled. "Son?" she said.

He understood her, took her hand.

"Clay," she said. Lynn and Alan in clay. "Bea?"

"Of course," Beatrice said. "Do you have an impression?"

"No!" It was the fastest that Naomi had answered anything. Then, almost childlike, she whispered, "Yes."

Beatrice laughed. "Touch them again if you like, Naomi. They don't mind."

We didn't. Alan closed his eyes, trusting her gentleness in a way I could not. I had no trouble accepting her touch, even so near my eyes, but I did not delude myself about her. Her gentleness could turn in an instant. Naomi's fingers twitched near Alan's eyes, and I spoke up at once, out of fear for him.

"Just touch him, Naomi. Only touch."

She froze, made an interrogative sound.

"She's all right," Alan said.

"I know," I said, not believing it. He would be all right, though, as long as someone watched her very carefully, nipped any dangerous impulses in the bud.

"Son!" she said, happily possessive. When she let him go, she demanded clay, wouldn't touch her old-woman sculpture again. Beatrice got new clay for her, leaving us to soothe her and ease her impatience. Alan began to recognize signs of impending destructive behavior. Twice he caught her hands and said no. She struggled against him until I spoke to her. As Beatrice returned, it happened again, and Beatrice said, "No, Naomi." Obediently Naomi let her hands fall to her sides.

"What is it?" Alan demanded later when we had left Naomi safely, totally focused on her new work—clay sculptures of us. "Does she only listen to women or something?"

Beatrice took us back to the sitting room, sat us both down, but did not sit down herself. She went to a window and stared out. "Naomi only obeys certain women," she said. "And she's sometimes slow to obey. She's worse than most—probably because of the damage she managed to do to herself before I got her." Beatrice faced us, stood biting her lip and frowning. "I haven't had to give this particular speech for a while," she said. "Most DGDs have the sense not to marry each other and produce children. I hope you two aren't planning to have any —in spite of our need." She took a deep breath. "It's a pheromone. A scent. And it's sex-linked. Men who inherit the disease from their fathers have no trace of the scent. They also tend to have an easier time with the disease. But they're useless to use as staff here. Men who inherit from their mothers have as much of the scent as men get. They can be useful here because the DGDs can at least be made to notice them. The same for women who inherit from their mothers but not their fathers. It's only when two irresponsible DGDs get together and produce girl children like me or Lynn that you get someone who can really do some good in a place like this." She looked at me. "We are very rare commodities, you and I. When you finish school you'll have a very well-paying job waiting for you."

"Here?" I asked.

"For training, perhaps. Beyond that, I don't know. You'll probably help start a retreat in some other part of the country. Others are badly needed." She smiled humorlessly. "People like us don't get along well together. You must realize that I don't like you any more than you like me."

I swallowed, saw her through a kind of haze for a moment. Hated her mindlessly—just for a moment.

"Sit back," she said. "Relax your body. It helps."

I obeyed, not really wanting to obey her but unable to think of anything else to do. Unable to think at all. "We seem," she said, "to be very territorial. Dilg is a haven for me when I'm the only one of my kind here. When I'm not, it's a prison."

"All it looks like to me is an unbelievable amount of work," Alan said.

She nodded. "Almost too much." She smiled to herself. "I was one of the first double DGDs to be born. When I was old enough to understand, I thought I didn't have much time. First I tried to kill myself. Failing that, I tried to cram all the living I could into the small amount of time I assumed I had.

When I got into this project, I worked as hard as I could to get it into shape before I started to drift. By now I wouldn't know what to do with myself if I weren't working."

"Why haven't you . . . drifted?" I asked.

"I don't know. There aren't enough of our kind to know what's normal for us."

"Drifting is normal for every DGD sooner or later."

"Later, then."

"Why hasn't the scent been synthesized?" Alan asked. "Why are there still concentration-camp rest homes and hospital wards?"

"There have been people trying to synthesize it since I proved what I could do with it. No one has succeeded so far. All we've been able to do is keep our eyes open for people like Lynn." She looked at me. "Dilg scholarship, right?"

"Yeah. Offered out of the blue."

"My people do a good job keeping track. You would have been contacted just before you graduated or if you dropped out."

"Is it possible," Alan said, staring at me, "that she's already doing it? Already using the scent to . . . influence people?"

"You?" Beatrice asked.

"All of us. A group of DGDs. We all live together. We're all controlled, of course, but . . ." Beatrice smiled. "It's probably the quietest house full of kids that anyone's ever seen."

I looked at Alan, and he looked away. "I'm not doing anything to them," I said. "I remind them of work they've already promised to do. That's all."

"You put them at ease," Beatrice said. "You're there. You . . . well, you leave your scent around the house. You speak to them individually. Without knowing why, they no doubt find that very comforting. Don't you, Alan?"

"I don't know," he said. "I suppose I must have. From my first visit to the house, I knew I wanted to move in. And when I first saw Lynn, I . . ." He shook his head. "Funny, I thought all that was my idea."

"Will you work with us, Alan?"

"Me? You want Lynn."

"I want you both. You have no idea how many people take one look at one workroom here and turn and run. You may be the kind of young people who ought to eventually take charge of a place like Dilg."

"Whether we want to or not, eh?" he said.

Frightened, I tried to take his hand, but he moved it away. "Alan, this works," I said. "It's only a stopgap, I know. Genetic engineering will probably give us the final answers, but for God's sake, this is something we can do now!"

"It's something *you* can do. Play queen bee in a retreat full of workers. I've never had any ambition to be a drone."

"A physician isn't likely to be a drone," Beatrice said.

"Would you marry one of your patients?" he demanded. "That's what Lynn would be doing if she married me—whether I become a doctor or not."

She looked away from him, stared across the room. "My husband is here," she said softly. "He's been a patient here for almost a decade. What better place for him . . . when his time came?"

"Shit!" Alan muttered. He glanced at me. "Let's get out of here!" He got up and strode across the room to the door, pulled at it, then realized it was locked. He turned to face Beatrice, his body language demanding she let him out. She went to him, took him by the shoulder, and turned him to face the door. "Try it once more," she said quietly. "You can't break it. Try."

Surprisingly, some of the hostility seemed to go out of him. "This is one of those p.v. locks?" he asked.

"Yes."

I set my teeth and looked away. Let her work. She knew how to use this thing she and I both had. And for the moment, she was on my side.

I heard him make some effort with the door. The door didn't even rattle. Beatrice took his hand from it, and with her own hand flat against what appeared to be a large brass knob, she pushed the door open.

"The man who created that lock is nobody in particular," she said. "He doesn't have an unusually high I.Q., didn't even finish college. But sometime in his life he read a science-fiction story in which palmprint locks were a given. He went that story one better by creating one that responded to voice or palm. It took him years, but we were able to give him those years. The people of Dilg are problem solvers, Alan. Think of the problems you could solve!"

He looked as though he were beginning to think, beginning to understand. "I don't see how biological research can be done that way," he said. "Not with everyone acting on his own, not even aware of other researchers and their work."

"It *is* being done," she said, "and not in isolation. Our retreat in Colorado specializes in it and has—just barely—enough trained, controlled DGDs to see that no one really works in isolation. Our patients can still read and write—those who haven't damaged themselves too badly. They can take each other's work into account if reports are made available to them. And they can read material that comes in from the outside. They're working, Alan. The disease hasn't stopped them, *won't* stop them."

He stared at her, seemed to be caught by her intensity—or her scent. He spoke as though his words were a strain, as though they hurt his throat. "I won't be a puppet. I won't be controlled . . . by a goddamn smell!"

"Alan—"

"I won't be what my mother is. I'd rather be dead!"

"There's no reason for you to become what your mother is."

He drew back in obvious disbelief.

"Your mother is brain damaged—thanks to the three months she spent in that custodial-care toilet. She had no speech at all when I met her. She's improved more than you can imagine. None of that has to happen to you. Work with us, and we'll see that none of it happens to you."

He hesitated, seemed less sure of himself. Even that much flexibility in him was surprising. "I'll be under your control or Lynn's," he said.

She shook her head. "Not even your mother is under my control. She's aware of me. She's able to take direction from me. She trusts me the way any blind person would trust her guide."

"There's more to it than that."

"Not here. Not at any of our retreats."

"I don't believe you."

"Then you don't understand how much individuality our people retain. They know they need help, but they have minds of their own. If you want to see the abuse of power you're worried about, go to a DGD ward."

"You're better than that, I admit. Hell is probably better than that. But . . ."

"But you don't trust us."

He shrugged.

"You do, you know." She smiled. "You don't want to, but you do. That's what worries you, and it leaves you with work to do. Look into what I've said. See for yourself. We offer DGDs a chance to live and do whatever they decide is important to them. What do you have, what can you realistically hope for that's better than that?"

Silence. "I don't know what to think," he said finally.

"Go home," she said. "Decide what to think. It's the most important decision you'll ever make."

He looked at me. I went to him, not sure how he'd react, not sure he'd want me no matter what he decided.

"What are you going to do?" he asked.

The question startled me. "You have a choice," I said. "I don't. If she's right . . . how could I not wind up running a retreat?"

"Do you want to?"

I swallowed. I hadn't really faced that question yet. Did I want to spend my life in something that was basically a refined DGD ward? "No!"

"But you will."

". . . Yes." I thought for a moment, hunted for the right words. "You'd do it."

"What?"

"If the pheromone were something only men had, you would do it."

That silence again. After a time he took my hand, and we followed Beatrice out to the car. Before I could get in with him and our guard-escort, she caught my arm. I jerked away reflexively. By the time I caught myself, I had swung around as though I meant to hit her. Hell, I did mean to hit her, but I stopped myself in time. "Sorry," I said with no attempt at sincerity.

She held out a card until I took it. "My private number," she said. "Before seven or after nine, usually. You and I will communicate best by phone."

I resisted the impulse to throw the card away. God, she brought out the child in me.

Inside the car, Alan said something to the guard. I couldn't hear what it was, but the sound of his voice reminded me of him arguing with her—her logic and her scent. She had all but won him for me, and I couldn't manage even token gratitude. I spoke to her, low voiced.

"He never really had a chance, did he?"

She looked surprised. "That's up to you. You can keep him or drive him away. I assure you, you *can* drive him away."

"How?"

"By imagining that he doesn't have a chance." She smiled faintly. "Phone me from your territory. We have a great deal to say to each other, and I'd rather we didn't say it as enemies."

She had lived with meeting people like me for decades. She had good control. I, on the other hand, was at the end of my control. All I could do was scramble into the car and floor my own phantom accelerator as the guard drove us to the gate. I couldn't look back at her. Until we were well away from the house, until we'd left the guard at the gate and gone off the property, I couldn't make myself look back. For long, irrational minutes, I was convinced that somehow if I turned, I would see myself standing there, gray and old, growing small in the distance, vanishing.

Afterword

"The Evening and the Morning and the Night" grew from my ongoing fascinations with biology, medicine, and personal responsibility.

In particular, I began the story wondering how much of what we do is encouraged, discouraged, or otherwise guided by what we are genetically. This is one of my favorite questions, parent to several of my novels. It can be a dangerous question. All too often, when people ask it, they mean who has the biggest or the best or the most of whatever they see as desirable, or who has the smallest and the least of what is undesirable. Genetics as a board game, or worse, as an excuse for the social Darwinism that swings into popularity every few years. Nasty habit.

And yet the question itself is fascinating. And disease, grim as it is, is one way to explore answers. Genetic disorders in particular may teach us much about who and what we are.

I built Duryea-Gode disease from elements of three genetic disorders. The first is Huntington's disease—hereditary, dominant, and thus an inevitability if one has the gene for it. And it is caused by only one abnormal gene. Also Huntington's does not usually show itself until its sufferers are middle-aged.

In addition to Huntington's, I used phenylketonuria (PKU), a recessive genetic disorder that causes severe mental impairment unless the infant who has it is put on a special diet.

Finally, I used Lesch-Nyhan disease, which causes both mental impairment and self-mutilation.

To elements of these disorders, I added my own particular twists: a sensitivity to pheromones and the sufferers' persistent delusion that they are trapped, imprisoned within their own flesh, and that that flesh is somehow not truly part of them. In that last, I took an idea familiar to us all—present in many religions and philosophies—and carried it to a terrible extreme.

We carry as many as 50,000 different genes in each of the nuclei of our billions of cells. If one gene among the 50,000, the Huntington's gene, for instance, can so greatly change our lives—what we can do, what we can become—then what are we?

What, indeed?

For readers who find this question as fascinating as I do, I offer a brief, unconventional reading list: *The Chimpanzees of Gombe: Patterns of Behavior* by Jane Goodall, *The Boy Who Couldn't Stop Washing: The Experience and Treatment of Obsessive-Compulsive Disorder* by Judith L. Rapoport, *Medical Detectives* by Berton Roueché, *An Anthropologist on Mars: Seven Paradoxical Tales* and *The Man Who Mistook His Wife for a Hat and Other Clinical Tales* by Oliver Sacks.

Enjoy!

Amnesty

THE STRANGER-COMMUNITY, globular, easily twelve feet high and wide, glided down into the vast, dimly lit food production hall of Translator Noah Cannon's employer. The stranger was incongruously quick and graceful, keeping to the paths, never once brushing against the raised beds of fragile, edible fungi. It looked, Noah thought, a little like a great, black, moss-enshrouded bush with such a canopy of irregularly-shaped leaves, shaggy mosses, and twisted vines that no light showed through it. It had a few thick, naked branches growing out, away from the main body, breaking the symmetry and making the Community look in serious need of pruning.

The moment Noah saw it and saw her employer, a somewhat smaller, better-maintained-looking dense, black bush, back away from her, she knew she would be offered the new job assignment she had been asking for.

The stranger-Community settled, flattening itself at bottom, allowing its organisms of mobility to migrate upward and take their rest. The stranger-Community focused its attention on Noah, electricity flaring and zigzagging, making a visible display within the dark vastness of its body. She knew that the electrical display was speech, although she could not read what was said. The Communities spoke in this way between themselves and within themselves, but the light they produced moved far too quickly for her to even begin to learn the language. The fact that she saw the display, though, meant that the communications entities of the stranger-Community were addressing her. Communities used their momentarily inactive organisms to shield communication from anyone outside themselves who was not being addressed.

She glanced at her employer and saw that its attention was focused away from her. It had no noticeable eyes, but its entities of vision served it very well whether she could see them or not. It had drawn itself together, made itself look more like a spiny stone than a bush. Communities did this when they wished to offer others privacy or simply disassociate themselves from the business being transacted. Her employer had warned her that the job that would be offered to her would be unpleasant not only because of the usual hostility of the human beings she would face, but because the subcontractor for whom she would be working would be difficult. The subcontractor had had little contact with human beings. Its vocabulary in the painfully created common language that enabled humans and the Communities to speak to one another was, at best, rudimentary, as was its understanding of human abilities and limitations. Translation: by accident or by intent, the subcontractor would probably hurt her. Her employer had told her that she did not have to take this job, that it would support her if she chose not to work for this subcontractor. It did not altogether approve of her decision to try for the job anyway. Now its deliberate inattention had more to do with disassociation than with courtesy or privacy. "You're on your own," its posture said, and she smiled. She could never have worked for it if it had not been able to stand aside and let her make her own decisions. Yet it did not go about its business and leave her alone with the stranger. It waited.

And here was the subcontractor signaling her with lightning.

Obediently, she went to it, stood close to it so that the tips of what looked like moss-covered outer twigs and branches touched her bare skin. She wore only shorts and a halter top. The Communities would have preferred her to be naked, and for the long years of her captivity, she had had no choice. She had been naked. Now she was no longer a captive, and she insisted on wearing at least the basics. Her employer had come to accept this and now refused to lend her to subcontractors who would refuse her the right to wear clothing.

This subcontractor enfolded her immediately, drawing her upward and in among its many selves, first hauling her up with its various organisms of manipulation, then grasping her securely with what appeared to be moss. The Communities were not plants, but it was easiest to think of them in those terms since most of the time, most of them looked so plantlike.

Enfolded within the Community, she couldn't see at all. She closed her eyes to avoid the distraction of trying to see or imagining that she saw. She felt herself surrounded by what felt like long, dry fibers, fronds, rounded fruits of various sizes, and other things that produced less identifiable sensations. She was at once touched, stroked, massaged, compressed in the strangely comfortable, peaceful way that she had come to look forward to whenever she was employed. She was turned and handled as though she weighed nothing. In fact, after a few moments, she felt weightless. She had lost all sense of direction, yet she felt totally secure, clasped by entities that had nothing resembling human limbs. Why this was pleasurable, she never understood, but for twelve years of captivity, it had been her only dependable comfort. It had happened often enough to enable her to endure everything else that was done to her.

Fortunately, the Communities also found it comforting—even more than she did.

After a while, she felt the particular rhythm of quick warning pressures across her back. The Communities liked the broad expanse of skin that the human back offered.

She made a beckoning motion with her right hand to let the Community know that she was paying attention.

There are six recruits, it signaled with pressures against her back. You will teach them.

I will, she signed, using her hands and arms only. The Communities liked her signs to be small, confined gestures when she was enfolded and large, sweeping hand, arm, and whole-body efforts when she was outside and not being touched. She had wondered at first if this was because they couldn't see very well. Now she knew that they could see far better than she could—could see over great distances with specialized entities of vision, could see most bacteria and some viruses, and see colors from ultraviolet through infrared.

In fact the reason that they preferred large gestures when she was out of contact and unlikely to hit or kick anyone was because they liked to watch her move. It was that simple, that odd. In fact, the Communities had developed a real liking for human dance performances and for some human sports events—especially individual performances in gymnastics and ice skating.

The recruits are disturbed, the subcontractor said. They may be dangerous to one another. Calm them.

I will try, Noah said. I will answer their questions and re-assure them that they have nothing to fear. Privately, she suspected that hate might be a more prevalent emotion than fear, but if the subcontractor didn't know that, she wouldn't tell it.

Calm them. The subcontractor repeated. And she knew then that it meant, literally, "Change them from disturbed people to calm, willing workers." The Communities could change one another just by exchanging a few of their individual entities —as long as both exchanging communities were willing. Too many of them assumed that human beings should be able to do something like this too, and that if they wouldn't, they were just being stubborn.

Noah repeated, I will answer their questions and reassure them that they have nothing to fear. That's all I can do.

Will they be calm?

She drew a deep breath, knowing that she was about to be hurt—twisted or torn, broken or stunned. Many Communities punished refusal to obey orders—as they saw it—less harshly than they punished what they saw as lying. In fact, the punishments were left over from the years when human beings were captives of uncertain ability, intellect, and perception. People were not supposed to be punished any longer, but of course they were. Now, Noah thought it was best to get whatever punishment there might be out of the way at once. She could not escape. She signed stolidly, Some of them may believe what I tell them and be calm. Others will need time and experience to calm them.

She was, at once, held more tightly, almost painfully—"held hard" as the Communities called it, held so that she could not move even her arms, could not harm any members of the Community by thrashing about in pain. Just before she might have been injured by the squeezing alone, it stopped.

She was hit with a sudden electrical shock that convulsed her. It drove the breath out of her in a hoarse scream. It made her see flashes of light even with her eyes tightly closed. It stimulated her muscles into abrupt, agonizing contortions.

Calm them, the Community insisted once again.

She could not answer at first. It took her a moment to get her now sore and shaking body under control and to understand what was being said to her. It took her a moment more to be able to flex her hands and arms, now free again, and finally to shape an answer—the only possible answer in spite of what it might cost.

I will answer their questions and reassure them that they have nothing to fear.

She was held hard for several seconds more, and knew that she might be given another shock. After a while, though, there were several flashes of light that she saw out of the corner of her eye, but that did not seem to have anything to do with her. Then without any more communication, Noah was passed into the care of her employer, and the subcontractor was gone.

She saw nothing as she was passed from darkness to darkness. There was nothing to hear but the usual rustle of Communities moving about. There was no change of scent, or if there was, her nose was not sensitive enough to detect it. Yet somehow, she had learned to know her employer's touch. She relaxed in relief.

Are you injured? her employer signed.

No, she answered. Just aching joints and other sore places. Did I get the job?

Of course you did. You must tell me if that subcontractor tries to coerce you again. It knows better. I've told it that if it injures you, I will never allow you to work for it again.

Thank you.

There was a moment of stillness. Then the employer stroked her, calming her and pleasing itselves. You insist on taking these jobs, but you can't use them to make the changes you want to make. You know that. You cannot change your people or mine.

I can, a little, she signed. Community by Community, human by human. I would work faster if I could.

And so you let subcontractors abuse you. You try to help your own people to see new possibilities and understand changes that have already happened but most of them won't listen and they hate you.

I want to make them think. I want to tell them what human governments won't tell them. I want to vote for peace between your people and mine by telling the truth. I don't know whether my efforts will do any good, in the long run, but I have to try.

Let yourself heal. Rest enfolded until the subcontractor returns for you.

Noah sighed, content, within another moment of stillness. Thank you for helping me, even though you don't believe.

I would like to believe. But you can't succeed. Right now groups of your people are looking for ways to destroy us.

Noah winced. I know. Can you stop them without killing them?

Her employer shifted her. Stroked her. Probably not, it signed. Not again.

"Translator," Michelle Ota began as the applicants trailed into the meeting room, "do these . . . these things . . . actually understand that we're intelligent?"

She followed Noah into the meeting room, waited to see where Noah would sit, and sat next to her. Noah noticed that Michelle Ota was one of only two of the six applicants who was willing to sit near her even for this informal question-and-answer session. Noah had information that they needed. She was doing a job some of them might wind up doing someday, and yet that job—translator and personnel officer for the Communities—and the fact that she could do it was their reason for distrusting her. The second person who wanted to sit near her was Sorrel Trent. She was interested in alien spirituality—whatever that might be.

The four remaining job candidates chose to leave empty seats between themselves and Noah.

"Of course the Communities know we're intelligent," Noah said.

"I mean I know you work for them," Michelle Ota glanced at her, hesitated then went on. "I want to work for them too. Because at least they're hiring. Almost nobody else is. But what do they think of us?"

"They'll be offering some of you contracts soon," Noah said. "They wouldn't waste time doing that if they'd mistaken you for cattle." She relaxed back into her chair, watching some of the six other people in the room get water, fruit or nuts from the sideboards. The food was good and clean and free to them whether or not they were hired. It was also, she knew, the first food most of them had had that day. Food was expensive and in these depressed times, most people were lucky to eat once a day. It pleased her to see them enjoying it. She was the one who had insisted there be food in the meeting rooms for the question and answer sessions.

She herself was enjoying the rare comfort of wearing shoes, long black cotton pants, and a colorful flowing tunic. And there was furniture designed for the human body—an upholstered armchair with a high back and a table she could eat from or rest her arms on. She had no such furniture in her quarters within the Mojave Bubble. She suspected that she could have at least the furniture now, if she asked her employer for it, but she had not asked, would not ask. Human things were for human places.

"But what does a contract mean to things that come from another star system?" Michelle Ota demanded.

Rune Johnsen spoke up. "Yes, it's interesting how quickly these beings have taken up local, terrestrial ways when it suits them. Translator, do you truly believe they will consider themselves bound by anything they sign? Although without hands, God knows how they manage to sign anything."

"They will consider both themselves and you bound by it if both they and you sign it," Noah said. "And, yes, they can make highly individual marks that serve as signatures. They spent a great deal of their time and wealth in this country with translators, lawyers, and politicians, working things out so that each Community was counted as a legal 'person,' whose individual mark would be accepted. And for twenty years since then, they've honored their contracts."

Rune Johnsen shook his blond head. "In all, they've been on earth longer than I've been alive, and yet it feels wrong that they're here. It feels wrong that they exist. I don't even hate them, and still it feels wrong. I suppose that's because we've been displaced again from the center of the universe. We human beings, I mean. Down through history, in myth and even in science, we've kept putting ourselves in the center, and then being evicted."

Noah smiled, surprised and pleased. "I noticed the same thing. Now we find ourselves in a kind of sibling rivalry with the Communities. There is other intelligent life. The universe has other children. We knew it, but until they arrived here, we could pretend otherwise."

"That's crap!" another woman said. Thera Collier, her name was, a big, angry, red-haired young woman. "The weeds came here uninvited, stole our land, and kidnapped our people." She had been eating an apple. She slammed it down hard on the table, crushing what was left of it, spattering juice. "That's what we need to remember. That's what we need to do something about."

"Do what?" another woman asked. "We're here to get jobs, not fight."

Noah searched her memory for the new speaker's name and found it. Piedad Ruiz—a small, brown woman who spoke English clearly, but with a strong Spanish accent. She looked with her bruised face and arms as though she had taken a fairly serious beating recently, but when Noah had asked her about it before the group came into the meeting room, she held her head up and said she was fine and it was nothing. Probably someone had not wanted her to apply for work at the bubble. Considering the rumors that were sometimes spread about the Communities and why they hired human beings, that was not surprising.

"What have the aliens told you about their coming here, Translator?" Rune Johnsen asked. He was, Noah remembered from her reading of the short biography that had been given to her with his job application, the son of a small businessman whose clothing store had not survived the depression brought about by the arrival of the Communities. He wanted to look after his parents and he wanted to get married. Ironically, the answer to both those problems seemed to be to go to work for the Communities for a while. "You're old enough to remember the things they did when they arrived," he said. "What did they tell you about why they abducted people, killed people. . . ."

"They abducted me," Noah admitted.

That silenced the room for several seconds. Each of the six potential recruits stared at her, perhaps wondering or pitying, judging or worrying, perhaps even recoiling in horror, suspicion, or disgust. She had received all these reactions from recruits and from others who knew her history. People had never been able to be neutral about abductees. Noah tended to use her history as a way to start questions, accusations, and perhaps thought.

"Noah Cannon," Rune Johnsen said, proving that he had at least been listening when she introduced herself. "I thought that name sounded familiar. You were part of the second wave of abductions. I remember seeing your name on the lists of abductees. I noticed it because you were listed as female. I had never run across a woman named Noah before."

"So they kidnapped you, and now you work for them?" This was James Hunter Adio, a tall, lean, angry-looking young black man. Noah was black herself and yet James Adio had apparently decided the moment they met that he didn't like her. Now he looked not only angry, but disgusted.

"I was eleven when I was taken," Noah said. She looked at Rune Johnsen. "You're right. I was part of the second wave."

"So what, then, they experimented on you?" James Adio asked.

Noah met his gaze. "They did, yes. The people of the first wave suffered the most. The Communities didn't know anything about us. They killed some of us with experiments and dietary deficiency diseases and they poisoned others. By the time they snatched me, they at least knew enough not to kill me by accident."

"And what? You forgive them for what they did do?"

"Are you angry with me, Mr. Adio, or are you angry in my behalf?"

"I'm angry because I have to be here!" he said. He stood up and paced around the table—all the way around twice before he would sit down again. "I'm angry that these things, these weeds can invade us, wreck our economies, send the whole world into a depression just by showing up. They do whatever they want to us, and instead of killing them, all I can do is ask them for a job!" And he needed the job badly. Noah had read the information collected about him when he first applied to work for the Communities. At twenty, James Adio was the oldest of seven children, and the only one who had reached adulthood so far. He needed a job to help his younger brothers and sisters survive. Yet Noah suspected that he would hate the aliens almost as much if they hired him as if they turned him down.

"How can you work for them?" Piedad Ruiz whispered to Noah. "They hurt you. Don't you hate them? I think I'd hate them if it were me."

"They wanted to understand us and communicate with us,"

Noah said. "They wanted to know how we got along with one another and they needed to know how much we could bear of what was normal for them."

"Is that what they told you?" Thera Collier demanded. With one hand, she swept her smashed apple off the table onto the floor, and then glared at Noah as though wishing she could sweep her away too. Watching her, Noah realized that Thera Collier was a very frightened woman. Well, they were all frightened, but Thera's fear made her lash out at people.

"The Communities did tell me that," Noah admitted, "but not until some of them and some of us, the surviving captives, had managed to put together a code—the beginnings of a language—that got communication started. Back when they captured me, they couldn't tell me anything."

Thera snorted. "Right. They can figure out how to cross light years of space, but they can't figure out how to talk to us without torturing us first!"

Noah allowed herself a moment of irritation. "You weren't there, Ms. Collier. It happened before you were born. And it happened to me, not to you." And it hadn't happened to anyone in Thera Collier's family either. Noah had checked. None of these people were relatives of abductees. It was important to know that since relatives sometimes tried to take revenge on translators when they realized they weren't going to be able to hurt the Communities.

"It happened to a lot of people," Thera Collier said. "And it shouldn't have happened to anyone."

Noah shrugged.

"Don't you hate them for what they did to you?" Pie-dad whispered. Whispering seemed to be her normal way of speaking.

"I don't," Noah said. "I did once, especially when they were beginning to understand us a little, and yet went right on putting us through hell. They were like human scientists experimenting with lab animals—not cruel, but very thorough."

"Animals again," Michelle Ota said. "You said they—"

"Then," Noah told her. "Not now."

"Why do you defend them?" Thera demanded. "They invaded our world. They tortured our people. They do whatever they please, and we aren't even sure what they look like."

Rune Johnsen spoke up, to Noah's relief. "What do they look like, Translator? You've seen them close up."

Noah almost smiled. What did the Communities look like. That was usually the first question asked in a group like this. People tended to assume, no matter what they had seen or heard from media sources, that each Community was actually an individual being shaped like a big bush or tree or, more likely, that the being was wearing shrubbery as clothing or as a disguise.

"They're not like anything that any of us have ever known," she told them. "I've heard them compared to sea urchins— completely wrong. I've also heard they were like swarms of bees or wasps—also wrong, but closer. I think of them as what I usually call them—Communities. Each Community contains several hundred individuals—an intelligent multitude. But that's wrong too, really. The individuals can't really survive independently, but they can leave one Community and move temporarily or permanently to another. They are products of a completely different evolution. When I look at them, I see what you've all seen: outer branches and then darkness. Flashes of light and movement within. Do you want to hear more?"

They nodded, sat forward attentively except for James Adio who leaned back with an expression of contempt on his dark, smooth young face.

"The substance of the things that look like branches and the things that look like leaves and mosses and vines is alive and made up of individuals. It only looks like a plant of some sort. The various entities that we can reach from the outside feel dry, and usually smooth. One normal-sized Community might fill half of this room, but only weigh about six to eight hundred pounds. They aren't solid, of course, and within them, there are entities that I've never seen. Being enveloped by a community is like being held in a sort of . . . comfortable straitjacket, if you can imagine such a thing. You can't move much. You can't move at all unless the Community permits it. You can't see anything. There's no smell. Somehow, though, after the first time, it isn't frightening. It's peaceful and pleasant. I don't know why it should be, but it is."

"Hypnosis," James Adio said at once. "Or drugs!"

"Definitely not," Noah said. At least this was something she could be sure of. "That was one of the hardest parts of being a captive of the Communities. Until they got to know us, they didn't have anything like hypnosis or mood-altering drugs. They didn't even have the concept."

Rune Johnsen turned to frown at her. "What concept?"

"Altered consciousness. They don't even go unconscious unless they're sick or injured, and a whole Community never goes unconscious even though several of its entities might. As a result, Communities can't really be said to sleep—although at long last, they've accepted the reality that we have to sleep. Inadvertently, we've introduced them to something brand new."

"Will they let us bring medicine in?" Michelle Ota asked suddenly. "I have allergies and I really need my medicine."

"They will allow certain medicines. If you're offered a contract, you'll have to write in the drugs you'll need. They will either allow you to have the drugs or you won't be hired. If what you need is allowed, you'll be permitted to order it from outside. The Communities will check to see that it is what it's supposed to be, but other than that, they won't bother you about it. Medicine's just about all you'll have to spend money on while you're inside. Room and board are part of the agreement, of course, and you won't be allowed to leave your employers until your contract is up."

"What if we get sick or have an accident?" Piedad demanded. "What if we need some medicine that isn't in the contract?"

"Medical emergencies are covered by the contract," Noah said.

Thera slapped her palms down against the table and said loudly, "Screw all that!" She got the attention she wanted. Everyone turned to look at her. "I want to know more about you, and the weeds, Translator. In particular, I want to know why you're still here, working for things that probably put you through hell. Part of that no drug thing was no anesthetic when they hurt you, right?"

Noah sat still for a moment, remembering, yet not wanting to remember. "Yes," she said at last, "except that most of the time, the people actually hurting me were other human beings. The aliens used to lock groups of two or more of us up together for days or weeks to see what would happen. This was usually not too bad. Sometimes, though, it went wrong. Some of us went out of our minds. Hell, all of us went out of our minds at one time or another. But some of us were more likely than others to be violent. Then there were those of us who would have been thugs even without the Communities' help. They were quick enough to take advantage of any chance to exercise a little power, get a little pleasure by making another person suffer. And some of us just stopped caring, stopped fighting, sometimes even stopped eating. The pregnancies and several of the killings came from those cell-mate experiments. We called them that.

"It was almost easier when the aliens just made us solve puzzles to get food or when they put things in our food that made us sick or when they enfolded us and introduced some nearly lethal substance into our bodies. The first captives got most of that, poor people. And some of them had developed a phobic terror of being enfolded. They were lucky if that was all they developed."

"My God," Thera said, shaking her head in disgust. After a while, she asked, "What happened to the babies? You said some people got pregnant."

"The Communities don't reproduce the way we do. It didn't seem to occur to them for a long time to take it easy on the pregnant women. Because of that, most women who got pregnant miscarried. Some had still births. Four of the women in the group that I was usually caged with between experiments died in childbirth. None of us knew how to help them." That was another memory she wanted to turn away from.

"There were a few live births, and of those, a few babies survived infancy, even though their mothers couldn't protect them from the worst and the craziest of our own people or from the Communities who were . . . curious about them. In all thirty-seven of the world's bubbles, fewer than a hundred such children survived. Most of those have grown up to be reasonably sane adults. Some live outside in secret, and some will never leave the bubbles. Their choice. A few of them are becoming the best of the next generation of translators."

Rune Johnsen made a wordless sound of interest. "I've read about such children," he said.

"We tried to find some of them," Sorrel Trent said, speaking up for the first time. "Our leader teaches that they're the ones who will show us the way. They're so important, and yet our stupid government keeps them hidden!" She sounded both frustrated and angry.

"The governments of this world have a great deal to answer for," Noah said. "In some countries, the children won't come out of the bubbles because word has gotten back to them about what's happened to those who have come out. Word about disappearances, imprisonment, torture, death. Our government seems not to be doing that sort of thing any more. Not to the children, anyway. It's given them new identities to hide them from groups who want to worship them or kill them or set them apart. I've checked on some of them myself. They're all right, and they want to be let alone."

"My group doesn't want to hurt them," Sorrel Trent said. "We want to honor them and help them fulfill their true destiny."

Noah turned away from the woman, her mind filled with caustic, unprofessional things best not said. "So the children at least, are able to have a little peace," she did say.

"Is one of them yours?" Thera asked, her voice uncharacteristically soft. "Do you have children?"

Noah stared at her, then leaned her head against the chair back again. "I got pregnant when I was fifteen and again when I was seventeen. Miscarriages both times, thank God."

"It was . . . rape?" Rune Johnsen asked.

"Of course it was rape! Can you actually believe I'd want to give the Communities another human infant to study?" She stopped and took a deep breath. After a moment, she said, "Some of the deaths were women killed for resisting rape. Some of the deaths were rapists. Do you remember an old experiment in which too many rats are caged together and they begin to kill one another."

"But you weren't rats," Thera said. "You were intelligent. You could see what the weeds were doing to you. You didn't have to—"

Noah cut her off. "I didn't have to what?"

Thera backpedaled. "I didn't mean you personally. I just mean human beings ought to be able to behave better than a bunch of rats."

"Many did. Some did not."

"And in spite of all that, you work for the aliens. You forgive them because they didn't know what they were doing. Is that it?"

"They're here," Noah said flatly.

"They're here until we find a way to drive them away!"

"They're here to stay," Noah said more softly. "There's no 'away' for them—not for several generations anyway. Their ship was a one-way transport. They've settled here and they'll fight to keep the various desert locations they've chosen for their bubbles. If they do decide to fight, we won't survive. They might be destroyed too, but chances are, they would send their young deep into the ground for a few centuries. When they came up, this would be their world. We would be gone." She looked at each member of the group. "They're here," she said for the third time. "I'm one of maybe thirty people in this country who can talk to them. Where else would I be but here at a bubble, trying to help the two species understand and accept one another before one of them does something fatal?"

Thera was relentless. "But do you forgive them for what they've done?"

Noah shook her head. "I don't forgive them," she said. "They haven't asked for my forgiveness and I wouldn't know how to give it if they did. And that doesn't matter. It doesn't stop me from doing my job. It doesn't stop them from employing me."

James Adio said, "If they're as dangerous as you believe, you ought to be working with the government, trying to find a way to kill them. Like you said, you know more about them than the rest of us."

"Are you here to kill them, Mr. Adio?" Noah asked quietly.

He let his shoulders slump. "I'm here to work for them, lady. I'm poor. I don't have all kinds of special knowledge that only thirty people in the whole country have. I just need a job."

She nodded as though he had simply been conveying information, as though his words had not carried heavy loads of bitterness, anger, and humiliation. "You can make money here," she said. "I'm wealthy myself. I'm putting half a dozen nieces and nephews through college. My relatives eat three meals a day and live in comfortable homes. Why shouldn't yours?"

"Thirty pieces of silver," he muttered.

Noah gave him a tired smile. "Not for me," she said. "My parents seemed to have a completely different role in mind for me when they named me."

Rune Johnsen smiled but James Adio only stared at her with open dislike. Noah let her face settle into its more familiar solemnity. "Let me tell you all about my experience working with the government to get the better of the Communities," she said. "You should hear about it whether or not you choose to believe." She paused, gathered her thoughts.

"I was held here in the Mojave Bubble from my eleventh year through my twenty-third," she began. "Of course, none of my family or friends knew where I was or whether I was alive. I just disappeared like a lot of other people. In my case, I disappeared from my own bedroom in my parents' house in Victorville late one night. Years later when the Communities could talk to us, when they understood more of what they'd done to us, they asked a group of us whether we would stay with them voluntarily or whether we wanted to leave. I thought it might have been just another of their tests, but when I asked to go, they agreed.

"In fact, I was the first to ask to go. The group I was with then was made up of people taken in childhood—sometimes early childhood. Some of them were afraid to go out. They had no memory of any home but the Mojave Bubble. But I remembered my family. I wanted to see them again. I wanted to go out and not be confined to a small area in a bubble. I wanted to be free.

"But when the Communities let me go, they didn't take me back to Victorville. They just opened the bubble late one night near one of the shanty towns that had grown up around its perimeters. The shanty towns were wilder and cruder back then. They were made up of people who were worshipping the Communities or plotting to wipe them out or hoping to steal some fragment of valuable technology from them—that kind of thing. And some of the squatters there were undercover cops of one kind or another. The ones who grabbed me said they were FBI, but I think now that they might have been bounty hunters. In those days, there was a bounty on anyone or anything that came out of the bubbles, and it was my bad luck to be the first person to be seen coming out of the Mojave Bubble.

"Anyone coming out might know valuable technological secrets, or might be hypnotized saboteurs or disguised alien spies —any damned thing. I was handed over to the military which locked me up, questioned me relentlessly, accused me of everything from espionage to murder, from terrorism to treason. I was sampled and tested in every way they could think of. They convinced themselves that I was a valuable catch, that I had been collaborating with our 'nonhuman enemies.' Therefore, I represented a great opportunity to find a way to get at them —at the Communities.

"Everything I knew, they found out. It wasn't as though I was ever trying to hold anything back from them. The problem was, I couldn't tell them the kind of thing they wanted to know. Of course the Communities hadn't explained to me the workings of their technology. Why would they? I didn't know much about their physiology either, but I told what I did know—told it over and over again with my jailers trying to catch me in lies. And as for the Communities' psychology, I could only say what had been done to me and what I'd seen done to others. And because my jailers didn't see that as very useful, they decided I was being uncooperative, and that I had something to hide."

Noah shook her head. "The only difference between the way they treated me and the way the aliens treated me during the early years of my captivity was that the so-called human beings knew when they were hurting me. They questioned me day and night, threatened me, drugged me, all in an effort to get me to give them information I didn't have. They'd keep me awake for days on end, keep me awake until I couldn't think, couldn't tell what was real and what wasn't. They couldn't get at the aliens, but they had me. When they weren't questioning me, they kept me locked up, alone, isolated from everyone but them."

Noah looked around the room. "All this because they knew —knew absolutely—that a captive who survived twelve years of captivity and who is then freed must be a traitor of some kind, willing or unwilling, knowing or unknowing. They x-rayed me, scanned me in every possible way, and when they found nothing unusual, it only made them angrier, made them hate me more. I was, somehow, making fools of them. They knew it! And I wasn't going to get away with it.

"I gave up. I decided that they were never going to stop, that they would eventually kill me anyway, and until they did, I would never know any peace."

She paused remembering humiliation, fear, hopelessness, exhaustion, bitterness, sickness, pain. . . . They had never beaten her badly—just struck a few blows now and then for emphasis and intimidation. And sometimes she was grabbed, shaken, and shoved, amid ongoing accusations, speculations, and threats. Now and then, an interrogator knocked her to the floor, then ordered her back to her chair. They did nothing that they thought might seriously injure or kill her. But it went on and on and on. Sometimes one of them pretended to be nice to her, courted her in a sense, tried to seduce her into telling secrets she did not know. . . .

"I gave up," she repeated. "I don't know how long I'd been there when that happened. I never saw the sky or sunlight so I lost all track of time. I just regained consciousness after a long session, found that I was in my cell alone, and decided to kill myself. I had been thinking about it off and on when I could think, and suddenly, I knew I would do it. Nothing else would make them stop. So I did do it. I hanged myself."

Piedad Ruiz made a wordless sound of distress, then stared downward at the table when people looked at her.

"You tried to kill yourself?" Rune Johnsen asked. "Did you do that when you were with the . . . the Communities?"

Noah shook her head. "I never did." She paused. "It mattered more than I know how to tell you that this time my tormentors were my own people. They were human. They spoke my language. They knew all that I knew about pain and humiliation and fear and despair. They knew what they were doing to me, and yet it never occurred to them not to do it." She thought for a moment, remembering. "Some captives of the Communities did kill themselves. And the Communities didn't care. If you wanted to die and managed to hurt yourself badly enough, you'd die. They'd watch."

But if you didn't choose to die, there was the perverse security and peace of being enfolded. There was, somehow, the pleasure of being enfolded. It happened often when captives were not being tested in some way. It happened because the entities of the Communities discovered that it pleased and comforted them too, and they didn't understand why any more than she did. The first enfoldings happened because they were convenient ways of restraining, examining, and, unhappily, poisoning human captives. It wasn't long, though, before unoccupied humans were being enfolded just for the pleasure the act gave to an unoccupied Community. Communities did not understand at first that their captives could also take pleasure in the act. Human children like Noah learned quickly how to approach a Community and touch its outer branches to ask to be enfolded, although adult human captives had tried to prevent the practice, and to punish it when they could not prevent it. Noah had had to grow up to even begin to understand why adult captives sometimes beat children for daring to ask alien captors for comfort.

Noah had met her current employer before she turned twelve. It was one of the Communities who never injured her, one who had worked with her and with others to begin to assemble a language that both species could use.

She sighed and continued her narrative. "My human jailers were like the Communities in their attitude toward suicide," she said. "They watched too as I tried to kill myself. I found out later that there were at least three cameras on me day and night. A lab rat had more privacy than I did. They watched me make a noose of my clothing. They watched me climb onto my bed and tie off the noose to a grill that protected the speaker they sometimes used to blast me with loud, distorted music or with old news broadcasts from when the aliens first arrived and people were dying in the panic.

"They even watched me step off my bed and dangle by my neck, strangling. Then they got me out of there, revived me, made sure I wasn't seriously injured. That done, they put me back in my cell, naked and with the speaker recess concreted over and the grill gone. At least, after that there was no more horrible music. No more terrified screaming.

"But the questioning began again. They even said I hadn't really meant to kill myself, that I was just making a bid for sympathy.

"So I left in mind, if not in body. I sort of went catatonic for a while. I wasn't entirely unconscious, but I wasn't functioning any more. I couldn't. They knocked me around at first because they thought I was faking. I know they did that because later I had some unexplained and untreated broken bones and other medical problems to deal with.

"Then someone leaked my story. I don't know who. Maybe one of my interrogators finally grew a conscience. Anyway, someone started telling the media about me and showing them pictures. The fact that I was only eleven when I was taken turned out to be important to the story. At that point, my captors decided to give me up. I suppose they could have killed me just as easily. Considering what they had been doing to me, I have no idea why they didn't kill me. I've seen the pictures that got published. I was in bad shape. Maybe they thought I'd die—or at least that I'd never wake all the way up and be normal again. And, too, once my relatives learned that I was alive, they got lawyers and fought to get me out of there.

"My parents were dead—had died in a car wreck while I was still a captive in the Mojave Bubble. My jailers must have known, but they never said a word. I didn't find out until I began to recover and one of my uncles told me. My uncles were my mother's three older brothers. They were the ones who fought for me. To get me, they had to sign away any rights they may have had to sue. They were told that the Communities were the ones who had injured me. They believed it until I revived enough to tell them what really happened.

"After I told them, they wanted to tell the world, maybe put a few people in prison where they belonged. If they hadn't had families of their own, I might not have been able to talk them out of it. They were good men. My mother was their baby sister, and they'd always loved her and looked after her. As things were, though, they had had to go into serious debt to get me free, repaired and functional again. I couldn't have lived with the thought that because of me, they lost everything they owned, and maybe even got sent to prison on some fake charge.

"When I'd recovered a little, I had to do some media interviews. I told lies, of course, but I couldn't go along with the big lie. I refused to confirm that the Communities had injured me. I pretended not to remember what had happened. I said I had been in such bad shape that I didn't have any idea what was going on most of the time, and that I was just grateful to be free and healing. I hoped that was enough to keep my human ex-captors content. It seemed to be.

"The reporters wanted to know what I was going to do, now that I was free.

"I told them I would go to school as soon as I could. I would get an education, then a job so that I could begin to pay my uncles back for all they had done for me.

"That's pretty much what I did. And while I was in school, I realized what work I was best fitted to do. So here I am. I was not only the first to leave the Mojave Bubble, but the first to come back to offer to work for the Communities. I had a small part in helping them connect with some of the lawyers and politicians I mentioned earlier."

"Did you tell your story to the weeds when you came back here?" Thera Collier asked suspiciously. "Prison and torture and everything?"

Noah nodded. "I did. Some Communities asked and I told them. Most didn't ask. They have problems enough among themselves. What humans do to other humans outside their bubbles is usually not that important to them."

"Do they trust you?" Thera asked. "Do the weeds trust you?"

Noah smiled unhappily. "At least as much as you do, Ms. Collier."

Thera gave a short bark of laughter, and Noah realized the woman had not understood. She thought Noah was only being sarcastic.

"I mean they trust me to do my job," Noah said. "They trust me to help would-be employers learn to live with a human being without hurting the human and to help human employees learn to live with the Communities and fulfill their responsibilities. You trust me to do that too. That's why you're here." That was all true enough, but there were also some Communities —her employer and a few others—who did seem to trust her. And she trusted them. She had never dared to tell anyone that she thought of these as friends.

Even without that admission, Thera gave her a look that seemed to be made up of equal parts pity and contempt.

"Why did the aliens take you back," James Adio demanded. "You could have been bringing in a gun or a bomb or something. You could have been coming back to get even with them for what they'd done to you."

Noah shook her head. "They would have detected any weapon I could bring in. They let me come back because they knew me and they knew I could be useful to them. I knew I could be useful to us, too. They want more of us. Maybe they even need more of us. Better for everyone if they hire us and pay us instead of snatching us. They can take mineral ores from deeper in the ground than we can reach, and refine them. They've agreed to restrictions on what they take and where they take it. They pay a handsome percentage of their profit to the government in fees and taxes. With all that, they still have plenty of money to hire us."

She changed the subject suddenly. "Once you're in the bubble, learn the language. Make it clear to your employers that you want to learn. Have you all mastered the basic signs?" She looked them over, not liking the silence. Finally she asked, "Has anyone mastered the basic signs?"

Rune Johnsen and Michelle Ota both said, "I have."

Sorrel Trent said, "I learned some of it, but it's hard to remember."

The others said nothing. James Adio began to look defensive. "They come to our world and we have to learn their language," he muttered.

"I'm sure they would learn ours if they could, Mr. Adio," Noah said wearily. "In fact, here at Mojave, they can read English, and even write it—with difficulty. But since they can't hear at all, they never developed a spoken language of any kind. They can only converse with us in the gesture and touch language that some of us and some of them have developed. It takes some getting used to since they have no limbs in common with us. That's why you need to learn it from them, see for yourself how they move and feel the touch-signs on your skin when you're enfolded. But once you learn it, you'll see that it works well for both species."

"They could use computers to speak for them," Thera Collier said. "If their technology isn't up to it, they could buy some of ours."

Noah did not bother to look at her. "Most of you won't be required to learn more than the basic signs," she said. "If you have some urgent need that the basics don't cover, you can write notes. Print in block capital letters. That will usually work. But if you want to move up a paygrade or two and be given work that might actually interest you, learn the language."

"How do you learn," Michelle Ota asked. "Are there classes?"

"No classes. Your employers will teach you if they want you to know—or if you ask. Language lessons are the one thing you can ask for that you can be sure of getting. They're also one of the few things that will get your pay reduced if you're told to learn and you don't. That will be in the contract. They won't care whether you won't or you can't. Either way it's going to cost you."

"Not fair," Piedad said.

Noah shrugged. "It's easier if you have something to do anyway, and easier if you can talk with your employer. You can't bring in radios, televisions, computers, or recordings of any kind. You can bring in a few books—the paper kind—but that's all. Your employers can and will call you at any time, sometimes several times in a day. Your employer might lend you to . . . relatives who haven't hired one of us yet. They might also ignore you for days at a time, and most of you won't be within shouting distance of another human being." Noah paused, stared down at the table. "For the sake of your sanity, go in with projects that will occupy your minds."

Rune said, "I would like to hear your description of our duties. What I read sounded almost impossibly simple."

"It is simple. It's even pleasant once you're used to it. You will be enfolded by your employer or anyone your employer designates. If both you and the Community enfolding you can communicate, you might be asked to explain or discuss some aspect of our culture that the Community either doesn't understand or wants to hear more about. Some of them read our literature, our history, even our news. You may be given puzzles to solve. When you're not enfolded, you may be sent on errands—after you've been inside long enough to be able to find your way around. Your employer might sell your contract to another Community, might even send you to one of the other bubbles. They've agreed not to send you out of the country, and they've agreed that when your contract is up, they'll let you leave by way of the Mojave Bubble—since this is where you'll begin. You won't be injured. There'll be no biomedical experiments, none of the nastier social experiments that captives endured. You'll receive all the food, water, and shelter that you need to keep you healthy. If you get sick or injured, you have the right to see a human physician. I believe there are two human doctors working here at Mojave now." She paused and James Adio spoke up.

"So what will we be, then?" he demanded. "Whores or house pets?"

Thera Collier made a noise that was almost a sob.

Noah smiled humorlessly. "We're neither, of course. But you'll probably feel as though you're both unless you learn the language. We are one interesting and unexpected thing, though." She paused. "We're an addictive drug." She watched the group and recognized that Rune Johnsen had already known this. And Sorrel Trent had known. The other four were offended and uncertain and shocked.

"This effect proves that humanity and the Communities belong together," Sorrel Trent said. "We're fated to be together. They have so much to teach us."

Everyone ignored her.

"You told us they understood that we were intelligent," Michelle Ota said.

"Of course they understand," Noah said. "But what's important to them is not what they think of our intellect. It's what use we can be to them. That's what they pay us for."

"We're not prostitutes!" Piedad Ruiz said. "We're not! There's no sex in any of this. There can't be. And there are no drugs either. You said so yourself!"

Noah turned to look at her. Piedad didn't listen particularly well, and she lived in terror of prostitution, drug addiction, disease, anything that might harm her or steal her ability to have the family she hoped for. Her two older sisters were already selling themselves on the streets. She hoped to rescue them and herself by getting work with the Communities.

"No sex," Noah agreed. "And we are the drugs. The Communities feel better when they enfold us. We feel better too. I guess that's only fair. The ones among them who are having trouble adjusting to this world are calmed and much improved if they can enfold one of us now and then." She thought for a moment. "I've heard that for human beings, petting a cat lowers our blood pressure. For them, enfolding one of us calms them and eases what translates as a kind of intense biological homesickness."

"We ought to sell them some cats," Thera said. "Neutered cats so they'll have to keep buying them."

"Cats and dogs don't like them," Noah said. "As a matter of fact, cats and dogs won't like you after you've lived in the bubble for a while. They seem to smell something on you that we can't detect. They panic if you go near them. They bite and scratch if you try to handle them. The effect lasts for a month or two. I generally avoid house pets and even farm animals for a couple of months when I go out."

"Is being enveloped anything like being crawled over by insects?" Piedad asked. "I can't stand having things crawl on me."

"It isn't like any experience you've ever had," Noah said. "I can only tell you that it doesn't hurt and it isn't slimy or disgusting in any way. The only problem likely to be triggered by it is claustrophobia. If any of you had been found to be claustrophobic, you would have been culled by now. For the nonclaustrophobic, well, we're lucky they need us. It means jobs for a lot of people who wouldn't otherwise have them."

"We're the drug of choice, then?" Rune said. And he smiled.

Noah smiled back. "We are. And they have no history of drug taking, no resistance to it, and apparently no moral problems with it. All of a sudden they're hooked. On us."

James Adio said, "Is this some kind of payback for you, Translator? You hook them on us because of what they did to you."

Noah shook her head. "No payback. Just what I said earlier. Jobs. We get to live, and so do they. I don't need payback."

He gave her a long, solemn look. "I would," he said. "I do. I can't have it, but I want it. They invaded us. They took over."

"God, yes," Noah said. "They've taken over big chunks of the Sahara, the Atacama, the Kalahari, the Mojave and just about every other hot, dry wasteland they could find. As far as territory goes, they've taken almost nothing that we need."

"They've still got no right to it," Thera said. "It's ours, not theirs."

"They can't leave," Noah said.

Thera nodded. "Maybe not. But they can die!"

Noah ignored this. "Some day maybe a thousand years from now, some of them will leave. They'll build and use ships that are part multigenerational and part sleeper. A few Communities stay awake and keep things running. Everyone else sort of hibernates." This was a vast oversimplification of the aliens' travel habits, but it was essentially true. "Some of us might even wind up going with them. It would be one way for the human species to get to the stars."

Sorrel Trent said wistfully, "If we honor them, maybe they will take us to heaven with them."

Noah suppressed an urge to hit the woman. To the others, she said, "The next two years will be as easy or as difficult as you decide to make them. Keep in mind that once the contract is signed, the Communities won't let you go because you're angry with them or because you hate them or even because you try to kill them. And by the way, although I'm sure they can be killed, that's only because I believe anything that's alive can die. I've never seen a dead Community, though. I've seen a couple of them have what you might call internal revolution. The entities of those Communities scattered to join other Communities. I'm not sure whether that was death, reproduction, or both." She took a deep breath and let it out. "Even those of us who can talk fluently with the Communities don't understand their physiology that well.

"Finally, I want to tell you a bit of history. When I've done that, I'll escort you in and introduce you to your employers."

"Are we all accepted, then?" Rune Johnsen asked.

"Probably not," Noah said. "There's a final test. When you go in, you will be enfolded, each of you, by a potential employer. When that's over, some of you will be offered a contract and the rest will be given the thanks-for-stopping-by fee that anyone who gets this far and no farther is given."

"I had no idea the . . . enfolding . . . would happen so soon," Rune Johnsen said. "Any pointers?"

"About being enfolded?" Noah shook her head. "None. It's a good test. It lets you know whether you can stand the Communities and lets them know whether they really want you."

Piedad Ruiz said, "You were going to tell us something—something from history."

"Yes." Noah leaned back in her chair. "It isn't common knowledge. I looked for references to it while I was in school, but I never found any. Only my military captors and the aliens seemed to know about it. The aliens told me before they let me go. My military captors gave me absolute hell for knowing.

"It seems that there was a coordinated nuclear strike at the aliens when it was clear where they were establishing their colonies. The armed forces of several countries had tried and failed to knock them out of the sky before they landed. Everyone knows that. But once the Communities established their bubbles, they tried again. I was already a captive inside the Mojave bubble when the attack came. I have no idea how that attack was repelled, but I do know this, and my military captors confirmed it with their lines of questioning: the missiles fired at the bubbles never detonated. They should have, but they didn't. And sometime later, exactly half of the missiles that had been fired were returned. They were discovered armed and intact, scattered around Washington DC in the White House —one in the Oval Office—in the Capitol, in the Pentagon. In China, half of the missiles fired at the Gobi Bubbles were found scattered around Beijing. London and Paris got one half of their missiles back from the Sahara and Australia. There was panic, confusion, fury. After that, though, the 'invaders,' the 'alien weeds' began to become in many languages, our 'guests,' our 'neighbors,' and even our 'friends.'"

"Half the nuclear missiles were . . . returned?" Piedad Ruiz whispered.

Noah nodded. "Half, yes."

"What happened to the other half?"

"Apparently, the Communities still have the other half—along with whatever weapons they brought with them and any they've built since they've been here."

Silence. The six looked at one another, then at Noah.

"It was a short, quiet war," Noah said. "We lost."

Thera Collier stared at her bleakly. "But . . . but there must be something we can do, some way to fight."

Noah stood up, pushed her comfortable chair away. "I don't think so," she said. "Your employers are waiting. Shall we join them?"

Afterword

"Amnesty" was inspired by the things that happened to Doctor Wen Ho Lee of Los Alamos—back in the 1990s when I could still be shocked that a person could have his profession and his freedom taken away and his reputation damaged all without proof that he'd actually done anything wrong. I had no idea how commonplace this kind of thing could become.

The Book of Martha

"IT'S DIFFICULT, isn't it?" God said with a weary smile. "You're truly free for the first time. What could be more difficult than that?"

Martha Bes looked around at the endless grayness that was, along with God, all that she could see. In fear and confusion, she covered her broad black face with her hands. "If only I could wake up," she whispered.

God kept silent but was so palpably, disturbingly present that even in the silence Martha felt rebuked. "Where is this?" she asked, not really wanting to know, not wanting to be dead when she was only forty-three. "Where am I?"

"Here with me," God said.

"Really here?" she asked. "Not at home in bed dreaming? Not locked up in a mental institution? Not . . . not lying dead in a morgue?"

"Here," God said softly. "With me."

After a moment, Martha was able to take her hands from her face and look again at the grayness around her and at God. "This can't be heaven," she said. "There's nothing here, no one here but you."

"Is that all you see?" God asked.

This confused her even more. "Don't you know what I see?" she demanded and then quickly softened her voice. "Don't you know everything?"

God smiled. "No, I outgrew that trick long ago. You can't imagine how boring it was."

This struck Martha as such a human thing to say that her fear diminished a little—although she was still impossibly confused. She had, she remembered, been sitting at her computer, wrapping up one more day's work on her fifth novel. The writing had been going well for a change, and she'd been enjoying it. For hours, she'd been spilling her new story onto paper in that sweet frenzy of creation that she lived for. Finally, she had stopped, turned the computer off, and realized that she felt stiff. Her back hurt. She was hungry and thirsty, and it was almost five A.M. She had worked through the night. Amused in

696

spite of her various aches and pains, she got up and went to the kitchen to find something to eat.

And then she was here, confused and scared. The comfort of her small, disorderly house was gone, and she was standing before this amazing figure who had convinced her at once that he was God—or someone so powerful that he might as well be God. He had work for her to do, he said—work that would mean a great deal to her and to the rest of humankind.

If she had been a little less frightened, she might have laughed. Beyond comic books and bad movies, who things like that?

"Why," she dared to ask, "do you look like a twice-life-sized, bearded white man?" In fact, seated as he was on his huge thronelike chair, he looked, she thought, like a living version of Michelangelo's Moses, a sculpture that she remembered seeing pictured in her college art-history textbook about twenty years before. Except that God was more fully dressed than Michelangelo's Moses, wearing, from neck to ankles, the kind of long, white robe that she had so often seen in paintings of Christ.

"You see what your life has prepared you to see," God said.

"I want to see what's really here!"

"Do you? What you see is up to you, Martha. Everything is up to you."

She sighed. "Do you mind if I sit down?"

And she was sitting. She did not sit down, but simply found herself sitting in a comfortable armchair that had surely not been there a moment before. Another trick, she thought resentfully—like the grayness, like the giant on his throne, like her own sudden appearance here. Everything was just one more effort to amaze and frighten her. And, of course, it was working. She was amazed and badly frightened. Worse, she disliked the giant for manipulating her, and this frightened her even more. Surely he could read her mind. Surely he would punish . . .

She made herself speak through her fear. "You said you had work for me." She paused, licked her lips, tried to steady her voice. "What do you want me to do?"

He didn't answer at once. He looked at her with what she read as amusement—looked at her long enough to make her even more uncomfortable.

"What do you want me to do?" she repeated, her voice stronger this time.

"I have a great deal of work for you," he said at last. "As I tell you about it, I want you to keep three people in mind: Jonah, Job, and Noah. Remember them. Be guided by their stories."

"All right," she said because he had stopped speaking, and it seemed that she should say something. "All right."

When she was a girl, she had gone to church and to Sunday School, to Bible class and to vacation Bible school. Her mother, only a girl herself, hadn't known much about being a mother, but she had wanted her child to be "good," and to her, "good" meant "religious." As a result, Martha knew very well what the Bible said about Jonah, Job, and Noah. She had come to regard their stories as parables rather than literal truths, but she remembered them. God had ordered Jonah to go to the city of Nineveh and to tell the people there to mend their ways. Frightened, Jonah had tried to run away from the work and from God, but God had caused him to be shipwrecked, swallowed by a great fish, and given to know that he could not escape.

Job had been the tormented pawn who lost his property, his children, and his health, in a bet between God and Satan. And when Job proved faithful in spite of all that God had permitted Satan to do to him, God rewarded Job with even greater wealth, new children, and restored health.

As for Noah, of course, God ordered him to build an ark and save his family and a lot of animals because God had decided to flood the world and kill everyone and everything else.

Why was she to remember these three Biblical figures in particular? What had they to do with her—especially Job and all his agony?

"This is what you're to do," God said. "You will help humankind to survive its greedy, murderous, wasteful adolescence. Help it to find less destructive, more peaceful, sustainable ways to live."

Martha stared at him. After a while, she said feebly, ". . . what?"

"If you don't help them, they will be destroyed."

"You're going to destroy them . . . again?" she whispered.

"Of course not," God said, sounding annoyed. "They're well on the way to destroying billions of themselves by greatly changing the ability of the earth to sustain them. That's why they need help. That's why you will help them."

"How?" she asked. She shook her head. "What can I do?"

"Don't worry," God said. "I won't be sending you back home with another message that people can ignore or twist to suit themselves. It's too late for that kind of thing anyway." God shifted on his throne and looked at her with his head cocked to one side. "You'll borrow some of my power," he said. "You'll arrange it so that people treat one another better and treat their environment more sensibly. You'll give them a better chance to survive than they've given themselves. I'll lend you the power, and you'll do this." He paused, but this time she could think of nothing to say. After a while, he went on.

"When you've finished your work, you'll go back and live among them again as one of their lowliest. You're the one who will decide what that will mean, but whatever you decide is to be the bottom level of society, the lowest class or caste or race, that's what you'll be."

This time when he stopped talking, Martha laughed. She felt overwhelmed with questions, fears, and bitter laughter, but it was the laughter that broke free. She needed to laugh. It gave her strength somehow.

"I was born on the bottom level of society," she said. "You must have known that."

God did not answer.

"Sure you did." Martha stopped laughing and managed, somehow, not to cry. She stood up, stepped toward God. "How could you not know? I was born poor, black, and female to a fourteen-year-old mother who could barely read. We were homeless half the time while I was growing up. Is that bottom-level enough for you? I was born on the bottom, but I didn't stay there. I didn't leave my mother there, either. And I'm not going back there!"

Still God said nothing. He smiled.

Martha sat down again, frightened by the smile, aware that she had been shouting—shouting at God! After a while, she whispered, "Is that why you chose me to do this . . . this work? Because of where I came from?"

"I chose you for all that you are and all that you are not," God said. "I could have chosen someone much poorer and more downtrodden. I chose you because you were the one I wanted for this."

Martha couldn't decide whether he sounded annoyed. She couldn't decide whether it was an honor to be chosen to do a job so huge, so poorly defined, so impossible.

"Please let me go home," she whispered. She was instantly ashamed of herself. She was begging, sounding pitiful, humiliating herself. Yet these were the most honest words she'd spoken so far.

"You're free to ask me questions," God said as though he hadn't heard her plea at all. "You're free to argue and think and investigate all of human history for ideas and warnings. You're free to take all the time you need to do these things. As I said earlier, you're truly free. You're even free to be terrified. But I assure you, you will do this work."

Martha thought of Job, Jonah, and Noah. After a while, she nodded.

"Good," God said. He stood up and stepped toward her. He was at least twelve feet high and inhumanly beautiful. He literally glowed. "Walk with me," he said.

And abruptly, he was not twelve feet high. Martha never saw him change, but now he was her size—just under six feet—and he no longer glowed. Now when he looked at her, they were eye to eye. He did look at her. He saw that something was disturbing her, and he asked, "What is it now? Has your image of me grown feathered wings or a blinding halo?"

"Your halo's gone," she answered. "And you're smaller. More normal."

"Good," he said. "What else do you see?"

"Nothing. Grayness."

"That will change."

It seemed that they walked over a smooth, hard, level surface, although when she looked down, she couldn't see her feet. It was as though she walked through ankle-high, ground-hugging fog.

"What are we walking on?" she asked.

"What would you like?" God asked. "A sidewalk? Beach sand? A dirt road?"

"A healthy, green lawn," she said, and was somehow not surprised to find herself walking on short, green grass. "And there should be trees," she said, getting the idea and discovering she liked it. "There should be sunshine—blue sky with a few clouds. It should be May or early June."

And it was so. It was as though it had always been so. They were walking through what could have been a vast city park.

Martha looked at God, her eyes wide. "Is that it?" she whispered. "I'm supposed to change people by deciding what they'll be like, and then just . . . just saying it?"

"Yes," God said.

And she went from being elated to—once again—being terrified. "What if I say something wrong, make a mistake?"

"You will."

"But . . . people could get hurt. People could die."

God went to a huge deep red Norway Maple tree and sat down beneath it on a long wooden bench. Martha realized that he had created both the ancient tree and the comfortable-looking bench only a moment before. She knew this, but again, it had happened so smoothly that she was not jarred by it.

"It's so easy," she said. "Is it always this easy for you?"

God sighed. "Always," he said.

She thought about that—his sigh, the fact that he looked away into the trees instead of at her. Was an eternity of absolute ease just another name for hell? Or was that just the most sacrilegious thought she'd had so far? She said, "I don't want to hurt people. Not even by accident."

God turned away from the trees, looked at her for several seconds, then said, "It would be better for you if you had raised a child or two."

Then, she thought with irritation, he should have chosen someone who'd raised a child or two. But she didn't have the courage to say that. Instead, she said, "Won't you fix it so I don't hurt or kill anyone? I mean, I'm new at this. I could do something stupid and wipe people out and not even know I'd done it until afterward."

"I won't fix things for you," God said. "You have a free hand."

She sat down next to him because sitting and staring out into the endless park was easier than standing and facing him and asking him questions that she thought might make him angry. She said, "Why should it be my work? Why don't you do it? You know how. You could do it without making mistakes. Why make me do it? I don't know anything."

"Quite right," God said. And he smiled. "That's why."

She thought about this with growing horror. "Is it just a game to you, then?" she asked. "Are you playing with us because you're bored?"

God seemed to consider the question. "I'm not bored," he said. He seemed pleased somehow. "You should be thinking about the changes you'll make. We can talk about them. You don't have to just suddenly proclaim."

She looked at him, then stared down at the grass, trying to get her thoughts in order. "Okay. How do I start?"

"Think about this: What change would you want to make if you could make only one? Think of one important change."

She looked at the grass again and thought about the novels she had written. What if she were going to write a novel in which human beings had to be changed in only one positive way? "Well," she said after a while, "the growing population is making a lot of the other problems worse. What if people could only have two children? I mean, what if people who wanted children could only have two, no matter how many more they wanted or how many medical techniques they used to try to get more?"

"You believe the population problem is the worst one, then?" God asked.

"I think so," she said. "Too many people. If we solve that one, we'll have more time to solve other problems. And we can't solve it on our own. We all know about it, but some of us won't admit it. And nobody wants some big government authority telling them how many kids to have." She glanced at God and saw that he seemed to be listening politely. She wondered how far he would let her go. What might offend him. What might he do to her if he were offended? "So everyone's reproductive system shuts down after two kids," she said. "I mean, they get to live as long as before, and they aren't sick. They just can't have kids any more."

"They'll try," God said. "The effort they put into building pyramids, cathedrals, and moon rockets will be as nothing to the effort they'll put into trying to end what will seem to them a plague of barrenness. What about people whose children die or are seriously disabled? What about a woman whose first child is a result of rape? What about surrogate motherhood? What about men who become fathers without realizing it? What about cloning?"

Martha stared at him, chagrined. "That's why you should do this. It's too complicated."

Silence.

"All right," Martha sighed and gave up. "All right. What if even with accidents and modern medicine, even something like cloning, the two-kid limit holds. I don't know how that could be made to work, but you do."

"It could be made to work," God said, "but keep in mind that you won't be coming here again to repair any changes you make. What you do is what people will live with. Or in this case, die with."

"Oh," Martha said. She thought for a moment, then said, "Oh, no."

"They would last for a good many generations," God said. "But they would be dwindling all the time. In the end, they would be extinguished. With the usual diseases, disabilities, disasters, wars, deliberate childlessness, and murder, they wouldn't be able to replace themselves. Think of the needs of the future, Martha, as well as the needs of the present."

"I thought I was," she said. "What if I made four kids the maximum number instead of two?"

God shook his head. "Free will coupled with morality has been an interesting experiment. Free will is, among other things, the freedom to make mistakes. One group of mistakes will sometimes cancel another. That's saved any number of human groups, although it isn't dependable. Sometimes mistakes cause people to be wiped out, enslaved, or driven from their homes because they've so damaged or altered their land or their water or their climate. Free will isn't a guarantee of anything, but it's a potentially useful tool—too useful to erase casually."

"I thought you wanted me to put a stop to war and slavery and environmental destruction!" Martha snapped, remembering the history of her own people. How could God be so casual about such things?

God laughed. It was a startling sound—deep, full, and, Martha thought, inappropriately happy. Why would this particular subject make him laugh? Was he God? Was he Satan? Martha, in spite of her mother's efforts, had not been able to believe in the literal existence of either. Now, she did not know what to think—or what to do.

God recovered himself, shook his head, and looked at Martha. "Well, there's no hurry," he said. "Do you know what a nova is Martha?"

Martha frowned. "It's . . . a star that explodes," she said, willing, even eager, to be distracted from her doubts.

"It's a pair of stars," God said. "A large one—a giant—and a small, very dense dwarf. The dwarf pulls material from the giant. After a while, the dwarf has taken more material than it can control, and it explodes. It doesn't necessarily destroy itself, but it does throw off a great deal of excess material. It makes a very bright, violent display. But once the dwarf has quieted down, it begins to siphon material from the giant again. It can do this over and over. That's what a nova is. If you change it—move the two stars farther apart or equalize their density, then it's no longer a nova."

Martha listened, catching his meaning even though she didn't want to. "Are you saying that if . . . if humanity is changed, it won't be humanity any more?"

"I'm saying more than that," God told her. "I'm saying that even though this is true, I will permit you to do it. What you decide should be done with humankind will be done. But whatever you do, your decisions will have consequences. If you limit their fertility, you will probably destroy them. If you limit their competitiveness or their inventiveness, you might destroy their ability to survive the many disasters and challenges that they must face."

Worse and worse, Martha thought, and she actually felt

nauseous with fear. She turned away from God, hugging herself, suddenly crying, tears streaming down her face. After a while, she sniffed and wiped her face on her hands, since she had nothing else. "What will you do to me if I refuse?" she asked, thinking of Job and Jonah in particular.

"Nothing." God didn't even sound annoyed. "You won't refuse."

"But what if I do? What if I really can't think of anything worth doing?"

"That won't happen. But if it did somehow, and if you asked, I would send you home. After all, there are millions of human beings who would give anything to do this work."

And, instantly, she thought of some of these—people who would be happy to wipe out whole segments of the population whom they hated and feared, or people who would set up vast tyrannies that forced everyone into a single mold, no matter how much suffering that created. And what about those who would treat the work as fun—as nothing more than a good-guys-versus-bad-guys computer game, and damn the consequences. There were people like that. Martha knew people like that.

But God wouldn't choose that kind of person. If he was God. Why had he chosen her, after all? For all of her adult life, she hadn't even believed in God as a literal being. If this terrifyingly powerful entity, God or not, could choose her, he could make even worse choices.

After a while, she asked, "Was there really a Noah?"

"Not one man dealing with a worldwide flood," God said. "But there have been a number of people who've had to deal with smaller disasters."

"People you ordered to save a few and let the rest die?"

"Yes," God said.

She shuddered and turned to face him again. "And what then? Did they go mad?" Even she could hear the disapproval and disgust in her voice.

God chose to hear the question as only a question. "Some took refuge in madness, some in drunkenness, some in sexual license. Some killed themselves. Some survived and lived long, fruitful lives."

Martha shook her head and managed to keep quiet.

"I don't do that any longer," God said.

No, Martha thought. Now he had found a different amusement. "How big a change do I have to make?" she asked. "What will please you and cause you to let me go and not bring in someone else to replace me?"

"I don't know," God said, and he smiled. He rested his head back against the tree. "Because I don't know what you will do. That's a lovely sensation—anticipating, not knowing."

"Not from my point of view," Martha said bitterly. After a while, she said in a different tone, "Definitely not from my point of view. Because I don't know what to do. I really don't."

"You write stories for a living," God said. "You create characters and situations, problems and solutions. That's less than I've given you to do."

"But you want me to tamper with real people. I don't want to do that. I'm afraid I'll make some horrible mistake."

"I'll answer your questions," God said. "Ask."

She didn't want to ask. After a while, though, she gave in. "What, exactly, do you want? A utopia? Because I don't believe in them. I don't believe it's possible to arrange a society so that everyone is content, everyone has what he or she wants."

"Not for more than a few moments," God said. "That's how long it would take for someone to decide that he wanted what his neighbor had—or that he wanted his neighbor as a slave of one kind or another, or that he wanted his neighbor dead. But never mind. I'm not asking you to create a utopia, Martha, although it would be interesting to see what you could come up with."

"So what are you asking me to do?"

"To help them, of course. Haven't you wanted to do that?"

"Always," she said. "And I never could in any meaningful way. Famines, epidemics, floods, fires, greed, slavery, revenge, stupid, stupid wars . . ."

"Now you can. Of course, you can't put an end to all of those things without putting an end to humanity, but you can diminish some of the problems. Fewer wars, less covetousness, more forethought and care with the environment. . . . What might cause that?"

She looked at her hands, then at him. Something had occurred to her as he spoke, but it seemed both too simple and too fantastic, and to her personally, perhaps, too painful. Could it be done? Should it be done? Would it really help if it were done? She asked, "Was there really anything like the Tower of Babel? Did you make people suddenly unable to understand each other?"

God nodded. "Again, it happened several times in one way or another."

"So what did you do? Change their thinking somehow, alter their memories?"

"Yes, I've done both. Although before literacy, all I had to do was divide them physically, send one group to a new land or give one group a custom that altered their mouths—knocking out the front teeth during puberty rites, for instance. Or give them a strong aversion to something others of their kind consider precious or sacred or—"

To her amazement, Martha interrupted him. "What about changing people's . . . I don't know, their brain activity. Can I do that?"

"Interesting," God said. "And probably dangerous. But you can do that if you decide to. What do you have in mind?"

"Dreams," she said. "Powerful, unavoidable, realistic dreams that come every time people sleep."

"Do you mean," God asked, "that they should be taught some lesson through their dreams?"

"Maybe. But I really mean that somehow people should spend a lot of their energy in their dreams. They would have their own personal best of all possible worlds during their dreams. The dreams should be much more realistic and intense than most dreams are now. Whatever people love to do most, they should dream about doing it, and the dreams should change to keep up with their individual interests. Whatever grabs their attention, whatever they desire, they can have it in their sleep. In fact, they can't avoid having it. Nothing should be able to keep the dreams away—not drugs, not surgery, not anything. And the dreams should satisfy much more deeply, more thoroughly, than reality can. I mean, the satisfaction should be in the dreaming, not in trying to make the dream real."

God smiled. "Why?"

"I want them to have the only possible utopia." Martha

thought for a moment. "Each person will have a private, perfect utopia every night—or an imperfect one. If they crave conflict and struggle, they get that. If they want peace and love, they get that. Whatever they want or need comes to them. I think if people go to a . . . well, a private heaven every night, it might take the edge off their willingness to spend their waking hours trying to dominate or destroy one another." She hesitated. "Won't it?"

God was still smiling. "It might. Some people will be taken over by it as though it were an addictive drug. Some will try to fight it in themselves or others. Some will give up on their lives and decide to die because nothing they do matters as much as their dreams. Some will enjoy it and try to go on with their familiar lives, but even they will find that the dreams interfere with their relations with other people. What will humankind in general do? I don't know." He seemed interested, almost excited. "I think it might dull them too much at first—until they're used to it. I wonder whether they can get used to it."

Martha nodded. "I think you're right about it dulling them. I think at first most people will lose interest in a lot of other things—including real, wide-awake sex. Real sex is risky to both the health and the ego. Dream sex will be fantastic and not risky at all. Fewer children will be born for a while."

"And fewer of those will survive," God said.

"What?"

"Some parents will certainly be too involved in dreams to take care of their children. Loving and raising children is risky, too, and it's hard work."

"That shouldn't happen. Taking care of their kids should be the one thing that parents want to do for real in spite of the dreams. I don't want to be responsible for a lot of neglected kids."

"So you want people—adults and children—to have nights filled with vivid, wish-fulfilling dreams, but parents should somehow see child care as more important than the dreams, and the children should not be seduced away from their parents by the dreams, but should want and need a relationship with them as though there were no dreams?"

"As much as possible." Martha frowned, imagining what it might be like to live in such a world. Would people still read books? Perhaps they would to feed their dreams. Would she still be able to write books? Would she want to? What would happen to her if the only work she had ever cared for was lost? "People should still care about their families and their work," she said. "The dreams shouldn't take away their self-respect. They shouldn't be content to dream on a park bench or in an alley. I just want the dreams to slow things down a little. A little less aggression, as you said, less covetousness. Nothing slows people down like satisfaction, and this satisfaction will come every night."

God nodded. "Is that it, then? Do you want this to happen?"

"Yes. I mean, I think so."

"Are you sure?"

She stood up and looked down at him. "Is it what I should do? Will it work? Please tell me."

"I truly don't know. I don't want to know. I want to watch it all unfold. I've used dreams before, you know, but not like this."

His pleasure was so obvious that she almost took the whole idea back. He seemed able to be amused by terrible things. "Let me think about this," she said. "Can I be by myself for a while?"

God nodded. "Speak aloud to me when you want to talk. I'll come to you."

And she was alone. She was alone inside what looked and felt like her home—her little house in Seattle, Washington. She was in her living room.

Without thinking, she turned on a lamp and stood looking at her books. Three of the walls of the room were covered with bookshelves. Her books were there in their familiar order. She picked up several, one after another—history, medicine, religion, art, crime. She opened them to see that they were, indeed, her books, highlighted and written in by her own hand as she researched this novel or that short story.

She began to believe she really was at home. She had had some sort of strange waking dream about meeting with a God who looked like Michelangelo's Moses and who ordered her to come up with a way to make humanity a less self-destructive species. The experience felt completely, unnervingly real, but it couldn't have been. It was too ridiculous.

She went to her front window and opened the drapes. Her house was on a hill and faced east. Its great luxury was that it offered a beautiful view of Lake Washington just a few blocks down the hill.

But now, there was no lake. Outside was the park that she had wished into existence earlier. Perhaps twenty yards from her front window was the big red Norway maple tree and the bench where she had sat and talked with God.

The bench was empty now and in deep shadow. It was getting dark outside.

She closed the drapes and looked at the lamp that lit the room. For a moment, it bothered her that it was on and using electricity in this Twilight Zone of a place. Had her house been transported here, or had it been duplicated? Or was it all a complex hallucination?

She sighed. The lamp worked. Best to just accept it. There was light in the room. There was a room, a house. How it all worked was the least of her problems.

She went to the kitchen and there found all the food she had had at home. Like the lamp, the refrigerator, the electric stovetop, and the ovens worked. She could prepare a meal. It would be at least as real as anything else she'd run across recently. And she was hungry.

She took a small can of solid white albacore tuna and containers of dill weed and curry power from the cupboard and got bread, lettuce, dill pickles, green onions, mayonnaise, and chunky salsa from the refrigerator. She would have a tuna-salad sandwich or two. Thinking about it made her even hungrier.

Then she had another thought, and she said aloud, "May I ask you a question?"

And they were walking together on a broad, level dirt pathway bordered by dark, ghostly silhouettes of trees. Night had fallen, and the darkness beneath the trees was impenetrable. Only the pathway was a ribbon of pale light—starlight and moonlight. There was a full moon, brilliant, yellow-white, and huge. And there was a vast canopy of stars. She had seen the night sky this way only a few times in her life. She had always lived in cities where the lights and the smog obscured all but the brightest few stars.

She looked upward for several seconds, then looked at God and saw, somehow, without surprise, that he was black now, and clean-shaven. He was a tall, stocky black man wearing ordinary, modern clothing—a dark sweater over a white shirt and dark pants. He didn't tower over her, but he was taller than the human-sized version of the white God had been. He didn't look anything like the white Moses-God, and yet he was the same person. She never doubted that.

"You're seeing something different," God said. "What is it?" Even his voice was changed, deepened.

She told him what she was seeing, and he nodded. "At some point, you'll probably decide to see me as a woman," he said.

"I didn't decide to do this," she said. "None of it is real, anyway."

"I've told you," he said. "Everything is real. It's just not as you see it."

She shrugged. It didn't matter—not compared to what she wanted to ask. "I had a thought," she said, "and it scared me. That's why I called you. I sort of asked about it before, but you didn't give me a direct answer, and I guess I need one."

He waited.

"Am I dead?"

"Of course not," he said, smiling. "You're here."

"With you," she said bitterly.

Silence.

"Does it matter how long I take to decide what to do?"

"I've told you, no. Take as long as you like."

That was odd, Martha thought. Well, everything was odd. On impulse, she said, "Would you like a tuna-salad sandwich?"

"Yes," God said. "Thank you."

They walked back to the house together instead of simply appearing there. Martha was grateful for that. Once inside, she left him sitting in her living room, paging through a fantasy novel and smiling. She went through the motions of making the best tuna-salad sandwiches she could. Maybe effort counted. She didn't believe for a moment that she was preparing real food or that she and God were going to eat it.

And yet, the sandwiches were delicious. As they ate, Martha remembered the sparkling apple cider that she kept in the

STORIES

refrigerator for company. She went to get it, and when she got back to the living room, she saw that God had, in fact, become a woman.

Martha stopped, startled, then sighed. "I see you as female now," she said. "Actually, I think you look a little like me. We look like sisters." She smiled wearily and handed over a glass of cider.

God said, "You really are doing this yourself, you know. But as long as it isn't upsetting you, I suppose it doesn't matter."

"It does bother me. If I'm doing it, why did it take so long for me to see you as a black woman—since that's no more true than seeing you as a white or a black man?"

"As I've told you, you see what your life has prepared you to see." God looked at her, and for a moment, Martha felt that she was looking into a mirror.

Martha looked away. "I believe you. I just thought I had already broken out of the mental cage I was born and raised in—a human God, a white God, a male God . . ."

"If it were truly a cage," God said, "you would still be in it, and I would still look the way I did when you first saw me."

"There is that," Martha said. "What would you call it then?"

"An old habit," God said. "That's the trouble with habits. They tend to outlive their usefulness."

Martha was quiet for a while. Finally she said, "What do you think about my dream idea? I'm not asking you to foresee the future. Just find fault. Punch holes. Warn me."

God rested her head against the back of the chair. "Well, the evolving environmental problems will be less likely to cause wars, so there will probably be less starvation, less disease. Real power will be less satisfying than the vast, absolute power they can possess in their dreams, so fewer people will be driven to try to conquer their neighbors or exterminate their minorities. All in all, the dreams will probably give humanity more time than it would have without them."

Martha was alarmed in spite of herself. "Time to do what?"

"Time to grow up a little. Or at least, time to find some way of surviving what remains of its adolescence." God smiled. "How many times have you wondered how some especially self-destructive individual managed to survive adolescence? It's a valid concern for humanity as well as for individual human beings."

"Why can't the dreams do more than that?" she asked. "Why can't the dreams be used not just to give them their heart's desire when they sleep, but to push them toward some kind of waking maturity? Although I'm not sure what species maturity might be like."

"Exhaust them with pleasure," God mused, "while teaching them that pleasure isn't everything."

"They already know that."

"Individuals usually know that by the time they reach adulthood. But all too often, they don't care. It's too easy to follow bad but attractive leaders, embrace pleasurable but destructive habits, ignore looming disaster because maybe it won't happen after all—or maybe it will only happen to other people. That kind of thinking is part of what it means to be adolescent."

"Can the dreams teach—or at least promote—more thoughtfulness when people are awake, promote more concern for real consequences?"

"It can be that way if you like."

"I do. I want them to enjoy themselves as much as they can while they're asleep, but to be a lot more awake and aware when they are awake, a lot less susceptible to lies, peer pressure, and self-delusion."

"None of this will make them perfect, Martha."

Martha stood looking down at God, fearing that she had missed something important, and that God knew it and was amused. "But this will help?" she said. "It will help more than it will hurt."

"Yes, it will probably do that. And it will no doubt do other things. I don't know what they are, but they are inevitable. Nothing ever works smoothly with humankind."

"You like that, don't you?"

"I didn't at first. They were mine, and I didn't know them. You cannot begin to understand how strange that was." God shook her head. "They were as familiar as my own substance, and yet they weren't."

"Make the dreams happen," Martha said.

"Are you sure?"

"Make them happen."

"You're ready to go home, then."

"Yes."

God stood and faced her. "You want to go. Why?"

"Because I don't find them interesting in the same way you do. Because your ways scare me."

God laughed—a less disturbing laugh now. "No, they don't," she said. "You're beginning to like my ways."

After a time, Martha nodded. "You're right. It did scare me at first, and now it doesn't. I've gotten used to it. In just the short time that I've been here, I've gotten used to it, and I'm starting to like it. That's what scares me."

In mirror image, God nodded, too. "You really could have stayed here, you know. No time would pass for you. No time has passed."

"I wondered why you didn't care about time."

"You'll go back to the life you remember, at first. But soon, I think you'll have to find another way of earning a living. Beginning again at your age won't be easy."

Martha stared at the neat shelves of books on her walls. "Reading will suffer, won't it—pleasure reading, anyway?"

"It will—for a while, anyway. People will read for information and for ideas, but they'll create their own fantasies. Did you think of that before you made your decision?"

Martha sighed. "Yes," she said. "I did." Sometime later, she added, "I want to go home."

"Do you want to remember being here?" God asked.

"No." On impulse, she stepped to God and hugged her— hugged her hard, feeling the familiar woman's body beneath the blue jeans and black T-shirt that looked as though it had come from Martha's own closet. Martha realized that somehow, in spite of everything, she had come to like this seductive, childlike, very dangerous being. "No," she repeated. "I'm afraid of the unintended damage that the dreams might do."

"Even though in the long run they'll almost certainly do more good than harm?" God asked.

"Even so," Martha said. "I'm afraid the time might come when I won't be able to stand knowing that I'm the one who caused not only the harm, but the end of the only career I've ever cared about. I'm afraid knowing all that might drive me out of my mind someday." She stepped away from God, and already God seemed to be fading, becoming translucent, transparent, gone.

"I want to forget," Martha said, and she stood alone in her living room, looking blankly past the open drapes of her front window at the surface of Lake Washington and the mist that hung above it. She wondered at the words she had just spoken, wondered what it was she wanted so badly to forget.

Afterword

"The Book of Martha" is my utopia story. I don't like most utopia stories because I don't believe them for a moment. It seems inevitable that my utopia would be someone else's hell. So, of course, I have God demand of poor Martha that she come up with a utopia that would work. And where else could it work but in everyone's private, individual dreams?

ESSAYS

Lost Races of Science Fiction

FOURTEEN YEARS ago, during my first year of college, I sat in a creative writing class and listened as my teacher, an elderly man, told another student not to use black characters in his stories unless those characters' blackness was somehow essential to the plots. The presence of blacks, my teacher felt, changed the focus of the story—drew attention from the intended subject.

This happened in 1965. I would never have expected to hear my teacher's sentiments echoed by a science fiction writer in 1979. Hear them I did, though, at an SF convention where a writer explained that he had decided against using a black character in one of his stories because the presence of the black would change his story somehow. Later, this same writer suggested that in stories that seem to require black characters to make some racial point, it might be possible to substitute extraterrestrials—so as not to dwell on matters of race.

Well, let's do a little dwelling.

Science fiction reaches into the future, the past, the human mind. It reaches out to other worlds and into other dimensions. Is it really so limited, then, that it cannot reach into the lives of ordinary, everyday humans who happen not to be white?

Blacks, Asians, Hispanics, Amerindians, minority characters in general have been noticeably absent from most science fiction. Why? As a black and a science fiction writer, I've heard that question asked often. I've also heard several answers given. And, because most people try to be polite, there have been certain answers I haven't heard. That's all right; they're obvious.

Best, though, and most hopeful from my point of view, I've heard from people who want to write SF, or who've written a few pieces, perhaps, and who would like to include minority characters, but aren't sure how to go about it. Since I've had to solve the same problem in reverse, maybe I can help.

But first some answers to the question, Why have there been so few minority characters in science fiction?

Let's examine my teacher's reason. Are minority characters

—black characters in this case—so disruptive a force that the mere presence of one alters a story, focuses it on race rather than whatever the author had in mind? Yes, in fact, black characters can do exactly that if the creators of those characters are too restricted in their thinking to visualize blacks in any other context.

This is the kind of stereotyping, conscious or subconscious, that women have fought for so long. No writer who regards blacks as people, human beings, with the usual variety of human concerns, flaws, skills, hopes, etc., would have trouble creating interesting backgrounds and goals for black characters. No writer who regards blacks as people would get sidetracked into justifying their blackness or their presence unless such justification honestly played a part in the story. It is no more necessary to focus on a character's blackness than it is to focus on a woman's femininity.

Now, what about the possibility of substituting extraterrestrials for blacks—in order to make some race-related point without making anyone . . . uncomfortable? In fact, why can't blacks be represented by whites who are not too thoroughly described, thus leaving readers free to use their imaginations and visualize whichever color they like?

I usually manage to go on being polite when I hear suggestions like these, but it's not easy.

All right, let's replace blacks with tentacled beings from Capella V. What will readers visualize as we describe relations between the Capellans and the (white) humans? Will they visualize black humans dealing with white humans? I don't think so. This is science fiction, after all. If you tell your readers about tentacled Capellans, they're going to visualize tentacled Capellans. And if your readers are as touchy about human races as you were afraid they might be when you substituted the Capellans, are they really likely to pay attention to any analogy you draw? I don't think so.

And as for whites representing all of humanity—on the theory that people will imagine other races; or better yet, on the theory that all people are alike anyway, so what does it matter? Well, remember when men represented all of humanity? Women didn't care much for it. Still don't. No great mental leap is required to understand why blacks, why any minority, might not care much for it either. And apart from all that, of course, it doesn't work. Whites represent themselves, and that's plenty. Spread the burden.

Back when *Star Wars* was new, a familiar excuse for ignoring minorities went something like this: "SF is escapist literature. Its readers/viewers don't want to be weighted down with real problems." War, okay. Planet-wide destruction, okay. Kidnapping, okay. But the sight of a minority person? Too heavy. Too real. And, of course, there again is the implication that a sprinkling of blacks, Asians, or others could turn the story into some sort of racial statement. The only statement I could imagine being made by such a sprinkling would be that among the white, human people; the tall, furry people; the lumpy, scaly people; the tentacled people, etc., were also brown, human people; black, human people, etc. This isn't such a heavy statement—unless it's missing.

From my agent (whose candor I appreciate), I heard what could become an even stronger reason for not using black characters in particular—not using them in film, anyway. It seems that blacks are out of fashion. In an industry that pays a great deal of attention to trends, blacks have had their day for a while. How long a while? Probably until someone decides to take a chance, and winds up making a damn big hit movie about blacks.

All right, forget for a moment the faddishness of the movie industry. Forget that movies about blacks are out. Movies, SF and otherwise, with a sprinkling of minority characters, but no particular minority theme, seem to do well. Yaphet Kotto certainly didn't do *Alien* any harm. In fact, for me, probably for a good many blacks, he gave the movie an extra touch of authenticity. And a monster movie—even a good monster movie —needs all the authenticity it can get.

That brings me to another question I hear often at SF conventions. "Why are there so few black SF writers?" I suspect for the same reason there were once so few women SF writers. Women found a certain lack of authenticity in a genre that postulated a universe largely populated by men, in which all the power was in male hands, and women stayed in their male-defined places.

Blacks find a certain lack of authenticity in a genre which postulates a universe largely populated by whites, in which the power is in white hands, and blacks are occasional oddities.

SF writers come from SF readers, generally. Few readers equal few writers. The situation is improving, however. Blacks are not as likely as whites to spend time and money going to conventions, but there is a growing black readership. Black people I meet now are much more likely to have read at least some science fiction, and are not averse to reading more. My extra copy of *Dreamsnake* (by Vonda McIntyre) had reached its fifth reader, last I heard. Movies like *Alien*, *Star Wars* (in spite of its lack), and *Close Encounters of the Third Kind*, plus the old *Star Trek* TV series, have captured a lot of interest, too. With all this, it's been a pleasantly long time since a friend or acquaintance has muttered to me, "Science fiction! How can you waste your time with anything that unreal?"

Now to those reasons people aren't as likely to give for leaving minorities out of SF: The most obvious one, and the one I feel least inclined to discuss, is conscious racism. It exists. I don't think SF is greatly afflicted with it, but then, racism is unfashionable now, and thus is unlikely to be brought into the open. Instead, it can be concealed behind any of the questions and arguments I've already discussed. To the degree that it is, this whole article is a protest against racism. It's as much of a protest as I intend to make at the moment. I know of too many bright, competent blacks who have had to waste time and energy trying to reason away other people's unreasonable racist attitudes: in effect, trying to prove their humanity. Life is too short.

A more insidious problem than outright racism is simply habit, custom. SF has always been nearly all white, just as until recently, it's been nearly all male. A lot of people had a chance to get comfortable with things as they are. Too comfortable. SF, more than any other genre, deals with change—change in science and technology, social change. But SF itself changes slowly, often under protest. You can still go to conventions and hear deliberately sexist remarks—if the speaker thinks he has a sympathetic audience. People resent being told their established way of doing things is wrong, resent being told they should change, and strongly resent being told they won't be alone any longer in the vast territory—the universe—they've staked out for themselves. I don't think anyone seriously believes the present world is all white. But custom can be strong enough to prevent people from seeing the need for SF to reflect a more realistic view.

Adherence to custom can also cause people to oppose change by becoming even more extreme in their customary behavior. I went back to college for a couple of quarters a few years ago and found one male teacher after another announcing with odd belligerence, "I might as well tell you right now, I'm a male chauvenist!"

A custom attacked is a custom that will be defended. Men who feel defensive about sexist behavior may make sexist bigots of themselves. Whites who feel defensive about racist behavior may make racist bigots of themselves. It's something for people who value open-mindedness and progressive attitudes to beware of.

A second insidious problem is laziness, possibly combined with ignorance. Authors who have always written of all-white universes might not feel particularly threatened by a multicolored one, but might consider the change too much trouble. After all, they already know how to do what they've been doing. Their way works. Why change? Besides, maybe they don't know any minority people. How can they write about people they don't know?

Of course, ignorance may have a category unto itself. I've heard people I didn't consider lazy, racist, or bound by custom complain that they did not know enough about minorities and thus hesitated to write about them. Often, these people seem worried about accidentally giving offense.

But what do authors ordinarily do when they decide to write about an unfamiliar subject?

They research. They read—in this case recent biographies and autobiographies of people in the group they want to write about are good. They talk to members of that group—friends, acquaintances, co-workers, fellow students, even strangers on buses or waiting in lines. I've done these things myself in my reverse research, and they help. Also, I people-watch a lot without talking. Any public situation offers opportunities.

Some writers have gotten around the need for research by

setting their stories in distant egalitarian futures when cultural differences have dwindled and race has ceased to matter. I created a future like this in my novel, *Patternmaster*, though I did not do it to avoid research. *Patternmaster* takes place in a time when psionic ability is all that counts. People who have enough of that ability are on top whether they're male or female, black, white, or brown. People who have none are slaves. In this culture, a black like the novel's main woman character would, except for her coloring, be indistinguishable from characters of any other race. Using this technique could get a writer accused of writing blacks as though they were whites in Coppertone, and it could be a lazy writer's excuse for doing just that. But for someone who has a legitimate reason for using it, a story that requires it, it can be a perfectly valid technique.

More important than any technique, however, is for authors to remember that they are writing about *people*. Authors who forget this, who do not relax and get comfortable with their racially different characters, can wind up creating unbelievable, self-consciously manipulated puppets; pieces of furniture who exist within a story but contribute nothing to it; or stereotypes guaranteed to be offensive.

There was a time when most of the few minority characters in SF fell into one of these categories. One of the first black characters I ran across when I began reading SF in the fifties was a saintly old "uncle" (I'm not being sarcastic here. The man was described as saintly and portrayed asking to be called "uncle") whom Harriet Beecher Stowe would have felt right at home with. I suspect that like the Sidney Poitier movies of the sixties, Uncle was daring for his time. That didn't help me find him any more believable or feel any less pleased when he and his kind (Charlie Chan, Tonto, that little guy who swiped Fritos . . .) were given decent burials. Times have changed, thank heavens, and SF has come a long way from Uncle. Clearly, though, it still has a long way to go.

Positive Obsession

M Y MOTHER read me bedtime stories until I was six years old. It was a sneak attack on her part. As soon as I really got to like the stories, she said, "Here's the book. Now you read." She didn't know what she was setting us both up for.

2

"I think," my mother said to me one day when I was ten, "that everyone has something that they can do better than they can do anything else. It's up to them to find out what that something is."

We were in the kitchen by the stove. She was pressing my hair while I sat bent over someone's cast-off notebook, writing. I had decided to write down some of the stories I'd been telling myself over the years. When I didn't have stories to read, I learned to make them up. Now I was learning to write them down.

3

I was shy, afraid of most people, most situations. I didn't stop to ask myself how things could hurt me, or even whether they could hurt me. I was just afraid.

I crept into my first bookstore full of vague fears. I had managed to save about five dollars, mostly in change. It was 1957. Five dollars was a lot of money for a ten-year-old. The public library had been my second home since I was six, and I owned a number of hand-me-down books. But now I wanted a new book—one I had chosen, one I could keep.

"Can kids come in here?" I asked the woman at the cash register once I was inside. I meant could Black kids come in. My mother, born in rural Louisiana and raised amid strict racial segregation, had warned me that I might not be welcome everywhere, even in California.

The cashier glanced at me. "Of course you can come in," she said. Then, as though it were an afterthought, she smiled. I relaxed.

The first book I bought described the characteristics of different breeds of horses. The second described stars and planets, asteroids, moons and comets.

4

My aunt and I were in her kitchen, talking. She was cooking something that smelled good, and I was sitting at her table, watching. Luxury. At home, my mother would have had me helping.

"I want to be a writer when I grow up," I said.

"Do you?" my aunt asked. "Well, that's nice, but you'll have to get a job, too."

"Writing will be my job," I said.

"You can write any time. It's a nice hobby. But you'll have to earn a living."

"As a writer."

"Don't be silly."

"I mean it."

"Honey . . . Negroes can't be writers."

"Why not?"

"They just can't."

"Yes, they can, too!"

I was most adamant when I didn't know what I was talking about. In all my thirteen years, I had never read a printed word that I knew to have been written by a Black person. My aunt was a grown woman. She knew more than I did. What if she were right?

5

Shyness is shit.

It isn't cute or feminine or appealing. It's torment, and it's shit.

I spent a lot of my childhood and adolescence staring at the ground. It's a wonder I didn't become a geologist. I whispered. People were always saying, "Speak up! We can't hear you."

I memorized required reports and poems for school, then cried my way out of having to recite. Some teachers condemned me for not studying. Some forgave me for not being very bright. Only a few saw my shyness.

"She's so backward," some of my relatives said.

"She's so nice and quiet," tactful friends of my mother said.

I believed I was ugly and stupid, clumsy, and socially hopeless. I also thought that everyone would notice these faults if I drew attention to myself. I wanted to disappear. Instead, I grew to be six feet tall. Boys in particular seemed to assume that I had done this growing deliberately and that I should be ridiculed for it as often as possible.

I hid out in a big pink notebook—one that would hold a whole ream of paper. I made myself a universe in it. There I could be a magic horse, a Martian, a telepath. . . . There I could be anywhere but here, any time but now, with any people but these.

6

My mother did day work. She had a habit of bringing home any books her employers threw out. She had been permitted only three years of school. Then she had been put to work. Oldest daughter. She believed passionately in books and education. She wanted me to have what she had been denied. She wasn't sure which books I might be able to use, so she brought whatever she found in the trash. I had books yellow with age, books without covers, books written in, crayoned in, spilled on, cut, torn, even partly burned. I stacked them in wooden crates and second-hand bookcases and read them when I was ready for them. Some were years too advanced for me when I got them, but I grew into them.

7

An obsession, according to my old Random House dictionary, is "the domination of one's thoughts or feelings by a persistent idea, image, desire, etc." Obsession can be a useful tool if it's positive obsession. Using it is like aiming carefully in archery.

I took archery in high school because it wasn't a team sport. I liked some of the team sports, but in archery you did well or badly according to your own efforts. No one else to blame. I wanted to see what I could do. I learned to aim high. Aim above the target. Aim just *there!* Relax. Let go. If you aimed right, you hit the bull's-eye. I saw positive obsession as a way of aiming yourself, your life, at your chosen target. Decide what you want. Aim high. Go for it.

I wanted to sell a story. Before I knew how to type, I wanted to sell a story.

I pecked my stories out two fingered on the Remington portable typewriter my mother had bought me. I had begged for it when I was ten, and she had bought it.

"You'll spoil that child!" one of her friends told her. "What does she need with a typewriter at her age? It will soon be sitting in the closet with dust on it. All that money wasted!"

I asked my science teacher, Mr. Pfaff, to type one of my stories for me—type it the way it was supposed to be with no holes erased into the paper and no strike-overs. He did. He even corrected my terrible spelling and punctuation. To this day I'm amazed and grateful.

8

I had no idea how to submit a story for publication. I blundered through unhelpful library books on writing. Then I found a discarded copy of *The Writer*, a magazine I had never heard of. That copy sent me back to the library to look for more, and for other writers' magazines to see what I could learn from them. In very little time I'd found out how to submit a story, and my story was in the mail. A few weeks later I got my first rejection slip.

When I was older, I decided that getting a rejection slip was like being told your child was ugly. You got mad and didn't believe a word of it. Besides, look at all the really ugly literary children out there in the world being published and doing fine!

9

I spent my teens and much of my twenties collecting printed rejections. Early on, my mother lost $61.20—a reading fee charged by a so-called agent to look at one of my unpublishable stories. No one had told us that agents weren't supposed to get any money up front, weren't supposed to be paid until they sold your work. Then they were to take ten percent of whatever the work earned. Ignorance is expensive. That $61.20 was more money back then than my mother paid for a month's rent.

10

I badgered friends and acquaintances into reading my work, and they seemed to like it. Teachers read it and said kindly, unhelpful things. But there were no creative writing classes at my high school, and no useful criticism. At college (in California at that time, junior college was almost free), I took classes taught by an elderly woman who wrote children's stories. She was polite about the science fiction and fantasy that I kept handing in, but she finally asked in exasperation, "Can't you write anything normal?"

A schoolwide contest was held. All submissions had to be made anonymously. My short story won first prize. I was an eighteen-year-old freshman, and I won in spite of competition from older, more experienced people. Beautiful. The $15.00 prize was the first money my writing earned me.

11

After college I did office work for a while, then factory and warehouse work. My size and strength were advantages in factories and warehouses. And no one expected me to smile and pretend I was having a good time.

I got up at two or three in the morning and wrote. Then I went to work. I hated it, and I have no gift for suffering in silence. I muttered and complained and quit jobs and found new ones and collected more rejection slips. One day in disgust I threw them all away. Why keep such useless, painful things?

12

There seems to be an unwritten rule, hurtful and at odds with the realities of American culture. It says you aren't supposed to wonder whether as a Black person, a Black woman, you really might be inferior—not quite bright enough, not quite quick enough, not quite good enough to do the things you want to do. Though, of course, you do wonder. You're supposed to *know* you're as good as anyone. And if you don't know, you aren't supposed to admit it. If anyone near you admits it, you're supposed to reassure them quickly so they'll shut up. That sort of talk is embarrassing. Act tough and confident and don't talk about your doubts. If you never deal with them, you may never get rid of them, but no matter. Fake everyone out. Even yourself.

I couldn't fake myself out. I didn't talk much about my doubts. I wasn't fishing for hasty reassurances. But I did a lot of thinking—the same things over and over.

Who was I anyway? Why should anyone pay attention to what I had to say? Did I have anything to say? I was writing science fiction and fantasy, for God's sake. At that time nearly all professional science-fiction writers were white men. As much as I loved science fiction and fantasy, what was I doing?

Well, whatever it was, I couldn't stop. Positive obsession is about not being able to stop just because you're afraid and full of doubts. Positive obsession is dangerous. It's about not being able to stop at all.

13

I was twenty-three when, finally, I sold my first two short stories. I sold both to writer-editors who were teaching at Clarion, a science-fiction writers' workshop that I was attending. One story was eventually published. The other wasn't. I didn't sell another word for five years. Then, finally, I sold my first novel. Thank God no one told me selling would take so long —not that I would have believed it. I've sold eight novels since then. Last Christmas, I paid off the mortgage on my mother's house.

14

So, then, I write science fiction and fantasy for a living. As far as I know I'm still the only Black woman who does this. When I began to do a little public speaking, one of the questions I heard most often was, "What good is science fiction to Black people?" I was usually asked this by a Black person. I gave bits and pieces of answers that didn't satisfy me and that probably didn't satisfy my questioners. I resented the question. Why should I have to justify my profession to anyone?

But the answer to that was obvious. There was exactly one other Black science-fiction writer working successfully when I sold my first novel: Samuel R. Delany, Jr. Now there are four of us. Delany, Steven Barnes, Charles R. Saunders, and me. So few. Why? Lack of interest? Lack of confidence? A young Black woman once said to me, "I always wanted to write science fiction, but I didn't think there were any Black women doing it." Doubts show themselves in all sorts of ways. But still I'm asked, what good is science fiction to Black people?

What good is any form of literature to Black people?

What good is science fiction's thinking about the present, the future, and the past? What good is its tendency to warn or to consider alternative ways of thinking and doing? What good is its examination of the possible effects of science and technology, or social organization and political direction? At its best, science fiction stimulates imagination and creativity. It gets reader and writer off the beaten track, off the narrow, narrow footpath of what "everyone" is saying, doing, thinking —whoever "everyone" happens to be this year.

And what good is all this to Black people?

Afterword

This autobiographical article appeared originally in *Essence* magazine under the *Essence* title, "Birth of a Writer." I never liked the *Essence* title. My title was always "Positive Obsession."

I've often said that since my life was filled with reading, writing, and not much else, it was too dull to write about. I still feel that way. I'm glad I wrote this piece, but I didn't enjoy writing it. I have no doubt at all that the best and the most interesting part of me is my fiction.

Furor Scribendi

WRITING FOR publication may be both the easiest and the hardest thing you'll ever do. Learning the rules—if they can be called rules—is the easy part. Following them, turning them into regular habits, is an ongoing struggle. Here are the rules:

1. Read. Read about the art, the craft, and the business of writing. Read the kind of work you'd like to write. Read good literature and bad, fiction and fact. Read every day and learn from what you read. If you commute to work or if you spend part of your day doing relatively mindless work, listen to book tapes. If your library doesn't have a good supply of complete books on audio tape, companies like Recorded Books, Books on Tape, Brilliance Corporation, and the Literate Ear will rent or sell you a wide selection of such books for your pleasure and continuing education. These provide a painless way to ponder use of language, the sounds of words, conflict, characterization, plotting, and the multitudes of ideas you can find in history, biography, medicine, the sciences, etc.

2. Take classes and go to writers' workshops. Writing is communication. You need other people to let you know whether you're communicating what you think you are and whether you're doing it in ways that are not only accessible and entertaining, but as compelling as you can make them. In other words, you need to know that you're telling a good story. You want to be the writer who keeps readers up late at night, not the one who drives them off to watch television. Workshops and classes are rented readers—rented audiences—for your work. Learn from the comments, questions, and suggestions of both the teacher and the class. These relative strangers are more likely to tell you the truth about your work than are your friends and family who may not want to hurt or offend you. One tiresome truth they might tell you, for instance, is that you need to take a grammar class. If they say this, listen. Take the class. Vocabulary and grammar are your primary tools. They're most effectively used, even most effectively abused, by people who understand them. No computer program, no

friend or employee can take the place of a sound knowledge of your tools.

3. Write. Write every day. Write whether you feel like writing or not. Choose a time of day. Perhaps you can get up an hour earlier, stay up an hour later, give up an hour of recreation, or even give up your lunch hour. If you can't think of anything in your chosen genre, keep a journal. You should be keeping one anyway. Journal writing helps you to be more observant of your world, and a journal is a good place to store story ideas for later projects.

4. Revise your writing until it's as good as you can make it. All the reading, the writing, and the classes should help you do this. Check your writing, your research (never neglect your research), and the physical appearance of your manuscript. Let nothing substandard slip through. If you notice something that needs fixing, fix it, no excuses. There will be plenty that's wrong that you won't catch. Don't make the mistake of ignoring flaws that are obvious to you. The moment you find yourself saying, "This doesn't matter. It's good enough." Stop. Go back. Fix the flaw. Make a habit of doing your best.

5. Submit your work for publication. First research the markets that interest you. Seek out and study the books or magazines of publishers to whom you want to sell. Then submit your work. If the idea of doing this scares you, fine. Go ahead and be afraid. But send your work out anyway. If it's rejected, send it out again, and again. Rejections are painful, but inevitable. They're every writer's rite of passage. Don't give up on a piece of work that you can't sell. You may be able to sell it later to new publications or to new editors of old publications. At worst, you should be able to learn from your rejected work. You may even be able to use all or part of it in a new work. One way or another, writers can use, or at least learn from, everything.

6. Here are some potential impediments for you to forget about:

First forget *inspiration*. Habit is more dependable. Habit will sustain you whether you're inspired or not. Habit will help you finish and polish your stories. Inspiration won't. Habit is persistence in practice.

Forget *talent*. If you have it, fine. Use it. If you don't have it, it doesn't matter. As habit is more dependable than inspiration, continued learning is more dependable than talent. Never let pride or laziness prevent you from learning, improving your work, changing its direction when necessary. Persistence is essential to any writer—the persistence to finish your work, to keep writing in spite of rejection, to keep reading, studying, submitting work for sale. But stubbornness, the refusal to change unproductive behavior or to revise unsalable work, can be lethal to your writing hopes.

Finally, don't worry about imagination. You have all the imagination you need, and all the reading, journal writing, and learning you will be doing will stimulate it. Play with your ideas. Have fun with them. Don't worry about being silly or outrageous or wrong. So much of writing is fun. It's first letting your interests and your imagination take you anywhere at all. Once you're able to do that, you'll have more ideas than you can use. Then the real work of fashioning them into a story begins. Stay with it.

Persist.

Afterword

I wrote this brief essay for the *Writers of the Future* anthology series (*L. Ron Hubbard Presents Writers of the Future IX*). This series showcases the work of new writers, and my essay is a compact version of a talk that I've given to groups of new writers.

The last word of the essay is its most important word. Writing is difficult. You do it all alone without encouragement and without any certainty that you'll ever be published or paid or even that you'll be able to finish the particular work you've begun. It isn't easy to persist amid all that. That's why I've called this mild little essay "Furor Scribendi"—"A Rage for Writing." "Rage," "Positive Obsession," "burning need to write" . . . Call it anything you like; it's a useful emotion.

Sometimes when I'm interviewed, the interviewer either compliments me on my "talent," my "gift," or asks me how I discovered it. (I don't know, maybe it was supposed to be lying in my closet or on the street somewhere, waiting to be discovered.) I used to struggle to answer this politely, to explain that I didn't believe much in writing talent. People who want to write either do it or they don't. At last I began to say that my most important talent—or habit—was *persistence*. Without it, I would have given up writing long before I finished my first novel. It's amazing what we can do if we simply refuse to give up.

I suspect that this is the most important thing I've said in all my interviews and talks as well as in this book. It's a truth that applies to more than writing. It applies to anything that is important, but difficult, important, but frightening. We're all capable of climbing so much higher than we usually permit ourselves to suppose.

The word, again, is "persist!"

The Monophobic Response

For all but the first 10 years of my life, writing has been my way of journeying from incomprehension, confusion, and emotional upheaval to some sort of order, or at least to an orderly list of questions and considerations. For instance . . .

At the moment there are no true aliens in our lives—no Martians, Tau Cetians to swoop down in advanced spaceships, their attentions firmly fixed on the all-important Us, no gods or devils, no spirits, angels, or gnomes.

Some of us know this. Deep within ourselves we know it. We're on our own, the focus of no interest except our consuming interest in ourselves.

Is this too much reality? It is, yes. No one is watching, caring, extending a hand or taking a little demonic blame. If we are adults and past the age of having our parents come running when we cry, our only help is ourselves and one another.

Yes, this is far too much reality.

No wonder we need aliens.

No wonder we're so good at creating aliens.

No wonder we so often project alienness onto one another.

This last of course has been the worst of our problems—the human alien from another culture, country, gender, race, ethnicity. This is the tangible alien who can be hurt or killed.

There is a vast and terrible sibling rivalry going within the human family as we satisfy our desires for territory, dominance, and exclusivity. How strange: In our ongoing eagerness to create aliens, we express our need for them, and we express our deep fear of being alone in a universe that cares no more for us than it does for stones or suns or any other fragments of itself. And yet we are unable to get along with those aliens who are closest to us, those aliens who are of course ourselves.

All the more need then to create more cooperative aliens, supernatural beings or intelligences from the stars. Sometimes we just need someone to talk to, someone we can trust to listen and care, someone who knows us as we really are and as we rarely get to know one another, someone whose whole agenda is us. Like children, we do still need great and powerful parent figures and we need invisible friends. What is adult behavior after all but modified, disguised, excused childhood behavior? The more educated, the more sophisticated, the more thoughtful we are, the more able we are to conceal the child within us. No matter. The child persists and it's lonely.

Perhaps someday we will have truly alien company. Perhaps we will eventually communicate with other life elsewhere in the universe or at least become aware of other life, distant but real, existing with or without our belief, with or without our permission.

How will we be able to endure such a slight? The universe has other children. There they are. Distant siblings that we've longed for. What will we feel? Hostility? Terror? Suspicion? Relief?

No doubt.

New siblings to rival. Perhaps for a moment, only a moment, this affront will bring us together, all human, all much more alike than different, all much more alike than is good for our prickly pride. Humanity, *E pluribus unum* at last, a oneness focused on and fertilized by certain knowledge of alien others. What will be born of that brief, strange, and ironic union?

Preface to *Bloodchild and Other Stories*

THE TRUTH is, I hate short story writing. Trying to do it has taught me much more about frustration and despair than I ever wanted to know.

Yet there is something seductive about writing short stories. It looks so easy. You come up with an idea, then ten, twenty, perhaps thirty pages later, you've got a finished story.

Well, maybe.

My earliest collections of pages weren't stories at all. They were fragments of longer works—of stalled, unfinished novels. Or they were brief summaries of unwritten novels. Or they were isolated incidents that could not stand alone.

All that, and poorly written, too.

It didn't help that my college writing teachers said only polite, lukewarm things about them. They couldn't help me much with the science fiction and fantasy I kept turning out. In fact, they didn't have a very high opinion of anything that could be called science fiction.

Editors regularly rejected my stories, returning them with the familiar, unsigned, printed rejection slips. This, of course, was the writer's rite of passage. I knew it, but that didn't make it easier. And as for short stories, I used to give up writing them the way some people give up smoking cigarettes—over and over again. I couldn't escape my story ideas, and I couldn't make them work as short stories. After a long struggle, I made some of them work as novels.

Which is what they should have been all along.

I am essentially a novelist. The ideas that most interest me tend to be big. Exploring them takes more time and space than a short story can contain.

And yet, every now and then one of my short stories really is a short story. The five stories in this collection really are short stories. I've never been tempted to turn them into novels. This book, however, has tempted me to add to them—not to make them longer, but to talk about each of them. I've included a brief afterword with each story. I like the idea of afterwords rather than individual introductions since afterwords allow me to talk freely about the stories without ruining them for readers. It will be a pleasure to make use of such freedom. Before now, other people have done all the print interpretations of my work: "Butler seems to be saying . . ." "Obviously, Butler believes . . ." "Butler makes it clear that she feels . . ."

Actually, I feel that what people bring to my work is at least as important to them as what I put into it. But I'm still glad to be able to talk a little about what I do put into my work, and what it means to me.

CHRONOLOGY

NOTE ON THE TEXTS

NOTES

Chronology

1947   Born in Pasadena, California, on June 22, to Laurice James and Octavia Margaret Guy Butler. Mother, born June 5, 1911, in Lafourche Parish, Louisiana, cleans houses; father, born May 9, 1910, in Tampa, Florida, shines shoes. Parents married in Los Angeles, California, on May 26, 1931. Father is drafted into the army in 1943; his draft papers record that he is separated from his wife at that time. He serves as a private in Battery B, 6th Field Artillery Battalion. Four brothers all died in infancy or in utero before she was born; Butler will later tell Charles Rowell, "I often wonder what kind of person I would have been if my brothers had lived."

1949   Meets, as she will later recall, her "first non-human being," a cocker spaniel named Baba who belongs to one of her mother's employers.

1951–52   Called Junie by her mother; known as Estelle growing up. An extremely shy child, with a learning disability she will later recognize as dyslexia, Butler suffers from low self-esteem and a desire to disappear; "instead," she will later write, "I grew to be six feet tall." Will later recall that she began telling herself stories at age four and began writing them down later in childhood when she realized she was starting to forget some of them. Father dies on February 16, leaving mother a widow and in poverty; due in part to Butler's own contradictory statements on the subject, father is sometimes said to have died anywhere from her infancy to age seven. Although they have a sometimes contentious relationship, Butler will later credit her mother in heroic terms with raising her and supporting her dreams. Spends time with her maternal grandmother Stella Guy, including months spent at her chicken ranch near the Mojave Desert, as well as with a beloved aunt, Hazel Guy, who works as a nurse and who, with good intentions, encourages Butler to seek the same sort of practical, well-paying work. Will later recall: "I was raised by strict Baptists whose views I never completely shared. Eventually, I became an ex-Baptist, but I never forgot the rousing services and the singing which I loved or the illogic and sometimes the religious bigotry which I hated." Enters kindergarten at James A. Garfield Elementary.

1953　Mother reads to Butler until she is six years old, at which time she is primed to love reading herself. "She didn't know what she was setting us both up for," she will later write. The Pasadena Public Library becomes her childhood second home. Among the books mother has at home is one by James Baldwin. Enters first grade at Abraham Lincoln Elementary.

1954　On a zoo trip with school class, realizes the chimpanzee is miserable in its enclosure as her classmates laugh and throw peanuts at him; later will say the experience taught her to hate cages of all sorts.

1957　Returns to James A. Garfield Elementary for fifth and sixth grades. Receives her first typewriter at Christmas, purchased for her by her mother; she will write her first five novels on it. Frequently writes stories at this time, often about magical horses. Purchases her first two books with money she'd saved herself, one about horses and one about outer space, from a used bookstore. Sees a horse trainer mistreating his ponies at a carnival, another experience of witnessing animal cruelty that will stick with her for life. Felix Salten's *Bambi: A Life in the Woods* is a favorite novel, along with *The Black Stallion* by Walter Farley, *King of the Wind* by Marguerite Henry, *Smoky the Cowhorse* by Will James, and the novels of Robert A. Heinlein and Edgar Rice Burroughs. Also reads juvenile science fiction novels in the Winston Science Fiction series.

1958　A teacher tells mother that Butler could not learn very well "because I was 'colored' . . . My mother came home angry and urged me to 'be somebody.'"

1959　Begins writing science fiction after watching a science fiction B-movie, *Devil Girl from Mars*, on late-night television. "As I was watching this film," she will later tell an audience at MIT, "I had a series of revelations. The first was that 'Geez, I can write a better story than that.' And then I thought, 'Geez, anybody can write a better story than that.' And my third thought was the clincher: 'Somebody got paid for writing that awful story.' So I was off and writing." The stories she begins writing will ultimately, after many permutations and transformations, become the basis for the Patternist books. Tall and "mature-enough looking at 12 to be mistaken for the mother of my friends," she will recount in an unfinished autobiography that she used this fact to her advantage to sneak into the adult section of the library and check out science fiction magazines and novels, leading to her lifelong love of the genre; she will frequently point to Robert A. Heinlein, Frank Herbert, Zenna Henderson, and later Ursula K. Le Guin as particular favorites. Attends William McKinley Junior High for seventh grade.

1960   Begins submitting stories to science fiction magazines, encouraged by a favorite science teacher. Swindled out of $61.20, more than a month's rent, by a fraudulent literary agent who wrote, "We think your story has merit and may sell, but it needs revision. For only $61.20, we will revise it." Butler's mother gives her the money; Butler will later note that "if the godawful little story had sold, it could not have brought more than $50." Aunt tells Butler that Black people cannot grow up to work as writers, and Butler worries that it is true: "In all my thirteen years, I had never read a printed word that I knew to have been written by a Black person." Moves to George Washington Junior High for eighth and ninth grades.

1961   Begins a fascination with the self-help discourse of both Napoleon Hill (creator of the "confidence formula") and Dale Carnegie (*How to Win Friends and Influence People*), whose work she types out verbatim and memorizes. This aphoristic style will later inform her own self-therapeutic practices as well as the poetic style of Lauren Olamina in the Parable series. Begins attending John Muir High School in Pasadena, California.

1964   Writes in high school journal: "I'm 17 now. I have an overpowering need to be just like everybody else—and a driving need to be as different as possible. . . . I may never get the chance to do all the things I want to do—to write 1 (or more) best sellers, to initiate a new type of writing, to win both the Nobel and the Pulitzer Prizes (in reverse order), and to sit my mother down in her own house before she is too old and tired to enjoy it."

1965   Graduates from high school. Receives a $50 graduation present from her mother, which she spends on a course in self-hypnosis, which she later credits with improving her habits as well as her writing. Enters Pasadena City College. Wins college literary contest for a short story titled "To the Victor" under the pen name Karen Adams; the $15 prize is the first money she has made from writing. Begins writing *Mary*, the novel that will eventually become *Mind of My Mind*. Will later recount getting the idea for *Kindred* from the radical declaration of a classmate who was part of the Black Power movement that "I'd like to kill all these old people who have been holding us back for so long. But I can't because I'd have to start with my own parents."

1966   Becomes an ardent fan of *Star Trek*, which she watches in its original airing on September 8 and sketches fan fiction for (developing a fierce crush on William Shatner). Asks a college creative writing professor to read an early draft of her first completed novel, which will ultimately become *Survivor*; the professor, Butler believes, reads only a few pages before replying, "Well, I don't know what to tell you." The same teacher will later ask her, exasperatedly, "Can't you write anything normal?"

1967   Wins fifth place in national Writer's Digest short story contest for short-short story "Loss." The congratulatory letter reads: "Your prize, a Sheaffer pen engraved with your name and the fact that you won a prize in this contest, will be sent to you within the next three weeks."

1968   In her last semester at PCC she takes a Black literature class; "that was when I became aware of people like Gwendolyn Brooks, Richard Wright, W.E.B. Du Bois, etc. Before that class, I had read James Baldwin, been aware of Langston Hughes, had read a few books about but not by Frederick Douglass and others who endured and escaped slavery." After the assassination of Martin Luther King, Jr., in April, reflects that despite her reservations about his conciliatory politics he can be a "drawing point, focal point, uniting force, more powerful in death than life." Graduates from Pasadena City College with an associate's degree in history; enrolls in California State University, Los Angeles, but does not complete the degree. In the next few years, her journals will frequently note her extreme loneliness, depression, and suicidal ideation (in 1974, she will imagine that "if I do suicide," it would not be planned but that she might find herself "in a place where it would be easy to die"), as well as her poverty, but the primary focus will always be on her devotion to her writing. Wakes up at two or three in the morning to write, and goes to work after, at low-wage clerk and factory jobs, of the sort held by the character Dana in her novel *Kindred*. Frequently unemployed, which she welcomes as time to write; much of her drafts are typed or handwritten on the back of company letterhead she takes from one workplace or another.

1969   Enrolls in a UCLA Extension creative writing workshop and subsequently enrolls in the Screen Writers Guild of America Open Door Workshop, led by Harlan Ellison, who becomes an early mentor and, for a time, a close friend.

1970   Attends Clarion Science Fiction Writers' Workshop in Clarion, Pennsylvania, where the teachers include Joanna Russ, Samuel R. Delany, Fritz Leiber, and Damon Knight; aside from a brief time living with her grandmother near the Mohave Desert, she has never before left California. Keeps a travel journal on the bus across the country, a habit she will keep up as she travels for the rest of her life. Lonely and frustrated at Clarion, where she is the only Black student, as well as by the pace of work demanded by her teachers, but makes lifelong friends and contacts, including author Vonda McIntyre. Attends her first science fiction convention, PgHLange, in Pittsburgh, Pennsylvania. Completes another draft of *Mind of My Mind*, now titled *Psychogenesis*.

1971   Sells story "Childfinder" to Harlan Ellison for *The Last Dangerous Visions* (the anthology is never published). "Crossover" is published in the Clarion collection edited by Robin Scott Wilson; the story is barely science fiction, and Butler considers it a lesser work. Loses a briefcase with a large part of an early novel, a memory that haunts her for the following decades; she will never keep just one copy of any of her works again.

1972   Moves out of her mother's house into the rental she will live in for the next two decades. Unsuccessfully attempts to sell a story set in the Patternist world about missionaries attempting and failing to settle on another world, titled "The Evening and the Morning and the Night"; as with the other elements of the Patternist series, she had been working on the story since the mid-1960s. Will later reuse the title, and ideas from the unpublished story will inform many later works, including "Bloodchild," *Dawn*, and *Parable of the Trickster*.

1974   Begins first work on *Kindred*; an early version of the novel places it within the Patternist series, but by the time of its publication it is Butler's first stand-alone novel, and the only one that she did not conceive of as part of a longer series. A period of unemployment after being laid off from a job as a telephone solicitor at Christmas allows her the time to finish a first draft of *Survivor* after she concludes that her writing habits, speed, and style will never allow her to make any sort of living writing short stories alone.

1975   Takes another UCLA class, this time with Theodore Sturgeon as instructor, which she will likewise remember as formative for her craft, even if she also recalled it as a site of "humiliation" and "long, painful thinking." Completes first draft, *Bondage*, of the book that will become *Patternmaster* and mails it to Doubleday in July. Receives nonbinding conditional acceptance from Doubleday in September and receives a contract, with an offer of payment of $1,750. Returns contract with a "yes" the same day it is received.

1976   Novel *Patternmaster* is published by Doubleday in July; *Kirkus Reviews* calls it "fine, old-fashioned sf," while *Publishers Weekly* calls it "consistently attention-holding." Temporarily moves to Maryland to research *Kindred* and tours plantation sites nearby, including Mount Vernon; the experience of seeing the mansions and recognizing the erasure in the tours of the slave labor that had built and maintained them is formative for the novel.

1977   Novel *Mind of My Mind*, the second in the Patternist series, is published by Doubleday in June. Butler negotiates a lower fee for the book in exchange for being allowed to use swear words and include a sex scene. *Kirkus Reviews* writes: "Despite some ragged moments, Butler is clearly on to a promising vein—something like Zenna Henderson's 'People' stories without their saccharine silliness. There's a lot of intrinsic energy in the Pattern idea, and one wants to see where this erratic, gifted storyteller will pick it up next."

1978   *Survivor*, the third Patternist novel, is published by Doubleday in March; *Kirkus Reviews* finds the book "cardboard" but says "one suspects that this author may give us something really first-rate one of these days." Butler herself will later view the book as her "*Star Trek* novel," considering it marred by the serious failure of having humanoid species that evolved on different planets be able to reproduce (like the half-human, half-Vulcan science officer Spock on *Star Trek*). She also feels the book was stronger before her last set of revisions, which were prompted by suggestions from Harlan Ellison. Butler will prevent the book's republication through the end of her life. Begins work on an ultimately unpublished novel called *Blindsight*, a Stephen King–esque horror novel centered on a cult leader with psychokinesis. Money troubles grow so acute that she is repeatedly on the brink of bankruptcy.

1979   Novel *Kindred* is published by Doubleday in July. The book is received extremely well; the cover of the 1981 Pocket Book reprint quotes Harlan Ellison's endorsement that the book is both "important" and "hypnotic" above the title, in letters nearly as large as Butler's own name. Short story "Near of Kin," which has no connection to *Kindred* despite the similar name and a misleading editor's note, is published in *Chrysalis 4*, edited by Roy Torgeson. Abandons work on *Blindsight* only a few months into the project; frustrated, she writes, "I feel on the verge of giving up."

1980   In March, is guest of honor at feminist science fiction convention WisCon in Madison, Wisconsin. *Wild Seed*, a fourth Patternist novel, is published by Doubleday in July; the book will eventually be shortlisted for a "retrospective" James Tiptree, Jr. Award in 1995, though at the time Butler is frustrated by what she perceives as a lack of promotion by the publisher. Elizabeth Lynn in *The Washington Post* praises the book's steady hand, finding Butler's prose "spare and sure" and "often grim, but . . . never casually brutal." Essay "Lost Races of Science Fiction" is published in the summer issue of the fanzine *Transmission*. Martin Greenberg approaches Butler regarding ultimately failed *Black Futures* anthology, intended as a collection of stories about positive futures for Black people. Wins a Creative Arts Award from the YWCA in Los Angeles. Receives a fan letter from Toni Cade Bambara, and the two strike up a correspondence that lasts several years.

1981   Completes the first version of *Blindsight*, which she had begun work on again the previous year. Frustrated with Doubleday and with her reception both inside and outside the science fiction community, feeling underpaid and not respected, she sends *Blindsight* to Houghton Mifflin (she receives a rejection letter: "one of this author's lesser works") and the Patternist novel *Clay's Ark* to Toni Morrison at Random House, hoping to use it to break into the more mainstream literary marketplace.

1982   Visits Finland and the Soviet Union in May with a group of science fiction writers (including Joe Haldeman, Forrest Ackerman, and Roger Zelazny); visits Moscow, Kiev, and Leningrad. Continues her efforts to sell *Clay's Ark* outside the science fiction market; writes in a letter to her agent, Felicia Eth at Writer's House: "[it] could be given away as standard sf the way *Wild Seed* was, but I see no reason to flush it down that particular toilet. Certainly, sf readers should be told about the book in ads and reviews in sf magazines, but I would be pleased if the words 'science fiction' appeared nowhere on the book itself. I love sf myself, but too much of the time, publishers see it as a step-child and reviewers see it as a bastard."

1983   Short story "Speech Sounds" is published in *Isaac Asimov's Science Fiction Magazine* in December. Returns to work on revisions of *Blindsight*. *Clay's Ark* is submitted to St. Martin's Press.

1984   *Clay's Ark* is published by St. Martin's Press in March; *Kirkus Reviews* gives it a somewhat backhanded endorsement: "Despite the basic triteness of its premise and its backdrop: another technically scintillating novel from the author of *Kindred* (1979) and the Patternmaster series." Short story "Bloodchild" is published in *Isaac Asimov's Science Fiction Magazine* in June. "Speech Sounds" wins the Hugo Award for Best Short Story, her first Hugo. Completes the second version of *Blindsight*, now focused more on the polyamorous love story among the three main characters.

1985   "Bloodchild" wins the Hugo, Nebula, Locus, and Science Fiction Chronicle Awards for Best Novelette. Takes part in a research trip to the Amazon rainforest in Peru as part of UCLA study group with botanist Mildred Mathias to do research for what will become the Xenogenesis trilogy; also visits ruins in the Andes Mountains as well as Cuzco and Machu Picchu. Begins teaching at Clarion West (and later Clarion as well). Continues to try to sell *Blindsight* but views the book as merely "saleable" and describes it in her journals as "thin and impoverished," even "boring."

1986   Unsure of what to do next, considers a return to the Patternist series with novels focused on Doro's life during the Roman Empire (including potentially an encounter with Jesus Christ, reimagined as one of Doro's children).

1987   *Dawn*, the first of the Xenogenesis or Lilith's Brood trilogy, is published by Warner Books in May. Short story "The Evening and the Morning and the Night" (different than the 1972 story of the same title) is published in *Omni* in May. Begins working with literary agent Merrilee Heifetz at Writer's House when Eth leaves.

1988   "The Evening and the Morning and the Night" wins the *Science Fiction Chronicle* award for Best Novelette and is also nominated for the Nebula, Locus, and Sturgeon Awards. Novel *Adulthood Rites*, the sequel to *Dawn* and the second book in the Lilith's Brood trilogy, is published by Warner Books in June; *Kirkus Reviews*, which had not reviewed *Dawn*, calls it "Butler in top form." Begins work on an early version of the Parables books called *Justice* or *The Justice Plague*, centered on a version of hyperempathy that spreads communally, including in at least some versions as a sexually transmitted disease. The notion that hyperempathy might be contagious was intended as the spark for utopian world formation, but Butler soon sees the potential for the mass pain and totalitarian social control that contagious hyperempathy could engender. At Christmas, pays off the mortgage on her mother's home.

1989   Autobiographical essay "Birth of a Writer" is published in *Essence* in May (and is later republished as "Positive Obsession" in *Bloodchild and Other Stories*). Novel *Imago* is published by Warner Books in May and concludes the Lilith's Brood trilogy. Sends a letter to literary agent Merrilee Heifetz in May detailing the plot for a story about an extrasolar colonization gone wrong, as the alien planet (a Gaia-like superorganism) rejects the human invaders like an immune system attacking a virus; she is describing a work she will never finish, *Parable of the Trickster*. In the letter she also asks Heifetz to throw out the earlier *Justice Plague* chapters as she will be "using the characters' names and the concept of contagious empathy but probably nothing else."

1990   Begins to suffer increasingly acutely from both health problems and the writer's block (which she often blames on her blood pressure medication) that would frustrate her next fifteen years.

1993   *Parable of the Sower* is published by Four Walls Eight Windows Press in October. *Publishers Weekly* praises the novel for its "uncommonly sensitive rendering of a very common SF scenario" and notes that Butler tells the story with "unusual warmth, sensitivity, honesty and grace." It is a 1994 *New York Times* Notable Book of the Year and nominated for a Nebula Award in 1995. Essay "Furor Scribendi" is published in *L. Ron Hubbard Presents Writers of the Future, Vol. IX*. Essay "Free Libraries: Are They Becoming Extinct?", celebrating the Los Angeles County public library system and its support of her self-education from childhood through adulthood, is published in *Omni* in August, after the destruction by arson of the L.A. Central Library.

1995   Awarded a John D. and Catherine T. MacArthur Foundation Fellowship in June. At the time the MacArthur Fellowship was a $295,000 award, giving Butler financial stability for the first time in her life. In a note in her journal she tries to prepare herself for public interviews: "1. What are you going to do? Write my novels. 2. Nothing special? Nothing I've planned so far. It will be great not to have to worry about money."

1996   The first edition of *Bloodchild and Other Stories*, collecting five stories and two essays, is published in August by Four Walls Eight Windows Press and becomes a *New York Times* Notable Book that year. Of her move to Four Walls Eight Windows, she will later tell an interviewer: "Some of [my publishers] wouldn't advertise me at all. And none of them would send me out on tour until I got to this very small publishing company. . . . My editor, Dan Simon, did see that it might be possible to send me out on tour, and he did do that. No one else had." Mother dies on November

18. Deeply distraught, Butler repeats to herself Olamina's slogan from *Parable of the Sower*: "God is change, and in the end, God prevails." She will later describe the completion of *Parable of the Talents*, on which she has been experiencing severe writer's block, as her mother's last gift to her, noting the paradox that her grief over her close relationship with her mother spawned a book about acrimonious and permanent mother-daughter alienation.

1997 Writes a letter to Heifetz apologizing that *Parable of the Talents* will never be finished and asks to return her advance. Eventually returns to work on and completes the book. Is honored guest at Intervention, the United Kingdom's national science fiction convention, in March. Receives honorary doctorate from Kenyon College in May. Finally switches from the typewriters she has used since childhood to word-processing software on a personal computer.

1998 Delivers speech "Devil Girl from Mars: Why I Write Science Fiction," reflecting on her early life and work, at "Media in Transition" forum at MIT in February. An early version of *Parable of the Trickster* is abandoned after José Saramago wins the Nobel Prize and Butler concludes her plan for the book is too similar to his novel *Blindness*. Considers, and briefly starts, a memoir titled "I Should Have Said . . ." *Parable of the Talents* is published by Seven Stories Press in October; *Publishers Weekly* singles it out as one of the best books of the year, and it is a *Los Angeles Times* best seller.

1999 *Parable of the Talents* wins the Nebula Award for Best Novel. It is also nominated for a James Tiptree Jr. Award. Moves to Seattle, where she will live for the rest of her life. Continues work on *Parable of the Trickster*.

2000 In spring, is guest of honor at the twenty-first meeting of the International Conference for the Fantastic in the Arts, an annual academic meeting for scholars of science fiction and fantasy, in Fort Lauderdale, Florida. Publishes "Brave New Worlds: A Few Rules for Predicting the Future" in *Essence* in May. Continues work on versions of *Parable of the Trickster*; in May, wonders why the version of the story she is working on now is so focused on men. Yet another version of *Parable of the Trickster* is abandoned after Butler concludes it is too similar to the plot of Kim Stanley Robinson's *Red Mars*. *Lilith's Brood* (an omnibus

and rebranded single-volume collection of her Xenogene-
sis trilogy) is published in June by Warner Books. Receives
Lifetime Achievement Award in Writing from the PEN
America Center in October.

2001   *Parable of the Talents* is shortlisted for the Arthur C. Clarke
Award. Publishes essay "A World Without Racism" at National Public Radio as part of the platform's special report
on the United Nations World Conference Against Racism, Racial Discrimination, Xenophobia and Related In-
tolerance in September. Continues work on *Parable of the
Trickster* with immense worldbuilding and reflection on
what life on the extrasolar colony will be like, but struggles
to develop the characters and plot. On 9/11, reflects, "I
now know . . . why [my character] leaves Earth." Several
abandoned versions of *Parable of the Trickster* spin off into
other potential writing projects, also mostly unfinished,
including *Paraclete*, a partially completed novel about a
woman with the power that anything she writes becomes
the truth; *Spiritus*, a mostly unfinished novel about a secret society of body-hopping immortals; and *Frogs*, an only
skeletal idea about a world where the gender balance of
the human species shifts off 50–50. Elements of these unfinished projects will inform "The Book of Martha" and
Fledgling.

2002   Publishes essay "Eye Witness" in *O: The Oprah Magazine*
in May.

2003   Short stories "Amnesty" and "The Book of Martha" are
both published at the website scifi.com.

2004   Completes *Fledgling* in September. In a private journal,
confesses that she identifies with Shori, and feels as if she
was forced to "re-educate myself—relearn my art, my craft,
the thing I love and need most." Says the book "isn't terrible, isn't even bad, really. But it isn't very good. I wrote it
because I was desperate to write a novel again, at last, and
it was the best I could do."

2005   *Fledgling* is published by Seven Stories Press in October;
Butler still considers the book unsuccessful and despairs
over its quality during proofreading. Nonetheless, begins
thinking about a sequel. In a *Guardian* review Junot Díaz
calls it his "book of the year . . . [a] harrowing medi-
tation on dominance, sex, addiction, miscegenation and

race that completely devours the genre which gave rise to it." The second edition of *Bloodchild* is published by Seven Stories Press in October, now including "Amnesty" and "The Book of Martha." Gives up caffeine in the face of ongoing and worsening health problems.

2006   Dies in Seattle, Washington, on February 24, following a fall outside her home. An omnibus collection of the Patternist series, from which she has excluded *Survivor*, is in the works; one of the last pages of her journal is a list of possible titles, from which *Seed to Harvest* is ultimately selected. It will be published by Warner Books in January 2007. The Octavia E. Butler Memorial Scholarship is founded by the Carl Brandon Society in Butler's memory to support the attendance of writers of color at the Clarion and Clarion West Writers' Workshops. Buried at Mountain View Cemetery and Mausoleum in Altadena, California, near her mother; her grave marker is inscribed with a quote from *Parable of the Sower*: "All that you touch, you change. All that you change, Changes you. The only lasting truth is Change. God is Change."

Note on the Texts

This volume contains several major works by Octavia E. Butler: the novels *Kindred* (1979) and *Fledgling* (2006), as well as the seven short stories and three essays gathered by Butler in the two editions of her only story collection, *Bloodchild and Other Stories* (1995, 2005). It also contains the short story "Childfinder," Butler's first major sale, which did not see publication until 2015, as well as two additional essays not collected by Butler.

Butler wrote *Kindred* primarily in 1976 and 1977. In 1976 she used the advance she received from the sale of her novel *Survivor* to travel to Maryland for a research trip, in which she visited the Maryland Historical Society and the Enoch Pratt Free Library to research the nineteenth-century Eastern Shore, and also toured Easton, Maryland, the setting for the historical portions of the novel. On her way home she visited Mount Vernon, the former plantation of George Washington, a site whose mix of opulence and cruelty struck her; at the time Mount Vernon did not yet have reconstructed slave quarters or use the word "slave" on its historical tours. Butler pinned a map of Mount Vernon on her wall as she completed the novel to keep what she had seen there in her mind as she wrote. In its first draft, *Kindred* was part of Butler's Patternist series. Besides *Survivor*, Butler had completed drafts of two other novels in the series, *Patternmaster* and *Mind of My Mind*, by this time; the Patternist series of novels concerns mutant telepaths bred by a semi-immortal being. But those trappings, including the science fictional time-travel elements, fell away in subsequent drafts, making it the first work published by Butler that was not part of the fictional world she had developed since she was a teenager.

In interviews later in her life she attributed the idea for *Kindred* to a conversation with a politically radical classmate at Pasadena City College, who had said during a heated conversation with other Black students, "I'd like to kill all those old people who have been holding us back for so long. But I can't because I'd have to start with my own parents." The novel, she often said, was an extended response to that provocation. As was common with Butler, the novel went through many possible titles, including "Canaan," "To Keep Thee in All Thy Ways," and "Guardian," before she settled on *Kindred*. The novel was also briefly advertised prior to publication as "Dana," a name Butler had insisted not be used; the mishap helped sour her relationship with her publisher, Doubleday, and contributed to her decision to seek a new publisher after *Wild Seed* in 1981. While all of Butler's works from the early portion of her career fell out of print at various times, *Kindred* only stayed out of print briefly, and it remains her most celebrated work; its current paperback publisher, Beacon Press, estimates that it has sold over 450,000 copies. *Kindred* was published in hardcover in July 1979 by Doubleday and in paperback in February 1981 by Pocket Books. A British printing was published as a trade paperback in October 1988 by The Women's Press, using the plates of the American edition. It was adapted into an acclaimed graphic novel by Damian Duffy and John Jennings in 2016. The first American hardcover edition is the source of the text used here.

Butler began composing *Fledgling* in 2003 after a long period of writer's block that predated her publication of *Parable of the Talents* in 1998. Much of the intervening period was spent working on multiple abandoned versions of a third book in the Parables trilogy, *Parable of the Trickster*, on which she never made much progress; some of the ideas from her *Trickster* drafts ultimately found an alternative form in late works such as *Fledgling*, "Amnesty," and "The Book of Martha," as well as her uncompleted and unpublished novels *Spiritus* and *Paraclete*. She viewed the novel as her "fun" novel, an escape from the "news burnout" she suffered during the height of the Bush administration. *Fledgling* was completed in September 2004 and was published in hardcover by Seven Stories Press in October 2005. *Fledgling* has not been published in a British edition. A trade paperback from Warner Books was published in January 2007. Butler was deeply unsatisfied with the book and acutely aware of what she believed were serious flaws, but she thought she had to publish it; she felt, like its protagonist Shori, that after years of writer's block and health problems she had been "forced to re-educate myself, relearn my art, my craft, the thing I love and need most." Nonetheless, despite her mixed feelings, at the time of her death in 2006 she was planning multiple sequels to the novel. The first American hardcover edition is the source of the text used here.

Butler struggled with the short story form, and due to the pace with which she wrote and revised and the diminished pay scale for short-form science fiction in the 1970s, she thought it made economic sense for her to focus on her novels. She sold two short stories immediately after her attendance at the Clarion Writers' Workshop in Pennsylvania in 1970: "Childfinder" and "Crossover." The stories "Speech Sounds," "Bloodchild," and "The Evening and the Morning and the Night" were all written in a creative burst in 1983, earning her multiple prizes that would permanently establish her as one of the major authors working in the science fiction genre at that time. "Speech Sounds" won the Hugo Award for Best Short Story in 1984 and was also nominated for a Locus Award. "Bloodchild" swept the Hugo, Nebula, and Locus Awards for Best Novellette. "The Evening and the Morning and the Night" (the second story by Butler with that name, though the first was never published) won the 1987 Science Fiction Chronicle Reader Award and was nominated for the Theodore Sturgeon, Nebula, and Locus Awards for best novelette. All three are frequently anthologized.

Of the eight short stories included in this volume, seven were gathered by Butler in her only short story collection, *Bloodchild and Other Stories*. The first edition of the collection, published in hardcover in August 1995 by Four Walls Eight Windows Press, contains the stories "Bloodchild," "The Evening and the Morning and the Night," "Near of Kin," "Speech Sounds," and "Crossover." A second edition, published as a trade paperback in October 2005 by Seven Stories Press, includes the additional stories "Amnesty" and "The Book of Martha." The second edition of *Bloodchild and Other Stories* from Seven Stories Press is the source of the text used here for those seven stories.

Information about the original publication of each of these short stories is given below:

"Crossover," *Clarion*, an anthology of speculative fiction from the Clarion Writers' Workshop, ed. Robin Scott Wilson (New York: Signet, 1971), pp. 140–45.

"Near of Kin," *Chrysalis 4: The Best All-New Science Fiction Stories*, ed. Roy Torgeson (New York: Zebra Books, 1979), pp. 163–75.

"Speech Sounds," *Isaac Asimov's Science Fiction Magazine*, Vol. 7, no. 13 (Mid-December 1983), pp. 26–41.

"Bloodchild," *Isaac Asimov's Science Fiction Magazine*, Vol. 8, no. 6 (June 1984), pp. 34–55.

"The Evening and the Morning and the Night," *Omni*, Vol. 9, no. 8 (May 1987), pp. 56–64.

"Amnesty," Sci Fiction webzine, ed. Ellen Datlow (scifi.com, January 22, 2003, no longer active).

"The Book of Martha," Sci Fiction webzine, ed. Ellen Datlow (scifi.com, May 21, 2003, no longer active).

The other story included in the present volume, "Childfinder," was written in 1971 and sold to Harlan Ellison for the science fiction short story anthology *The Last Dangerous Visions*, but the anthology, and the story, were never published. Posthumously, the story appeared in *Unexpected Stories*, a collection of two unpublished stories by Butler brought out as an e-book by Open Road Integrated Media in June

2014. The e-book edition is the source of the text used here, but the text has been corrected with reference to the draft of the story at the Huntington Library in the Octavia E. Butler Papers (mss OEB 288–291) in the following places: 577.9, 855 South Madison; 577.26, filthy even; 578.29, Valerie have is ten years or so; 578.31–2, helped those slaves to get; 579.2, evenings of entertainment; 579.13, *Push.*; 579.21, the rest of Harriet's; 582.6, cripple kids; 582.6, kill them.; 582.13, growing up, and; 582.18, who's likely; 583.23, attacker.; 584.5, four!; 584.15, ought to have been; 585.33, slightly, less; 585.36, they could see it; 585.40, work for long.; 586.4–5, about it, thinking about forgetting,; 586.12, deserved a chance.; 586.20, *Whatever the cause, we*; 586.31–32, *sure that this is one civilization that was destroyed.*

The first three of the five essays in this volume were collected in both editions of *Bloodchild and Other Stories*, the second edition of which is the source of the texts used here. Information about the original publication of each of the essays is given below:

Preface to *Bloodchild and Other Stories*, *Bloodchild and Other Stories* (New York: Four Walls Eight Windows, 1995) and second edition (New York: Seven Stories Press, 2005).

"Positive Obsession," Butler's longest published autobiographical statement, was first published as "Birth of a Writer" (a title she did not like) in *Essence* in May 1989 (Volume 20, Issue 1, p. 74).

"Furor Scribendi," Butler's advice for beginning writers, was published in *L. Ron Hubbard Presents Writers of the Future, Volume IX* (Los Angeles: Bridge Publications, 1993), pp. 324–27.

"Lost Races of Science Fiction" was published in the only issue of the fanzine *Transmission* (Summer 1980), pp. 16–18, which is the source of the text used here.

"The Monophobic Response" first appeared as "Journeys" in *Journeys*, a limited-edition anthology published by the PEN/Faulkner Foundation, collecting talks by fourteen authors delivered at the PEN/Faulkner Awards for Fiction on October 30, 1995 (Rockville, MD: Quill & Brush, 1996), n.p., and then was reprinted under the author's preferred title in *Dark Matter: A Century of Speculative Fiction from the African Diaspora*, ed. Sheree R. Thomas (New York: Aspect/Warner Books, 2000), pp. 415–16, which is the source of the text used here.

This volume presents the texts of the original printings chosen for inclusion here, but it does not attempt to reproduce features of their typographic design. The texts are presented without change, except for the correction of typographical errors. Spelling, punctuation, and capitalization are often expressive features, and they are not altered, even when inconsistent or irregular. The following is a list of typographical errors corrected, cited by page and line number: 18.1, drawn; III.1 and .4, La Canada; 112.2, into the white; 142.17, DeBow; 142.30, County was; 144.5, disappointment and; 156.20, Tom Weylin in; 162.21, hearth and; 194.29, surprsied; 203.35, coudn't; 219.24, straring; 224.4, "pleasure"; 233.13, and me; 236.33, sell the; 238.34, awhile; 249.13, June 19,; 279.18, instead wandering; 279.30, here. How; 282.20, been first; 283.19, said because; 283.28, to passenger; 286.3, in mental; 295.22, sleep?; 309.31, shoes were; 310.33, live it; 326.9, What's; 332.15, though; 333.18, it side; 336.39, want it to; 337.15, moment. In; 341.34, thing."; 342.11, an Iosif; 343.30, makes; 344.9, to want; 345.7, half the; 354.5, away."; 360.2, not let; 364.21, may older; 364.23, ago.; 367.21, turn off; 368.20–21, from it; 368.37, it healing; 369.3, telltale; 375.20, Had be; 375.22, whoever; 377.35, the said,; 378.36, than; 386.29, into house; 387.14, and I; 406.24, can."; 412.27, we traveling; 415.37, brothers Gordon; 419.3, much I; 423.3, the how; 424.1, asked surprised; 429.29, that; 438.9, a uneven; 450.29, us.; 450.30, "Eighteen."; 458.33, time adjust; 459.2, that; 460.32, who's idea; 462.13, A instant; 468.26, said. They're; 475.30, be to just; 477.35, it this; 480.21, both to; 481.10, then accept; 483.31, walk it in; 485.21, effects; 491.22, one the you; 499.34, how use; 501.23, whom; 511.5, captive human captives; 514.30, a hour; 524.31, barabaric; 524.35, symbionts, "I; 524.38, into to the; 526.40, on a such; 527.30, Katherine; 532.31, that; 535.38, us kill; 537.29, descendent,; 541.6, killed of my; 541.37, advocate said,; 543.7, inured."; 545.7, human, then.; 545.33, were lies.; 546.22, I'd had done; 547.29, looked; 549.8, You're; 550.28, begin tell; 555.4, trying kill; 555.19, spoke; 566.26, most their; 569.15, for while; 571.11, to bed; 574.1, mattered Theodora; 579.12, shot; 585.11, *Jordon*; 585.12, *to for me*,; 609.34, Figuroa; 613.20, scrapping; 622.38, ¶ "Nothing; 623.29, time; 660.12, Of course,"; 660.14, whispered.; 664.16, them." He; 668.3, wide glided; 669.14, it's; 670.1, messaged,; 673.22, choose; 675.5, Another; 675.19, Translator,"; 679.25, contract."; 682.36–37, here." She; 685.12, interrogator,; 692.40, Kalahari the; 693.7, of years; 693.30, well."; 693.32, I'll I; 695.4, "Shall; 697.12, twice-live-sized; 698.30, they do; 703.8, who's; 706.15–16, want do; 708.28, work.; 709.11, happen."; 709.33, indeed her; 712.34, them.; 713.6, maturity.; 713.19, consequences?; 715.1, someday.; 721.25, faddishness; 721.28, seems; 721.34–35, conventions,; 722.16, unreal?" Now; 723.3, ned; 723.5, cutom; 723.12 and .14, biggots; 723.30, decided; 726.23, out. In; 734.9, work can; 737.17, will being.

Notes

In the notes below, the reference numbers denote page and line of this volume (the line count includes chapter headings). No note is made for material included in the eleventh edition of *Merriam Webster's Collegiate Dictionary*. Biblical references are keyed to the King James Version. For further background, see Gerry Canavan, *Octavia E. Butler* (Champaign: University of Illinois Press, 2016); Rebecca J. Holden and Nisi Shawl, *Strange Matings: Science Fiction, Feminism, African American Voices, and Octavia E. Butler* (Seattle, WA: Aqueduct Press, 2013); Gregory Hampton, *Changing Bodies in the Fiction of Octavia Butler: Slaves, Aliens, and Vampires* (Lanham, MD: Lexington Books, 2010); Jane Donawerth and Kate Scally, "'You've Found No Records': Slavery in Maryland and the Writing of Octavia Butler's *Kindred*," *Extrapolation* 58.1 (2017).

KINDRED

2.1 *To Victoria Rose*] A close friend of Butler's from her youth. In a letter to Rose from the Clarion Writers' Workshop in 1970, Butler implored her friend: "Write me and reassure me that there are still Negroes around somewhere." Butler would later use Rose as one basis for the character of Tate Marah in the Xenogenesis/Lilith's Brood series.

6.2 June 9, 1976] Butler's own birthday was June 22, giving her the childhood nickname Junie. Dana was three years younger than Butler, born in 1950 to Butler's 1947. 1976 was the bicentennial celebration of America's founding, as well as the year the first version of *Kindred* was completed.

6.8 Los Angeles] Like most of Butler's early novels, *Kindred* is set in Southern California. Prior to moving to Altadena, Dana lives in a Los Angeles apartment not unlike Butler's own.

16.1 the South] In fact, Dana is in Maryland, which is located south of the Mason-Dixon Line but which would not secede from the Union during the Civil War. Butler chose Maryland as her location because she believed a story set deeper in the South would have made the fugitive slave plotline later in the novel impossible.

19.33 The Second Book of Kings] Cf. 2 Kings 4:18–37, in which Elisha raises the Shunammite's son from the dead.

19.37–38   nigger] Prior to Rufus's use of this slur Dana's racial identity is unmarked in the text. Butler used the word rarely and quite deliberately; she had
originally intended for it not to appear in *Kindred* at all.

20.39   Nero] The infamous Roman emperor (37–68 C.E.), who many Romans
believed instigated the Great Fire of Rome in 64 C.E. to clear land to build a
palace.

22.26   eighteen fifteen] Maryland's slaves would not be freed until the end of
the Civil War in 1865.

23.34   Hagar] In the book of Genesis, Hagar is Sarah's slave, who bears Abraham his son Ishmael; later, after Sarah, who had been thought barren, bears
Abraham a son at the age of ninety, Hagar and Ishmael are cast out. Sarah's
son Isaac was said to be the patriarch of the twelve tribes of Israel, and Ishmael
was said to be the patriarch of the Arab people. In both the nineteenth and
twentieth centuries, Hagar was taken up as a figure for the plight of enslaved
African Americans in the United States, especially African American women.

25.16–17   She thought you were a man at first] Butler's protagonists frequently disguise themselves or are misidentified as men, reflecting Butler's own
experiences of being misgendered.

25.26–27   You don't talk right or dress right or act right.] In her plans for
Kindred Butler was preoccupied with the sense that a twentieth-century African American would possess too much confidence and sense of self to be mistaken for a slave, were they somehow to travel back in time. She believed this
was especially true of twentieth-century Black men, who she believed would
be quickly killed by slave-owners out of fear.

26.23   Edana] Edana is a Gaelic name meaning "fire."

27.22   Easton] Butler used the city of Easton, Maryland, which she visited
during her research trip to Maryland in 1976, as her model for the area surrounding the Weylin estate. The published epilogue of *Kindred* was actually
written in Easton while Butler waited for a bus back to Baltimore.

30.29   free papers] Also referred to as a "pass." A certificate issued to freed
slaves, without which they were at risk of re-enslavement.

33.9–10   Ku Klux Klan] The KKK would not be founded until 1865, as a social
club that eventually morphed into a terrorist network; after mostly disappearing in the wake of anti-Klan legislation in the early 1870s, the organization was
refounded in 1915 in Stone Mountain, Georgia.

42.13   Highway Patrol] The California Highway Patrol is the law enforce-
ment agency that in other states is colloquially known as state police or state
troopers.

46.7–8   Pennsylvania Railroad] The Pennsylvania Railroad would eventually
become the largest railroad company in the country and would persist until the

twentieth century; it was only merged into the Consolidated Rail Corporation (Conrail) in April 1976, several months before the events of the novel.

49.24–25 Uncle Sam's share] Taxes.

49.25–28 You swept floors, . . . merchandise] These are all jobs that Butler herself took on during her lean years in the 1970s as she worked to establish herself as a writer.

49.34–36 At one or two . . . working on my novel] This detail too is borrowed from Butler's life.

50.2 zombie] A word of Haitian creole origin, *zombi* originally referred to the folkloric tradition of a dead person revived by a witch doctor, essentially a fantasy of slavery that continues even after physical death. The concept of the zombie as a mindless ghoul feasting on the living would be a staple in American horror fiction and film of the 1950s and after.

50.35–36 He was an unusual-looking white man] Butler reflected in her private notebooks that she often wrote about interracial couples in a spirit of imagining a less oppressive, less race-dominated future.

52.22–23 I'll convince myself . . . right] Butler received the same advice from her own family elders.

53.9 extension classes at UCLA] Butler also took these classes.

58.28–29 where we come from, whites and blacks can marry] The *Loving v. Virginia* Supreme Court case that legalized interracial marriage across the United States was decided in 1967, making this state of affairs less than ten years old for Dana and Kevin.

61.35–36 But you'd have made a good Missourian] The unofficial nickname of Missouri is the "Show-Me State." The name comes from an 1899 speech by U.S. Congressman Willard Duncan Vandiver.

62.34 muzzleloader] A gun that loads through the muzzle.

65.6 Georgian Colonial] The "Georgian" in Georgian Colonial refers not to the state but to the reigns of George I, II, III, and IV of England, from 1714 to 1830. The style is marked by symmetry and by restrained (or completely absent) ornamentation.

65.20 Marse] Master.

71.24 Free state?] There were eleven free states in 1819, New York among them; slavery was legally prohibited in these states, though the federalist legal system of the United States would make the status of enslaved persons who entered free states a highly contested question until the final abolition of slavery in 1865, and in many cases (as in New York) the abolition of slavery even in "free states" was a complicated, decades-long legal process that had not yet been fully completed.

72.4   Polyester] Polyester would not be invented until 1941.

78.19–20   Educated slaves aren't popular around here.] While Maryland would never formally forbid literacy to its enslaved persons, such laws were passed between 1740 and 1850 in Alabama, Georgia, Louisiana, Mississippi, Missouri, North Carolina, South Carolina, and Virginia. Many individual slave-owners forbade the people they enslaved from learning to read or write even without formal legal sanction.

82.14–15   cornshuck mattresses] A bed with a mattress stuffed with dried corn husks, common in the era.

82.15–17   I'm not being treated any worse . . . field hands] The distinction in treatment between enslaved persons working in the house and those working in the fields has been a staple of slavery narrative since the nineteenth century and is frequently conflated with the idea that enslaved persons working in the house were more complicit with their white slavers than those working outside.

83.26–27   Potiphar's wife and Joseph] Cf. Genesis 39, in which Joseph is jailed under a false rape accusation after his master's wife attempts unsuccessfully to seduce him.

83.34   look more like Weylin than Rufus does] Under the prevailing legal doctrine of *partus sequitur ventrem* (that which is brought forth follows the belly/womb), the children of women raped by their slave-owners were enslaved themselves; such offspring were sometimes euphemistically known as "children of the plantation."

85.31   *Robinson Crusoe*] The famous castaway novel of a man stranded by himself on a desert island, written in 1719 by Daniel Defoe (c. 1660–1731). In the novel, the protagonist Crusoe's relationship with the slave trade spans his entire career.

85.37   f's for s's] The "long s" (ʃ) was a staple of English-language printing in the seventeenth and eighteenth centuries, falling out of favor around 1800 and more or less disappearing entirely by the middle part of the nineteenth century.

89.25   You say that like you're sure.] Because records were not kept, many enslaved persons did not know their exact birth date or even birth year, including, famously, Frederick Douglass.

90.8   cipher] An archaic term for arithmetic.

102.22–23   *Pilgrim's Progress . . . Gulliver's Travels*] Like the other novels read by Rufus, both *The Pilgrim's Progress* and *Gulliver's Travels* use the literary device of a fantastical journey to provide cover for political and moral critiques of their time. Published in 1678 by English Puritan preacher John Bunyan (1628–1688), *The Pilgrim's Progress* is a religious allegory about an everyman who seeks to avoid iniquity and sin on his journey to the Celestial City (Heaven). *Gulliver's Travels* is a bitter, misanthropic satire of British society written by Irish clergyman Jonathan Swift (1667–1745) and published in 1726.

105.12   speller] A book for teaching spelling.

108.3–4   I had a sardine-can sized apartment on Crenshaw Boulevard] Crenshaw Boulevard was a major thoroughfare in the Crenshaw neighborhood of Los Angeles, which was a predominantly African American area by the early 1970s.

111.1   La Cañada] La Cañada Flintridge is a predominantly white suburb of Los Angeles and the site of the NASA Jet Propulsion Laboratory.

111.14   any children we have will be light] The discriminatory preference for lighter-skinned African Americans is frequently called "colorism."

111.40   Pasadena] Butler's hometown and the place where she spent nearly all of her life prior to moving to Los Angeles.

112.9   Las Vegas] Vegas's lax marriage laws, requiring neither a blood test nor a waiting period, with marriage certificates issued cheaply and quickly, made it the "Marriage Capital of the World."

112.9   gambled away a few dollars] Then, as now, Las Vegas was a resort town famous for its casinos.

112.12   *The Atlantic*] Founded in 1857, *The Atlantic* is one of the oldest continuously published literary magazines in the United States. Butler may have selected this as the place for Dana's first major publication because of the magazine's early abolitionist politics; it also gives Dana's work an imprimatur of literary quality and seriousness that Butler's own writing would not receive till much later in her career.

116.1   Volvo] A Swedish make of small car.

117.6   even *Gone with the Wind*] The 1936 novel by Margaret Mitchell (1900–1949) was made into a 1939 film that (adjusted for inflation) is still the highest-grossing film of all time. Both the book and the film have been criticized as overly sympathetic to slave-owners while depicting enslaved persons in stereotyped and demeaning terms.

117.6   happy darkies in tender loving bondage] The slur "darkies," applied to the Black characters, is used in both the novel and film versions of *Gone with the Wind*.

117.22   for eight days] This puts the date of Dana's next travel back in time at June 19, commonly called Juneteenth, a day commemorating the end of slavery. The holiday was originally a celebration in Texas of the day emancipation was announced in Galveston, Texas, in 1865, but later spread nationally.

120.19   sell Isaac South] Because the legal rights afforded enslaved persons generally worsened the farther South one went, and the prevailing treatment became even crueler, the idiom "sold South" (or "sold down the river") suggested a dramatic worsening of a slave's quality of life, often tantamount to a death sentence.

133.32 They're called aspirin] Aspirin would not be invented until 1899.

134.27–28 Didn't have to jump no broomstick] The full origins of this custom are not well understood, but it is widely believed that the custom of jumping over a broomstick became a way to signify the marriage compact where legal marriages between enslaved persons were forbidden (perhaps growing out of a Ghanaian tradition, or perhaps in reference to a British legal idiom describing unofficial marriages dating back to the 1760s). Although the custom mostly faded into obscurity after emancipation, it received renewed attention in the African American community after its depiction in Alex Haley's *Roots* (novel 1976, TV film 1977).

139.39 a purgative] A laxative.

142.13 Sojourner Truth] An African American abolitionist and women's rights activist (c. 1797–1883) and, with Harriet Tubman, a frequent source of inspiration for Butler when creating her characters.

142.17 J. D. B. De Bow] Magazine publisher and superintendent of the U.S. Census James Dunwoody Brownson De Bow (1820–1867). Butler likely refers here to an 1860 pamphlet penned by De Bow titled "The Interest in Slavery of the Southern Non-Slaveholder," in which De Bow notes, in part, "The non-slaveholder of the South preserves the status of the white man, and is not regarded as an inferior or a dependant."

142.28 Frederick Douglass] Douglass (1818–1895) was a national leader in the abolitionist movement after his escape from slavery in 1838. Douglass's *Narrative of the Life of Frederick Douglass, an American Slave* (1845) remains one of the most read and most influential slave narratives ever written.

142.31 Harriet Tubman] An antislavery activist (c. 1822–1913) and organizer of the Underground Railroad who made more than a dozen missions into the South to rescue enslaved persons, Tubman was a hero of Butler's, on whom she based multiple characters in her novels, including both Lilith Iyapo of the Xenogenesis books and Lauren Olamina of the Parables books.

142.34–35 a man named Nat Turner was biding his time] Nat Turner (1800–1831) led one of the most successful slave rebellions in American history in 1831, which killed sixty white people before it was put down after four days.

143.11 Denmark Vesey] After his conviction for plotting a slave revolt, Vesey (c. 1767–1822) was executed by hanging in Charleston, South Carolina.

145.8 follow the North Star] The North Star (also called "the drinking gourd," referring to its place on the Big Dipper constellation) was frequently used by fugitive slaves and those helping them to navigate toward freedom in the absence of detailed maps or compasses.

147.26 "mammy"] By the 1970s, this stereotypical term for a motherly Black woman was used almost exclusively in a negative sense, as a critique of white racism. See also note 117.6 for *Gone with the Wind*, in which the primary Black character is named "Mammy."

147.28–29 handkerchief-head] A term in 1960s slang among Black activists advocating for natural hairstyles like the Afro over straightened or processed hair; the wearing of straightened hair under a handkerchief or headscarf was seen as a politically suspect concession to white standards of beauty.

147.29 Uncle Tom] The character from *Uncle Tom's Cabin* (1852) by Harriet Beecher Stowe (1811–1896) is commonly used in African American culture to signify a traitor beholden to white people.

148.32 antiseptic?] Antiseptic would not be invented by Dr. Joseph Lister until 1867.

166.2 five years!] This puts this portion of the story in 1824.

172.31 johnnycake] A cornmeal flatbread.

190.11 flintlock] "Flintlock" refers to the ignition mechanism of the firearm; such rifles were in common use in the nineteenth century.

200.21 the war in Lebanon] The Lebanese civil war lasted nearly fifteen years, from 1975 to 1990, with approximately 120,000 casualties and massive displacement of civilians and refugees both within and outside Lebanon. The United States was not a formal participant in the war; President Gerald Ford ordered the U.S. Embassy to evacuate all nonessential personnel from the country following the assassination of the U.S. ambassador to Lebanon, Francis E. Meloy, Jr., on June 16, 1976.

200.28 South Africa] The apartheid government in South Africa, which saw a majority Black population ruled by a white minority without equal rights or representation in government, would not fall until the early 1990s.

203.40 Levi's] The Levi's company would not be founded until 1853, and denim jeans would not be invented until 1871.

206.31 ague] A severe illness marked by recurrent periods of chills, fever, and sweating; the term is most frequently associated with malaria.

206.37–38 bleeding and blistering and purging and puking] All archaic medical techniques based on the nineteenth-century theory that disease originated in overstimulation; bleeding, blistering, purging, and vomiting were all used to restore the body's natural equilibrium through the deliberate infliction of controlled injury.

207.23 six years] Six years from Dana's previous trip puts this portion of the story in 1830.

208.1–2 mosquitoes] British doctor Sir Ronald Ross (1857–1932) would not discover that mosquitoes transmit malaria to humans until 1897.

208.11   mumps] The vaccine for the common childhood disease mumps first became available in the U.S. in December 1967.

209.3–4   microorganisms] The germ theory of disease would not be widely accepted until the end of the nineteenth century, following experiments by Louis Pasteur from 1860 to 1864.

213.38–39   Cardiopulmonary resuscitation] More commonly known as CPR.

222.9   laudanum] Laudanum is a narcotic medicine derived from opium, with addictive properties. Prior to the twentieth century it was in common use and could be sold without a prescription; it is rarely used today.

223.28   the Sermon on the Mount] Matthew 5–7.

230.22   dengue fever?] Dengue fever is a mosquito-borne illness similar to malaria; reinfection with dengue is typically much more serious than the initial infection due to a phenomenon called antibody-dependent enhancement, which prevents the immune system from properly repelling the disease.

231.1   Windsor chair] A chair with a wooden seat with the legs and back pushed into drilled holes. The modular construction technique made the Windsor chair amenable to factory production, which in turn made it very common in the nineteenth-century United States.

234.13   shorthand] A system of abbreviated writing common in the midcentury United States prior to the invention of recording devices, dictation machines, and word processing. It was commonly taught in high schools in the 1960s.

239.25   Miriam and Aaron] In the Bible, the sister and brother of Moses.

239.29   Ishmael] See note 23.34.

239.29–30   In the Bible, . . . didn't have to stay slaves] Hereditary, chattel slavery of the sort practiced in the United States is a historical anomaly; slavery in antiquity did not typically pass from parent to child, nor was it usually lifelong.

241.28   a bit on a horse] A bit is a metal mouthpiece used to control a horse in horseback riding; used incorrectly or by an inexperienced rider, it can hurt the animal.

246.18   Andrew Jackson] Jackson (1767–1845) was the seventh president of the United States, in office from 1829 to 1837. Jackson spent most of the years from 1819 to 1824 in Florida and Tennessee, although he served in the U.S. Senate from 1823 to 1825.

249.13–14   reverse symbolism, . . . July 4] The two-hundreth anniversary of America's founding, July 4, 1976.

253.14   Rose Bowl] The stadium in Pasadena, not the football game of the same name (which was played in January in 1976).

258.26–27 my father who had died before . . . know him] Another detail from Butler's life that she attributes to Dana.

258.32–35 Man that is born . . . continueth not] Job 14:1–2.

269.9–10 schools with Black kids and white kids together] School integration remained a fiercely contested political issue in 1976, despite the more than twenty years since the 1954 *Brown v. Board of Education* Supreme Court decision that mandated school integration nationwide.

270.17 Maryland Historical Society] This was one of Butler's primary research sites during her trip to Maryland to research *Kindred*.

FLEDGLING

287.31 You're a vampire] Originating in folklore, the figure of the vampire as an undead, blood-drinking predator is best known to most Americans through its presentation in horror fiction, television, and film. Butler's Ina are not vampires: they are not undead, and do not have many of the mystical weaknesses attributed to vampires, such as vulnerability to garlic and silver.

287.37 Jailbait.] A colloquial term describing a girl viewed as a potential sexual partner who is under the legal age of consent for sexual relations.

288.21–22 A friend of mine told me it meant 'reborn.'] Butler was interested in the meanings of names and considered publishing a dictionary of name-meanings during a period of prolonged writer's block in the mid-1990s.

290.5 Seattle] Butler moved permanently to Seattle, Washington, in 1999.

293.31 brown-skinned person] This is the first reference to Shori's skin color in the novel, which, as in *Kindred*, comes several chapters in.

305.8 His computer] The description of the computer and the process Wright uses to access the Internet place the narrative in the late 1990s or early 2000s.

305.33 a huge amount of nonsense about vampires] Butler was a fan of at least some of these cultural productions, including Joss Whedon's *Buffy, the Vampire Slayer* (1997–2003).

306.3 anthropology] Butler enjoyed her studies of anthropology (both in her formal education and as an autodidact) and at one point considered going back to school for a Ph.D. in the subject.

306.5–6 so allergic to sunlight that they only go out at night] This may be porphyria or perhaps solar urticaria.

306.7–8 a disease . . . people think they're vampires] Often called clinical vampirism or Renfield Syndrome, named after Dracula's follower R. M. Renfield in the 1897 novel by Bram Stoker.

314.20 the national forest] Most likely Mount Rainier National Park, the closest national park to Seattle.

335.16   Iosif Petrescu] This spelling of Joseph strongly suggests Iosif's Eastern European heritage; Petrescu is a common family name in Romania. Most of the Ina family names presented in the novel similarly suggest Eastern European or Russian origin.

336.8–9   the vampire creatures Bram Stoker described in *Dracula*] While not the first vampire novel in English, *Dracula* (1897)—set in the Transylvania region of Romania—became the primary template for the century of vampire fiction and film to follow.

336.37   mutualistic symbiosis] This biological formulation—of a mutually beneficial relationship rather than host and parasite—was central to Butler's thought; she relies on it as a structuring idea in the Xenogenesis books as well.

341.38   Darrington] Darrington is seventy-five miles northeast from Seattle.

361.32–33   "Invite me in."] In many vampire narratives, the vampire cannot enter a home without first being invited inside.

376.17   Arlington] Arlington is approximately twenty-eight miles west of Darrington and approximately forty-seven miles north of Seattle.

384.32   the shakes] A reference to delirium tremens, a symptom of alcohol withdrawal.

396.11   a semiautomatic Beretta] Beretta is a manufacturer of semiautomatic pistols; the gun is a popular choice for espionage novels, including the early James Bond novels by Ian Fleming.

404.36–37   Punta Nublada] Spanish: "Cloudy Point."

409.4   *The Thomas Guide: King and Snohomish Counties*] Published by Thomas Brothers Maps, which was acquired by Rand McNally in 1999.

419.17   melanin] Melanin is the chemical responsible for the pigmentation of human skin, and is frequently used as a synecdoche for nonwhite skin tones.

419.19–20   Hatfields and McCoys] Two feuding families of West Virginia, who bitterly and often violently opposed each other for generations in the nineteenth century.

429.38–39   I didn't want to join with a man] The idea throughout *Fledgling* that men are less able to accept nonheterosexual and nonmonogamous pairings than women, particularly ones that put them in a subordinate power position, is also a theme in Butler's Xenogenesis series, as well as her unpublished novel *Blindsight*.

436.23   Hummer] A brand of extra-large, military-grade sport utility vehicles (SUVs).

452.6   Toyota Sequoia] Another model of large SUV.

458.25   Tigris and Euphrates] The Tigris and Euphrates Rivers are often referred to as "the cradle of civilization," as the Mesopotamian civilizations that emerged there (especially the Sumerians and the Babylonians) were the planet's first literate cultures and considered by later Western cultures as ancestors.

462.27 Los Angeles] The Silks' presence in Los Angeles County returns Butler to the region where she spent nearly all of her life prior to her move to Seattle.

476.9 Jeep Cherokees] Another model of sport utility vehicle.

487.19 germ line] The sex cells (eggs in females and sperm in males). This will make the alterations to Shori's genome inheritable by her children.

499.8 Gypsies] The word is now widely considered a slur, especially outside the United States; "Roma" or "Romani" is preferred today.

500.2 "Break a leg."] A common idiom from theater, used in place of "good luck!"

505.7 contralto] The lowest of the female vocal ranges.

514.6 'ESP.'] Extrasensory perception.

563.8–9 They will be Silk no longer] Butler's ideas for a sequel to *Fledgling*, still fragmentary at the time of her death, mostly hinge on at least some of the Silks refusing the terms of their sentence. These Silks, Shori is told, have "escaped before they could be adopted by their new families. We thought they would try to go back to the Silk Community. Instead, they've come after you."

STORIES AND ESSAYS

577.3 psionic] Psychic, as in psychic powers.

577.9 835 South Madison] A Pasadena, California, address.

577.20 pre-telepath] "Childfinder" is written in a version of Butler's Patternist series, which focuses on mutant psychics whose powers fully develop (in a fairly disturbing mental and physical ordeal called "transition") around puberty. The series was still in development at the time "Childfinder" was sold to Harlan Ellison for his third (and never published) *Dangerous Visions* anthology, so some details from the story do not align with the Patternist series as it was eventually published.

578.40 Harriet Tubman] The earliest reference in Butler's published work to the figure on whom she based multiple heroines.

584.8 Watusi man] A historical name for the Tutsi ethnic group of East Africa, today associated more with Rwanda than with Kenya due to the genocide against the Tutsi in that country in the 1990s. The reference here is likely to the group's reputation for being unusually tall.

594.1 *Near of Kin*] As Butler notes in her Afterword (see pp. 602–3 in this volume), despite the closeness in name to *Kindred*, and an editor who promoted "Near of Kin" as being linked to the novel at the time of its first publication, the story in fact has no connection to *Kindred*.

595.40   She had had four miscarriages before you] This is a biographical detail from Butler's mother's life. See also the Chronology for 1947.

597.1   Knott's Berry Farm] A popular Los Angeles–area theme park.

603.4–5   Lot's daughters] Cf. Genesis 19:30–38.

603.5   Abraham's sister-wife] Sarah. Cf. Genesis 20:1–16.

603.5–6   the sons of Adam with the daughters of Eve] Butler here references the well-known problem that all of Adam and Eve's children would have been brothers and sisters; the precise phrasing may be a reference to C. S. Lewis's series of children's novels The Chronicles of Narnia, which uses this wording repeatedly.

604.2   Washington Boulevard bus] A bus route in Los Angeles. Butler did not have a driver's license, because, she said, of her dyslexia, and was a bus rider throughout her life.

618.15   Clay's Ark] Clay's Ark would be published by St. Martin's Press in 1984, the same year Butler won the Hugo for "Speech Sounds."

620.24   Terrans] From the Latin terra, or earth, this word is frequently used in science fiction to refer both to human beings and to our home planet.

621.10   "Lien, . . . Gan's egg."] Lien is a Vietnamese name meaning "lotus flower"; Gan is a Vietnamese name meaning "near," though its Hebrew meaning, "garden," might fit better with the naming theme for the other Terran characters in the story.

623.12   Xuan Hoa] Xuan means "spring" and Hoa means "flower."

625.23   Qui] A Vietnamese name meaning "turtle," traditionally feminine but here assigned to a male.

642.1   The Evening and the Morning and the Night] This is the second story Butler completed with this title, the first being set in her Patternist storyworld, which she attempted to publish in the 1970s but never sold.

642.4   Duryea-Gode] Duryea-Gode disease is Butler's invention, but as she explains in the Afterword, elements of the condition exist in the real world: the inheritability and cognitive decline of DGD are a reference to Huntington's disease, the special diet of DGD sufferers is a reference to phenylketonuria, and the violent self-mutilation comes from Lesch-Nyhan disease.

642.10   old Roman style] Butler refers not only to the historical and literary association of Rome with suicide, often to avoid dishonor or public disgrace, but also specifically to the method used by Lucius Annaeus Seneca (c. 1 B.C.E.–65 C.E.), who slit his wrists and entered a warm bath after being ordered to commit suicide by the emperor Nero.

649.37   Hedeonco] The mechanism described here recalls the drug Thalidomide, a morning-sickness drug that caused severe birth defects in the late 1950s and early 1960s. Butler would use this figuration again in her Parables books, in the intelligence-enhancing drug Parateco, which causes hyperempathy in the children of the people who took it.

674.6   Mojave] Butler spent some of her childhood at her grandmother's house near the Mojave Desert, the only portion of her life she spent outside Pasadena and the greater Los Angeles area prior to the Clarion Writers' Workshop in Pennsylvania in 1970.

682.40   Thirty pieces of silver] Judas's payment for betraying Christ in the book of Matthew.

683.15   Victorville] A city in California in the San Bernardino Valley.

695.8   Wen Ho Lee] Wen Ho Lee (born 1939) is a Taiwanese-American scientist who worked at the Los Alamos National Laboratory and was accused by the U.S. government of espionage for the People's Republic of China in a highly publicized case in 1999. Federal prosecutors were ultimately able to convict Lee on only one of the original fifty-nine counts, improper handling of restricted data, to which he pled guilty as part of a settlement. The case was widely considered an abuse of power by the Department of Justice, an opinion held by both the judge presiding over the case and President Bill Clinton.

697.15   Michelangelo's Moses] The sculpture is located at the church of San Pietro in Vincoli, in Rome.

707.3–4   The Tower of Babel] Cf. Genesis 11:1–9.

710.13   Twilight Zone] A popular early science fiction television series, which aired from 1959 to 1964.

721.4   Back when *Star Wars* was new] "Lost Races of Science Fiction" was first published in the summer of 1980, so Butler is referring to an event only three years prior. Given that *The Empire Strikes Back* was released in late May 1980, Butler had most likely not seen the film (which introduces a Black character named Lando Calrissian to the core cast, played by Billy Dee Williams) before writing this essay. The workshop teaching notes in her archive from later in the 1980s indicate she was not impressed with the character.

721.28   Yaphet Kotto] Kotto (born 1939) played Technician Dennis Parker in *Alien* (1979).

722.10   *Dreamsnake*] *Dreamsnake* was published by Houghton Mifflin in 1978 and won the 1978 Nebula, 1979 Locus, and 1979 Hugo Awards. McIntyre was a personal friend of Butler's; they attended the Clarion Writers' Workshop together in 1970.

722.12   *Close Encounters of the Third Kind*] The 1977 film directed by Steven Spielberg.

724.26   Harriet Beecher Stowe] See note 147.29.

724.27   Sidney Poitier movies] Butler is likely thinking of films such as *In the Heat of the Night* (1967), a detective film that was the winner of the 1967 Academy Award for Best Picture and the first film to be lit specifically to complement its Black star's skin tone rather than those of his white costars, and *Guess Who's Coming to Dinner* (1967), a dramedy about interracial marriage.

724.30   Charlie Chan] A fictional Hawaiian detective in the mystery novels of Earl Derr Biggers (1884–1933) initially lauded for their positive portrayal of Asian Americans, but which later became viewed as stereotype-laden and racist.

724.30   Tonto] The American Indian sidekick of the Lone Ranger in the radio and television series of the 1930s, '40s, and '50s.

724.30–31   that little guy who swiped Fritos] The Frito Bandito, the official corporate mascot for the Fritos company from 1967 to 1971.

728.20   *The Writer*] Founded in 1887, it is the nation's oldest magazine for writers.

730.29   Last Christmas] Christmas 1988.

731.6   Samuel R. Delany, Jr.] Delany (born 1942) is the author of myriad works of science fiction and is, with Butler, widely considered one of the founders of Afrofuturism. Delany was one of Butler's instructors at the Clarion Workshop (see Chronology for 1970).

731.7   Steven Barnes] Barnes (born 1952) is a prolific writer of both prose (including both original works and *Star Trek* and *Star Wars* tie-in novels) and television.

731.7   Charles R. Saunders] Saunders (born 1946) may be best known for *Imaro* (1981), a sword and sorcery novel that spawned multiple sequels.

734.23   *L. Ron Hubbard Presents Writers of the Future IX*] Scientology was not as controversial at the time of this essay's publication as it is today; Butler had no connection with it, and the Writers of the Future contest, mostly associated with Hubbard as science fiction author rather than as Scientology founder, is generally seen positively by the science fiction community.

736.7   Tau Cetians] Tau Ceti is a star that has frequently been cited in science fiction as a possible location for nonhuman intelligent life, in part because it is within the same general size and type of star as Earth's sun. The most famous example of Tau Cetians in science fiction literature may be from Ursula K. Le Guin's *The Dispossessed* (1974), a favorite novel of Butler's.

*This book is set in 10 point ITC Galliard Pro, a face
designed for digital composition by Matthew Carter and based
on the sixteenth-century face Granjon. The paper is acid-free
lightweight opaque that will not turn yellow or brittle with age.
The binding is sewn, which allows the book to open easily and lie flat.
The binding board is covered in Brillianta, a woven rayon cloth
made by Van Heek–Scholco Textielfabrieken, Holland.
Composition by Dianna Logan, Clearmont, MO.
Printing and binding by LSC Communications.
Designed by Bruce Campbell.*

THE LIBRARY OF AMERICA SERIES

Library of America fosters appreciation of America's literary heritage by publishing, and keeping permanently in print, authoritative editions of America's best and most significant writing. An independent nonprofit organization, it was founded in 1979 with seed funding from the National Endowment for the Humanities and the Ford Foundation.

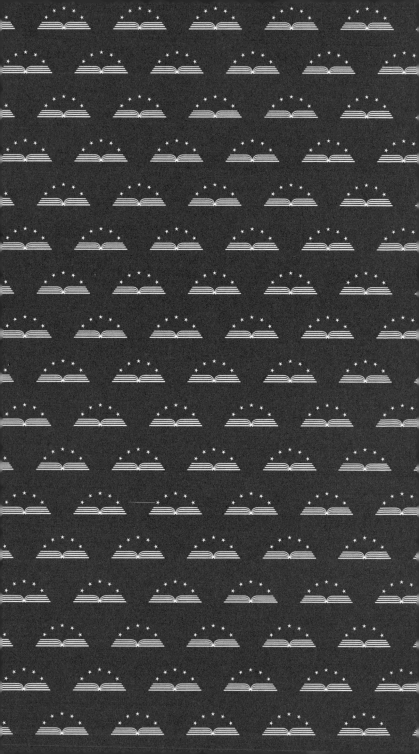